PRAISE FOR
BLACKWATER SPIRITS:

*The third book in the critically acclaimed
Glynis Tryon historical mystery series.*

"Satisfying historical fare whose proto-feminist spin feels just right."
—*Kirkus Reviews*

"Glynis [Tryon has] a substantial personal history that gives credibility to the choices she makes." —*The Drood Review*

"Rich in historical background and Native American lore, vibrant with characters who are as engaging as they are individualistic . . . *Blackwater Spirits* is one of the most marvelously written mysteries I have ever read." —*Kate's Mystery Books*

"Ms. Monfredo demonstrates a real appreciation for the drama of our history, and is very skilled at translating the social and political ferments of the times . . . into immediate problems for her characters."
—*Mystery News*

"Excellent courtroom scene . . . A very fine historical novel."
—*The Poisoned Pen*

"Monfredo excels at capturing the mood and spirit of the times, especially in her delineation of what it meant to be a woman of that day." —*The Purloined Letter*

"One of the most historically accurate, compelling series I've found . . . Just as with the two previous books which preceded this, *Seneca Falls Inheritance* and *North Star Conspiracy*, I didn't put this down until I'd finished." —*Meritorious Mysteries*

"A marvelous eye to historical detail . . . a beautiful read. If you have not yet read this author, then you are missing out."
—*The Merchant of Menace*

continued . . .

PRAISE FOR
SENECA FALLS INHERITANCE:

Amidst the bustle of the Women's Rights Convention of 1848, a body turns up in a nearby canal. Now Glynis must put her talent for sleuthing to work and take a stand against a murderer . . .

"An exceptional first novel . . . from its exciting opening right up to the revelation of a well-concealed murder in a gripping courtroom scene."
—Edward D. Hoch, Past President,
Mystery Writers of America

"An engaging mystery . . . Monfredo has given us a taste for a dynamic time in the history of women's rights."
—*Mostly Murder*

"Blends history and mystery in an unconventional murder story."
—*Rochester Times-Union*

"A meticulously researched, first-class mystery that evokes, with charm and vividness, rural life in the Empire State a century and a half ago."
—*Buffalo News*

"A wonderful evocation of time and place, a heroine worth cheering for, and an involving, well-crafted plot—a recipe that any mystery reader can savor."
—Stephen F. Wilcox, author of the
T.S.W. Sheridan and Hackshaw mysteries

"A page-turning suspense story . . . historically authentic and cleverly entertaining."
—*Publishers Weekly* (starred review)

Berkley Prime Crime Books by Miriam Grace Monfredo

SENECA FALLS INHERITANCE
NORTH STAR CONSPIRACY
BLACKWATER SPIRITS
THROUGH A GOLD EAGLE

THROUGH A GOLD EAGLE

A GLYNIS TRYON MYSTERY

Miriam Grace Monfredo

BERKLEY PRIME CRIME, NEW YORK

THROUGH A GOLD EAGLE

A Berkley Prime Crime Book / published by arrangement with the author

PRINTING HISTORY
Berkley Prime Crime hardcover edition / July 1996
Berkley Prime Crime mass-market edition / July 1997

All rights reserved.
Copyright © 1996 by Miriam Grace Monfredo.
This book may not be reproduced in whole or in part, by mimeograph or any other means, without permission. For information address: The Berkley Publishing Group, 200 Madison Avenue, New York, NY 10016.

The Putnam Berkley World Wide Web site address is http://www.berkley.com

ISBN: 0-425-15898-5

Berkley Prime Crime Books are published by The Berkley Publishing Group, 200 Madison Avenue, New York, NY 10016. The name BERKLEY PRIME CRIME and the BERKLEY PRIME CRIME design are trademarks belonging to Berkley Publishing Corporation.

PRINTED IN THE UNITED STATES OF AMERICA

10 9 8 7 6 5 4 3 2

In Memory of
Shawn Warren Monfredo
1963–1994

ACKNOWLEDGMENTS

The novelist who works to credibly recreate a historic period must rely heavily on research facilities and experts in varied and sometimes esoteric fields. To the following I offer my profound gratitude.

Rachel J. Monfredo, of the Museum of Fine Arts, Boston, Department of American Decorative Arts and Sculpture, was the first to suggest the numismatic theme, as she prepared a display of colonial and United States Mint coins at the MFA. She has since assisted in many and varied aspects of my research, and has helped to bring *Through a Gold Eagle,* as well as previous novels in the Glynis Tryon series, to realization by her willing, cheerful, and creative contributions. And it was she who fortuitously introduced me to the following numismatic authority.

Q. David Bowers is the author of *The History of United States Coinage* (1979); *United States Gold Coins* (1982); and *Silver Dollars & Trade Dollars of the United States: A Complete Encyclopedia* (1993). He has graciously given permission to quote from the above; in fact, Mr. Bowers's staggering wealth of knowledge is exceeded only by his generosity. In addition to readily answering scores of questions, he read an early draft of this work and offered many helpful suggestions. Needless to say, any errors that might have crept into the final version are solely my responsibility.

Others to whom I owe grateful thanks are Carol Sandler, director of The Strong Museum Library, Rochester, New York; Janice Estey, archivist and curator, Remington Arms Company, Ilion, New York; Ron Pytko and his wife, Fran, the Utica Connection; Horst J. Heinicke, M.D.; Nicholas E. Nicosia, D.D.S.; Toni Hicks and Jeff Bowers, park rangers at the Harpers Ferry National Historical Park; Kathy Stewart; and Nancy Woodhull and Bill Watson for the loan to Glynis Tryon of their historic Cayuga Street house in Seneca Falls. Also, Frank R. Monfredo, problem solver (legal and otherwise), cartographer, and first reader extraordinaire.

And to my son Shawn, the first and most beloved coin collector of my acquaintance.

AUTHOR'S NOTE

The major characters in *Through a Gold Eagle* are fictitious, but actual historic figures do appear from time to time. Interested readers will find them annotated in the Historical Notes in the back matter of this and the other books in the Glynis Tryon series.

In the autumn of 1859, a small, heretofore unremarked town in Virginia exploded into the American consciousness. This town stands on a promontory where the Potomac and Shenandoah rivers meet; the land was purchased in the mid 1700s by Robert Harper, who subsequently began operation of the Potomac ferry. The town itself was established in 1783 by the Virginia General Assembly and named "Shenandoah Falls at Harper's Ferry," but was commonly referred to as *Harper's Ferry*. Although the possessive form has since been abandoned, it appears in all contemporary nineteenth-century accounts of the events that occurred there. For this reason, I have retained the possessive form in the novel.

On the other hand, American baseball in the mid-nineteenth-century was written as two words—*base ball*—but to avoid the reader's possible bewilderment, and since the sport appears infrequently in the novel, I have used the familiar compound. This is also the case with the Adirondack mountain that is today written as Whiteface, but in the nineteenth century was *White Face*.

The maps of New York State and Seneca Falls contain only *actual* locations; fictional entities, such as Black Brook Reservation and Painter Creek, are not included.

The plainest print cannot be read through a gold eagle; and it will be ever hard to find many men who will send a slave to Liberia, and pay his passage while they can send him to a new country, Kansas for instance, and sell him for fifteen hundred dollars.

—ABRAHAM LINCOLN

THROUGH
A
GOLD EAGLE

PROLOGUE

❧

For the love of money is the root of all evil.
—I TIMOTHY 6:10

APRIL 1859

THE GOLD OF a western New York sunset glinted off the surface of Painter Creek. John Fairfax stood on one of many large boulders strewn beside the creek bed while he gauged the amount of remaining daylight. Restlessly shifting his feet, the young man glanced with a frown at the rented bay horse which grazed a few yards away. He knew the animal needed rest. It was, if possible, more tired than he. Fairfax tried to restrain his impatience by lowering himself to a seated position, and concentrating on the whisper of water as it flowed over the creek's rough stones. Yet at the same time he listened for the drum of hoofbeats.

All at once the bay horse brought up its head with a sharp cry, straining at the rope looped around the trunk of a birch. Then it reared, struggling to free itself. Fairfax slid off the boulder as he drew his knife from its sheath. His eyes raked the surrounding rocks before they moved to the mouth of a nearby cave. He could find nothing that would alarm the horse. But he recalled another agent's warning: "Painter Creek was named for the mountain lions—'painters' they're sometimes called hereabouts—that hunt the area. Not too many left these days. All the same, watch out for them."

Fairfax knew the horse could smell a big cat long before he himself could see it. Grabbing the rope, he unlooped it from the birch, and holding the horse's bridle to check its rearing, he made for the cave. Just what he needed right about now was a mountain lion attack. Mountain lions, panthers, painters, cougars, pumas—or catamounts, as they were called down in his neck of the woods—they were all the same animal. The cats just assumed the entire country was their God-given territory. But maybe they should. Who was to say? Fairfax shrugged and allowed himself a tired smile.

Just ahead of him, the cave yawned more than large enough to let man and horse enter side by side, but a sudden growl overhead made Fairfax release the bridle and slap the nervous bay's flank to urge it ahead of him. Then he crooked his neck to look up at the outside roof of the cave. He straightaway sucked in his breath, not daring to move. It stood directly above him, large paws and long muscular legs beneath a massive creamy chest and triangular tawny head. Amber eyes outlined in black gazed at Fairfax with cool appraisal. Not for nothing were these animals called the consummate predators. The lion's heavily muscled shoulders began to slant toward the man, and its claws extended as if it were about to spring.

Fairfax lunged into the cave, where he sank to a crouch with his knife ready. The mountain lion leapt without effort, as graceful as a dancer, to a boulder beside the cave entrance and again stood motionless, staring unblinking at the man for what seemed an eternity. Then it glided off soundlessly in the direction of the creek. Not until it disappeared did Fairfax let out his long-held breath.

After remaining in a crouch until his legs ached, Fairfax finally rose, taking the precaution of another glance out the cave. No lion in sight. Unless cornered, the cats were ordinarily wary of men, so he was not overly concerned that it would return. He lit a globe lantern hanging from an upright railroad tie that abutted the cave roof, then went toward the rear of the deep cavern. He found the horse, still somewhat jittery, near the printing device that he'd discovered earlier.

The seven-foot-tall, lever-operated hand press made mostly of steel rested on four spindly cast-iron legs; one of these heron-like front legs had running through it a diagonal crack. Thus Fairfax eyed the press with misgiving and kept his distance—the weight of it could easily be more than a ton. It must have been brought into the cave piece by piece and assembled there.

The entire apparatus resembled a bookbinding press. Far from having anything to do with books, though, this press was used to print banknotes. Thin damp paper would be laid in the waist-high press bed, over a hand-engraved, rectangular copper printing plate that had been rolled with black ink, then pressed with a padded leather top plate by means of the lever. Fairfax had earlier removed the notes that had been placed to dry on a rack of narrow lath-like wood strips, as well as the notes to which a counterfeiter had added serial numbers and forged two signatures. Most of the notes were for two, three, or five dollars. They were now stowed in Fairfax's saddlebags. So were the ten-dollar gold eagle coins he'd found cached nearby in a heavy wooden chest along with the plaster molds for making the coins.

In the dim light of the lantern, Fairfax looked around one more time. Then he brought the horse forward to the front of the cave. After tethering the animal to the railroad tie, he pulled a watch from his trouser pocket. Two more hours before catching the New York Central Railroad train to take him and the evidence to Washington. Fairfax hoped in the meantime a counterfeiter would return—return to be captured, as such criminals were rarely if ever violent. With luck, it might even be the engraver, without whom the whole operation could fold.

Then it was home for Fairfax. Home at last, after days of tracking these thieves to their den. The trick now would be to stay awake. God, he was tired.

THIN GOLD BANDS of cloud that trailed the sunset had long since dulled. The North Star glittered like a beacon over the sleeping New York countryside, while darkness brought the chirp of crickets, the hoot of owls, and the rustle of other nocturnal predators. And to John Fairfax, grown increasingly tense as he waited inside the cave, every sound registered an alarm. Another look at his watch reassured him he wouldn't need to wait much longer for the train. It looked now as if the counterfeiters had somehow been warned, and they'd taken off.

The soft murmur of Painter Creek outside made him drowsy, and more than once Fairfax had to shake himself alert. Even had he dared to sleep, dreams of death would bring more torment than the minutes of rest would be worth. He couldn't remember when he had last slept without the dreams. He wondered if he ever would again.

Then, suddenly, from outside the cave came something that fell on his ears like shrieks of terror and the screech of iron wheels on iron track. Fairfax leapt to his feet. Fighting fatigue and fear that verged on panic, he struggled to see ahead to the cave entrance. The flickering light of the lantern showed him nothing. Maybe he dreamed after all. But behind him, and giving his fear reality, the horse snorted and reared on its hind legs, as its forelegs flailed the air in a pantomime of flight.

Fairfax shook off his dread and, drawing the knife from its sheath, once again crept forward to the boulders at the mouth of the cave. He squatted with the knife poised.

His racing pulse began to clear his mind. He then recognized the shrieks, growls, shrill whistles, and even, improbably, loud purring to be the mating cries of mountain lions. With a rush of expelled breath, he slumped against the cave wall, willing his heart to slow. Then, after attempting to calm the horse, he bent forward to listen. He thought he'd caught the sound of a train whistle. All he could hear now were the caterwauling lions, their noise like the back-fence yowling of domestic felines magnified tenfold.

The one he'd seen earlier must have found an eager partner. "The pair of them are probably right overhead," he muttered, gazing up at the cave roof, "having themselves a grand time." Relaxing slightly, Fairfax leaned against the wall, and he almost smiled.

Some minutes later the shrieks overhead diminished, in volume if not intensity, as though the cats were gradually moving away. They must be; the horse was quieting. Fairfax resumed his crouch. Not long after, the distant wail of a train whistle brought him to his feet. The mournful wails came one after another.

The cave lay two miles from the railroad crossing. It was nearly time to go. Fairfax reluctantly extinguished the lantern, which had provided as much solace as light, then stood staring into the blackness, hearing in the depths behind him the eerie ticking *whirr* of waking bats. He took several steps forward, inclining his head while he listened for other, less innocent sounds and rubbed his moist palms against the rough homespun of his trousers. Beside him, the horse nickered softly, though beyond the cave entrance the now quiet darkness seemed benign enough. Yet Fairfax found himself shifting his feet, troubled. It was not the cats. Something else, something that felt wrong.

Seeking reassurance, he reached into the breast pocket of his shirt to finger a small gold frame and the smooth oval of glass over an ivory portrait miniature. He did not withdraw it. There was no need. In his mind's eye the luminous watercolor image of the miniature surfaced: the fine features, a slope of lush breasts concealed by ruffles, and skin that surpassed the ivory itself. Beneath the glass of the miniature's reverse lay strands of fine hair that were the silvery brown of ash-tree bark and bound with gold thread. The portrait did not reveal the swelled belly that cradled an unborn child.

Fairfax let his fingertips stroke the spidery engraving on the frame: *"To my Johnny with Love."* He experienced a longing so intense it hurt him to draw breath.

Again the train's wail reached him, deeper and closer. The fingers that had caressed the miniature now fumbled for the bridle of his horse. Before Fairfax mounted, he carefully checked the leather saddlebags. He shrugged aside the gnawing anxiety as fatigue. Just tired nerves, and he should be used to them by now, but he had been jumpy ever since he got involved in this damn thing.

A glance from the cave's mouth assured him that clouds still covered the nearly full moon. After checking his saddlebags one last time, he swung himself astride and guided the horse forward. They emerged from the cave at the base of the boulder-strewn drumlin hill, cool night air bracing after the cave's dank warmth, and the smell of it sweet with the coming spring. The big cats were nowhere to be seen. Fairfax felt his confidence begin to return. Once shallow Painter Creek was crossed, he prodded the horse past the few final boulders to level ground. All seemed to be well.

Moments later a shaft of moonlight hurtled through the clouds, striking man and horse with its cold white beam. Fairfax winced, cursing his luck. He urged the horse eastward, and hunkered down over its neck as if that might conceal him, though he knew it was not likely—not while traveling an open sweep of greening fields.

At the crest of the next drumlin hill, and concealed by an outcrop of boulders, another man stood watching. He apparently saw that for which he had waited, since he plunged recklessly down the slope. His smile was one of satisfaction. After sidestepping more boulders at the base of the hill, he leapt to his horse, spurring the animal to a gallop. His horse was fresh and steadily gained ground on the bay.

When Fairfax heard the pounding hooves behind him, he jerked upright in the saddle, then quickly told himself it was happenstance. Simply another night-rider. He had been told that no one knew he was an agent, no one even suspected, so there could be no danger. Of what was he afraid? he had been asked with barely disguised scorn. He had not forced the issue further.

Fairfax twisted around in the saddle and recognized pursuit, although it was too dark to identify the pursuer. He could see just one horse being whipped forward by its rider, but there might be more. There was small chance of making it back to the village; Seneca Falls lay to the northwest a good three miles. And his horse, too tired to be ridden hard, had already begun to flag.

When Fairfax scanned the moon-washed surroundings for possible cover, he saw at some distance to the south the squat outline of the local militia armory. No doubt there would be a night watchman, another weapon at the very least. Fairfax turned the horse south while his right hand groped for the buckle of a saddlebag. He might be able to leave a message. As he yanked the bag open, coins spilled out over his wrist; involuntarily he leaned to one side to grab at them. The maneuver threw him off-balance. He heard a bullet wing over his head, then another fly past his shoulder. He righted himself intending to flatten his torso against the horse. Before he could do it, the next bullet found its mark.

The terrified bay galloped on with Fairfax slouched sideways in the saddle. In his mind the watercolor image swam through dizzying whorls of red. Blood spurted from the wound in his side and ran over his fingers as he fumbled with the buckle of the other saddlebag. Damn thing wouldn't give—he had to get it open. He clenched his teeth against the pain, holding on to consciousness, while he wrestled the bag open and thrust a hand inside. Then another bullet found him.

Some time later, after the bay horse had been unburdened of the saddlebags, it circled closely the figure splayed on the ground. Its muzzle lowered with nostrils dilating. The horse then lifted its head and called, a shrill keening cry, but shied away as, still gripped in the man's fingers, a banknote fluttered.

After searching the air for the scent of home, the horse veered northwest and loped toward the village of Seneca Falls. From beneath its hooves flew several gold eagle coins; they came to rest a short distance from the dying Treasury agent John Fairfax. Another banknote sailed upward. Then it slowly floated down like a dry crumpled leaf.

ONE

The Mint Act of April 2, 1792, originally written in the Senate, proposed that: . . . the reverses of the gold and silver coins were to bear the figure or representation of the eagle with the inscription THE UNITED STATES OF AMERICA.
—Q. DAVID BOWERS, THE HISTORY OF UNITED STATES COINAGE

MAY 1859

IT WOULD BE a hazardous passage. She might break an ankle. Possibly both ankles, which would be a steep price to pay for the gluttony aroused by the smell of fresh-baked bread. Thus did Glynis Tryon speculate, standing in laced high-heeled boots before the cobblestones that lay between herself and the promised land of the public market. That this scriptural allusion leapt so readily to mind surprised her, reminiscent as it was of a conservative Protestant upbringing she'd thought leavened by this time. But after scores of mind-dulling hours aboard the train from Illinois, and these served up with soggy sardine sandwiches and weak tea, the sudden aroma of the market's fresh bread had come to her as manna from heaven. There was no better, secular, way to describe it.

Glynis had left her niece Emma asleep on the train, and had climbed from the passenger car to the station platform to stretch her cramped limbs. It was there she had smelled the bread. She'd then walked through the elegant arches of the Rochester railroad terminal, and on a short block farther to the noise and bustle of the market. Where she now confronted the cobbled paving.

With reluctance Glynis lifted the long skirt of her silk day dress and several muslin petticoats to pick her way gingerly forward. Even with square heels this demanded the agility of a mountain goat. At last the cobblestones gave way to the market's less perilous brick paving.

She stepped to the bricks and paused to get her bearings. Directly in front of her stood a roan mare that regarded Glynis with eyes serene, while behind the horse a yellow-painted, four-spring dray wagon, mounded with fresh produce, was being unloaded by two farmers. Beyond them swirled the shoppers. They were mostly determined-looking farm women carrying deep wicker baskets, wearing plain white aprons over dresses of calico and checked gingham, sturdy flat-heeled shoes, and cloth sunbonnets with large protective ruffles in back to shade their necks. Or bright-colored kerchiefs they had tied like turbans.

As the day had dawned warm and sunny, the market also became the place in which to see and be seen. In consequence, there were younger women who merely strolled. They glanced coquettishly from under round-brimmed bonnets of lace and straw and ribbon, while their long flounced skirts over hoop-framed petticoats made them resemble noiselessly swinging bells. Their silk-fringed parasols bobbed overhead. Amidst the women—although not too close, due to the forbiddingly wide skirts—sauntered men in gray- or fawn-colored trousers, long flared redingotes, frock coats, or shorter box coats. These men, Glynis decided, looked much like leafless twigs of winter mingled with bright spring flowers.

At the far edge of the brick paving a man wearing a ragged straw hat—which from a distance made him resemble a scarecrow—stepped up onto a wooden crate and lifted a fiddle to his shoulder. He paused before playing, and appeared to send a searching glance over the shoppers. Then, tucking the instrument under his chin, he began a lively Irish jig. Young people instantly burst from the crowd, paired off, and began to dance to the music's compelling six-eight time. Glynis stopped to listen and watch the dancers, but was reminded of her mission when she smelled sausage. She could hear the sizzle of frying eggs from where farmers stood eating around barrel stoves, their deep laughter rolling over the sound of the fiddler. Perhaps, Glynis speculated, the farmers' good humor resulted from the coins jingling in the pockets of their overalls. Then the renewed fragrance of fresh bread swept all else from her mind.

She rose up on her toes to try to see, over the heads of those surrounding her, the location of the elusive bakery stall. Suddenly she found herself flailing to keep her balance. She'd been shoved from behind by a slender, well-dressed man who was looking back over his shoulder. His head swung around, and after a quick, mumbled apology, he rushed on past. For a moment Glynis watched him zigzag through the crowd, struck by his obvious agitation. He gave her the distinct impression that he was pursued. But she saw no pursuer, and the man himself soon disappeared among the shoppers.

She pivoted slowly, determined to find the bakery. Color and movement swirled around her like a kaleidoscope, but though she felt disoriented, she could still smell fresh bread. It had to be *somewhere* in the shifting patterns of this maze.

She went past crates displaying fresh rhubarb and asparagus, barrels of pickles, sausages and sides of smoked pork, and spring lamb suspended from hooks on stall roofs. At last, there it was: the bakery stall. Glynis managed to make her selection without much deliberation. After handing over her coins, she received not only a paper sack of sugared waffles from the jaunty young vendor, but a frankly admiring grin, which gave her an unexpected twinge of pleasure. She felt her cheeks redden, a response that hadn't occurred in some time, and quickly turned away. Shaking herself slightly in embarrassment as she opened the sack, she loosed a shower of powdered sugar. While she brushed at the white dust clinging to her dress, she heard behind her a soft, male chuckle. She smiled ruefully, conceding she had earned the chuckle, and took a bite of the warm buttery waffle. Then she glanced around for a clock. One in a nearby church tower revealed just enough time to return to the train before it departed for the last leg of the two-day journey home. She'd been away from Seneca Falls for close to a year. It felt more like half a lifetime.

Again attempting to rid herself of sugar dust, Glynis shook her skirts briskly, and once more glanced at the clock. To cover the remaining forty miles, with stops, would take at least another hour and a half; she should buy some more waffles for Emma, who was probably still asleep on the train. After turning back to the pastry table and opening her purse for coins, she felt herself suddenly forced up against the wooden slats of the stall by two men jostling past her. One she recognized—the slender man who had run into her earlier. Although their voices were muffled by the babble around them, it looked from their expressions and gestures as if they were arguing—rather heatedly, Glynis thought with a pang of misgiving. They halted a few feet beyond her.

Not the one she recognized but a mustached man—in shirtsleeves with cap pulled low over his forehead—suddenly grabbed the lapels of the other's immaculate gray frock coat and shoved him against the slats of the adjoining stall.

Glynis backed away, watching them and feeling at the same time alarmed and fascinated. The mustached man now stood with his back to her, but she had an unobstructed view of the other's angular, clean-shaven face. His eyes, clearly reflecting fear, swept past his assailant's shoulder and caught hers for a moment. She backed farther away, more alarmed but still curious. Suddenly the man facing her did something which made the mustached man double over with a sharp cry. The slender man twisted sideways, wrenching his frock coat from the other's grip, and disappeared into the crowd.

Glynis again found herself staring after him. All at once she remembered the time and swung back to the pastry table to pay for Emma's waffles. When she turned to leave, she saw that the mustached man had likewise disappeared. Weaving her way back through the market, she hurried toward the train station.

GLYNIS WALKED ALONG the platform to the second passenger car where she found others before her in line to board. While she waited she glanced around and saw—several yards down the platform—a handsome, elegantly dressed young man who looked vaguely familiar, although she couldn't place him. He stood with a strikingly beautiful woman. The woman's hand, held by her companion, was raised to his lips, and Glynis caught the glint of several large gold rings on her fingers. A gold filigree necklace that resembled a band of lace circled her throat. Several times the man started to walk toward the train steps, but returned again and again to take the woman's hand.

A polite cough behind Glynis made her realize she was holding up those in back of her. She went up the train steps, still wondering why the man on the platform looked so familiar. When she looked back, he still hadn't boarded.

She found her niece seated by the window, bent over her thin steel knitting needles, and Glynis slipped into the aisle seat beside her. Emma accepted the waffles with softly voiced thanks, and characteristic lack of enthusiasm, but did listen with some attention, or possibly just courtesy, to Glynis's account of the curious scuffle she had witnessed at the market.

"How strange," Emma murmured between bites of the waffle, and then made a face, as motion of the accelerating train caused the troublesome sugar to sprinkle her lace-trimmed gray dress. Glynis bit her lip, remembering her embarrassment at the vendor's, while nodding agreement with Emma's words. But she now questioned the wisdom of relating the disturbing incident. Emma still seemed so very frail.

Glynis began to unfold the Rochester *Times-Union* newspaper she'd bought on her way to the train. Then, instead of reading it, she laid her head back against the upholstered seat, and stole a sideways look at Emma—at the delicately boned profile, heart-shaped face, and wings of smooth dark-brown hair pulled back over her ears and into a neat coil at the nape of her neck. Glynis's hands went to her own topknot, where she sensed wisps of reddish hair were escaping with untidy abandon. She pushed a few loose hairpins firmly back in place, while Emma, as if realizing she was under observation, put down her knitting and turned to Glynis the large gray eyes that mirrored those of her aunt. Emma's brows lifted slightly in question, and she fingered the ivory lace of her collar.

Briefly touching her niece's pale cheek, Glynis smiled to reassure her, and looked beyond her through the window to the passing spring landscape. Clouds of white dogwood and wild cherry and the pink of wild plum flowed past. Alongside the track ran freshly tilled fields. Occasionally a farmer could be seen walking a furrow behind a horse and triangular iron plow.

"They aren't working the fields yet in Springfield," Emma murmured, following Glynis's gaze. "It must be warmer here."

Glynis didn't think New York winters were any shorter or

milder than those of Illinois, but didn't say this. Emma so rarely offered comment on anything that it seemed best not to disagree when she did.

Glynis took another quick glance at her niece, who had returned to her knitting. She wondered, once again, if uprooting Emma was a wise response to her despondency. But her father, Glynis's brother Robin, had thought it might be, and given the circumstances, Glynis agreed that something certainly needed to be done.

Several times in Springfield, Glynis had gone into her niece's bedroom and seen the silent dulcimer, which, she later imagined, had eyed her with rebuke—as if she would somehow overlook the sketches she then discovered beside it. Sketches of coffins, and black-robed figures in graveyards—even a gallows scene that made her skin crawl. As Emma had talent, though no interest in art for its own sake, the sketches had been vivid and more than a little unsettling. They had not been in the least concealed, but looked as if they'd deliberately been put on display. As if Emma, perhaps without realizing it, wanted them to be seen.

"But what can she be thinking of?" Robin had asked in alarm, after Glynis finally went to him with the sketches. She had hesitated for some time before she told her brother that what Emma was thinking seemed appallingly clear.

It was mostly for her niece's sake that Glynis extended what had been planned as a short visit into nearly twelve months. When she first arrived in Springfield, it quickly became obvious that Emma's mother—Robin's wife, Julia—was in failing health. And then, three weeks ago, the woman succumbed to the consumption she had suffered so long.

For a few days the two younger children grieved loudly. But they had long since grown accustomed to their mother's confinement; thus, finding their daily routine essentially undisturbed, and aided by the self-absorption of the young, they began to heal. Not so Emma. Silent, dry-eyed, she moved about the house as if nothing unusual had taken place. Her dulcimer remained silent. She spoke of her mother not at all, attended the funeral only at her father's insistence, and had not since visited the gravesite. It was as if, for Emma, the refusal to openly acknowledge death meant that it had not occurred.

Then came the sketches.

It was several days ago that Robin had asked, "Glyn, would you consider taking Emma back with you to Seneca Falls? For a time at least? She has a strong affection for you, always has. I've employed a housekeeper, and I think the younger children will be all right, but Emma . . ."

His voice had trailed off as if he couldn't bear to think of the consequences. And Glynis had agreed readily to his request. "Maybe," Robin had said then with palpable relief, "you could interest her in something . . . something other than clothes, that is, which are the only things she's enthusiastic about. But she can't exist on a dressmaker's pittance. Not if she doesn't marry, she can't. And she's dead set against that! Maybe you could talk to her about it, convince her that marriage is the only reasonable course for a woman—"

He had broken off with an embarrassed smile.

"No, Robin, I'm probably not the one to talk to Emma about marriage." And Glynis, too, had smiled.

"Have you ever been sorry, Glyn? That is, are you happy being unmarried?"

"Most of the time I'm content," she had said. Not always, she wasn't. "But that was my own choice," she had added, "and doesn't mean that Emma would be content unmarried. She doesn't seem as determined as I was to be independent."

The only way for a woman to achieve independence was to remain single. Glynis had gone to Oberlin College, and had become a librarian. But education did not appear to be a course in which Emma would be interested; the young woman showed no disposition whatsoever to spend more time in school than was required.

The whisper of Emma's steel knitting needles, which resembled stiff thin wire, now caught Glynis's attention, and she wondered what her niece was creating. But if the slowly increasing length of knitted silk—*very* slowly due to the fineness of its gauge—hadn't told her, the color did: stockings, of the same odd but attractive shade of dark garnet-hued brown as the day dress Glynis now wore. The one Emma had made for her in secret, using one of Glynis's other dresses as a pattern. Only when it was ready for the final fitting, a week ago, had Emma disclosed it.

Her work was flawless—though that wasn't surprising, because Emma had sewn expertly for years. Although Glynis at first had doubts about the color, to avoid wounding her niece she'd said only, "What an unusual shade of brown. I don't believe I've ever seen anything like it."

"No, you wouldn't have," Emma explained as Glynis slipped the dress over her head, and the diffident voice of her niece became a voice of authority. "It's *raisin d'Espagne*— new and very *chic*." Emma took a step back and cocked her head to scan the effect. "It's splendid, Aunt Glynis! You shouldn't wear so much black—*Godey's Lady's Book* says it's not fashionable this year."

Glynis, who had climbed onto a footstool so Emma could pin the unfinished hem, stood there gaping at her niece, who had just displayed more conviction, and certainly enthusiasm, than Glynis had ever hoped to hear from her. And the dress *did* look splendid, from its wide bishop's sleeves to the ruffled flounce at the hem.

"Just one, Aunt Glynis. I know you don't like ruffles, but flounces are *de rigueur*, so you must have at least *one*."

"I can see," Glynis had said by way of consent, "that you didn't neglect your French at school."

"No, I didn't." Emma had plucked another straight pin from the cushion tied to her wrist, then rocked forward on her knees to catch up the hem. "I wanted to read *Le Moniteur de la Mode,* and the other fashion magazines from Paris."

But *naturellement,* Emma's tone implied; didn't everyone study French for that reason?

Her father's evaluation had been correct. Emma was interested in clothes. Period.

And so, here they were, Glynis mused, with yet another glance at her niece: a librarian of forty-one and a seamstress all of seventeen, rolling along the rails toward Seneca Falls, where Glynis needed to face a situation she'd too long avoided. And where, perhaps, Emma might begin to loosen the grip of despondency.

*   *   *

FROM ROCHESTER, THE train headed southeast, and Emma
continued to knit while Glynis read the newspaper. The only
item that involved Seneca Falls was a report of an attempted
break-in at the Seneca County Militia Armory. A night watchman and another as yet unidentified man had been killed in the
attempt—the most recent in a series of armory break-ins and
weapon thefts in the area. The Seneca Falls attempt had been
thwarted by the constable, Cullen Stuart. Glynis put down the
paper and stared out the window, her thoughts on Cullen and
what might be his reaction to her return.

After a short stop at the resort town of Canandaigua, the train
turned east toward Seneca Lake and, at its head, the town of
Geneva.

"Ten years ago," Glynis told her niece, "Elizabeth Blackwell went to medical school in Geneva." Emma didn't respond.
The only sound was the soft click of the knitting needles.

"She was the first woman in America to become a physician," Glynis added, and now received a small, polite nod. She
tried again. "Since Dr. Blackwell, a small number of other
women have managed to become physicians, despite being
barred from most medical schools. And I think it's remarkable
that the majority of those women came from New York State.
There's a woman physician in Seneca Falls—well, you'll meet
Neva, Dr. Cardoza-Levy, soon enough."

She paused and waited. Finally Emma lowered the knitting
and turned to say in a soft voice, "I don't understand why
anyone would want to be a doctor. All they do is watch people
die. Besides, if it's not proper for women to go to medical
school—and Mama said it is not—then why would they want
to do it?"

Glynis caught her lower lip between her teeth. The last thing
she wanted was to argue with Emma, but she had heard this
kind of thing for nearly a year. And they weren't in Springfield
anymore. "I suppose," she said carefully, "that women want
to be doctors for the same reasons that men do."

Emma did not reply. And Glynis didn't press the issue further.

As the train left Geneva, she said only, "There's one more
stop, Waterloo, before Seneca Falls."

Again Emma nodded politely, but ignored the passing scene to concentrate on her knitting. Her niece's lack of interest did not prevent Glynis from experiencing her own surge of excitement. *Home.* After so long away, how much had changed?

She'd received letters, of course, from her landlady Harriet Peartree. Most of those had been simply chatty, reassuring Glynis that she was missed, and that her library was surviving under the care of her assistant, Jonathan Quant. Glynis had been sure it would. But that was before Jonathan had gone into mourning; while Harriet's letters usually didn't contain anything earthshaking, one carried the dreadful news that Aurora Usher had died.

Glynis could still scarcely believe it. Aurora had seemed a constant in life. Always there, always sweet and unassuming. Like Emma's mother, Aurora had died of consumption; or, as doctors were lately calling it, tuberculosis.

Glynis's thoughts were now interrupted by a loud noise at the far end of the railroad car. She glanced up and saw that the door had been flung open and was banging against the car wall. Just outside, on a wildly swaying platform between the car ahead and the one in which Glynis and Emma rode, two men stood facing each other. They looked antagonistic, but the clamor of the train wheels covered whatever they might have been saying.

All at once, after the train had rounded a curve of track, both men stumbled, then fell toward each other. Arms swinging, they grappled momentarily, then separated. One man lunged forward again, grabbed the other, slighter man by the shoulders and gave him a shove. His victim staggered backward, reaching out in a frantic attempt to catch the guardrail before being thrown from the train. Somehow he managed to grab hold of it and hang on. Glynis watched in horror as his assailant rained blow after blow on his hands to loosen his grip.

Suddenly she recognized the would-be victim as the slender, well-dressed man she had earlier seen accosted in the market. Although he wore the same gray frock coat, his current opponent had the denim trousers and shirt of a workman, and a battered, black, wide-brimmed hat. The only feature Glynis

could see of his face was a shaggy dark beard. And now, in
his hand, there appeared a long-bladed knife.

She glanced around, but the other passengers were just staring dumbly, apparently as horror-struck as she. Emma, too,
seemed paralyzed, except for her hands, which moved to knot
together in her lap. The bearded man raised his knife; then the
wicked-looking blade descended. With a howl that rose over
the noise of the train, the slender man let go the railing and
slumped forward on his knees. One arm shot up to ward off
another knife thrust. At that moment, the train's motion again
threw the attacker off balance; he lurched backward. The other
scrambled upright and gave his reeling attacker a desperate
shove. Then he grabbed for the doorjamb. The bearded man
tottered backward to disappear from view, and his quarry half-
fell through the doorway into the car.

Staggering as if he were intoxicated, he started down the
aisle. He'd made it halfway when behind him a woman
screamed. At the far end of the car, a bloodied hand was reaching for the door handle.

The slender man glanced back, saw his assailant appear with
raised knife, then turned to look frantically over the seated passengers. His eyes swept the car, went past Glynis, stopped, then
darted back. She saw in them a momentary flash of recognition.
Then he stumbled down the aisle toward her.

The left sleeve of his frock coat had been slashed and he
dripped blood with each step. His right hand fumbled in his
coat pocket. The bearded attacker followed him down the aisle.
Swaying from side to side with the motion of the train, man
and knife moved determinedly forward.

At this point, despite the rocking car and the swiftness with
which the fight had escalated, two male passengers managed to
climb from their seats as if to intervene. But they shrank back
when confronted by the bearded man's long blade. He flailed
the knife viciously, back and forth, until he slashed the back
of a leather seat. The leather split open like a ripe melon, and
stuffing of straw and cotton batting exploded upward, then descended like airborne seeds.

The victim now came level with Glynis. She raised terrified
eyes to his, and he held them for just an instant before dropping

in her lap what looked like a small leather tobacco pouch. With his hand on the back of her seat, he whispered something that sounded like, "The trouble's in Seneca Falls," then pushed himself farther down the aisle. By this time his pursuer was only five seat lengths behind. His knife still moving back and forth, he stumbled past Glynis. She tried to get a good look at him, but it happened so fast, his face was a blur except for the beard. The battered hat, pulled down over his forehead, concealed even his eyes.

While staring dumbfounded at the object in her lap, Glynis heard the car's rear door open. She spun around to see the wounded man slip through it onto the platform leading to the last car. Close behind was his assailant. For a moment there was only the deafening roar of the train wheels, then the car door slammed shut.

Over the rising cries and shouts of the other passengers, Glynis became aware of a bell ringing, and looked up to see several persons yanking the overhead alarm cords. But it seemed to her as if hours passed before the train actually ground to a stop.

She felt something tugging at her arm and glanced down. Her fingers had clamped themselves around Emma's hand. She took in her niece's frightened face, her gaze then going past Emma to the window to see where they had stopped. And she realized why it had taken so long. Beyond the window appeared the low wooden roof of the Waterloo station. The engineer, when he heard the alarm bell, had likely figured they were so close that he decided to continue to the station. Glynis desperately hoped this decision had not cost a man his life.

As passengers rushed toward the exit door, she released Emma's hand. "Are you all right?"

Hesitantly Emma nodded, then shook her head, then nodded again. Which, Glynis thought, was about as lucid an answer as she deserved. "I'm sorry, Emma, that was a stupid thing to say. Of course you're not all right!"

At this Emma nodded with more conviction. "Yes, I am, Aunt Glynis. But do you think they'll catch him?"

"The one with the knife?"

Another nod.

"I hope so, though I'm more concerned about the other man."

"That one looked as if he knew you," Emma said doubtfully, "but he couldn't have . . . could he?"

"He was the man at the public market, Emma—the one I told you was attacked. And he saw me, then, watching. So, yes, in a manner of speaking, he did recognize me."

Emma stared at her with eyes wide. "And the other man . . . ?"

"No, he wasn't the same one—the man at the market didn't have a beard."

Emma now looked pointedly at Glynis's lap. "What *is* that?"

Startled, Glynis realized she'd all but forgotten the leather pouch. She lifted it from her skirt. "I don't know—"

She broke off as a man she assumed was the Waterloo stationmaster, followed by the engineer, came through the door of the car. Outside the window, porters could be seen herding passengers toward the train.

The stationmaster addressed those still seated. "Did any of you see what happened after the two men left this car?"

A unit of shaking heads answered. The stationmaster started down the aisle, asking each person the same thing. As he drew near, Glynis impulsively tucked the pouch under the folds of her skirt. She felt Emma's gaze and turned to her niece with a shake of her head. Emma remained silent.

While passengers moved up and down the aisle, Glynis felt a strong reluctance to remove the pouch from where she had concealed it. There were no law enforcement officers present, and she thought the pouch should be protected until one showed up. With luck, it might even be Cullen Stuart.

When the stationmaster moved on to the next car, Glynis estimated it had been close to fifteen minutes since they'd stopped. Her fingers curled around the small pouch under her skirt folds. She could feel inside it two hard objects. Aching for a look at them, she began surreptitiously drawing it forth, when some sort of commotion broke out on the station platform—several loud shouts, followed by a medley of agitated voices. Glynis nudged Emma, who immediately understood and casually slipped her hand under Glynis's skirt, then slid the pouch across the seat until it lay hidden under her own skirt. Looking straight ahead the whole time, she gave a slight nod when the transfer was complete.

Glynis, somewhat bemused by Emma's cool complicity, left her seat and walked to the door of the car, where below her stood the stationmaster, the engineer, and several porters involved in an intense discussion. The stationmaster then announced, with tones so emphatic that Glynis could hear, "O.K., I'll send a wire ahead. Constable in Seneca Falls, he can meet the train. And since there's no one here has the authority to deal with this . . ."

Glynis missed the end of it as his voice lowered. The group now broke up quickly, and a stubby, round-faced porter came aboard to wave her back to her seat. Shortly thereafter the train pulled out.

Glynis waited, as did Emma, until they were well under way for the six-mile trip east to Seneca Falls. She glanced over the car, then turned to Emma and gestured. Out came the pouch, while Glynis turned sideways in her aisle seat to obstruct the view of any passerby, and Emma, at her aunt's nod, pulled apart the drawstring opening. With a puzzled look, the young woman drew forth what appeared to be a crumpled banknote, then upended the pouch to pour numerous flakes of tobacco and two bright objects into her aunt's open palm. One was a heavy coin, and Glynis disregarded it for the moment to examine the other, a large signet ring, the carved agate set into a gold band.

"It isn't a cameo," she whispered rhetorically.

To her surprise, Emma whispered back, "No, I don't think so," while her fingers reached out to trace the heraldic shield that had been engraved below the flat surface of the agate. Emma now said more confidently, "I think it's called *intaglio*."

Glynis raised her eyebrows, then handed the ring to her niece. After glancing over Glynis's shoulder to check the aisle, Emma turned the ring toward the window. Heads close together, both squinted at the carving: a pointed Norman shield on which the profile of a bear appeared. Rearing on its two hind legs, the bear had its forelegs raised, one above the other, as if ready to deliver a blow.

"That bear's stance—it's called the rampant position," Emma said quietly.

Glynis was impressed. Then she remembered the heraldry manual in her library, and said, "I've read that lions or stags are common. But I've not heard of bears being used—although they might be in Berne, Switzerland," she added, recalling their recent stop in Geneva.

"I guess they're not usual," Emma agreed with a shrug.

"So why—never mind, Emma. Look inside the band to see if there's any engraving."

Emma turned the ring, squinted inside the band, then handed it to her aunt. Glynis, after herself checking the aisle behind, held up the ring and found the date "1820," and the words "Yale College."

"What do you think?" Emma asked. "Could it be a family ring with the coat of arms?"

"I don't know," Glynis replied. "There's a volume in my library that identifies English family crests—and a lawyer in town who went to Yale. But until we get to Seneca Falls . . ." She dropped the ring back into the pouch. Then she smoothed the crumpled note. It had been issued by the Bank of Central New York in Utica for ten dollars. Glynis turned it over several times, but finding nothing out of the ordinary, she then picked up the coin. It was a twenty-dollar gold piece.

"A double eagle," she murmured.

TWO

❧

The eagle or $10 gold piece, first minted in 1795, was America's largest denomination until the advent of the double eagle in 1850.

— Q. DAVID BOWERS, *UNITED STATES*
GOLD COINS: AN ILLUSTRATED HISTORY

AFTER ANOTHER GLANCE about the passenger car to make certain she would be unobserved, Glynis Tryon tucked the leather tobacco pouch deep inside her carpetbag, concealing it under books and a wool shawl. Emma said nothing during this procedure, and her face revealed little about how she viewed her aunt's intentions.

"I'll turn it over to the constable," Glynis whispered in explanation, "when we get to Seneca Falls." Emma merely nodded.

When Glynis had asked, the moonfaced porter refused to talk about the condition of the injured man. She wondered if he had even survived the brutal attack. An attack apparently begun— by a different assailant—in the Rochester public market. And what about the contents of the pouch he had for some reason dropped in her lap? The banknote and gold coin seemed ordinary enough, but the ring surely was not. Perhaps all would be made clear when the man's identity was known.

The final miles rolled by. Close upon freshly tilled fields, the first outlying houses of Seneca Falls appeared. In the meantime, Emma had stowed her needles and skeins of silk in her knitting bag and, although silent, gave more attention to the passing scene than she had previously done.

During their two-day trip from Springfield, Glynis had attempted to acquaint her niece with the approaching western New York village, trying to recall from her own girlhood just what excited a seventeen-year-old girl's interest. It was an effort. She steered Emma's attention to the Seneca River, running in a shallow channel with gentle slopes on either side. The river flowed around small islands, where it became the Cayuga and Seneca Canal, dividing the village of Seneca Falls north and south. Through the village the canal banks were walled, while east of town the river swung north to join the Erie Canal system. As the train drew nearer, Glynis pointed out packet boats hauled by mule teams plodding the clay and gravel towpath as they made their way through the Waterloo lock. Her niece appeared indifferent.

Along the towpath swayed aspen and birch with newly green leaves fluttering in a soft spring wind. The wind came not only off the river but from nearby Seneca and Cayuga Lakes as well. The village of Seneca Falls and the Seneca County seat of Waterloo sat between these two slim bodies of water. All the Finger Lakes had been formed, so legend said, when the hands of the Iroquois' Great Spirit once pressed upon the earth. But geologists reasoned that the lakes' elongated north-south beds were gouged by retreating polar ice sheets, which, in an earlier age, had covered most of western New York.

"I myself have always liked the Iroquois version better," Glynis said.

"I do, too," Emma unexpectedly agreed. "What do you think might be on those boats down there?"

"The packet boats? Could be they've come from New York City," Glynis guessed, restraining a smile, "and they might be carrying dry goods, such as, oh, things like hats and shoes and bolts of fabric . . ."

"Fabric?" said Emma, her attention riveted on the canal. "That's right, you mentioned a dress-making shop in town."

"It just recently opened. My landlady wrote that soon after I left for Springfield, a store on Fall Street—that's our main thoroughfare—went up for sale. As luck would have it, the store was directly next door to the widow Coddington's millinery shop. So Fleur Coddington purchased the vacant space, and she's apparently expanded her business to include dressmaking."

Immediately Emma turned to her with a look of eagerness. "Do you think she might need someone to do piecework?"

Caught unprepared, Glynis shook her head. "I've no idea."

The carelessness of this response was evident as Emma's shoulders drooped, and just as she had begun to show enthusiasm. Glynis hastily added, "But you certainly can ask her—Fleur Coddington, that is—and see what she says."

This brought from Emma only an apathetic murmur. And Glynis, with the stark memory of her own youthful shyness, imagined the prospect of asking a stranger for work would be too intimidating for Emma to even consider.

Steam puffs from the train engine grew farther apart as it gradually slowed. Ahead Glynis saw the small, brick railroad station of Seneca Falls. And the chimneys and church spires of home.

THE TRAIN HISSED to a full stop. Glynis craned her neck to see the platform where a group of men were gathered. To her pleasure, the first familiar face she found was that of Zephaniah Waters, Cullen Stuart's muscular young Negro deputy. A lively alertness overlaid Zeph's usual somber expression, though he rocked back and forth on his feet with typical impatience. Glynis smiled with affection. While over the past months, several letters had passed between them, she hadn't realized until now how much she had missed Zeph.

"Aunt Glynis, who's *that?*" Emma asked, indicating the rangy man just emerged from the station house. Glynis watched as Cullen Stuart approached the train, the short-legged station-master beside him nearly running to keep up. Seeing Cullen again provided more of a jolt than she'd reckoned on, and her vision instantly blurred. She reached into her sleeve for a hand-kerchief, but while dabbing surreptitiously at her eyes, she managed to keep her tone casual. "That's Constable Stuart."

"Oh, yes," Emma said, and Glynis caught her sidelong glance. "You got some letters from him."

Some letters. Yes, Glynis supposed they could be called that; short notes in Cullen's firm uniform handwriting, they had contained nothing much more than perfunctory wishes for her continued good health. As if she were someone he had met only briefly, and to whom he owed some brief acknowledgment. No mention of the years, the many years, they had known each other. One would never guess, for instance, that Cullen

had once asked her to marry him. And he referred not at all to
their estrangement, occurring some weeks before she left for
Springfield; the estrangement which had been, in fact, the reason she'd left. She had needed time to think things through, if
she could, and to put some distance between herself and those
in Seneca Falls.

But then she had found her brother's wife so seriously ill,
her brother himself distraught, and Emma clearly troubled: it
was not a circumstance from which one could walk away. At
least, *she* could not. And she rejected out of hand the idea posed
in a letter from her friend Neva Cardoza-Levy, one that suggested Glynis had discovered, in Springfield, the perfect excuse
not to confront her dilemma.

Just then, Emma, who'd been gazing out the window, said
shyly over her shoulder, "Constable Stuart's very good-
looking, Aunt Glynis." In Glynis's state of mind, this sounded
to her vaguely like a reproach, although Emma's opinion did
not differ from most women's.

Glynis looked down to the platform where Cullen stood talking to the engineer and porters. Even in the sunlight, his thick,
sand-colored hair showed as yet no gray. His mustache still
looked as soft and shaggy as she remembered. The lines that
weather had creased in his face emphasized what Neva Cardoza-Levy referred to as his "Texas Ranger" look. When
Glynis had inquired as to just where the young woman from
New York City might have seen a Texas Ranger, Neva had
retorted, "Those popular magazines in your own library!"

Glynis turned her gaze from Cullen and sought Zeph. He
stood some feet away, positioned at the bottom of the passenger
car's steps. His square jaw was set while his jet eyes combed
the train cars. It looked to Glynis as if no one was being allowed to get off. She rose and moved to the window to see the
car behind. Guarding those steps was a young man who, from
his red hair and abundant freckles, must be a member of the
town's multitudinous Cleary clan. She could see no one leaving
the first car either. Were they all being held there like prisoners?

While the passengers fidgeted, arguing among themselves as
to when they might be allowed to leave, from behind the station
came the clattering wheels of a dray wagon drawn by a big-

footed draft-horse. Glynis and Emma watched it pull up to the steps of the car behind them. Several men jumped from the wagon and, carrying a canvas stretcher, boarded the third car. Minutes later they emerged, the stretcher sagging with the motionless blood-soaked body of the slender, gray-suited man. Glynis sat down abruptly.

Beside her, Emma gave a small moan. She quickly covered her mouth with her hands, then hunkered down into the seat. "If you feel faint, drop your head between your knees," directed Glynis, torn between concern for her niece and the scene outside.

Emma shifted, and then straightened. "I'll be all right," she said, the words muffled behind her hands. "I'm not going to faint, or something silly like that." She stated this with a remote expression, as disturbing in its lack of emotion as it had been the day of her mother's funeral.

"It's not silly to be distressed, Emma. *I* certainly am!"

"Perhaps so, but I'm *not*." And it was true that Emma, now looking straight ahead, showed no anxiety. Not reassured by this, Glynis gave her niece worried scrutiny before she got up again to look out the window. The stretcher was being hoisted into the wagon.

Cullen motioned to the driver. The wagon rattled over the cobblestones as it headed, Glynis guessed, toward Fall Street and the office of Dr. Quentin Ives. As she stood there at the window, watching the wagon depart, something made her glance down. On the platform below, Cullen Stuart stood gazing directly up at her. He passed a hand over his eyes, as if not quite believing what he saw, then disappeared up the train steps.

He reappeared seconds later, and came quickly down the aisle toward her, then stopped just a few feet away. Even at that distance she could smell his pipe tobacco and the clean spicy scent of the soap he used. She concealed her hands, inexplicably trembling, in the folds of her skirt.

"Glynis . . ." He paused, as though he'd forgotten what he was going to say. His eyes, dark and unreadable, didn't leave her face. "I had no idea you were coming back," he said. "Coming back now, that is."

"No," Glynis agreed, "no, you wouldn't have . . . any idea, I mean." They stood there, looking at each other, and Glynis had the sensation of blood leaving her head—somewhat akin to the canal being drained prior to the winter freeze. Then someone in the car coughed sharply. Cullen moved his shoulders, almost as if shaking himself, and crossed his arms over his chest. He casually leaned back against a seat before he asked, "Did you see what happened here? To him?" He motioned toward the departing wagon.

Glynis lowered herself to the seat. "Yes, we saw him being chased through the train. I guess he's . . . is he . . . ?"

"Yes," Cullen said. "Yes, he's dead."

A quick intake of breath beside her made Glynis realize she'd forgotten her niece. Emma, deathly pale and remoteness gone, was gaping at Cullen with large frightened eyes.

"Cullen, this is my niece, Emma Tryon, and I think she needs some fresh air. Probably everyone does," she added, gesturing at the surrounding passengers, some of whom nodded their agreement vigorously. But as they began to rise, Cullen motioned them back into their seats.

"Sorry, folks, but we have to keep you here. It shouldn't be too long." It was typical of him. The easy manner belied the fact that, when he chose, he could wield power as harshly as anyone. But harshness was rare, and ordinarily Cullen wore his lawman's badge lightly. It was one of the things about him that Glynis respected.

With some unhappy muttering, most of the passengers remained seated. When one woman began to complain, Cullen said to her, "We need to ask a few questions, ma'am. Just your name and place of residence—so we can get in touch if we need to. Nothing to fret about." His languid smile accompanied this, and the woman seemed quite satisfied. Indeed, she now appeared ready if necessary to sit there all afternoon.

"Please, Aunt Glynis, I really do need some air." The plaintive voice made Cullen turn to study Emma.

"Yes, I know you do," Glynis replied. "We've had a long trip from Illinois, Cullen. When do you think we might get off this train?"

Cullen leaned over Emma to peer out the window. "Soon

as we question everybody on the last car," he said, straightening and turning to the other passengers. "You folks will be next."

To Glynis he said quietly, "You and your niece can leave, but wait for me by the station house." When Glynis reached for her carpetbag, Cullen added, "I'll see you, soon as I finish here. So far nobody in that last car, or probably this one either, knows anything useful—like the dead man's name, for instance. He didn't have any identification on him. Of course, it's possible nobody'll admit to knowing anything even if they do."

"I may have something, Cullen, that could be of use." His eyebrows shot up, and Glynis went on quickly, "But I think it can wait. Please let me get Emma out of here."

She'd immediately regretted saying anything, because for a moment it looked as if he would refuse. But although he frowned slightly, he gave her a short nod. "All right—so long as you're sure that whatever it is can wait."

For a second, Glynis had the nagging sense she'd forgotten something. It passed, however, and she gestured for Emma to follow her. It wasn't until they'd reached the platform, and she saw people waiting to board, that she remembered.

She hurriedly told Emma to wait by their baggage. When she turned back to their car, Cullen, who had apparently watched her from the window above, appeared at the top of the steps. At the same time, Glynis saw that passengers on the last car were being allowed to leave. Some had already headed toward the street. They included the young man she'd seen on the platform in Rochester—the elegantly dressed one so reluctant to leave the woman with the gold jewelry.

As Cullen came toward her, Glynis gestured at the man's back. "Who is that, do you know, Cullen?"

"It's Alan Fitzhugh, the new dentist in town. Alan *junior*—remember his father?"

"So that's why he seemed familiar." Glynis now looked carefully at each departing person. "I've just recalled, Cullen, that no one got on the train at the stops between Rochester and here. No one. So the killer must have either boarded at Rochester, or some stop before that."

"You mean you saw him?"

"Everyone on the train, or at least in my car, saw him." She described what little she'd viewed of the bearded man with the battered hat. "And he couldn't very well have gotten off at Waterloo," she went on, "or someone would have seen him leaving. As I said, the entire car saw him attack that poor man. And while people did dash off the train in a panic when we stopped, the stationmaster and porters herded them all back on. At least, I think they did."

Cullen nodded. "Yes, I asked about that. The engineer and porters swore nobody from the train had left the vicinity of the Waterloo station." However, he looked as dubious as she herself probably did. But suddenly his eyes went past her. "Glynis, see him—over there?" He gestured toward another departing passenger, a sturdily built, middle-aged man with curly graying hair. "Did you see him get on in Rochester?"

Glynis shook her head. "But I easily could have missed him. Especially since he was in the last car. Why, who is he?"

"Name's Valerian Voss. He moved back to town about the time you left. He's originally from around these parts, but he'd been living for some years in San Francisco. And now he's vice-president of Farmers and Merchants Bank."

Again she shook her head. "Well, I guess the killer either somehow escaped without anyone noticing, or he was still on board when we pulled in here." That thought sent an unpleasant sensation down her spine.

"And he's already long gone," Cullen said. "We did find an open window in the back of that last car. So, he could have jumped off the rear of the train as it pulled in, although I was watching for that." And he shrugged as if to say, Who knows?

Glynis surely didn't know, and gripped her carpetbag with both hands, since it contained the only information, albeit slim, they had about the murdered man.

"I'll see you in a few minutes," he said. "Right now I want to keep an eye on these passengers."

When Cullen went back up the train steps, Glynis hurried toward the station house, in front of which porters were piling baggage onto a growing mountain of trunks, band boxes, barrels, satchels, crates, cartons, and carpet bags. With some difficulty, Glynis located Emma. She had crouched beside a wooden crate overflowing with wads of soft fleece; some of it had fallen out at her feet to resemble small drifts of snow. Emma was in the process of returning to the crate a trapezoidal-shaped, hinged case. As she carefully tucked the fleece back around it, a satisfied expression indicated that her dulcimer had arrived safely. But then she stood up, casting her eyes over the baggage. By the time Glynis reached her, Emma's expression had changed to one of concern.

"I don't see it, Aunt Glynis. Almost everything seems to have been unloaded," she motioned toward the train, "but I haven't found my sewing machine."

"Oh, it must be here," Glynis told her, looking around herself. "You saw it put on the train in Springfield."

"I know, but what if someone took it, or—" She broke off as porters dragged a large packing case off the train, then heaved it unceremoniously to the platform. "Careful of that!" Emma cried, rushing toward the porters. "It's not very heavy, but it's fragile!"

She hovered nervously beside the men, wheedling and coaxing them to "Please be careful—please!" while they carried the cumbersome packing case to one of the side-seated, four-wheeled platform wagons used to convey passengers and baggage. When they'd finally deposited the machine, after removing a back seat of the wagon, the porters looked no less relieved than did Emma.

While watching this, Glynis concluded there was hope for her niece; that evidently Emma's reticence could be overcome if the inducement was strong enough. That had been true of Glynis's own shyness—although it still surfaced often enough to distress her.

"Miss Tryon?" Glynis turned at the low-pitched, familiar voice and found Zeph Waters coming toward her.

Glynis took several steps forward to meet him, but then stopped a few feet short. Her impulse had been to embrace him. But white women did not embrace black men. At least not with others looking on, they didn't. No matter their ages—separated by decades, Zeph's and hers. No matter how long they had known each other—since he'd been a troubled boy. Or how great their affection. Thus Glynis extended her hand.

"I'm glad to see you, Zeph—we'll talk later. Right now I have to find a way to get my niece and myself home." He stepped aside to let her pass, and she whispered, "I'll give you a more enthusiastic greeting later."

With a smile, unusual for him, Zeph just nodded. He knew the rules even better than she. "I can drive you," he said. "You going to Mrs. Peartree's boardinghouse?"

"Yes. Could you, Zeph?"

"Right, let me ask the boss." He moved toward the train just as Cullen again came down the steps, shoving a notebook into his trouser pocket.

Zeph said a few words to him. "Yes," Cullen said to Glynis as they walked toward her, "yes, Zeph can take you. So," he said when he stood beside her, "what have you got for me?"

Glynis glanced at the people milling around the station house. "I think we should find somewhere a little less public. And Zeph, would you please go and introduce yourself to my niece, Miss Emma Tryon? She's over there by the wagon with her sewing machine, and I know she won't leave it, not for a minute. I'll be along shortly."

Zeph started toward the wagon, while Cullen guided Glynis around the side of the building. It felt strange, Cullen's hand on her arm, after all this time. She recalled, with a twinge of nostalgia, that he was one of the few men who could walk beside a woman—walk as closely as he did now—without tangling himself in petticoats and full skirts. He looked down at her and, apparently thinking the same thing, said, "You haven't changed your mind about those contraptions."

Glynis smiled. He must mean the fashionable hoops; whalebone, wire, or—the most recent—steel watch-spring hoops known as cages. They were designed to swell skirts to dimensions rounder and fuller than could even multiple, starched or crinolined petticoats. "No, Cullen, I said I wouldn't wear hoops. I meant it. I'm told that the New York City omnibuses are getting so crowded with billowing skirts that they've raised certain of their prices. There are now signs saying 'Ladies with Hoops, twelve cents.' "

"Those things *are* damned silly," he said with disgust.

"Women won't even be able to walk if their skirts get much bigger. They're dangerous."

"I know," Glynis agreed. "And at least twice in Springfield, which is more fashionable than Seneca Falls, I heard of women being horribly burned. They were standing with their backs to fireplaces, and their skirts caught fire. They didn't even know they were ablaze until too late."

Cullen shook his head, but surprisingly refrained from further comment on feminine vanity. He had let go of her arm and now walked less closely to her. Glynis wondered if the distance was purposeful. She had missed Cullen. Perhaps, as with Zeph, she hadn't realized just how much. But after all, when she left Seneca Falls the bond between them had been severely strained.

When they reached the rear of the station house, Cullen gestured to a slatted wooden bench. And Glynis related what she had first seen of the murdered man: her impression in the market that he was fearful of pursuit, the subsequent scuffle at the bakery stall, and, finally, what had occurred on the train. Then she drew the tobacco pouch from her carpetbag.

"He just dropped this in my lap, Cullen," she said, handing it to him. "He'd seen me before, in the market, and I may have been the only person on the train he recognized. If he feared for his life, perhaps it's a hastily constructed clue to his killer. But who was he? And why on earth would they—two men— want to kill him?"

Cullen shook his head, and studied the banknote, the ring, and the double eagle coin he now had in his hand. "Don't know yet. Only thing we do know is that his frock coat had a label from a Utica tailor. And now there's this banknote from the Bank of Central New York in Utica. Could be he was on his way there."

"Perhaps that's where his home was," Glynis ventured.

"I'll check with the Utica constable's office, see if they've got a missing person's report on him. It's about all I can do right now." Cullen hefted the ring and coin, tossing them back and forth in his hands several times. "Weight feels like they're real gold," he said. "Got any ideas about them? About why a total stranger, fearing he'd be killed, would turn them over to you?"

"Only the reason I just gave, and what Emma and I discussed on the train. Since the ring has 'Yale College' engraved inside, I thought Jeremiah Merrycoyf might offer some explanation. Remember, he went to law school there."

"Good idea." Cullen held up the ring to look inside the band. "I'll ask Merrycoyf and the other lawyer—oh, that's right. You wouldn't know him."

"Who?"

"New man in Merrycoyf's law office—besides Adam MacAlistair, that is. By the way, did you know Merrycoyf made young MacAlistair his partner?"

"Both Harriet and Neva wrote to tell me, yes. But who is the new man?"

"Name's Doggett—Cyril Doggett. Law school classmate of Merrycoyf's. Landed in town about four months ago. He's not a partner yet in Merrycoyf and MacAlistair—" Cullen gave a smile to this weighty name "—but I expect he will be. And since he went to Yale, too, I'll ask him about this." He again looked inside the band. "Could be this man was simply worried about being robbed."

"Well, I think the double eagle is genuine enough. But to kill a man for twenty dollars?" She shook her head. She didn't believe it.

Cullen had turned to look squarely at her. "How do you know the coin is genuine? Why not counterfeit?"

"Well, of course, I can't be absolutely certain." She took the coin from him, bouncing it in her hand. "It's heavy enough for gold. The gold-washed brass commonly used by counterfeiters is lighter—has a different feel to it." She turned the coin over and studied its reverse side. "And this coin really looks all right."

She stopped because Cullen was staring at her in bewilderment. "You don't remember, do you, that I know a little something about coinage?" she asked him.

"Wait a minute," Cullen said, his face beginning to clear. "Wasn't there something about an uncle of yours, went to California during the 'forty-nine gold rush?"

"Yes." Glynis smiled, recalling her uncle with affection. "My father's brother, Ned Tryon. He did go west, but he didn't find the fortune in gold that he planned on. He ended up in San Francisco . . .'' She paused and looked narrowly at Cullen.

"Yes, I told you Valerian Voss lived in San Francisco.'' He shrugged. "So have thousands of other people.''

"Not from around here,'' Glynis commented, but then went on, "Anyway, Uncle Ned eventually became a banker there. Over the past years he's sent me a number of small coins— half dimes and three-cent pieces—which I've saved, and I have a few of the old copper pennies that were discontinued several years ago. And while I was in Springfield, my nephew Peter— he's Emma's younger brother—began collecting copper half cents, so I bought Hickcox's *Historical Account of American Coinage,* published last year in Albany. Then, seven or eight months ago, Uncle Ned went to work for the San Francisco Mint, and for my birthday he sent me a double eagle that was struck there. Here, Cullen, look at this.''

She stretched out her hand, palm open with the dead man's coin. "See the tiny *o* on the reverse? It's right under the eagle's tail, and above the word 'TWENTY.' That *o* means this particular double eagle was coined at the Mint in New Orleans. The 'o' is for Orleans,'' she explained. "If, on the other hand, it had been coined at the Mint in San Francisco, it would carry a small *s*. If it had been coined at the Dahlonega Mint in Georgia, it would have a—''

"A *d* for Dahlonega,'' Cullen broke in. He fished in his trouser pocket and extracted several coins. Sorting through them, he picked out one and handed it to her. "What about that? No mintmark at all.''

"That's because it's from the Philadelphia Mint,'' Glynis explained. "It was the first United States mint, and, for a time, the only one in operation, so it didn't need a mark to designate its coins. The other mints' marks are to avoid confusion with Philadelphia. Except I'm not sure that all the mints coin the double eagles.''

"Can you find out?'' Cullen asked.

"Yes, I think I know of someone I can ask, but I am sure about New Orleans. And this coin that belonged to the dead man. Like all coins, it's dated.'' She turned it over. "This is the obverse side. See the date, right below the head of Liberty—1856?''

"The date it was minted."

"Yes, and that's fine in this case. But if it had been a date older than 1850, it would *not* be fine. It would be counterfeit."

She waited for his question, hoping she wasn't sounding too full of herself.

"O.K.," Cullen said, grinning. "Why would it be counterfeit?"

"Because double eagles didn't exist before 1850—that was the first year the denomination was struck!"

"How did you learn *that?*"

"I really don't know all that much," she said. "However, I do know where to go for answers—or rather, who the experts are, because just last year the American Numismatic and Archaeological Society was formed. And there's a coin collectors' group in Philadelphia. But, Cullen, now I think I'd better go and find Emma. We can talk about this again."

She looked at him, expecting a comment or two, something like, "Sure we can" or "How about tomorrow?" What she got was silence. A silence that lengthened until it became embarrassing.

Glynis didn't know what else to say, and Cullen just sat there bouncing the ring and coin in his hand. Finally, he dropped them back into the pouch. The silence stretched on. This was the first time they'd been alone together, Glynis realized, since resolution of the tragic events of a year before. Events that involved not only the Black Brook Reservation north of the village, but Cullen's former deputy, the half-blooded Seneca Indian, Jacques Sundown. And shortly after that, she'd left Seneca Falls.

But it appeared that Cullen wasn't going to bring up their past, because he got to his feet, sliding his hands into the pockets of his denim trousers, then stood idly staring off at the sky. He behaved as if being with her made him uncomfortable. Had he been like this earlier? There was so much going on, she might not have noticed.

She rose and said, "Cullen, don't you think there's something that we—"

"Got to go along to Doc Ives," he broke in, "and see if an autopsy will cast some light on the dead stranger." He took a few steps and turned, looking back as if he'd suddenly remembered she was there. He still said nothing. And although she felt bewildered by the distance he'd imposed between them, and disturbed by the memories she'd just awakened, Glynis didn't know what else to do but walk beside him—no hand on her arm now—around to the front of the station house.

What should she have expected? That she would return after a year's absence, and she and Cullen would just pick up where they had left off? Which, for that matter, was where—where *had* they left off? She didn't even know that.

She was troubled enough that she didn't look at Cullen, didn't know if he still walked somewhere beside her or not. She kept her eyes on the stones underfoot, and headed in the direction of the baggage wagon, where she hoped Emma and Zeph were still waiting. Then, without warning, her ankle turned. The heel of her boot had slipped between the stones, and when she stumbled, it was Zeph, not Cullen, who caught her arm to steady her. At that point, she glanced around. Cullen was already astride his black Morgan, and as he rode off in the direction of Fall Street, he did not look back.

THE WAGON JOUNCED over the railroad tracks, causing Emma to throw a dark look at Zeph, who was driving; with her dulcimer case awkwardly cradled on her lap, she braced both of her laced boots against the packing case to steady it. I.M. SINGER & CO. was etched on a silver-colored plate fastened to one side of the case, the side that would face the one sewing, because it had been designed to double as a table on which the machine would sit.

Months ago, Emma had purchased her Singer for one hundred and twenty-five dollars—Glynis still wondered from where this considerable amount had come—when the innovative, relatively lightweight, family model had first been offered for sale. When the Singer machines had initially appeared, early in the decade, they were heavy cumbersome affairs intended only for use in factories. Glynis had recently read, though, that demand for the new machines, nicknamed "turtle backs," was

enormous. During a protracted and highly publicized legal battle over patent rights between Isaac Singer and inventor Elias
Howe—who had built the first unsophisticated machine—the
market for all sewing machines had mushroomed. From a handful sold before 1850, there had been over a hundred thousand
manufactured in the last year by seventy-some American companies.

But Singer's, although one of the most expensive, was generally considered to be the best.

"Could you please go a little slower?" Emma now called to
Zeph. He threw an amused glance over his shoulder at Glynis;
the horse was *walking,* the glance seemed to say. Glynis raised
her hands to him, palms upward, in a plea for patience. But
when they rounded the corner from Clinton Street, Emma leapt
forward, the dulcimer case sliding from her lap, as the sewing
machine's packing case began to rock. After steadying it, she
returned to the seat, retrieved the scuttled dulcimer, and sucked
at knuckles scraped by the wagon's rough floor. The back of
Zeph's shoulders received a withering glare.

As they left the station, Zeph had asked if they would mind
going a few blocks out of their way. He needed to deliver
several packages of patent medicine, come on the train from
Rochester, to Dr. Neva Cardoza-Levy's recently opened Clinton Street refuge and clinic for homeless women and their children. Glynis had agreed readily, despite the small frown of
fatigue that shirred Emma's straight dark brows.

"It's just around the corner," Glynis had told her, "and I'd
like to see the new refuge—and Neva. We won't stay long."
Emma had nodded, resignation etched across her features.

The refuge was in a small, previously abandoned warehouse
just one block south of the railroad depot. As they approached
and Glynis first saw it, she had to struggle to conceal disappointment. She could find no windows at all, just expanses of
stark brick walls that evoked an image of the prison in nearby
Auburn. The wooden entrance step had rotted through, although
someone had shored it up with loose bricks; the roof sagged
precariously, and the area directly bordering the warehouse was
nothing more than hard-packed dirt. Over this she could see
that a few planks laid end to end served as a walk from the

street. But when it rained, the refuge must be encircled by a moat.

A dozen or so children, all of them dressed in faded overalls, seemed to be wandering around aimlessly. A few more ambitious ones carved figures in the dirt with twigs or threw a ball back and forth. One little boy sat with his arms wrapped around a gaunt, long-eared dog. What struck Glynis most was how quiet it was, without the usual shouts and hollers of youngsters at play. But then, this really didn't look like play. More like enforced activity. Several women, probably their mothers, stood watching, a few with arms crossed over their chests. The women were for the most part very thin, eyes hollow in their haggard faces. Some might once have been healthy-looking, or even pretty. Now any sign of youthful bloom had been overcome by what seemed a collective look of despair.

However, the small-statured Dr. Cardoza-Levy, in comparison to her bleak surroundings, looked not only high-spirited but remarkably content. At least on Neva contentment looked remarkable. As she took the packages of medicine Zeph handed her, Glynis noted that the doctor's cheeks were ruddy, her eyes were sharp as ever, and she'd bobbed her crinkly brown hair. Her marriage a year before to Seneca Falls shop owner Abraham Levy had clearly succeeded. Nonetheless, her affectionate embrace was accompanied by characteristic bluntness. "So, Glynis, you finally decided to come back and face the music! I must say, it's about time. In fact, it may be too late, as you'll soon find out."

Before Glynis could ask what this meant, Neva went on, "But the first thing you'd better do is look into the recent library acquisitions—your assistant's bought nothing but romantic novels. By the wagonload!" She wrinkled her narrow Spanish nose in distaste, while Glynis felt her own heart sink.

Emma, after being introduced, shrank back against the wagon at the invitation to "look around." Her reluctance could hardly have been missed by Dr. Cardoza-Levy, forcing from Glynis the excuse that, "Emma and I are both worn out from the train trip, Neva. We'll come back for the grand tour after we've settled in, and just take a quick look for now."

A quick look was all Glynis could bear anyway. From the

entrance she could see a huge open expanse of stone floor, unbroken by a single inner wall, and again the impression of no windows. What light there was proved so dim, in fact, that she could make out practically nothing of the refuge's interior, save a wood-burning stove, and a scarred wooden table. A row of mattresses, some with straw spilling out, lay on the floor. One of these looked to be occupied by a sleeping woman, although Glynis couldn't be sure—it might have been a child.

As her eyes grew accustomed to the dimness, she could see, standing behind the table, a tall, severe-looking woman of indeterminate age. She wore thick spectacles and was folding what looked to be wide cotton strips, either for bandages, or diapers, or the cloths that were women's monthly necessities. She was introduced by Neva as her new assistant, Margaret Taylor. The woman threw Glynis a brief peremptory nod, and continued folding her cloths.

"Margaret's spent some years in England," Neva said. "And she tells me that Florence Nightingale—that woman should be certified a saint!—has just published a book, a collection of her papers. What was the title again, Margaret?"

"*Notes on Nursing,*" said Margaret crisply, not raising her head or spectacled eyes from her task.

"It's been published in England," Neva said. "Glynis, do you think you could somehow get it here to us?"

"Yes, I can certainly try," she answered, while watching with admiration Margaret Taylor's adept hands. Suddenly the figure sleeping on the mattress gave a soft groan. Margaret Taylor went to kneel beside the mattress. "Mrs. Roarke, are you awake now?"

As Neva watched, her face turned to stone. "That woman over there, Fiona Roarke, has been beaten to within an inch of her life. I swear, if I see her husband . . ." Her voice trailed off in restrained anger.

When they returned to the outside, it seemed astonishingly bright after the gloomy interior of the refuge. Neva seemed unfazed by her surroundings, however. While they walked back to the wagon, she told Glynis, "As you no doubt observed, we're desperately in need of basics here. But relief should come next month—with a barn dance at the fairgrounds to raise money for the refuge.''

To Glynis's surprise, Emma gave a small cry of pleasure. She hadn't said one word during the "tour." Immediately she blushed and turned to climb into the wagon. In reply to Neva's puzzled expression, Glynis whispered, "Emma's ordinarily shy, but the prospect of a barn dance seems to have made her temporarily forget that.''

When they were again seated in the wagon, Zeph suggested that they take the long way around, by way of Fall Street, to reach Harriet Peartree's boardinghouse. "So," he had said, "you can take a look at what's new in town.''

Emma had acquiesced after a long sigh, as if she knew it would do no good to protest. And it would not have, Glynis thought, as they now started down Fall Street. Once Zeph decided on a course of action, straight dynamite couldn't shake him loose from it.

While pointing out to Emma various shops and dry goods stores, Glynis suddenly spotted attorney Jeremiah Merrycoyf and his young partner, Adam MacAlistair. They stood on the front stoop of their law office, under an elongated sign that read: MERRYCOYF & MACALISTAIR, ESQS., ATTORNEYS-AT-LAW. Glynis asked Zeph to stop. When Adam turned, saw, and immediately started toward them, Glynis noticed another man, previously concealed by Merrycoyf's considerable girth, opening the office door. She didn't get a good look at him, as he stepped inside just as Merrycoyf, apparently hearing Adam's greeting, turned toward the street.

"Miss Tryon, you're back!" Adam came forward with his customary friendliness and wide attractive grin. When he reached the wagon, he took Glynis's outstretched hand in an enthusiastic grip.

"Didn't know you'd be back today," he said, "otherwise we'd have been at the station with a brass band." Measuring her response to this, Adam cocked his head of sleek, dark brown hair to one side like an alert otter breaking the surface of water. "So how was Springfield," he went on, "and your family . . ." He left off, apparently having just noticed Emma, and his bright hazel eyes widened.

Glynis glanced sideways at her niece, noting that Emma's own eyes had enlarged before she lowered them to gaze at the wagon floorboards. Her cheeks flared a violent color. She seemed to be inching downward, giving the impression that she intended to disappear beneath the seat.

Glynis sympathized, but made the introductions. Adam was forced to speak to the top of Emma's bowed head. "Pleased to make your acquaintance, Miss Tryon." His glance skipped over the mound of luggage. "Are you planning to be in Seneca Falls for some time?"

Emma's stifled murmur was lost to Glynis when, appearing behind Adam, Jeremiah Merrycoyf said, "You mean we're to have *two* Miss Tryons gracing our small town?"

"Jeremiah." Glynis smiled, catching the pudgy hand held out to her. Resembling more than ever the spirit of Clement Moore's Christmas poem, Merrycoyf peered up at her from behind his small, wire-framed spectacles.

"My dear Miss Tryon," he said, "I'm happy that you've returned, as things have been rather uneventful—that is to say, dull—since you left us. But I've just now talked with Constable Stuart. And it seems your arrival has been accompanied by some rather spectacular unpleasantness."

Since he'd made it sound as if Glynis were somehow the cause of the "unpleasantness," Emma, with a small gasp, swung her head first to her aunt, and then to Merrycoyf, as if she couldn't believe she'd heard what she had.

"Mr. Merrycoyf!" Adam said, his voice a little too outraged to ring true, Glynis thought—even *she'd* known Jeremiah was being droll—until she saw his warm glance at Emma. "Sir, how can you imply such a thing?" he went on with a tone of high dudgeon. "Why the Misses Tryon have only just arrived and—"

"Indeed so," Merrycoyf interrupted, "exactly as I have observed. Well, Miss Tryon," he now said to Glynis, "do come pay me a visit when you've a moment. We can discuss class rings . . . and things. It seems you've returned at an auspicious time, and we'll put to good use your skills in detection."

Glynis had known Merrycoyf a long time. He was an inquisitive old elf, probably as curious as she about the murdered man on the train, and she gave him a quick, conspiratorial nod.

Zeph flicked the reins over the horse's back, and as the wagon moved forward, Adam MacAlistair walked alongside. "Miss Tryon . . . Miss *Emma*," he said while, to keep abreast, his pace necessarily increased to a trot, "allow me to say that if you should ever need legal assistance, I am at your disposal." With that, he fell behind.

Since Emma stared at her lap, Glynis wondered if perhaps she hadn't heard Adam. But she then saw that, although it didn't seem physically possible, her niece's cheeks had flushed still more violently.

Glynis suppressed a smile and looked down Fall Street, pointing out Carr's Hotel at the corner of State, then, a few minutes later, drew Emma's attention to the shop coming up on their left. Glynis abruptly sat forward, and looked again. Whither had gone the modest millinery shop of the widow Coddington? Black curliqued letters on the sign above a large plate glass window read: "La Maison de Fleur."

Glynis found it hard to credit what she saw. What had formerly been two rather small shops now stood joined as one; the plain wood exterior had been painted a lovely shade of pale green, while the window, its frame and shutters black, displayed interior drapery that fell in swags of gleaming satin, matching exactly in color the shop's exterior. This provided startling contrast to the prosaic brown storefronts on either side; in point of fact, not another such facade existed on all of Fall Street. Nor, Glynis would wager, in all of Seneca Falls.

"Zeph, stop the wagon!"

And the three of them sat there, simply staring.

"Really something, isn't it?" Zeph finally offered. To which Glynis nodded dumbly.

Elaborate wrought-iron railings ran down steps that looked to be slabs of green marble. Over these steps swooped a green-and-white-striped canopy, spanning the distance from two glossy black entrance doors to the street, where the canopy was supported by two slender Doric columns. Beside them, fat brass urns held pink tulips.

Glynis leaned forward. "Zeph, how long has Fleur Coddington's shop looked . . . ah . . . like *that?*"

"That?" he repeated in a peculiar voice. "The mayor says it looks like a house of ill repute." She caught a muffled chortle before he said, "Oh, *sorry*, Miss Tryon!" Glynis was sure he was not. And the mayor was wrong. The shop looked exquisite.

Emma, in the meantime, had shot bolt upright from her previous slump and was fixing La Maison with hungry eyes. She had just turned to her aunt when the two entrance doors suddenly swung open. A young woman in ice-blue linen, who looked not much older than Emma, started down the steps. A straw bonnet covered her hair. She concealed her face, at least partially, with a lace handkerchief clutched in a white-gloved hand. Then she tripped on the bottom step, grabbed at the railing, and lifted swollen red eyes to give the wagon occupants a startled look.

Following a strangled gasp, she dropped the handkerchief and fled. Her laced high-heel shoes left indentations like small animal tracks in the dirt of Fall Street.

As Glynis and Emma exchanged baffled looks, the doors again swung open, this time to allow the passage of Fleur Coddington herself. Tall, as slim as a birch branch, she descended the steps, her cream-colored silk dress and petticoats making the *swish* of wind through wheat. Despite an immense, dark green velvet hat from which ostrich feathers waved, she raised her parasol. Then, as if indecisive, she stood gazing up and down Fall Street.

As Glynis remembered, Fleur Coddington had never been a beautiful woman. She was, in fact, taken feature by feature, rather plain. But with elegant bearing and clothes, a slow enigmatic smile worthy of da Vinci's masterpiece, and a voice reminiscent of soft gray smoke, she created an illusion of beauty that far overshadowed what, in other women, was the real thing.

Glynis felt Emma tugging at her arm and received from her niece a desperate look. Reluctantly, she gathered her skirts to climb from the wagon. "Mrs. Coddington!" she called. "Fleur, I wonder if I might have a word with you . . ."

Her voice trailed off. Fleur Coddington, after she'd stared directly at Glynis, had whirled around, and was now moving rapidly in the opposite direction. She did not walk so much as float, her hooped skirt swaying from side to side like a bell of which the slender Fleur herself was the clapper.

But the woman had seen her—Glynis was sure of it. What on earth could be the matter?

Glynis looked at her niece, who gazed wistfully after the retreating figure. "I'm sorry, Emma. I guess she didn't hear me." That was, of course, a fiction for Emma's benefit. The woman had heard.

"It's all right, Aunt Glynis. Thank you for trying." And then, unexpectedly, Emma suggested coyly, "Perhaps the oh-so-stylish mistress of La Maison doesn't speak *l'Anglais! N'est-ce pas?*" She laughed softly.

Zeph twisted in his seat to look at Emma, then urged the horse forward, while Glynis sat wondering when she'd last heard her niece laugh. With that sobering thought, she tried to forget Fleur Coddington's inexplicable rudeness, and pointed out her library to Emma just before they turned onto Cayuga Street.

"Miss Tryon?" Zeph asked over his shoulder. "Miss Tryon, you ever heard of someone named John Brown?"

Startled, Glynis responded, "You don't mean the abolitionist John Brown, do you?" She hoped this was not the case.

"Yes, he's the one. He's coming here to Seneca Falls, sometime next month. Wait 'til you hear him talk! Believe me, you've never heard the likes."

No, from what she'd read about John Brown, she supposed not. But she'd been thinking about something else entirely, and realized that the question she had wanted to ask Zeph, ever since they'd started out, would have to come now or never. They would reach the Peartree house in a few minutes.

"Zeph, have you . . . that is . . . have you been out to Black Brook Reservation? Recently?"

His head turned toward her, and he nodded. "A couple weeks ago."

"I see." Oh, just spit it out, Glynis prodded herself. "Was everything at the reservation all right? I mean, have there been any changes since I left?"

"Nope. But if what you really mean is, Was Jacques Sundown still there . . ."

"I didn't exactly—"

"Then, no. He'd left. I don't know for where, or for how long." He twisted in his seat to give her a long silent stare.

Glynis, embarrassed, lowered her eyes. Fortunately, Emma didn't seem to have heard this exchange. And Zeph turned to face front, then a few minutes later reined in the horse. They had arrived at 33 Cayuga Street.

As Glynis and Emma climbed from the wagon, the front door of the white federal-style house opened, and Harriet Peartree stepped to the porch. She stood for a moment, sunlight glinting off her gold-and-silver hair, then came down the stairs to meet them with outstretched arms. Like a mother hen, she gathered in Glynis and Emma under her wings, and when they separated, Harriet smiled and patted Emma's cheek. Then she turned to Glynis. She was still smiling, but Glynis, having known her for many years, saw immediately that beneath Harriet's smile lay something else.

And whatever it was, it was not good.

THREE

YOUNG ANNIE BROWN, her hands clamped on the patched knees of her overalls, bent down to glare at a stringy rhubarb stalk. It was the last of the clump, and up to now it had bested her. She brushed her overalls before she straightened to glance with resentment at the others, the ones she'd already pulled and tossed into a heap at the edge of the garden plot. They had stained her hands blood-red. The stalks were vile things, clinging stubbornly to roots that were barely alive in the poor, rocky soil, like children clinging to the hands of those who would sooner see them gone.

Without thinking, Annie wiped a hand over her perspiring forehead, then gazed ruefully at her reddened dirt-caked fingers. She'd better rid her face of smudges before Father saw. If, as he said, cleanliness was next to godliness, she would hear herself named Satan's child, pure and simple.

But first she was going to pull this rhubarb! She planted both bare feet firmly, placed her fingers close to the stalk's base, took a deep breath, and yanked. The stalk separated from its roots with a moist *plop*. The sudden release sent Annie tumbling over backward, the stalk and its huge single leaf held aloft in her hands like a flag. She now sprawled half-on, half-off the meadow grass encircling the garden; but with a certain amount of satisfaction, she sat up and threw the rhubarb stalk on the heap with the others. Cooking them, though, would be still another battle. It could take hours.

The small garden plot had been dug on a hill, so she had to

wriggle upward until she got clear of the dirt. She sat a moment, looking off at the horizon jagged with mountain peaks, then threw herself back into the tall grass to lie with arms spread wide, and eyes closed against the hazy spring sun.

She lay there, breathing in the clean sharp scent of balsam and spruce and listening to the drone of bees in the grass, an occasional birdsong, the murmur of spring peepers. If she opened her eyes and shaded them with her hand, she could see the wild berry bushes along the edge of the woods. There'd be raspberries soon. Beyond the bushes stood yellow birch trees whose leaves quaked gently though there was barely a breeze. And the clouds like goose-down pillows hung overhead as if dangling from unseen fishing line.

It was good to be alone. By herself, without the noise of the younger children, or the insistent demands of her older brothers, or the sorrowful voice of her mother. How long before one of them realized she hadn't come back with the rhubarb?

Annie closed her eyes again. She dragged her hands through the grass until they lay at her sides, then she ran them over her stomach, growling with emptiness, then over her chest that in recent days had begun to change from its familiar flatness. She had known they would come, but not so soon. As her fingers explored them, something streaked through her like a shiver of dread.

She sat up, quickly, to gaze at the mountains looming around her, and around the isolated crossroads of North Elba below, and below that, the town of Lake Placid. The mountains rose like giants that had climbed from the center of the earth. They stood tall and dark with fir and pine, brown with tree bark and pinecones, and newly green with the leaves of spring. Only old Whiteface, rising at the head of the shimmering lake, looked different, with its pale gray blotch that had been caused, Annie was told, by a landslide. But other than the green, which came and went, the mountains always looked the same. For all she knew, they'd looked that way forever. Not like her, changing every day. She wished she could stay the same. Like the mountains did.

She turned her head at the distant clang of cowbells and the rumble of a wagon coming from far down the hill toward North

Elba. It must be Father. The uneasiness that felt like fear, but love too, shot through her as it always did when he came home.

She'd better get back to the house, and wash. Her heart skipping, she jumped to her feet, snatched the rhubarb from beside the garden, and ran with it down the hill. When she got to within a few yards of the log house, she paused to watch as Father pulled the wagon to a stop behind the big oxen. When he clambered down, she noticed again that he seemed thinner than he had before he'd gone to Kansas, and he stooped a little. But he still looked strong. He went around to the back of the wagon and lifted its false bottom to let a black-skinned man and woman climb out. They stood blinking in the sunlight, and they looked frightened and cold. It was a curious thing, the way Father made runaway slaves hide themselves like that, all cramped up in a little space. No slavecatchers ever came here. They knew better. The mountains could be the death of strangers.

ANNIE BACKED UP to the rough wood cupboard that stood beside the fireplace. Her father and seven older brothers, and stepbrothers, and the visitors, sat eating at the long table. She watched them until she was sure no one watched *her*. Then, reaching behind, she pulled the cupboard drawer open a crack and reached in to snatch a corn-cake. She tucked it into her apron pocket at the same time she grabbed the handle of the wooden bucket. Quiet as a hare in a carrot patch, she slipped out the door.

She ate the corn-cake on the way to the well. But she was so hungry that it didn't help much. Whenever there were visitors, the womenfolk—even little Sarah—had to wait for them to finish before they themselves could eat. There was simply not enough room at the table. It had been explained to her that, since women did the cooking, if they got hungry, they could always "sample" the food. They were the ones closest to it. But somehow this never worked out. There wasn't time. Annie and her mother and sisters were always too busy; falling over one another in the small space, they pulled iron pots from the fire, kettles off the stove, and then put the food on the table to be eaten as fast as it got set down. Or, as happened this night, there were just too many mouths to feed. There was nothing left over to sample. But her mother could sometimes tuck corn-cakes away so they wouldn't go without.

Father had, as usual, brought the visitors. Two of them were the Negroes, Mr. and Mrs. Jones, who'd come from North Carolina by way of the Underground Railroad. Mrs. Jones looked scared and shy and cold, seated there with all the men. It was plain she had never been spoken to or treated like this before. She'd wanted to help in the kitchen, but Father insisted she sit at the table.

Annie hoped Mrs. Jones and her husband would do better than the others who came from the South. They wouldn't be used to the winters, so long and so cold that many escaped slaves sickened and died. One of her brothers claimed that was why the slavecatchers didn't come up here—they figured slaves they were tracking would likely be dead by the time they were found.

Two white men at the table had come in the wagon, come with the crates of rusty guns. Another man, with a high forehead and long thin nose and eyes that looked out as if from deep caves, had ridden on his horse up from Lake Placid. That was Mr. Smith—Mr. Gerrit Smith, his name was—who last year ran for governor of New York State. He'd lost the election, but Father said he was still a rich man. And Gerrit Smith owned all the land around North Elba. Including theirs until just recently, when two of Father's secret friends had given him the deed to the farm, so that Annie's mother would always have a place to live. Annie still didn't understand why Father called some of his friends the secret ones, but he did.

It was a good thing, Annie thought, while she cranked the handle to bring the bucket up from the well, that her brother Jason had gone fishing in the creek that ran through the farm. Lucky that he'd come home with five speckled trout. Otherwise, they'd have had to feed all those people on just bread and butter and corn-cakes. There was milk; their cows were a sorry lot to look at, but they did give milk. And there was rhubarb. A tin kettle full of it. She had used half a sack of sugar, much more than she was supposed to, and her mother, when she'd found out, just stared at Annie with sad eyes. But the rhubarb still tasted so sour it made everyone's mouth pucker. Annie had seen one of the visitors spit it out in his hand when he thought nobody was looking.

She lugged the bucket back inside the kitchen where the smell of fish stayed on, and would for some time. She found her mother hunkered beside the washtub loaded with dirty tin plates, and both her arms wrapped around her stomach. Annie felt an inner lurch, and put down the bucket. Not another baby. But it couldn't be—Father had been back from his last trip for only a week. And all told, he'd been gone, off and on, for six years, moving between Kansas and the northeastern states, and the settlements of former slaves in Canada. So there had been no baby for a long time. But before that, there had been thirteen, including Annie. Not reckoning the seven from Father's first marriage.

"Mother, go upstairs," Annie said quietly.

Her mother shook her head. "Ruth's already up there, nursing her babe. Somebody got to help clean up."

"That's all right. I can do it alone," Annie said as forcefully as she could without Father hearing. "You go now. You can be asleep before the others get up there." They didn't have enough straw mattresses, so when there were visitors, everybody just lay down where they could find a place.

Her mother turned her pale face to Annie and nodded. She winced when she straightened up to walk past the men. No one, except Annie's brother Salmon, seemed to notice her; his were the only troubled eyes besides Annie's own to follow their mother up the stairs. Otherwise she might have been invisible.

Annie heard the slow footsteps overhead as her mother crossed the floor of the upstairs loft. There was just the one room under the slope of the roof, and when she finally got there herself, she knew she'd find her mother on Annie's own mattress under the window. Her mother always slept curled on her side like a child, legs pulled up, knees hugged against her chest as if to protect her worn hurting womb.

After she'd poured water into the tub, Annie plunged in her arms up to her elbows to rinse the dishes. She was supposed to first heat the water on the stove, but she'd have to get more wood to burn and it'd take too long. She wanted to hear what the men in the other room were saying.

"Pa, you know it's going to take time from spring planting to clean those guns," Annie heard Salmon protest. "We still got the west quarter to finish, and Ma and the girls can't do it."

"Then let it be," Father said. "The guns are more important—they've got to be ready for when we go to Virginia."

"We leave off planting now, Pa, even the buckwheat won't ripen before first frost." That was her brother Henry's voice.

"What's the family supposed to eat next winter, Pa?" Salmon added. "We can't eat guns."

This brought a roar of laughter. But Annie was sure Salmon hadn't meant it to be funny. The winters when Father and her brothers had been in Kansas, the ones left behind near hungered to death.

"Listen, Pa," Annie heard Jason say, "I don't think we should go off again until next spring. There's work got to be done here."

"It can wait! Freeing the slaves can't." Father's voice now had that sharp edge. Annie felt a ripple of fear and wished her brothers would stop baiting him.

"Well, sir," Jason continued, "then I guess I better tell you: I'm not going to Virginia. Had enough of that kind of thing in Kansas."

Annie's breath caught. Jason shouldn't have said that. Didn't he know yet that he shouldn't say things Father didn't want to hear? He and the others used to get strapped, strapped bad, when they did that. Once, after, Salmon couldn't walk for close onto a week. Father'd never had to strap her, though. She was careful.

Annie heard Father start to say something, but Salmon got there first. "And I'm not going either. We can't leave Ma alone again. She's not strong, and—"

"Enough!" Father half-rose out of his chair to cut Salmon off. "Enough of this kind of talk in front of our visitors!"

And Annie had wondered what poor Mr. and Mrs. Jones were thinking. Gerrit Smith would be used to it, and so would the men who brought the guns. But the Joneses?

By the time she'd finished the dishes, and poured the dirty water over a scrawny lilac bush outside the door, the Joneses had gone upstairs. The two men had headed back to North Elba, and Father and Mr. Gerrit Smith sat, talking quietly in front of the cold fireplace. She'd heard a few snatches of what they were saying, and now she crept to perch on the bottom step of the stairs.

"... and to pay for more arms, I've got to have the money soon," Father was saying. Annie looked at him, with his grave, gaunt face, and the long beard streaked with gray that he'd grown since Kansas. His eyes, one of them drooping now he was tired, held a blue-gray fire. That meant he was talking slavery. And she'd caught the words "Harper's Ferry" again.

Gerrit Smith began to say something, but stopped when he spied Annie. "You can talk in front of the girl," Father told him. "I trust her. Always have. Annie doesn't repeat things she's told not to."

Gerrit Smith shrugged, then took another draw on his pipe before he said, "John, you have to be careful. Since the Kansas wars, lawmen are watching you closely, you know that." He paused to give Father a long look. "And, John, there's something I need to know. My cousin Elizabeth—you know, Judge Cady's daughter, married to Henry Stanton—"

"Stanton's anti-slavery," Father interrupted, "not abolitionist. And he's lily-livered. Says the law should be the tool to wash the sins of this nation away. Well, just you take a look at Kansas. Wasn't the law that stopped the heathen slaveholders there. It was blood!" And Father made a deep sound in his throat.

Gerrit Smith said quickly, "Yes, all right, I agree, but as I've told you before, my involvement, as well as that of the others, has to be kept quiet. No one can get wind of where your financial support is coming from—you *do* understand that, John?"

Father set his thin straight lips, in that way he did when he was getting riled, but he didn't say anything. Annie had noticed that Father didn't raise his voice to Mr. Smith. Maybe it was because he'd owned their farm.

"In any event," Gerrit Smith went on, "as I was saying,

Elizabeth Stanton told me, the last time I was in Seneca Falls, that a group of marauders made an attempt to rob the local militia armory. They got scared off by the constable, but not before they'd killed an elderly watchman. John, I hope, and indeed pray, that this wrong had nothing to do with you.'' Gerrit Smith fixed Father with a solemn gaze.

''Mr. Smith, I've been more than three years now recruiting volunteers, and collecting guns. When the trumpet of Gideon sounds, we got to have men. We got to have weapons!'' Father explained in a rising tone. Then he lowered it somewhat. ''I don't hold, though, with killing innocents. And I didn't authorize any robbery of any armory.''

Gerrit Smith continued to look solemn. ''I hope that's true, John. Or you, and maybe some of us, too, will end up in prison. Might even be put on trial for treason. So let's have no more of these raids in the North—those tactics might be all right in Kansas, and in the South, but not here. If for no other reason than the abolitionists could turn against you. The anti-slavery party already has; most of them feel that violence is not the way—''

''It's the *only* way!'' Father broke in, and got up to pace across the room. ''Those anti-slavery yellowbellies—all of them! Leave slavery alone in the South, they say. Just keep it from spreading into the territories, they say. No! It's got to be abolished altogether!'' His voice had begun to reach higher, and he walked back and forth, swinging his arms. ''*I* say we got to wash out this evil completely. This abomination of slavery is against God's will. So we got to purge this land with blood! There is no other way!''

Annie felt her heartbeat quicken. *Whose blood?* she wanted to ask. *Yours, Father? Or my brothers'? John Jr.'s and Oliver's and Owen's and Watson's?* She felt the fear creeping up her spine. Poor Frederick was already dead, lying somewhere under Kansas soil. *Now, Salmon and Jason, they say they're done with it, the killing, Father—but will you let them be done?*

Gerrit Smith, who had been staring at Father, at last said, ''I'll get you the money you need, John. I said I'd talk to the other five, and I will. And there's something else—we've been contacted by the agent of a foreign power who wants to make a sizable contribution to the cause.''

"That so? How will I get it?"

"The plan is to have it ready when you come through Seneca Falls. Now, tell me how far the Virginia plan has progressed since last I saw you. Is it to be Harper's Ferry, then?''

Annie saw Father's eyes flare bright. And he nodded vigorously. "Harper's Ferry—the federal armory and arsenal. I am convinced, *convinced,* I tell you, that black people are ripe for insurrection. Given just half a chance they'll join us—I figure between two hundred and five hundred slaves the first night. We arm them, then make a dash against the arsenal. I'll destroy whatever arms I can't carry off, then we move into the Allegheny Mountains.''

Father paused for breath, and he stopped striding back and forth to face Gerrit Smith as he spoke. "Slaves all over Virginia and Maryland will join us. They'll rise in holy wrath against their captors, and they'll come! If U.S. troops come after, we stay in the mountains.'' Father's voice had the high excited ring that frightened Annie the most. The ring had a dangerous shrill to it, like the sharp notes of a fire bell.

And she could see the other man's deep-set eyes were now flaring, too. "Yes, by God," Gerrit Smith said in a loud whisper. "Yes, it can be done!'' He stood as if to make leave. "I'll see you next month, John, in Seneca Falls. We can . . .''

Annie didn't want to hear more. She got up quickly and climbed the stairs. And found her mother curled up on her mattress. It was quiet in the room, the younger children sleeping, and only a few scattered snores from the others. Before Annie slipped in beside her mother, she went to kneel by the window. Clouds had gathered, and it had started to rain, so there was no moon. She couldn't see the mountains. But they were there.

She closed her eyes. No matter what happened, to Father, to her brothers, or to anyone else in the world, the mountains would be there. Whatever Father did.

It gave her a kind of peace. Even he couldn't move mountains. But she wondered, suddenly, if that was true. Her eyelids snapped open, and she stared into the darkness, straining to find the lost mountains. And her heart began to race with dread.

FOUR

The law "establishing a mint and regulating the coins of the United States," received the president's approval on the 2nd of April, 1792. . . . President Washington proceeded at once to carry out the intentions of the act, and as Philadelphia was then the seat of government, he there caused the necessary buildings and machinery to be provided and put in a condition for the purposes of coining.

—JOHN H. HICKCOX, *An Historical Account of American Coinage* 1858

AFTER DESCENDING THE Peartree porch steps, Glynis paused to stand as if planted in the front walk, and she sighed deeply. There was, she supposed, no putting off the library. Not after what she had been told by Harriet the night before. And while she'd been told a great number of things by Harriet, this particular one required more urgent attention than the others.

Glynis sighed again before she adjusted the large brim of her straw hat for protection against a dazzling noonday sun. She then started resolutely down the walk. The flagstones were edged with flowerbeds that now burst with regal pink and white tulips and blue iris. At their feet lay mats of white rock cress. Any other day she would have cut some for her library desk, but given what she had learned, she supposed she'd better arrive with both hands free. Thus, at the end of the walkway, she headed for Fall Street with only a book bag slung over her shoulder.

She wondered again where Emma had gone. It was curious, her niece leaving the house an hour before with no explanation. All she'd said was, "I have something to do." Coming as this did from shy Emma, it had sounded tantamount to an adventure. Glynis hadn't pressed her to be more specific; Emma was not a child and was not a prisoner, either. Now Glynis worried that she might get lost—which was absurd! Lost in a village far smaller than Springfield? Still, Emma had been so mysterious.

When Glynis passed by the Usher house, she increased her pace and stared straight ahead. The last thing she wanted was to confront Vanessa Usher, and according to Harriet, a confrontation it would necessarily be. And all because of Aurora Usher's last will and testament—which her sister, Vanessa, was fighting tooth-and-nail. Well, Glynis thought, she would simply have to visit Jeremiah Merrycoyf sooner than she'd anticipated.

In fact, seeing Vanessa was not the worst that could happen. Seeing Cullen Stuart would be. It had taken hours to pry the truth from Harriet—in fact until after midnight, by which time Glynis had all but given up trying to find the source of her landlady's evasiveness.

"Harriet, *what is wrong?*" she had said, determined to make a last attempt before leaving the familiar kitchen for bed. "Is it something you haven't told me about Jacques Sundown? Has anything happened to him?"

"No, Glynis, nothing that I know of. Only that, as I've already said, he stopped by here several weeks ago."

"Yes, to tell you he'd be gone for a few months' time. But is that all?"

"Just that he'd signed on as guide for some western expedition. Glynis, this is not about Jacques Sundown." Harriet paused, frowned, then apparently made up her mind. "It's about Cullen Stuart."

"Cullen? What about Cullen? I saw him earlier today, and he didn't mention anything . . ." Her voice trailed off as she remembered their scene at the train station; his odd discomfort and the distance he had placed between them. Then slowly a light began to flicker. "Harriet, is Cullen . . . is he keeping company with someone?"

Harriet, looking miserable, nodded. "He's been seen squiring Fleur Coddington."

Abruptly the light grew brighter. That was the explanation then, Glynis realized. Cullen hadn't acted much differently with her until they had talked of hoop skirts—reminding him no doubt of the fashionable Fleur. And Fleur's heretofore baffling rudeness was made clear; probably triggered by her shock in realizing that Glynis had returned. Because surely the woman knew something of Cullen's history—and that Glynis had been part of it.

Last night, when she should have been sleeping, Glynis had gone over the past again and again, finally reaching the inescapable conclusion that she had brought this on herself. Such reasoning did not comfort her in the least. But she couldn't cope with it right now. She just prayed she wouldn't run into Cullen until she had recovered herself.

Thus, when she reached Fall Street, Glynis again kept her eyes straight ahead and fixed on her library. *Her* library? Apparently there was some question about that.

As she went down the few steps from the road to the small fieldstone building set on the slope between Fall Street and the Seneca River below, she heard a babble of voices. More voices, all at one time, than had ever issued forth from the library in its entire history, she was sure. Glynis pulled open the door, and gazed upon a scene reminiscent of Hoskin's Dry Goods Store two days before Christmas. Many of those crowded into the large sunny room she did not immediately recognize. As her initial shock receded, she found she could pick out a few faces. But most were not regular library patrons, or hadn't been at the time she'd left for Springfield.

As she weaved her way through the noisy room, she finally came upon her assistant, Jonathan Quant, in conversation with seven or eight people swarming around his desk. He appeared to be extremely pleased with himself.

"Jonathan!"

He looked up. Looked again. "Miss Tryon! I just heard you were back—and you are." He jumped from his chair, knocking several books off his desk. Then he ran a hand through his hair in a habitual effort to smooth it into something that didn't resemble a rat's nest. And he straightened his lopsided neck cloth. "You're back," he repeated.

"Indeed, Jonathan."

His color had gradually faded until his face now looked bleached. In the meantime, Glynis responded briefly to several greetings, her mood being such that she thought it better not to say much. But she somehow managed to grind out, "Jonathan,

I need to speak with you. Now. In my office." She gestured toward the back of the room. "That is," she could not refrain from saying, "if it isn't already occupied. To capacity."

"Oh, no," Jonathan hurriedly assured her. "But I . . . that is, I mean, we can't leave the room unattended."

Glynis glanced around to locate a patron. "Morwenna," she called to Liam Cleary's older, redheaded sister, who had three small children clinging to her skirts. "Could you please keep an eye on things for a few minutes? Mr. Quant and I need to have a short business discussion. And please do not allow books to be signed out in our absence."

Morwenna's bright head bobbed, making her freckles seem to dance. "Sure 'n I'll be glad to watch things, Miss Tryon. And a welcome home t'you."

Glynis saw with grateful surprise that her office appeared to be exactly as she had left it. She sank into her cushioned chair beside the window, momentarily calmed by its familiar contours. Jonathan remained standing by the door as if unwilling to abandon a position that afforded a fast retreat. "Very well, Jonathan. Suppose you tell me: *what exactly is going on*?"

His face underwent several changes of expression, and finally settled into one of contrition. "I'm sorry, terribly sorry, that I didn't have time to write you about . . . well, all of this," he said, waving an arm in the direction of the library proper. "But I didn't expect you back . . . yet."

"Obviously. Go on." Glynis knew how angry she sounded—but she *was* angry. "Why don't you start from the beginning. From the time you made the decision to open this library, this *subscription* library, to the general public."

"Oh, you've heard then," Jonathan said, exhibiting some relief. He probably thought he would be spared the task of attempting to explain the unexplainable. But of this he had not a prayer.

"I want to hear it from you," Glynis said, and sat back in her chair, hands tightly folded in her lap.

Jonathan appeared to rally. He told her, as she'd already been informed by Harriet, that he had recently instituted "an experimental variation in policy." For those who could not afford the full price of subscription membership, he'd offered something he called an associate membership for half the price. It allowed these members limited use of the library, consisting of two specific afternoons a week—Glynis assumed today was one of them—and they were restricted to borrowing two books at a time.

"It's been in effect for just six weeks, Miss Tryon," he concluded. "And you can see for yourself how popular it's proved to be." His anxiety seemed to have vanished, and he beamed at her as if expecting a standing ovation.

"What I can see," Glynis responded, "is that the Seneca Falls Library is being used for other than what its charter defines. Or have you, perchance, cleared this revolutionary plan of yours with the board of directors, who are, as you well know, the stockholders? Did you consult with them, Jonathan?"

"Well, no . . ."

"No. I thought not, since I've heard nothing from them. Which is surprising. Do they, in fact, even know about it?"

"Uh, some of them do."

"Jonathan, there are only five board members. How many do you mean by 'some'?"

"One."

"One. And that might be . . . ?"

"Mr. Gould."

"Ah." Seabury S. Gould was so occupied with his burgeoning Gould Pumps business that he rarely appeared at even the annual board meeting. On the other hand, he *was* the library's principal contributor.

"Mr. Gould seemed interested in the plan," Jonathan ventured. "Especially for his employees. He really thought it had the earmarks of a winning idea."

"Did he, now."

Jonathan nodded. "Of course, Miss Tryon, I told him I merely wished to give the idea a trial run, so to speak. I wouldn't have dreamed of instituting such a program on a permanent basis until you got back and approved it." He gave her a tentative smile.

"Oh, I see," Glynis replied. "You have allowed these people to come in and use the library under false pretenses—and left to me the job of telling them that they haven't the right to use it at all. Correct?''

"But why can't they? Isn't it better that the library be used by more people? Why should use be confined to only those who have money?''

"Because they pay for the books, Jonathan—and the building, and *your salary!* And mine. Plus assorted other items such as supplies, and—but you know these things!''

"Miss Tryon, if you'd just give me a chance to show you the financial schedule, I think you'll agree it can be done.''

Glynis turned to look out the window. When Harriet had told her about this last night, she'd tried to think of ways it might be made to work. It wasn't that she opposed Jonathan's premise; she had, in fact, thought of it a time or two herself. It would be in the best interest of the village to have people better informed. However, more people meant more books, more periodicals, more newspapers—paid for by whom? How? The obstacle was—always had been—money. Except that she now remembered something else.

She turned back to him. "Jonathan, putting the financial question aside for the moment, what kind of books have you been ordering to fill this new demand?'' She knew the answer, having been assured by Harriet that Neva Cardoza-Levy's comment of the day before carried some truth, even though wagonloads of romantic novels might be a tad excessive. At least Glynis certainly hoped so.

"Well, it's true we have more volumes in some categories now than we used to—more, that is, than we used to order,'' Jonathan admitted, looking unhappy.

"Than *we* used to order?'' Glynis repeated. "I know what *I* used to order. And it was not romantic novels! I don't read them myself, and you read them regularly, so in the past I left those choices to you, Jonathan. I've had no objection to the acquisition of a few of them. But my understanding is that you've concentrated on those to the exclusion of perhaps more worthy things.'' She knew she sounded pompous, but couldn't seem to stop herself.

"Oh, no,'' Jonathan protested. "That's not precisely true. I *have* increased the number of romantic novels, but not to the exclusion of everything else." He seemed quite put out by this accusation. "But, Miss Tryon, if romantic novels are what people most want to read, why shouldn't we have more of them?"

"Because other things are—" Glynis did stop herself this time. It wasn't fair to disparage the entire category. That *would* be pompous. Besides, some romantic novels were not badly written, and a few were quite good. One or two were better than good. She knew because, despite what she'd said, she had read a few herself—had enjoyed Rachel Merino's *Spinning Shadows of New York* so much she'd even recommended it to Jonathan. "All right," she conceded. "Perhaps I have overstated this. Tell me what you've ordered other than the romantics."

"Just last week," he said eagerly, "we got in a novel titled *Adam Bede;* it's by that British author—I know you like him. It's his second book, and I ordered it right away."

"Except for the fact that George Eliot is not a 'him,' Jonathan, I applaud your choice. What else?"

But after several minutes, Jonathan had not convinced her that his acquisitions had been evenhanded; the romantics definitely had the upper hand and then some, as the number of total books and periodicals ordered for the library seemed far larger than usual. Glynis did some rapid mental calculation. Her exasperation with Jonathan soared.

He opened the office door, peered into the library room from behind his thick spectacles, and announced hopefully, "People are waiting to sign out books, Miss Tryon." He edged into the doorway.

"Just a minute. I want to know where you found the money to order additional books."

"Well, I didn't precisely find it. That is . . ."

Glynis waited.

Jonathan fidgeted. "Can we discuss this later?"

"No. We'll discuss it now."

Jonathan's shoulders slumped. He suddenly seemed to be lost for words. "Have you heard," he at last said softly, "about Miss Usher's will?" The question seemed to bring him close to tears.

"Yes, I've just heard. Of course, I feel terrible about Aurora's death. I know how fond of her you were, so it must have been a terrible blow, Jonathan. But what does her will have to do with this? Other than what I understand included a bequest to the library?''

"She left ten percent of her estate to the library . . . for the purchase of books. So I . . .''

As his voice faltered, Glynis rose to her feet. ''Jonathan, you *didn't* rely on that money to pay for the books you ordered! You didn't, did you?''

Jonathan nodded glumly.

Glynis again sank to her chair. ''How *could* you? Aurora's will is being contested. We may never see that money.''

"I know that now," he said, his voice so nearly despairing that Glynis almost—*almost*—took pity on him, ''but I never imagined such a thing could happen,'' he explained, shaking his head as if still mystified. ''To think that anyone would suggest that Dr. Cardoza-Levy and I exerted undue influence on poor, dear Aurora—why, it's unthinkable.''

"No, it's not!" Glynis replied emphatically. ''And if you had any awareness of how Vanessa Usher's mind works, you wouldn't say that. You certainly would not have acted on it. When it comes to Vanessa, nothing is unthinkable.''

"But it's not the bequest to the library she's challenging," Jonathan protested. ''It's the ninety percent Aurora left to the Women's Refuge.''

And that, of course, had been the reason for Neva's buoyant spirits the day before. The worth of Aurora Usher's estate must be considerable, it having been left to her and her sister Vanessa by their aunt, Rebecca Usher, heir to the Usher canalboat-building business in Lockport. ''Yes, I know about that ninety percent,'' Glynis said, ''and it will keep the will from being probated for who knows how long. In the meantime, just how do you propose to pay for all the books you've ordered?''

Jonathan looked so distressed that Glynis waved him out of the office before she could say more. There was nothing to be gained at this juncture by further berating him. Besides, Jonathan's heart was in the right place; what was wrong had been the way he'd gone about his project. Regardless, the question remained. How would they pay for the books? And just what was she to inform the library board of directors? That they, the stockholders, now had a more egalitarian library—albeit one involuntarily subsidized by themselves—and that, to this purpose, they had just acquired on their line of good credit a wagonload of romantic novels?

INTERIM

❦

SOME FORTY MILES *north of Seneca Falls was the busy port of Oswego. A city built by traders, it stood astride the Oswego River where it flowed into Lake Ontario. Both Britain and France had recognized early the strategic value of a port on the southeastern edge of a Great Lake, and one just a short sail from British-held Canada. Later, Oswego had been of crucial importance during the American Revolution and the War of 1812. Indeed, the British had not willingly given up control of the fort they had erected there, but had been finessed by John Jay's Treaty of 1795. And there were those who feared the British meant to have Fort Ontario back.*

Bathed in warm afternoon sunshine, a tall man stood alone at the end of a pier. He seemed oblivious to the bustle around him of little one-masted sloops flitting in and out of the harbor, the larger schooners and occasional three-masted ships that came to rest at the wharves, the clanging of bells on the buoys, and the shouts of dockworkers loading and unloading cargo. The man appeared to prefer watching the sun play off the water. He had been standing there for some time. The only indication that he might not be as tranquil as he looked was the recurrent flexing of his wrists, followed by intervals of rubbing his thumb over the ink-stained fingertips of his right hand.

When, from due north, a two-masted schooner flying a Canadian flag glided in to dock at the next pier, the man seemed to take no notice. In fact, he turned away casually, indifferently, when from the ship a lone passenger disembarked. Then the tall man on the pier began to amble, in seemingly aimless fashion, back up to the shoreline.

The ship's passenger, a smooth-shaven man of medium height and build, strolled up the other pier toward shore. There was no overt communication between the two men. Even when their paths crossed some distance down the shoreline from the wharves and the river, it looked to be an entirely random encounter.

"Warm down here," said the former passenger, passing a hand over his smooth-shaven jaw. "Kingston's much cooler." He glanced around with sharp eyes that belied his nonchalance—the glance was a quick but thorough scan of the surroundings. "So, Mr. Brockway," he addressed the other man, after satisfying himself that they would not be overheard, "what is this all about? Your message sounded urgent."

"I think," said Brockway, while continuing to flex his wrists, "that we have a problem in Seneca Falls."

"How so? I thought all was proceeding smoothly."

"Well, it's not. Your boy has been a little too eager to dispose, as he puts it, of 'possible complications.' So there's been another 'accident'—that's three in as many weeks—and this time it wasn't even one of the other side's. Just a minor player, a banker. I don't like it. Besides, the constable has to be suspicious." Brockway glanced around somewhat uneasily.

"And if he is? The dead have no connection with us. So how can the constable know anything?"

"Cullen Stuart's not stupid, you know, so anything at all is too much. What happens if he starts to add things up? I'm concerned we may have a loose cannon there in Seneca Falls— if we can't predict what your boy'll do next. I'm telling you, he's unreliable, maybe unstable. He could put the whole operation in jeopardy."

"No, he won't do that. Although I agree that he's apparently been overzealous. Perhaps a bit too cocky for his own good."

"For mine either. Damn it, man, can't you see that he may be more trouble than he's worth?" Brockway rubbed his thumb over his fingertips.

"No, I confess I cannot see that. We've waited a long time to place someone in the position he is in now. And the patience will be well rewarded. We would be fools to dismiss such a stroke of good fortune. But I'll have a talk with him, settle him down."

"Not good enough."

"I'm the one who decides that," responded the smooth-shaven man pleasantly.

"And if you're mistaken? I tell you, there's something doesn't smell right about him."

"*That's your imagination. Admit it, my good Brockway, you've been uncomfortable with him from the start.*"

"*All right, I admit it! But I didn't sign on for murder—and I don't like it. The money is one thing, but killing . . . ?*"

The smooth-shaven man smiled darkly. "*There is much more at stake here than the lives of a few men. Don't exercise yourself. Just do what you're being paid to do—*" the man paused "*—paid in good,* bona fide *United States coin. Now, I mean to stay here in New York for a while to keep an eye on things. I need to make sure nothing comes to pass that would interfere with a certain Mr. Brown's ambitions.*"

Brockway made a disparaging sound. "*Brown's another loose cannon as far as I'm concerned. Sometimes I think this whole damn scheme is insane—crazy as old John Brown.*"

"*Brown can be useful, I assure you. In regard to that money for him—I want you to use the Farmers and Merchants Bank plates—*" the man chuckled "*—the ones we acquired from our friend in Seneca Falls.*"

"*That could be dangerous—*"

"*I'll take that chance,*" the other interrupted. "*And don't waste any more thought on Brown. We can influence but we can't control the outcome of that piece of business. The end result doesn't matter in any event. Brown's a convenient wild card—win, lose, or draw, he's going to provide the agitation we need. And again, there's no possible connection can be made from him to us. So stop worrying!*" The smooth-shaven man again scanned their surroundings. "*I shall be in contact shortly,*" he said before he turned toward the road that led into the city of Oswego.

Brockway's face reflected no small amount of skepticism, and he moved off at a faster pace.

Each man went in a different direction, distancing themselves in purposeful strides. If anyone chose to watch, all that would be seen was two men out walking, who had met by chance and merely paused to pass the time of day on their routes into Oswego.

Of the two men, as they moved away from the harbor, only Brockway stopped and looked over his shoulder.

FIVE

∾

There are now in circulation nearly four thousand counterfeit or fraudulent bills. . . . These spurious—more properly altered—bills are generally the notes of broken or exploded banks, which were originally engraved and printed by bank note engravers for institutions supposed to be regularly organized and solvent. . . . During the past year, the circulation of these spurious notes has increased to an alarming extent.

—AN 1859 ISSUE OF *NILES' WEEKLY REGISTER*

AFTER THE SCENE with Jonathan, Glynis spent the remainder of the afternoon reviewing the library's inventory. It proved worse than she had feared. Moreover, several periodical subscriptions had lapsed, books lay in piles on the floor for want of space on the shelves—all those romantics!—and two booksellers in New York City and Lippincott in Philadelphia had refused to send more items on credit until overdue bills were paid. By four o'clock she had resolved to fire Jonathan—it was only a shame she could do so but once. Not, of course, that she would do so at all. He was a good librarian, just a dreadful administrator. And most of this predicament had come about because she had left him in a position for which he was unsuited. It was, therefore, *her* fault. And she had warned herself that morning, even before she'd started out from home, that she would arrive at this inevitable conclusion.

She glanced over at him now, standing by the shelves, being listened to with adoration by two well-dressed elderly women. Jonathan could recommend anything to them—say, *The Farmers' Guide to Diseases of the Sheep*—and they would take it home and read it cover to cover even if there was not a sheep within a mile. He might have single-handedly educated more people in Seneca Falls than the entire school system. How could she fire him?

She looked at her Skeleton clock under its glass dome, after moving aside clutter that had somehow accumulated on her desktop in the course of a single afternoon—unlike Jonathan's desk which was invariably tidy—and thought she might have time to see Jeremiah Merrycoyf. Her stomach churned every time she thought of acquainting him with the financial state of the library, especially since he was himself a board member. However, it had to be done.

As she left, Jonathan was signing out to one of the elderly women a copy of Adam Smith's *Wealth of Nations*. The very thing with which to curl up on a fine spring afternoon!

As Glynis went up the steps to Fall Street, she heard a number of raised voices. When she paused to listen, she realized the voices weren't only raised, they were angry. Once on the road, she saw that a small crowd—although gaining members by the minute—was gathered at the entrance of Farmers and Merchants Bank. Even from a block away she could hear shouted phrases. The words almost seemed to carry an element of hysteria.

When she drew nearer to the bank, she saw Cullen Stuart approaching from the opposite direction; Zeph Waters and Liam Cleary were beside him, their young faces looking worried. Glynis firmly told herself to leave, to go directly home, and to see Merrycoyf another day. With these good intentions, she had just turned back toward Cayuga Street, when she heard a number of loud shouts. They were followed by the blast of a rifle.

She flinched and involuntarily ducked. But then, as a second blast did not come, she cautiously turned to look. Cullen stood with the rifle pointed skyward, and Glynis couldn't tell if he'd fired the warning shot himself or had just wrested the rifle from someone else. Moreover, Zeph and Liam Cleary each had hands resting on the revolvers in their holsters.

The rifle shot had been immediately followed by silence, but now the angry shouts broke out again. Glynis, still transfixed and a block away, could hear cursing, the oaths directed at the Farmers and Merchants Bank and its president, Thomas Bingham. At first, all present seemed to be men, and it wasn't until Glynis saw several women join them that she ventured forward. As she neared the crowd, she could hear more clearly, and her apprehension increased when she realized the accusations being leveled at the bank involved a possible failure.

"What's happened?" she inquired of a thin, agitated-looking woman at the fringe of the crowd.

"Been a run on the cursed bank—they got no more money, that's what!" the woman snapped, then turned small shrewd eyes on Glynis. "You got *your* money in there?"

Glynis backed away without answering. She could hear Cullen saying, "Farmers and Merchants Bank is closed for now, so you might as well all go home."

"Who says it's closed—by whose authority?" came the furious question.

"By *my* authority," Cullen answered, his voice steady. He now stood on the bank's front step, blocking the way of anyone who tried to get past. And he still had the rifle stock in one hand, the barrel resting in the crook of his other arm—not precisely threatening, but there.

"When will it reopen?" asked one man, slightly less irate-looking than most.

"I can't say. Why don't you folks all head on home, then I'll have a talk with the bank's president, Tom Bingham. We should know more tomorrow."

No one moved. And Glynis didn't sense any lessening of the crowd's hostility.

"Look," Cullen said, his voice level and reasonable-sounding, "you're not any of you getting in there. Not now, anyway. So you might as well clear out. Unless you plan to stand here all night."

Glynis felt someone behind her. She turned to find Zeph Waters scanning the crowd as if searching for someone, but his eyes flicked constantly back to Cullen. "You see anybody else who's armed?" he asked her in a near whisper.

Glynis, who had been concerned about the same thing, shook her head. "No one that I can see."

"C'mon, my friends," a new and distinctive voice urged from somewhere to the far side of the bank. "Let's give the constable room to do his job. Won't be anything gained by hot tempers right now.''

Everyone turned toward this voice, mostly, Glynis thought, because it held a compelling friendliness. And, as the crowd shifted, a youngish, sturdily built man appeared. From where Glynis stood, the man seemed to have no particularly outstanding features, just light blond hair, somewhat shaggy, and a square clean-shaven face. He nodded affably to those closest to him, and Glynis felt the tension lessen a notch.

"Afternoon, Constable," the blond-haired man said. "Got yourself quite a crowd here." Glynis found herself again struck by the husky warmth of the voice, and it seemed to be this quality, more than anything else, that made the difference: a palpable lessening of tension.

"Afternoon to you, Mr. Fox." Cullen smiled as he spoke. "Think you can help convince these folks to wait—before they jump to conclusions about their money?"

"Sure would like to accommodate you, Constable Stuart." The man grinned. "This is too nice a town to be in such an uproar, leastways until we find out what's going on. Listen, folks—" he turned to those standing around him "—my money's in that bank, too. Guess we'll all just have to worry together."

And now many of those standing there, while they didn't by any means look happy, at least seemed to lose their belligerence. Several even began to move away. They muttered still, but their antagonism sounded much subdued. And most important, it was not directed at Cullen.

"Who is he, that man?" Glynis asked Zeph, who now stood beside her. His own face had lost some of its tenseness, although he seemed surprised by her question.

"You don't know him?"

"No," Glynis said. "Does he live in Seneca Falls?"

"Not exactly. Guess he must have first come here after you'd left. His name's Fox, Grandy Fox. He's a peddler—you know, what they call a Yankee peddler? Travels with his wagon."

Glynis looked around, but the man Zeph called Grandy Fox seemed to have disappeared. However, Cullen was coming toward her, nodding pleasantly to the few people still anxiously gazing at the bank door.

"It's no good, folks," he said to them. "We won't have any answers until tomorrow at the earliest."

"Constable Stuart, I got most of my life's savings in that bank." The speaker was a frail-looking man of indeterminate if considerable age. He seemed to be fighting tears. Cullen put his arm around the old man's shoulders and talked to him quietly. Then together they walked a little way up the street. The remainder of the greatly diminished crowd straggled after them, some obviously still hopeful that their money was safe.

Glynis, distressed by the old man's plight, and berating herself for not heeding her initial instinct to leave, stood watching Liam Cleary. He'd begun meandering around the near side of the bank, peering without much apparent interest into the windows as he went. But then he stopped, suddenly. And Glynis heard an anguished, "Oh, sweet Lord! *Oh, Lord!*"

Zeph, on his way to the road, swung back and ran to where Liam stood with eyes staring as he gestured a shaky hand toward the window. Zeph pressed his own face against the pane. Glynis saw his shoulders stiffen before he turned and went past her. "Constable! Constable Stuart, better come have a look!" His tone carried no discernible distress, nothing that would alarm the few stragglers still dispersing.

She started toward the gray-faced Liam, but he waved her back. "Better not look, Miss Tryon. It's not good."

When Cullen rounded the building with Zeph, Liam moved aside to let him look in the window. Cullen's shoulders, like Zeph's, drew taut. Then he backed away.

"It's Tom Bingham," he said, his voice strained. "Looks like he's hanged himself."

Glynis took a startled step backward. "Hanged himself?" she echoed. "In there?" She motioned toward the window, although, like the rest of her, her arm felt numb.

But Cullen and Zeph had already disappeared around the back of the building. A minute later, she heard scraping noises inside, like chairs being moved, then silence. Liam Cleary stood with his back against the side of the building, and Glynis thought his color looked worse. Even his freckles had paled beneath a sheen of perspiration. "Liam," she suggested, "perhaps you'd feel better if you sat down."

Just then, Cullen and Zeph reappeared. "Liam," Cullen directed, "you go get Doc Ives. If he's not around, get Dr. Cardoza-Levy. And Zeph, get a wagon from the livery."

Zeph turned to go, but Liam Cleary stood as if paralyzed. He gave Cullen a desperate look, then stumbled toward the back of the bank building, where he bent over and vomited. As he continued to retch, Zeph threw up his hands. "I'll get the wagon and the doctor, Constable Stuart." He shot a disgusted look toward the other deputy.

"Yes, go ahead." Cullen didn't look much more sympathetic to Liam than did Zeph. Glynis took a step toward the stricken boy, but Cullen stopped her with a hand on her shoulder. "Don't embarrass him any more—he'll feel bad enough as it is."

When she nodded, Cullen said, "Bingham's dead, all right. I need to go back inside, and you'd best wait out here."

Glynis had no intention of going inside. On the contrary, she wanted to leave. "What do you mean by *wait*, Cullen? I'd like to go home."

"And I'd like you to wait," he answered. "I got some news about the man who was killed yesterday—and I need to ask you a few questions."

"Won't they hold until tomorrow?" she asked, dismayed that her voice sounded so shaky.

He just shook his head and went striding off to the back of the bank again. Glynis stood there wondering if she couldn't simply ignore Cullen and leave; on the other hand, she did want to hear what he'd learned. Then Neva Cardoza-Levy's voice made her turn toward the road. "What's happened?" she asked as she came toward Glynis.

Following her, Zeph glanced around for Cullen. "I found the doctor on Fall Street, and I told the livery to send a wagon."

Neva was clearly impatient for an answer, and again asked Glynis, "Do you know what's going on? Deputy Waters said I was to come here, but he wouldn't say more."

"It seems, Neva, that Tom Bingham has committed suicide."

Neva stared at her. "But that can't be," she said flatly.

"Yes, I'm afraid it can. The bank is in trouble," Glynis added, "and may have failed. I suppose that could be the reason."

"No, it just can't be," Neva argued. "I saw Bingham this very morning." She paused, then said, "Although, now that I think about it, he did look disturbed about something. But I can't imagine he'd kill himself over money."

Zeph grunted. "I think that'd be the best reason in the world to kill yourself. Especially if you're a banker."

"You've suddenly become very worldly," Neva said to him with a scowl. "You're now an expert on suicide?"

Glynis couldn't begin to speculate as to why someone she hardly knew would take his own life. But people had been known to kill themselves for all manner of reasons. As she now said to Neva.

"But it's a spineless thing to do," Neva said with revulsion, almost as if she were taking Bingham's suicide personally. And she might have said more, but Cullen reappeared. As well as a few other people on Fall Street who, apparently realizing something of interest was going on, had started to gather.

"Guess we don't need an autopsy, Doctor," Cullen said, "but I will need a certificate of death."

"Why don't you need an autopsy?" Glynis asked.

"Doesn't seem to be much question of how he died," Cullen answered. To Neva he added, "But why don't you go take a look? Show her where he is, Zeph." Then he leaned close to Neva's ear to whisper something, and Glynis caught the word "autopsy."

Neva nodded, and followed Zeph in the direction from which Cullen had come.

The arrival of more onlookers and the rattle of an approaching wagon made Glynis hold her next comment. But she still wanted to go home.

SHE WAITED, AS Cullen insisted she do, until Thomas Bingham's body was on its way in the livery wagon to Dr. Quentin Ives's office. It was accompanied by Neva and Zeph, with a group of the curious following them. Meanwhile, Cullen sent the hapless Liam Cleary back to the constable's office in the lockup. "After you pull yourself together, Liam, see if you can locate Valerian Voss. Funny, he isn't around—vice-president of the bank, you'd think he'd show some concern about its difficulties." Cullen turned to Glynis. "All right," he said, "I'll walk you back to Peartree's."

She started to object, but bit her lower lip, thinking that Cullen must not realize that she'd have heard, by this time, about Fleur Coddington and himself. But since she certainly wasn't going to bring it up, she could find no excuse not to walk with him.

They started down Fall Street, and Cullen said nothing until they turned onto Cayuga. Then, "Good thing Tom Bingham didn't have a family. At least I don't think he did—he was a widower."

As Cullen himself was, although it had been years since his wife and infant son died in a wagon accident. "How long had Mr. Bingham lived in Seneca Falls?" Glynis asked him, mostly to keep the awkward silence at bay.

"About five years, I'd guess—didn't you know him?"

"Not really. I probably saw him on the street a few times, but he didn't use the library, and I didn't use his bank." Thank goodness, she nearly added.

"Good thing," Cullen said. "That bank's probably failed like a lot of others. I couldn't say that to the crowd—I didn't want a riot on my hands. And I need to get more information about it—that is, if I can find out where the hell Voss has got to."

"Is there any hope of those people getting their money back, Cullen?"

"I doubt it. But this is nothing new. The country's got one helluva problem with its banks."

"But doesn't each state have its own banking requirements?"

"Pretty much so, yes," Cullen said, giving her a strange look that she saw from the corner of her eye. Maybe he *did* think she knew about Fleur. But he continued, "The banking problems really started when good old Andy Jackson vetoed the reauthorization of the United States Bank—by that, I mean a national bank. So now there are no federal requirements for setting up a bank, and no reserve funds are necessary to maintain a bank once it gets started. You're right, of course, that each state has its own banking rules and ways of enforcing them. And it's been a disaster. As long as there are genuine-looking engraved banknotes, anybody can open a bank. Why, even *you* could . . ."

"I doubt it," Glynis inserted. "How many women bankers do you know, Cullen?"

She caught his startled glance; he probably wasn't certain she was joking. Rather than assure him that she was not, she just smiled, enigmatically she hoped, recalling Fleur Coddington's *Mona Lisa* impersonation.

Although he looked puzzled, Cullen went on, "In any event, the situation is ready-made for counterfeiters and their bogus banknotes. I think that's what did in Farmers and Merchants Bank. In fact, I'm sure of it."

Glynis stopped walking. "You mean counterfeit notes of credit—with no actual money behind them—were cashed by the bank?"

"Right. There's an epidemic of that going on in this country, but nobody seems to care much unless it's his own bank that goes belly up."

"Could it be that people don't seem to care because they don't know it's happening, Cullen? I certainly didn't. And how do *you* know so much about it?" They began to walk again.

"Any lawman knows. But I learned more than most because of working for Allan Pinkerton—that's how Pinkerton's detective agency got started, you know, by collaring counterfeiters. But counterfeiting isn't a new activity in America. It started in the colonies . . ." He left off to smile at her. "But you know that!"

He must be referring to what she'd told him about her ancestor, the British colonial governor of New York, William Tryon. As handed down through the family, the story went something to the effect that, during the Revolutionary War, the British tried to depreciate the colonists' money by printing forgeries and false bills of credit. The eminent Governor Tryon himself, while aboard ship in New York Harbor—a ship that just happened to be carrying a printing press—hired a notorious counterfeiter to engrave currency plates. The British then stuffed the bogus Continental bills of credit into burlap bags meant to carry clothing to British prisoners of war. The bags were subsequently loaded on humanitarian wagon trains and sent into the colonies. The Trojan horse revisited.

Glynis found herself smiling until she realized that Cullen did not look amused. "There, you see," he said, "you think it's humorous, and that's the posture most people take toward counterfeiting. It's acquired a romantic veneer it doesn't deserve."

"I suppose you're right," Glynis conceded, "but it's that I have a vision of old Great-Grandfather Tryon aboard his ship, feverishly cranking out counterfeit—" She paused, suddenly shamed as she recalled another old man, the one who earlier had stood bereft in front of Farmers and Merchants Bank. "I guess it's not in the least amusing," she murmured.

They had by now reached the Peartree house. As they went up the front walk, Glynis realized Cullen was heading for the porch stairs, which had in the past been a favorite place to sit and talk. But things had changed. However, as Cullen stood aside waiting for her, and since she didn't know what else to do, Glynis climbed the stairs. Cullen followed, moving past her to promptly settle into a wicker chair. Glynis remained standing on the top step, feeling increasingly uncomfortable.

"Come sit down," Cullen said, unnerving her even more. Surely he didn't intend to tell her about Fleur Coddington and himself. Or perhaps he did.

"He was a banker," Cullen announced.

"What?" Her thoughts muddled, Glynis sank into the nearest chair. "Who was a banker . . . Bingham? No? Oh . . . you mean the murdered man on the train?"

Cullen nodded. "Got a wire this noon, in response to the one I sent yesterday. Constable's office in Utica had a missing person's report on him, filed just yesterday."

"You said he was . . . *another banker?*"

"Another banker. Vice-president of the Bank of Central New York in Utica, where the ten-dollar note in his pouch had been issued. Name of Edward Barrymore."

"Barrymore?" Glynis groaned. "Of course! That's why the ring had a bear . . . at least, I'd guess so. Although, it could be just a terrible pun, and it *was* a signet ring engraved with Yale College! But when you talked to Merrycoyf, did he know the man—this Edward Barrymore?"

"Haven't talked to Jeremiah since I got the wire. But I will. In the meantime, I want to talk to you about something else."

Glynis winced. She did not want to hear about Fleur Coddington. "Cullen, I don't think this is the time."

"Why not?" He pulled out his pocket watch—the watch she had given him for Christmas several years back—glanced at it, and said, "It's not even six yet, Glynis. And I want you to start thinking about this."

For the moment, all she could think about was the watch. Did he wear it when he was courting Fleur?

"Glynis?" Cullen leaned forward to say, "Did you hear me? I said, I'd like you to think about this. See if you can come up with any ideas."

She swallowed hard, and focused her eyes on an ancient coffee stain on the porch floor. "Any ideas?" she repeated faintly.

"Glynis, are you all right?" Cullen asked, a frown appearing under the thick sand-colored hair tousled over his forehead. "I just want you to listen." He seemed to be watching her warily for signs of wool-gathering. "In the past month," he went on, "we've had three violent deaths, either in or near Seneca Falls. And that doesn't even include your banker, Barrymore."

Glynis recoiled, then sat forward with a creak of wicker, thinking she could not have heard correctly. "By violent deaths, do you mean murders?"

"I mean murders."

Three—in a month? "Cullen, how can that be?"

"You think I don't wish I knew? The one thing I'm fairly certain about is that the murders are connected—to money, bogus money. Which, of course, could also link the two bankers."

"So you don't believe Thomas Bingham took his own life?"

Cullen shrugged. "Remember you asked about an autopsy? Just as curiosity-seekers were beginning to arrive? Well, I told Neva to do one, and said to keep it to herself. I'd just as soon everybody in town believes it was suicide—so the murderer, if there *was* murder, will think I believe it, too.''

''So you assume all the murders have been committed by the same person?'' Glynis paused, then said, ''Well, yes, I guess you do if you think the motive is the same.''

''No, there could be more than one person involved. Could be several. But Glynis, let me tell you what's been happening here, O.K.?'' Again he looked at her closely.

''All right, Cullen, go ahead. But I can't imagine how I can help. I just deposited my money in the Globe Bank, and hope it's safe—I know next to nothing about banking.'' Nor did she particularly want to know much, but this she did not say.

''You will,'' Cullen told her. Glynis sighed, and nodded. But now she found a perverse disappointment in the fact that she was not to hear about Fleur Coddington. ''I think, Cullen, that before we get into this—''

''Glynis,'' Cullen interrupted, with rather unnecessary force she thought, ''I'd like to discuss it before anybody appears from in there.'' He motioned toward the front door.

Glynis decided not to fight a losing battle. ''It's just that I'm not eager to get involved in murder, again,'' she said. ''If these recent killings have to do with money and banking, well, don't I recall reading that some government agency was formed to handle it? On the federal level, I mean?''

''If you'll listen, that's what I intend to explain,'' Cullen said, by now clearly impatient. When she reluctantly nodded, he went on, ''You're right about an agency. It's the Special Detective Service, and its agents are under the authority of the United States Treasury Department.''

''Well, why can't they deal with this?''

''Because,'' Cullen said, his expression seeming to be one of surprise at her question, ''the killing is being done in Seneca County. Which is under my jurisdiction. I take that kind of personally. And I'd just as soon not have to find any more dead men!''

''I'm sorry, Cullen, of course you don't. But still, if there are Treasury agents to—''

''The problem, Glynis, is that two of those agents have turned up dead!''

Six

❦

That it shall be the duty of the superintendent of the banking department . . . to destroy, or cause to be destroyed, all bank note plates, in his custody, of banks, banking associations or individual bankers which have failed or given notice of closing their business . . .

—CHAPTER 189, SECTION 5, EIGHTIETH
SESSION OF THE LEGISLATURE OF THE
STATE OF NEW YORK MARCH 1857

"TREASURY AGENTS HAVE been murdered—here in Seneca Falls?" Glynis knew she sounded incredulous, but she had assumed that kind of thing happened only in big cities. That rural western New York was somehow not susceptible.

"Afraid so," Cullen said. "A couple of months ago counterfeit money began showing up in large quantities in western and central New York—by that, I mean places like Rochester and Syracuse, Albany and Utica. We've always had *some* bogus money floating around, but this was a helluva lot more than some. It was almost as if the stuff originated here in Seneca Falls. I myself found it hard to believe we had a counterfeit ring operating in this area, but I wired the Treasury Department in Washington anyway."

Glynis sat forward in the chair. If Cullen wanted her full attention, he certainly had it now. And she could appreciate why he sounded skeptical. A counterfeiting ring here?

"Treasury wasn't particularly surprised," he continued. "There had been bogus coins and bills and forged banknotes showing up for months in the eastern part of the state, including New York City. They thought in Washington that it was only a matter of time before the counterfeits surfaced here."

"And what did the Treasury Department do?"

"Sent out an agent, name of Paul Trent. Good man. He

nosed around for a few weeks, then he thought he was on to something.''

The something that Agent Trent was on to, Cullen explained, included a possible link between local coney dealers—counterfeit brokers—and a number of recent raids on western New York armories as well as break-ins and robberies at several Finger Lakes rifle and gun manufacturers.

''Did this Agent Trent know who was involved?'' Glynis asked.

''Thought he knew a few who were 'passers.' They're the ones who exchange bad money for good and pass it on to the unsuspecting—like shopkeepers, for instance. But he wasn't ready to tell me what he knew until he found the ones involved in actually making the counterfeit. Said it was Treasury policy, which I can understand. They wouldn't want some inept, or crooked, local lawman tipping off the higher-ups.''

''This sounds like a bad dream, Cullen. But was Agent Trent successful?''

He shook his head. ''Trent had managed to infiltrate a gang that was breaking into local armories—he said it wasn't all that hard to do, if you were cautious. Trent, unfortunately, wasn't cautious enough. At any rate, he twice alerted me to a robbery, but we didn't have enough time to catch them red-handed. We'd get there, and they'd have disappeared.''

''Who is 'we'?'' Glynis asked. ''You and Zeph and Liam Cleary?''

''Yes, although Liam Cleary's not . . .'' Cullen's voice trailed off. Then he went on, ''A couple weeks ago, Trent really thought he had this gang of marauders set up for a fall. But they apparently changed their plans at the last minute, because we got there a little too late.''

The item in the Rochester newspaper came back to Glynis as she watched Cullen's expression turn grim. ''We got there too late,'' he repeated, ''not only to capture the gang, but to keep Paul Trent alive. He'd been shot, along with an old watchman—both of them dead when we rode up. My guess is that one or more of the men involved suspected Trent of a double cross, and killed him.''

''Cullen, I know I keep questioning this,'' Glynis apologized, "but why on earth would anyone around here want to collect weapons? To what purpose?"

"Oh, I expect there are plenty of purposes, mainly resale."

"It seems rather a risky enterprise."

"I agree," Cullen said, "but I haven't come up with anything better. Unless some group is stockpiling weapons—who knows why?"

"But what could be the reason for it?" Glynis asked with a sense of dread. "Could they be plotting some kind of outlaw activities? Something, for instance, like those train robberies in the western territories?"

Cullen shrugged. "Maybe. But there's more to the story of that armory break-in. While Zeph and Liam were taking the weapons back inside, I went for a look around. Just after I saw a couple of mountain lions bounding up a drumlin hill, I found another dead man—maybe a mile from the armory. Shot in the side and back, but he was clutching a banknote. And there were a few gold coins nearby. He had no identification on him—just a portrait miniature of a woman—but I played a hunch and wired the circumstances and his description to the Treasury. They wired back that he'd been an agent, all right—a John Fairfax. And I forgot to mention that Trent, when we found his body inside the armory, was holding a ten-dollar gold piece."

"A gold eagle," Glynis said, drawing in her breath. "Cullen, the man on the train—Barrymore—he had a double eagle in his pouch."

"Yes, but I doubt there's any connection, unless his double eagle turns out to be bogus—like the eagle that Agent Trent had when we found him."

"It was counterfeit?"

"Yeah, and so was that banknote the other dead agent, John Fairfax, had clutched in his hand. And the coins, too: they were all spurious—you know what that means?"

"Spurious?" Glynis echoed. "False, or counterfeit?"

"Yes, counterfeit, but the term *spurious,* in this context, means banknotes that have been altered, or raised, from a low value to one higher. Say a ten to a one hundred, just by adding a zero. Or a note printed from an original bank plate that *should* have been destroyed when the bank closed—New York law demands that. It's complicated, Glynis, and there's more to it, but I'll save it for another time. All you need to know now are the basics.''

And that was enough! Her mind was already reeling. But the deaths . . . ''Cullen, did the Treasury Department send other agents here—after the two you mentioned were killed?''

''No, not as yet. They said they couldn't spare anyone else right now, and it might be a few months before they can. But it could be they simply don't want to disclose there's another agent here. Hell, for all I know, they may be suspicious of *me*. In the meantime, we've got a dead banker—make that two— who may or may not be connected in some way to the counterfeiters. But by tomorrow I'll have that double eagle of the Utica banker Barrymore checked out—and his banknote too. If they're genuine, then there's probably no link between the counterfeiters and him.''

Glynis wondered if this might be wishful thinking on Cullen's part. But, she remembered, he'd always chided her about seeing malignant patterns where none existed. ''And Thomas Bingham?'' she asked.

''Doctor said she'd do the autopsy tonight.''

Glynis, stiff from sitting in one position for so long, shifted in her chair and winced at the sound of complaining wicker. ''But Cullen, I don't see what I can possibly add. In the past, when I've figured things out, it's been mostly a matter of proximity, and luck. When it involves someone I don't even know . . .'' She paused, then asked with alarm, ''You don't think someone I know *is* involved, do you? Someone here in town?''

''I don't know what to think, Glynis, but you've said exactly the same thing before—and it hasn't been just luck on your part. We'll talk more after I get the autopsy report.''

He looked up as Harriet opened the door and came out onto the porch. She greeted Cullen, then looked to Glynis. ''Emma's not back yet?''

''Harriet!'' Glynis jumped to her feet. ''Do you mean Emma's been gone since morning? All day?''

''No, she came back, and then left again. I just thought you might have seen her on Fall Street, is all.''

"But where is she? Did you find out what she was up to?"

Harriet seemed to hesitate, then nodded, but with a guarded expression. "Yes, she finally told me."

"Well?" Glynis prodded. "*Harriet,* why won't you—"

"She went to see about getting work," Harriet broke in, her expression now one of exasperation.

"What?" Glynis felt some exasperation of her own. "You mean that Emma—*shy Emma*—went alone to find work? Where . . . where did she go?"

Harriet scowled. "To the dress shop." As if the words had caught in her throat, she cleared it and added, softly, "Fleur Coddington's dress shop."

Instinctively, Glynis glanced at Cullen. She looked away immediately, but not before seeing that his face revealed nothing. But then, he was considered to be the best poker player in Seneca County.

Harriet was gazing at Glynis with something like you-forced-me-into-it written across her face. And Cullen, who had stood up when Harriet came through the door, now moved to the top of the porch steps. But at the clatter of distant wagon wheels, they all three looked down the road. Near the Fall Street end of Cayuga Street, a large draft horse had appeared, drawing an odd-looking wagon. Emma walked alongside it, and beside her was the man Glynis had been told was the peddler Grandy Fox. What in the world was Emma doing with him?

"I'll be going along now," Cullen said. But as he started down the steps, Glynis recalled something he'd begun to tell her earlier. "You mentioned Liam Cleary, Cullen," she said, "about him not being . . . not being what?"

"Just that he's not as rugged as I'd like, that's all. But he's still young, and maybe he'll grow a tougher skin along the way. In any event, I need him."

"You mean because of the—" Glynis stopped herself, sure Cullen would not want Harriet to know what they'd been discussing.

But he shook his head. "I mean," he said, "because Zeph isn't reliable anymore."

"Zeph unreliable? No." Glynis came down the steps to where Cullen stood, while she protested, "No, surely not."

"Yes," he answered her. "Zeph's gotten himself all wound up in abolition. I never know when he's going to take off to a meeting somewhere. He's already been to Canada a couple times this year."

"I know he has a cousin there," Glynis said. "And there are several communities of escaped slaves in Canada. Is Zeph still involved in the Underground Railroad?"

"That, and other things." Cullen frowned. "I'm afraid he's come under the influence of a real troublemaker. An abolitionist, name of Brown. John Brown. You ever heard of him, Glynis?"

"Yes," she said, recalling Zeph's same question, "I've read about Brown in the newspapers. I can't remember it exactly— something to do with the civil war in Kansas—but I'm certain whatever I read wasn't good."

"No, it wouldn't have been. And I don't mind telling you, I'm concerned about Zeph. Maybe you can talk some sense into him." Cullen looked toward the road at the jangle of harness bells. A muscular chestnut horse, fetlocks and feet like big white fringed boots, drew the wagon up to the Peartree walk.

"Evening, Constable," Grandy Fox said. He had the horse's reins looped over his right hand, and he deftly transferred them before offering the hand to Cullen. And then said to Glynis, "You must be the young lady's aunt who I've been hearing about." He smiled, and looked down at Emma standing beside him. She colored faintly, but nowhere near as much as usual, Glynis marked with interest. And this peddler, seen close up, looked a good deal more interesting than she'd noticed earlier.

"Yes, I'm Glynis Tryon, Mr. Fox," she said, offering her own hand. He took it in a warm firm grip, and when he smiled again, Glynis saw lines around his mouth. He was slightly older than she'd thought. His eyes, however, held the brightness of the young, and the deep green of summer leaves.

Cullen again announced that he had to leave. Whereby Grandy Fox quickly said, "You going to be at the barn dance, Constable?" Not waiting for the answer—which Glynis was interested in hearing—Grandy now turned to her, saying, "I'm trying to convince your niece to bring along her dulcimer, Miss Tryon. I've put together a group of string players, but for a dance we could certainly use another. I know," he said, his eyes now dancing themselves, "that your neighbor Miss Usher plays dulcimer, but I don't think we can count on her attending—not a benefit for the refuge. Do you?"

It wasn't so much what he said as the ingenuous way he'd said it that made Glynis laugh. And behind her she heard Cullen's pleasant chuckle. "No, I don't think so, Mr. Fox," she agreed. "I see you've come to know this town quite well." She looked at her niece. "What do you think, Emma, about playing? It sounds like fun."

Emma made a face and shook her head.

Cullen now looked as if he were actually going to leave. In fact, he'd gone as far as the road, when Grandy Fox, with a mischievous smile, said, "Constable Stuart, I think you'd best plan to come. I hear there's to be gallons of brew—no telling what might happen."

"I've already made plans to be there," Cullen answered, his voice suddenly sounding almost irritated. He quickly walked off.

Glynis felt her face grow hot; she wondered if the others were aware of it. Cullen had certainly made it clear—he would be at the dance all right, but with someone else. To cover her discomfort, she feigned preoccupation with Grandy Fox's wagon. And found it definitely worthy of study. The wagon was for the most part painted a forest green, with its wheels and trim a brown that matched the chestnut horse. So well did the vehicle blend with the dirt road and the trees that Glynis had not at first appreciated its intricate gear. She was amazed, in fact, that a single horse could pull it.

Grandy Fox apparently read her mind. "It's not as heavy as it looks, Miss Tryon. I know, the clutter makes it appear that it weighs more than a locomotive, but it doesn't—I wouldn't do that to my friend here." And he gave the horse's white-blazed muzzle a few affectionate pats.

"You should see what's in there," Emma whispered to Glynis, a stage whisper that Grandy Fox evidently heard as he moved to the side of the wagon, unfastening a padlock, then several hooks at the bottom of what looked like doors. He swung the doors up and out on long hinges. The rectangular box that sat on the wagon bed looked to be some five feet in height and eight feet in length. After the peddler had pulled down a wooden arm to prop open the doors, Glynis could only gape at what had been revealed.

"Brought your scissors back, Mrs. Peartree," Grandy Fox told Harriet. "Sharpened up nicely, they did." He reached into one of many small, open, box-like cubbyholes and extracted Harriet's long-bladed pair of tailoring shears, as well as several smaller pairs of scissors.

"Thank you for your swiftness." Harriet smiled and leaned over the porch railing for her scissors. She extracted coins from her apron pocket, handed them to the peddler, and turned toward the front door. "It's nearly seven o'clock, Glynis. I'm going in to check the oven, and mind you aren't out here too long or the lamb kidneys will toughen."

Glynis nodded, somewhat indifferent to the condition of Harriet's meat when confronted with the treasure trove that was Grandy Fox's wagon. The top half of the opened side held rows of hooks, from which hung large buckets and small pails, National washboards, Universal coffee grinders, muffin tins, strainers, kettles, and sundry other kitchen goods. The lower half consisted of shelves heaped with crocks and cans, and cubbyholes sprouting long-handled spoons, knife handles, and various size spatulas, even elongated boxes of Gates matches.

Glynis walked slowly around the wagon, skirting the fishing rods that protruded from rear cubbyholes. With the flourish of a seasoned showman, Grandy Fox swung open the hinged doors on the opposite side of the wagon to reveal shelves. Stacked on these shelves, amidst straw and woodshavings for protection, were bowls—more bowls than Glynis had seen in one place in her entire life. Big bowls nested inside bigger bowls. There were tiny, medium, and mammoth bowls. Punch bowls, finger bowls, mixing, butter, and salad bowls. Enameled tin, copper, wood, pottery, and cut glass. Plain and decorated and silver-plated. Green, magenta, blue, and brown transfer-printed, ceramic bowls with scenes of the Hudson River Valley.

"I can't resist them," Grandy Fox said, his grin admitting that he knew such explanation to be unnecessary. "Don't know why, I just like bowls."

His sheepish admission made Glynis smile. "So I gathered. Are you a collector, Mr. Fox, or do you sell these bowls?"

Grandy Fox shrugged. "Some I sell. But not all, not if I don't have to. As I said, I like them."

Emma, who'd been following Glynis around the wagon, now asked the peddler, "Where do you keep your concertina and violin, and the tin-whistle and banjo?" She said to Glynis, "He plays them all." Whereupon Emma tilted her head to one side, and gave the peddler a coy smile. "At least he says he does."

Glynis was so taken aback by the appearance of this flirtatious Emma that she barely registered Grandy Fox's laugh.

"You don't believe me? You'll see." He grinned, adding, "And come the dance, I want to see your dulcimer, Miss Emma."

Behind them, a front window opened and Harriet's voice called, "You're welcome to stay for supper, too, Grandy Fox, if you like."

"Thank you, no, Mrs. Peartree. Got myself an earlier invitation. And I'll be heading out now." He pulled down the sides of the wagon, much like lowering the curtains on a stage, and fastened the padlock before clambering up into the narrow driver's seat. He smiled at Emma. "I'll look for you at the dance. And you, too, Miss Glynis Tryon."

All this while the chestnut horse had been standing quietly, seeming content to nuzzle the flowerbed and occasionally sample the rock cress. But with a flick of the peddler's reins over his broad back, the horse tossed his head, making the bells on his harness jingle. After the chestnut's first few prancing steps, the wagon began to move slowly back down Cayuga Street. Grandy Fox raised his hand to wave, and in return, Emma's shot into the air.

"I've never seen anything like that wagon," she said to Glynis as they went up the porch steps.

Nor anything like Grandy Fox either, Glynis guessed.

GLYNIS PAUSED ON the landing between the first and second floor of the Peartree house. She'd heard a faint *click-click-click* coming from behind the closed door of an upstairs bedroom, and now she identified the sound as the treadle foot of Emma's sewing machine. So *that* had been why her niece vanished so quickly after supper. Glynis climbed the remaining steps, knocked, and heard a muffled "Come in." She opened the door on "La Maison de Peartree."

Remnants of fabric, yards of ribbon and lace trim, spools of cord and thread, and boxes of buttons covered every available inch of floor space. Unfinished sections of what looked to be skirts lay over the poster bed and bureau top, and several more hung from the drapery rod. From the open doors of the wardrobe cabinet swung hangers holding a finished bodice and sleeves. The Singer stood diagonally across one corner of the room with Emma wedged behind it, seated on a straight-backed chair. Through the window, the faint light of early evening came over her shoulder. This and a wavering candle flame provided the room's only illumination.

Subduing her initial shock, Glynis stepped into the room quickly, closing the door behind her so Harriet wouldn't see what had become of her bedroom. The clicking stopped as Emma removed her foot from the treadle and looked up from the task of feeding satin fabric through the Singer. Her lips appeared to bristle with straight pins.

"Emma," Glynis said, standing in front of the door and searching for an unoccupied space to put her feet, "it's dark in here. How can you see?"

"My lamp's over there, but I haven't got around to lighting it," Emma mumbled around the pins, then removed them to a plump pincushion.

Glynis stepped gingerly over several yards of fabric to reach a lace-maker's lamp with a large blown-glass globe that Emma had brought from Springfield. "Is this one lamp going to be enough?"

"It'll have to do for now. I asked Grandy Fox if he had any lamps I could hang in the corner here, and he said he'd find some for me."

"Will it bother you if we talk while you work?"

"No; sit down, if you can find a spot."

Glynis turned to the four poster and cleared a small portion to expose a crocheted coverlet, then sat on its edge. "You seemed reluctant to talk at supper, Emma,'' she ventured. ''I mean about your search for work.''

Emma tossed aside a scrap of pink satin she'd just trimmed away from the seam of what looked like a sash, and nodded at Glynis with obvious embarrassment. ''I was ashamed that I hadn't told you where I was going today,'' she said quietly. ''But I didn't want you to feel you had to look after me.''

''And you were probably also concerned, with good reason, about Fleur Coddington's response to me yesterday?'' Glynis asked.

Emma flushed, her answer obvious.

''Yes,'' Glynis said, ''I thought so.'' She debated the wisdom of giving her niece the reason. It seemed only fair, especially since Emma was bright and would likely figure it out for herself sooner or later. ''Harriet told me last night,'' Glynis explained, ''that Fleur Coddington has . . . well, has recently been seen with Constable Stuart—seen socially, that is.''

She paused as Emma's look had become one of mortification. ''Oh, Aunt Glynis, I had no idea. I'm so sorry,'' she said with a great deal more sympathy than Glynis felt she deserved or was comfortable in accepting.

''There's no cause for you to be sorry, Emma. And I hope it didn't interfere with your gaining a position at the dress shop.''

Emma shook her head. ''No, I don't think Mrs. Coddington even saw me in the wagon with you. She didn't act as if she had. But she did say she couldn't hire me. At first, she told me that she already had two seamstresses—one of them is the girl we saw crying, yesterday. Remember her?''

''Yes, I remember.''

''Her name's Sally Lunt. She seems a bit of a ninny, though. She was there today, and she was still crying. I imagine if she keeps that up, she'll stain a lot of silk fabric.'' Emma paused, then added wryly, ''And then I expect I can get her job. In the meantime''—she went on before Glynis could do more than blink at her niece's Machiavellian logic—''Mrs. Coddington finally said she'll give me some piecework. That was after I came back here, and collected some of my dresses, including the one I made for you—it's a good thing she didn't know that!

Anyway, I took the dresses, and some of the design sketches I'd made in Springfield, back to the shop to show her. Then Mrs. Coddington decided she might use me after all. But just for piecework in the beginning." Emma gestured toward the layers of fabric on the bed.

"Emma, that's wonderful! You should be proud of yourself, persisting like that."

"It was Grandy Fox's idea," Emma said, "to show her what I'd made."

"Grandy Fox? How did you happen to meet him?"

"He was at the shop returning some dress-making shears he'd sharpened. And he overheard what Mrs. Coddington said about not needing me."

"How nice of him to take an interest," Glynis remarked, hoping her voice sounded neutral while she pondered how concerned she should be about the peddler's interest. After all, Emma was still young and naive—although her comment about replacing Sally Lunt seemed to somewhat refute this. "But, Emma, going to the shop, alone, was something I could never have done at your age. I was just too shy."

With a slight shake of her head, Emma gave her aunt a skeptical glance. "But you went off to college alone," she argued, "when nobody wanted you to. Papa said he remembered everyone telling you it was wrong for a woman. But you did it. That was brave—I think it was *very* brave. It's what made me decide, coming here on the train, that I had to overcome my shyness too. Or I'd never be able to do what I want. I'd just have to get married like everybody else."

Glynis could scarcely believe what she'd heard. This, coming from Emma, was so unexpected. She studied her niece a moment before asking, "And do you know what you want, Emma?"

"Yes! Yes, I do know! Someday I want to have my own dress shop."

Not anticipating such a decisive response, Glynis didn't know what to say. Or even how to offer encouragement. But Emma, her head bent again over her sewing machine, pumping the treadle with an even rhythm, didn't seem to need encouraging. "Aunt Glynis," she said, without looking up, "could you give me that spool of ribbon on the bed there—the pink grosgrain?''

While Glynis looked for the ribbon, Emma added, ''I wish Mrs. Lincoln wouldn't insist on wearing *pink*. It's not a good color on her, but she loves it.''

''Is that what you're working on now?'' Glynis asked, handing Emma the spool of wide grosgrain ribbon. ''A gown for Mary Lincoln?''

Emma nodded. ''Remember how she had forty fits when she found out I was leaving Springfield? So I said I would still sew for her—I've got all her measurements—and mail the gowns back there. Well, the night before you and I left, she came dashing over to the house with this pink satin, all in a dither because she needed a new dress for some party she and Mr. Lincoln are going to next month.''

Glynis smiled. It wasn't hard to imagine the vivacious and impulsive Mary Lincoln dashing down the street in a dither. She and her husband, and their three small boys, lived at the corner of Eighth and Jackson streets, just two doors down from the Tryons. The large two-story Lincoln house, surrounded by a low black iron fence and no discernible greenery—she had heard that Mr. Lincoln attempted and failed at several gardening projects—was a boisterous one. More so when Mr. Lincoln was away as he often was, and Mary had to cope alone with her brood of ''dear, sweet angel boys.'' Most of Springfield took issue with this idyllic portrayal, and William Herndon, Mr. Lincoln's law partner, made no bones about calling the boys ''the brats.''

Glynis thought that Mary's leniency with her children might stem from nine years before, when she lost a four-year-old son. Little Edward's had been a hard death, after weeks of suffering from consumption, and the neighbors still talked of Mary's terrible grief. She told of writing in her diary that she herself had wanted to die, and that she hoped ''never to endure such anguish again.''

Glynis, now watching her niece twist the pink ribbon into small rosettes for Mary's gown, recalled the day she had first gone to the Lincoln house with Emma, who was unable to carry alone all the garments she'd just completed. When they arrived,

Mr. Lincoln was apparently at his office, four blocks away in the courthouse square. Glynis had finally grown restless after watching an hour's worth of fittings in a second-story bedroom, and had come down the stairs to leave. In the front hall, she'd found Mary's husband dressed in a rumpled but well-tailored linen suit and lying stretched out on the floor, his head propped against an overturned chair while he read the *Springfield Journal*. When he'd gotten to his feet—"he just sort of unfolds, in long sections," was the way Glynis's brother Robin had described it—she found the most extraordinary thing about the man's size to be his enormous boots, and hands that looked as if they should belong to a giant.

All he'd said was, "Well, howdy," and taken her hands in both of his huge ones, his gray eyes conveying great good humor. From her brother's accounts, Glynis knew enough not to be misled by the man's rustic exterior; that Abraham Lincoln's intellect made him an extremely successful lawyer, but one who was at first often underestimated by legal adversaries—until in defeat they learned otherwise. However, Glynis decided, even his adversaries must find it next to impossible to dislike this amiable-looking man, and standing with him there at the foot of the stairs, she believed Mary Lincoln to be one of the most fortunate of women. As Mary herself did.

Glynis now slid off Emma's bed and moved toward the door of the bedroom, unnoticed by her niece, who sat scowling at an unruly knot of pink ribbon. As she closed the door behind her, she heard a murmured, "Good night, Aunt Glynis."

She stood outside the door going over their conversation. Something appeared to have happened to her niece since they'd left Springfield—whatever it was had changed her mood, her demeanor, and, apparently, her previous dearth of ambition. Emma seemed a different young woman. But that was improbable. Most people did not change all that much, not even in the course of a lifetime. Certainly not in a few days. So what had happened here? Could the very act of leaving Springfield, the town where she'd lived all her life, have had that profound an effect on Emma?

Glynis shook her head in bewilderment as she went down the hall to her own room. After lighting the lamp on her dresser, she turned to gaze at the walking stick resting against the far wall. The stick's shank was walnut, a rich chocolate color, varnished and buffed to the sheen of Emma's satin. Above a ringlike silver collar was the horn grip, or handle, of a milky soft brown. The horn had been carved into the head of a wolf. Thus, the night before, as soon as Harriet handed the stick to her, Glynis had known its maker.

"He brought this here before he left town, and asked me to give it to you," Harriet had told her. "As usual," she added, "he didn't say much. Except that you should be careful when you turned the wolf. Do you know what he meant by that?"

Glynis had nodded. She knew what he'd meant; she'd seen enough of his lethal, carved walking sticks. But she also knew, then, that he would come back. The wolf was spirit and protector of Jacques Sundown.

EMMA HEARD THE hall clock strike eleven times. She slumped back in the chair, and rubbed her eyes with the heel of her hand. The light was so dim that her head throbbed with the effort of straining to see; nonetheless, the pink gown was close to completion. But even if she sent it off to Springfield tomorrow, and Mary Lincoln mailed her a banknote straightaway, Emma still couldn't cover the last installment payment on the Singer. The *lost* payment, that was. She had sent the money from Springfield in April, now almost two months past.

Since then she'd received three demand letters for the "overdue amount" from a Mr. Archibald Throckmorton of the Singer Company. She'd written back to Mr. Throckmorton twice, explaining that the payment had been sent. That in the meantime, it must have gone missing in the mail, or been mislaid, or even stolen. Mr. Archibald Throckmorton had not been sympathetic. On the contrary.

She'd not answered the last demand from him because it had so frightened her. Mr. Throckmorton's letter stated that she would very likely be sent to jail because of the delinquent payment. Almost as bad, Emma thought with her stomach lurching, was his threat that the sewing machine would be repossessed. And this was after she'd faithfully made all the payments, on time, plus interest. She had no idea what she was going to do. Obviously she had to do something!

She couldn't tell Aunt Glynis about it—she couldn't. Not after her aunt had so generously given her the chance to escape Springfield. Had kept Emma from being ensnared by burdens her aunt had had to assume at an even younger age than Emma. And how capable would Aunt Glynis think her of having her own dress shop if she couldn't even make sewing machine payments on time?

Emma knew her aunt had been surprised when told of her ambition. Probably didn't know what had come over her. But Emma knew. And this was her opportunity—she couldn't forfeit it to some horrid little man with a name like Archibald Throckmorton. Who, for all Emma knew, had likely "mislaid" her money for himself.

But what could she do about it?

SEVEN

❧

*I believe there are better times dawning, to my sight at least.
I am not now laboring and waiting without present reward
for myself; it is for a future reward for mankind, and for you
all. There can be no doubt of the reward in the end, or of the
success of a great cause which is to earn it.*

—JOHN HENRY KAGI, AN 1858 LETTER TO
HIS FATHER AND SISTER

THE AIR OF the Great Northern Woods was sweet with honey
locust and wild plum blossoms. The breeze bearing their scent
from the trees below the log house carried with it a distinct and
unexpected male voice. Annie Brown heard it as she stood at
the well. The hand with which she had been reaching for the
bucket handle stopped in mid-air. That must be his voice that
came to her. It couldn't be, but it *was*.

Earlier she had seen from the upstairs loft window two men
on horseback coming up the long rise from North Elba. They'd
been too distant to identify. A short time later Father saw them,
too, and called for her to make coffee. But she'd first had to
get the water.

She lifted a hand to shade her eyes against the sun, her bare
toes curling in the mud beside the well where she had just
spilled the water. Spilled it because now the man's voice came
to her more clearly. And it *was* his. John Henry's.

He hadn't been to North Elba for five months and three days.
Annie had believed he was still a newspaper correspondent in
Kansas, reporting on the happenings there. But there must not
be any more happenings there, if he was here. Father hadn't
mentioned that John Henry was coming, which was why, she
now told herself, her heart had begun leaping like a fish, as if
she were afraid. And maybe she was.

He was smart. Smarter than anyone she knew. Smarter even
than Father. John Henry had studied mathematics and law and

philosophy. He could argue like a lawyer, or talk like a school-teacher, which is what he had been in Virginia. And his large watchful eyes seemed to look straight into her head, to know what she was thinking now, and what she had thought in the past. That was reason enough to be afraid.

The first time he had come to North Elba, she'd been scared of him because he had just spent four months in a Kansas jail for taking part in the anti-slavery war there. She had also heard he once shot and killed a man. But he told her why one day, up on the hill behind the house. "Are you afraid of me, serious little Annie Brown?" he had asked.

How had he known? Could he see her mind?

"Why do you think that?" she'd answered. She had been weeding the garden plot when he appeared and, at his question, she took a few quick steps backward. But she could smell the faint evergreen scent of him, like balsam firs when they stood covered with snow.

"Because you act like a skittish colt whenever I try to talk to you," he said. "Just as you're doing right now. What have you heard about me? I give you my oath that I would never harm a young lady."

Young lady? Annie had never thought to be called that! And she'd been forced to smile. She didn't want to, and it was a small one, but smile she did. And he'd laughed then, a bright ripple of sound like the Raquette River when it tumbled over rocks, and that was when her heart had begun the leaping she couldn't seem to check.

"I heard you killed a man," she said, mostly to quiet his laugh, and her heart.

It did quiet. He looked at her with a somber face, and said, "Yes, I did kill a man. He was a big man, and he had a bludgeon, and he hit me with it, and he was going to keep hitting me with it until I died. So I shot him."

Now the men on horseback crossed the narrow bridge over the creek. Annie stood by the well, watching them, then bent down and grabbed the handle of the bucket and started at a run for the house. She hardly felt the water sloshing over her feet.

*   *   *

ANNIE HAD MADE the coffee and given it to the men who
were in the front room with Father. John Henry didn't seem to
notice she was there. At least he didn't say anything to her. It
was as if she were invisible, like her mother.

Her sister Ruth called from upstairs that her baby was sick,
although Annie didn't think it was. Ruth always fretted about
her baby, maybe because ten years ago she'd spilled boiling
water on their little sister Amelia, and Amelia had died. Ever
since then, Ruth prayed that she wouldn't be forsaken by the
Lord. But it had been an accident. Annie thought that if the
Lord was as all-seeing as Father said, He would know this.
And if the Lord wasn't all-seeing, then He probably missed the
whole thing, and Ruth should stop worrying about it. But Annie
took warm willow-bark tea upstairs for the baby anyway. When
she came back down, the last step creaked and John Henry
looked over at her. He didn't smile, although his eyes seemed
to say something she couldn't make out, and after a moment
he looked away.

Her mother was feeling poorly and needed to stay upstairs,
so Annie made pig hocks and dandelion greens and cornbread
for supper. While they ate, the men and her brothers and Father
talked about slavery and how the Lord hated it, and how the
Lord would hate them, too, if they didn't do something about
it. Annie didn't think they tasted the food; they just shoveled
it in as if it were porridge. She might as well have made that.
And John Henry still didn't take notice of her—she must have
been wrong about his eyes saying something. So her heart had
stopped leaping. It felt instead like a great heavy lump in her
chest.

While Annie cleaned up after supper, Father began to talk
about Virginia. And again she heard the words "Harper's
Ferry." John Henry murmured something then, so low that Annie couldn't make it out. In reply, Father's voice took on the
shrill pitch of a preacher, and she could hear every word
plainly. He was talking to John Cook, the other man who had
come on horseback, and Father said, "You were down in Harper's Ferry to study the town and the layout of the armory.
Collect information, not draw attention to yourself." Father's
voice rose higher. "You put our work for the Lord in danger

by indulging in fornication! And what did you do to put things right?''

John Cook's tone sounded blustery. "I married her, that's what. There's no harm done!"

The voices lowered, and the next thing Annie heard was her brother Oliver saying, "How we going to buy arms if we don't have money? We've got to have money."

It was always money. They had never had any, Annie reasoned as she scrubbed the tin kettle, so why did they expect it to be different now? She didn't hear an answer.

After a time, John Cook came swaggering into the kitchen and Annie knew she'd have to hear him talk about himself, like he always did. About how he'd gone to Yale, so it was a natural thing that he'd know more than anyone else. And then he'd toss his long blond hair, and grin with his mean little blue eyes, and Annie would remember how she'd heard that John Cook "had a way with women." She guessed that proved she was still a girl, no matter what her body told her, because she didn't like him. Especially now after she'd heard he had to marry someone in Harper's Ferry because he got her with child. Seemed like John Cook didn't know as much as he thought he did.

When the men's voices in the other room started to get louder, John Cook left the kitchen to join them. Mostly Annie heard Father's voice, shouting at Salmon and Jason because they still wouldn't agree. to go to Harper's Ferry. Then other voices chimed in—although none of them was John Henry's—and after a frightening roar from Father, followed by a howl of rage from someone, probably Salmon, Annie grabbed up the wash basin and went with it through the doorway. After she splashed the lilac bush with the dirty water, she set the basin down and moved a few feet away from the house. But she could still hear the men's voices.

She walked toward the creek in the warm, sweet-smelling darkness. Then she hitched up her coarse-woven cotton dress to climb onto a huge boulder that the mountains left behind when they rose from the earth. When she twisted around on the boulder to sit, she felt a seam in the dress give way. Likely from pulling too tight across her new chest.

The sickle-shaped moon floated over the shoulder of old Whiteface, and Annie threw back her head to gaze at the black sky. The North Star shone with a cold light, and she shivered to think of escaped slaves following it, through marshes and bogs, across rivers and streams, and over the tall rounded mountains of Pennsylvania that she'd seen on Father's maps. The slaves had no maps, only their star. Father said that after he went to Harper's Ferry, there would be no more slavery. But Annie thought that first, before the death of slavery, there would be many other deaths. Men didn't seem able to give up what they had without killing. They were not like women, who gave up with only a sigh, or a cry of pain.

She heard the door of the house swing open, then close quietly. She didn't turn to look, thinking it was one of the men going to the outhouse. But then she heard firm footsteps on the slope behind her. Before she got turned around, she smelled balsam under snow.

"Thought I might find you down here," said John Henry, coming to lean against the boulder. "Saw you creep out earlier, during the wrangling."

Annie said nothing. What could she say that would be louder than the sound of her heart banging against her chest? She wrapped her arms around herself to muffle the noise. But John Henry didn't seem to hear anyway, and just stared up at the sky.

After a while he straightened and moved to within a few feet of her. "Nice out here," he said, "but I have to go in and get some sleep. Thought I would say good-bye to you now, because there won't be time in the morning. I leave at dawn."

She hadn't thought he had even remembered her, but he had. She slid off the boulder to ask, "Are you going to Harper's Ferry in Virginia?"

"Yes, I'm going first, because I know the territory. Your father and the others will follow, later in the summer, after I've found a place for them."

"I wish you . . ." Annie cut herself off, not even sure what she'd been going to say.

"What do you wish, Annie Brown?" When she couldn't answer, because she didn't know, John Henry said, "That was a fine supper you cooked for us. I expect one day you'll make some man a good wife."

"No!" It was out of her mouth before she knew it was coming.

"No? Why not? A smart young lady like you, even if you *are* too serious. You'll see. Some young man will come riding up that hill to carry you off. Make your heart leap at the sight of him. Here now, let me take a good look at you, and see how soon that might happen."

He moved back a little, putting his head to one side to see her. She watched the moonlight dance off his cap of shiny hair. And even if there had been no moon, just starlight, she would have known that he wasn't looking only at her face. Her heart raced with . . . with what she didn't know, but it didn't feel like fear. Then, all of a sudden, he looked away with a long shuddering sigh.

He took a few quick strides away from her, before he turned and said, "Good-bye, Annie Brown. If we don't meet again, you keep yourself safe for that young man."

Then John Henry turned and walked back toward the house.

Annie looked up at the dark silent mountains. They would always be there. There just under the North Star.

EIGHT

❦

Madame de Montespan invented the robe battante, or hooped skirt, to conceal an accident in her history; which, however, occurred at such regular periods that people soon began to guess the cause when they perceived the effect.
—THE FEBRUARY 1859 ISSUE OF *HARPER'S NEW MONTHLY MAGAZINE*

GLYNIS CARRIED A furled umbrella as she walked toward Fall Street, slowing as she passed the Usher house. Vanessa's gardener kneeled before a newly turned bed of earth, setting out dark-faced pansy plants, while behind him lilac bushes with blooms from white to pink to darkest purple stood swaying under dense gray clouds. The gray was an appropriate color for such a morning as this might prove to be, Glynis speculated, glancing up at the sky directly overhead. It was concealed, however, by elms rising like tall stately urns on either side of Cayuga Street; above the center of the road their branches merged to form a green cathedral arch all the way to Fall Street.

When she reached the intersection, Glynis hesitated, then decided that instead of going to the library, she would walk directly to Jeremiah Merrycoyf's office. The lawyer, always an early riser, would undoubtedly be there. She might as well get this over with now. As she headed up Fall Street, dodging farm wagons and buggies and carriages, her eyes were drawn to a solitary black Morgan horse. When she got closer, she recognized that, as she had guessed, the horse was indeed Cullen's. It was tethered to a post beside the striped canopy of La Maison de Fleur.

She quickly crossed the road. It was none of her concern. Cullen certainly had every right to go where he pleased, and if where he pleased was Fleur Coddington's, no matter the hour— and it was either very early, or very late—that was his affair. *Affair* being hardly the word she wanted to bring to mind, she concentrated on the plank sidewalk underfoot, and hurried on to the law office.

When she reached the front stoop of Merrycoyf and MacAlistair, Esquires, she paused to shake dust from the hem of her dress, a pale green, embroidered muslin with flounced skirt and petticoats—Emma had insisted on the flounces. And Glynis, with only token resistance, had concluded that to encourage her niece's dressmaking ambitions, she should bow to Emma's fashion dictates. As a result, her wardrobe was being thoroughly overhauled.

Although she now heard the door behind her swing open, Glynis had no time to move before nearly being toppled by the man emerging from the law office. She swayed on the edge of the step before he reached out and grasped her elbow to steady her. She looked up into a face dominated by eyes as black as obsidian, then felt a sharp pain from the talon-like grip on her elbow. She winced, and with "Please, sir!" tried to pull her arm from his grasp.

Her release was immediate. "My dear lady, I do beg your forgiveness. I fear that I have made a very poor first impression. Tell me, are you quite all right?"

While noting his unmistakable British accent, Glynis rubbed her tingling elbow—the man was strong!—and smiled ruefully. "Yes, I'm fine, thank you. It was foolish of me to perch on the step to begin with." Her smile, she hoped, was a persuasive one, as he looked so solicitous. Paradoxically, he also resembled a bird of prey with the shiny dark eyes and sharp features, and the double-breasted gray morning coat he wore with a distinction not ordinarily seen in Seneca Falls. The coat sat on his shoulders as if he'd been born in it, and his white cuffs and high turned-down collar were immaculate. The small black cravat and black silk vest, as Glynis had seen in *Harper's Monthly,* were the most currently fashionable. Emma would approve.

"Allow me to introduce myself," he said with a hint of courtliness. "I am Colonel Dorian de Warde. At your service," he added, smiling pleasantly.

"Glynis Tryon," she answered, and extended her hand with caution. This time his grip was merely firm. And then, behind him, Jeremiah Merrycoyf appeared in the doorway.

Colonel de Warde touched the brim of his gray top hat with the ebony walking stick he carried. "Good day, then, Miss Tryon. I trust we shall meet anon," and he walked briskly away.

Merrycoyf looked after the Englishman briefly before ushering Glynis through the doorway and into a small waiting area. "Was that gentleman a client of yours, Jeremiah?" she asked.

"No, my new associate's," he said, leading the way to his inner office.

After being seated opposite his desk, Glynis forced herself to meet his inquisitive spectacled eyes. "Jeremiah, as I'm too troubled to make small talk, I'll come straight to the point. I must discuss with you something very painful. It's about the library."

She then told him of the impending financial crisis, ending with, "I feel responsible for this, and in no way does it reflect on my assistant's trustworthiness. Very simply put, I stayed away too long. And if the board desires my resignation, although I certainly hope it doesn't—"

"My dear Miss Tryon," Merrycoyf broke in, "I trust things will not come to that. However, I agree there is most definitely a problem here."

"What is the possibility," she asked with small hope, "that Aurora Usher's estate will be probated soon?"

"At the moment, I'd say the odds are not in your favor. Unless—" Merrycoyf peered at Glynis over his spectacles "—unless someone can convince Miss Vanessa Usher that her sister was not unduly influenced in the last days of her life."

"That is an absurd accusation, Jeremiah."

"Nonetheless, the fact that Aurora Usher insisted on changing her will only three weeks before she died does not bode well for either Dr. Cardoza-Levy's refuge or your library."

"I just don't understand this. How could Aurora be 'unduly influenced' by Neva or Jonathan?"

"Perhaps you weren't aware that Dr. Cardoza-Levy was Miss Aurora's attending physician. That Aurora Usher spent the last four weeks of her life in the house of the doctor and her husband Abraham. And that Jonathan Quant was often a visitor there."

"But *you* know, *everybody* knows, how Vanessa detests illness or infirmity of any kind—she's very nearly phobic about it. Neva was taking care of Aurora because Vanessa couldn't—or wouldn't. And of course Jonathan was there. He'd been enamored of Aurora for years!"

Merrycoyf nodded. "Yes, *we* know that."

Glynis sat forward. "Jeremiah, I don't wish to sound churlish, but *you* are the lawyer here. Can't you do something?"

"Yes, possibly, but it may take time, which you have just informed me that you do not have."

Glynis sank back into the chair.

"However," Merrycoyf began, "perhaps we might speak with Seabury Gould, and ask—"

He paused, as a knock sounded at the door. "Yes?"

The door opened, and a gaunt face appeared around its edge. But the face quickly withdrew, and only a voice remained. "Forgive me, Jeremiah—I didn't know you had someone in there."

"It's quite all right, Cyril. Come in and meet Miss Tryon."

The door swung open to admit a tall stooped man with a frame as emaciated-looking as his face—an elongated face made more so by a receding hairline.

Merrycoyf rose to say, "Allow me to introduce my associate, Mr. Cyril Doggett."

As Glynis extended her hand to the other attorney, Merrycoyf came around his desk. Seeing the two men together, side by side, it crossed Glynis's mind that if Merrycoyf resembled the spirit of St. Nicholas, then Cyril Doggett must be the ghost of Jacob Marley. When he stepped forward to grasp her hand, she expected a rattle of chains. Instead, she felt the slight pressure of a metal band, and looked down. "A family signet ring, Mr. Doggett?" she asked, extracting her hand from his to gesture at the ring. It looked something like the one Merrycoyf wore. As had the murdered Utica banker's.

"Yes, it was my father's—he went to Yale also," Cyril Doggett answered in a surprisingly deep voice, and he gave Merrycoyf a sad smile.

"You and Jeremiah were in the same class there, I understand," Glynis said.

Both men nodded, and Merrycoyf said, "Constable Stuart has already been here with questions, and neither Cyril nor I can recall the man Edward Barrymore. If that's what you were about to inquire, Miss Tryon."

"Yes, it was," she admitted. "It's possible you both were at Yale earlier than Mr. Barrymore."

"Very possible," Cyril Doggett agreed.

"But you do have reunions," Glynis said. "Might you have seen him then?"

"I don't travel to New Haven but every four or five years," Merrycoyf answered. "And if Barrymore hadn't attended the law school, there's no reason I would run into him in any event." To which Cyril Doggett added his nod of agreement.

"There is an alternative explanation," Merrycoyf stated, "to the effect that the ring bestowed upon yourself by Mr. Barrymore might not have been his own. Perhaps a family member's?"

Cyril Doggett frowned, wrinkling his high forehead like a bloodhound, which, possibly due to his name, was what Glynis had begun to think he most resembled. "Or," he suggested, "it's possible that Barrymore might have acquired the ring by, shall we say, illegitimate means."

"You think he might have stolen it?" That didn't match the impression she'd had of the man; still, it hadn't been the best of circumstances under which to form an opinion. So as Doggett shrugged his hunched shoulders, she said, "Well, gentlemen, I guess Edward Barrymore's possession of that ring may raise more questions than it answers. Unless, of course, the answer is a very simple one. That, fearing for his life, Mr. Barrymore thought if the worst were to happen, then the ring might serve to identify him."

Both Merrycoyf and Doggett seemed to consider this a distinct possibility. As did Glynis, who had thought about it at some length. But the banknote and coin Barrymore had included in his pouch—did they too represent some clue to his identity? Or to his killer's?

She got to her feet and thanked them for their conjectures.

"I'm sorry we can't be of more help," Cyril Doggett said to her with his lugubrious smile. She had just reached the door when he added, "Miss Tryon, are you, by some chance, a descendant of General William Tryon?"

"Yes, I am—though it's not something of which I'm overly proud. Are you interested in history, then, Mr. Doggett?"

"Not particularly. But I am a native of Connecticut, a state that during the Revolution, as you may be aware, staunchly supported the Continental cause. You may not know that New Haven was sacked by Loyalist forces under the command of your illustrious ancestor—an event which, I assure you, has not yet been forgotten." Another sad smile accompanied this.

Glynis nodded politely, but in regard to Great-Grandfather Tryon's activities, she refused to accept responsibility for a man who had lived three-quarters of a century before. And certainly not a man engaged in war as a profession.

"It's interesting," Merrycoyf said as he escorted her through the waiting room to the door, "that Cyril brought up your ancestor, Miss Tryon, in view of what I remarked to him just this morning—that the British have never ceased sticking their fingers into American pies."

Glynis must have looked bewildered, but Merrycoyf simply went on, "Rest assured that I will look into that financial matter we discussed, my dear, and consult with Mr. Gould about possible remedies."

She thanked him, and stepped to the plank sidewalk. Just as Merrycoyf closed the door after her, she became aware of a sound, somewhere between a high-pitched moan and the gurgle of someone drowning, that issued from the office directly next door. She glanced at the large window on which was lettered: DR. ALAN FITZHUGH, JR—PAINLESS DENTISTRY. That, she thought, must either spring from the wit of a sadist, or be, at best, an unintentional oxymoron. The senior Dr. Fitzhugh had practiced in Seneca Falls for a number of years, but he did not advertise his services as painless—lest he be laughed out of town—and he did not locate his office on the main street of the village with, no less, a large window! Apparently this son was a braver soul than his father. Or was perhaps more eager for the money he thought such exposure would bring.

She couldn't resist a closer look, and had just opened the office door and stepped inside, when a small object flew in an

arc across the room simultaneously with a blood-curdling
shriek. Ah, yes, painless dentistry. Glynis looked for the source
of the shriek. A small boy, squirming on a tall rounded chair,
held both fists bunched against his mouth.

"My tooth," he wailed, "my tooth hurts terrible!"

"It *can't* hurt," declared the good-looking young man wield-
ing forceps and in the process of retrieving the flown object
from a far corner. "It can't hurt, because it's not in your mouth
anymore. You even kicked it out of my hand. Now here, look!"

He waved at the boy a minuscule, slightly bloody tooth held
fast in the forceps, which brought even greater wails of anguish.
The comely plump woman who stood alternately wringing her
hands and patting the boy's shoulder, gazed at the dentist with
reproach. "But you promised it wouldn't hurt Willy, Dr. Fitzhugh," she reminded him.

"And it didn't, I'm sure of it," Alan Fitzhugh said confidently, his smile featuring teeth so white Glynis had to wonder
if he soaked them each night in Best-Begone Household
Bleach. "It's only fear that your son is expressing."

But fear, it seemed to Glynis, was a worthy enough substitute
for pain. It was true that the sign which hung above a magnif-
icent walnut desk did promise: TEETH EXTRACTED, POSITIVELY
WITHOUT PAIN, 50¢, adding in somewhat smaller print: GOLD
FILLINGS OUR SPECIALITY. The sign admittedly mentioned nothing about fear.

At this point, the boy leapt from the chair and pushed past
Glynis to hurl himself against the door. "Help!" he yelled at
the top of his lungs. "Help, someone—I'm being tortured!"

"Willy, dear," said his mother pleadingly, "please, darling,
don't shout so—the whole town will hear you."

"Good!" was Willy's yelped response, and he hammered at
the door with clenched fists. "Help! Let me out of here!"

"Willy, please come away from the door," Dr. Fitzhugh said
quietly, and with laudable restraint, Glynis acknowledged while
trying not to laugh. Anyone else might have been expected to
say something stronger to this little dramatist, as Willy was
clearly playing the scene for all it was worth. She had just
decided to wait for another day to introduce herself to the dentist, when Willy managed to yank the door open and fling him-

self outside. His mother gasped and rushed after him.

"I hope you received your payment in advance, Dr. Fitzhugh," Glynis said with as straight a face as she could muster.

Fitzhugh seemed to see her for the first time. He smiled a bit tentatively, although his reply was delivered in the most sober of voices. "Oh, yes. Oh, with children I must." He gestured toward the door as if to express, You can see why. "Forgive me," he said, "but I don't believe I recall your name."

"Glynis Tryon. I knew your father slightly because he occasionally used the library. Is he still practicing?"

"He retired last year. I think I remember you—you're Miss Tryon, the librarian."

"Yes, though I've been away for some time. In fact, on my return trip, I saw you while waiting to board at the Rochester train station."

A faint crease appeared in the smooth forehead. "I'm sorry, I don't believe I recall that."

No, Glynis supposed not, given that he'd been so preoccupied with the bejeweled hand of his companion. "I really just stopped to introduce myself," she said. And added, thinking he might find it amusing, "Though I confess to being intrigued by what I overheard coming from in here."

He gave her a tight smile. "Yes. Well, if I can be of assistance to you in the future, Miss Tryon, please don't hesitate to come in." As he spoke, Alan Fitzhugh removed his blue smock, under which he wore the most beautifully tailored silk shirt Glynis had ever laid eyes on. She also noticed that his fawn-colored trousers were of soft fine wool, as was the satin-lapeled morning coat for which he reached. After bringing to mind his elegance at the Rochester train station, Glynis decided the man was rather a dandy.

And she knew when she was being dismissed. Apparently, she had wounded his pride—or not worn enough jewelry—but thought apologizing for her misguided attempt at humor might make things worse. Perhaps after he gained more experience, he would develop a more finely honed sense of the absurd. As in young Willy's histrionics.

When she stepped to Fall Street, she saw Cullen approaching. She was wondering how she could avoid him, short of ducking back inside Dr. Fitzhugh's for a painless extraction, when he called to her. "Glynis! Glynis, I just stopped by the library to see you. Need to talk to you about something—have you got a toothache?"

"No, and I'm late to work, as you've discovered, Cullen."

"The autopsy on Tom Bingham showed something interesting," he said as if he hadn't heard her. "Just came from Dr. Ives's—thought you'd want to hear about it."

He had certainly been busy that morning, what with Fleur Coddington's La Maison and Quentin Ives's medical office. She began walking toward the library, and Cullen swung into step beside her.

"First, I should tell you," he began, "that I've just had a wire from the New York State banking superintendent. The banknote, the one in Barrymore's tobacco pouch, was a forgery. The superintendent's wire said its number was one in a series that had been destroyed several weeks ago."

"Destroyed because the bank had failed?"

"Not this time, although Barrymore's bank *is* in trouble. No, it seems that Barrymore—a few days before his death—had alerted the superintendent that several other spurious notes with numbers from that series had surfaced. He'd indicated he was going to investigate them himself."

"Do you think that's why he was killed? Because he'd discovered something dangerous to the counterfeiters?"

"I suspect that's exactly why he was killed. Problem is, we don't have any idea what or who he'd uncovered."

"I've just now remembered something," Glynis said, slowing her pace. "On the train, when Barrymore dropped the pouch in my lap, he whispered something about Seneca Falls. Given the circumstances, it didn't seem to be important—I probably assumed he was telling me what his destination was. But perhaps he wasn't. Perhaps he was saying that here, Seneca Falls, was where he'd discovered counterfeiters were forging the banknotes."

"Or that the town is their distribution point. But as far as the double eagle in the pouch, it checked out—it's genuine."

"Then my original guess about the coin could be correct; that it had already been in the pouch when Barrymore dropped in the ring and the banknote, and it had no significance—except to indicate he was in a hurry.''

Cullen nodded. ''Certainly could be the case if Barrymore knew he was being followed. And by the way, our elusive banker Valerian Voss has finally surfaced. Says he came back into town this morning. He claims that—believe it or not—he'd been in Utica. And he apparently didn't know about Tom Bingham's death until he got here. Someone told him at the rail station, which is why he came to see me. That and to have me open the bank; after we found Bingham, I had it padlocked.''

''Voss was in Utica? What a coincidence—or was it? Did he say why he was there?'' Glynis asked, then stopped and looked around her, thinking she'd heard Cullen's name being called. They had reached the corner of Fall and Clinton. The Farmers and Merchants Bank stood directly across the street and its entrance door stood open.

''Speak of the devil,'' Cullen said as Valerian Voss came rushing out through the doorway.

''Constable Stuart! I need to speak with you!'' the banker shouted in an urgent voice. He ran a hand through his crisp graying hair, and stood plucking at abundant sideburns as Glynis and Cullen crossed the road.

''What's the matter, Voss?'' Cullen asked when they reached the bank.

Valerian Voss gestured vigorously to the door. ''Come inside, Constable.'' He whirled around and went back through the doorway, his stocky, barrel-chested frame moving with more agility than one might expect.

When Cullen started to follow him, Glynis said, ''I should get to the library, Cullen, so . . .''

Her voice trailed away because Cullen took her arm and propelled her inside the bank. After a hasty introduction, Valerian Voss gave Glynis no more notice. He didn't seem to care that she heard what he had to say—if, in fact, her presence even registered, he was so obviously distraught. Moreover, Glynis wasn't sure herself why she was there.

''See this safe over here in the corner, Constable?'' the banker asked as he went toward a square gray vault.

Cullen nodded. "I see it. What's the problem?"

"The problem is that it's been broken into!" The swarthy skin of Voss's face darkened. "When I got here, the safe's door was ajar. I saw immediately that they were missing!"

"*What* was missing?"

"The banknotes! The forged notes from the Rochester and Syracuse banks—they're gone!"

"Wait a minute, Voss, slow down. You want to tell me what you were doing with forged banknotes?"

Voss lowered himself into the nearest chair and pulled at his sideburns. "They were notes that had been redeemed by us, unfortunately, before we discovered they were bogus. I was holding them for the state banking authorities. But someone has stolen them, Constable."

"Besides the state, have you been in touch with the Treasury in Washington about this?"

"Yes, of course! That is, Tom Bingham was—" Voss broke off his speech as he got up and went behind a glass and polished wood partition. Glynis heard the sound of wooden drawers being pulled open, then slammed shut. "Damn!" issued from behind the partition several times. And Voss soon reappeared to say, "It's gone, too!"

Cullen sighed. "What's gone?"

"The report that came from the Treasury. It arrived just as I was leaving to catch the train for Utica, and I didn't have time to read it."

"Do you know if Bingham read it?"

"Yes, that's why I came back, Constable. That is . . . well, Tom wired me that the report had something important in it. In fact, his wire used the word 'urgent.' "

"Let me get this straight, Voss. When you were in Utica, Tom Bingham wired about a Treasury report sent to this bank, and now you're saying the report's not here?"

Voss nodded impatiently. "Yes, yes, don't you see, Constable? It must have had to do with the forged notes we'd been receiving—and redeeming," he added sourly. "I know where Tom kept all the papers regarding this, because we were going to deliver them to Albany. I've just gone through the file drawers, and the report's not there."

"O.K., Voss, let's think about this. The bank's big enough for things to get lost, misplaced, misfiled, whatever. Why don't we take another, thorough look."

Glynis began to edge toward the door, still wondering why Cullen had dragged her in there—she guessed she'd just have to wait for the results of bank president Thomas Bingham's autopsy. When she reached the bank entrance, she glanced back to see, as she expected, that both Valerian Voss and Cullen had disappeared behind the partition.

Once again she stepped to Fall Street, determined this time to ignore interruptions and to actually reach the library. Nevertheless, when she crossed State Street, Glynis was drawn to the window of W. F. Williams' Watchmaking and Jewelry store. It was the glint of gold that had caught her eye. She stopped to admire the display of gold rings, necklaces, bracelets, and earrings that gleamed on yards of black velvet. The jewelry had reminded her again of Alan Fitzhugh's gold-bedecked Rochester companion, and the sign in the dentist's office that advertised gold fillings. Did he make gold teeth as well? This led her to wonder from where counterfeiters obtained the gold they used to make fraudulent coins. Who would have a more legitimate reason for buying gold in quantity than dentists? And jewelers, she revised, drawing away from the window and returning a wave from the elderly Mr. Williams inside his store.

Any further speculation was cut short by the wet drops that splattered the plank sidewalk. Hurrying to avoid the rain, she at last arrived at the library. She had no sooner settled at her desk than in rushed Neva Cardoza-Levy and her husband, hardware store owner Abraham Levy. One look at their faces—especially that of the ruddy-cheeked Abraham, who could ordinarily be depended upon for calm and reason—told Glynis she would have to forgo her work for what was obviously yet another crisis.

"What is it, you two?" she asked, while Abraham kept tugging at his short curly beard.

The young doctor shook her head, but her eyes glittered alarmingly. Since Neva practically never reached the state of tears, Glynis braced herself.

"There's a problem with the benefit for the Women's Refuge—the barn dance," Abraham said.

"A *problem?*" snapped Neva. "That's what you call it? A *problem?*" This response of Neva's made Glynis feel somewhat encouraged. It was more like her and meant that her tears were born of anger, not impotence.

She waited while Neva hoisted her small frame to perch on the corner of Glynis's desk; on its surface her blunt fingers tapped a staccato cadence. Abraham, meanwhile, had folded his arms across his chest before he said, "Yesterday afternoon, a Mr. Alvin Blum—he's secretary of the Seneca County Agricultural Society—came to me with a letter—"

"Please take note," Neva interrupted, "that this Blum person didn't have the courtesy to come to *me.*"

Or, perhaps, Glynis guessed, the Blum person didn't have the necessary nerve. Abraham continued, "To make this brief, the letter stated that the society had decided not to allow use of the fairgrounds for the benefit."

"But I thought that was all arranged with them weeks ago," Glynis protested. "How can they do that at this late date—the dance is to be this Saturday, isn't it?"

"They *said,*" Neva retorted, "that the fairgrounds were *suddenly* in need of reseeding. Do you believe they came up with something as insultingly banal as that? You know what this is about, don't you—I mean *really* about?"

Glynis sighed. "Yes, I suppose so, Neva. The Agricultural Society has had second thoughts about the refuge?"

"That's part of it," Neva retorted. "But, yes, this organization, which consists solely of *men,* has suddenly realized that the Women's Refuge might be for mistreated wives—maybe even their own. But even worse—and you know this is true, Glynis—is that these women and their children might be treated by a *woman* doctor. God forbid!"

Glynis knew it was true. When Neva had first arrived in town, she'd trained with Dr. Quentin Ives. Because of Ives's long-held position in town, she had been grudgingly accepted—although Glynis guessed that many thought she was simply paid help, some sort of domestic. But now, with Neva starting her own practice, Glynis had learned—by way of Harriet's letters to Springfield—that there had been ample vocal opposition to a woman practicing medicine. Although, on one recent occasion, it hadn't been only vocal: someone had scribbled WE DON'T WANT NO LADY JEW DOCTOR! on an outside wall of the warehouse.

"There's more to this whole thing, though," Neva declared. Abraham looked as if he might try to discourage her from saying more, but then closed his mouth with a sigh.

"What else?" Glynis asked.

"It's not only that I'm female." Neva's cheeks were flushed, and again her eyes began to glitter. "It's because they know—"

"That you're Jewish," Abraham pronounced with satisfaction. It had taken him, Glynis was well aware, some time to initiate his new wife to the idea that she couldn't just renounce her religious heritage as if it were a choice as easily changed as, say, dietary habits, because she believed Judaism to be patriarchal, and therefore unjust to women. And Glynis herself had said to Neva, "Tell me of a religion that *isn't* patriarchal and therefore unjust to women."

But Abraham said now, "You shouldn't be so naive, as if you can't imagine that your being a Jew would be used against you." When Neva opened her mouth to reply, he said, "And no, let's not get into *that* again."

Neva's combative look had heightened, but surprisingly she murmured, "You're right, Abraham." Her voice grew louder. "Of course, you're right. You're a man, Abraham, therefore you are always right—forever and ever *you are right!* So," she turned to Glynis, "what do we do now? I refuse to cancel the benefit. Even if I have to hold it in the middle of Fall Street—not that anyone will come now, anyway."

"I doubt the mayor, or Cullen Stuart either, will think much of the main street of town as a site," Abraham said dryly.

"But the refuge needs the money desperately, and now, or we'll have to close it." Neva threw Glynis a desperate look. "You're always ripe for an idea or two."

"Not this time, Neva. The one person in this town who can usually come up with something creative is our friend Vanessa Usher."

Both Neva and Abraham groaned. Glynis said hurriedly, "Yes, I know. If it weren't for Vanessa you probably wouldn't need this benefit so much."

"Vanessa Usher is an obnoxious spoiled brat!" Neva declared. "Don't frown at me, Abraham. You agree, I know you do."

"Actually," Glynis said, "I agree with you, too. Because if Vanessa weren't blocking the probate of her sister's will, for no good reason, the library wouldn't—" She left off, deciding that particular issue was not relevant here. But, then again, perhaps it *was*.

"You know, it's really too bad," Glynis said, thoughtfully, "that we can't somehow join forces on this." Her eyes flew to the tall library windows. Neva and Abraham stood watching her, their faces expressing doubt when she got to her feet and walked to the windows. She stood looking out at the rain-pocked water of the canal.

Why should they not join forces?

IT WAS SEVERAL hours later when Jonathan, just leaving for his dinner, opened the library door and collided with Cullen Stuart.

After a mumbled apology to each other, Jonathan trotted off and Cullen asked Glynis if they could talk in her back office.

"Yes, for a few minutes," she answered, looking to see how many patrons might be expected to need her. She spoke to the several present, then led the way to her office.

"What a nightmare this counterfeiting thing is!" Cullen said, after lowering himself to the only chair other than her own. "It's creating hell on earth for everybody. But you know, there's something about Valerian Voss that makes me uneasy. Can't put my finger on what it is, though." He looked at Glynis. "You were quiet in the bank—never said a word in there."

"What was there for me to say? But you have something to tell me about Thomas Bingham's autopsy?"

"Actually there are several things. First off, late yesterday a train porter who works the Rochester-to-Utica run came into my office with a laundry bag. It had a bloody shirt and trousers in it. Porter said he found them stuffed under a trunk in the baggage car, just after the train pulled out of here the day you and Barrymore's corpse arrived.''

"Were the shirt and trousers those of a workman—blue denim?'' Glynis asked.

Cullen nodded. "That sound like your killer's outfit, then?''

"Yes. I don't suppose there was also a black hat?''

"No hat. Just the two items.''

"So if Barrymore's killer had concealed extra clothes on the train—'' Glynis paused to consider ''—that implies premeditation, doesn't it, not simply a chance encounter with Barrymore. Then the killer just blithely walked off the train here in Seneca Falls. Even if there hadn't been a lot of confusion that day, no one would recognize him. After all,'' she added, ''at one point on the train I was right beside him and couldn't really see his face. And if, when he discarded his bloody clothes, he'd also removed his hat, I'd likely never have known him.''

And all of this didn't help to explain the *other* man, the one in the Rochester public market, who had attacked Barrymore. Glynis didn't think it safe to assume the two assaults were related to each other—or that the assailants were coconspirators, although it certainly looked that way.

"The porter told me,'' Cullen said, ''that he rearranged the baggage during the stop in Rochester. So the shirt and trousers, if they'd been under the trunk then, would have been discovered. That means they were hidden after the attack, all right. But just to be sure they're the clothes you saw on Barrymore's killer, would you stop by the lockup and have a look at them?''

Glynis didn't answer. Cullen apparently didn't notice, because he went on to say, ''Now, about the autopsy—for a couple reasons both Neva and Quentin Ives don't think it's likely that Tom Bingham hanged himself. One is that Bingham should have had some bruises or rope burns around his neck, which he didn't. Another reason is that if he'd died by hanging, his blood would've drained into his lower extremities, and it hadn't. So they think Bingham was killed before he was strung up.''

"So what *do* Neva and Quentin think killed Thomas Bingham?''

"He had a fractured bone above his larynx—which could mean he'd been throttled. Mind you, they won't guarantee, positively, that Bingham didn't hang himself, but it doesn't look like it."

"You didn't think he did, anyway," Glynis murmured. She took a deep breath and said, "I've come to a decision about something, Cullen. I don't feel I can get mixed up in this. . . . No, please, wait and hear me out before you object. We both know that, in the past, I've gotten involved with crimes here because I was trying to help someone I cared about, someone I knew. This is altogether different."

His eyes grew dark. "I see," he said sharply. "If this had involved someone you *knew*"—the meaning behind his emphasis on *knew* was painfully clear without him adding— "someone like Jacques Sundown . . ."

"I think that's enough, Cullen." Glynis glanced toward the office door. "It's also unfair, since there was Harriet's son Niles, too, if you will recall."

"Yes, but obviously since this involves—" His mouth clamped shut, and without finishing, he got up and strode out of her office. She sat there for several minutes, hoping he might think better of it and come back. When he didn't, Glynis finally stood up and took a few steps toward the library proper. Then she paused with her hand on the door.

Cullen had told her that Valerian Voss last lived in San Francisco. It wouldn't hurt, she supposed, to send a letter to her uncle at the mint there. Perhaps he might know, or could find out, something about the vice-president of the failed Farmers and Merchants Bank.

INTERIM

✑

FORTY MILES TO the north, at the lively port of Oswego, the rain had stopped late in the afternoon, and the sun now flared through hazy clouds above Lake Ontario. Amid the bustle and noise of the wharves, the dockworkers heading home or shipboard, the two men standing together at the end of an isolated pier seemed in no danger of being overheard. Still, before they spoke, each glanced about with a practiced eye.

"I've had word regarding Mr. Brown's ambitions," said the smooth-shaven man. "It is to be the federal arsenal at Harper's Ferry in Virginia. An inspired choice."

"I don't think so," Brockway argued. "I know that region, and Harper's Ferry is a rotten choice—a potential trap if ever there was one."

"Exactly!" The other man smiled, saying, "Brown's plan will undoubtedly fail, and fail spectacularly, but that might be just the spark to ignite the South. Southerners will blame Northern abolitionists for backing Brown and inciting slaves to revolt—they've been terrified of another slave uprising since the Nat Turner massacre several decades back—and Virginians are the most terrified, and that includes even those who aren't slaveholders. As well they should be. Do you have any idea how many more Negroes than whites there are in that state? Yes, indeed, when Brown's activities come to light, I dare say any further effort toward political compromise between North and South will be doomed."

"Listen, I don't give a damn about political issues."

"Do you mean to say, my dear sir, that you don't want to see your government under fire, the agitation for bank reform lost in the confusion? Think of the possibilities for your profession—why, they're endless. And in the meantime, all your thriving mills here in the North will creak to a halt. And England's mills will have your southern cotton to spin into gold!" He chuckled at the image.

"Whatever you say. That's not why I wanted this meeting.

Are you aware that your boy's been very busy—that there's been another murder?''

"Yes, unfortunate. And you will now say that you didn't get into this—"

"I didn't," Brockway interrupted. "I didn't get into this to face a hangman! Now unless you get that loose cannon under control, I'm out of it. O-U-T! You hear me?" His thumb moved nervously over his ink-stained fingertips.

"My good Brockway, you excite yourself unnecessarily over trivial matters. These things happen. Espionage has always been a game of chance. One must learn to extemporize when the situation calls for it."

"I'm not in espionage. I'm just a simple engraver who—"

"Simple engraver!" The soft controlled laughter interjected itself. "Oh, Mr. Brockway, you are far too modest. And please, let us hear no more talk of 'getting out.' For you to attempt such a breach of faith would be a serious miscalculation. Now, let me take care of my boy, and don't further concern yourself with him."

Brockway looked frustrated, and somewhat apprehensive, but said in a subdued tone, "And what if he blows his cover?"

"Then we remove him. We simply remove him."

"You think that's going to be easy—without him implicating some of us?"

"Stop worrying! Your job is very simply to make money. Now, I will be out of touch for a short time. I need to line up more arms for Mr. Brown's project—to move him along a bit faster. I'll contact you when I get back."

"Hold on! What if something goes wrong while you're away?"

"Extemporize, my good man. Extemporize."

The smooth-shaven man waved his hand and walked away. Brockway stood scowling after him, flexing his wrists until they hurt. After a time, he moved off in the opposite direction.

NINE

❦

*Fine dancing, I believe, like virtue, must be its own reward.
Those who are standing by are usually thinking of something
very different.*
—JANE AUSTEN, *EMMA*

SALLY LUNT EXPERIENCED another surge of anxiety, one so
strong it verged on nausea. She very nearly turned and ran back
to her boardinghouse, but instead, as if to protect herself against
imaginary demons, she took several deep breaths. Still, she hesitated in the alley behind the shop, looking uneasily about her,
before going forward to unlock the rear door of La Maison de
Fleur. Now, in addition to fear, she felt more than a little guilt.
Her employer had provided Sally with a key to open the shop
mornings; the widow Coddington certainly did not envision it
being used for an activity such as Sally now intended.

The young woman clenched her teeth and tried to avoid
frightening herself further. After all, it was extremely unlikely
that anyone would come to the shop at this late hour, even
more unlikely that Fleur Coddington herself would return. Not
with the benefit dance that evening. Madame Fleur would spend
the next hours dressing, curling her hair, and primping for Constable Cullen Stuart. Sally shivered as she thought of the constable, a person she once believed she could trust. But now she
feared even he might be a threat. And the lawyer had said to
confide in *no one.*

Sally slipped inside the shop, carefully closing the door behind her. She had worried about this nigh unto death for days,
and at last, that very morning, had made up her mind. She'd
been told exactly what she needed to do. Going straight to the
tall mahogany wardrobe cabinet standing along one wall of the
fitting room, she pulled open the two cabinet doors. But her
next intended move was arrested, and she stood motionless with

dread. What had that been? That muffled scraping that seemed to come from just outside the shop's rear door.

She remained frozen in place, although now she heard nothing but the thudding of her heart. Then, glancing wildly about, she realized that a hiding place was close at hand. She quickly climbed into the wardrobe cabinet, pulling the doors closed as best she could from the inside. Then she squeezed herself behind the large white cotton bags that contained finished gowns, hanging from a horizontal pole. The drawstring garment bags, covering untold yards of fabric used in the voluminous hooped skirts, felt like bloated apparitions as they swung around her before she managed to catch and yank them together in front of herself. Concealed thus, she crouched there in utter darkness, trying not to breathe, her heart hammering against her chest.

After a long minute or two, and despite the blood pounding in her ears that made it difficult to be absolutely certain, Sally concluded there had been no further sounds from outside. And, overwrought as she was, she might easily have imagined the one. It had probably been a dog rummaging in the trash barrels placed outside the shop's door. Yes, that *must* have been it. After all, she reassured herself, who could possibly suspect she was in the shop—to say nothing of what she had in mind?

Feeling somewhat silly, she nonetheless again strained to listen from behind the smothering bags. No, there was nothing. She had simply imagined it. Now she would suffocate if she didn't get some air.

With fresh determination, she pushed her head between two bags, then leaned forward to place her ear against the crack separating the doors. In doing so, she almost lost her balance, but recovered herself inches before falling heavily against the wall of the cabinet. However, to her horror, one of the doors swung open with a shrill rasp. Yet as she crouched, listening intently, she heard nothing else. She cautiously stepped out of the wardrobe cabinet, then stood for a moment longer in the quiet room. When she turned back to the cabinet, she stood on her toes to reach the inside pole and untie the blue drawstring of one of the garment bags. Rapidly sliding the loosened bag down to uncover the bodice of the dress it contained, she put her hand inside a huge puffed sleeve. Her fingers searched between the fabric of the sleeve and its cambric undersleeve; nothing there. She reached into the other sleeve—and found that for which she had hoped. Withdrawing it with a sense of elation, she had just reached into the cabinet for another blue-stringed bag, when she felt a movement of air, a draft where there should have been none. And then she heard something. Several things all at once. A soft intake of breath, the sound of coarse fabric brushing against itself, and then a footstep. Unmistakable this time, and directly behind her.

Sally Lunt gasped and whirled around. Her fright receded almost immediately. "Oh, it's you!" she said, her voice heavy with relief.

This relief was cut short by powerful hands that suddenly encircled her neck, making it impossible for her to say more. Her surprise almost as great as her terror, Sally struggled wildly against her assailant.

The struggle did not last long.

THE SUN STILL sat well above the horizon when Glynis walked with Harriet down Cayuga Street, each of them carrying an unlit lantern and a covered plate of cherry tarts. And as they were joined by several others heading toward town, the number of lanterns and pastries grew. It seemed that everyone had followed the suggestion made in the *Seneca County Courier*.

Several days before, after conferring with Merrycoyf, Glynis and Neva had dashed to the newspaper office, where the *Courier* editor had cheerfully agreed to insert an item announcing a change of location for the Women's Refuge benefit. He had even included their request that those attending bring food and light.

As she and Harriet now crossed Fall Street, Glynis could hear musical instruments tuning up—a cello, guitar, banjo, and, unless she was greatly mistaken, a dulcimer. As they drew nearer, the transformation of the library grounds became visible. Two large green-and-white-striped awnings had been raised in the space between the library building and the stone church to the east. People had already seated themselves on bales of hay which had appeared earlier in the afternoon, and here and there, on the shallow grassy slope to the canal, plaid horse blankets had been spread.

The musicians of a string band stood on a platform—or, as young people had recently begun to call it, a bandstand— erected at the very edge of Fall Street. Dancing would take place on a stretch of grass nearby. The musicians at the moment were milling about, waiting for Grandy Fox and his fiddle.

Green-checked tablecloths lay fluttering over trestle tables that looked remarkably like the ones to be found in many Seneca Falls kitchens—and on them plates of fresh-baked berry pies, chocolate cakes and fruit slumps and gingerbread, short-cakes, jumbles, cookies, and bowls of cherries were accumulating. While Harriet added their tarts to the collection, Glynis glanced around for the casks she knew would be somewhere close by. Despite Neva's fierce opposition to beer at the Women's Refuge benefit—it would be, she'd said, like handing out matches at the Fireman's Ball—others had convinced her that, the dance being held in the open, it would be near impossible to prohibit. Or if they did succeed in banishing beer, most of the men would leave. Glynis decided the young doctor had mellowed considerably when Neva's final comment was only, "I don't want to know about it!"

Without much effort Glynis deduced, by the number of men who kept disappearing around the side of the building to emerge minutes later with contented grins, that the casks were on the far side of the library. It was a piece of great good fortune that the weather was fair; a fine balmy July evening that wouldn't require her to open the library for shelter. The night before she'd had nightmares of books drenched with beer, and been sorry she'd ever thought of the library grounds.

The first strains of a Celtic jig came drifting toward her. When she got to the bandstand, she found Emma standing behind an upended barrel labeled SUGAR, and on which sat her dulcimer; earlier she'd explained that an empty barrel would amplify the sound. Emma was using hammers with heads of bare wood, and the dulcimer rang brightly. The softer, warmer tone Glynis was more accustomed to hearing came from heads that Emma wrapped with strips of leather. As Glynis gazed up at her niece, she now understood why Emma had stayed all but sequestered in her bedroom for the past two days. She must have been sewing nonstop to complete the creation she wore.

At first glance it appeared to be a simple frock of red-and-white-checked gingham with full flounced skirt. But as Glynis studied it, the dress proved to be anything but simple. Its design and construction clearly reflected the skill of a clever seamstress.

Currently, the wide full skirt regarded as fashionable could conceal almost anything, from bowleggedness to pregnancy, if the wearer's torso was constricted by a long-boned corset laced tightly enough to severely compress the waist. This might result in a well-endowed woman billowing above and below like plump feather pillows, but it was stylish! Walking, even with mincing steps, was difficult, bending over virtually impossible. This torturous practice could, and often did, result in serious damage to a woman's health; impaired respiration, digestion, and circulation, collapsed lungs, and the prolapsed uterus for which the devices of treatment—such as insertion of wood, ivory, or glass pessaries to support the womb—rivaled those of the Spanish Inquisitors.

But this was of no particular concern to those who set the trends. And too often, Glynis had to admit, middle-class women followed like sheep rather than risk the embarrassment that might result from appearing ignorant of, or too poor to afford, the fashionable. Neva, who saw firsthand the consequences of this slavish obedience to fashion, railed against it long and loud. "I've come to believe," she'd said on many an occasion, "that women are often their own worst enemies." But Glynis didn't think this was bred in female bones. It had been spread, she thought, like a disease by the institutions—churches, professions, universities—which had much to gain, and to retain, by keeping women penned in their clothing, in their homes, in their place. Like so many docile infected sheep.

But every so often a shrewd woman would resist, and find a way out.

Emma had constructed a bodice which did not end at the natural waistline but instead extended to a lightly boned point below the waist. The effect was to flatten the front fullness of the long skirt and make the waist appear smaller. The fullness of the skirt itself came not from cumbersome hoops or pounds of stiff petticoats, but from lightweight muslin underskirts made full at the hem, not waist, by yards of white eyelet lace flouncing. Emma had accomplished much the same sought-after wasp-waisted effect as would tight lacing, but without the discomfort and rigid wooden look of a long-boned corset.

The neat prim bun at the back of her head was gone and the fall of smooth dark hair had been caught back with white ribbon. Perhaps because of her heart-shaped face, Emma resembled nothing so much as one of the curvaceous beauties who graced the romantic ruffled valentines said to be popular in Queen Victoria's Britain.

This seemed a view shared by the number of young men who lolled below the bandstand, and whose eyes frequently came to rest on the dulcimer player. Most of them were unfamiliar to Glynis, but one she did know was Merrycoyf's law partner Adam MacAlistair. The young man's gaze seemed fixed on Emma. Emma's own eyes, however, seldom strayed from Grandy Fox, who, with fiddle tucked under his chin, was leading the others in a lively jig Glynis knew as "The Irish Washerwoman."

A cluster of women had gathered to the side of the bandstand. From their gestures and the occasional comment that reached her, Glynis gathered they were discussing her niece's dress. She smothered a smile. It now seemed obvious why Emma, despite protestations of shyness, had at last agreed to play. What better showcase for her dressmaking than this! In addition, Glynis thought she displayed pluck and inventiveness. Emma just might have her dress shop one day. Although probably not if she were to marry. From the tail of her eye, Glynis gave Adam MacAlistair a searching look.

Apparently he saw it. "Your niece looks very fetching up there," he said. "I trust at some point Grandy Fox can do without a dulcimer long enough for Miss Emma to dance. With me, that is," he added with his self-confident grin. Glynis was about to reply when, over Adam's shoulder, she saw Cullen, with Fleur Coddington at his side, coming toward the bandstand. She gave Adam a quick smile, turned, and hastened off in another direction.

*   *   *

GLYNIS SURVEYED THE crowd several hours later as she stood alone under an ancient white oak, its lower branches spread like wings over the sparse, sun-starved grass beneath. For her the momentary solitude had a soothing effect. Crowds invariably became oppressive after a time, and it was then she felt most keenly the old burden of shyness.

Emma, on the other hand, seemed almost exhilarated by the movement and noise of the crowd. And Glynis again wondered at the sudden change in her niece. Perhaps it was not change in Emma, but change in her surroundings that made her appear to be different. But why had her niece been locked into what seemed not only shyness but sadness? Her mother's death couldn't have been the cause; it had started long before, when Emma was still a child. Glynis had begun to wonder how much Emma's mother Julia had contributed; she had been a demanding parent, one not at all sympathetic to something like shyness. Julia would have undoubtedly perceived her daughter's bashfulness as a self-indulgent weakness. A weakness to be corrected by any means necessary.

Glynis shook her head, then brought her attention back to the present. The view before her was lit by scores of lanterns augmented by a radiant three-quarter moon. Thus illuminated, the library grounds took on a bucolic character. The hay bales, the trestle tables heaped with fruit and pastries, the townspeople dressed in the colorful cottons of summer and gathered together around punchbowls gave the scene a muted pastoral cast not seen in the glare of sunlight.

A number of couples had begun to form lines at right angles to the bandstand. Men and women stood opposite each other for what was called contra dancing, an Americanized version of the wildly popular French *contradanse*, which had itself developed from the English country dance.

Emma, in the meantime, had bent over her dulcimer pins with a small T-shaped wrench. According to her, tuning the instrument was a constant necessity. Grandy Fox waited for her to finish, then moments later the string band launched into the lively reel called ''Arkansas Traveler.'' The lines of dancers

moved to the fast two-four time in a blur of revolving color
and flash of white petticoats.

Not for the first time that evening did Glynis, while watching
Grandy Fox's bow skip over the strings of his violin, have the
peculiar sensation that she'd seen him play before—but of
course she couldn't have. As Zeph had told her, the peddler
first came to Seneca Falls while she'd been in Springfield.

By this time, there looked to be more people on the library
grounds than Glynis had anticipated, although not as many as
Neva had hoped; the heap of coins in the collection basket,
however, continued to grow. As she looked around, Glynis realized that some of those there she was seeing for the first time
since she'd come back from Springfield, those like Elizabeth
Stanton with her husband, Henry. Rochesterian Susan Anthony
was also in town but due to leave shortly on a tour of speaking
engagements.

In the lines of dancers, Glynis could pick out Neva and Abraham, and Dr. Quentin Ives and his wife, Katherine, as well as
a number of the Cleary clan, which had extended itself over
the length and breadth of Seneca County. Seated nearby on a
hay bale was Lacey Smith, escaped slave and lace-maker who
now, Emma had told Glynis, was responsible for the beautiful
collars and cuffs and shawls of La Maison de Fleur. Lacey's
good-natured husband, Isaiah, and Zeph Waters were, at that
moment, in the process of putting away gigantic slabs of cake.

Jeremiah Merrycoyf had appeared a short time before, accompanied by his new associate Cyril Doggett and, to Glynis's
surprise, the Englishman, Colonel de Warde. The dentist Alan
Fitzhugh stood talking to Valerian Voss, while hanging on Fitzhugh's arm was a lovely woman who gazed at him with adoring
eyes; her jewelry was only slightly less conspicuous than that
of the dentist's Rochester companion. Glynis wondered if Fitzhugh collected exclusively women with jewels, or was it the
other way round—that women who fancied jewels collected
them from him. If the latter, his must be an expensive pastime.

The majority of the younger people had come, she supposed,
simply because it was a party, as they would come to any such
doing that offered food and drink and music and dancing. This
was likely true of many of the others. Still and all, these people

were knowingly donating to the Women's Refuge—run by a woman doctor. And even if, like Merrycoyf, they had reservations about a female practicing medicine, most were at least willing to give Neva Cardoza-Levy the benefit of the doubt.

It gave Glynis a moment of extreme uneasiness to recall that somewhere among these decent folk of Seneca Falls a killer could be concealed. Or possibly not, if, as she hoped, the murderer came from outside the town and struck at just those men who, because of their relationship with money, were unfortunate enough to cross his path. Where that path might next lead was what concerned her.

Thus her following thought was of the potential danger to Cullen. As she glanced around for him, she was startled to see that, from some short distance away, he was looking at her. Now he detached himself from a small group and started in her direction.

She'd not tried to avoid him, not after that first glimpse with Fleur Coddington. Although it had taken her some effort, Glynis had concluded that, given the long history she and Cullen shared, it would be unthinkable to lose his friendship entirely. She would simply have to readjust, accept things as they were now. It was true that after she had once refused him, he'd never again spoken to her of marriage—but now perhaps he thought he needed a wife. And if he'd made up his mind as to Fleur . . . well, so be it.

She had too much sense, she hoped, to battle the inevitable. One of the very few times in her life when she had almost lost that good sense was with Jacques Sundown. That she had been only human was an explanation she could accept. And she missed Jacques, even now. As for the attraction he held for her, she had ultimately resisted it, and thus did not feel there was something for which to forgive herself. She couldn't know of course if Cullen, not witness to the fact but suspecting the worst, had forgiven her. It would seem not.

"Glynis." Cullen pushed aside a low branch of the oak to stand beside her. "Nice night. And a good crowd. Neva seems satisfied."

"I hope so. I haven't seen her for several hours, but you're right, it's a good crowd."

"Abraham gathered up the money baskets a while ago. Looked to be a fair sum, but after he'd stashed it away, Colonel de Warde insisted on donating more, and that started another round of contributions. At least now Neva should be able to afford some windows for that place."

"You noticed that."

"Hard not to." Cullen smiled at her, and with relief she saw that his anger of several days ago seemed to be gone. Granted that they were just making small talk, not something at which either was particularly good, but it didn't feel as uncomfortable as it might have done.

"Cullen, what do you know about Colonel de Warde? I only just met him last week."

"He's a merchant, buys and sells for British firms. Some of them have offices in Montreal and Oswego. He's legitimate, if that's what you mean—I asked about his Canadian affiliations when he opened his office here."

"I didn't know he had an office in town."

"It's across the river on West Bayard Street. He told me that, among other transactions, he's negotiating with Gould to ship pumps to Australia, and said the arrangements could take some months to complete. He's also, I've heard, begun negotiations with the Remington Arms Company—you've heard of them, they're near Utica."

"Remington Arms? Why would a British merchant be dealing with them?" Now Glynis turned, as Cullen had, to watch a bespectacled woman who was walking down the slope toward the canal. "Isn't that Neva's assistant?" she asked. "I've only seen her once, at the refuge, and the light, as you know, was very dim. Now I can't think of her name."

"Taylor," Cullen said. "Margaret Taylor. Don't know much about her, except that Neva said the woman has some experience in nursing. She's odd, though."

"Why odd?" Glynis asked, watching Margaret Taylor begin to walk along the towpath toward the bridge.

"She's unfriendly. Has that severe expression, almost forbidding, and she doesn't mingle with—"

He broke off because Margaret Taylor had stumbled but, before falling, caught herself with surprising agility. She then whipped off her spectacles and, while seeming to clean them between a fold of skirt, stared off across the channel of moonlit water.

As a voice hailed Glynis, she turned back toward the library grounds. "Here you are, Miss Tryon!" Colonel de Warde dodged the oak branch, saying, "You are an elusive lady. I've been looking for you to further apologize for very nearly causing you grievous injury the other day." He smiled, not looking, Glynis thought, really apologetic. He was as beautifully dressed as he'd been that morning, and despite his predator's face, he seemed quite charming—at least by moonlight, he did.

"Please think nothing of it, Colonel de Warde," she said. "As I told you, it was more my fault."

"No, I won't hear a word against you. In truth, Miss Tryon, I confess that I was searching for you with the intention of asking for a dance. Your American jigs are a bit daunting—I believe it was your President Jefferson who called them 'a necessary accomplishment although of short use.' However, they've just announced a quadrille. May I have the honor?"

He offered his arm, which Glynis accepted with an inner sigh of gratitude. Fleur Coddington was just coming across the grass, a vision in embroidered white silk. The colonel, who had seen Fleur, waited courteously until she reached them.

"Good evening, Glynis. Colonel de Warde," Fleur said pleasantly. "A lovely evening."

"Lovely," Glynis repeated, while watching Fleur slip her hand around Cullen's arm, then look up at him with the *Mona Lisa* smirk—now stop being nasty, Glynis told herself. Despite her previous lofty intentions, she felt a twinge of something she chose to interpret as impatience. As well as the realization that in pale yellow muslin, with merely two unflounced petticoats, she looked rather drab—or as Emma might say, *frumpy*—in contrast to Fleur Coddington's fashionably wide-hooped silken gown. Indeed, Emma had wrinkled her nose at the yellow muslin, but was left with no time to supply what she put as "a more stylish alternative."

Thus it was with relief that Glynis heard Colonel de Warde say, "I was just escorting Miss Tryon to the bandstand, Mrs. Coddington. Won't you and Constable Stuart join us in a qua-

drille?'' While he spoke, he seemed to be eyeing Fleur Coddington speculatively.

Perhaps it was her imagination, but Glynis thought Cullen
also showed some relief. Well, it *was* awkward, there was no
getting around it.

The four of them strolled toward the music, Fleur's hand
resting proprietorially on Cullen's arm. Ahead of them, Glynis
saw Grandy Fox lift Emma from the grass to the bandstand,
then jump up beside her. Adam MacAlistair stood just below
them. Glynis took one look at Adam's face, then Emma's, and
knew without question that her niece would rather be somewhere else.

''. . . and there's no reason,'' Adam was saying rather loudly
to Grandy Fox, ''why you can't do one number without a dulcimer.'' Adam was smiling while he said this, but his tone of
voice would not lead one to think so. ''Now, look here, my
man . . .''

''Mr. MacAlistair,'' Emma leaned over to say softly to him,
''please, don't.''

''There you see, my good fellow,'' Grandy Fox said affably,
''you're embarrassing the young lady.''

''Is that true, Miss Tryon?'' Adam, though still smiling, demanded of Emma. While heads of those around them turned in
amusement, Glynis cringed in sympathy for her niece. ''Because,'' Adam continued, ''if it is—''

''Nonsense!'' Colonel de Warde broke in with a hand on
Adam's shoulder. ''The only one who should be embarrassed
is this slave-driving fiddler, who clearly doesn't want the young
lady to stray from his side.''

Grandy Fox grinned broadly, but Emma, who had previously
looked as if she wished the earth would open and swallow her,
now sent a glare of such withering proportions to both Adam
and Colonel de Warde that Glynis very nearly applauded.

''It's quite all right, Mr. Fox,'' Emma announced to Grandy
in a surprisingly firm voice. ''If the only way to keep these
gentlemen quiet is to dance with Mr. MacAlistair, then I shall!''

She closed the dulcimer cover with a decisive gesture, and
Adam lifted his arms to swing her down from the bandstand.

Emma gave him another glare as she landed on her feet beside Glynis.

"I'm sorry," Glynis mouthed behind her hand.

Emma shook her head slightly, and smiled determinedly. "It's nothing, Aunt Glynis, really." Then, her lips close to Glynis's ear, she whispered, "You can't imagine how many women have inquired about this dress—that's all that matters!" She shot her aunt a conspiratorial smile, then resumed a look of indignation before she turned to Adam.

As the quadrille required four couples arranged in a square, Neva and Abraham joined them. While they stood waiting for the music, Colonel de Warde said to Glynis, "Are you familiar with Shakespeare, Miss Tryon? 'When you do dance, I wish you / A wave o' th' sea, that you might ever do / Nothing but that.' "

Glynis smiled. "*The Winter's Tale,* I believe," and was rewarded with his look of surprise.

"Ah, yes," he said then, "I quite forgot—you are, of course, a librarian."

Implying what? she reflected. That in America only librarians read Shakespeare? But she nodded, now wondering if Colonel de Warde was aware of what Americans had done to the European quadrille, often called simply a square dance. Once the dancing began, however, she saw that he'd done this before. He went through the five main figures flawlessly.

The string band first played a New England fiddler's tune called "Smash the Windows," followed appropriately enough by "Farewell to Whiskey." The music's exuberance and irresistible six-eight meter worked its customary magic, and Glynis, passing hand to hand from the colonel to Cullen to Adam to Abraham, began to feel a lightness of spirit absent for too long. When the colonel effortlessly swung her round and round, she could see that Emma too was hard pressed not to smile.

But all at once the reliable rhythm flagged, as various instruments straggled off into silence. The reason for this remained obscure even when Glynis looked up at the bandstand and saw, for the first time that evening, Cullen's young deputy Liam Cleary. She had assumed the boy was on duty—since

Cullen and Zeph Waters clearly were not—but now Liam stood beside Grandy Fox, his eyes anxiously scanning the dancers below. From the crowd, Zeph suddenly materialized to gesture toward Cullen. And Liam jumped from the bandstand. Cullen, who by this time had seen both deputies and broken from the square, took Liam by the arm and walked him rapidly away from the others. After listening to Liam only a moment or two, Cullen suddenly turned and motioned to Dr. Quentin Ives. Then he took off at a run, Zeph and Liam beside him.

Glynis moved quickly to the bandstand to ask Grandy Fox, "Do you know what's happened—why Liam wanted the constable?"

Grandy's face was grim as he dropped to one knee, bending forward to say quietly to Glynis, "Some girl's been found lying on the towpath—this side of the canal. The deputy thinks the girl's dead."

Glynis stared at Grandy Fox, disbelief rocking her like a violent wind. A girl? Grandy had said *a girl?*

She had seen Cullen's expression when he motioned to Dr. Quentin Ives, and she'd had a terrifying intuition. But because of the previous pattern what she'd expected was a *man's* death—if death on such a tranquil night could come as expected. But a girl?

Did this death, then, not relate to the others? Perhaps the result of a tragic brawl at the nearby tavern—not common but not unknown? Glynis's questions came nearly too fast to form.

She asked the most important of Grandy Fox. "Did Liam know who the girl was?" Still resting on one knee above her, Grandy shook his head. Aware of the chorus of questions from those standing behind her, Glynis made an attempt to gather her scattered wits.

"I think you should continue playing," she said to him. "Then most people won't suspect anything—Cullen doesn't need a swarm of people down there at the canal."

"My thoughts exactly," Grandy agreed, and rose quickly to wave his fiddle bow at those beginning to crowd around the bandstand. They smelled blood, Glynis thought, then cast aside the thought as uncharitable. They were simply curious—as she herself had been.

"Listen up, folks!" Grandy called over their heads. "Folks, the constable's had to leave—got a small problem down by one of the taverns. Certainly nothing to worry any of us on this fine night." He smiled reassuringly, then continued, "And there's nothing new about trouble at the taverns—right, my friends?"

While Glynis was admiring his deft sidestepping, Grandy added, "Now, we'll give you another tune and get back to more important business here!" He immediately turned to the band members, gesturing with his bow. The musicians, with a mild amount of confusion, resumed the "Farewell to Whiskey" they had abandoned.

Emma, in the meantime, had been standing to one side of the bandstand with Adam, and Neva and Abraham, none of whom looked eager to continue dancing. In fact, Glynis realized, they were all staring at her with doubt written across their faces. Fleur Coddington, on the other hand, was engaged in conversation with Colonel de Warde, and Glynis was surprised that the woman's expression looked almost as grim as had Grandy's. Glynis supposed it was concern for Cullen that Fleur was exhibiting.

"Aunt Glynis," Emma said, "what really happened? I saw your face when Grandy Fox was talking to you, and I don't believe—"

"Emma, please," Glynis interrupted, "let's go somewhere else and discuss this."

"Yes, I think something's very wrong," Neva agreed, "because I saw your face, too."

And with blunt accuracy, Adam MacAlistair added, "You'd best not play poker, Miss Tryon—you'd lose your shirt!"

"All right!" Glynis conceded. "Let's go over there, by the oak tree. But in the meantime, please be quiet." She saw with relief that no one else seemed to pay much attention as they crossed the grass to stand beneath the tree's winged branches.

"You're all going to be disappointed," Glynis told them, noticing that Fleur Coddington, but not Colonel de Warde, had joined them, "because I don't know much. I only moved away from the others to forestall a mass exodus from here to the towpath. And Constable Stuart—" she watched Fleur's eyes narrow slightly ''—well, the constable doesn't need more people than he already has down there.''

''But what's the trouble that Grandy Fox mentioned?'' Fleur Coddington suddenly asked, and now her face seemed to hold genuine apprehension.

''It's nothing the constable can't handle, Fleur,'' she said, uncertain as to why she should be reassuring Cullen's romantic interest. She instantly felt petty, and hastened to add, ''Someone was found . . . well, I'm afraid the person might be badly injured.''

''Or dead?'' Fleur exclaimed in a much harsher tone than Glynis had ever heard her use. ''Someone *else* is dead? Oh, my God!''

''No, no, Liam wasn't certain about that,'' Glynis said to her, but realized the words had been drowned in the others' questions.

''Who is it?'' Emma asked, eyes very wide.

''. . . and is Miss Hathaway involved?'' Adam was asking, which reminded Glynis that Serenity Hathaway, proprietor of the tavern-cum-brothel, had once been Adam's client—his first client, as a matter of fact. That would likely not be something for Emma to learn. Glynis declined to answer him.

''Glynis, do you *know* who it *is?*'' Neva said, sounding thoroughly exasperated.

''No. No, I don't know who, except that apparently Liam Cleary said it was *a girl*.''

Stunned silence was followed by another round of questions, none of which Glynis could answer. Finally Neva announced, ''Well, I'm relieved they don't need me. I dislike autopsies. And thank you, Glynis, for not allowing the dance to be disrupted—a stampede to the canal would probably have caused more catastrophe.''

Emma's face, meantime, had gone very white, and Adam, hovering over her protectively, took her hand in his and began rubbing it vigorously. Emma didn't even seem to notice.

Glynis thought it odd that Fleur Coddington looked so shaken. Her long white fingers were fumbling with a lacy handkerchief. Emma, after all, was still very young, but Fleur must have heard her share of shocking news. And yet, the woman looked sincerely distraught. Glynis was about to ask if she was all right, when Fleur pivoted on her heel and walked rapidly away.

Emma, her cheeks suddenly suffused with color, said abruptly, "Mr. MacAlistair, my hand—why are you scrubbing it?" Without waiting for an answer, she yanked her hand from his. Adam did not look at all taken aback by this rebuff. On the contrary, he seemed somewhat amused.

"I think we should all go back and rejoin the others," Glynis suggested. "I expect we'll hear soon enough what's happened."

"Nothing would surprise me, considering what goes on down there by the canal," Neva said. "Although, I pity the tavern women who believe they must earn a living that way." She stopped at a sound from Abraham, who shook his head in Emma's direction.

Emma, however, picked up her skirts, gave them a purposeful shake, and—with Glynis's gratitude—announced, "I don't know about the rest of you, but I'm going back to my dulcimer."

Glynis watched Adam's determined efforts to change Emma's mind.

He didn't succeed.

THE BELLS IN church towers were tolling midnight by the time Cullen reappeared. Most of the crowd had left; those few who had not were, like Glynis, helping to clean up. She had assumed that Cullen *would* come back, although Fleur Coddington had been escorted home some time ago by Colonel de Warde.

Glynis, who had been folding tablecloths with Emma and Neva, felt her niece draw closer to her, and remembered that despite a startling sophistication about some things, Emma was still young. Her maturity, like all young people's, was far from uniform. She took Emma's hand, and they waited for Cullen to cross the grass. Abraham and Grandy Fox had been heaving hay bales into an open wagon, and the two men now joined them, along with Adam MacAlistair, who'd just returned from walking Katherine Ives home.

"Thought you all would have left by now," Cullen said as he came up to them. His face looked drawn with fatigue and his stride was not as easy as usual. The moonlight gave his sun-ruddy skin a pallor, his hair a silvery cast, and Glynis had a sudden rush of sympathy for him as she asked, "Cullen, who was it? And is she alive?"

He shook his head. "No, and what's worse, Quentin Ives is almost sure she was strangled." He looked at Neva, when he explained, "Quentin said the structures in her neck—the hyoid and cricoid, he called them—were fractured, consistent with the way they would be if she were throttled. And the bruises on her neck looked like they'd been caused by pressure."

Neva nodded, almost absently, as though this was to be expected. Glynis thought immediately of the banker Thomas Bingham—and so apparently did Cullen, from the pointed way he was looking at her.

She had felt Emma beside her stiffen, but her niece said nothing. None of them did, at first. Then Neva asked, "Was it someone we know . . . knew?"

"I think so," Cullen said. "It was the seamstress who worked for Fleur Coddington—name of Sally Lunt."

Emma made a choking sound, and pulled free of Glynis to put her hands over her face. Adam took a step toward her, but then had the good sense to leave her alone. And during this, while everyone else just stood with their mouths open, Cullen studied Emma with a thoughtful expression.

"You knew the girl, then?" he finally asked her.

Emma's head went up and down like a floppy doll's. "I . . . I wanted her job!" she choked, with hands still covering her face and fingers glistening wetly.

Glynis put her arm around Emma's shoulders.

"Why on earth would someone kill that girl?" Neva said. "And *what* was she doing down by a tavern? I knew her, only very slightly, but she didn't impress me as . . . well, as that kind of girl."

"I don't think she was," Cullen said. "In fact, I'm almost certain of it. And then, too, I check the taverns often, and I never saw Sally Lunt down there at Serenity's—or any other tavern."

"So, *why?*" Adam MacAlistair asked in a tight voice. "Why would someone kill her? Was it during some kind of drunken fight down there?"

Cullen shook his head. "Serenity Hathaway claims she doesn't know a thing about it. Says there was no fight."

"And you believe her?" Neva retorted, being no supporter of the tavern owner whose business she had once tried to shut down.

"Don't know," Cullen answered. He looked off toward the canal, and Glynis had the distinct impression that he was deliberately not saying what he *did* know.

"Look," Abraham said, "it's late. We all need to go home. Cullen, is there anything more to tell us?"

"No. But if you recall anything about the girl that could be useful, let me know."

Grandy Fox went to Emma, now herself staring off at the canal, and said, "You made good music tonight. We'll do it again." He brushed Emma's cheek with his fingers, then walked toward his wagon waiting on the far side of Fall Street.

Emma looked after him, until Adam said to her, rather emphatically, and as if he expected her to object, "I'll walk you and your aunt home now."

"It's all right, Adam," Cullen said, his tone decisive enough to preclude any argument, "I'll walk them home."

Adam shot Cullen a dark look. At any other time but this, Glynis would have wanted to laugh.

The walk was a silent one. Glynis had more questions, but sensed that Cullen not only wouldn't respond to them, but didn't want to talk, period. Emma seemed to be deep in thought, and kept shaking her head slightly, as if arguing with herself. Now and then she would wipe her eyes.

Feeling her niece's misery to be somewhat misguided, Glynis finally said, "Emma, the wish does not make the deed." Where she'd picked up this homily she had no idea, but like so many hackneyed phrases it seemed ever apt. "I hope you aren't thinking yourself somehow responsible for Sally Lunt's death."

This seemed to have no effect whatsoever on Emma until Cullen unexpectedly asked her, "Why would you think that?"

Emma started, gaped at him, then moved away to walk at the edge of the road.

"I asked you a question, Miss Tryon," Cullen said, "and I'd like an answer."

"Please, Cullen!" Glynis protested. "She's upset enough."

"I need to find some answers, Glynis. If your niece knows something . . ."

"What could she possibly know?" Glynis argued. "Emma and the girl had barely met each other."

But Emma suddenly burst out, "I told you earlier, Constable Stuart, I wanted to work at La Maison de Fleur! And I've been wishing"—here she threw Glynis an agonized look—"that something would happen to Sally Lunt so I could have her job. And now see what's happened!" She clenched her fists and Glynis could see she was making tremendous effort not to cry. Recalling how many times in the past month she'd hoped Emma *would* cry, Glynis wondered if the fact that she was now doing so should be considered an improvement.

Unfortunately, Cullen seemed intent on continuing his interrogation. "Did you ever talk to Mrs. Coddington about working there?" he asked Emma.

Emma nodded. Cullen started to ask something else, but Glynis broke in and said firmly, "That's enough for tonight, Cullen—surely tomorrow is soon enough for more questions." She looked at him, her anger mixed with bewilderment; she'd never known him to be callous. He seemed to be taking Sally Lunt's death personally.

The Peartree house, with a lamp glowing in a front window, was reached in a few more uncomfortable minutes. Harriet was already home, and it was with considerable relief that Glynis managed to prod Emma up the porch stairs and inside. Then she turned back to Cullen.

"I don't know what's troubling you about Emma," she said to him, "but I'm disturbed at your attitude. It almost sounds as if you think she had some involvement in that girl's death." She was standing on a porch step looking down at him. The moonlight might be unreliable, but still, she felt certain she saw him wince. "Cullen?"

"I don't know what to think," he said. "But I believe your

niece knows something. No, don't protest—you don't have as much to go on as I do.''

"Such as what?'' Glynis felt a chill streak down her spine. "You don't think this Sally Lunt's death is connected to the others, do you?''

"I'm almost sure of it.''

"Cullen—''

"Good night, Glynis. And keep an eye on your niece, O.K.?''

Before she could ask what that meant, he turned, and strode back up Cayuga Street.

Frustrated, and upset by his manner, she opened the front door and stepped inside. As she closed the door behind her and was reaching for the bolt, she suddenly paused, recalling Fleur Coddington's earlier distress. It had been *before* the identity of the victim was known. All anyone knew was what Grandy had told Glynis: that Liam Cleary said it was "a girl." No name, nothing else.

Glynis threw the bolt and went to the foot of the stairs, but again paused. Could Fleur Coddington possibly have guessed it was her seamstress to whom Liam referred? But supposing, just supposing this were true. Then why—why, out of all the girls in Seneca Falls, would Fleur even begin to think the unfortunate girl might be Sally Lunt?

TEN

❧

Why was Eden so pleasant to Adam,
    So rid of connubial ills?
Because his ingenuous madam
    Never bored him with milliners' bills.

No bonnets had she for her tresses,
    No silks did her person enroll;
So cheap were her costliest dresses,
    For a fig one had purchased the whole.
    —THE JULY 1859 ISSUE OF
    HARPER'S NEW MONTHLY MAGAZINE

WARM HAZY SUNSHINE streamed through the open window of Emma's bedroom, while Emma herself sat on the edge of the bed, trying to determine if this bright summer morning might be more bearable than the two days and nights she'd just passed. She had barely slept at all. How could she? Reality had not altered over time; Sally Lunt was still dead, and the wretched Mr. Throckmorton of the Singer Company still lived. The unhappy Sally, whom Emma had talked about so flippantly to her aunt, was no longer unhappy . . . was no longer anything. Though of course Aunt Glynis had been right: Emma herself had had nothing to do with the girl's death. But she couldn't shake the sense of guilt for her ill will toward Sally.

And why on earth had Sally been anywhere near a tavern? Even Constable Stuart had said she wasn't that kind of girl—but then, how could he know? There had certainly been something very distressing in Sally's life, of that Emma was certain. All that crying! And Emma had the nagging sense of having forgotten an item of importance, something that she'd seen or heard in connection with Sally. But since she couldn't remember what it was, why did she feel so strongly that it had to do with a man?

When no answers came, Emma sighed and went to stand at the window; however, the view of Mrs. Peartree's flower garden below gave her no joy. In fact, she resented the cheerful blooms. She turned away and stared instead at the opposite wall. She needed to concentrate. What *was* she going to do about Mr. Throckmorton's most recent threat, something called a show cause order.

It had been handed to her last Saturday by a man who said he was a process server from Waterloo. The one thing for which she would be eternally thankful was that Aunt Glynis had been at the library, and Mrs. Peartree at the market when the man arrived. Emma had been able to get rid of him and run up to her room to read the fearfully official-looking thing. When she'd finally sorted through all the confusing and intimidating legal mumbo jumbo, the gist of it was that she'd been commanded to appear in court to *show cause* why an order should not be granted the Singer Company to repossess her sewing machine. The order was upon application of an Orrin Makepeace Polk, Esq., local counsel for the Singer Company. It had been signed by a Seneca County court judge.

Clearly she couldn't just pretend this hadn't happened. And even if she was terrified, she had to talk to *someone* about it. If only so that Aunt Glynis would know why when her niece was dragged off to jail.

Emma felt her stomach heave, as it had been doing since Saturday. The only time she'd really managed to forget Mr. Throckmorton and the Singer Company was when she'd been playing her dulcimer. Did they, she wondered, allow musical instruments in jails?

She had to stop scaring herself or she would retch. There was one person with whom she could imagine discussing this— but it would be so humiliating! On the other hand, it would probably humiliate her even more to be arrested. She could hear her mother's voice as clear as a bell, saying: What have you done now, you selfish girl?

And, upon hearing that, Emma decided that even if a judge said she deserved to go to jail—and she didn't think she did— then the least she could do was try to spare Aunt Glynis the embarrassment.

Emma went to the wardrobe cabinet and pulled open the doors. She stood there looking at the dresses she'd made with her Singer, and tried to determine just what one should wear when declaring oneself a fugitive.

AN HOUR LATER, Emma stood dawdling on the stoop of the law office, while attempting to find an excuse, any excuse, not to go through with this. She brushed dust from the hems of her prettiest white lawn, puff-sleeved summer frock and lace-edged petticoats. Running a finger inside the high frilly collar under her chin, she glanced at the tiny pearl buttons down her front to make sure they weren't undone. She retied the blue ribbon of her flower-trimmed straw bonnet, and tucked back an errant strand of hair. There—she surely looked as pure and innocent as she could manage. Unfortunately, she could think of nothing else to delay her.

She took several deep breaths, and knocked on the door with a white-gloved hand. After waiting for what seemed like hours, while barely resisting an impulse to run down the slope and throw herself into the canal, she rapped again. When there was still no response, she opened the door, and stepped inside. She entered a waiting room, and heard voices coming from behind an open door down the hall. She stood there quietly, her resolution wavering, mostly because the voices sounded so combative. But that was probably the way lawyers *should* sound. Emma drew in a shaky breath and called, "Hello? Is anyone here?" When there was no reply, just the contentious voices, she called again, this time more loudly. "HELLO?"

The voices stopped. A moment later a tall gaunt man, who was vaguely familiar, peered at her around the door. "Yes? Yes, my dear, may I help you?"

"Oh, no!" She must be in the wrong place. "Oh, no, please excuse me, sir."

She took several steps backward, ready to turn and flee, when she heard a more familiar voice. "Miss Tryon? Can that be you?"

The gaunt man was jostled aside by Adam MacAlistair as he came dashing through the doorway into the hall. Emma was so relieved to see him that her knees threatened to buckle, and she reached for something to steady herself.

Adam's initial grin dissolved as he leapt forward to take her arm. "My dear Miss Emma, are you all right? Here, take my arm. Now, come with me."

Emma was not so enfeebled that she didn't catch the hostile look he directed at the other man, who then hurried off down the hall while Adam MacAlistair led her into his office. Once through the doorway, the first thing she noticed was the colors, because they surprised her; she'd expected something more austere than the lemon yellow walls and matching drapery over the window, and the thick wool carpet of dark pumpkin. On one wall hung a hand-colored print of a painting by Thomas Cole—an artist Emma liked herself—called *Voyage of Life*. There were also two landscapes resembling some she'd seen in Mrs. Lincoln's parlor; one was of Harper's Ferry, Virginia, the other the Catskills of New York State.

Another wall held shelves of books, which Emma studied rather carefully as she sat down in an upholstered pumpkin-colored chair. Two shelves held law books, including one by a Blackstone that Mr. Lincoln also had in his Springfield office. And since Aunt Glynis insisted that the books people read were a good clue to their character, she wondered what her aunt would think of the person whose books included Thoreau's *Walden;* Mill's *The System of Logic;* Aristotle's *Ethics;* and then several that even Emma recognized with some astonishment, *The Faerie Queen, Sir Gawain and the Green Knight,* and Malory's *Morte D'Arthur*. Lying open, face down, at the edge of an impressively large cherry desk, was a new book, one Aunt Glynis herself had just received for the library, called *Idylls of the King* by someone named Tennyson.

Emma looked up to see Adam MacAlistair standing over her, and her cheeks grew hot, as if she'd just been caught peeking into someone's windows.

"Would you like some water?" he asked. "You look extremely . . . pink. It's very fetching, needless to say, but are you feeling feverish?"

"No, thank you, I'm fine. And no, I don't want any water; it's just the heat," lied Emma, wishing she'd never thought of coming here. Adam MacAlistair thought her a silly goose *now;* what would he think when he heard her story? No, she couldn't go through with this.

She stood up. "I'm sorry, Mr. MacAlistair, for taking your time. But I think I should leave now. I . . . I forgot something I need to do."

Adam, who had begun to round the desk to his chair, instantly turned and shot forward to stand in front of the door. Was he going to bar her way? "Please," she began, "I—"

"No, you can't leave until you've told me why you came." He was smiling, but since he'd also been doing this when he'd argued with Grandy Fox and embarrassed her in front of half the town, she didn't believe the smile to be sincere. He was definitely not as nice as he looked. Pretended to look.

But almost as if he'd read her thoughts, he stepped aside. The smile vanished. Looking down at her, he said with what Emma considered proper contrition, "I apologize, Miss Tryon. I've been told that I'm sometimes arrogant. Perhaps this is so. But I think you came here for a reason, and I would like to hear it." Then he smiled at her again.

And Emma, with a vivid recollection of Mr. Throckmorton's latest threat, decided she'd better believe him.

She reseated herself and withdrew from her purse the dread Throckmorton letters and the show cause order. "It's about these, Mr. MacAlistair." She felt her lower lip start to quiver, and she caught it between her teeth; it occurred to her that she'd seen her aunt do this. Now she knew why. More determined than ever not to start weeping, Emma moved to hand over the documents to the lawyer.

Seated behind his desk, he leaned across it to take them from her, and she said, "Before you read them, Mr. MacAlistair, you must tell me how much you charge. I don't have much money, and I don't know if I can afford you . . . I mean, it . . . that is . . ."

"How much did you think I would charge?" Adam asked her. She felt enormously grateful that he was no longer smiling, but looked quite serious. As she thought a lawyer should.

"Well, I don't know," she answered. "I've never been to a lawyer before. But I could pay you two dollars. Would that be sufficient?'' She knew her voice sounded unsteady, but she couldn't help herself.

"Yes, I believe that would be the right amount," Adam said briskly. He opened the letters, then the order, and began to read. And as he read he began to scowl. Emma, sitting there quietly and watching him, thought his eyebrows might meet, he was scowling that fiercely. Oh, she'd known it! He thought she was a ninny. Or worse, a thief. Why had she ever come here?

"Very well, Miss Tryon," Adam said finally, and put the papers down on the desk. "To begin with, how old are you?"

"Excuse me?"

"How *old* are you? Your age?"

"Yes, I heard you. But what does that have to do with those?" She gestured to the letters.

"It may have a great deal to do with those. With your case."

Her case? That sounded grim. As if she were going to jail . . .

"Miss Tryon! *Your age.*"

"Seventeen. Well, almost eighteen. I'll be eighteen in a month. That is, next month."

He sat back in the chair and folded his hands across his vest, and for a moment he just smiled at her. "Well," he said, pulling himself upright again, "that is extremely important. It may well be that you were not old enough to enter into a contractual agreement with the Singer Company. It's likely the odious Mr. Throckmorton was not aware of that."

"You think he's odious, too?"

"Definitely odious. A man who could direct such threatening dispatches to a young woman such as yourself is hardly worthy of living. Now, did you answer these letters?"

"Yes, the first two, I did." She explained the fact that she'd sent the final payment, and that it must have gotten lost.

"I hope you believe me," she said. "I truly did send it." She bit her lower lip again.

"Of course I believe you! And this should be a very simple matter to resolve. I assume you kept a receipt of the bank draft?"

"I didn't send a bank draft."

"Your personal check, then."

"I didn't send a check, either," Emma said, sinking lower into the chair.

"No? What did you send?"

"Coins! I sent two half eagles." She saw his face, and wanted to drop through the floor. "That wasn't good, was it?"

Adam shook his head. "No, that wasn't good. You should never send—well, but that's water over the dam, isn't it? However, in future, you should—"

"I know," Emma broke in. "Never send coins. I was afraid you'd say that, and I feel very foolish. Does that mean you can't help me?"

"Oh, no, no, it doesn't mean anything of the kind. It will just take a bit more time to sort out. But have no fear, Miss Tryon. You are in good hands, and you needn't worry yourself about a thing."

"How can I not worry? That order there says I have to appear in court in Waterloo. *In court!*"

"Please let me reassure you. You don't need to go to Waterloo—I'll appear in court on your behalf."

"Really? But what about jail? Mr. Throckmorton's letter said I would go to jail."

"Miss Emma, we have already agreed that Throckmorton is a contemptible individual, yes? He used the threat of jail merely as a ploy—to make you send another ten dollars."

"The rat!" Emma said with feeling, then immediately blushed. "So I'm not in danger of being arrested?"

"Absolutely not. I will not allow you to be arrested. I would go to jail myself rather than permit such a thing to happen to you."

Since he was again smiling, Emma didn't know whether to believe this. "I expect you will need to charge me more, though, won't you?" she asked.

"Charge you more? Why no, the sum you previously mentioned will be quite adequate."

Although Emma was doubtful about this, she certainly wasn't going to argue when she had no more money. But she didn't want him to think she expected charity. "Mr. Mac-Alistair, I think I may have some regular employment soon. If I do, I will be in a position to pay you more if necessary."

"I assure you, no more will be necessary. But where do you think you might be working?"

"At La Maison de Fleur. It's very sad that it has to come about this way, but yesterday Mrs. Coddington offered me a position, now that Sally Lunt is . . . is gone."

"You're a seamstress then?"

"That's why I bought the sewing machine, Mr. Mac-Alistair."

"Oh, yes. Yes, of course. But how did you manage to make the payments—the one hundred and fifty dollars that you paid the Singer Company."

"I earned it by sewing!" Emma thought this was a trifle impertinent of him. Where did he *think* she'd gotten the money? Oh, yes, there was something else. "Mr. MacAlistair, I have a very great favor to ask of you. Please don't mention this to my aunt. I haven't told her anything about it."

Adam looked puzzled. "Naturally, anything that passes between lawyer and client is entirely confidential, Miss Tryon. But your aunt—"

"Doesn't need to know," Emma said emphatically. "I got myself into this, and with your help I must get myself out. Aunt Glynis has done more than enough for me already. And I need to show her that I'm a responsible person." She stopped, upset that she'd revealed so much to this relative stranger.

Adam was studying her with the bemused expression she'd seen last Saturday night. "Forgive me for asking, Miss Emma," he said now, "but has someone suggested that you *aren't* a responsible person?"

"My mother did—all the time!" she blurted, before she even knew it was coming. Aghast at herself, she clapped her hand over her mouth, and felt the sting of tears compound her embarrassment.

Mercifully, Adam MacAlistair turned away and looked out the office window. With any luck, he'd been thinking about something else and perhaps hadn't heard her.

Emma swallowed hard, and said, "May I please have your promise on it—not to tell Aunt Glynis?"

"Of course, you may," Adam said as he swung back around to face her. He looked very serious, almost as if she'd insulted him by asking again. That would be too bad, she thought, but she'd learned a lesson from the Singer Company: Don't trust anyone to whom you owe money.

She rose, and started for the door. "Thank you, Mr. MacAlistair. I'm very grateful that you will take my case. . . ."

She stopped, as a sudden sound like a faraway scream made her jump. Emma turned in alarm toward the wall from where it had seemed to come.

Adam MacAlistair, however, was grinning. "That's from the office next door—just our neighbor the dentist plying his grisly trade."

Emma stood at the door, frowning in concentration. Something had just nearly surfaced in her mind. When she'd walked past it, she recalled seeing a name painted on the big plate-glass window of the office next door, but it hadn't really registered.

"What is the dentist's name?" she asked.

"Fitzhugh. Dr. Alan Fitzhugh, Junior." He was still grinning. "And I hope you don't have to make his acquaintance any time soon."

Emma barely heard his last comment. Fitzhugh! Yes, she'd heard the name before and now remembered when. It had been the first day she'd gone to Fleur Coddington's shop. She was positive the name had been "Alan Fitzhugh" that the voice had been saying over and over again. The sobbing voice—belonging to Sally Lunt.

A SHORT TIME later, Jeremiah Merrycoyf stood in the door of his office, watching Adam MacAlistair usher his new client, with seemingly undue ceremony, out the front door. When Adam returned to the hall, Merrycoyf said, "Come into my office if you would, Mr. MacAlistair."

As Adam entered and sat down opposite Merrycoyf's desk, the older man asked, "Was the delightful voice I just heard that of the young Miss Tryon?"

"Yes, yes, it was. Jeremiah, you couldn't imagine the shoddy tactics to which that young woman has been subjected."

Merrycoyf's eyebrows rose. "By whom?"

"The Singer sewing machine company. She apparently purchased one of its machines on an installment payment basis; since then she has paid ten dollars every month for fifteen months. That's a total of one hundred and *fifty dollars* for a machine whose cost was one hundred and *twenty-five dollars!* Jeremiah, that's an interest charge of twenty-five dollars—or one-fifth the price of the machine! It's unmitigated exploitation!''

''Miss Tryon is unwilling to pay the total interest charge?''

''No, not at all, that's what is so outrageous. She sent Singer the final ten dollars—in coin, I'm afraid—and the company claims it never was received.'' Adam slouched back in the chair, arms crossed behind his head, and stared at the ceiling. ''I think to begin with, I'll sue Singer for usurious practices; then for harassment, then defamation of character, then—''

''Just a minute, my eager young colleague. Did Miss Tryon agree to the Singer Company's contract when she purchased the machine?''

''Well, yes, but she was naive and didn't understand, I'm sure, what it entailed. The company probably counted on that.''

''That excuse will not hold up in a court of law, as you well know. In addition, do you believe she actually sent that last ten-dollar payment?''

''Yes, I believe it—she said she did! Jeremiah, the Singer Company is abusing innocent young women with that kind of usurious practice. It, and its practices, must be stopped!''

Merrycoyf sighed mightily. The impulse to mount a white horse and gallop off to rescue fair damsels had left him some time ago. ''Very well, Adam—but that is not the reason I asked you in here. We need to discuss a matter of some concern to me.''

Adam, his crusading fervor so abruptly intruded upon, looked over the desk at Merrycoyf with some surprise. ''What matter is that?''

''The one of Cyril Doggett becoming our law partner.''

Adam bolted upright. And Merrycoyf saw the young lawyer's face, ordinarily the very essence of good humor, assume a truculent expression. ''That is a matter whose time I feel has not yet come,'' Adam replied, his voice carrying a certain coolness hard for Merrycoyf to miss.

"I don't agree."

"Yes, I'm aware you don't," Adam said evenly.

"Cyril has been with us for some time," Merrycoyf reminded Adam unnecessarily. "How much more is required before you will consider the issue?"

Adam frowned and shook his head. "I'm not sure exactly what it is about Doggett, Jeremiah, but I just don't trust the man. I'm sorry," he said quickly, apparently seeing Merrycoyf's dismay. "I know he was a law school classmate of yours, and I know you spent years in New Haven together, but . . ." His voice trailed off.

"Adam, I must confess I am mystified by your attitude. And it's not at all like you. Why, precisely, do you not trust Cyril? Precisely, Adam."

Adam twisted in the chair, resettling himself at length, before he said, "There are just too many things we don't know about him."

"For example."

"He's evasive about his past to the point of secrecy—his past, that is, after law school."

"He practiced in New Haven," Merrycoyf replied, a small frown beginning to form. "That's hardly a secret."

"But where did he practice? Did he have partners? If so, who were they? I can't find any record of a law firm with Doggett listed as a partner."

"You've investigated it?" Merrycoyf asked, the frown deepening.

"Yes, I have. Because whenever I question him about it, I get an evasive answer. He implies he was in a firm. When I ask him with whom, he sidesteps the question and changes the subject. Jeremiah, as you are well aware, partners in a law firm are responsible for acts of the other partners. For that reason alone I find Doggett's secrecy worrisome."

Merrycoyf sat silently, and stared at the younger man. Then he said, "Go on, what else worries you."

Adam looked off, as if debating with himself, then turned back to Merrycoyf. "All right, there's the business of his new client, Colonel de Warde. How did Cyril Doggett acquire him? De Warde came into town not long ago, and suddenly Doggett's his attorney, right off the bat. It seems strange.''

"Mr. MacAlistair! This is truly not worthy of you. There are any number of ways in which Cyril and Colonel de Warde might have become acquainted. Or perhaps they knew each other in the past.''

"And that's just what I assumed. But when I asked Doggett, just casually in passing, if he'd known de Warde previously, he quickly, and forcefully, denied it. Just the vehemence of his denial made me suspicious, so—''

"Why, I believe you're envious," Merrycoyf interrupted, smiling. "Just because the colonel sought counsel from someone else other than yourself.''

"I hadn't finished what I was saying." Adam's tone was brusque. "May I?''

Merrycoyf nodded.

"I did some more checking, this time on de Warde. And what do you think, Jeremiah? It just happens that the good colonel has an office in New Haven! Has had for some time.''

Merrycoyf sat forward. "I am afraid this excessive distrust of Cyril Doggett has clouded your reason. Why shouldn't Colonel de Warde have an office there? He's a merchant! New Haven, Connecticut, is a busy trading town—or were you unaware of that?''

Adam's following silence spoke loudly. Merrycoyf sighed with some frustration, realizing that this discussion would go no further than had those in the past. He well knew that Adam believed him blinded by friendship and old school ties. But there was nothing, *nothing,* about Cyril for Adam to so excessively distrust.

"Adam, we must overcome this stalemate. I find your attitude toward Cyril to be unwarranted, to say the least. Now, if you cannot base your objections to him on something more concrete than vague suspicions, then we are at a most unfortunate impasse. Nonetheless, I must insist that we arrive at some conclusion on this question of Cyril's partnership.''

Adam rose, but remained standing in front of Merrycoyf's desk while he again stared off into space. Then, "Very well, Jeremiah. I have too much regard for you to question your demand for a resolution—no, please allow me to finish.

Therefore, I suggest the following: If I do not find grounds—substantive grounds—on which to base my conviction that Doggett should not become our partner, then I will withdraw my objections. If, on the other hand, I find grounds which to my satisfaction disqualify him, and you are still not convinced, then you may have my resignation.''

"My dear man, that is entirely unnecessary."

"No, Jeremiah, that is only fair. To us both. Shall we put a time limit on it? Say, three months?"

Merrycoyf witnessed the firm set of the jaw, the resolution in the direct hazel eyes, and he nodded. Not happily.

As Adam reached the door, and began to pull it open, Merrycoyf said, "One more thing. Didn't I hear you and Cyril having an unpleasant discussion—to put it mildly—just before Miss Tryon came in?"

The young lawyer stepped back into the room and started to close the door, but then swung it open wide. "Yes, we were having a discussion, Mr. Doggett and I." Adam made no effort to keep his voice down. In fact, he raised it. "I'd asked him if he had told Constable Stuart yet about Sally Lunt—about her being in this office last Friday. The day before she was killed."

"Sally Lunt was here?" Merrycoyf asked. "But why? About what did she come here?"

"That's a good question, Jeremiah, at least I thought so. But—" Adam looked out into the hall and then said, certainly more loudly than was called for "—when I asked Mr. Doggett that question, I was informed that the matter about which Sally Lunt saw him was confidential. And when I explained—as if I needed to—that confidentiality no longer applied because the girl had been murdered, your old classmate told me, in so many words, that it was none of my concern!"

Adam gave Merrycoyf a curt nod and went through to the hall, leaving the door behind him open.

ELEVEN

It was like standing on a powder magazine, after a slow match had been lighted.
—ANNE BROWN, RECOLLECTIONS

ANNIE STOOD AT the kitchen window of the log house, looking up at the garden plot where she'd just been tugging weeds from the hard, parched earth. Only mid-July and there had been no rain for several weeks. It looked to be a hot dry summer. She lifted her apron to wipe her face.

"Would you go for water?" her sister-in-law Belle asked her.

Annie hid a tired sigh behind her hand, nodded, and went back out the door. She walked to the well, lowered the bucket, then slowly drew it up, pulling hand over hand on the frayed creaking rope. Only after she had placed the bucket beside her on the ground, taking care not to slosh any of the water, did she wipe her forehead with the back of a hand.

She picked up the bucket, and while she lugged it down the hill, Annie guessed that with one arm stuck up in the air for balance she looked like the windmill behind the rickety old barn. Before she went into the house, she gazed in the direction of the stream to where, just this side of the bridge, three wagons were standing. One of them was already loaded and covered with canvas. Several of her brothers, carrying supplies, walked back and forth between the other two wagons.

They were getting ready to leave. Father and her brothers Oliver and Watson were leaving to free the slaves. Or, Father had said, they would die trying. Watson's wife Belle was going to have a baby in a few weeks, and Annie guessed that Belle, if she had the strength, would try to talk Watson out of going. But it would likely be for nothing. Watson was what her mother called a firebrand.

One of the wagons had been standing there by the bridge

since two days ago, when Oliver brought it by mule from the Lake Placid rail station. The wagon had come by train and it was loaded with guns. Annie's brothers were worried about where the wagon came from, but Father insisted it didn't matter. The arrival of the guns, he said, was a sign sent by the Lord that he should go forward with his mission. And now there was another wagon being loaded with "freight," as Father called the rifles, revolvers, swords, powder, and caps. All three wagons would be pulled to the South by mules. Annie didn't envy them.

John Henry Kagi had written from Chambersburg, Pennsylvania, saying that Father should stay in the mountains of Maryland, along with the other men who would come there to join him. In Maryland, farmhouses could easily be rented under a false name, and then, while they waited, they would be just a short distance from the Harper's Ferry arsenal. But hidden safely away. The town of Harper's Ferry perched on a slim strip of land at the junction of the Potomac and Shenandoah rivers in Virginia's Blue Ridge Mountains. John Henry said it was secluded and a pretty place. Annie had read his letter many times; there was one sentence that said: "*Mr. Brown, you may tell your daughter Anne that the mountains of Pennsylvania and Maryland are almost as beautiful as her own mountains at home, and the North Star is just as bright.*"

When Annie got inside the house with the water, her mother and Belle were still shelling peas at the kitchen table. Belle's white ankles were so swollen with the heat that they looked like misshapen peeled potatoes, and her belly was so full of child it seemed as if a down pillow had been stuck under her apron. Belle and Annie's mother looked as tired as Annie felt, and her mother had dark half-moons under her eyes. Her lips pressed tight together in a thin straight line. The women—Annie and Ruth and their mother, and Belle, and Martha, who was Oliver's new wife—had spent the past days from sunup to late night, sewing and cooking and pickling, to make ready for the men to go. But that hadn't been all to make them tired; mostly it was Father arguing with Annie's brother Salmon.

Jason and Henry Thompson, who was married to Annie's sister Ruth, had given up fighting after the Kansas civil wars.

Annie's brother Frederick had been killed by pro-slavery men at the battle and burning of Osawatomie, and the others had been forced to bury him hurriedly in Kansas soil. Far from home, in a solitary grave, he lay there still. Jason said that Father stood over Frederick's body and trembling with rage he had said, "I will die fighting for this cause. There will be no peace in this land until slavery is done for." But Jason and Henry had had enough fighting. And now Father couldn't accept that Salmon had, too. He just couldn't believe Salmon would refuse to go with him and help free the slaves.

Father began working to change Salmon's mind, and wheedled and raged at him, but Salmon was big now, and stronger than Father, so he couldn't be strapped anymore. And he was almighty stubborn. Annie thought Father would give up sooner than he did, because in a battle of stubbornness Salmon was more than a match even for *him*. Their arguing went on night after night until finally, two nights ago, Father told Salmon that he was a great disappointment as a son. The arguing had stopped. And now Father hardly spoke to Salmon at all.

They would leave tomorrow. After traveling through western New York, Father would go on to Ohio, where there was a cache of weapons that needed to be moved in secret to Virginia; then he would go to Chambersburg to John Henry, who was now Father's secretary of war. On the way to Chambersburg, Father would meet with supporters, including a Negro man named Frederick Douglass, who owned an abolitionist newspaper in Rochester; he hadn't yet agreed to take part in the Harper's Ferry plan. But Father was certain he could convince Mr. Douglass to join them. Annie wasn't so sure. She'd once met Frederick Douglass, and thought he was a man who couldn't be talked into much.

Annie's oldest stepbrother, John Jr., was traveling through Ohio and western New York to raise money. He said he'd meet up with the others at Chambersburg, but Annie had her doubts about him, too. John Jr. acted very strange the few times he'd come back east after Kansas. He looked sad, and didn't remember things very well, and sometimes he seemed to be mumbling to himself. Bad things had happened to John Jr. in Kansas. He was captured and chained and beaten with rifle butts until, he said himself, he was a raving lunatic. Then he was made to march, still in chains, for hundreds of miles on foot. He was driven like a beast, he said. And after that he remained in jail for months.

Annie believed that Frederick hadn't been the only Brown to die in Kansas. It was just that John Jr. . . . well, he maybe didn't know it yet.

But the most troubling thing in the past days—leastwise to Annie it was—had been Father saying that, after he'd found a place to stay, her mother should come to Maryland and keep house for all the men. It terrified Annie, his saying that. She was afraid it might kill her mother, her being sick and with no strength anymore. Her mother didn't say no to Father. She didn't say anything. And Annie decided that they would just see about who was going to Maryland. After Father had gone.

THE NEXT MORNING, mist lay over the mountains and spread like thin gray smoke into the valley below the log house. While Annie and her sisters packed food for the men to take, Father stomped in and out of the house with last-minute orders. Earlier Salmon had gone to the barn, and he hadn't come back. Annie wondered if he was afraid Father could somehow talk him into leaving North Elba.

When they'd finished loading the last wagon and everything seemed to be ready, they all stood outside in the mist, all but Salmon. Annie thought of going to the barn to tell him it was time, but then, he could probably see that from the loft window. It worried her that Salmon wasn't there, because what if he never saw Father again? There were some things that once they were done, they couldn't be undone. Like staying in the barn until it was too late.

Father stood alone by the wagons. He gazed off at the mountains with his arms folded over his chest, his arm muscles looking like bumps of twisted rope under his thin shirtsleeves. He'd gained a little weight since coming home, and he'd cut his beard short to help disguise himself. But really, he still looked like the same man. His birthday had been last month, and now he was fifty-nine. Watching him standing there by himself, Annie felt her chest tighten.

For some reason, she brought to mind the night her little sister had been dying of consumption. Father had walked up and down with baby Ellen in his arms, the whole time talking to her in a quiet voice about God and afflictions. When he saw that baby Ellen was dead, he closed her eyes, and crossed her hands over her small hollow chest, and calmly laid her in her cradle. When they buried baby Ellen, he cried and cried as if he would never stop.

And then Annie remembered the cold winter morning when twin lambs had been born. They'd had a hard time coming, and the ewe was too tired to raise her head to lick them, so Father took off his shirt and used it to rub them dry. Then he very gently picked up the shivering lambs and held them close to his chest for warmth. He stroked them, all the while talking softly to them like they were little scared children before he put them back down with their mother.

Annie's sight blurred, and her chest felt as though it had shrunk to a small hard knot. She swiped at her eyes and looked toward the barn. Salmon wasn't coming. Then Father and Oliver and Watson each climbed up into a wagon and slapped their reins over the backs of the mules. The wagons groaned and their wheels clattered as they started slowly down the hill to North Elba.

Annie watched them pass through the wispy veils of smoke-gray until they disappeared into the mist as if they were ghosts. She didn't go back to the house right away, but stood listening for some time to the echo of rumbling wagons.

And she thought Salmon would one day be very sorry that he hadn't said good-bye.

TWELVE

〜

There are some questions which should never be drawn into the political vortex. Religion is one of these; temperance another; we believe slavery another. We see no result from twenty years' discussion of slavery except domestic disturbance, ill-temper, sectional jealousy, and general alienation.
—THE MARCH 1859 ISSUE OF *HARPER'S NEW MONTHLY MAGAZINE*

GLYNIS HAD STEPPED outside the Stanton house just moments before to escape the argumentative voices of anti-slavery and abolitionist supporters alike. But the residence at 32 Washington Street had apparently reached overflow capacity, as these same people now began spilling down the front porch steps and into the yard. A move made all the more inviting by a soft breeze off the river below. The summer Sunday afternoon was very warm.

The land on which the house stood had been given to Elizabeth Stanton by her father Judge Cady and overlooked the village and the Seneca River. While Glynis gazed at the placid scene below, she absently rolled an empty iced-tea glass between her palms and narrowed her eyes against the glitter of sun skimming across the water. The village of Seneca Falls had been founded along what were once white-frothed rapids, a series of waterfalls that extended a mile in length with a combined drop of forty feet. The resulting power ran flour and saw mills, textile factories, and tin and sheet-iron plants.

Glynis turned as Emma and Elizabeth Stanton walked toward her across the summer-browned grass. When, in March of that year, Elizabeth had given birth to her seventh child, she was forty-three years old. Elizabeth had not been the same since, Glynis thought as her friend moved rather gingerly toward her. Despite a difficult pregnancy, Elizabeth had found the wherewithal to assist in petitioning the New York legislature on behalf of a Married Women's Earnings Act—one that would allow women to keep the wages they had earned rather than, as the prevailing law would have it, turn the money over to their husbands. Added to this was an even more controversial section which would at last grant women joint guardianship of their own children, putting them on an equal basis in this regard with their husbands. But although the bill had been introduced and passed in the Assembly, it failed to reach a vote in the Senate. And while the phrase "Perhaps next year" had become a common and recurrent one in the struggle for women's rights, Glynis wondered if the legislative failure hadn't added to Elizabeth Stanton's recent melancholy turn of mind.

Glynis reached to clasp the woman's outstretched hands. Elizabeth seemed almost fragile, drawn and pale with exhaustion. Not at all like the driving force who had led the women's rights movement until now. But fortunately, Susan Anthony was willing to take on that position, at least for the time being.

"My dear Glynis, what a delightful young woman your niece is," Elizabeth said with a wan smile.

Emma blushed and turned toward the river, as Elizabeth gestured toward the house. "It's certainly become contentious in there," she said. "I came outside to avoid saying something terribly rude, hardly the proper function of a hostess. But I do wish Cousin Gerrit and Mr. Brown would arrive. I wonder what's keeping them?"

Emma gave her aunt a troubled look. "Aunt Glynis, some of the men were arguing that the women's anti-slavery petitions are hurting the abolition cause. How can that be?"

Glynis was surprised at the question only because she'd had to work so hard at getting Emma here to Stanton's in the first place. Her niece's reaction earlier had been, "I'm not interested in slavery or politics—they're boring. After all, what do they have to do with me?"

Thus Glynis now said bluntly, "Because women want rights most men don't think they should have, Emma. And so the opponents of abolition are using female petition activity to demean not only women but the entire movement to abolish slavery."

Elizabeth's forehead creased in a frown as she nodded agree-

ment. "There is such hostility, inside and outside the movement," she said, "that women are withdrawing from petition
campaigns. And I suppose this peaceful means will be abandoned."

"I certainly hope not," Glynis replied. "If that happens,
women will be left with only prayers to keep men from deciding to resolve the slavery issue with war."

Elizabeth's eyebrows rose. "Then perhaps you won't like
what Mr. Brown has to say, Glynis."

"From what I've read of John Brown, I imagine you could
be right. But I want to hear him, then decide for myself if he's
as much of a rabble-rouser as the newspapers have made him
out."

Elizabeth Stanton gave Glynis and Emma both a brief smile
before she moved on. Glynis ran her eyes over those standing
on the grass, trying to locate Zeph Waters, whom she'd seen
arrive some minutes before, accompanied by an unfamiliar
young Negro man. She wanted to ask Zeph what more had
been learned, if anything, about Sally Lunt's death, as Cullen
wouldn't be there at Stanton's. A lawman would not participate
in an assembly that criticized the law of the land—and slavery
was legal. In fact, a northern lawman could himself be arrested
and fined for not enforcing the Fugitive Slave Law, which directed that runaways be returned to their southern owners.

Although Cullen spoke of it seldom, and had on more than
one occasion ignored the law and the runaway, he tended toward the anti-slavery persuasion, which said: Leave slavery
alone in the South, where it was already established—lest the
southern states secede from the Union as they'd threatened to
do—but don't allow it to spread into the new western territories. Abolitionists, on the other hand, were those committed to
abolishing slavery altogether. Then there were those considered
the moderates, such as lawyer Abraham Lincoln in Springfield,
who, while believing slavery to be morally untenable in a country that trumpeted equality for all men, felt that in due time the
practice of slavery could be eliminated by continued compromise with the South. Or by assistance to the new African country of Liberia where Negroes could resettle.

None of those categories, of course, included the great majority of northerners, who claimed no position on slavery; who, if they thought about the issue at all, simply wished it would go away. If it didn't directly affect their own lives, then, like Emma, they weren't interested. This attitude seemed to Glynis to be one of extreme shortsightedness—if the southern states did secede from the Union over slavery, then all northerners would be affected, whether they liked it or not. And even now, talk of war had begun to surface with some frequency. Glynis had heard enough horror stories from her Grandmother Tryon about the 1812 War with Britain to believe that path should be avoided at nearly any cost.

Still looking for Zeph, Glynis hadn't succeeded in finding him when a carriage wheeled into the yard and interrupted her search. Two men clambered down and walked toward the Stanton house.

"Who is that?" Emma asked.

"One of them, the man with the frock coat and top hat, is Elizabeth Stanton's cousin, Gerrit Smith. The other, I presume, is John Brown."

"He looks like . . ." Emma's voice trailed off.

"Looks like what?" Glynis asked, curious as to Emma's impression of Brown.

"I don't know exactly," Emma answered feebly. "He . . . well, I wouldn't want to cross him, that's all."

Glynis agreed. It wasn't just the stern countenance, but the evangelical cast in the man's gray eyes that gave her pause.

"Don't tell me he's finally here!" said a voice behind her. "It's been like waiting for an audience with God."

Glynis turned at the familiar throaty voice and scent of rose perfume. Vanessa Usher had come up behind them, and the woman now stood with her violet gaze fixed on Emma. Glynis introduced her niece, adding, "I didn't know you were interested in the slavery issue, Vanessa."

"Oh, I'm not," she said with an airy wave, "but one just doesn't turn down an invitation—any invitation—certainly not after being isolated in mourning as I've been for months on end. However"—she turned back to Emma—"I *am* interested in you, Miss Tryon. I'm told by my friend Fleur Coddington that you are an exceptional seamstress, and if that frock you're wearing is a sample of your work, she was correct. Is it?''

Emma, her cheeks pink, nodded. "I made it, yes."

Vanessa then scanned Glynis's soft muslin day dress—of a blue-green shade Emma called *verdigris*, like the patina on exposed copper—her eyes moving from the graceful bishop's sleeves to the lace-edged flounce at the skirt hem. "And you made your aunt's, too?" When Emma again nodded, Vanessa said, "Yes, I guessed as much. It's a good color on you, Glynis, and I don't believe I've ever seen you look so fashionable before, dear."

Emma's eyebrows shot up, but Glynis merely smiled. What other rational response was there after years of acquaintance with Vanessa Usher?

With a downward sweep of arm, Vanessa indicated her own dark gown, saying, "I've worn this beastly black long enough! It won't bring my poor sister Aurora back from the dead, and the lack of color and style is thoroughly depressing me. I need a new wardrobe—and I've just decided to tell Fleur that you must make it for me," she announced, bestowing this laurel wreath on a stunned-looking Emma. "When can you start?"

Glynis took the opportunity to move away. She had sympathy for Emma—though not quite enough to linger—and directed a glance of commiseration over her shoulder. However, Emma missed it entirely. Her recovery had been rapid, evidenced by hands that sketched in the air what must be an hourglass gown, while the lovely Vanessa watched with rapt attention.

Poor Emma. She would learn soon enough that Vanessa brought out the worst in even the most saintly. It remained a source of mystery as to how anyone—especially someone who resembled a Renaissance angel, as did Vanessa—could create such fiendish reactions in others. The fair Miss Usher seemed a slap in the face to the orderliness of the universe. To say nothing of refuting the explosive, just-published theories of Mr. Charles Darwin.

And it was, Glynis thought with relief, a very good thing that Neva Cardoza-Levy wasn't there. She supposed, too, that she should be grateful Aurora's contested will hadn't been brought up by Vanessa. Even if only because she'd surely forgotten about her sister's bequest to the library.

Glynis walked to the shady side of several huge willows, their slender, leafy branches flowing to the ground like green waterfalls. She still hadn't located Zeph when Henry Stanton emerged from the house. He stood at the edge of the porch to introduce the Negro editor of Rochester's *North Star* newspaper, Frederick Douglass.

Mr. Douglass was a friend of both Elizabeth Stanton and Susan Anthony. And he was much in demand at anti-slavery and abolition rallies. Glynis had met him on several occasions, including the time she'd taken a runaway slave—which Douglass himself had once been—to shelter at his home in Rochester. Just how involved Douglass had become with the abolitionist John Brown she didn't know.

But some minutes later, as Douglass completed his introduction of Brown, Glynis decided he had chosen his words with even greater care than usual. While he praised John Brown's hatred of slavery, Douglass seemed to take a position at some figurative distance from the man himself.

As John Brown began to deliver his speech, his voice reedy and somewhat irritating, Glynis finally located Zeph standing just below the porch and the speaker. The young deputy gazed up at Brown with an uncharacteristic expression, his ordinarily sober face displaying what Glynis would describe as adulation. Or, as the eighteenth-century British had called it, hero worship. An unpleasant tingle slid down her spine.

Brown's delivery held the intensity of the zealot. What disturbed Glynis most was Brown's "any means to an end" posture about ending slavery. On the other hand, she didn't agree with Mr. Lincoln's premise that slavery could be phased out gradually. She did realize, though, that Abraham Lincoln was, among other things, a superb politician who might be trying to calm Northerners; those who feared that a sudden end to slavery would mean an unmanageable influx of freed Negroes into the North.

John Brown's voice had been growing louder, and the speech promised to be long. Glynis was congratulating herself for being some yards from the porch, when she saw a sudden move-

ment at the far side of the willows. The trees, though, were too
thick to identify what it might be. However, when Brown's
voice soared, then paused for dramatic effect, into the silence
Glynis heard a distinctly male voice say, "... and Brown's got
the guns, what else does he need?"

"Keep it quiet!" ordered another male voice.

Glynis whirled and peered toward the voices, which seemed
to come from the other side of the willows. Guns? He'd said
guns? She inched closer to the source, moving cautiously into
a thicket of willow branches. She could hear a murmur of talking, but no specific words. Then came, "... the cave ... maybe
suspicious ..."

Scattered applause for Brown covered whatever came next,
and Glynis, with willow branches brushing her face, strained
to hear. But now the voices had quieted. It had been at least
two men talking, but how could she see who they were without
exposing herself? Then again came the demand, "Be quiet!"
Hardly a sinister turn of phrase.

She craned her neck through the branches. Hoping what
she'd overheard was random gossip, Glynis started to turn back
to the speaker, but then, from the corner of her eye she caught
a flash of something. Warily, she moved a few feet farther
around the tree. Standing there was Neva's assistant, Margaret
Taylor. The woman wore a green frock that came close to cam-
ouflaging her, although not completely, because the flash
Glynis had seen came from the thick glass of the woman's
spectacles glinting in the sun.

Suddenly, Margaret backed away from the willows. Her head
turned, and for a moment her gaze seemed to be straight at
Glynis, although the spectacles made it all but impossible to
see her eyes. Glynis didn't move. What interest could Margaret
Taylor have in John Brown—or in the odd conversation she'd
obviously tried to overhear?

Then the woman abruptly pivoted on her heel and walked
past the others in the Stanton yard, and on toward Washington
Street. Shortly after, she disappeared under the dark beeches
bordering the road. Glynis's impulse was to go after the
woman. But she could hardly ask Margaret if she'd overheard
something of more importance than she herself had managed.

Not without giving away her own eavesdropping. She stood trying to think what to do when her attention was drawn back to John Brown, who was now using biblical references from the Old Testament prophets of doom.

"We must smite the demon of slavery," Brown shouted, his arm outstretched due South, "lest the Lord of the prophet Isaiah 'come with fire, and with His chariots like a whirlwind, to render His anger with fury, and His rebuke with flames of fire.' "

Brown paused to gaze heavenward with the haunted eyes, then faced his listeners again and intoned, " 'Thus saith the Lord; Behold, waters rise up out of the north, and shall be an overflowing flood, and shall overflow the land and all that is therein; the city and them that dwell therein. Then the men shall cry, and all the inhabitants of the land shall howl.' "

Book of Jeremiah, Glynis identified with uneasiness and no small sense of awe at the power with which Brown delivered the doomsday quotations. He had certainly brought to this warm summer afternoon the chill of bitter wind. Those closest to him in the Stanton yard reacted accordingly. Glynis saw some not-so-veiled looks being exchanged, heard a few anxious titters of laughter, and sporadic rumbles of indignation.

But Mr. Brown had not alienated quite all of his audience. Glynis now looked with concern at Zeph. His hands were clenched into fists at his side, and at his shoulder the other young Negro stared at John Brown with the selfsame expression of adulation.

When she felt herself shiver, Glynis knew it was not from a chill wind but from fear.

THE MONEY BASKETS passed for donations might have been fuller, their worth greater, but John Brown gave no sign that he was dissatisfied. He stayed only a few minutes after completing his speech. But Glynis saw a short and intense-looking conversation between Brown and Zeph and the other young man. Then John Brown strode toward the waiting carriage. After climbing in, he stood with his arm lifted straight into the air as if about to offer a benediction. But it was not a blessing he delivered: "For these are the days of vengeance, and there shall be great distress upon this land."

He sat down with shoulders rounded, jaw set, eyes looking straight ahead as if he wore blinders. The carriage driven by Gerrit Smith rattled out of the Stanton yard.

Glynis listened to the mixed comments of those around her while she studied Zeph, who stood staring after the departed carriage. He was young and impressionable, and while his history had made him skeptical in many respects, he still carried within him the hopes of the idealist. And although not enslaved himself, Glynis remembered all too well Zeph's terrible encounter with the consequences of slavery. The scars were surely still there.

She started toward him, and was halfway across the yard when Vanessa Usher came hurrying up to her. "Glynis, I'm just mystified about your niece—why has she been hidden away from me all this time?"

"She's been growing up in Illinois, Vanessa. It was nothing personal."

"No, no, I meant since your niece has been here in Seneca Falls. There's been all this time wasted—why, she could have made an entire wardrobe for me."

"Yes, well, thank heavens you've found her at last," Glynis said, trying to edge away.

"And just in the very nick of time. I tell you," Vanessa said, her face tragic, "I've almost succumbed to madness, I'm so bored with mourning. Well, it's been six months and that's enough! Wasn't that man simply depressing?" Glynis still found herself startled by Vanessa's sudden leaps. But she had to agree with the woman's assessment of Brown.

"Yes," Vanessa repeated, "depressing! I can't understand why Elizabeth Stanton would invite someone so disagreeable on such a lovely afternoon. Do you know, Glynis, I've heard tell that Mr. Brown has failed at every single business venture he's ever tried? And yet here he is, running around the country, stirring up trouble over slavery, while his scores of children are starving to death. Charity begins at home, I always say."

But wasn't that exactly what her sister Aurora's bequest to the Women's Refuge was about? thought Glynis, staring at Vanessa. Besides, most zealots tended to ignore the mundane aspects of life, such as taking care of their own. But Brown's effect on Zeph was worrisome.

Glynis left Vanessa and again started toward the young man. She found him in conversation with his companion, a man of medium height with a short neat beard, and large unhappy eyes. The man's skin color resembled that of Zeph—the dark amber of buckwheat honey.

"What did you think?" Zeph asked her.

"I thought Mr. Brown was . . . impressive. Very impressive."

Zeph nodded and turned to introduce the man beside him. "This is Osborn Anderson. He's my cousin—my second cousin from Canada."

"Really?" Glynis said, shaking Osborn Anderson's hand. "I do recall hearing that you had relatives in Canada, Zeph."

Anderson smiled, briefly relieving the sadness of his eyes, and said, "But we didn't know each other. Not until we met up in Chatham last year."

"How did that come about?" Glynis asked him.

Zeph answered for his cousin with a trace of defensiveness. "It was a convention called by John Brown. A *secret* convention," he added, his intent to curb any further questions obvious.

But Osborn Anderson added, "Brown wanted to meet the escaped slaves who'd been fugitives—which is about one-third the town of Chatham. But he spoke mostly about his experiences in Kansas."

Glynis nodded. "Yes, I understand Mr. Brown and his sons were arrested there, in connection with some—"

"They were let go!" Zeph jumped in. "There was no evidence to link them to those killings."

Glynis knew about *those killings* from newspaper accounts. They involved three pro-slavery men at Pottawatomie, who, in the middle of the night, had apparently been pulled from their beds, taken outside their cabins and, in full view of their wives and children, shot to death or hacked to death with broadswords. Broadswords! And Zeph was right—although Brown and his sons had been identified and arrested, they were subsequently released. But did Zeph know their release was said to have occurred only because of some inexplicable legal blunder? That a warrant had since been issued in Kansas for their arrest?

As if Zeph read her mind, he said, "You can't believe everything you see in the newspapers, Miss Tryon. You know that. Besides, you can't understand this."

"This? You mean the issue of slavery?"

"Yes."

"Because I've never been a slave, myself? But neither have the other whites who've helped runaways to reach Canada, often at great personal risk. I don't think people have to actually experience a circumstance themselves to know that it's wrong. That's why we have laws—"

She knew immediately she had bungled when Zeph scoffed loudly. "Laws! Slavery is legal, Miss Tryon!"

"Yes, and it's wrong," she answered softly. "And yes, perhaps I can't understand." Nonetheless, she no longer agreed with Elizabeth Stanton's oft-quoted statement that a married woman's position in America was like that of the slave in the South. Glynis had since been to Virginia, and now well knew that the two were not alike. And it didn't surprise her that the statement gave offense to those like Zeph.

"Miss Tryon, I know you mean well," Zeph offered, "but no, you just can't understand. And I guess I better tell you that I'll be leaving Seneca Falls, soon now—because I'm going with John Brown."

"Going where?" Glynis asked, her fear for him overcoming the caution she knew was needed with Zeph on this subject.

He shrugged. "South. To help free the slaves. Osborn here is going, too."

Osborn Anderson nodded.

Glynis tried to think what she could say that might make Zeph pause and reconsider.

"It's settled," Zeph declared, although she hadn't said a word. "Oh, and I've got a message for you from Constable Stuart. He said he needs to talk to you, sometime today if possible."

"About Sally Lunt's murder?" Glynis asked, having decided

that she wasn't going to get far discussing John Brown with Zeph right then.

"Yeah, Constable Stuart says he thinks she might have been moved after she was killed."

Glynis frowned. "Well, please tell him I'll be by a little later, then."

Zeph and his cousin sauntered off toward the street, and Glynis realized that while they'd been talking, she had dimly registered the sound of a violin. Looking around, she saw Emma at the foot of the porch steps. Beside her stood Grandy Fox with his fiddle tucked under his chin, playing Stephen Foster's "My Old Kentucky Home." It's sweet poignant strains were rather at odds, Glynis thought, with the prevailing emotions of the day. Or perhaps that was the point. As she watched the peddler, something flitted through her mind. She recalled having the same sensation at the benefit dance.

Looking now at the people who had come ostensibly to hear John Brown, she was somewhat surprised to see Colonel de Warde. The man was certainly making every effort to become familiar with those in Seneca Falls. With de Warde was Cyril Doggett, his face no less lugubrious than when Glynis had first met him. Talking to Henry Stanton was dentist Alan Fitzhugh.

Glynis immediately recalled what Emma had told her; that she'd overheard a weeping Sally Lunt mention Fitzhugh's name. It probably meant only what it appeared to mean: a feared visit to the dentist. Although Emma seemed to doubt this. It was true that Alan Fitzhugh did appear to like the company of young women—which was hardly a crime.

But when she saw Cullen she would pass on Emma's comment, as well as one of her own.

She had received the day before a letter from her uncle in San Francisco, replying to her request for whatever he might know about Valerian Voss. And Uncle Ned did, in fact, have some rather disturbing information. It seemed that Voss, like Glynis's uncle, was employed by the San Francisco Mint—until some eleven months before. When Voss resigned his position at the mint, there were rumors that he'd been involved in some shady activity. That he was about to be fired when he'd resigned. Glynis's uncle was careful to say this was *only* rumor, but that he would try to learn if there were more solid details.

"Miss Tryon?"

Glynis turned to find Adam MacAlistair beside her. "Adam, I didn't realize you'd come today."

"Seems as if almost everybody's come," he said, tilting his head toward the porch, and scowling as he did so.

Glynis swallowed a smile and avoided looking in the direction of Emma and Grandy Fox. "Yes, I suppose everyone wanted to hear John Brown."

"What do you think of him?"

"I think he has all the qualities of a fanatic, Adam. What do you think?"

"Much the same, but since I'm not as courteous as you, I'd say he's a madman. And dangerous."

"Yes, I think he's potentially dangerous. Fanatics often are," Glynis added, thinking with uneasiness of Zeph and his cousin—and overhearing the word "guns" in connection with Brown.

"Look at the history of the man," Adam said. "In Kansas, for instance. But even so, there are abolitionists who seem to admire him greatly. There's a rumor going around that he has some very powerful men backing him."

Glynis looked at Adam with skepticism. "Backing him financially?"

When Adam nodded, she asked with concern, "To what purpose? What is Brown planning to do—other than public speaking, I mean?"

"There's been talk, and maybe it's just talk, that Brown wants to form a new state for slaves down in the Appalachian Mountains. That he's got a constitution he wrote up himself, and a plan to set the slaves free."

"How—by insurrection?"

Adam shrugged. "How else? The slaveholders aren't going to just roll over and let their slaves walk away. But as I said, maybe it's only talk. Nobody seems to take Brown very seriously. After all, the man hasn't been able to do much of anything right, so I hear. He's got a string of lawsuits pending against him by former business partners—whom he's either cheated out of their money or lost it due to simple ineptness. I doubt Brown's going to get very far no matter what harebrained scheme he comes up with.''

''Perhaps you're right,'' Glynis said, but she knew her voice lacked conviction. She had seen the faces of Zeph and Osborn Anderson. And she wondered how many more young men there were, black and white, who could be persuaded to follow John Brown.

A violin's strings rasped, followed by peals of feminine laughter. Glynis looked up to see that someone, possibly Emma, had clapped a ragged straw hat on Grandy Fox's head. With a start, Glynis gazed at the scarecrow likeness as an elusive memory finally emerged. She *had* seen Grandy Fox previously—and before she'd ever set foot back in Seneca Falls. She was very nearly certain: it was he who had been the fiddler at the Rochester public market.

THIRTEEN

❧

A wonderful fact to reflect upon, that every human creature is constituted to be that profound secret and mystery to every other.

—CHARLES DICKENS, *A TALE OF TWO CITIES* 1859

•

THE SUN STILL sat high above the horizon when Glynis, after knocking several times without result, pulled open the door of the constable's office. She found Liam Cleary seated behind Cullen's desk. His elbows were propped on its surface and his head rested in his hands.

"Liam?"

His head came up with a jerk, then he quickly got to his feet. The tautness of his shoulders and face seemed to indicate considerable distress.

"Liam, are you all right?"

He opened his mouth as if to reply and began to shake his head, then nodded and simply collapsed back into the chair. "No, I don't guess so," was what finally emerged.

Where was Cullen, and why had this lad been left by himself when he was in such a miserable state? "Are you ill?" she asked him.

"Not yet, anyway." Liam sighed, and Glynis then noticed that his pale lashes were moist.

She lowered herself to the seat of the only other chair. "Would it help to tell me about it, Liam? Perhaps I could suggest something useful." Although she doubted this, it seemed the least she could do was offer to listen.

He looked at her with such abject misery that Glynis repeated her offer. But he shook his head at her, saying, "No, I probably shouldn't talk about it."

"About what? Does it have to do with your job?" she asked,

recalling Cullen's reservation about Liam's fitness for police work.

"Not exactly. Course, I don't think Constable Stuart's any too happy with me. I throw up very easily," he explained with such seriousness that Glynis nearly choked, whether from sympathy or something less admirable.

Observing Liam's dismayed expression, she said with haste, "Oh, I'm sure that's just temporary. You'll overcome it, I'm certain, when you grow more accustomed to . . ." To what? Dead bodies? The violence that people committed against one another? How could anyone get accustomed to that?

"Liam, I don't know what to say—especially since I don't know what's wrong. But can you tell me where the constable is?"

"Huh? Oh, yeah, he's at the hardware store with Mr. Levy. Said if you came in, you should meet him there."

Glynis got to her feet, speculating as to just how long Liam would have let her sit there if she hadn't asked. "Thank you," she said. She hesitated, waiting for him to say something more. He didn't. "Well, I'll just go along now."

"Uh, Miss Tryon?" Liam ventured with obvious reluctance as she pushed open the door. "I wonder if you could—no, I guess not."

Glynis, lingering in the doorway, said, "Could I what, Liam? Is this to do with some family problem?" She thought that might be a fair guess, since there were so many Clearys it would be a miracle if all were trouble-free at the same time.

"I reckon you could call it a family problem," Liam agreed, although he sounded uncertain.

Glynis smothered a sigh, and stepped back into the office; Cullen apparently hadn't indicated there was any hurry. "Yes, Liam, what is this problem?" she asked him, not hopeful of receiving a definitive reply.

But he surprised her. "It's my sister—my sister, Fiona. I think she's getting beat up."

Beat up? Did he know what he was saying? Glynis frantically searched her mind for Fiona, something to differentiate the girl from the other red-headed females of the family. "Isn't she a little older than you, Liam? Very pretty, I remember."

Though that didn't help distinguish her, as all the Cleary women were pretty. But then Fiona surfaced. "Didn't I hear she was married a year or two ago?"

"Yep, that's Fiona. I think the ape she married is the one beating her up. I don't know what to do. Pa's no use—you know him!—and my sister Morwenna isn't sure what to do either."

That sounded ominous, Glynis decided, as Morwenna Cleary Ryan had always known what to do—till she married, she had for years taken care of her widowed, perpetually inebriated father and all her siblings. "Liam, shall *I* have a talk with Morwenna? Perhaps we can figure something out."

"Would you, Miss Tryon? I'd be real grateful. But I don't 'specially want Constable Stuart to know—I think he'd be mad that I got you into it."

"I can't see that it's really any of Constable Stuart's concern. I'll try to see Morwenna soon, sometime this week," Glynis promised as she again opened the door.

Liam nodded, not looking overly optimistic.

WHEN GLYNIS FINALLY arrived outside Levy's Hardware Store, she could see Cullen and Abraham through the windows that faced the road. Forced to skirt a clutter of farm implements and sacks of fertilizer, wooden barrels, and tall milk cans, she reached the front door just as it was swung open by Cullen. His first words were, "I'd decided you hadn't gotten my message. Don't tell me that even John Brown could talk all this time!"

Very well. Despite its near truth, she wouldn't tell him that. Glynis just shook her head and went through the doorway, and immediately tripped over a washboard leaning against a butter churn, which fell, knocking over a hayfork and long-handled waffle iron, which in turn came perilously close to dropping on an open crate of pickle jars. Glynis watched this with dismay, but Abraham Levy, standing behind his long, waist-high counter, looked implausibly unconcerned. As Glynis and Cullen went about putting things to right, Abraham picked up a small leather pouch, upended it, and poured a number of coins into his palm. He separated one from the others, and held it out to Glynis.

When she reached for it, she had to stretch on her toes over stacked crates of the new glass Mason jars that were the latest thing for home canning; beside the crates stood columns of boxed, zinc lids with their innovative ring sealers. Harriet Peartree was already experimenting with these reusable jars. In the past weeks she'd preserved peas and asparagus from her own garden, spring vegetables previously available only when in season or sold at high cost in tin cans. And even at a price these cans, with their metallic-tasting contents, were not always available in Seneca Falls. But it was tomatoes, Harriet predicted—which, once they began to ripen, quickly reached astronomical abundance—that would make the Mason jars forever indispensable.

Glynis took the coin from Abraham, and bent over slightly to rest both forearms on the stack of crates while she inspected it. Cullen looked over her shoulder, asking, "Know what that is?"

"Yes, Cullen, it's a gold dollar."

"Take the time to look at it carefully," Abraham instructed.

They both behaved as if she were simpleminded. Glynis dutifully studied the obverse—the head side of the coin, with its left-facing profile of an Indian princess wearing a feathered headdress, nearly circled by the words "UNITED STATES OF AMERICA." Seeing nothing untoward other than the Indian—who, she thought, looked suspiciously Anglo-Saxon—she turned the coin over to see its reverse. A wreath of leaves and berries enclosed the number "1" above the word "DOLLAR." Beneath "DOLLAR" was "1856," the date the coin was minted.

She turned the coin in her fingers several ways to catch the light from the store windows. There was no mintmark, meaning it had been struck at the Philadelphia Mint.

Glynis twisted the coin back and forth in the light. She then ran her finger around the edge with its ornamentation, or reeding, designed to keep coins from being shaved or clipped for the gold and thus reducing their value.

She was aware that Cullen and Abraham were watching her

with rapt expectation, and that they anticipated she would pronounce the coin genuine. Why would she not?

She straightened and handed the coin back to Abraham. "It's counterfeit," she stated, denying herself for the moment the satisfaction of a smug smile—although both men deserved it.

Abraham gaped at her, and Cullen muttered, "I thought you said you didn't know much about coinage."

Now she smiled, as she hadn't been absolutely certain until they'd reacted. She could have gotten her dates confused.

"C'mon, Glynis," Cullen prompted her, while still looking surprised, "what makes you think so?"

"Oh, it isn't too hard to see," she said, smiling as yet. "It's the wreath that gives it away."

"The wreath," Abraham echoed as if too stunned to come up with anything more original.

"I don't believe it," Cullen said. "You're just guessing."

Glynis allowed herself another smile. "If you say so, Cullen."

"No, no," Abraham protested, "I want to hear this. Just how did you know?"

Glynis took the coin back from him and retreated with caution from the crates of glass jars. "All right—the wreath design on this coin is leaves and berries. But the wreath was redesigned using corn, cotton, tobacco, and wheat, and that style was approved in '54. And the Philadelphia Mint began producing coins with the heavier wreath late in that year. This coin is dated 1856! Made by a counterfeiter who didn't know about the change in design!" She leaned back against the cold iron stove behind her, and waited for them to say something.

At last Cullen found his voice. "O.K., Glynis, that was quite a display, and I'm sure you enjoyed yourself."

She had, indeed. "The really odd thing here," she said, "is that the Indian princess design is also a change from the earlier Liberty head. How could any self-respecting counterfeiter get it only half right?"

"I thought you said you just started getting interested in coins."

"And I've been educating myself. The day we had a . . . well, a disagreement, Cullen, I wired the Treasury Department and asked them to direct me to an appropriate reference on United States currency. A Mr. William DuBois, the keeper of the Mint Collection, sent back a very nice letter suggesting that I contact a numismatist, Dr. Dickeson, who has just finished writing a book on United States coins—*The American Numismatical Manual,* it's entitled. Since then, I've continued to correspond with Mr. DuBois, and I've also read the Hickcox book I bought in Springfield.''

"Read it, and obviously committed it to memory, word for word," Cullen said, now conceding to smile himself. "Very resourceful woman, you are."

"Well, thank you, Constable. Is this the first time you've noticed that?" She'd intended it as banter, just a flip remark, the kind of thing she might have said to him a year or two ago. She'd momentarily forgotten how much things had changed. So it was with surprise that she saw Cullen looking at her with warmth. And he shook his head.

"No, it isn't the first time," he said.

She felt herself coloring under his gaze, and to cover her embarrassment she said, "It's a good thing you didn't give me anything smaller than a gold dollar—or I couldn't have performed. I've concentrated on the larger denominations because I thought that's what counterfeiters would produce the most of—but I've since found that isn't necessarily true."

When she glanced at Abraham, he appeared to be watching her with some amusement. "Where did you get that coin?" she asked him. "It's a fair amount of money."

His amusement vanished. "It was in a donation basket from the Women's Refuge benefit, just mixed in among the others."

"Who would have put it there?"

"Could have been just about anybody who's well-to-do," Cullen said. "Probably someone who'd been passed it and didn't realize it was counterfeit. I can't imagine the counterfeiter himself being so stupid as to use it, at least not intentionally, and not when it would be handled again—when it was counted."

Glynis nodded. "The coin could initially have been passed on in the same manner as the other bogus coins and banknotes that have appeared in Seneca Falls.'' She turned to Abraham. ''What made you suspect it was counterfeit?''

''It seemed a little lightweight for gold. It's hard to tell with a coin that small, but I thought maybe it could be brass—these days everyone who's a shopkeeper is suspicious. So I went to Cullen with it. He came up with the same thing you did—but, after all, he's in the police business, so it wasn't as impressive as your exhibition,'' Abraham said, grinning. ''And it *is* brass, just washed with gold.''

''But wait. I still don't understand how a counterfeiter could make a mistake with the reverse of the coin like that?'' she said to Cullen. ''After all, he got the obverse right, and that design was changed at the same time.''

''Glynis, how many do you think would catch it? Most folks don't look closely at coins. And unless they'd educated themselves as you did . . .'' He shrugged, his voice trailing off.

''But I don't think that's the point,'' she argued. ''It's dangerous—all it takes is for one person to recognize it. I can't believe a forger would knowingly allow that kind of error.''

''Maybe, as you said, he didn't know about the wreath design change,'' Abraham offered. ''Just hadn't heard.''

Glynis shook her head. ''I know I said it, but it doesn't sound feasible in this case. Oh, I've learned that a lot of counterfeit money is sloppily done. So I suppose it's possible, but wouldn't *good* counterfeiters make it their business to be careful?''

''You'd think so, but they don't need to. Most of these guys aren't artists, you know. And this one simply missed it, somehow,'' Cullen answered.

''I suppose,'' Glynis agreed halfheartedly. Then she brightened. ''Although it certainly might be possible if he was, for instance, serving time in prison. Or isolated for some other reason.''

''He'd had to have been in Australia, or else living in a cave to be isolated these days,'' Abraham said dryly. ''At least around here. Town gets more crowded every week.''

Glynis, musing on this, suddenly said, ''Wait! You know what might have happened? If, for some reason, he *had* been out of circulation—'' she smiled at their groans and went on ''—now, listen for a minute. Say the counterfeiter is sequestered—in prison or by illness or for whatever reason—and, when he begins making bogus money again, he happens to have for a model a gold dollar minted before the design change in '54. Why would he assume anything had changed? He wouldn't. But then, after making the reverse sides of the coins, he discovers his error.''

"But he goes ahead anyway," Cullen said, nodding, "because to make another mold, then print all the coins over, would take too much time and effort. So he makes the obverse correctly, and hopes no one will notice the wreath mistake on the reverse—at least not until it's too late.''

"Exactly!"

"And you know, Glynis, that's not a bad idea of yours, either—about serving time. I think I'll find out which convicted counterfeiters have been released from jail lately. Or," he grimaced, "those that have escaped. Not particularly uncommon.''

"Really?" Glynis found this somewhat unnerving. "You mean the prisons aren't . . . aren't . . . ?''

"Secure," Cullen said, "that's the word. Jails often aren't, at least in small towns. Even Auburn Prison has had its share of escapes. And, as I told you before, the public generally doesn't get all that excited about counterfeiting *or* counterfeiters.''

Glynis went around the end of the counter and picked up the coin pouch. "Anything else in here that looks suspicious?" She emptied the dozen or so coins into her palm. "This isn't *all* that was donated?''

"No," Abraham smiled, "I deposited the rest in the bank earlier. But I just found this particular pouch this morning. Funny thing is, it must have slipped down between some of the stuff on the counter here.'' He motioned to "the stuff" which included a coffee bean roaster, potato mashers, boot jacks, tobacco cutters, a rug beater, and rolls of brown wrapping paper. And those were just the things directly in front of Glynis.

"You mean, otherwise, you might have missed this coin," she said, "if it had been mixed in with the entire lot?''

He nodded. "Easily. It was just luck I spotted it.''

"In that case, how do we know there weren't more of them?''

"We don't, but I'll go back to the bank about it," Abraham said.

Glynis looked through the coins she had, picking out a small shiny one of copper, dated 1859—rather, copper-nickel, she corrected herself. Would it be unseemly to show off a bit more? "Cullen, isn't this the new Indian head cent? Just issued this year?"

Cullen gave her a look of mock annoyance. "Think you're pretty smart, don't you? Yes, you're right."

"Aside from the Indian princess not resembling any Indian I've seen, don't you think using it is rather odd—even hypocritical?" she asked. "After all, look at what's happening in the western territories. There's constant war with the Indians."

Both men gave her a look clearly bespeaking their bafflement with the policies of government.

Then Cullen, who had turned to the window, abruptly turned back to Glynis. "I'd like you to come to the lockup with me. Take a look at those clothes the porter turned in. It'll be dark soon, so we should leave now."

A FEW MINUTES later, when they emerged from the store into the summer evening, the sun sat round and glowing just above the horizon. Against it were silhouetted old men and boys who sat fishing from the canal bank, while their motionless poles pointed to the sky like thin fingers. The earlier breeze had stilled and the warm air held the scent of roses. Altogether a perfect summer evening, Glynis thought with a twinge of nostalgia; she and Cullen had spent many a summer evening walking together as they did now. But that was before. Before Jacques and before Fleur. She shouldn't think about it.

"Cullen, I received an interesting letter from my uncle in San Francisco." She told him about the rumors concerning Valerian Voss.

"Well, now, imagine that," Cullen said. "That *is* interesting. Especially since I've found out from several former bank employees that Voss and Tom Bingham began having some violent arguments about a month before the bank failed. Wonder if Bingham found out Voss was up to some—how did your uncle put it?—shady business!"

"But he said it was just rumor, Cullen."

"Good enough for me to do some thorough checking on Voss. Find out what he was doing in Utica, for instance."

Glynis nodded. A bank vice-president would certainly have the opportunity to change bad money for good; to say nothing of secretly holding onto plates supposed to be turned into the state banking commission and destroyed—and she knew Cullen was thinking the same thing.

"By the way," she asked as they neared the firehouse, "how is Liam Cleary working out?"

Cullen sighed long and loud. "Answer enough?"

"Is it that he's too sensitive?"

"Oh, he's sensitive, all right. I can't see him in this job much longer if he continues to vomit every time there's a tough situation. And then, to further distract him, there's his sister's troubles."

Glynis was immediately wary. She thought Liam had said Cullen didn't know about Fiona. "What's that?" she asked.

"The poor kid doesn't know I'm aware of it," Cullen explained, "but his sister's gone and married a bad one. *Had* to get married, is my understanding. Husband uses her for a punching bag. Matter of fact, right now she's at Neva's refuge. Again."

"Oh, no—does her married name happen to be Roarke? If it is, I saw her there some time ago."

"Well, she's there again. Yes, she's Kerry Roarke's wife. This time Roarke gave her a black eye, split lip, and likely a broken rib. Reason I got involved was a neighbor's kid came flying into the office, saying the man next door was killing his wife." Cullen shook his head.

As they rounded the firehouse and walked toward the office in the back, Glynis decided she'd talk to Morwenna the next morning.

When Cullen pulled open the door, Liam Cleary didn't look up. He didn't move. He was slumped over the desk, his head on his arms, snoring softly.

"That's what I like," Cullen said, "an alert, ever vigilant deputy. Keeping the jail *secure!*" He went over and shook Liam's shoulder, not gently.

"Cullen," Glynis protested, "he's asleep."

"He's on duty! Or supposed to be. Liam, wake up!"

Liam's head bobbed, and he looked around groggily. "Oh, it's you, Constable Stuart. Well, I'm sure glad of that."

"You should be! What if I'd been a prisoner, just escaped from the holding cell back there?"

"We haven't got a prisoner back there," Liam said, blinking. "Have we?"

Cullen expelled his breath, and gave Liam a long look. "Go on home," he said at last. "If you need sleep that badly, you'd better get it. You're no use to me like this."

Poor Liam, Glynis thought, watching the boy shuffle out of the office with his head down. When the door closed behind him, she said, "Don't you think that was a little harsh? Not, I guess, that it's any of my concern."

"You're right, it isn't. And I'm not sure what exactly's wrong with Liam. Maybe he's dim-witted, although I doubt it. Or maybe I'm just spoiled by Zeph, who's sharp as a tack. What a contrast!"

Glynis wondered if he knew about Zeph's intentions. She wasn't going to ask.

Cullen disappeared into a back room of the lockup, and she settled into the chair opposite his desk. She was still debating whether or not to tell him about seeing Grandy Fox in Rochester the day she'd returned to Seneca Falls or, more pertinent, the day the Utica banker, Barrymore, had been killed. Certainly, the most likely explanation was simply coincidence. After all, Grandy was a peddler, presumably traveling all over western New York. Why shouldn't he be in Rochester? In addition, he looked nothing like the men—*either* of the men—who'd attacked Barrymore at the public market and on the train.

Cullen returned with two large laundry bags, one of which he deposited on his chair. He loosed the drawstring top of the other and turned it upside down to empty its contents. Denim trousers and a jacket fell out onto the desk. There was no battered black hat such as Barrymore's assailant on the train had worn, nor the cap of the man at the market. There were, however, several large rust-colored stains on the jacket. Glynis drew back from the desk as some small coarse black hairs drifted to the floor, reminding her that the man on the train had a black beard. "Those clothes were found by the train porter?" she asked Cullen.

"Yes. You recognize them?"

"Well, yes, although the stains—they're blood I suppose—would lead me to think so, anyway. You know, I can't for the life of me remember what-all the man in the market, the one who accosted Barrymore there, was wearing. Just that he had a cap—no, wait: he was in shirtsleeves."

"Could it have been the same man, Glynis? Maybe he just threw on a jacket over the shirt before he boarded the train."

"No. No, it wasn't the same man. The one on the train had a beard, a shaggy beard. And the black hat. The first, the one at the market . . ." It all seemed so long ago, it was hard to recall. She couldn't bring back a clear picture of the market episode. "I can't remember much about it, Cullen. But I do know what was my immediate reaction on the train—that here was *another* attacker."

"O.K. I didn't think these few things would give us much information. There's no knife here, for example, like the one you described that killed Barrymore."

"It may be a fine line to draw, but I didn't actually see Barrymore killed, remember."

Cullen smiled grimly. "You're beginning to sound like a lawyer, Glynis, splitting hairs like that. You *did* see him stabbed, didn't you?"

"Yes, but only the one time. Maybe the other man, the market man, was also on the train, and he finished it." She threw up her hands. "I just don't know!"

As he was stuffing the items back into the laundry bag, he said, "It's all right. Don't give up, not yet anyway. Here, take a look at this." He upended the other bag.

With a haunting whisper, pale blue silk spilled onto the desktop. It must have been Sally Lunt's dress. Glynis closed her eyes, because even though there weren't any bloodstains, she could see rips in the fabric, probably indicating that Sally had struggled with her killer.

"Look at this," Cullen directed. "See the back of this dress?"

She left the chair reluctantly and moved closer, frowning as she brushed away a few more black hairs that had apparently been stirred up from the floor by her movement. Or maybe not; maybe they came from the dress. She looked closely but could find no hairs on the garment itself.

Cullen had picked up the dress, turning it so Glynis could see the back bodice and, below it, shirred into the waistband, the long full skirt. Very distinct stains, long streaks of green, ran more or less up and down the skirt and bodice.

"Are those grass stains, Cullen?"

"Looks like it to me. To Quentin Ives, too. And see the small tears at the bottom of the skirt?"

Glynis picked up several inches of the hem and examined the jagged tears. "From stones or gravel?" she guessed.

"That's what I think. Looks like after she'd been killed, she was then, for whatever reason, dragged to where she was found—behind offices backing up to the canal towpath."

"Offices! I thought she was found near one of the taverns."

"That's the conclusion everybody leapt to last Saturday night. And I decided to let them go on thinking so."

Glynis could understand why. Sad to say, a death resulting from a brawl at a tavern would be more tolerable and less frightening to the town than the intentional murder of a young girl. But that's what it had been, and it didn't seem fair or decent to Sally not to set it straight. And she said so now to Cullen.

"Not yet, Glynis. I know what you're saying, and I agree, but not until I have the killer. I want him put off guard, by letting him think we all believe the tavern story."

So concerned had she been with Sally that she'd nearly ignored the most important thing he'd said. "You just told me that Sally was found behind *offices*. Whose offices?"

"That's the strange thing. She was right between Jeremiah's law office, and the one next to his—the dentist's."

"Alan Fitzhugh's, you mean?" When he nodded, she made for the chair and sat down.

"You all right?" Cullen's forehead creased with concern. "I know this is rough."

"Yes, it is. Do you think," she asked, "that Sally might

have been killed *in* one of those offices, and then dragged outside? But why leave her so close to the murder scene? Why not take her body farther away to divert suspicion?''

''Maybe that's what the killer originally intended to do,'' Cullen said thoughtfully, ''but was interrupted for some reason—remember, it was the night of the benefit dance and people started gathering early. So he might not have had time to move the body without someone spotting him.''

''Him? You're sure it's a man?''

Cullen shrugged. ''Took a fair amount of muscle to strangle a struggling girl—though I suppose it could have been done by a strong woman. But there's something more here.''

Glynis sighed, and waited while he opened another desk drawer and withdrew an envelope. ''Here, take a look.''

He handed the envelope over the desk to her, and she pulled out a banknote. Frowning at it, she said, ''Is this what I think it is?''

''Yes, and we found it down inside a sleeve of Sally Lunt's dress. Notice that it's issued by Farmers and Merchants Bank. Now why would she have that, do you think?''

''Because her killing might somehow be linked to the others?''

Cullen didn't answer, and she noticed that his face had become closed, almost guarded. She'd known him so long she knew what it meant. ''Cullen, you aren't telling me everything, are you?''

''There's a couple of things I don't want to go into right now.''

When she started to protest, he said, ''Look, I have to leave town for a time, and I don't want you putting yourself in danger over this. Sally Lunt's death . . . well, this thing has gotten more complicated. In fact, I should never have brought you into it to begin with, and I regret that I did. But since you *are* now aware of the situation, I'd like you to confine yourself to speculation. Speculation *only!* Glynis, don't go poking around while I'm gone. Promise me that.''

''I can't imagine where I would go poking around, anyway. But can you at least tell me where you're going?''

''Sure. To Albany and the state banking commission with

that note you're holding. And the one I found on the dead agent, John Fairfax. I need to check the serial numbers, and I can't sit around waiting for next month's issue of *Hodges Bank Note Safeguard,* or even *Niles' Weekly Register*. I need to find out whether or not the plates of this particular series—'' he reached for the note ''—have been turned in as the law demands. And see if any more of these notes have been found floating around New York State.''

''You mean counterfeiters have been forging notes of the Farmers and Merchants Bank,'' Glynis asked, ''and that could be why it went bankrupt? Tom Bingham found out, and so he was killed. But where do you think Valerian Voss fits in?''

''I can't think anything until I find out more. And while I'm in Albany I'm going to follow up on your idea—the status of convicted counterfeiters.''

''Do you know when you'll be back?'' She asked because it occurred to her that Zeph might choose to leave during this time, and, in which case, who but Liam Cleary would be in charge.

''Could be a week or two. While I'm in the vicinity, I'll stop in Utica and check on Voss's story, and the Bank of Central New York. And maybe take a side trip south to the Remington Arms plant in Ilion. See if I can find out something more about Colonel de Warde's dealings with them.''

''I thought you already checked on him.''

''Won't hurt to check some more, will it?''

''Is there something you suspect?''

''Look,'' he said with some impatience, ''I'm not going to say more until I've checked into these things. So please don't ask me for specifics.''

''Well, then,'' Glynis said, getting up from the chair, ''I think I'll go on home. Since you aren't going to divulge anything more, there's really no point in my staying, is there?''

''You're annoyed.''

''Why would you think that?''

''Because I've known you too long *not* to think that.''

How could she argue with this logic? And yes, she was annoyed. He'd asked for her ideas, and aroused her curiosity, and now had decided to be secretive. Why wouldn't she be annoyed?

She pushed open the door and stepped into the dusk. Cullen, she realized, was right behind her. "It's all right," she told him, "I can get home by myself. It's not dark yet."

He said nothing, but walked along beside her. From the corner of her eye, she could see the muscle in his cheek working, a sure sign of either concentration or vexation. At the moment, she really didn't care which.

They came to Boone's Livery, and Cullen said, "Wait a minute, while I get my horse."

"I'll just go along," she said. "I hope your trip is fruitful." She bit her lower lip, and said nothing more.

Cullen also said nothing, but went on through the livery's two large open doors. As Glynis passed the building's far side, she saw a distinctive green wagon parked in back. Grandy Fox's wagon. She wondered where he slept. Perhaps in the wagon?

She'd reached Cayuga Street and just turned the corner, when she heard horse's hooves behind her, and shortly the black Morgan drew alongside. Cullen dismounted, and swung into step beside her, the reins held loosely in his hands.

"Glynis, I'm sorry if you're angry."

"I'm not, just puzzled. And, I suppose, my feelings are hurt."

"Why?"

She stopped and turned to face him. "Because you obviously don't trust me!"

"You think that's the reason I'm not telling you everything? It's not. I'm worried, that's why. As I said before, Sally Lunt's death changes things. This is no longer solely about counterfeiters. Something more sinister's going on. You certainly can see that!"

Since no reply seemed called for, they reached the Peartree house in silence. As she started to go up the stone walk, Cullen reached out and grasped her arm. He looked down at her and said quietly, "Glynis, I don't like this wall between us."

She started to shake her head, and then blurted, "Well, Cullen, who put it there?"

His expression changed abruptly. He let go of her, and stepped back. "I was under the impression that you did. You and Jacques Sundown. And I haven't heard anything different."

"I don't believe you've ever asked, have you? And what about Fleur Coddington, Cullen? Isn't she a part of this?" There! But she would probably be sorry she'd said it.

Nonetheless, she could have sworn he looked startled, just before his face closed. "Why don't we continue this when I get back?" he said, his voice and gaze steady.

She turned and walked quickly to the house. As she opened the front door, she heard behind her the Morgan's hoofbeats fading down Cayuga Street. She told herself she didn't care; these quarrels with Cullen were becoming altogether too frequent.

She suddenly realized she hadn't mentioned seeing Grandy Fox in Rochester. Or Emma's belief that there was some link between Sally Lunt and dentist Alan Fitzhugh. Probably neither of the items were critically important, but they might be.

She stepped back out to the porch, but Cullen and the Morgan had disappeared. She thought, sadly, that perhaps it was just as well.

FOURTEEN

❦

The men generally did not know that the raid on the Government works was part of the plan until after they arrived at the [rented] farm. . . . It was Father's original plan to take Harper's Ferry at the outset, to secure firearms to arm the slaves, and to strike terror into the hearts of the slaveholders; then to immediately start for the plantations, gather up the negroes, and retreat to the mountains . . .
—Anne Brown, Recollections.
Richard J. Hinton, *John Brown and His Men.* 1894

ANNIE OPENED HER eyes in an unfamiliar attic room. Still half-asleep, she scrambled to a sitting position before she remembered where she was: a dilapidated farmhouse in Maryland, some five miles from Harper's Ferry, Virginia. She and her brother Oliver and seventeen-year-old Martha, married to Oliver the previous year, had arrived there only five days before from the Adirondack Mountains of New York.

Annie had come because Father's letter to North Elba, written in the first week of August, had said her mother must join him in Maryland. Annie could still see that letter in her mind's eye: "I find it indispensable to have some women of our own family with us for a short time. I don't see how we can get along without, and on that account have sent Oliver at a good deal of expense to come back with you and Martha."

Annie could remember, too, her mother's expression while she stood reading Father's words, and the way she had swayed before sinking into a rickety kitchen chair and letting the piece of paper flutter from her hand to the floor. Annie had picked it up and read it, her eyes going back and forth from her mother's face to the words on the page.

"I can't do it. I can't go, I just can't go there," her mother kept saying, over and over, her voice hollow with despair. Annie had taken her hand and said, "You don't have to go. I will. Martha and I can do everything Father needs done. You don't have to go."

"No, Anne. No, you can't go either. There's work to be done here, and it's too much to care for all those men."

"Mother, I want to go," she had said, not really certain at first that she did. But then, with the thought that she had never seen anything but home and might never see anything more, had never ridden a train through countrysides and mountains, and that at the end of the ride John Henry would be there, she had to go. She had to.

"No, Anne," her mother had said, "I can't let you."

"But Mother—"

"No!" The uncommon harshness of her mother's voice, the severity of the word itself, startled Annie into retreat. And her mother just covered her face with her hands, while her body shook with silent weeping.

Later that day, Annie had gone up the stairs to pack some things to take to Harper's Ferry. She was going. It felt shameful and frightening to go against her mother's will, but what else could she do? This was her chance, her one chance to have and to do something she really wanted. She had wanted to go to school, pleaded to go, but Father had said no, she was needed at home to take care of the younger children. She had wanted, just one time, to have a new dress that was all her own, not a worn hand-me-down, but there was never even enough money for food. And she had wanted a dog so much, but when she carried home a small shaggy puppy from the neighboring farm, Father had made her take it back. It would grow up and be one more mouth to feed, and it might attack the sheep, he had said.

So she was going to Harper's Ferry.

When she had come back down to the kitchen that day, her mother was holding a small square tin box that made a clinking sound.

"Put out your hand," her mother told Annie. Then she opened the box, and counted out the coins from her hidden cache of egg money collected over more than two years' time. When Annie protested, her mother said, "No, take it. You'll need shoes to travel—you can't go in bare feet."

A week later, the train pulled out of the tiny station at North Elba, bearing Annie with sturdy second-hand leather shoes, and Oliver and Martha.

It was late in the afternoon several days later when they came out of Maryland's Blue Ridge Mountains on the Baltimore and Ohio Railroad. Just ahead, the train track ran through a long covered bridge over the place where the Potomac and Shenandoah Rivers met, then on to a promontory just below the town of Harper's Ferry. As the train emerged from the bridge, Annie questioned Oliver about the large two-story brick buildings that looked like factories built alongside the track.

Oliver had glanced furtively around the railroad car before he answered, in a low voice, "That group of workshops, twenty of them, is the musket factory that's part of the armory. The weapons they make are stored not far from here in two large arsenal buildings along the Shenandoah. That four-story building—over there on Virginius Island in the river—is the cotton factory, and there's another gun shop. The rifle factory is some ways up the river on another island. And over there"—he'd gestured, still keeping his voice down—"is the engine house, more arms shops, and the storehouse."

After the train stopped and they got off in air that smelled like fireplace soot, they went to wait on a bench in front of the stationhouse for John Henry to meet them with a wagon. For the past days, Annie's stomach had fluttered like dry leaves in a storm. Now she tried to ignore her innards by making a closer study of the town that had absorbed Father for the past years. Harper's Ferry didn't look like a place to be worth so much trouble. Taverns, whose rowdy occupants she could plainly overhear, and a number of hotels and inns crowded the nearby promontory. There appeared to be countless small houses and stables and smokehouses and sheds that were crammed so close together they reminded her of a jumble of wooden matchboxes, through which here and there a church spire poked. All had been built on the slope above where the Potomac and the Shenandoah merged to flow as one river.

Restless—they had been days on one train or another—Annie got up from the bench. Martha had her head on Oliver's shoulder, and they both looked to be asleep. Annie took a few tiptoe steps away from them. When her brother didn't open his eyes, she walked around the stationhouse to see better the blue-green mountains above the town and the rivers running at their feet. She skirted several hogs rooting in manure and the stagnant water that covered much of the cobbled street, and after walking some distance farther she paused at the edge of a dirt side road to let the sun fall warm on her back. Beside her, the water of the rivers rolled with stately grace.

She heard behind her the rattle of a wagon. She felt her heart lift and she knew, she knew even before she turned to look, that it would be John Henry she saw. After he pulled up the mules, he jumped down to come and stand a few feet from her.

"Annie Brown!" he said, his voice rough with what must be surprise. His hair was longer, curling over the collar band of his yoked shirt, and she leaned forward a little to catch the balsam smell of him. He came closer, then just stood there, looking down at her. "I never thought to see you here," he said finally with a slow smile.

"No, I guess not," she said, not knowing what else to say, and with her chest hurting because she felt so glad.

He cleared his throat, and asked, "Did your mother come?"

"No. I came instead."

"But you're just a girl." For a moment John Henry stopped, then shook his head. "No, maybe not." And he smiled again. "You didn't come alone, did you?"

"Oliver and Martha are on the other side of the stationhouse. I think they're sleeping."

"Then we'll let them sleep. Come along with me," he said and reached for her hand. They walked along the dirt road, and Annie felt her blood race up and down her arm from the hand he held, flowing faster than the mingled rivers below them.

"Your father's in a farmhouse," John Henry said, "off that direction." He pointed northeast. "He rented it from a Dr. Kennedy. Didn't use his own name of course, so now we have to remember to call him Smith, Mr. Isaac Smith. It's not very big, the house, and it's old and neglected, but it has two kitchens. And there's a cabin across the road."

Annie hoped there was an attic where she could sleep away from others. If there *were* others.

When she asked him about this, he answered, "Yes, men have been slowly coming in for several weeks now. And the house has an attic," he answered, even though she hadn't asked him, "just made for a young lady to sleep in, if she wants some privacy."

There he went again, seeing into her mind. But it didn't seem frightening anymore, not with her hand so safe inside his.

They paused to stand in the shade of sycamores with peeling white bark to look down at shallow pools created by the river's shale ledges. Mayflies hovered over them. Every so often they would see flashes of what John Henry said were Shawnese sunfish and perch and smallmouth bass.

And then Annie heard voices coming up behind them.

John Henry grabbed her and turned her around so she faced the voices, while he stood with his back to them. Then he pulled her into his arms and buried his face in her hair. "Stand still," he whispered, as if she might run away. Why would she? He was hiding himself, she was sure, from those who belonged to the voices. She wouldn't have moved if her life had depended on it.

The voices came nearer. Although her heart was striking her ribs like a hammer, she put her arms around his waist and felt him stiffen against her. Then he crushed her to him even tighter, making a muffled sound as his face moved to hide in her neck. The voices were right behind them now, but Annie couldn't see past his shoulder. His hand moved up under her hair, holding her close against him. She could feel the heartbeat in his neck, fast and strong, and all at once, her own heart stopped pounding. It felt so light in her chest she wondered if it might have escaped to fly like a caged bird set free. John Henry's mouth was soft on her throat, and she thought she could stand there forever, even if they turned into stone.

She heard the voices fade, and then they were gone. John Henry released her, but before he moved away he brushed her mouth with his. "Annie," he said softly, "Annie Brown."

He stepped away from her then, and turned to look in the direction the voices had gone. "They know me here," he said. "At least some of them do. It was foolhardy, walking around like this, but . . .'' He shook his head. "We'd best leave town, right now."

"Are you staying at the farmhouse?" Annie asked him as they walked quickly back to the stationhouse.

He stopped walking and looked down at her. "I was," he said. "But now . . ." His eyes moved over her face and his fingers reached up and touched her cheek. Then he pulled his hand back. "No, I'd better not stay there now."

It was all he said. He didn't speak to her again, not once after they got Oliver and Martha, and rode in the wagon five miles to the farmhouse in the hills above the Potomac River. It was only after he picked up his carpetbag to leave that he really looked at her. He looked at her for a long time, and then he walked away. Annie watched him heading up the road, north into the mountains, until he was just a speck against the blue-green peaks.

That had been five days ago. Annie now swung herself off the bed to stand on the rough wood attic floor. She felt sticky all over from the humid heat, and wished she could sleep without a shift, but she couldn't, not with all the men there. She tugged off the sleeveless garment and washed herself quickly in the tepid water from a pail she'd brought upstairs the night before. By the time she pulled her faded-blue calico dress over her head, she could hear faint noises below. The men must be getting up. There were eleven of them, not counting Father, and he expected many more to arrive in the next few days. Although Frederick Douglass wouldn't be coming. Father had met him in Chambersburg, and Watson, who'd been there too, said Mr. Douglass told Father that if he attacked federal property it would "array the whole country" against him. Father was still upset that Mr. Douglass wouldn't be there.

Annie tied an apron around her waist, then went down the attic stairs. The smell of bacon and coffee rose to meet her. Martha was in the small kitchen off the second-floor porch, bent over a cookstove and frying eggs and potatoes—and unless the money that Father was expecting came soon, eggs and potatoes would be all they would eat for some time. The ground floor of the house was used only for storage, as they'd found that, all too often, strangers passing on the road would stop and ask for water. It would create suspicion to refuse them. Since secrecy was of great importance, someone had to be on watch at all times to see that no one detected the presence of the men. It was usually Annie who sat on the porch or just inside the door. Father had directed that she not let work interfere with "constant watchfulness."

She tried to help Martha as much as she could at mealtimes because Oliver's young wife had just discovered she was pregnant. That morning while she set the table, Annie kept an eye on the road from the windows and open porch door. The men—the white men, that was—were coming from the cabin across the road to gather in the room they used for eating; the Negroes had to keep out of sight at all times, so they stayed in the basement or in the loft over the kitchen. The house was already beginning to feel crowded.

After the men had finished eating, Annie and Martha ate the leftovers while they washed dishes and swept the room, including the floor around the boxes of rifles loaded against the wall; they'd been placed so they could be sat on like benches. Father called them their furniture. The boxes of pistols were kept in Martha and Oliver's bedroom.

Annie had almost finished the sweeping when Father appeared and told her to go to the porch. "The men are going to wash their clothes today, so you have to keep a close watch for strangers. Sing out loud, you hear anyone coming. Except for John Henry—he's coming down from Chambersburg with the mail. I have everything sent to him there for safety's sake."

He might have said more, but Annie didn't hear. She'd fastened onto the fact that John Henry was coming that day.

"Annie! You paying attention to me?"

"I'm sorry, Father. I'll watch for John Henry."

"You don't need to bother about *him*. You just keep your eyes open for strangers."

Annie nodded, and waited until Father went back inside before she picked up her sewing basket. At least she could darn some socks while she watched. She crossed the porch floor to sit in an ancient rocking chair, and looked down in the direction of Harper's Ferry. Although she couldn't see the town, the air above it hung in a yellow haze with a smell like hot metal that carried for miles.

There was no one coming up or down the road. All there was for her to watch were a few scrawny chickens scratching in the dirt, and a puffy-chested rooster strutting among them. On the sparse grass at the foot of the porch steps, a brown goat with curved horns appeared and rolled a yellow eye at her, as if getting ready to test her mettle. Then he put one hoof on the bottom step.

"Don't! Don't you try it! Shoo now," Annie scolded, starting to rise. The day before, when she'd still thought of the goat in friendly terms, he'd come clambering up the steps, and before she could stop him he'd stuck his head into her basket and made off with a ball of yarn. When she tore down the stairs after him, she'd found herself being laughed at by the men standing at the windows. But she didn't really mind. They were nice men and they probably needed to laugh at something.

The goat looked up at her now and shook his head back and forth, all the while making an irritable sound. Then he bucked a few times, showing off, and wandered away.

She wished John Henry were staying here at the farm instead of up in Chambersburg. And then she felt ashamed that she'd thought about him, when she should be thinking about the slaves, who Father and the men were going to free. Father had said that, right now, hers was the most important job, and he was depending on her. No one in the town could be allowed to get wind of what was going on, or they could be arrested, and all the years of Father's work, all his speeches, all the planning—all would be for nothing.

Even so, when Annie finally saw a tiny speck appear from the north, then move down the road between the mountains, she couldn't keep her heart from leaping like a hooked trout.

FIFTEEN

❦

*We sometimes form our judgment on what seems to us strong
evidence, and yet, for want of knowing some small fact, our
judgment is wrong.*
—GEORGE ELIOT, *ADAM BEDE* 1859

GLYNIS STOOD INSIDE the door of her library to supervise the
Saturday morning delivery by Zeph, Jonathan, and Mr. Eberly,
the carpenter, of long planed oak boards from the Seneca Sawmill. She had purchased the wood from Rosie MacNamara, who
ran the mill; Rosie's husband Paddy believed that *he* ran it, but
everyone in town knew better. Word of the library's inadequate
shelving had somehow reached Rosie, and she'd offered the
wood to Glynis at cost. Glynis had accepted quickly, although
the money would have to come from her own bank account—
but shelves for the romantic novels must be built.

Jonathan had been correct about their popularity—the
women readers were grabbing them like hot cakes—although
their appeal continued to elude Glynis. Most romantics were
variations on the same theme: the unbearable consequences of
becoming a Fallen Woman! This usually happened at the hands
of some archfiend who had been not too subtly disguised as
everywoman's secret daydream. Glynis mused that this fantasy
must be widespread among female readers; thus the fact that
the readers themselves had not fallen, nor were they ever likely
to do so, made the reality of their own humdrum lives seem
virtuous in comparison. And therefore bearable.

There was no question that the number of library members
had increased rather sizably of late. It suddenly occurred to
Glynis that Rosie MacNamara might be one of them.

"Miss Tryon," Zeph said now, "when we finish unloading
the wagon, I'm going on to the Women's Refuge—promised
Abraham Levy I'd help with the new windows."

"Of course, Zeph. Mr. Eberly and Jonathan can manage.

Actually, I need to go to the refuge myself. I'd appreciate it if you'd help me carry some books.''

Zeph nodded and went back outside to the wagon for another load of boards. He seemed to be involved in a great many things these past few days—as if he was putting not only his own house in order, but everyone else's as well. It worried Glynis that Zeph might believe he would not return from his mysterious mission with John Brown.

Minutes later she and Zeph removed what volumes had been placed in the donation box. There were many more than Glynis had expected when she'd requested used books, especially children's literature, for the refuge. The vision of those children, standing listlessly in the dirt yard as she had seen them on her first day back in town, had disturbed her ever since.

"Do you know when Constable Stuart might be back?" Zeph now asked as they trudged together up Fall Street. Zeph was pulling a small two-wheeled dump cart bearing the books.

"No, I don't. I thought he might have told you."

"Nope. Course he didn't know I planned on going away. And I need to get moving, but I sure can't leave Liam Cleary here alone. If something happened—well, he could be throwing up while the whole town burned down."

Glynis refrained from smiling. Poor Liam's affliction, if that's what it should be called, certainly wasn't humorous. "Zeph, why didn't you tell Cullen about joining John Brown?"

"Are you serious? He'd have had a fit, probably thrown me in the lockup so I couldn't go. He's not too keen on John Brown, if you've noticed."

"I've noticed. And I'm afraid I'm not either, Zeph."

"Yeah, I know. But Brown's the only one nowadays who's willing to *do* something about slavery. Everybody else just talks. What good does that do? No good!"

Glynis wished she could disagree with some conviction. But nothing said or done after the Supreme Court handed down the *Dred Scott* decision had loosened the grip of slavery. Even Abraham Lincoln had conceded that, as long as there was money to be made in slaves, no legislation proposed by the North's anti-slavery men would get past the southerners in Congress. "The plainest print cannot be read," he had written, "through a gold eagle." So the country was locked in a stalemate.

But John Brown might try to tip the precarious balance by doing something that could provoke the southerners past the point of compromise and into secession. Brown had very nearly accomplished this in Kansas. As one politician had recently put it, their young country was sitting on a powder keg.

Glynis looked sideways at Zeph and again felt a sense of foreboding.

When they drew near the refuge, Glynis could hear the din of saws and hammers and, happily, the boisterous noise of children at play. After another block she was able to see the piles of bricks stacked below square openings in the warehouse walls that announced the coming of glazed windows. A score of men in shirtsleeves were climbing up and down ladders; a few of them Glynis recognized, such as the blacksmith, Isaiah Smith, and Adam MacAlistair, and, of course, Abraham Levy.

Five or six women and their young children were seated off to the side of the construction on what scrubby grass grew in the hard-packed clay around the refuge. Glynis was surprised to see Emma there, kneeling in front of several little girls. Only when she got close could she tell that Emma was pinning up the hem of one girl's pinafore. The child stood fidgeting, and Emma's forehead looked slick with perspiration.

Glynis smiled down at her niece. "I didn't expect to see you here."

"I didn't expect to be here this long," Emma answered. To the child she said, "Please stop wiggling, or I'll stick you with these pins." The little girl screwed up her face and Glynis expected a protest. Apparently so did Emma, as she quickly said, "You do want me to finish your new pinafore, don't you?"

The others who were standing by nodded eagerly, but the one being asked just plugged the impending wails by sticking a thumb in her mouth. And kept wiggling.

Emma sighed, and reached around the child to untie the pinafore's large bow. "All right, Mandy, I can finish the rest of it without you. Go along then."

Mandy slid her arms out of the garment and stood there in

her overalls with her eyes glued on the pinafore that Emma held, a pink-and-white-checked gingham trimmed with eyelet ruffle. Emma stood up, wiped her forehead, and said, "I'll bring it back finished tomorrow, Mandy, along with the other girls'." Mandy looked doubtful. But Emma said to her with great seriousness, "I promise. And then you can wear it every day if you want to."

Mandy gave Emma a skeptical frown, and finally ran off with the others.

Glynis sensed someone behind her, and turned to find Adam MacAlistair; he obviously didn't see her as he was gazing at Emma with an age-old look in his eyes.

"How many of those pinafores are you making, Emma?" she asked.

"Oh, a half dozen. They go very fast with the sewing machine." At this, she shot Adam what Glynis thought to be a cryptic glance. Then Emma went on, "I thought it was too bad those little girls didn't have anything pretty to wear. I always wanted a ruffled pinafore when I was that age." She frowned slightly, as if the memory were more significant than she had made it sound.

"Your mother didn't sew for you, did she?" Amazingly, this came from Adam.

Emma looked startled, and Glynis, equally startled if not more so, wondered what insight on Adam's part could have prompted this. She thought he wouldn't receive a response from Emma, but unexpectedly she said, "No; my mother thought pretty clothes were frivolous."

That did sound like Julia, Glynis had to admit. But how bitter a pill for Emma, especially Emma, to swallow. And indeed, her tone had sounded bitter. Then Glynis's reflection was abruptly interrupted by an all too familiar voice.

"My dear Miss Tryon, how relieved I am to find you." Vanessa Usher, sweeping across the dirt like visiting royalty, clearly meant Emma by this. She ignored everyone else there.

Adam quickly retreated up a nearby ladder, and Glynis, after catching her breath at seeing Vanessa there in the enemy camp, made for the refuge door.

The window openings had transformed the interior, and a far

more cheerful expanse now stretched before her. Abraham
Levy stood holding in place what looked like a large wooden
frame, while another man hammered above him. Neva stood
watching, her face radiant.

"What is that?" Glynis indicated the frame.

"It's going to be a partition, so the sleeping quarters will be
separate. What do you think, Glynis?"

"I think it's splendid."

"That's all very well," Abraham said, "but the construction
crew has to stop and eat." He stepped back from the secured
frame, and glanced at his wife as if expecting an argument. As
he and the other man went toward the door, he told Neva,
"We'll be outside—but not for long. You'll have your wall
and windows soon enough."

Neva nodded with a smile of affection. "And I thank you,
my husband."

"Thank you, my wonderful, talented, and generous husband," Abraham amended, and went through the door.

"He is that," Neva, still smiling, said to Glynis, "but don't
tell him I said so. What brings you here today?"

"Zeph and I brought some donated books I've been collecting at the library. Also, I wanted to find out something about
Fiona Cleary—or Roarke, I guess it is. I didn't see her outside—she is here, isn't she?"

Neva made a sound of frustration. "She *was* here. She left
late last night when that brute she married showed up to 'fetch
her home where she belongs,' as he put it. Glynis, I put four
stitches in the woman's face and a few in a split lip. She has
multiple bruises and a possible concussion. Now I ask you—
would you go back to a man who'd done that to you?"

"That's really beside the point, isn't it, Neva? I wouldn't
have married him in the first place. So you've met her husband?"

"Kerry Roarke. A big beautiful Irishman who, when he
drinks, has the disposition of a mad bull. Fiona's going to get
herself killed or permanently maimed. But why did you want
to see her?"

"I promised Liam Cleary I'd talk to their sister Morwenna
about this. Before I did, I wanted to see for myself if things

were as bad as Liam claims. Apparently they are.''

"I tried to talk her out of going home—talked until I was hoarse. You can see where it got me.''

"Fiona's probably terrified of him, Neva. Besides, she has a child—''

"Yes, she has,'' Neva broke in, "and she's obviously afraid for her little girl, too. But Cullen Stuart can tell you that in the past she's refused to press charges against her husband. Not that it would do any good. A judge would just shake his finger at *Fiona* and tell *her* to behave herself! And that would be the end of it. Until the next time.''

Glynis knew Neva was right. She returned her friend's look of frustration.

Neva sighed deeply. "Glynis, speaking of mistreated women, did Cullen Stuart tell you what Sally Lunt's autopsy showed?''

"That she was definitely murdered—yes, he told me.'' But seeing Neva shake her head, she added, "Was there something more?''

"Sally Lunt was pregnant,'' Neva stated with stunning bluntness. "About four months' pregnant.''

"Pregnant? But she wasn't—''

"Married?'' Neva completed. "Come now, Glynis, you aren't anywhere near that naive.''

"No, but I hadn't heard that Sally was serious about anyone, and I'm wondering if the pregnancy might have had a bearing on her murder.''

She hoped this satisfied Neva, as Glynis didn't want to explain her real concern: that Alan Fitzhugh might well be the man with whom Sally had been so intimate, hence her tears. In addition, the scenes that Glynis had witnessed between Fitzhugh and at least two other women now held new implications. If Alan Fitzhugh was seriously courting others—others with what he might consider the requirements of beauty and kind of money the women's jewelry suggested—a pregnancy resulting from a mere dalliance with a shopgirl like Sally could prove disastrous to him. But surely Fitzhugh wouldn't murder for that. Although it would not be an unprecedented motive; the lurid plots of Jonathan Quant's romantic novels could attest to it.

Sally's body *had* been found behind his office. But wasn't that a bit too neat? Glynis couldn't believe Alan Fitzhugh stupid enough to leave his victim's body anywhere near his own office. Unless, as Cullen said, he'd been interrupted when trying to move it.

This disclosure of Neva's put another cast on Sally's death. If it hadn't been for the banknote found on her body, Glynis wouldn't believe the girl's murder was connected with the others. As it was, at this point she could believe anything.

Neva interrupted her speculation. "Glynis, did I just hear, by any stretch of the imagination, the voice of Seneca Falls's *grande dame*—Mistress of the House of Usher? Tell me it isn't so."

"I confess I was surprised to see Vanessa."

"'Surprised'? What an understatement! What is she doing here? Spying on us? Hoping we'll have to close down without her money—or rather, her sister Aurora's money?"

"She said that she was looking for Emma," Glynis answered as Neva went to peer around the door. "Is she still here?"

"Still here," Neva said with disgust, "and she's talking your niece's ear off. Something about the richness of eggplant and the subtlety of *pensée*, whatever that means."

"I think those are stylish new shades of purple, Neva."

"Good God, Glynis! Here I am worrying about where and how I'm going to get food for these people to eat, and That Woman is going to be *wearing* eggplant!"

It had been a sound at the far end of the room that made Neva stop to draw breath. Glynis turned to look back at the two women seated there—the refuge had apparently been the recipient of several straight-backed wooden chairs. She'd seen the women earlier, when she first came in. One was the severe-looking and reclusive Margaret Taylor, but the other did not look familiar. Or did she? There was something about her. . . . Glynis walked toward the door where Neva still stood, to ask quietly, "Neva, who is that woman back there?"

"I assume you don't mean Margaret Taylor. I don't know who the other woman is—I was rather hoping you might tell me. She came here several days ago, dehydrated and very weak, and asked for shelter. Couldn't even keep food down at first.

She was literally starving to death. I don't know how she managed to get here.''

"Yes, I noticed how painfully thin she is. But no, I don't recognize her."

"That woman, Glynis, has obviously been accustomed to much better things. There's something about her, a certain elegance, for want of a better word. And she refuses to give her name. Not that she needs to."

"Refuses to give her name—because she's ashamed?"

Neva shrugged. "Most women who come here are. They're ashamed of being destitute, even ashamed of having been beaten—like Fiona Roarke. They think they've done something to deserve it, so at first they won't say who they are. Before long most of them do, but not this woman. Her sense of shame is profound."

The sudden rustling of silk made Neva draw back from the doorway just before Vanessa swished through it, saying, "Glynis, I must speak to you about your niece. She needs to go to Rochester for me—that is, for my gowns. There are fabric shops there that—"

"Vanessa," Glynis interrupted, "I don't think this is quite the place to discuss it."

Vanessa looked irritated, but she did glance around. After a perceptible shudder, she said, "Oh, yes. Well then, come outside so we *can* discuss it."

Vanessa had not so much as looked at Neva, much less acknowledged her presence, although Glynis could feel hostility generating from both women. Vanessa now took several steps forward to peer at the two women in the back of the room, suddenly gasping, "Oh, my Lord! It can't be—"

She broke off as Neva stepped into her line of vision. "Miss Usher, you'd best leave here!"

Glynis saw that Vanessa's face had blanched, and she had backed up against the brick wall as if for support. "I can't believe it," she said, voice muffled by her hand at her mouth. She turned to Neva. "Do you know who that is? Or, at least, who I think it is?"

"I don't care who you think it is," snapped Neva, "because

it's none of your business. Now, do I have to call someone to remove you bodily?''

Before Neva or Glynis saw what she intended, Vanessa had picked up her skirts and rushed through the open frame toward the two seated women. ''Beatrice? Beatrice, is that you?'' Vanessa's voice echoed in the near empty warehouse, and the woman with Margaret Taylor looked up and flinched, then tried to stand. She wobbled alarmingly before Margaret caught her arm and helped her back into the chair. By that time, Vanessa had reached them.

''Beatrice—Beatrice Whitaker,'' Vanessa whispered. ''Oh, my poor, dear woman! What has happened to you?''

The woman whom Vanessa had called Beatrice Whitaker shrank back against her chair. The slack skin of her face took on a gray hue, and it was obvious that only with great control could she remain seated upright. But the control did not extend to her pale blue eyes, which began to fill.

''That's it!'' Neva said, arriving to grip Vanessa's arm. ''Out!''

''No, no, you don't understand,'' Vanessa moaned, and Glynis decided that for once she wasn't acting.

''Beatrice Whitaker was my mother's dear friend,'' Vanessa said in a voice which held none of its characteristic haughtiness. ''She comes from a distinguished family, a very wealthy family. What is she doing *here?*''

''It doesn't matter,'' Neva said, her tone a trifle less sharp. ''Miss Usher, it does not matter why someone comes here. If a woman needs shelter, she gets it!''

At this point, Vanessa looked ready to burst into tears, and Beatrice Whitaker's anguish seemed to retreat somewhat. ''It is true that I came here for shelter,'' she said to Vanessa, in a voice remarkably steady despite her evident weakness. ''And I received it.''

Vanessa's eyes filmed as Beatrice Whitaker took a deep breath, or tried to, but was hindered by a spasm of dry coughing. When Margaret Taylor looked as if she would intercede, the woman moved her hand in a frail wave. ''No, it's all right, Margaret. Now that I've been discovered—or perhaps the word is *uncovered*—it comes almost as relief.''

She turned to Vanessa. "You wouldn't know that my husband left me some months ago. You couldn't have known, because naturally I tried to conceal it from everyone. I hid myself away, but failed to take into account that one must eat." It was hard to watch the effort with which she said, "As you see, I have nothing."

"No," Vanessa protested, "that's not possible! My dear Beatrice, there's your beautiful house—why, it's been in your family for generations."

"I have nothing," Beatrice Whitaker repeated. Glynis was relieved that the woman appeared to be rallying, and held herself erect although tremors shook her frame. Neva had been right, in that Mrs. Whitaker did possess a certain elegance which even her condition and shabby clothes could not take from her.

Vanessa kept shaking her head. "But your clothes, your gardens, your servants—we were all so envious of you, Beatrice."

"Your money and property must have been in your husband's name," Glynis now said to Beatrice Whitaker, "so when he left . . ."

"When he left," she said, nodding, "I lost them all. He sold my house," she added, her voice soft with something that Glynis heard as defeat, "and several weeks ago, I was evicted."

"But why didn't you tell someone?" Vanessa persisted. "Why didn't you ask for help?"

"That is an absurd and insensitive question," Neva stated. "Why do you think someone like Mrs. Whitaker wouldn't ask? Or don't you ever think?"

Vanessa ignored this. "Beatrice, you must allow me to give you money to find your husband, so you can leave here. It's not the place for you."

"Yes, it is, because as far as locating my husband, Vanessa—you can't possibly imagine that Roger would have left alone. No, he found someone more to his taste—younger, attractive, more . . . more what I no longer am. So I am quite fortunate to be here. To be anywhere at all." And Beatrice Whitaker sagged slightly in the chair.

Margaret Taylor stood up and declared in a tone that would

brook no argument, "Mrs. Whitaker needs rest. Suppose y'all continue your discussion outside." It was only the second time Glynis had heard Margaret Taylor speak, and the slight but unmistakable southern drawl came as a surprise.

"Yes, of course," Glynis answered, taking Vanessa's elbow to steer her toward the door. "We'll talk about this somewhere else." Vanessa did not resist.

Once outside, she seemed to recover herself. Frowning deeply, Vanessa glanced around, her eyes stopping overly long on the women and children on the grass before she said to Neva, "I had no idea what was going on here. But I think that's to have been expected, since I was never invited to see for myself."

Neva looked as if she might erupt, but Glynis sent her a quick shake of the head. She knew Vanessa. Knew that between long periods of self-centered oblivion, there had been brief moments when Vanessa displayed generosity. Her noble moments were infrequent, but Glynis prayed this might be one of them.

Vanessa now pointed to several children playing in the dirt. "Why do they look like urchins?" she asked somewhat piously.

"Because they *are* urchins," Neva replied, her face now empty of expression, as if that might make Vanessa more receptive. "Only one of them has a father—a known father. And their mothers are usually sick or injured, or they've starved to death. Fortunately, your mother's friend Beatrice Whitaker had the strength and will to avoid that. But some women prefer to die. They see that as the only way out of their misery."

"That's monstrous!" Vanessa retorted. "How can they do that to their children?"

"Their children die, too. But sometimes—" Neva gestured at those playing "—sometimes the children, like your Mrs. Whitaker, take it into their heads to survive."

Vanessa turned to watch the youngsters, and she looked at them for a long moment. When she turned back to Glynis and Neva, her expression was inscrutable, certainly a first of its kind for her. Then her eyes narrowed. "This, I suppose"—her arm swept over the warehouse and grounds—"is why my sister wanted you to have her money. Is that correct?" She looked at Neva, but would still not unbend enough to use her name. Nevertheless, Glynis began to sense in Vanessa a sea of change in approach. If only because the woman ordinarily didn't ask questions of those she considered inferior. And she actually waited for Neva's reply.

"Yes, that's correct," Neva said, smart enough to keep her tone neutral, her answer short.

Vanessa now stared at the bleak warehouse walls. Then her eyes went back to the children. After a drawn-out sigh, she said with obvious reluctance, "Very well. I will not stand accused of preventing hungry children from eating, or abandoned women from finding shelter." She paused and lifted her chin slightly to announce, "I withdraw my objection to probate of my sister's estate."

Glynis glanced at Neva, who swallowed hard before replying with a simple, "Thank you."

Glynis silently gave thanks as well. Probate of Aurora Usher's will would mean the library's debts could be paid and the romantic novels might now reside on shelves not financed from the librarian's own pocketbook.

Neva turned, sent Glynis a small smile of triumph, then walked toward the refuge door.

"Wait!" Vanessa called to Neva, her eyes dancing back and forth over the warehouse. "Wait," she said again, "I've just had a marvelous idea."

Glynis and Neva exchanged worried glances.

"I'm certain," Vanessa stated after Neva turned to her, "that your little barn dance didn't raise much in the way of funds. And anyone in town can tell you what a superb hostess I am." She paused, and looked at Glynis with the raised eyebrows that required confirmation.

"Oh, superb," Glynis said quickly. "You are indisputably without equal, Vanessa, when it comes to that." It happened to be true.

"Therefore," Vanessa declared, her tone conveying the weightiness of her next words, "I propose to hold a grand ball at the Usher Playhouse, with this place—" she gestured at the brick walls of the refuge "—to receive the proceeds."

She stood there expectantly, her glance going from Glynis

to Neva and back. Glynis wondered just what, short of kneeling down before her with foreheads to the ground, would satisfy Vanessa.

Neva, however, looked genuinely impressed. "I think that would be very generous of you, Miss Usher. Very generous, indeed."

"Good. Then it's settled. Now let's see—we can't have the ball too soon, certainly not before autumn, else there won't be time for Fleur Coddington, and dear Emma, to make gowns. I think, however," Vanessa said, apparently unaware that Neva had already turned and gone back inside, "that I shall need a theme. What do you think, Glynis?"

"Oh, yes, by all means, Vanessa. A theme to be sure," Glynis answered, envying Neva her swift exit.

"I have it!" Vanessa clapped her hands together. "A masquerade ball. Yes! And in keeping with the occasion's poverty-stricken recipients—" Lady Bountiful fluttered a delicate hand over the refuge grounds—"those attending will be required to come in the costume of someone they themselves would like to be, someone successful they admire. That will provide examples for these poor unfortunates to follow."

Glynis couldn't resist, "Oh, then you'll be inviting the women and children here at the refuge to your ball, Vanessa?"

"Good heavens, no, Glynis! What a thought!"

Glynis was spared a response by a sudden yell from blacksmith Isaiah Smith. "It's time!" he bellowed from a ladder's top rung. "C'mon now—we got to go!"

An intense rush of male activity followed this announcement. It seemed to Glynis that every man within the sound of Isaiah's voice began gathering up tools and stowing ladders, all the while grinning broadly.

She stopped Zeph as he hurried by with several lengths of what looked to be wood molding. "What's going on?" she asked.

Zeph's face creased in an unusual smile. "Baseball—up at Isaiah's farm. We're playing a baseball game against the Seneca Falls Grange. And we'll whip the tar out of 'em."

"I see. And who's 'we'?"

"Smith's Iron Works." He frowned slightly. "Least I hope

we're going to win. But"—and now he shook his head—
"without Constable Stuart here, it's not a sure thing."

"You mean Cullen . . . that is, the constable plays town
ball?"

"It's not town ball anymore, Miss Tryon. It's *baseball*. We
play with bases." Zeph gave her a sidelong glance that bor-
dered on shock at her ignorance. "And sure, Constable Stuart
plays. Everybody does!"

"Everybody? I didn't know there were women on ball
teams." Of course she did know this.

"Miss Tryon!" Now his shock was unmistakable. "Naturally, *girls* don't play. How could you think such a thing?" But
Zeph knew she didn't from the chuckle in his voice as he went
past her to join the others headed at a fast trot in the direction
of the blacksmith's farm.

Glynis was on her way to Fall Street and the library when
she sensed someone coming up behind her. Margaret Taylor
brushed past. "Mrs. Taylor?"

The woman slowed, then stopped and turned. "We seem to
be going in the same direction," Glynis said lamely. It was
plain the woman did not welcome friendly overtures. But curiosity about Margaret Taylor overcame Glynis's reluctance to
chance a rebuff. "Please excuse my asking," she said, "but
am I correct in addressing you as 'Mrs.'?"

"Yes." Then she added quietly, "I'm widowed."

"I'm sorry, Mrs. Taylor." She assumed the woman would
continue on by herself as before, but instead Glynis thought
she was now being scrutinized, although the thick spectacles
made it difficult to be sure. Margaret Taylor fell into step beside
her.

They walked in silence for a block before Glynis remarked,
"Neva—Dr. Cardoza-Levy—says you're a godsend to her,
Mrs. Taylor."

Margaret Taylor just nodded.

Glynis was beginning to regret her earlier impulse, but tried
again. "She also told me that you'd once trained with Florence
Nightingale. Was that in England?"

"Yes."

Glynis restrained a frustrated sigh. And told herself that if

Margaret Taylor wanted to talk in monosyllables, and to remain an enigma, it was certainly the woman's right to do so.

They reached Fall Street, and Glynis said, "Good-bye," sure that Mrs. Taylor would be relieved to see the last of her. Thus she was astonished when the woman said unexpectedly, "Miss Tryon, have you noticed how often the peddler leaves town without his wagon?"

Glynis was so taken aback she could only repeat, "The peddler? You mean Grandy Fox?"

Margaret Taylor nodded. "He almost always takes the train and leaves his wagon at the livery. Don't you think that's odd?"

"I'd never noticed," Glynis answered—and why should she have?

"It's something you *should* notice," Mrs. Taylor said. "It's strange, that wagon business. I'd look into it if I were you." And she walked away.

Glynis, with the anxious sense that she'd missed something crucial, watched the woman turn onto a side street off Fall. As Glynis continued walking toward the library, she slowed as she passed the livery. The peddler's green wagon was there, parked in back. The peddler himself was nowhere to be seen.

What had Margaret Taylor just insinuated—and why was she interested in Grandy Fox? On the other hand, Glynis herself was interested in just what Grandy Fox had been doing in Rochester, besides playing his fiddle at the public market, the day the banker Barrymore was murdered. Glynis now suddenly remembered seeing the fiddler climb up onto a crate—he would be able to see over the crowd much better from there. And Barrymore had looked over his shoulder as if afraid someone was pursuing him.

If that were the case, did the man have time to deliberately place the ring and banknote and coin in the pouch—and if so, were the items simply to identify himself, or had he been clever enough to point to his killer?

SIXTEEN

❦

With fingers weary and worn,
With eyelids heavy and red,
A woman sat, in unwomanly rags,
Plying her needle and thread,
Stitch! Stitch! Stitch!
In poverty, hunger, and dirt;
And still with a voice of dolorous pitch—
Would that its tone could reach the rich!—
She sang this "Song of the Shirt"
    —THOMAS HOOD, "SONG OF THE SHIRT"

We know of no class of workwomen [shirt sewers] who are
more poorly paid for their work or who suffer more privation
and hardship.
    —AN 1853 ISSUE OF THE *NEW YORK*
    HERALD

EMMA STOOD ALONE at the window of Adam MacAlistair's law office, waiting for the lawyer to appear. Minutes earlier, Jeremiah Merrycoyf had ushered her in, explaining that Mr. MacAlistair was down the hall in conference with their associate, Mr. Doggett. She had been told that her wait should not be long.

So far, it hadn't been. But just a minute or two in the close room had been enough to send Emma to the window, trying to blot with a lace handkerchief the perspiration which beaded her upper lip. Since midsummer heat had set in with a vengeance, it occurred to her that the outside air would be as uncomfortable as that inside. Nevertheless, she flung open the window as far as it would go. Then, after pushing up the full sleeves of her ivory silk frock, she rested her elbows on the sill to gaze out— and found it impossible to repress a shudder when her eyes moved irresistibly to the canal towpath where Sally Lunt's body was reported to have been found. Pulling her gaze away, Emma stood there wondering why Adam MacAlistair had sent word that he wanted to see her. Dare she hope that he had good news? She sighed heavily, letting drop the fringed ends of the blue silk sash she'd been nervously running through her fingers. The heat had made gloves unthinkable.

Determined to keep her eyes from the towpath, she leaned out the window. All at once, loud, angry voices seemed to come from nowhere. Emma jumped, before she realized the words came not from the room behind her but from outside. There must be an open window in an office down the hall from the one in which she stood, because she now thought she recognized Adam MacAlistair's voice. Although it sounded somewhat unlike him in that it held such intensity. Emma leaned out farther to catch the words.

"... and it's no longer a matter of client confidentiality!" Adam was saying. "The girl was murdered!"

Emma flinched and jerked herself back inside. But when it came to her that he probably was referring to Sally Lunt, she was unable to contain her curiosity and again thrust her head outside.

Another voice, equally angry-sounding, was now speaking. "... furthermore, you can be sure that I'm quite able to make that determination for myself!"

"I'm not at all sure of that, Doggett"—it was Adam's voice again—"and frankly, I'm becoming more than uneasy about your clandestine past activities."

"Now, listen here!"

"No, Doggett, *you* listen! Jeremiah may take you at face value, but I don't! Keep that in mind. And as far as Sally Lunt is concerned, you leave me no choice but to go to Cullen Stuart. Tell him that the girl was here—here in this office with you the day before she died."

Emma drew in her breath, and, in her zeal to hear every last word, had to grab the wooden frame to keep from plunging headlong through the window opening.

"Do what you like, MacAlistair. I'll simply refuse to discuss it with Stuart. I also refuse to continue this—"

The voice abruptly dropped, and Emma heard a door open. She started to whirl around, almost braining herself on the window frame, but stopped herself just in time. Once she was safely back inside the room, she found it was not the door to this office that had been opened. And then, somewhere down the hall, a door slammed sharply. Emma rushed to a pumpkin-colored chair and threw herself into it, then fumbled in her reticule for the lace handkerchief with which to wipe telltale windowsill smudges from her hands.

She needn't have hurried. A full three minutes passed before the office door swung open and Adam MacAlistair came in. His attractive clean-shaven face was flushed. And although he was smiling, an unmistakable glimmer of anger lingered in his eyes. Once again, she had the feeling that this man was more complicated, and, considering what she'd just overheard, less good-natured than he appeared.

"Ah, Miss Tryon," he said, standing before her chair and taking the hand she offered him. "I apologize for keeping you waiting. I'm afraid it was unavoidable. But now I am here, and I have good news for you. Very good news." He pressed her fingers, giving rise to a sensation which Emma found unexpectedly pleasant. Quickly, she withdrew her hand from his, aware of some unnamed tension.

But as he rounded the desk to his chair she sat forward eagerly. Had he somehow managed to better the contemptible Mr. Throckmorton? "Good news, Mr. MacAlistair?"

"Yes. I have corresponded with the Singer Company's local attorney, Orrin Polk, and have advised him of the futility, to say nothing of the offensiveness, of Singer's pursuing its claim against you. And I have just received a reply, to the effect that Singer would be agreeable to negotiating a settlement. The terms the company proposes will, I'm certain, meet with your approval."

"What are they?" Emma asked, frowning in confusion, as she did not follow this professed "good news," and she added, "The terms, I mean?"

"Well," Adam said, leaning back in his chair, "after doing some research on the subject, I found a seldom used, but entirely relevant, legal remedy for just such a situation as yours.

And I then apprised Mr. Polk of the circumstances—''

''Excuse me,'' she broke in, ''but I don't understand. Just what *are* the circumstances?''

''That, Miss Tryon, you were not of sufficient age to enter into a binding contract with the Singer Company. That is why, if you recall, I questioned you so carefully about it—not something I would ordinarily do to a lady.''

Yes, she remembered thinking that rude. And if she could just understand precisely what he was saying, it was no doubt very clever of him. ''So just what does my age have to do with this, Mr. MacAlistair?''

He sat forward to give her an expansive smile. ''It means that when you agreed to Singer's terms, you were too young to know what you were doing. Just a sweet young girl who couldn't possibly have been expected to understand, much less fulfill, the terms imposed upon you. Why, you were practically still in infancy—''

''Infancy!'' And she had too understood the terms.

''—and so,'' he went on, apparently unaware of her outburst or the look she was directing at him, ''the remedy for your dilemma is quite simple, really.''

Mercifully, he stopped talking, so Emma could begin to gather her wits. He continued to gaze at her with a broad smile, and she was almost afraid to ask. ''Mr. MacAlistair, what exactly *is* this remedy you speak of?''

''It's nothing complicated. You simply disaffirm the contract and return the sewing machine. And—''

Her gasp went unnoticed.

''—if we take this option, Singer will return your money. All of your money.'' Adam MacAlistair sat back in his chair, clearly expecting something in the way of accolades, if not sustained applause.

Give up her sewing machine? Emma rose to her feet without volition, keeping her eyes fastened on him as if he might suddenly transform into the fairy-tale Rumpelstiltskin demanding next her first-born child. Surely she hadn't heard him correctly. He *couldn't* have said what he did.

She reached out to grasp the edge of the heavy desk because she felt weak at the knees. ''Mr. MacAlistair,'' she began, summoning more courage than she believed she owned, "I do hope, indeed I pray, that I have misunderstood what you just said."

Ever so slightly, his smile began to waver. "What is it you don't understand, Miss Emma? I assure you, there is no question of the Singer Company pursuing you any further."

"Mr. MacAlistair! Do I understand you to say that *I must return my sewing machine?*"

He now dispensed entirely with the smile, and also got to his feet. His hands planted flat on the desk, he leaned toward her and said, "Why, yes, that is the answer I—"

"No, that is *not* the answer. I need my machine. I bought it in the first place because I needed it, and I need it now more than ever, and what in the world made you think otherwise? *I cannot give it up!*" Emma paused for breath.

She found herself nearly panting, she was that angry. For this betrayal she was paying him money? Besides, what he was proposing didn't make sense. "Mr. MacAlistair, I don't see why the Singer Company would offer to return all my money. They said they didn't *receive* all my money. If they admitted they had, there would be no reason for any of this—because I've already paid in full for my machine."

Again she was forced to breathe. During this pause, he jumped in to explain with a patience undoubtedly reserved for the feeble-minded, "But Miss Tryon, don't you see? When Singer returns your money, you can simply buy a new machine. From another company. Singer's are supposed to be the most expensive anyway."

With a moan, Emma lowered herself back into the chair. "You don't understand," she said, with a foundering feeling that she was getting nowhere. "Singer sewing machines may be the most expensive, but they are the best. At least for my purpose. I know because I looked at every make available. Besides that, they're not sold everywhere—only in big cities like Boston and Philadelphia. In Springfield I had to order mine, and then wait forever for it to arrive. But I can't afford that kind of time now. I've got dress orders to complete immediately. And I don't *want* another machine!"

To her intense distress, Emma found she was wiping furiously at her eyes to keep from crying. While praying Adam

MacAlistair hadn't noticed, she stole a look at him. And supposed it was somewhat to his credit that he appeared almost as distressed as she.

"My dear Miss Tryon—Emma—it does seem I didn't fully understand. I thought that—"

"I know what you thought," she interrupted, sniffing to keep back tears while she searched for her handkerchief. "You thought I was a feather-brained female, who didn't even know not to send cash through the mail. That if I had been stupid enough to do that, then . . ."

"Not true! Not at all!" He dashed around the desk to hand her his own immense snow-white handkerchief. "I merely exercised my judgment as to what would be best for you. And clearly, this was a mistake. I failed. Failed abysmally."

Emma looked up at him in surprise. She hardly knew how to respond to this display of contrition. Moreover, Adam MacAlistair looked completely sincere. She had to admit, he was almost likable in this condition. "Well," she said, sniffing, "then what can I do?"

"*You* don't have to do a thing. I'll—"

"Wait, please!" Emma broke in. "Maybe you'd better not do anything—not until you understand why I can't give up my sewing machine."

Adam, who had been hovering at her side, now nodded, and moved back behind the desk. "All right," he said, "then explain it to me."

Emma eyed him suspiciously for signs of sarcasm, but found none. She cleared her throat, but before she could begin, Adam said, "Please take your time. As I said before, I know I'm prone to arrogance—but I hope you believe I would never do something intentionally to harm you. Before doing that, I would cut off my right arm."

"Have you agreed to their terms?" Emma asked anxiously, not wanting to be the cause of any further such excessive pledges.

"No! No, of course not!" Adam MacAlistair's contrition clearly had its limits. "Never would I agree to something without first consulting my client."

"That's good," Emma responded with relief. "Then, perhaps there's another way?"

"I assure you, I will find another way! Now tell me, did you manage to obtain employment from Mrs. Coddington? Is that why you need the machine?"

"Well, I'm not exactly employed. That is, I've entered into an arrangement with her." At this, she saw with irritation that he'd stiffened instantly and looked alarmed. No doubt thought that she'd botched things again.

She straightened, and went on with some warmth, "It's just that I don't want to work for hourly wages. They're always unfair—do you know about seamstresses in New York City?" Receiving a puzzled look, she explained, "A tailor, a male tailor, gets five dollars for something that takes him just two days, but a female shirt sewer gets paid, at most, one and a half dollars *per week,* and for that she has to work twelve or fourteen hours a day."

She stopped as he was frowning at her with what appeared to be disbelief. "It's the truth!" she declared emphatically.

"So what is your arrangement with Fleur Coddington?"

"I asked Mrs. Coddington for forty percent of the price she would charge her customers for the garments I make."

"That's all? Forty percent?" Adam was scowling. "I hope you didn't—"

"Yes," Emma interrupted, "yes, I did. Because," she continued before he could contest this, "Mrs. Coddington's agreed that I can keep *sixty* percent of what I charge my own customers. Most important, I'll be able to use the facilities of La Maison de Fleur. That's a very real benefit because I certainly can't continue dressmaking at my aunt's boardinghouse. Almost as important, I can buy the fabric for my own designs at Mrs. Coddington's wholesale cost. So I hope you can believe," she finished, "that it's a very useful arrangement."

The lawyer had been studying her with an odd expression. Emma wasn't sure it was approval. Then, with an even odder note in his voice, he said, "Yes, Fleur Coddington must think highly of your work. You've done well for yourself, Miss Tryon." He was silent for a moment, and when he spoke again, his tone didn't sound as patronizing. "But tell me this," he asked, "does a sewing machine actually allow you to work that much faster?"

At least he didn't seem to think her an infant! "Oh, yes! With the Singer I can sew a wool dress in little more than two hours. The same dress sewn by hand used to take me eight or nine."

"I see." He looked appropriately impressed. "Well, in that case, we have to find a way for you to keep your machine."

Emma let out the breath she'd been holding, which brought a smile from Adam. "While you were talking," he said, "I had a thought. I know that the Singer Company has been besieged with lawsuits over patents. Isaac Singer might like a chance to avoid yet another lawsuit—yours, that is—and obtain an endorsement of his machine in the bargain. I have an idea, and while I can't guarantee it will work, I think it's worth a try." He paused. "Well, what do you think, Miss Tryon?"

So startled was she at being asked an opinion that she blurted, somewhat rudely she supposed, "I'm sure I don't know, Mr. MacAlistair. Just what *is* your idea?"

Remarkably, he not only didn't seem offended, he even smiled. "It's probable that Isaac Singer doesn't even know of this situation. Perhaps Throckmorton simply takes it upon himself to intimidate women. Therefore, I think you might write a personal letter to Mr. Singer. Legally, I can't communicate directly with him myself, but I would be delighted to assist you in this effort."

"But what should I say? He wants my machine!"

Adam leaned back in his chair, and after a moment of staring at the ceiling, he answered, "You might explain to him that I, as your attorney, have advised you otherwise, but since you like your machine so much, you don't want to give it up. Even to accept his generous offer! So, with the approval of your attorney, you decided to contact him directly to see if this 'misunderstanding' could be resolved out of court!" Adam sat forward to add, "If Isaac Singer is a stubborn curmudgeon, this likely won't work. On the other hand—" he shrugged "—we can always sue. Not ever the best remedy, certainly not when speed is of the essence. So now, what do you think?"

"I think . . . I think you have a splendid idea. And yes, I do think it's worth trying. Can we do it soon?"

Adam pulled open a desk drawer, and extracted a sheet of heavy white paper. "Right this very minute," he said. He stood up and came around the desk, and drew up the other pumpkin-colored chair very close to her own.

AN HOUR LATER, as he prepared to usher her out of his office, Adam said, "So you are a women's rights advocate, Miss Tryon?"

"Me? Oh, no, I don't care anything about politics. That is . . ." She hesitated.

"Yes," Adam said, "all of life is politics, isn't it? What have we been talking of here, if not the power a Mr. Throck-morton exercises when he threatens an innocent young woman? And I assure you, Miss Emma Tryon, that with most women his threat would have worked. Since I undertook the research into your case, I've learned that Singer, along with other man-ufacturers, has repossessed any number of machines from women who couldn't make the final payments. And not only that, they kept those women's money as well. Perhaps, in de-manding fair treatment, you're more of a feminist than you think."

Perhaps so, Emma thought with an odd but agreeable sense of pride. Aunt Glynis, if she knew, might be amused—certainly she'd be surprised. And it was to Emma's own surprise that she'd found composing the letter with Adam MacAlistair rather enjoyable. Since he'd begun to treat her as more than a child, well, he was really quite nice. But while she imagined she could come to like this man, she had more important things with which to concern herself.

For one, worrying about whether that letter to Mr. Singer would prove successful.

JEREMIAH MERRYCOYF WAITED until Emma was well out the front door. Then he said, "Mr. MacAlistair?" and nodded to-ward his own office.

When both men were inside the room, and Merrycoyf had firmly closed the door behind them, he didn't mince words.

"Again, you and Cyril have been arguing, and quite loudly I might add. It's a wonder the charming Miss Tryon didn't leave. Which would have been a shame, considering the prodigious amount of time and effort you've spent researching her case, the likes of which I've never quite seen. But these quarrels between you and Cyril cannot continue, Adam."

"I agree, Jeremiah. And I expect they will end shortly. Perhaps we'd better sit down," Adam suggested. When they'd done so, he said, "I'd wanted to wait for more information before I talked to you, but now is probably as good a time as ever."

Merrycoyf folded his hands over his stomach, lacing his fingers together so as not to exhibit the concern he felt by drumming them on the desk. He had known Adam MacAlistair since he was an eager young pup, and had watched him grow into a potentially fine attorney. But his obsession with Cyril Doggett, Merrycoyf found not only inexplicable but alarming in its implications. With no proof—with nothing, in fact, but perverse intuition—Adam had determined that Cyril Doggett must be guilty of something! Hardly the desirable stance for a lawyer. But he was entitled to have his say. "Very well, Adam, I am listening."

"Thank you, Jeremiah. I know this will be difficult for you, and I sincerely wish there were another way."

"Please, if you have something concrete, do get on with it." Merrycoyf knew he sounded irritable. He was also becoming impatient.

"All right," Adam said, sitting forward at the edge of his chair. "Would it interest you to know why your former classmate is not practicing law in Connecticut?"

Merrycoyf said nothing. Clearly, he didn't need to, since Adam would answer regardless.

"The reasons for this," Adam went on, "are very telling, Jeremiah. I've communicated with a friend, Samuel Tremain, who now practices law in New Haven—he's a former William and Mary classmate of mine, as a matter of fact. I've just received a reply from Sam about my inquiries. So, first, do you recall Doggett giving me, although only under duress, the name of his previous law firm in New Haven? Well, wonder of wonders, it seems there *is* no law firm in New Haven by that name. Never has been!''

Merrycoyf sighed deeply. ''Is it possible there's been some mistake on the part of your friend?''

''That's extremely doubtful. I asked him for specific information, and indicated it was important, and confidential. Please hear me out, Jeremiah. Because this is only the beginning. Sam Tremain's inquiries have disclosed that our Mr. Doggett is the subject of an investigation by the New Haven district attorney's office. Sam doesn't know exactly what the investigation entails, but he did find out that the federal Treasury Department is involved.

''The Treasury agents connected with the investigation are also looking for a counterfeiter named William Brockway. Several years ago, Brockway got himself arrested here in upstate New York, was tried and convicted despite someone's attempt at extravagant bribery, and served time in prison. However, last year he escaped! The man has a fascinating history, if you'd care to hear it.''

Merrycoyf suppressed a desire to unlace his fingers. ''I should say not—not unless you are claiming he has some far-fetched connection with Cyril.''

Adam's eyes narrowed, and Merrycoyf found himself the subject of his junior partner's intense study. And suddenly, for the first time, he began to sense within himself a powerful misgiving. Adam MacAlistair might be impetuous, sometimes arrogant, and occasionally over-enthusiastic, but he was as honest as the day was long. Of this, Merrycoyf had not a doubt. He would never fabricate, never. ''Very well, Adam; you may advise me of the background of the—as you put it—fascinating Mr. Brockway.''

''Brockway was born''—Adam began, and he watched Merrycoyf—''in Connecticut, some forty or so years ago. Lived there a number of years.''

Merrycoyf's eyebrows went up, and his misgivings increased twofold.

''During his adolescence, Brockway apprenticed with a New Haven jeweler-engraver who was also a printer,'' Adam went on. ''And his life took an unexpected turn. Brockway's employer gave him permission to sit in on classes at Yale College, classes in a new science called electro-chemistry. They were taught by a Professor Silliman.''

''*Benjamin Silliman?*'' Merrycoyf nearly choked on it.

''The same. And while those chemistry classes were undoubtedly the most important ones to Brockway's future occupation, he also attended classes at Yale Law School.'' Adam sat back in his chair and directed a level noncommittal look at his senior partner.

Merrycoyf, primarily to engage his hands in purposeful behavior, removed his spectacles and rubbed the bridge of his nose. ''I see,'' he said at last. ''Well, that is all very interesting, Adam. But what, pray tell, does that have to do—''

''Jeremiah!''

''—with Cyril Doggett? Except''—Merrycoyf hurried on before Adam could again interject himself—''that this Brockway and Cyril were at once in the same Connecticut town. For that matter, I was there myself. You are building, Adam, an entirely circumstantial case. As you must be aware.''

''There's more.''

Merrycoyf again sighed. Yes, that there was more was something of which he'd been uncomfortably certain. ''Go on.''

''Jeremiah, I *am* sorry. I don't enjoy this, I can assure you.''

''Shall we skip the nonessentials? Please continue.''

Adam frowned at Merrycoyf's harsh tone, but he continued, ''At some point, it appears Brockway became dissatisfied with his work and his wages. So, after making wax impressions of the locks on the front door and the safe, he looted his employer's shop and made off with diamonds and silver and gold jewelry. At the time there was a great stir about the robbery, but it seems that young Brockway had up to that time led such an exemplary life that no one, including his employer, suspected him. Not even when he made numerous trips to New York to sell his loot.

''Meanwhile, he was engaged in another endeavor. Under the guidance of the same printer, Brockway was learning to run off the notes of local banks on his employer's printing press. And when this unsuspecting man's back was turned, Brockway sent through the press a thin sheet of lead that took the impressions of five-dollar banknotes. Then the enterprising Mr. Brockway simply stashed the plate under his apron—until he could leave the shop undetected.''

Merrycoyf shifted uneasily in his chair as Adam explained, ''After Brockway had his lead plate, it became a matter of transferring the design to plates of copper—the techniques for which he had picked up in the electro-chemistry classes at your alma mater, Jeremiah.''

Adam got to his feet and went to the window. Merrycoyf watched and began to accept, from the sag of the young lawyer's shoulders, that Adam indeed was not enjoying this. ''And I suppose,'' Merrycoyf offered, ''that he then forged the appropriate signatures on the counterfeit bills. Were there many?''

''Many,'' Adam echoed. ''One thousand of them, or five thousand dollars. And one guess as to how he planned to pass these bills.''

Merrycoyf cleared his throat. ''I'd rather not speculate, since you're going to tell me anyway. But if I must, I would guess that Brockway probably had an accomplice.''

''And you would be right. Trouble is, this accomplice disappeared—along with the five thousand dollars. Leaving our intrepid young entrepreneur holding the empty bag, so to speak.''

''Tell me,'' Merrycoyf said, his eyes behind the spectacles glittering with hopeful expectation, ''was Brockway's accomplice a woman?'' Surely this was not impossible, he thought. Since women were daily pressing for legal rights—thus, why not illegal ones as well? Although Miss Glynis Tryon, whose intelligence Merrycoyf admired, might suggest that women engaged in counterfeiting could have been forced into it by men.

''Jeremiah? Did you hear me?''

''Forgive me, Adam, I was woolgathering. The accomplice?''

''A male accomplice.''

''Ah. And what happened to young Mr. Brockway then?''

''Not much. Apparently, Brockway simply printed another five thousand, managed to pass some off on his own, and then left town. Left, that is, before the New Haven bank discovered the scheme when the notes began to come back to them for redemption into coin. And then the hunt for Brockway was on.

"He's had Treasury agents after him ever since, but that hasn't stopped him from counterfeiting money all over the eastern seaboard. Brockway has only been caught once. He was sentenced to Sing Sing and later transferred to Auburn Prison here in western New York. But as I said earlier, he escaped and his whereabouts are unknown."

"Is that all of it, then?" Merrycoyf sincerely hoped so. But when Adam said, rather dispiritedly, "That's all about Brockway," Merrycoyf sensed there was still worse to come. "I trust," he said, "that you have not spent the past minutes regaling me with tales of a thief—even a thief so admittedly ingenius—to no purpose, Mr. MacAlistair." Take the bull by the horns, he told himself, and thus added, "How does this in any way concern Cyril Doggett?"

"I've told you that he's under investigation, and there's strong indication that Brockway's original accomplice was a Yale law student."

"There were scores of Yale law students that could have been involved!" Merrycoyf said sharply.

"But not whom William Brockway was seen with, and seen with often, as he was with Doggett," Adam answered quietly. He waited, then said, "I think you had better face it. Something is very, very wrong here."

"I'm willing to admit that there *appear* to be some rather unfortunate coincidences—"

"Jeremiah," Adam broke in, "you can't argue with what we know to be fact. First, there's no question Doggett lied about his New Haven law firm—a nonexistent firm. Check on it yourself if you don't believe me. Second, he's being investigated by the Treasury Department—granted, we don't know for precisely what, but I suggest we find out. Third, and even more important than our law firm's interest, we have bogus money being passed here in Seneca Falls, accompanied, so it seems, by several murders. And one of the victims, need I remind you, was here, *here,* with Doggett the day before her death. For reasons he refuses to disclose."

"Adam, it is merely your conjecture that Cyril is somehow implicated. You have presented me with circumstantial evi-

dence that wouldn't hold up in a rainstorm, much less a court
of law!''

"This is not a court of law," Adam protested. "Won't you
at least agree that there's reason to inquire about these matters?
Look into this further before we take a viper into our midst?"

Merrycoyf's limbs had grown stiff, thus it was with considerable trouble that he extricated himself from the chair. He
needed to think. Needed to acquaint himself with the possibility
that his old friend might be other than honorable.

He walked to his office door and opened it. "Some time,
Adam—I need some time."

INTERIM

❧

LIGHT RAIN WAS falling at the port of Oswego, and the shore-line of Lake Ontario lay hidden in heavy mist. Foghorns blew their warnings in a steady mournful cadence. All of which added to the considerable anxiety of the man who had for some time been pacing up and down the length of a pier.

Brockway paused to look down at the water, and decided he would wait only a few minutes longer. It was all too possible that something had gone wrong. That something more *had gone wrong, he corrected himself. Like the fog that surrounded him, events were closing off his alternatives, much like the stark cellblock walls of Auburn Prison. Brockway allowed himself a fragmentary smile, recalling the weeks he'd spent planning his escape from the state's oldest jail. It just proved that Auburn, supposed to be a model of penal efficiency, was only secure if every guard remained immune to bribery; it took just one who did not. But Brockway had vowed then, during his first minutes of freedom, that he would never go back inside.*

His heart slammed against his ribs when, directly in front of him, a figure suddenly stepped out of the mist.

"Ah, Mr. Brockway. Been waiting long?"

"Too long. A minute more and I'd have been on my way east. I told you, I didn't sign on for murder."

"Quite so, Mr. Brockway. And I can understand your reluctance to—"

"No, I don't think you can," Brockway interrupted. "I warned you a couple months ago that the man was a loose cannon. You said you'd take care of it. You didn't."

The other man's smooth-shaven face reflected a momentary sadness. "You're absolutely right. But my good man, you're not in any danger. You've never shown your face in Seneca Falls. No one there knows you exist. However, I concede that the situation has become of some concern."

His agreement took Brockway by surprise. "You know about his latest victim, then?"

"Yes, I do. Most unfortunate."

"Most insane, you mean. Killing a young girl? What kind of man is he, anyway?"

"An imprudent man, it seems. However, he did assure me that it was necessary. Sally Lunt posed a threat to our entire operation."

Brockway scoffed loudly. Then quickly looked around. But they were alone on the end of the pier. He lowered his voice, however, when he asked, *"What kind of a threat could she have been?"*

"She'd discovered something that had dangerous implications. And she'd solicited advice on how she should proceed. Most unfortunate," he said again.

"Unfortunate? I'd say it's downright evil. And I'm done with it. Find someone else to take your risks. I'm out!"

"Now I believe it is you who are being imprudent, Mr. Brockway. This whole phase will be coming to a conclusion very shortly. And I do assume you want to be paid? In genuine money, that is?"

"Now look—"

"No, I'm afraid it is you who must look," the other man said, his voice tinged with regret. *"I cannot allow you to put the entire plan in jeopardy. John Brown should be getting ready to move on Harper's Ferry any day now. But he won't move an inch without a sign from God."*

"What?" Brockway said incredulously. *"Are you telling me that everything hinges on that bloodthirsty lunatic's getting 'the word' from on high?"*

"That's what I'm telling you. Which means one more job. Just one more short run of double eagles, Mr. Brockway, consisting of, oh, six hundred dollars should do. Then you can leave this vicinity for parts unknown, and with a substantial amount of reward in your pocket. I give you my word."

"I don't know. It's more dangerous than it was, thanks to your homicidal friend. I got word that Constable Stuart's been seen in Albany, snooping around. Sooner or later he's going to track those bogus notes back to Seneca Falls."

"And by that time you'll be long gone. We both will. In any event, it's not Stuart I'm worried about."

"Oh, so now you're *worried?"*

"There are, admittedly, some unpleasant signs that things are coming unraveled, yes. I'm rather troubled by several women in Seneca Falls. And one in particular. But you needn't concern yourself with—"

"I am concerned!" Brockway almost shouted. He lowered his voice again, and said, *"Who is she? Somebody else your boy's going to get rid of because he decides she knows too much?"*

"I shall hope it does not come to such unpleasantness. It would be a shame, as I rather like the woman in question. I just wish she weren't quite so inquisitive—she has a reputation for that. But, as I said, you needn't concern yourself with her. Just six hundred dollars, dear Mr. Brockway, and you can leave western New York behind, knowing you have done your share. When the South goes to war, as she assuredly will, and Britain comes to her aid, then you will be generously rewarded for the small part you have played. Believe that, my good man!"

"Six hundred. Then I'm gone."

"With my blessings, Mr. Brockway. With my blessings."

The clean-shaven man moved back into the mist. Brockway stood for some time, staring at the spot where the man had just been, before he himself went down the pier to the shore. He rubbed his ink-stained fingers together as he walked.

He didn't trust the smooth-shaven man. Nor did he believe his future lay with the British. No, after this one last job, he'd head east to the coast. Maybe go on south, although only as far as Philadelphia, until he could read which way the wind would blow. Because, after being caught and sent to prison, he no longer believed in luck.

But in one thing Brockway did believe: there would be war.

SEVENTEEN

❦

Thou large-brained woman and large-hearted man, Self-called George Sand! whose soul, amid the lions Of thy tumultuous senses, moans defiance And answers roar for roar, as spirits can.

—ELIZABETH BARRETT BROWNING,
TO GEORGE SAND. 1844

GLYNIS STOOD ON the train station platform, looking up at the window of a passenger car through which she could see her niece settling into a seat. Emma smiled down at her and waved with a nonchalance Glynis found somewhat disconcerting, as if the young woman started off alone on a journey every afternoon. But there was no reason why Emma should not go to Rochester. She would be met at the station there by her Aunt Gwen, Glynis's sister, and Gwen's four children. Although one purpose of Emma's trip was to visit her cousins, Glynis knew very well that another purpose held as much if not more appeal: Emma would choose and order the fabrics for Vanessa Usher's new wardrobe. A far greater selection would be available in the larger city than in Seneca Falls. And, too, Emma wanted to establish an association with Rochester fabric merchants. For the future, she'd said.

Her shopping trip would be for more than Vanessa's gowns. Word had begun to circulate about the masquerade ball to be held in the autumn, and Emma was receiving orders from a number of those confident of receiving invitations. Glynis herself was one of them. After much deliberation, she'd nearly made up her mind to go as Amandine Aurore Lucile Dudevant, better known as the French author George Sand, whose controversial novels protested the social conventions that oppressed women. Although Sand's early and current novels were in the Seneca Falls library, Glynis trusted that the author's personal life was not familiar to western New Yorkers. She would certainly look into this before committing herself to impersonate a woman who, while extolling the virtue of fidelity, had engaged in numerous love affairs. But surely no one in Seneca Falls would know that—except possibly Vanessa, who loved Frédéric Chopin's music, and therefore might conceivably have heard that he and Sand had been lovers.

Vanessa should, however, be easy enough to sound out. The attraction of this particular impersonation to Glynis was that she could spend an evening in the comfort of Sand's distinctive trousers. An entire evening without the awful confinement of full skirts. Although, Glynis told herself with a regretful sigh, perhaps she was too old to do something as daring as that, even though she, like everyone else at the ball, would be masked. Still, she would have to consider it more.

As the train now chugged out of the station, Glynis sent a last wave to Emma and began to walk toward Fall Street. The town suddenly seemed smaller: Cullen was still somewhere in central New York; Harriet Peartree had left several days before to visit her son Niles and his wife and child in Montreal, and Emma was now on her own journey. Glynis found the sensation of being alone in the Peartree house rather pleasant, even liberating. How long it would remain so she couldn't predict.

When she turned onto Fall Street she saw ahead, in front of Carr's Hotel, its owner, British-born Thomas Carr, and Colonel Dorian de Warde. The Englishmen were engaged in what looked to be intense, even heated, conversation. Then, suddenly, Colonel de Warde turned on his heel and strode off in the opposite direction. Carr stood with his arms folded over his chest, staring after the other man.

"Good afternoon, Mr. Carr," Glynis said, with every intention of continuing on her way. But Carr's answering "Afternoon!" was abrupt, and his face so indignant that Glynis paused.

"Sorry, Miss Tryon," Carr said quickly. "Didn't mean to growl at *you*." He sent a glare down the street. "It's just some people—they don't know when they're well off."

Glynis followed his gaze. "Doesn't Colonel de Warde stay here at the hotel when he's in town?" she asked, not even sure why she was curious about Carr's obvious annoyance.

"Oh, he does that. Has the largest room in the place—very grand, the colonel is. Yes, indeed." Now there was no mistaking the dislike in Thomas Carr's voice, and Glynis wondered how she might politely ask why. Carr then volunteered, "Don't care for the man, myself."

"I see," Glynis replied, her voice carefully neutral.

"No, I don't care for those who come to this country to make money and then have nothing decent to say about it. This country's been very good to me. And I don't like the colonel's insinuations."

"Insinuations?" Glynis echoed. What could Colonel de Warde have said to provoke the good-natured hotel owner? But apparently she was not going to find out, as Carr gave her a nod and withdrew inside his establishment.

A moment later, Neva Cardoza-Levy appeared, hurrying out of the telegraph office just a few doors down the street. She had a basket over her arm that looked to be filled with cotton cloths and small rolls of lamb's wool.

"Glynis, am I glad to see you! Would you have a minute to do something for me? It's Margaret Taylor's day off—could you take this to her?" Neva pulled a telegram from a side pocket of her skirt. "Mr. Grimes in there—" her head bobbed toward the office "—saw me going past and asked if I'd give it to Margaret. But I've got to go right back to the refuge. A woman who came in last night has gone into labor."

"Certainly I'll do it, but where does Mrs. Taylor live?"

"Down that side street there," Neva answered, pointing it out. "She's on the top floor of the green house, number twenty-eight. And thank you, Glynis."

She rushed off, and Glynis, now bearing the telegram, turned down the street.

After she'd gone through the front door of number twenty-eight, Glynis picked up her skirts and climbed a steep flight of stairs to be met by a door at the landing. She knocked several times without response. Margaret Taylor must be out. Glynis crouched down in front of the door to slip the telegram underneath it. As she started to rise her skirt caught under the toe of her shoe and she stumbled forward against the door. It swung open. She nearly tumbled into the room, but caught herself just as a gasp and sudden movement by the window told her the room was occupied.

Regaining her balance, though not her composure, Glynis began to sputter an apology to the person at the window, but was interrupted by, "It's all right, Miss Tryon. I apparently neglected to lock the door."

Only the voice was familiar. Otherwise, Glynis thought in astonishment, she might never have guessed it was Margaret Taylor who stood there. The severe bun had been unpinned to loose a thick mane of brown hair that swung halfway down the woman's back. Gone were the heavy spectacles, and the deep-set eyes which now gazed at Glynis with mild annoyance were the color of summer sky.

"I'm so sorry, Mrs. Taylor. I fell against the door through sheer clumsiness." Glynis bent down to retrieve the telegram. When handing it to Margaret Taylor, she couldn't miss seeing the woman's anxious expression. "Neva Cardoza-Levy asked me to bring it to you," Glynis explained and took several steps backward toward the hall. The least she could do now was leave quickly and allow Margaret Taylor the privacy she so clearly desired when she had declined to open the door.

"I do hope it isn't bad news," Glynis offered as she went out to the landing. When she received no reply, she took a glance back into the room before she closed the door. Margaret Taylor was standing there reading the telegram, her anxious expression unchanged.

"No, I wouldn't say that, Miss Tryon," she responded, her head still bent over the piece of paper. "And thank you," she said, finally lifting her eyes, "for bringing it to me."

As Glynis turned to leave, the door behind her closed gently. Once outside the house, she made a quick scan of the second-floor windows and saw a curtain fall across the one that would have been Margaret's. Had the woman realized what Glynis had seen? Or, rather, not seen: the thick spectacles were no-where in evidence. Not even on the small table beside a chair where a newspaper lay spread, and Glynis now recalled hearing the rustle of paper as the door had flown open. Then, too, Margaret Taylor had obviously read the telegram without them. Just as she hadn't needed them, Glynis now recalled, to gaze over

the canal the night of the Women's Refuge benefit. But if she
didn't need spectacles, then why on earth wear such cumbersome things? Indeed, they and the bun that concealed the luxuriant hair altered Margaret Taylor's appearance dramatically.
Without them, she looked quite another woman.

Glynis kept herself from glancing back at the window as she
went down the street. Besides, there was certainly much there
that did not meet the eye. She'd have to think about it later,
though, as she now planned to see Morwenna Ryan. However,
when she reached Fall Street, she paused to reconsider. It would
take only a few minutes to stop at the telegraph office. Almost
everyone in town, including herself, had at some time or another complained about Mr. Grimes's penchant for gossip. Perhaps it could be put to good use.

She walked to the telegraph office and opened the door on
a small musty-smelling cubbyhole of a room.

"Miss Tryon, a good day to you!" Mr. Grimes, a spare man
whose outstanding feature was a nose resembling a parsnip,
gave Glynis quick scrutiny along with a facile smile.

"Mr. Grimes, I've just taken a telegram to Margaret Taylor—the one you gave to Dr. Cardoza-Levy?"

"Just came in for her."

"Yes, the one from—" Glynis made a quick guess based
on Mrs. Taylor's very slight southern drawl "—from Maryland."

Mr. Grimes took on the look of a school teacher who believed his student to be hopelessly dull. "No, Miss Tryon, it
was from *Washington!* Even had a government sender address."

"Ah, yes, of course, I should have recognized the sender's
name."

"Why, do you know him? Are you a close friend of Mrs.
Taylor's? If so, would you mind telling me if she's a widow?"

"I know Margaret well enough, and yes, Mr. Grimes, she is
a widow. That's why the telegram from Mr. . . . . Mr. . . . . ?

"Mr. Bevan," the operator said smoothly. "I imagine he's
a friend of hers—of Mrs. Taylor's, I mean."

Glynis merely nodded. Bevan. Bevan. The name meant nothing to her. But since she was receiving such cooperation, she

said evenly, "Mr. Grimes, I know you have a prodigious, indeed remarkable, memory—everyone in town has commented on it."

She waited momentarily while he basked in this. "But I wonder . . ." Glynis paused, then shook her head, "No, I'm sure it was too long ago for even *you* to remember the telegram, also sent from Washington, that Thomas Bingham picked up a day or two before his death?"

"Oh, I remember all right." Mr. Grimes seemed put out by her lack of faith, thus he said with unmistakable glee, "But it was Mr. Voss picked up that telegram."

Glynis shook her head. "No, I mean the telegram that *Mr. Bingham* received from Washington."

"I told you, Miss Tryon, Mr. Voss picked up that telegram—said he'd give it to Mr. Bingham. Made me wonder, afterwards it did, if the message meant bad news. Didn't seem to, I recall—it was just about Treasury agents. But it came the very morning that Mr. Bingham died."

Glynis closed her gaping mouth quickly. "Mr. Voss picked up the telegram that morning, on the day Mr. Bingham died? Are you sure of that, Mr. Grimes? Might there have been another wire?"

"Of course I'm sure!" His voice projected irritation. "And no! Before that one came, Mr. Bingham had received no other telegram for a week or more."

So Valerian Voss had lied about being in Utica that day. And if he'd lied about that, what else might he have made up?

WHEN SHE ARRIVED at the small brick house of Morwenna Cleary Ryan, Glynis found Fiona there as well. And what seemed to be a half-dozen small children underfoot. Morwenna managed to shoo them all outside while directing Glynis to the cluttered but immaculate kitchen. Morwenna's younger sister Fiona sat at one end of a table over a cup of what smelled like chamomile tea. Glynis saw instantly that the left side of Fiona's face had been very recently injured. It blazed a fiery red and her eye was swollen almost shut. In contrast, the older bruises on her other cheek were bluish green, and the stitches Neva had put in made Fiona's situation look even more heartbreaking. Glynis didn't know whether to try to shake some sense into the young woman or to join in her tears.

"Fiona, why on earth did you leave the refuge?" she asked.

"I had to," Fiona said, sobbing into her hands. "Kerry came to get me. He said he'd hurt the baby if I didn't come home. What could I do?"

What indeed? Glynis sank into a chair, experiencing an impotent rage. Morwenna reappeared with a small infant nursing at her breast and joined them at the table.

"I thought your youngest was almost a year now," Glynis said to her with surprise. Despite the unhappy atmosphere, she found herself smiling at the tiny fists clenched against Morwenna's swelling breast, the eyes shut fast in concentration.

"Oh, sure'n it's not my babe," Morwenna explained. "He's almost weaned now. But my milk was still flowing strong, so I took this wee girl of Fiona's. She can't nurse the babe—how could she?" Morwenna sent her sister a worried frown.

"Fiona," Glynis began tentatively, "everyone is concerned for you. For your safety and that of your little girl. How can we help you?"

Fiona moved her head slowly back and forth in what Glynis interpreted as a gesture of despair. Morwenna said quietly, "My Tom's threatened him, but it does no good. When Kerry's been at the drink there's no talking sense to him. He's like a man possessed."

Morwenna now put the baby over her shoulder and absently patted the tiny girl's back, while giving her sister another worried look. "Fiona, tell Miss Tryon when the worst of it started. When Kerry got himself mixed up with those other men."

"Other men?" Glynis repeated. "Who are they, Fiona?"

Fiona began to shake her head, but then groaned softly and answered Glynis. "I don't guess it makes any difference. He said he'll kill me if I tell, but he's near done it anyway."

She choked slightly, but she'd stopped sobbing. And when she turned her red eyes to Glynis, Fiona's face had taken on the cast of one inexorably doomed. And indeed she probably would be, Glynis thought with distress, if they didn't find the means to keep her husband away from her. Even jailing Kerry Roarke would prove futile, as it would be only temporary.

Judges did not find wife-beating to be a serious offense—in fact, most judges believed the woman probably deserved it, and thus it was a husband's right and obligation to discipline her—so Kerry would be released and, like others, return to further punish the wife who'd had him arrested.

Fiona drew a deep breath and said with a resigned voice, "It wasn't so bad before Kerry started keeping company with those rough men. They're out all night sometimes, and when he does come home he's tired and dirty, and he smells like gunpowder. And he's got money. I think they must be stealing things." Fiona shuddered as if saying this assured her further pain.

"You mean you think the money is stolen," Glynis prodded gently, "or that it's some kind of payment?"

Fiona again started to shake her head, but Morwenna put a hand on her sister's arm and said firmly, "Tell her, Fiona! Tell her what Kerry makes you do."

Glynis waited silently, afraid to say what might be the wrong thing and earn Fiona's distrust.

"Go on!" Morwenna urged her sister.

Fiona eyed Glynis with some wariness. Then, "He makes me take the money," she blurted at last, "and he drives us in the wagon to Auburn or Geneva, and he makes me buy things. I have to spend all the money. All of it. He won't let me save any. I don't know why." Her tears flowed again, and Glynis surmised that Fiona did at least suspect why.

"This money," Glynis said, "is it in coin?"

Fiona nodded.

"Have you ever looked at the coins closely?"

Again Fiona nodded, but now sucked in her breath, her fear painful to see.

"What do you think the reason is—the reason why your husband makes you spend the money, and spend it *out of town,* Fiona? No, please don't shake your head, because I think you've guessed, haven't you?"

"He'll kill me if I tell," Fiona sobbed.

"He'll kill you if you don't tell," Morwenna said sharply, bringing a whimper from the baby on her shoulder. Fiona didn't seem to notice, and didn't respond when Morwenna stood up, saying "I'll tuck the wee one away for a nap. Be right back."

As Morwenna left the kitchen, Glynis bent toward Fiona and covered the woman's hand with her own. "If you can bring yourself to tell me, Fiona, I think Constable Stuart will help you. Now, tell me—you think that coin is counterfeit, don't you?"

Fiona sobbed against her hand but brought forth a muffled "Yes. Yes, I think so, and I'm going to jail, aren't I? What will happen to my baby, and . . . ?"

"No, you won't go to jail, Fiona, not if you were forced into passing counterfeit money by your husband. But who are the men he's been with on these all-night forays?"

"I don't know them, and he wouldn't tell me. But I've seen him go to the livery a couple of times. And that peddler, what's his name?"

"Grandy Fox?" Glynis asked, catching her breath. "What about him?"

"He's been at the house a few times, even though we haven't bought anything from him. I thought it was strange."

Yes, very strange, Glynis agreed. Grandy Fox did seem to keep showing up under odd circumstances. It suddenly occurred to her that a peddler would be in a near-perfect position to circulate counterfeit money. He could travel all over western New York without anyone thinking it suspicious. But if Grandy *was* involved in the counterfeiting ring, did that mean the recent murders weren't related? The knife-wielding man on the train hadn't been Grandy Fox, and neither had the one who assaulted banker Barrymore in the Rochester public market. She'd seen both those men with her own eyes. On the other hand, she now remembered that the night Sally Lunt had been killed, the night of the refuge benefit, Grandy Fox had come late to the library grounds—the other musicians had been there some time before he arrived.

Fiona was still sobbing softly, and Glynis pressed the young woman's hand. "Constable Stuart's not in town right now, but you know I have to tell him about this when he comes back, don't you, Fiona?"

There was no response other than the sobs. Morwenna returned to the kitchen and stood looking with question at Glynis. "When *will* the constable be back?"

"I don't know. But after I leave here, I'll try sending a wire to the Albany and Utica constables' offices. Maybe they can track him down. But Morwenna, I'm sure you realize this is serious—what Fiona's been telling me. Why didn't you come forward with it yourself?"

"She didn't know," Fiona choked.

"No, I didn't," Morwenna said. "Not until this morning. And I knew Constable Stuart wasn't in town, so I couldn't figure out what to do. Liam's my brother and I love him most dearly, but he's too green to handle this. And I don't dare tell my Tom—he'll go after Kerry sure'n certain, and who knows what might happen. Fiona says that Kerry's got a store of guns out there at the house. Nobody keeps that many guns unless he intends to use them for something bad."

Fiona nodded. "He brings home guns all the time. I'm so scared he's going to use them to kill the baby and me."

"Can you stay here for now, Fiona?" Glynis asked. "That is, if you won't go to the Women's Refuge?"

"She's better off here," Morwenna said. "At least Tom and I can protect her. The other way, she puts everyone at the refuge in danger."

"But then *you're* in danger," Fiona protested. "That's why I went to the refuge to begin with."

"I'll tell you what," Glynis said, having racked her brain to come up with some solution, "why doesn't Liam stay here nights—just until Cullen Stuart gets back. Zeph Waters can handle the constable's office for the time being."

And that just might keep Zeph in town a while longer, too. Maybe John Brown would have given up any wild schemes by the time Zeph joined him.

JONATHAN HAD LONG since left the library, and when Glynis next looked up from her desk, she saw that daylight was fading. She'd not paid attention to the time, as there was no one at home expecting her for supper. She didn't feel particularly hungry, though she attributed that to the bread and sausage Morwenna had insisted she eat before leaving.

Glynis leaned her elbows on the desk and gazed at the dying light beyond the windows. The circumstances surrounding

Fiona Cleary Roarke were more than disturbing. It seemed likely, though by no means certain, that her husband Kerry was involved in the counterfeiting operation which had plagued western New York. And that Fiona had been an accomplice, albeit a reluctant one. Glynis felt confident, however, that when Cullen had the facts, he wouldn't hold the poor woman responsible for something in which she'd been compelled to participate. Notwithstanding that Glynis, through her correspondence with Mr. DuBois at the Philadelphia Mint, had learned to her surprise that women were sometimes *willing* accomplices and even, though less often, engaged in producing counterfeit money themselves. But this was clearly not the case with Fiona.

Kerry Roarke's increasing hoard of guns was alarming. It seemed possible, given Fiona's disclosures, that Roarke had taken part in the raids on western New York armories. It was difficult to picture the temperamental, hard-drinking Roarke as a ringleader in either counterfeiting or gun theft—but he must know who *was* in charge. He just might provide the key for which Cullen was searching.

On her way back to the library from Morwenna's, Glynis had stopped at the firehouse to tell Zeph what she'd learned about Fiona. Zeph had immediately sent Liam to his sister's, and then urged Glynis to send the wires to Albany and Utica in search of Cullen. At her suggestion he would go to Fleur Coddington to see if she knew how to reach Cullen—but it could still be several days before he was located. In the meantime, whoever was behind the counterfeiting might somehow hear of Fiona's confession. And the result of that could be more perilous, at least to Fiona, than the counterfeiting itself.

Or the perpetrator might leave town.

The more Glynis thought about it, the more credible it became that Grandy Fox was involved. Margaret Taylor must, for some unknown reason, also suspect him of something, as Glynis recalled the woman's cryptic comment about the peddler's wagon.

Another thing to consider, although how important it might be Glynis couldn't yet tell, had been Emma's report of the argument she'd overheard between Adam MacAlistair and

Cyril Doggett. Why would Sally Lunt have visited Doggett the day before she died? Just as curious was Doggett's refusal to relay this to Cullen. What could have been so serious, or incriminating, that Doggett persisted on maintaining his client's confidentiality, even when that client had been brutally murdered? Might Sally have told him she was pregnant, possibly by Alan Fitzhugh? And that Fitzhugh had thrown her over for a more desirable alliance? But why would Sally Lunt tell Cyril Doggett all of this? It didn't make sense. Unless Doggett himself was involved with her in some manner. Glynis decided she should talk to Jeremiah Merrycoyf, who surely knew the man better than did anyone else in town.

She got to her feet and hurried out of the library, thinking she might catch Merrycoyf before he left the law office. It was rapidly growing dark, however, and she began to have misgivings. Then, when she reached the office, no one answered her knock. She had turned and stepped back to Fall Street when she caught a sudden movement to her right. A man had appeared at the near side of the livery. It was too dark to be certain, but she thought, from his height and his rounded shoulders, that the man could be Cyril Doggett.

Glynis peered ahead into the gathering gloom. The man's behavior looked furtive as he slipped alongside the wooden structure, stopping often to glance back toward the street. Had it not been for such suspicious behavior, she might have paid no attention and just gone on home.

The man now disappeared down an alley that ran alongside the livery. Glynis found herself moving toward it at the same time a voice in her head urged her to stop immediately. Whoever it was did not wish to be seen. But all she wanted was to discover why Doggett was acting the way he was. Then she would leave.

She inched cautiously into the narrow alley between the adjacent store and the livery. A lantern inside the livery cast its dim light through a grimy window. That meant the owner John Boone was still on the premises and could be summoned if for some reason she should need him. Fortified by that thought, Glynis moved down the alley a bit farther. Now she could see to the end of it. She pulled back for a moment, then hugged the wall of the store, as she thought she heard faint noises coming from just behind the livery. There was a series of ringing *pings,* followed by a sharp *crack.*

What was he doing back there? And how could she see without disclosing herself? She certainly wasn't brave enough to proceed down the alley any farther. As she stood debating what to do, she spied ahead of her, at the rear corner of the building, a number of ash cans. She just might be able to conceal herself behind them. Guardedly, she moved forward to slip between the cans and the wall. As she squeezed behind them, one of the empty cans tipped and started to go over. She grabbed it just before it tilted beyond her reach, and held her breath while she righted it.

Had the man heard? She waited, counting to ten, then craned her neck to peer warily around the corner. Another lantern swung from a nail, its light feeble but enough for her to see Cyril Doggett—and Glynis was now practically certain it *was* Doggett—with his back to her while standing beside Grandy Fox's wagon. He abruptly took a few steps backward, then swung the side of the wagon up and out. Glynis could make out a broken padlock on the ground; the source of the sounds, she guessed.

She leaned forward, straining to see what the opened wagon had revealed, other than a multitude of bowls, when suddenly she felt something run across her shoe, followed by the faint but unmistakable—if one had heard it one never forgot it—angry clicking of a rat's teeth. She managed to muffle her gasp, but flinched and took a quick instinctive step backward. As she did, her skirt snagged on the rough wood of the store wall, forcing her off-balance. She stumbled forward against one of the ash cans. A brief metallic bang led to a sustained crash as the several cans she'd set in motion tipped over onto the alley's cobbles.

The side of the wagon fell back into place with a loud *whack.* Glynis dropped to the ground like a stone and a split second later the man sprang into the alley and hurtled past her, making for Fall Street. It happened so quickly she almost missed a close-up look at him. If it hadn't been for his emaciated frame, she couldn't have been positive that it was Cyril Doggett. But she was. And now he had vanished.

She remained in a crouched position, waiting for John Boone to come charging out of his livery. When it seemed that he wasn't going to appear, she rose and stepped to another window of the building. There was no one inside she could see, and it suddenly occurred to her that Boone might be elsewhere. She had not even considered that—had just assumed the livery owner was within hailing distance. A foolhardy assumption only a fool would make!

Glynis quickly skirted the fallen cans and started for Fall Street. Then it came to her that the padlock Doggett broke made the wagon accessible. As long as she was already there, and now obviously alone, she should take a look at what had been worthy of a forced entry. What danger could there be in a quick look?

Glynis turned back and swiftly rounded the corner of the livery to Grandy Fox's wagon. She had a glimmer of an idea as to what Doggett might have been after; it would take only a minute to see if she was right. Then she would leave. After checking the alley to be sure Doggett hadn't come back, Glynis lifted the hinged door. Then she swung it up and out as she'd seen both Doggett and Grandy do and propped it open with its wooden arm.

The lantern light was weak, but she could see the shelves with their scores of nested bowls. During the past minutes, she'd thought about those bowls, especially the ones which she remembered Grandy Fox telling her he wouldn't sell because he liked them. His possessiveness seemed a peculiar quality for a peddler whose wagon had only limited space—unless the bowls had a more utilitarian purpose. Such as doing what bowls did best: holding something.

She glanced around her—where *was* John Boone?—before she lifted two bowls from a shelf, dusting herself with wood chips and sawdust as she did so. She examined each as closely as she could in the meager light. Nothing about them seemed unusual. They were simply bowls. As she began to replace them, she accidently struck a large wooden bowl at the back of the shelf; Glynis was certain she heard a sharp clinking.

She stepped back, suddenly aware of an increase in light. For a moment her heart stopped, then she looked up to see a half-moon just appearing over the roof of the adjacent store. She quickly looked around again. It remained eerily quiet.

She turned back to the wagon and stretched both arms toward the wooden bowl—it had to be two feet across—but as she started to lift it down, its weight proved more than she'd expected; even a dense wood like black locust couldn't account for it. She very nearly dropped the bowl on the cobblestones, but somehow managed to hold it against herself, then kneeled under it while she slid it off her lap onto the ground. Nested inside it was a just slightly smaller wooden bowl.

However, when she tried to lift the smaller one out, it refused to budge. Almost as if it was fastened somehow to its larger cousin. Kneeling beside it, Glynis grasped the rim of the smaller bowl and tugged at it. All at once the rim moved sideways. She peered at it for a moment, then wiggled it again. And now it moved counterclockwise with a soft scraping sound. She kept turning the smaller bowl inside the larger one, much as if she were unscrewing a lid from a canning jar.

Suddenly, from behind her, Glynis heard a thud. She jumped to her feet and whirled around, but could see nothing. Then another sound just like the first reached her, and she strained toward the livery, her anxiety lessening some when she realized it was simply a horse kicking the side of its stall. But she should hurry.

A few more turns and the small bowl wobbled in her hands. She pulled the rim upward and it came free of the larger bowl. Placing it on the ground beside her, she caught the flash of metal and looked down into the hollow that was now revealed in the large bowl. Before her lay a hoard of shiny gold coins. She picked one up and turned it to the moonlight; it was a twenty-dollar piece—a double eagle. The other coins all appeared to be eagles, both singles and doubles. It was impossible to determine exactly how many were there, but it had to be a substantial cache. And if there were more bowls designed the same way, possibly each with a like amount of coins, Grandy Fox had himself a small fortune in the wagon.

However, Glynis would wager that the coins were most

likely not genuine, as the double eagle in her hand didn't feel heavy enough to be real gold. What an inspired hiding place for counterfeit!

As Glynis glanced up at the wagon shelves with their scores of bowls, she told herself not to be greedy—she had found enough, and needed to get out of there. When she began to replace the small bowl, she hesitated for only a moment before she took one of the double eagles and thrust it deep into a skirt pocket. She would need some evidence. Then, glancing around, she rescrewed the smaller bowl into its nest, and lifted the heavy receptacle to place it back on the shelf. Suddenly, she heard male voices coming from inside the livery.

She didn't dare stop to think. With strength born of desperation, she heaved the bowl, with an accompanying jangle of coins, onto the shelf and grabbed the others to place in front of it. There was no time to worry about whatever dirt from the ground might be going with them, or in what order they might have originally been stored. She had to get them back on the shelf, close the overhead door, and get away. And the voices were becoming more distinct. One of them she could now recognize as John Boone's. The other could easily be that of Grandy Fox.

Her hands shook so severely that the pottery bowls nearly slipped from her fingers. She had just put the propping arm back in place and brought the wagon side down over the shelves when she heard a door open at the far side of the livery. They would be there in seconds.

There was no excuse for her presence that Grandy Fox would find credible. Even if Boone could protect her at that moment, she would be in danger from then on. Grandy Fox, or someone else involved in the counterfeiting, would come after her. Too many had already died for her to doubt that.

Glynis could think of only one feasible way to save herself.

She scooped up the broken padlock, then hoisted her skirts to her knees and ran into the alley and over the cobblestones as fast as she could manage. She counted on the wagon looking as usual to Grandy, if it *was* him, until he came to notice that the padlock was missing. But he would have seen this instantly if she'd left it there on the ground.

Her heart slamming against her rib cage, she didn't slow until she reached Fall Street. Then, her breath coming in gasps, she crept forward, hugging the storefronts and slipping in and out of doorways, while a stitch developing in her side threatened to double her over. And soon, in order to reach home, she must cross Fall to Cayuga Street—without being seen.

When the pain in her side became intolerable, she stopped, crouching in a doorway in the moon shadow of a shop awning. Even now, Glynis could scarcely credit what she'd found in the wagon. It was difficult to accept that the charming Grandy Fox was a criminal. And she could hardly believe him a murderer. The more she thought about it, the more unlikely this seemed, as she had witnessed two other men in pursuit of the banker Barrymore. No; Grandy Fox might well be involved in counterfeiting, if, as she guessed, the coin in her pocket proved bogus, but that didn't prove he was a killer.

The pain had subsided, and she looked across Fall Street toward Cayuga, then took a small, cautious step out from under the awning. Fall Street appeared deserted. She had gone several yards to the street corner, when the sound of male voices coming from the direction of the livery made her duck back into another doorway. But now at the corner, she was even more exposed. How long could she stay there without being discovered?

A sudden sound behind her made her start violently. She whirled around, fully expecting to meet a killer. What she met were the velvet eyes of a distinctively marked, black-and-white paint horse.

For a long moment she thought she must be imagining it. But the wet mouth of the horse nuzzling her shoulder was real enough. As was the familiar voice of its laconic rider that said, "Kind of late to be out. You in trouble again?"

"Jacques!"

Jacques Sundown sat there on the paint horse, calmly looking down as if he'd last seen her only a few hours before. While at that distance she couldn't gauge his eyes, his voice didn't reveal the least surprise at finding her cowering in a doorway. The strong features held their usual lack of expression. The smooth skin, gleaming in the moonlight like the frosty surface of a newly minted copper coin, caused Glynis to wonder why it was that nothing about Jacques ever seemed to change. Not after all the time that had passed since she'd last seen him.

"You nearly scared me to death, Jacques. What are you doing here?" This certainly wasn't the first thing she'd planned to say to him when he returned to Seneca Falls.

"Looks like I'm watching you being scared. What's going on?"

"You mean you don't know?" The question just tumbled out. Because she'd naturally assumed that he did know; he had always seemed to—where she was, what she was doing. That was absurd now, of course, but it had so often appeared to be the case in the past.

"Well, then you guessed right," she said limply, "I'm in trouble again."

"Somebody chasing you." A statement, not a question.

Glynis leaned out of the doorway and peered down the street. It was empty. "Not at the moment, I guess," she replied, hearing relief in her voice. "It seems, Jacques, that you don't have to rescue me this time. I apparently did a pretty fair job of taking care of myself."

She thought she saw the trace of a smile cross his face. He smiled so rarely she couldn't be sure.

"Looks like you did. Figured you'd learn how." He dismounted with the easy fluid motion she remembered—like a cat he moved—and stood for a moment, listening. "Somebody down there by the livery," he said finally. "That where you came from?"

She nodded. "But I don't want to talk about it now. I'd very much like to get out of here. Without being seen."

"Go to the other side of the horse."

She saw what he intended, and slipped around the paint. Jacques began walking, reins in his hand, the horse plodding between them while Glynis walked at the paint's far side, concealed from anyone at the livery who might be watching.

Without speaking they went across Fall Street and some distance down Cayuga before Jacques paused, looked back, then let the horse trail behind them. Now that they walked side by side, the only thing she could find different about him was that his glossy black hair was longer than she remembered, almost to his shoulders. She recalled her niece Katy, Emma's cousin in Rochester, once saying that Jacques Sundown was "the most beautiful man" she'd ever seen. This must be a matter of taste, however, because Glynis thought Jacques a little too dangerous-looking to be "beautiful"; there was about him something of the red-tailed hawk. In fact, before their estrangement, Cullen used to call him "Dagwunnoyaent," an Iroquois wind spirit.

Jacques now said to her, "The walking stick I made—did you get it?"

"Yes, of course I did. And I knew what you meant by the message that went with it. Thank you, Jacques. It's beautiful work and I treasure it."

"So why don't you have it tonight?"

"Because I never expected to find myself in a dangerous situation. But you're right—I should keep it with me."

When they reached the Peartree house, Jacques tethered the paint to the front post and followed her halfway up the walk. There he stopped, and said, "No."

Glynis stood stunned for a moment, then realized what he meant. No, Jacques wouldn't go into the house. He never had. She'd seldom seen him at ease in an enclosed place, other than his own cabin at the edge of Black Brook Reservation. She gestured toward the back yard. "No one else is here," she told him as they rounded the house, "but I understand."

Jacques Sundown straddled two worlds—that of his white father and that of his Seneca Indian mother—but he belonged to neither. Glynis still found it surprising that he'd drawn as close to her as he had. And she to him. It was some strange alchemy that she had given up trying to understand; she didn't think Jacques understood it either. Over time, it had simply happened.

She seated herself on a stone bench under a birch clump, conscious of the sound of crickets and katydids, and the smell of late summer roses and herbs in Harriet's garden. Jacques stood with his back against the white birch bark, and looked for a time at the sky. A few clouds trailed like long silk scarves over the face of the moon.

"When did you get back?" she asked him.

"Yesterday. Not staying long."

"But you just got here," Glynis protested, swallowing hard against the sudden lump rising in her throat. She waited for him to say more. He looked down at her, the flat brown eyes warming to liquid gold, and she wanted to pull him into the house and into her bed—and knew she couldn't do that. In the past, she'd gone over in her mind the reasons why a thousand times, and they hadn't changed. Much as she might wish they had.

This must have shown on her face. Jacques shifted his eyes and said, "Came by to tell you—I'm heading west. Oregon's a state now, so the military needs scouts. The pay's good." His eyes moved back to her face, and he seemed to be studying her closely when he added, "Expect it's no place for a woman, though."

No, she didn't suppose it was. If Jacques had wanted her to argue this, she couldn't, because while Oregon had been admitted to the Union earlier in the year, by all accounts it was still wild dangerous country. If what Jacques meant to imply was that a western trek was no place for *her,* he was right again. She was not an adventurer, had no need to explore new worlds. The world she knew was challenge enough.

"How long do you expect to be gone?" The question was out of her mouth before she realized she didn't want an answer—didn't want to hear that he wasn't coming back.

"Don't know. There's trouble with the Indian tribes out there—you know how Indians are."

"Yes, they resent having their land taken," Glynis said quietly. "I can't imagine why."

This time she caught the smile that flickered across his face. It had disappeared by the time he said, "How's the constable?"

"Cullen's fine, I guess. He . . . he's involved with someone. I don't suppose you knew Fleur Coddington, but Cullen has been seeing her."

"No."

"No? I assure you he has been, Jacques."

"No. He's not involved with her."

"And how do you know that?"

"I know, that's all. Cullen Stuart's never wanted any woman

but you. Trouble is, you still don't know what you want.''

Trouble was, she did know. She wanted things the way they once were—before Cullen had brought up the subject of marriage, and before Jacques had drawn her to him. She didn't want to be forced to choose, not only between Cullen and Jacques, but between marriage and the freedom she could have only if she remained single. And she would not, *could* not, live openly with a man without marriage, as did George Sand. Seneca Falls was not Paris. For though Paris might display some disapproval, Seneca Falls would simply not stand for it.

Not only would she lose her position at the library by becoming the object of scandal, but there was, as well, another factor: the possibility of conceiving a child. In this respect, Glynis felt her body had betrayed her. She was forty-one years old, past the point of fertility for many women. Still, every month she was reminded that she had not yet been released from the threat of pregnancy.

So yes, she did know what she wanted. To be someone else, someone who could cast caution and consequence aside. But she was who she was. Caught in a woman's body, in a woman's rigidly defined place, with a vivid appreciation of what would be the result if she scorned the standards assigned her by her community.

The irony there, of which she was well aware, arose from her belief that standards were, for the most part, necessary to a community.

She became conscious of a sprinkle of wet drops on her upturned face. Dark clouds began gliding over the moon, and now the air had the heavy warm feel of impending rain. Jacques, still standing against the birch, looked steadily at her and now, holding his eyes, she felt the tension streak between them like lightning charges in a summer storm.

She said at last, with a candor that was new to her, ''I wish things were different for us, Jacques. That I were different. Perhaps someday they, and I, will be. Do you think that's possible?''

''Maybe.''

Glynis rose from the bench. ''When are you planning to leave?''

"Tomorrow."

"So soon?"

He took several strides toward her until he was within arm's reach. "You get things straightened out with Stuart. One way or the other."

"Why are you saying that to me?"

"You think he's involved with somebody else, then there has to be a reason. But it doesn't have anything to do with you and him."

Glynis felt confusion, and a kind of dread, sweep over her. "Even if that's true—and I'm not saying it is—I don't understand why you . . . unless . . . Jacques, are you telling me that you're not coming back here?"

She fought the anxiety that had brought the question. After all, why *should* he come back? He knew, they both knew, that if she ever were to make a choice, Cullen was clearly the appropriate one. *Appropriate*. How very telling. But it had been her feelings for Cullen that had kept her from this man once before.

"Jacques, please come back. I know I have no right to ask that, but I just can't imagine never seeing you again." And now that she had said this, he could do with it as he liked. Walk away for all time, or tell her he would come back.

He said nothing. Her eyes welled, despite her every effort, and, scarcely aware of what she did, she brushed at them furiously. Silent, Jacques stepped forward and took her hands in his. He gripped them against his chest, then pressed them hard against his mouth before he lifted her arms and placed them around his neck. And pulled her to him, still saying nothing but waiting, she knew, for her to make a decision. And even as she raised her face, even as his mouth came down on hers, it was for the moment only.

She could promise nothing beyond it.

EIGHTEEN

*The season requires that special attention should be given to
out-doors costumes. From among many novelties adapted for
the carriage or promenade, we select one. The PARDESSUS
is composed of black taffeta and lace, trimmed with rich pas-
samenterie and tassels. Another novelty is composed of
applique lace, with two lace flounces. . . .*

——THE MAY 1859 ISSUE OF
HARPER'S NEW MONTHLY MAGAZINE

EMMA CLAMPED HER teeth together so as not to scream. The
train porters were tossing the large boxes containing her fabrics
from Rochester onto the Seneca Falls station platform as if they
were so much rubbish. It had taken her three whole days to
choose just the right things, and now to watch them treated
with such contempt. . . . What if the boxes had contained fine
crystal? She reminded herself they did not, and that a few
bumps wouldn't hurt the rich velvet and taffeta and silk and
buttery-soft challis wool. It had taken an anxious week to arrive.

She had not purchased in Rochester any of the lace currently
so popular. Nothing could match the work of Lacey Smith, who
lived right here in Seneca Falls. Emma had spent hours with
Lacey the day before to determine how many yards of her lace
trim would be needed for Vanessa Usher's new wardrobe—in
addition to the orders Emma had received to fashion costumes
for the masquerade ball.

The porters now announced that everything had been unloaded, and Emma hurried to count the boxes before they were
stacked onto the baggage wagon. Just a few minutes more,
conveying them to Fleur Coddington's shop, and Emma could
finally get to work! At least while she'd been waiting for the
fabric to come she had been able to take Miss Usher's mea-

surements, and to make the muslin patterns. With her glorious new sewing machine!

The machine had been delivered in an enormous crate to Mrs. Peartree's house, arriving just after Emma's return from Rochester. The card inside had read: *"For Miss Emma Tryon, with the sincere compliments of Mr. Isaac Singer."* The letter she and Adam MacAlistair composed had worked magic.

She'd been assured by Mr. MacAlistair that she owed the Singer Company no money; that, in fact, the Singer Company wanted to pay *her* for her "splendid endorsement" of its machines. And now she had two of them. But that wasn't all. The Singer Company had retained Adam MacAlistair to be its western New York counsel—apparently impressed, he had told her, by his avoidance of a lawsuit and the accompanying bad publicity. They had both, she and Mr. MacAlistair, been so deliriously giddy with this turn of events that he'd picked her up and whirled her around his office. This had ended abruptly when Mr. Merrycoyf opened the office door just as Adam was giving her a friendly embrace—although, if truth be told, it had been somewhat more than friendly. She thought she would never forget the look on Mr. Merrycoyf's face. Even now she blushed to think of it. But she smiled, too. Even now.

The driver she'd hired had just started off for La Maison de Fleur with the baggage wagon. Emma walked behind, watching her precious cargo jounce down Fall Street. She could see in the rear of the wagon one box labeled VELVET, and prayed it still contained the lush gold-colored fabric for Aunt Glynis's George Sand trousers and long, fitted coat—or, rather, *pelisse,* Emma corrected herself. She must remember to use the French words, as they seemed to impress her customers.

When the wagon reached the dress shop, Emma told the driver he could unload the fabrics from the back alley. She went on through the Fall Street entrance to unlock the rear door. Fleur Coddington wasn't there, but after going through the shop to the sewing room, Emma did find Lacey Smith.

The woman sat bent over a pillow, on which lay a square of ivory lace she was making, her spectacles perched halfway down her nose. She didn't look up at Emma's greeting, but nodded, then mumbled something unintelligible through the

pins she had between her lips. By the time the driver had unloaded all the boxes, restacking them in the back room, Lacey
had finished her square.

"Child, what you goin' to do with all that stuff?" Lacey
asked, gesturing at the boxes. "You got enough cloth there to
dress everybody in this here town twice."

Her round-cheeked ebony face glistened with perspiration.
She ran a handkerchief over her forehead, then picked up a
long section of the delicate lace. "This here's for your Aunt
Glynis. You wanted it for a blouse you making, that right?"

Emma reached out and carefully took the cobweb of lace.
"It's lovely, Mrs. Smith. And yes, I'll use it on her costume
for the masquerade ball."

Lacey nodded with a slight frown. "You still tellin' me that
lady is goin' to a ball dressed as a *man?*"

Emma smiled. "Well, she's going as a woman who dresses
like a man."

Lacey gave Emma a narrow-eyed look. Then she threw back
her head and laughed. "Your aunt won't fool nobody, mask or
not—she's too good-lookin' to be a man!" Her laugh rang as
brightly as brass chimes swung by the wind. "Well, I got to
be off now, child, to make supper. Isaiah's been working all
day, and he got a baseball game tonight. He's goin' to be hungry."

Lacey had worked all day, too. Emma didn't suppose Isaiah
Smith ever made supper for his wife, however.

"You best remember to lock up tight after me," Lacey called
as she went through the shop. "Town's not safe these days—
not with a murderer runnin' loose and all."

Emma didn't think Lacey needed to worry. Who in the world
was going to commit murder in a dress shop? But she locked
the front door before she went back to her boxes of fabric.
There were so many of them. She glanced around to see if any
shelf space was empty. Since there wasn't, she went to the
wardrobe closet to see what might be available.

At first glance, the wardrobe seemed to be crowded with
dresses and cloaks. But that was odd, because there weren't all
that many hangers. When Emma started to push the garments
to one side, she met some resistance: their hems were not fall-

ing free but seemed to be catching against one another. What kind of fabrics had Fleur Coddington used that would be so bulky? Emma peered into the closet. They were not winter gowns of velvet or corduroy, but lightweight summer dresses of lawn and gingham and muslin.

As Emma tugged at the hangers, several dresses slipped to the wardrobe floor. She noticed that from the different hangers were dangling tags that said "Rochester" and "Lockport" and "Buffalo"; Mrs. Coddington's business must have suddenly mushroomed.

Emma reached down to retrieve a blue embroidered-lawn evening dress. When she withdrew it from the wardrobe to place it back on the hanger, the deep flounces of the skirt caught her eye. They *were* bulky, almost stiff. But how could a layer of feather-weight lawn and sheer lining create that thickness— some new kind of interfacing, perhaps? In which case, Emma told herself, *she* certainly wouldn't use it. Curious, she held the dress up to the light coming in the window. The flounces, even lined, should have been almost transparent, or at least translucent. They were not.

She reached into the wardrobe and lifted out a short white cashmere cloak. Even with its pink silk lining it should have weighed very little. But again Emma had the impression of bulk. Not only that, the cloak did not fall gracefully from the hanger but hung in heavy accordion-like folds. Next she pulled from the wardrobe a cage crinoline petticoat, its hoops in multiple tiers made with watch-spring steel; each casing section holding one of the hoops was made from lightweight, honeycomb-woven Welsh cloth. And now Emma noticed something else.

The petticoat casings, ordinarily designed like slim envelopes to hold the hoops, were much wider than necessary and seemed to contain more than just a circle of watch-spring steel. And it was not sheer lining fabric either, but something stiffer, something that slightly crackled when Emma handled it. She grabbed the tiny sharp-pointed scissors that Lacey had used for her lace, knelt on the floor, and turned out the underside of the crinoline's hem. Now she could see some unaccountable faint print showing through the Welsh cloth. Trying to ignore her misgivings, she very carefully opened with the scissors a side seam of the bottom casing. And sucked in her breath.

Emma couldn't keep her hands from shaking as she withdrew the dozens of banknotes that had been sewn inside. Each was redeemable for one hundred dollars in coin. With growing dread, she counted the hoop casings of the one petticoat: ten of them. So in this dress alone there could be notes worth thousands of dollars. And inside the other bulky garments?

But why on earth would anyone hide banknotes this way? Whatever for? Unless . . . maybe they weren't genuine. What if they were counterfeit, like the ones Constable Stuart and Aunt Glynis had been talking about over the past weeks?

At a sudden sound outside in the alley, Emma sprang to her feet. Had she locked the back door? No, she'd forgotten! She flew over to it and thrust home the bolt, then flattened herself against the adjacent wall, panting in terror. Again came the sound, a metallic scraping. Emma willed herself to inch toward the window. Peeking around the drapery, she saw several dogs rooting in the ash cans. At the same moment, Emma had a sudden and horrifying vision of Sally Lunt discovering in the dresses the same thing that she herself had just found.

And a faceless killer who had then found Sally. Had it been here in the dress shop? Aunt Glynis said Sally's body had apparently been moved to the canal towpath.

Who could have done such a thing? Surely not Mrs. Coddington. Emma just couldn't believe that. But how could those dresses be full of money without Mrs. Coddington knowing?

Emma glanced down at her hands, which continued to tremble. What should she do? What would Aunt Glynis do in this situation? She or any other sane person would get out of the shop! But Emma couldn't get her feet to move. She knew she had to stop thinking about the money—and a killer—because she wasn't going to stay there and let herself get strangled like Sally Lunt.

Emma made herself step forward. After cautiously checking that the draperies were completely closed, she returned to the petticoat lying on the floor where she had dropped it. When she reached for a spool of thread, her hands were shaking so hard she dropped the spool twice, and it took forever to thread the needle. But she had to sew the money back in the petticoat casing so no one would notice anything amiss.

She somehow managed to reline the casing with the banknotes and stitched the seam—in between going back and forth to the window to check the back alley. Then she hurriedly hung the petticoat back on a hanger and replaced the other garments that had slipped off. From the bulk and weight of them, she realized they must all be stuffed with notes. How could Fleur Coddington not know? She must.

As Emma closed the wardrobe cabinet it suddenly occurred to her. Maybe Mrs. Coddington was being made to do this. Someone could be forcing her to transport counterfeit money out of Seneca Falls in the garments. But even so, she would still be guilty of some crime, wouldn't she?

After a last glance around to make certain everything looked as it had—except for her stack of fabric boxes—Emma crept forward through the shop to the front entrance. She was not going out by way of the alley! She warily peered around the draperies of the large window facing the street, then waited while a group of shoppers passed and several carriages rolled by. Finally, when she could see no one coming down Fall Street, she dashed out the front door. After fumbling to lock it, she ran down the steps and set off for Cayuga Street as fast as she dared without looking conspicuous.

She didn't know what she was going to do. If she told Aunt Glynis, then *she* would tell Constable Stuart. He'd probably arrest Mrs. Coddington. And then La Maison de Fleur would close down, and that would be the end of Emma's dressmaking venture. Put out of business before she even got started. But if she waited and said nothing, just for a short time, maybe Constable Stuart would catch the counterfeiters. Then no one would have to know about the banknotes.

In her preoccupation, Emma had nearly reached the front walk of the Peartree house before she noticed the black Morgan horse tethered to the hitching post.

GLYNIS SAT AT the kitchen table and gripped a coffee mug, determined not to show her impatience. Cullen was demonstrating the action of a new revolver that he'd acquired at the Remington Armory in Ilion, and his enthusiasm brooked no interruption.

"They've just come out with it this year, Glynis. Amazing, isn't it?"

"Amazing."

Cullen gave her lackluster response a knowing smile. "You just don't appreciate how revolutionary this double-action mechanism is. Now watch carefully."

"Cullen, you've already shown me that twice."

"But you don't seem to understand the implications. How *fast* this is. Watch!"

And once again he demonstrated the weapon, designed in such a way that when the trigger was pulled it turned the cylinder, cocked the hammer, and fired the gun in a single movement. "Revolutionary," he said again. "They haven't produced enough of them yet to offer for sale, but Eliphalet Remington wanted me to try out this one. Think of it, Glynis— the first ever double-action revolver!"

Glynis nodded with something less than the veneration she knew Cullen expected, while asking herself, not for the first time, why men found guns so endlessly fascinating. Even Cullen, ordinarily the most sensible of persons, behaved like a child with a new toy—yet he complained constantly about the increasing number of firearms owned by the general public.

"Cullen!" she said now, rather more emphatically than she'd intended. "We need to talk about something that's important."

He looked at her closely, then said with some irritation, "Glynis, all you had to do was say so. I didn't realize I was boring you."

"I'm sorry if I was rude—I'm upset about what I discovered while you were gone."

He immediately became serious. " 'Discovered'? I thought you promised me that you wouldn't go poking into things."

"No, actually, I didn't promise. I guess you just assumed, because you'd ordered me not to, that I wouldn't."

"I don't recall *ordering* you to do anything. I *asked,* that's all. I asked because I was worried about you. And it appears I had reason to worry. But why are we arguing about this, anyway?"

She had been wondering the same thing. It was no doubt her fault, as she'd been edgy now for days, and perhaps Cullen would understand when she explained. Although she couldn't explain away Jacques Sundown. If Cullen asked her outright she wouldn't lie about it, but there was a good chance he didn't even know Jacques had been back, however briefly.

"Cullen, please, I don't want any unpleasantness between us. I'm just very concerned about a number of things. Now may I tell you about them?"

He nodded. She started with Sally Lunt's probable connection with Alan Fitzhugh, Valerian Voss's lie about Utica, and ended with what Emma had told her about the overheard conversation between Adam MacAlistair and Cyril Doggett.

"Interesting," Cullen said, "especially since there was a message at my office saying that Adam MacAlistair wants to see me. Must be about the girl visiting Doggett the day before she died. And I knew that Voss didn't go to any banks in Utica, because I checked. That he didn't go to Utica at *all* is even more interesting."

"Cullen, there's something else a great deal more interesting than that."

She paused as his eyes moved past her to the hall beyond the kitchen. Glynis had barely registered the sound of the front door opening and closing, but now she turned in her chair. Emma had appeared in the kitchen doorway.

"I'm back," she said, hovering there as if only momentarily pausing in flight to somewhere else. "Good afternoon, Constable Stuart." She took several quick steps backward. "Well . . . that is . . . I hope you'll excuse me. I'm going upstairs now."

"Emma," Glynis asked, "did your fabrics arrive safely?"

"Oh, yes! Yes, just fine . . . they arrived, that is."

Glynis studied her niece with some concern. "Emma, are you feeling all right? You look rather pale." And sounded more than a little rattled, Glynis thought.

"I'm fine. Just fine. Well, perhaps a trifle tired. Unloading all those boxes, you know. I thought I'd just go up and rest a bit." Emma whirled toward the stairs.

"Would you please wait a minute?" Glynis asked, frowning slightly. "I've just told Constable Stuart about what you overheard at the law office regarding Sally Lunt. Perhaps you'd like to add something?''

"Oh, I'm sure you did a better job of telling him than I could, Aunt Glynis. But I really am tired, so if you don't mind . . .''

Her voice trailing off behind her, Emma made quickly for the stairs.

Glynis looked at Cullen and saw that he, too, was frowning. "What was that all about?" he said. "Your niece acted like she couldn't get away from me fast enough. Is she still upset that I questioned her so closely the night Sally Lunt was killed?''

"I don't know, Cullen. But I agree that Emma acted peculiarly.''

"So tell me what you'd started to say. What's so interesting?''

His face became grim as she talked, and when she got to the part about Fiona and Kerry Roarke's participation in passing counterfeit money, plus Roarke's probable involvement with the militia armory break-ins, Cullen swore softly. "And I didn't believe Roarke.''

"Didn't believe what?''

"Glynis, Kerry Roarke came to my office the night before I left town. He appeared to be so drunk I discounted what he said.''

"Which was what?''

"That he knew who killed the watchman and treasury agent Paul Trent the night of the armory break-in. That he, Roarke, thought he was going to be framed for it, but that he didn't do it. He was drunk, so naturally I didn't believe him. You know what drunks are like—they'll say anything. But Glynis, when you found out about Roarke from his wife, why didn't you or Zeph get in touch with me?''

"How? Maybe you can tell me, Cullen, because I certainly tried. I even had Zeph go to Fleur Coddington and ask her—'' Her voice broke off, and she felt a flush creep over her face.

"Now listen to me.'' Cullen's voice had lost its irritation and he now sounded almost as upset as she did. "There's something I need to tell you about that,'' he went on, "but I can't do it yet. You'll just have to accept that . . . that I may do things for reasons that aren't always clear to someone looking on.''

''Is that what I'm doing—simply *looking on?*''

''No. No, of course not. I didn't mean that. But I can't explain any more right now.''

She didn't much like it. Secrets kept from each other had not been part of their bond in the past. Nonetheless, she had no intention of acquainting him with Jacques's visit, so she could hardly complain about Cullen's lack of candor.

''I haven't yet told you the most important thing, Cullen.''

While she related the discovery of concealed coins in Grandy's wagon, Cullen's face grew darker with each word. ''That bastard!'' he finally exploded. ''So he *is* the one. And he probably killed both Treasury Agents Trent and Fairfax, and maybe even the bankers as well, although I imagine there's going to be a hell of a time proving it.''

''Cullen, I don't know about the agents, or even Thomas Bingham, but Grandy Fox couldn't have killed Barrymore. I was there, remember?''

''But you said yourself that you didn't see Barrymore actually die. And Fox might have been somewhere on that train without you spotting him. It's possible, isn't it?''

''Yes, it's certainly possible—especially since he was in Rochester at the public market that day. But even so, who were those other two men that I *did* see attack Barrymore?''

Cullen started to shrug, then said, ''They were probably accomplices. Fox couldn't have engineered the counterfeiting operation all by himself. There had to have been others; for instance, passers—like the Roarkes—and an engraver who did the banknotes. That reminds me, Glynis. I found out in Utica and Albany that we've been on the right track as far as those notes are concerned. A series of plates from the Bank of Central New York had been turned into the state banking department for destruction a few weeks before Barrymore's death. When bogus bills from those series surfaced at banks here in western New York, Barrymore got word of them. His associates at the bank indicated that he'd been very concerned before he left Utica. And the reason he left was to try and track down some information about those notes.''

"It appears as if he found something," Glynis said, sighing deeply. "As we already suspected, it's probably why he was killed."

"Probably," Cullen agreed. "I've relayed this to the Treasury Department in Washington, but I haven't heard back from them yet. They did confirm, though, that there have been several known counterfeiters released from jail recently. Or, in the most significant instance, an engraver who escaped from— guess where—Auburn Prison some months ago. Name's William Brockway, and because of the proximity I'd say he's a likely suspect in this operation."

"None of which has anything to do with Sally Lunt, though, does it?"

"No, doesn't seem to. But all the murders occurring in a given area don't have to be connected, Glynis. In fact, most of the time they aren't."

"No, I suppose not. So, what are you going to do now?"

"Take a look at Fox's wagon. If he hasn't passed those coins on yet, we'll have him red-handed."

"That reminds me—I have one of the coins, Cullen, a double eagle. I took it with me that night. There was always the possibility that they weren't counterfeit after all. . . ."

She stopped as Cullen was regarding her with a look of some surprise. "You *took* one? As in *stole* it?"

"Well, yes . . . that is, I sort of borrowed it . . . for evidence. And, instead of looking at me as though I were a habitual criminal, Cullen, aren't you more concerned with whether the coin is counterfeit?"

"Well, is it?"

"Yes. Mr. Williams the jeweler confirmed it for me. It's gold-washed lead. And whoever poured the lead—most likely into a sand mold, according to my expert Mr. DuBois—was careless while the lead was cooling, and the print on the coin is blurred. Not a very good job."

"Maybe a hurried job," Cullen added. "In which case we need to worry that they suspect we're onto them. So," he said, pushing away from the table, "I think I'd better go pay Mr. Fox a visit."

"Can't he refuse to let you look in the wagon?" Glynis asked.

"He can try," he said grimly, picking up the new revolver that had been on the table all this while.

"Please be careful, Cullen. If Grandy Fox has really killed all those men, he won't think twice about—" She left off, as Cullen was giving her an odd look.

But "I'll be careful," was all he said. Then, as he was going out the kitchen door, he paused on the threshold and turned back to her. "I heard Jacques Sundown hit town while I was gone."

Stunned by the suddenness of it, Glynis just sat there, assuming he would next ask if she'd seen Jacques. And knowing she couldn't lie to him.

"I also heard," Cullen said, smiling faintly, "that he left again the next day." He stepped out onto the back porch and said over his shoulder, "I'll let you know what happens with Fox." He closed the door firmly behind him.

THE NEXT MORNING Cullen strode into the library to tell her he hadn't found either Grandy Fox or the wagon. "It's possible he could have got wind I was on to him and took off permanently," he said, standing in front of her desk, "but John Boone at the livery said Fox left two days ago and was supposed to be back in a day or two. And I've wired the Treasury Department to see if they have anything on him."

Jonathan, seated at his desk across the room, seemed to be straining to hear the conversation, so Glynis lowered her voice when she asked, "Does that mean we just have to wait?" This did not seem to be an adequate response if Grandy Fox was indeed a killer. Who might he target in the meantime?

"No, I've already alerted the U.S. Marshal's offices in Syracuse and Buffalo to watch for him. And if Fox doesn't show up here in town today, we'll start after him. Although it appears I'm about to be short one deputy."

"Zeph has told you, then."

"He told me. He's hell-bent to go tilting at windmills with John Brown! How that lunatic expects to right the wrongs of slavery with a bunch of youngsters like Zeph and his cousin is beyond me. I hoped you'd be able to talk the boy out of it, Glynis.''

''I tried, but as you've reminded me several times, Zeph is no longer a boy. He's convinced Brown's the only one willing to fight slavery with other than words. And since words have been spectacularly unsuccessful, you and I can't fault Zeph for that.''

''Except that Brown's crazy. He's the kind of zealot who craves a cause—if it wasn't slavery it would be something else. Who knows what he's going to do, and that it won't blow the whole country sky high? Men like Brown don't care about consequences so long as they get notoriety, and their names in the newspapers.''

''I agree that Zeph could get caught in—'' Glynis stopped as the library door flew open and crashed against the wall. She and Jonathan jumped to their feet, and Cullen whirled around as a woman, doubled over and with her hands clutching her abdomen, staggered through the door.

''Fiona!'' Glynis gasped, rounding her desk as Cullen leapt toward the stricken woman. Fiona swayed on her feet, and when she reached out a hand to grasp at Cullen, her terrible injury became all too apparent. Blood spread over her lower body from waist to thighs, while every move she made brought more pumping out in life-draining quantity.

Cullen lowered Fiona to the library floor, while Glynis sought a pulse in her neck. The one she finally found was thready and erratic, clearly failing.

''Should . . . should I get a . . . a doctor?'' Jonathan's quavering voice was aimed at the ceiling to seemingly question God.

''My little . . . girl . . .'' Fiona's broken reply came so faint they had to bend close to her ashen face to hear it. ''The baby,'' she got out.

''All right, Fiona,'' Cullen said to her. ''We'll see to your baby, but tell me what happened. Did your husband do this?'' He looked up at Glynis and mouthed, ''Looks like a shotgun wound.''

Fiona's eyes suddenly rolled back and Glynis thought they had lost her when the pulse in her neck barely fluttered. But astonishingly, Fiona answered, through lips white with shock, "Kerry didn't . . . didn't mean it . . ." Abruptly her mouth went slack and a rush of air was expelled.

And now Glynis, her fingers probing frantically, could find no pulse at all. She tried several times, at wrist and neck, to no purpose. Fiona would say no more.

"Jonathan, please go and get Dr. Cardoza-Levy," Glynis told him. "Tell her, though, that Mrs. Roarke has already died."

Jonathan didn't move, and as Glynis got up from her position beside Fiona's body, she wondered if he'd heard her. In the meantime, Cullen had gone to the door. Before he went out, he said, "I'm going to their place to pick up Roarke." He started out the door, then came back to say, "She made it here to you for a reason, Glynis—do you know what it is?"

"Her little girl, I suppose—she probably wasn't thinking clearly. I think I'd better come with you, Cullen. I feel obligated now to see that Fiona's baby is safe. Perhaps her sister Morwenna can take the child."

"No, I don't want you there now. Roarke's more than likely to resist and I don't want you in danger."

Glynis decided not to argue. She just nodded as he left, Jonathan right behind him but moving stiff-legged, as if in a trance.

After staring down at the destruction that had been Fiona, Glynis realized she wasn't particularly surprised, and the realization itself brought revulsion. That men like Kerry Roarke were not prevented by courts or clergy from mistreating their wives meant that, to society's institutions, women like Fiona had no value. A man could be jailed, even hanged, for stealing another man's horse, but not even reproached for beating his wife. So why should the result be surprising?

She stood a few moments longer, then went to her back office for a shawl to cover the body. While there, Glynis heard the library door open. She came out half-expecting to see Kerry Roarke with a shotgun, there to finish the job in case Fiona had somehow survived. Instead, Dr. Quentin Ives came across the room, shaking his head at the still form.

"Quentin, how did you hear?"

"I was on Fall Street, just going home for lunch, when Jonathan Quant told me what happened."

"Yes, well, I'm glad you're here," Glynis said, handing him the shawl. "I didn't want to leave her alone . . . and I need to get to her house and see to her child."

She left Ives bending beside the body, still shaking his head.

As soon as she crossed the bridge, Glynis could hear a babble of voices, and an occasional shout. A fair-sized number of people were gathering at the Roarke place, a wooden shack erected along the canal, and in the midst of the crowd she could see the green and brown peddler's wagon. The first person she recognized was Morwenna, who had Fiona's baby in her arms. Morwenna's face, when she turned to Glynis, was set in a stony expression; it might have been rage or grief, or both.

"She's passed on, then? Like the constable said?"

"Yes, Morwenna. I'm so sorry."

Morwenna stared straight ahead. "Can't say as I'm all that surprised," she stated with no inflection in her voice.

"No," Glynis agreed, "that was my reaction. And it makes me angrier than anything else—that we're not surprised. But how did it happen, do you know?"

Morwenna shrugged slightly, her mouth fixed in a straight line. "I wasn't here." She turned to her husband.

"Constable's tryin' to sort it out now," Tom Ryan said, pointing to Cullen, who was standing in front of the house. He was surrounded by men and women all talking at once.

Glynis moved closer, looking for but not finding Liam Cleary. Then she saw Zeph, rifle in his hands, his face grim, standing with legs apart. And a moment later Glynis saw why: he straddled the prone body of a man. For a moment Glynis thought it must be Grandy Fox. But as she drew nearer, wedging herself between shoulders of the crowd, she could see that the man's hair was dark, not the blond of the peddler.

"Who is it?" she asked a man nearby.

"Roarke," came the terse reply. "Kerry Roarke. He's dead."

"All right, folks!" Cullen's voice abruptly rose over the crowd. "Folks, you're going to have to back off some here.

And quiet down, so we can hear what's being said. C'mon now, back off—don't make the deputies get rough.''

With a great deal of muttering the crowd did shift some, and then Glynis saw Liam, hands gripping the stock and barrel of his rifle and holding it out horizontally to push back those who resisted moving. He appeared extremely pale, but to Glynis's relief, seemed to be in complete control of himself. Although he looked to have aged half a century.

Glynis struggled forward to those standing closest to Cullen. And now she could see that Grandy Fox was indeed there, positioned close by Cullen's shoulder, and with a revolver held in the hand at his side. He did not look like a man about to be arrested.

Cullen nodded his head at Glynis, while she moved closer to Zeph. "What happened?"

"Not quite sure yet," Zeph said from the corner of his mouth. His eyes stayed on the crowd, scanning back and forth, while he stood over Kerry Roarke's body. And now, looking down, Glynis could see the bullet hole in Roarke's forehead.

"O.K., let's go through it again," Cullen said now, addressing two people, a man and woman, who stood in front of him.

"Like we said, Constable," answered the man whom Glynis recognized as sawmill owner Paddy MacNamara, "we heerd all this shouting and gunshots and me and the wife come to see this here Roarke waving his shotgun and he was ranting like a madman and—"

"Be still, Paddy!" Rosie MacNamara said firmly. Paddy gave his wife a look of gratitude. "What do you want to know, Constable?" Rosie asked, her callused hands planted on broad hips, her face like a granite block.

"I want to know who fired first," Cullen said.

"Oh, sure'n it was him all right—Roarke," Rosie answered, pointing at the body. "That there peddler, he ducked just in time. Or else he'd 'a' been lyin' there instead."

"You, over there," Cullen said to a slight man wringing his hands at the far edge of the crowd, "you said you saw it all?"

"Yes, sir, Constable Stuart, sir. I did that. Something terrible, it was."

"Go on," Cullen directed.

"Well, sir, I was just out on my front stoop there," the man explained, gesturing toward a small well-kept house directly across the street, "and I saw that peddler fellow pull up in his wagon. And Kerry Roarke, he comes a-running out of his place there, yelling his head off. And waving his shotgun, too, he was. Peddler, there, he says something I can't hear, and Roarke keeps yelling. Then the missus—Roarke's missus, that is—she comes a-running out behind Roarke, begging him like, to come back inside, you know?"

Cullen had infinite patience, Glynis thought, wondering how long this man could ramble on without getting to the point. And Cullen just stood there, looking deceptively relaxed and as if he had all day to listen.

"Then Roarke he lifts his shotgun up, ready to fire at that there peddler," the man went on, "and his missus, she steps in front of him. I 'spect, least from the ways it looked, that she was trying to get that shotgun away from him, 'cause she grabbed the barrel and pulls it down. And it went off, right into her stomach, it did."

Glynis felt a sudden lightheadedness and took a deep breath as Cullen asked the slight man something she didn't catch.

"No, Constable," the man answered, "there was nobody else here, cept'n the MacNamaras. And no, I didn't hear what the peddler there said. He didn't talk loud. But it sure riled Roarke, whatever it was."

"Constable," said Rosie MacNamara, "Roarke was drunk as a skunk. I mean, he shoots his own wife, and he doesn't turn a hair. When I tried to get to her, Roarke waves that shotgun at me, tells me to move off. And the poor girl, she stumbles across the yard toward the bridge, holding her belly, and he still wouldn't let me go after her. Then he turns his gun on the peddler there."

Glynis had been watching Grandy Fox closely, waiting for some reaction. His hands swung at his sides, one still holding the revolver, and although he looked concerned, he didn't exhibit any of the fear Glynis would expect to see in his circumstance. And it amazed her that he hadn't as yet been disarmed. But perhaps Cullen hadn't had the opportunity. Or, more likely, he trusted the crowd even less than he did the peddler.

"It was self-defense, all right, Constable," said the slight man. "Roarke would've killed him—the peddler there—sure and certain, if'n he hadn't got his own gun and fired. But Roarke, he fired first, and that's the God's honest truth."

Cullen looked over at Rosie and Paddy MacNamara, who nodded their agreement without his asking. "It's the truth," Paddy said. "Peddler, he *had* to shoot."

"O.K., folks, that's all," Cullen said. "Everybody go on home, now."

"So what're you going to do, Constable?" someone asked.

"I'm going to take Mr. Fox here to jail," Cullen answered. "And you all can just move along." He gave Zeph and Liam both a short nod. The two young deputies stepped forward, moving the crowd before them, and gradually people began to wander toward the road, muttering and shaking their heads, and looking back over their shoulders.

"You got anything to add to those accounts, Fox?"

Grandy stared directly at Cullen a moment, then shook his head, before saying, "No. But you heard them, Constable. Roarke fired first. He shot his wife, and I had every reason to think he was going to shoot me."

"Yes, that's what it sounds like." Cullen seemed to agree. "But he—Roarke—is not the reason I'm taking you in. The charge is counterfeiting, at least for now, it is."

Grandy looked genuinely surprised, Glynis thought. And once again she found it hard to believe that this man was a criminal of any kind, much less a murderer.

He said nothing more. He made no protest when Cullen took his revolver, and he stood quietly while his wrists were manacled. Cullen directed him to walk toward the bridge, which he did, again without protest. It was only when Cullen told Liam Cleary to drive Grandy Fox's horse and wagon to the lockup that the peddler made comment.

"You're making a mistake, Constable."

It was all he said.

LIAM PARKED THE wagon alongside the firehouse and tethered the chestnut horse to a hitching post. Glynis felt a flush of embarrassment when Cullen motioned her forward, this after

Grandy had willingly given him the key to a shiny new padlock, and the side of the wagon had been unlocked and propped
up. She pointed to the shelved nests of bowls. Zeph and Liam
took them down while she felt Grandy staring at her with what
seemed an expression of rebuke, and something like disappointment in his eyes. She tried to ignore it.

Zeph unscrewed the smaller wooden bowl, separating it from
the larger one, and as he lifted it out Glynis stepped forward
to identify the counterfeit coins.

The bowl was empty. There were no coins, there was nothing
there at all. She looked up at Cullen in dismay. "They were
there," she protested. "I saw them, scores of them."

Cullen didn't seem to doubt it. "O.K., Fox, where'd you get
rid of them?"

Grandy just shook his head, silent and stoic-looking.

"Should we take apart the others?" Zeph asked, gesturing
to the various bowls.

"Yes," Glynis said. "Please, Cullen."

The bowls were removed from the shelves and while the
still-manacled Grandy stood quietly, Zeph and Cullen went
through them, one by one. All were empty. Glynis began to
feel more and more uncomfortable, sure that Zeph thought she
had imagined finding the coins, and perhaps by then Cullen
did, too.

When they stood surrounded by empty bowls, it seemed obvious to her that the coins had been dispersed elsewhere, very
probably on Grandy's recent trip out of town.

And Cullen, as if reading her mind, said, "Where'd you go
in the past couple days, Fox?"

"Just up to Syracuse," he answered readily enough. "Then
Skaneateles and Auburn. You're welcome to check on it—I
can give you the names of the customers I saw."

Then it must be true, Glynis figured, because it would be so
easy to verify. But had he passed on all the coins? As she stood
there gazing at the wagon's empty shelves, she thought of
something else. She rounded the wagon to its other side and
motioned Zeph to pull up the door. But confronted with the
sundry kitchen goods, she hesitated, watching Grandy sideways. She pointed to the crocks and milk cans on an upper

shelf and, as she did, she caught the peddler's minuscule shift of feet. It wasn't much, but enough to make her hopeful.

Down came the crocks and the milk cans. It was Cullen who suddenly said, "Well, well. What have we here?" He'd opened a milk can, and now he reached in and withdrew from its interior a thick bundle of banknotes tied with string. He riffled through them, then handed the bundle to Glynis while he disappeared through the door of his office. Moments later he reappeared with a sheet of paper on which Glynis could see written several columns of numbers.

"Read me the serial numbers on those first notes, would you?" he directed her.

She began to read, while he scanned the paper, and then, almost immediately, he told her she could stop. "That's it, Fox," he said. "Got you dead to rights. What Miss Tryon read off are the serial numbers for the notes issued by Farmers and Merchants Bank. Their plates were surrendered to the state banking authority for destruction the day after the bank closed. So where—" he took the sheaf of notes from Glynis and waved it in front of Grandy Fox "—just where did these come from?"

Grandy Fox said nothing. And Liam Cleary, who'd been slumped dejectedly against the firehouse wall, now straightened and took several determined steps toward the prisoner.

"Hold it, Liam!" Cullen's voice sliced the air, and Liam hesitated.

"He got my sister killed, Constable." The boy's hands twitched at his side.

"Kerry Roarke killed your sister, lad," Grandy Fox said quietly. "Not me."

"But you said something that made him mad," Liam replied, and the steadiness of his voice frightened Glynis more than if he had stammered. "And you're the one got him mixed up in your rotten business."

"Did your sister tell you that, Liam?" Glynis asked him.

"She told me she found out Fox here was holding something over Kerry's head," Liam answered. "I told her to tell Constable Stuart, but she said she was afraid of him—she wanted to tell you, Miss Tryon."

That must have been the reason why Fiona, in a confused and desperate state, had come to the library.

"Do you know *what* Fox was threatening Kerry Roarke with?" Cullen asked now.

"There was nothing, Constable," Grandy said. "The man was deranged from drink. I hardly even knew him."

"Then why were you at his house?" Cullen demanded.

Grandy sighed. "To return the scissors his wife wanted sharpened. They're right up there, Constable, on that top shelf. Take a look."

But that was safe enough to say, Glynis thought, as there *were* scissors there, and who could possibly identify them as Fiona's? Scissors all looked pretty much alike. Nonetheless, Liam Cleary had moved away from the peddler as if now doubtful about his accusation. Which was to the boy's great credit, since there were many men who by this time would have blown the peddler's head off.

"Since you've decided to talk, Fox," Cullen said, "suppose you make a stab at explaining these bogus banknotes."

Grandy shook his head. "I can't."

"Can't what?"

"I can't explain."

"You do realize you're in one hell of a position, don't you?" Cullen asked him. "I've wired your description to the Treasury Department."

Grandy Fox just nodded. His composure made Glynis extremely uneasy, and she glanced at Cullen to see his reaction. But Cullen, too, looked calm, just staring levelly at his prisoner. Then he said briskly, "O.K.! Guess you'll just have to wait in jail, Fox, until we can find a court date for you. I'm charging you with counterfeiting, aiding and abetting the robbery of the Seneca County militia armory, and suspicion of murder. Anything I missed?"

"Murder? Whose murder?" Grandy Fox asked.

"Don't you mean *how many?*"

Again, Grandy Fox fell silent. And he remained silent as Cullen took him inside the lockup. Liam followed a moment later, but Zeph remained outside with Glynis. He had a look on his face she'd seen there before—one of unyielding intent—

and she had a helpless feeling that she knew what he would say.

"Miss Tryon, I've got to go now."

"Please, Zeph—"

"No, I got to do it. Constable's back, and Liam . . . well, Liam's changed some. You can see that for yourself."

Glynis felt her eyes fill, and although she knew the last thing to move Zeph would be tears, she couldn't help herself. She had to try to dissuade him. "Zeph, I truly believe that something terrible could happen to you, if you insist on throwing in with John Brown. Please don't go."

"I told you before, I have to." He started toward the street. Then he stopped, turned, and said, "Hey, you know me— Zephaniah! Remember what my name means? 'Hidden by the Lord.' I'll be O.K., Miss Tryon. Don't you worry yourself."

He took several quick strides toward her; then, shaking his head a little, as if he'd just recalled who and where he was, he paused and extended his hand. But it didn't matter, not now, just who might be watching. Glynis put out her arms to gather him in, and held him close.

"Then go with God, Zeph. And come safely home."

INTERIM

❦

THE THICK GOLDEN haze of late summer had settled over the port of Oswego. It was a Sunday afternoon, and heat appeared to have plunged the entire town into a drowsy languor in which only the waters of lake and river moved, and they in desultory fashion. Hemp ropes creaked occasionally, and the bows of moored vessels nudged the docks with soft thuds. Even the dogs dozing along the waterfront roused themselves only enough to follow the shadow of the piers.

Brockway stood on the shore in the shade of a wide-spread maple, his yoked shirt damp and clinging to his chest, and his palms slick. He continually eyed the nondescript valise that perched just above his head in a fork of low branches.

Where the hell was the Englishman? And why did he, Brockway, always have to be the one to wait? But this would be the last time. He'd fulfilled his part of the deal. The only reason he waited there now was because he wanted payment.

"Ah, Mr. Brockway. Good afternoon."

Brockway swung around to face the smooth-shaven man who had come up behind him. "Damn, you startled me!"

"You've become a bit tense, my good man. But why? Your role is finished. Provided, that is, you have brought me something."

Brockway motioned with his head to the valise. The other man looked up and nodded, giving Brockway a broad smile. "Well done."

"Don't you want to look at them? Six hundred dollars in our new gold coin?"

"Not at all. I am confident you are aware of the consequences should you try to effect a betrayal. The coins are worthless—but only to us. The recipient of them won't know that."

"Who is the recipient?"

"Mr. Brockway, you know I am not at liberty to divulge that. Sufficient unto the day is the fact that he is the nephew of a *prominent abolitionist, and although he is somewhat limited in intelligence, we have arranged that he will have no trouble in locating Mr. Brown. And delivering to him a sign that the revolution should commence. A sign from the Lord.''*

"Six hundred dollars of bogus money.''

"Six hundred dollars in gold coin, Mr. Brockway.''

"Right. Now where's my money—the real kind.''

The smooth-shaven man reached down behind the trunk of the maple and retrieved a brown valise that resembled closely the one above in the branches. "Here you are. And by all means, do count it.''

"I intend to!'' Brockway opened the valise's clasp and withdrew five packets of banknotes. He thumbed through them with a practiced eye, his lips moving silently in count. When finished he said, "Speaking of betrayal, do you swear the Ontario Bank is still solvent?''

"Mr. Brockway! Are you impugning my honor, sir?''

Brockway smiled coldly. "Of course I am. This is a dishonorable business we're in. But you must know better than to double-cross me.''

"Indeed. That would hardly bode well for future collaborative ventures, would it now? Yes, the bank is quite solvent. You may of course look it up in your current counterfeit detector newspaper.'' The man gave a short laugh.

"There won't be any more 'cooperative ventures,' as you put it,'' Brockway responded, replacing the packets in the valise. "You people are a bloodthirsty bunch—and I told you before, I don't hold with murder.''

"I don't care for it myself. But unpleasantness is occasionally necessary as the means to achieve vital ends. You know, my dear man, you Americans are squeamish about the most extraordinary matters. You have no hesitation in jailing an indigent man for stealing a few dollars, yet you allow your Congress unlimited opportunity to do the same, and much worse, under the auspices of your Supreme Court. Look at the Dred Scott *decision; handed down by the Court's southern justices and supported not by law, certainly not by morality, but on the money to be made in slavery! This fair country of yours, Mr. Brockway, is about to engage in a conflict that will tax your*

citizens' resources unmercifully. And the highest legal authority in your land has made it all but inevitable.''

"And you and your cronies are helping to make it possible,'' Brockway stated.

"But we are not causing it. That your southern states are doing with their intractable greed, while your Supreme Court is supplying them the ammunition. We are simply taking advantage of the situation.''

"You know,'' Brockway said, frowning, "a few more chats like this one, and you might make an ex-patriot out of me.''

The smooth-shaven man laughed again. "And what will you do now?''

"I leave. Go as far from western New York as I can get. I should think you would, too.''

"No, I must linger in this part of the country for some short time yet. My affairs here are not quite concluded.'' He extended his hand. "It's been a pleasure doing business with you, Mr. Brockway. You are a man of your word, such a rarity these days. I am quite certain we will meet again.''

"Don't bet on it.'' Brockway pulled the valise from the fork of the tree, tossed it to the smooth-shaven man, and, picking up the other valise, tipped his cap and walked away.

The other man stood watching as Brockway made his way into the sleeping town. Then he patted the brown valise under his arm. Yes, things were proceeding nicely. And now Mr. Francis Jackson Meriam of Boston, their one-eyed, dim-witted courier, was about to receive his marching orders.

The smooth-shaven man looked out to Lake Ontario, where a British sailing ship—a man-of-war as evidenced by the Union Jack flying at its bow—strained at anchor some distance from shore. His face assumed an almost wistful expression. Then he shrugged lightly and, with seemingly reluctant steps, he began to walk in the direction of the Oswego train station.

NINETEEN

◦❧◦

The organization spread out until a line was formed, reaching in every direction through the New England and Middle States. There were many judges, justices, and sheriffs who were contaminated. The company not only consisted of thieves, but counterfeiters of both coin and paper money.
　—STILE DOTY, *THE LIFE OF STILE DOTY,*
　　COUNTERFEITER.
　COMPILED BY J. G. W. COBURN 1880

GLYNIS GLANCED AROUND the courtroom, noticing that, on this second day of Grandy Fox's trial, those gathered in the Seneca County Courthouse at Waterloo numbered less than for previous courtroom proceedings she had attended. The time of year might be in part responsible, September being the start of harvesting season. More than likely, however, the reason was simply lack of interest. The trial of an accused counterfeiter would not generate enough excitement to keep men from their fields or women from their kitchens, whereas a murder trial could cause the hay to molder and the bread to burn.

Glynis turned to her niece, seated beside her on the aisle, knitting with thread of violet silk some stockings for Vanessa Usher's new wardrobe. And, in fact, Emma had pleaded too much work to attend yesterday's opening session, which consisted of picking a jury and opening statements from the opposing lawyers. Neither the young district attorney nor Grandy Fox's defense lawyer were familiar to Glynis. Both Jeremiah Merrycoyf and Adam MacAlistair had refused Grandy's request to represent him, but Merrycoyf did suggest he might look for someone out of town. Which advice Grandy had apparently taken to heart, as his attorney came from Syracuse.

Judge Endicott, a thickset, straightforward man, spoke briskly when asking the district attorney to call his first witness.

"The People call Miss Glynis Tryon," the young attorney called out loudly.

Glynis thought the man looked unduly impressed with his role, an observation that did not cheer her as she rose unhappily from her chair. Still, she'd known it was coming; she was, as far as anyone knew, the first person to have witnessed a tangible connection between Grandy Fox and counterfeit money.

She had just edged past Emma and into the aisle when a commanding male voice came from the rear of the room. "If it please the court, may I have permission to come forward?"

Glynis saw that the owner of the voice, a stranger to her, had already made it halfway down the aisle before the judge had time to say, "And who, sir, might you be?"

The man's answer, presumably his name, was lost to Glynis in the noise of chairs scraping and people muttering as they turned to see this intruder.

Judge Endicott held up a hand, saying, "Just a moment, sir, before you go any further."

The man's springy steps came to a halt just a few feet from where Glynis stood.

"To exactly what purpose are you interrupting this proceeding?" Judge Endicott inquired, a faint scowl wrinkling a broad forehead. "And before you answer, let me assure you it had better be a good one."

"Yes, your honor," the man replied, "I have good reason, I promise you that. If you will but let me speak, I can greatly shorten this day."

Glynis thought she heard in his voice a slight accent, and an inflection that was surely British. While he was facing the judge, she could see a tracery of lines fanning from the outer corners of his eyes—so he was not as youthful as his buoyant gait had suggested. Closer to her own age, she guessed, and she was rather intrigued by his boldness.

Then, uncertain as to what to do with herself, she looked back to the bench for direction, but Judge Endicott was staring straight ahead, sizing up the interloper. And behind her, Emma's voice, no doubt intended as a whisper but resounding in the courtroom's quiet, said, "I'll move over into your seat, Aunt Glynis, so you can sit down."

The man in the aisle abruptly turned his head, and Glynis found herself the focus of intensely blue eyes. "Yes, Aunt Glynis," he said under his breath, "you'd best sit. This could take a bit of time." And he sent her a puckish smile before he turned back to face the judge.

Glynis heard Emma's quick intake of breath, while she lowered herself into the aisle seat her niece had just vacated. "Who *is* he?" Emma whispered, this time very softly. Even so, Glynis caught the stranger's responding smile. He clearly owned very good ears.

Judge Endicott had apparently made up his mind, as he said, "Very well, sir. You may approach the bench."

As the man moved quickly up the aisle, Glynis could see better the long shape of his head, the smooth dark brown hair, and slim but well-proportioned frame of more than average height. She glanced sideways at Emma, who also seemed to be taking this man's measure. And she whispered again, "Who do you think he is, Aunt Glynis?"

Glynis just shook her head, not wanting to miss what might happen next as the man had reached the front of the room to stand before the judge. Judge Endicott leaned over his bench and said a few words to him, which did not carry to the rest of the room. The stranger appeared to reply briefly. "Bailiff," Judge Endicott then directed, "swear this man in, if you please."

The bailiff stepped forward with the Bible. "State your name for the record."

"It's Rhys Bevan."

Glynis could now place the Celtic hint in the man's speech. But *Bevan* . . . where had she heard the name Bevan?

"*What* is his name?" Emma asked, this time so softly Glynis barely heard it.

"It's spelled *R-h-y-s*," she whispered to her niece, "and it's pronounced 'Reese.' He's Welsh, as were some of your ancestors, Emma. Your father's and my maternal grandparents came from Wales. As a matter of fact, the name *Glynis* is Welsh."

Emma looked somewhat amused by this sudden infusion of genealogy, and she actually put her knitting down on her lap to study Rhys Bevan while he was being sworn. The judge had also leaned forward to watch. And by this time, both the district attorney and Grandy Fox's defense lawyer were poised on the edge of their chairs as if making ready to leap up with objections. It seemed obvious that neither attorney knew this man and both were concerned that what he might say could influence the jury. However, Judge Endicott's next words were, "Bailiff, please escort the gentlemen of the jury from the room."

While the jury filed out, Rhys Bevan was directed into the witness chair. The man moved with a lithe sureness that bespoke either athletics or the theater, Glynis speculated, and she watched him with curiosity, as did most everyone else in the courtroom.

The jury now safely beyond earshot, Judge Endicott addressed the witness. "You stated that you have something to say which will be of vital interest to this court. Very well—but are you an American citizen?" So the judge, too, had noted the faint Celtic lilt.

"I am, Your Honor. For some years now."

"Then you do understand, Mr. Bevan, that the law provides you with certain rights. For instance, you are not required to incriminate yourself."

"I have no intention of incriminating myself. I am here solely to protect the interests of the United States government—by which I am employed."

Glynis immediately sat forward, the better to hear over the courtroom chatter that followed Rhys Bevan's statement. The man no longer looked the least bit puckish.

Judge Endicott banged his gavel once, and glared out over the room. The noise ceased. And the judge turned again to the witness. "You say you are employed by the government, Mr. Bevan. In exactly what capacity do you serve?"

"By the authority of the Solicitor of the Treasury, Your Honor, I am chief detective of the Special Detective Service." As he said this, Rhys Bevan reached into an inner pocket of his frock coat and withdrew several folded sheets of heavy vellum, then handed one of them to the judge.

"You're a *detective?*" Judge Endicott asked with manifest skepticism while he unfolded the paper. He scanned it, during which time his expression gradually changed. "All right, Mr. Bevan, this document from the Treasury Solicitor confirms that you are indeed a detective."

"We're more commonly called agents, sir."

"To what purpose are you employed as a Treasury agent, Mr. Bevan?"

"Most Treasury agents are in the business of finding and apprehending counterfeiters. Unlike myself, the majority of those in the field work undercover, meaning they are disguised as someone other than who and what they are."

"Is that cloak-and-dagger approach necessary?"

Rhys Bevan's smile appeared and disappeared in an instant. "It does cause some problems, sir. But yes, we think it's necessary. Counterfeiting's a serious problem these days, and it has a long reach. There are all manner of folks involved—" for the first time the man seemed to hesitate, then continued "—and sometimes they are bankers or constables or lawyers . . . or judges."

Judge Endicott looked dumbstruck, and Rhys Bevan had to wait until the noise that greeted his statement died down before he went on. "These are people not ordinarily suspected of breaking the law, Your Honor, so secrecy is often the only way to ferret them out. And it has to be done—it's been estimated that over one-third of the nation's currency is now bogus."

Instead of the clamor that Glynis might have expected to follow this, the courtroom became utterly still. In shock, she imagined, like herself; and she resisted the urge to pick up her reticule and examine her money. Suddenly a sound rang out that might have been large pins dropping into the silence. Emma blushed furiously while she bent to retrieve her knitting needles. As Glynis smothered a smile, she looked up to find Rhys Bevan's eyes on her. It so startled her that it took her a moment to look away.

"And what does all of this have to do with your presence here today, Mr. Bevan?" Judge Endicott asked, his voice sounding somewhat strained.

"It has to do with the charges brought against the defendant, Your Honor. The need for secrecy I mentioned—often requiring agents to work undercover—has brought about the present situation." Rhys Bevan now handed to Judge Endicott the other sheet of vellum he'd been holding. "This document will verify," he said, "that the man on trial here is my colleague, Treasury Agent Granville Fox."

Glynis drew in her breath at the same time the rest of the spectators drew in theirs, thus while the judge scanned the new document the courtroom delivered itself of a prolonged sigh. Then voices rose steadily. Rhys Bevan had dropped his bombshell not only with aplomb but with close to theatrical timing. However, he did not give any indication that he was particularly enjoying himself. He looked down at Grandy Fox with a somber expression, and he sat without moving as noise grew in the courtroom.

While Judge Endicott's gavel descended, Glynis craned her neck around the heads of those in front of her to see defendant Fox's reaction. Grandy looked relieved; a snatched-from-the-jaws-of-death relief. And where Rhys Bevan remained serious, Grandy Fox now smiled broadly, at his attorney, at the judge, at the witness. Then he turned and smiled back at her. And at Cullen in the rear of the room.

His attorney rose and addressed the judge. "Your Honor, in light of this witness's testimony, I move that the charges against my client be dismissed."

Judge Endicott nodded, then said to Rhys Bevan, "Why did it take the Treasury so long to come forward with the information you've just given us, Mr. Bevan?"

"We didn't know what had happened here until the description of Agent Fox came by wire from Constable Stuart—and along with it was Stuart's request for information. By that we knew Fox hadn't, and wouldn't, reveal himself to be an agent and jeopardize his cover identity. Frankly, sir, we hoped the matter might not come to trial. Not a realistic hope, as it turns out."

While Glynis listened to Rhys Bevan she recognized that Grandy Fox's presence in western New York as a Treasury agent, and one working undercover disguised as a peddler, meant that any number of things were now explained. But the two most urgent, most crucial, questions were ones apparently neither agent could answer. Since Grandy Fox wasn't a counterfeiter, then who in Seneca Falls was? And since he hadn't killed those other agents, and the bankers Barrymore and Bingham, and poor Sally Lunt, then who had?

SOME TIME LATER, when Glynis came down the courthouse steps with Cullen, she saw that a small group of people, which included Grandy Fox and Rhys Bevan, were standing on the nearby green, engaged in what appeared to be lively conversation. She looked up at Cullen. "Well, what now?"

He shook his head. "Guess we start over. And Rhys Bevan says the Treasury wants Grandy Fox to stay on here, despite the loss of his cover, until the counterfeit operation is broken— if it can be. At least Fox didn't seem to be holding a grudge after the judge dismissed the charges."

"Why should he, Cullen? You were doing your job, and after all, Grandy looked—as you would say—as guilty as sin."

He shot her a quick smile, which was a welcome change from the scowl he'd been wearing all morning. They'd stopped at the bottom of the steps amid tethered horses and carriages, and now both looked across the cobbled drive to the green.

"That's the trouble, though, with circumstantial evidence," Cullen said. "It can make an innocent man look guilty. And as Fox himself just explained, the evidence we thought we had against him could be turned around and, when seen from another direction, look very different."

"Yes," Glynis agreed as they began to stroll toward the grassy area. "But how could we know that he'd sent those coins I discovered on to the Treasury as evidence, or that he was going to do the same with the banknotes we found? And, too, once he'd been unmasked as a Treasury agent, then his being at the Rochester public market that morning made sense. Since, as he said, he was keeping an eye on Barrymore to see if anyone was following him; but then Grandy lost him in the crowd."

"Or he was watching to see if Barrymore himself was someone to be suspicious of," Cullen added. "Apparently they suspected me, too, which is why they didn't let me know, after Agents Trent and Fairfax were killed, that they had another agent already in place here."

"Did Grandy say what it was that he knew about Kerry Roarke?"

"Yes, Grandy said he'd become certain that Roarke was one of the gang that had been stealing weapons, and he confronted Roarke with it. Agent Paul Trent had earlier infiltrated the gang, and had been on the last several forays; it was Trent who initially fingered Roarke—and got himself killed for it. At first, Grandy thought maybe *I'd* done it to keep them quiet. It makes sense, Glynis. I never did catch up with the gang—and it could have been, again from another point of view, because I didn't *want* to catch them."

"I understand that, Cullen, but none of it changes the fact that there's still an unknown killer loose. Or do you and the Treasury agents believe that Kerry Roarke was responsible for all the deaths?"

"I can't speak for Fox or Bevan, but I sure don't believe it. And I don't suppose you do either."

"No, I don't. Kerry Roarke was not the man I saw in the market, nor was he Barrymore's attacker on the train. It would be a terrible mistake to blame Roarke for both the bankers' deaths."

"I agree—we've still got a killer to find. But since Zeph went off, I'm shorthanded, so I'll be glad to have Fox's help. By the way, have you heard anything from Zeph?"

Glynis waited to answer until they'd seated themselves on the stone steps of the Presbyterian church facing the green. The small crowd around the two agents was a few hundred yards away, and Glynis was surprised to see Emma talking to Rhys Bevan. She was more surprised to realize they both were looking her way.

She quickly turned back to Cullen. "I got a letter from Zeph just yesterday, mailed several weeks ago in Philadelphia. He wrote that he and his cousin were staying with someone there involved with the Underground Railroad, and were waiting for word on John Brown's location. But they expected to hear anytime, so I don't know where he is now. Heading south, most likely. Cullen, I hope Zeph's cautious—he could be picked up as a runaway. The slavecatchers don't care whether or not any Negro is actually an escaped slave. You know that."

"Zeph's aware of it, Glynis. He'll be careful."

But she could see that Cullen's expression belied the confidence of his words.

Wanting to distract herself from worry about Zeph, she said, "Perhaps we should rethink the events of the past months. There might be something we've overlooked that would point to the killer."

"Far as I can see, it has to be someone here in Seneca Falls who's mixed up in the counterfeiting operation. At least that seems to be the motive for the bankers' and the agents' deaths. It might easily be Valerian Voss—who better than a bank vice-president to know the time period between a bank surrendering its plates to the state, and those plates' series numbers appearing in the various banknote detector registers. In other words, the interval of time when it would be safe to pass bogus notes with numbers of the discarded plates."

"Or it could be Alan Fitzhugh. You were right, Glynis, about the man having expensive tastes. And I've just found out that Fitzhugh's been buying an amount of gold no dentist could use even if he planned to replace every tooth in Seneca Falls."

"Cullen, I just now thought of something. Could Alan Fitzhugh be buying that gold not only for counterfeiting but to have it made into jewelry for his various women friends? That would require a huge sum of money. Perhaps it's worth talking to Mr. Williams, the jeweler."

"Maybe, but right now I'd say our best suspect is Cyril Doggett—I told you what Adam MacAlistair had to say about him. And Rhys Bevan confirmed that the Treasury is investigating Doggett's activities when he was in New Haven. It's probably why Doggett left there."

"And there's a possible connection between Doggett and Colonel de Warde," Glynis added, "as de Warde also has an office in New Haven, remember? But Cullen, why do you think Sally Lunt went to see Doggett before she was killed?"

Cullen's face abruptly closed, and Glynis felt again the absolute certainty that he wasn't telling her something of importance. She couldn't curb her annoyance, and rose from the steps. Cullen didn't seem to notice that she now stood with her back to him as he went on, "I think you're right to be suspicious of de Warde. Man's too damn closemouthed whenever I try to pin him down about what his actual business is here in Seneca Falls, or in New Haven. And he travels a lot. . . . Glynis? What's wrong?''

He'd apparently noticed. But only because she'd started to walk away. She took several steps back to him before she said quietly, "You *know* what's wrong, Cullen. Because we've been through this before. You don't want to tell me certain things, and you're not subtle about it. At this point, I am more than just hurt by your attitude, I'm angry—and I'm disturbed by our quarreling. So from now on, I think you should leave me out of your investigation.''

She turned back to the green and started toward Emma, who had broken away from the group and was now walking toward her.

"Aunt Glynis,'' she asked with a smile as they met, "were your ears burning?''

"Why?'' Glynis really didn't care, she was so upset with Cullen.

Emma's smile broadened to a grin, and her newly acquired maturity dropped away as she clapped her hand over her mouth to unsuccessfully stifle a giggle.

"Emma?''

"I'm sorry,'' Emma blurted, before giggling again. "It's just that I felt like a captured spy. I was being interrogated about you.''

"By whom?'' Glynis asked, although she thought she could guess, and looked past Emma's shoulder to see Rhys Bevan watching her with his intense blue gaze. He caught her eyes before she could look away, and he nodded briefly.

Glynis turned quickly to her niece. "Emma, I'm going to our carriage. Are you coming?''

"Aunt Glynis, please don't be mad. It's just so funny—I mean, you're my *aunt!* That man is certainly curious about you.''

"I don't want to hear any more,'' Glynis stated, although not very convincingly she feared, and she started walking toward the carriage with purposeful strides.

"You don't really?'' Emma asked, a little breathlessly as she trotted to keep up. "But Aunt Glynis, he's so . . . so attractive! Don't you want to hear just a little, if I promise not to laugh?"

This was obviously a promise Emma would have difficulty keeping, because her hand again flew to her mouth. Glynis said nothing and continued walking.

"Well, Mr. Bevan said," Emma began, clearly undeterred, as Glynis thought would be the case, "that he wondered if my Aunt Glynis was *the* Glynis Tryon."

Despite her best intention to ignore this, Glynis stopped in her tracks to stare at her niece. "Why on earth would he say that?"

"Because he said he'd heard about you. He didn't say how, but it must have been from Grandy Fox, don't you think?"

"I have no idea."

"And then he, Rhys Bevan, said that—" Emma's face contorted with effort but in spite of it the giggle escaped.

Glynis resumed walking. Emma caught up with her, saying, "I'm truly sorry, Aunt Glynis. I can't stop myself."

"Try."

When they reached the carriage, stationed in front of the courthouse steps, Glynis motioned for Emma to get in while she untied the horse from the hitching post. She didn't dare look at her niece, as she was, herself, on the verge of breaking into hysterical laughter. It must be the accumulated strain of the past weeks.

She was about to climb up into the carriage when Emma, her whisper deafeningly loud, said, "I think he's coming over here, Aunt Glynis! Rhys Bevan—he's walking in this direction."

Glynis hoisted her skirts and, with a deliberate effort at composure, climbed into the carriage while Emma, not to be denied, whispered, "He told me that he'd heard of my Aunt Glynis, but that he *hadn't* heard how—" Emma broke off as laughter choked her. Nevertheless, she managed to gasp, "But that he hadn't heard how . . . how fetching she was!" And no longer making a serious attempt to restrain herself, Emma collapsed against the seat with peals of laughter.

Glynis clenched her teeth against the infection of Emma's hilarity, and lifted the reins to urge the horse forward. However, the reins were caught by a hand that shot forward, and she turned to meet again the direct gaze of Rhys Bevan. His eyes then moved beyond her to rest on Emma, who'd buried her face in her hands, but still shook with silent laughter.

"You'll have to forgive my niece, Mr. Bevan. She's become slightly delirious with . . . with the strain of the trial, I'm afraid."

This brought forth a strangled sound from Emma, and a quick grin from the man, who, Glynis decided with embarrassment, was far too observant, to say nothing of his being sharp-eared, not to guess what had occasioned Emma's behavior.

"But since there's been no trial," he commented, the corners of his eyes creasing with humor, "I have to think your niece has passed on to you what I said." He looked again at Emma, who suddenly quieted and peered at him through her fingers. "I hoped she might do that," he added.

"You're very forward, Mr. Bevan," Glynis replied, although it didn't come out as tartly as she'd intended.

"I'm working against time, Miss Tryon. I don't know how long I'll be here in western New York. But I've heard that—" He stopped as Emma, for the past moments mercifully restrained, now erupted again. This time Glynis directed a reproving look at her niece while, in a helpless gesture, Emma plunged her face into the leather of the seat.

When Glynis looked back at Rhys Bevan, she had to credit him for laughing himself and, in so doing, easing her embarrassment. And then, to her astonishment, he narrowed his eyes at Emma of the hidden face and said sternly, " 'Haste thee, Nymph, and bring with thee /Jest and youthful jollity /Quips and Cranks and wanton Wiles /Nods and Becks and wreathéd Smiles.' "

Emma raised her head, her eyes wide, and Glynis was aware that she herself was gawking at him, but it was so startlingly: a United States Treasury agent quoting Milton? But then again, this agent was Welsh.

Rhys Bevan just smiled at her surprise and said, "Now, let's try this again—I've heard that if anyone knows the people in Seneca Falls, it's you, Miss Tryon. I'd like to ask you some questions, if I might. But—" he stopped, looked again at

Emma with narrowed eyes, and said "—this is probably not the best place for it. May I call on you in the next day or two?"

"I can be found at the Seneca Falls Library, Mr. Bevan," Glynis answered, and then flicked the rein to get them out of there before Emma again lost control.

Rhys Bevan nodded, and stepped back as the carriage moved forward.

THEY WERE WELL on the road to home before Emma finally spoke. "Oh, Aunt Glynis, I'm so sorry—I just couldn't seem to stop laughing. And you probably didn't see Constable Stuart while you were talking to Rhys Bevan. The constable kept looking over at you. And he was frowning something fierce."

"Men can be that way, Emma," Glynis said casually, while wondering why it was true. "Constable Stuart and I have been friends for a long time. We're having a disagreement at the moment, but it's nothing we can't resolve." She wasn't as sure of that as she sounded.

"I don't know," Emma said, her eyes dancing. "Wait until he finds out Rhys Bevan is coming to call on you."

"Emma," Glynis began, then gave it up. Still, she thought, Cullen's behavior was maddeningly unfair. Whatever he was keeping from her had something to do with Fleur Coddington; now she was sure of it. And she was sure it had to do with the murders.

But how were they to find the guilty one—and before he possibly killed again? Glynis felt a sudden chill, because it now occurred to her that *if* Fleur Coddington was involved in some way, then perhaps at least one murder could be connected to the dress shop.

Glynis looked sideways at Emma, and fear took her breath away as surely as the hands that had closed around young Sally Lunt's throat.

TWENTY

❦

I, John Brown, am now certain that the crimes of this guilty land will never be purged away but with Blood. I had as I now think: vainly flattered myself that without very much bloodshed it might be done.
—JOHN BROWN. 1859

ANNIE BROWN'S ROCKING chair creaked softly. She moved in it restlessly, back and forth, while the yellow-eyed goat, curled up like a large dog on the porch floor, occasionally roused himself enough to butt his horns against the chair runners. Annie took a deep breath to try and quiet herself. And smelled woodsmoke in the fall air.

Her brothers' voices coming through the window from inside the rented Maryland house went on and on, as they'd done now for hours. Ever since John Henry had arrived from Chambersburg. Would they never get done with talking? It would begin to get dark soon. The late-September nights came quickly enough, and the sun this day seemed to be moving even faster than usual across the sky. But then, in the past week everything had taken on the feel of urgency. It started when that sad, half-blind man, Mr. Francis Jackson Meriam, arrived there from Boston with the gold coins. It didn't matter that Mr. Meriam said the six hundred dollars came from the purses of abolitionists; Father saw the gold as a sign from God. The sign he'd waited for that would tell him it was time to make ready.

And now all the men were there. The men who were going with Father to free the slaves. He had expected more, although two young Negro men arrived only yesterday. One of them said he'd been a lawman, a deputy constable, in a small town in western New York. He frowned most of the time, and it seemed as if he didn't trust Father's plans for the raid on Harper's Ferry, because he asked so many questions. It got so that, finally, the other black men told him to stop asking. After that, the deputy just rocked on his feet and scowled all the time. He was quiet about it, though.

Annie looked anxiously toward the window, praying the men would stop talking soon. What if she didn't have a chance to see John Henry alone? She and Martha were leaving next morning. Father had said they must go back to North Elba, that it would be dangerous for them to stay here longer. Why it should be more dangerous now than before, Annie didn't know. She did know she didn't want to leave.

The door suddenly opened and Father came out onto the porch. The goat scrambled to its feet and went jumping down the stairs as if it had forgotten something it had to do. Father watched it prance away, then said to Annie, "I have to go into town with a few of the men. You get to bed now—you leave tomorrow on an early train."

Annie's heart plunged like a stone tossed into a pond. But she couldn't ask Father if John Henry was one of the men going to town with him. Then John Henry himself came out on the porch. He didn't look at her, hadn't once since he got there. She guessed he had more on his mind than to think of her.

Next some of the white men with their heavy boots came clumping out the door, so Annie got up and stood against the porch wall. She wasn't going inside until she saw John Henry leave. He would walk away and she would watch him, maybe for the last time in a long time. She closed her eyes so they wouldn't spill over again, like they did earlier when John Henry hadn't seemed to notice her.

Father had gone to the edge of the stairs, and stood there talking to a few of the men. She felt something prickly then, and when she looked around, sure enough, John Henry's eyes were on her. He pointed to the porch floor and his lips moved silently: "Stay here." He pointed again. Annie nodded once to let him know she understood. And her heart came leaping up from where it had been lying cold and heavy.

Father and the men trooped off, John Henry with them, while Annie sat back down in the rocker. She wouldn't move from that spot if the Lord Himself came to fetch her. That was because in the time she'd been there, waiting for Father's word from God and taking care of the men, she found out there was nothing in the world she wanted so much as John Henry. And there never would be. She wanted to marry him and live with him and have his children. That's all she wanted. She guessed John Henry would be enough for anybody, even a rich girl who had gone to school and could have anything she wanted. He would be more than enough for Annie. If anything good was ever going to happen to her, she prayed it would be that.

Now she saw a sudden movement down the road. She jumped up and ran to the edge of the porch. It was John Henry, and his arm was raised and beckoning her. Annie stood there a moment, wondering if she should tell Martha she was leaving. But Martha could take forever trying to talk her out of it, saying Father would be furious, and Father would be this and Father would be that. It would just waste time, because Annie was going no matter what. Wherever John Henry wanted to take her, she was going.

She ran toward him across a field of goldenrod, sending the flower heads flying in clouds of pollen that coated her bare arms and legs. When she got to John Henry, he picked her up in his arms and whirled her around while the pollen flew until they were covered, both of them, with fine gold dust.

John Henry put her down and began to brush himself off. ''I couldn't let you go without saying good-bye, Annie Brown.''

''No,'' she said. ''I was afraid, though.''

''You afraid? I don't think you're afraid of much,'' he said, starting to brush the pollen from the hem of her blue calico dress.

''I am,'' Annie said again. ''I'm afraid.''

John Henry didn't ask her of what. He probably knew. He just kept brushing at her dress, moving his hand higher and higher until he touched her breast. He let his hand stay there, touching her, until he shook his head and let his hand drop to his side. Then he stood back and just looked at her for a long time. It troubled Annie that his eyes had turned so sad.

''Let's walk some, Annie Brown.'' John Henry took her hand, and they went through woods of sycamore and black walnut and slender dogwood nipped by frost and changed to scarlet tongues of fire. Wild geese winged across the sky, and the air smelled of apples and burning leaves and new-mown hay. They walked to where the land dipped to a rocky bluff above the two rivers. When they stood looking down from the bluff they could see the Baltimore and Ohio tracks and the long, covered railroad bridge, and the Shenandoah and Potomac merging at the promontory of land that bore the town of Harper's Ferry.

"That's where it will happen," John Henry said softly, pointing down to two brick armory buildings. "The beginning of the end of slavery. We'll do it, Annie Brown, or we will die trying."

"Yes," Annie said. "That's why I'm afraid."

"Don't be afraid. Be proud. You've been part of it," he said, looking at her with eyes that were now as bright as two gold coins. "You've been part of the history that will be made here. See there?" He pointed, turning her so she looked straight down. "See that building way over there, on that strip of land between the canal locks and the Shenandoah? That's the rifle factory. It's where I'll be, after we capture the railroad bridge and the armory."

Annie didn't want to see it. She turned into him, pushing her forehead against his chest, and breathing in the snowy balsam scent of him. "I'm afraid, John Henry. I'm sorry, but I am."

And she was, more afraid than she'd ever been before. Now that she could see it, see exactly where it would happen, it terrified her with its realness. Up until then, it had been just lines and crosses and squares on Father's maps. Not something that was true. And her brothers and the other men had been together so long, she hadn't thought of what might happen to them when they weren't just eating and sleeping and talking. But that was before, and now she could see John Henry down on that strip of land with all the rifles. And he was alone.

He seemed different now, too, and that made her afraid.

"There's nothing for you to be afraid of," he said, bringing his hand up under her chin. He lifted her face and stroked her cheek. "You won't be here when it happens. You'll be up in your northern mountains, and you'll be safe. That's why I told your Father he had to send you back, you and Martha."

"*You* told him? That's why we're leaving tomorrow?"

"You can't stay here, Annie. If something goes wrong, they'll find you at the Kennedy farm and . . ." His voice broke as Annie wrenched away.

She backed off the bluff, then turned and started to run toward the woods. She'd gotten into the first stand of trees when John Henry caught her. "Annie! You *can't* stay here," he said, gripping her arms. "How could you believe I'd let you? Or that your Father would, either?"

Annie shook her head, trying so hard not to cry that her eyes squeezed shut. And then she couldn't see him.

"Annie, look at me. *Look* at me!"

Her eyes flew open and the tears came spilling out like the rivers of Harper's Ferry. The rivers where John Henry would die. He would die if she left; she knew this with absolute certainty, caught in a rising southern storm with great howling winds that even now chilled her through to her bones. He would die.

She stood shivering in John Henry's grasp, while behind him the setting sun turned the sky to fiery red, the red of blood and battle. Her mother's words came back, the words she'd said to Annie just before the train pulled out of North Elba: "A man will do what he wants to do. Right or wrong, clever or stupid, he will do it. And no woman can stop him. She can only watch and wait. You will have to learn that, Anne, and learn it now. Before your heart gets broken."

Annie guessed she hadn't learned quick enough. She reached up and pulled John Henry's head down to hers and kissed his mouth as hard as she could. When his arms closed around her, she pressed herself against him so tight she could feel every part of him. If she burned herself into him like a brand, then she might keep him from harm. Keep him with her forever.

John Henry took hold of her shoulders and gently pushed her away. "No. We can't do this, Annie. It wouldn't be right. I might have to die, you know. I'm not afraid of that . . . well, not very." He smiled down at her and she knew it was so she would stop crying. She tried.

"I'm not so afraid of dying now," he went on, "but I would be afraid if we did something that could hurt you in times to come."

He smiled again and said, "I want to think of you safe up there in your mountains under the North Star. If something happens to me . . ." He stopped because she started to cry again. "Annie, please listen. If something happens and I have to die, you'll be what I'm thinking of at the last. So I need to know you're safe. But Annie, if things go well, when it's all over—"

"Will it ever be over?" Annie interrupted to ask.

"It might be a while, I grant you that. But when it is, then I'll come up that road from North Elba. And when you see me coming, I pray your heart still leaps."

THE TRAIN PULLED slowly out of the station. Annie didn't look up; she just kept staring at her lap. John Henry wasn't there. He'd said the night before that he wouldn't come to the station. It would be too hard, he had said. So why should she look around? She didn't want to see any more of Harper's Ferry.

The train chugged into the covered bridge, and when it came out again, Annie had to look. And there, on the road heading into the mountains, she saw a speck moving against the cloud-filled sky. It could be John Henry.

And she felt her heart break.

TWENTY-ONE

The Harper's Ferry invasion has advanced the cause of Disunion more than any other event that has happened since the formation of the government.

— AN 1859 ISSUE OF THE *RICHMOND ENQUIRER*

GLYNIS WAS VAGUELY aware of the warm sunshine that streamed through the library windows, but she shivered as she gazed again at the newspapers of the day previous. The October 17th headlines blared: "NEGRO INSURRECTION AT HARPER'S FERRY"—"FIRE AND RAPINE ON THE VIRGINIA BORDER"—"SLAVES LOOT AND BUTCHER IN THE STREETS OF THE SOUTH." And those were the more restrained. The wire reports coming out of Washington, so Rhys Bevan had told her, were a morass of confusion, one conflicting story after another. The only thing on which the various sources agreed was that a raiding party had attempted to capture a United States armory in the small, heretofore little known town of Harper's Ferry, Virginia. None of the perpetrators had as yet been identified. And what exactly had occurred around midnight of Sunday, October 16th, as well as what had taken place since—it was now more than thirty-six hours later—remained obscure. But every recent dispatch seemed to indicate that a pitched battle was being waged between the renegade band and militia companies from Maryland and Virginia.

Glynis had asked herself over and over why she feared this was John Brown's doing. Had Zeph mentioned a location before he'd gone that might lead her to think that? She'd racked her brain, trying to disregard the overwrought newspaper stories spinning through her head. Virginia, Virginia—had Zeph mentioned *Virginia?* She slammed her open palm down on her desk, and saw Jonathan, across the room, jump three feet into the air.

"I'm sorry, Jonathan. I'm just so terrified that Zeph is down there, mixed up in that . . . that bloodbath. And I can't remember what he said before he left—just that he was heading south. We know by his letter that he was in Philadelphia. But where is he *now?*"

"I can go to the telegraph office again for you," Jonathan offered. "Maybe something new has come in."

"No; thank you, anyway. Rhys Bevan said he would try to get a wire through to Washington, and that he'd let me know if he found out anything. But from the newspaper accounts, the entire South seems to have been thrown into a frenzy. As if the slave owners hadn't brought this on themselves!"

Jonathan's face held a grim look not typical of him. "I'd imagine they probably remember Nat Turner's uprising in '31, Miss Tryon. A lot of white southerners got slaughtered, so you can hardly blame them for being scared now."

"I certainly *can* blame them, Jonathan! Or, more accurately, blame the men—the plantation owners and the congressmen and those southern justices on the Supreme Court—for their unyielding position on slavery!" With sudden dismay, Glynis realized her voice had risen nearly to the level of shouting. She shook her head, at the same time thinking she should probably apologize to Jonathan, again. While she was contemplating this, Rhys Bevan came through the open library door.

Even before he said anything, Glynis felt her cheeks grow hot. She'd forgotten the door was open. And he must have heard her—how could he have helped it?

"The sound of passion ringing forth from your library, Miss Tryon? And a noble sound it was, although I scarcely can believe I heard it."

The puckish smile was all that kept him from a mortal wound, Glynis thought, twisting her letter opener between her fingers. "I'm sorry you overheard that, Mr. Bevan. I apologize to you—and to you, too, Jonathan."

Rhys Bevan appeared disappointed. "Miss Tryon, are you aware of what your own George Sand has said—"

"*My own George Sand?* Has Emma been talking to you?"

"Talking about what?" he asked, affecting such a look of innocence that she knew he'd not confess to anything. "I know you have a fondness for Sand—you have every last one of her works, after all. But what I was about to say was, in George's own words: 'The capacity for passion is both cruel and divine.' ''

Since he was watching her so closely, as was Jonathan, Glynis merely smiled. She certainly would not admit to being impressed—not only that Rhys Bevan knew Sand was a woman, but that he'd read enough to quote her. The man was just full of surprises.

But then, as he pulled what were obviously several telegrams from his frock coat pocket, Glynis quickly got to her feet. ''What have you heard?''

''Not a great deal,'' he said, now serious, ''except it does appear that the attack on Harper's Ferry is all but over. I'm sorry to have to tell you though . . .'' He stopped and took a step toward her as she sucked in her breath.

''No, go on, please! It *is* John Brown who's responsible, isn't it?''

''It would seem so. But I don't have definite word on who the others are. So let's not assume your young friend was involved. Not just yet.''

He looked at her with such genuine concern that she felt compelled to nod agreement. But she found this compulsion disconcerting. Rhys Bevan himself was disconcerting. Although he'd indicated he wouldn't stay long in western New York, he was still there. Grandy Fox's aborted trial had been over three weeks ago, and while Rhys Bevan had shot off every so often to chase down possible evidence in the counterfeiting case, he always returned to Seneca Falls. During the past weeks he'd questioned her closely about her train trip from Rochester the day Barrymore had been killed; her proximity to the argument in the market, and the second man with the knife. Again and again he had demanded, if pleasantly, descriptions of the two men she'd seen in conflict with the Utica banker. At last she'd said with exasperation, ''No, I've told you two dozen times, Mr. Bevan, that I can't be more specific. I couldn't see either man very well. The only person I could later identify was Grandy Fox, and then only because of the straw hat and fiddle. Without those, I doubt if I'd have known even him!''

Rhys Bevan had given her a long searching look; so long, in fact, that Glynis had the uneasy sense he might suspect her of lying to him. And he'd then interrogated Emma—this done with his mischievous smile, but it was interrogation nonetheless. While she too pleaded ignorance, she had been far more flustered than her aunt.

"He acts like he thinks I did something illegal," Emma fretted. "And here I thought he was a nice man."

"We don't know yet that he's not, Emma. Don't forget that Rhys Bevan is first and foremost a detective, and no doubt accustomed to people lying, so he's skeptical of everyone."

Emma, though, appeared so agitated that Glynis began to worry that her niece might be concealing something. And despite Rhys Bevan's solicitous manner, he was a man about whom she really knew very little. And it troubled her.

"I'm truly all right, Mr. Bevan," she now assured him. "What else have you learned about Harper's Ferry?"

"President Buchanan sent in a contingent of U.S. Marines who were stationed in Washington, plus two cavalry units from Virginia under a Colonel Robert Lee. John Brown's been captured after another skirmish in Harper's Ferry, during which he was wounded. The reports don't say how badly. But one of his sons has already been killed, the other's apparently dying of injuries. So far those are the only ones who've been identified."

"Do you know whether any others were killed, though?"

"Yes, there were others, and there's a preliminary casualty count—Miss Tryon?"

Glynis had reached for her desk to steady herself. But Rhys Bevan, before she could protest, grasped her shoulders and literally lifted her into her desk chair.

"Why don't you wait to worry until some names come in?" Despite the casual words, his voice held compassion.

"There are still *no* names?"

He shook his head. "None other than Brown and his sons, Watson and—" he paused to scan one of the telegrams "—and the other son's name is Oliver. As we suspected, the first reports from Virginia were greatly exaggerated. There was no slave uprising. None at all, anywhere. In fact, the first person killed by the raiders seems to have been, ironically, a free Negro baggage master who worked at the Harper's Ferry rail station—and whose bad luck it was to be in the wrong place at the wrong time. But the press reports have so inflamed white southerners that they're now hunting down blameless Negroes.''

Glynis sank back against her chair, despairing for Zeph if he had indeed managed to locate John Brown.

Rhys Bevan lowered himself to sit on the edge of her desk before he went on. ''The Treasury sources report that nine or ten of Brown's men were killed during the time they occupied various buildings in the town. And a handful more were captured. A few might have escaped—there's a manhunt on for them. I doubt they can slip through the dragnet that's been cast—certainly no white southerners will help them.''

Jonathan, who had been listening without a word, now said, ''Were any of the townspeople killed?''

''The reports say three, including the mayor. Plus a slave-holder, and one Marine. And there's some nine or ten wounded. Those are the best estimates that Treasury has as of now. The final numbers may change, but probably not by much.''

Glynis reached for hope, although there wasn't much on which to base it. Those captured would most surely be hanged for treason, but if a few had escaped? Zeph was smart and resourceful. In addition, he was not, as far as she knew, either a martyr or in the least suicidal. She clutched at this thin thread of optimism.

Still, she wouldn't accomplish anything more in the way of work this day. She pushed aside some clutter to unearth her desk clock. ''I think we can close the library now, Jonathan. Harvest season's at its peak, so we won't get more patrons, not at this time of day.''

As Jonathan began to clear off his desktop—a daily ritual that irked Glynis unreasonably—and as she shifted some papers from one pile to another, Rhys Bevan asked nonchalantly, ''Are you going to the dress shop now?''

She turned to him warily, guessing that his question wasn't as offhand as it sounded. ''As a matter of fact, I am. How did you guess?''

"No amazing deduction on my part, Miss Tryon. That's where you go every night after closing here."

So he *was* spying on her, or Emma, or both of them. But why? She sincerely hoped he was also watching others surely far more worthy of attention than herself and her niece; people such as Cyril Doggett and Alan Fitzhugh, or Valerian Voss and Colonel de Warde. Even the enigmatic Margaret Taylor. And were they, Agents Rhys Bevan and Grandy Fox, still suspicious of Cullen?

She desperately wished she knew more about this man: wished she could confide in him, explain why she went to La Maison de Fleur every night. But she sensed there was in Rhys Bevan an engaging exterior joined with the inner control of a good actor.

When they left the library, he remained beside her as she walked toward the dress shop. "I think," he began in the most casual way, "that you're right to concern yourself with your niece's safety." Glynis must have looked startled, as he added, "Until we find out exactly what's going on in this town, I worry about people putting themselves in danger."

Glynis stopped walking. "Exactly *whom* are you worried about, Mr. Bevan?"

"You, for one. I'm afraid you may know more than you think you do."

"Oh, then you don't believe I'm deliberately lying to you?"

Rhys Bevan actually laughed. "I didn't say *that*. I believe you'd lie to protect someone you cared about. After all, Miss Tryon, why should you tell me anything? What do you know about me? Not very much."

"My thoughts precisely, Mr. Bevan." She again began to walk a little faster.

He laughed. "So we're at a standoff, aren't we? Not a good place to be, especially since you're the one person most likely to have seen the killer."

Glynis began to protest, but then silenced herself. She did have the nagging sense of having overlooked something of importance—or perhaps more than one thing.

They had stopped by the canopied entrance of the dress shop, and Glynis found Rhys Bevan studying her with what might have been amusement. "You believe I've seen the killer, Mr. Bevan. Do you mean other than on the train from Rochester?"

"I think it's possible. And since you're an intelligent woman—with a history of solving puzzles—I think eventually you're going to find a crucial piece of this one. Or something will happen to jog your memory, or someone will reveal more than he intended—"

"*He?* So you're sure it's a man?" Glynis interrupted.

"I'd willingly wager on it. What about you?"

"Yes, I think so. Although I'm not so sure that all the members of the counterfeiting ring have to be male."

Ever so slightly his eyes narrowed as he said, "And you're right about that. In the past, women have been very successful counterfeiters, primarily because they're the last to be suspected. It's true even when they're the ringleaders, as they occasionally are, although I'm not saying that's the case here."

"But some local woman might have been forced into taking part, as Fiona Roarke was—I assume you heard about her?"

He nodded. "And you think there's another woman as well, don't you, Miss Tryon? Fleur Coddington?"

Glynis struggled to keep her expression neutral, but had been told more than once that she failed miserably in these attempts. "I don't know," she said finally, while looking into his sharp blue eyes. He didn't miss much, she feared.

"I think you do know," he countered. "However, since you don't trust me, you'll not say. And thus we're back where we started. But one of these days, you'd better consider confiding in me. . . ."

He left off as Fleur Coddington came through the entrance doors and down the marble steps. Her head was lowered, watching her feet, so she didn't immediately see the two people standing in the road. Glynis took note of the recent change in the woman; an unbecoming loss of weight and a pale haggard look that evidenced lack of sleep. When Fleur looked up and saw Glynis and Rhys Bevan, she halted on the bottom step. For a moment, Glynis had the impression that Fleur was debating whether to retreat into her shop. But Glynis could have imagined it.

"Afternoon, Mrs. Coddington," Rhys Bevan said with a

noncommittal smile. Glynis watched Fleur's face carefully, and was rewarded by the fleeting look of distress that crossed it before the woman composed her own smile and answered with a soft greeting. She acknowledged Glynis with simply a nod.

"You must excuse me," she said to Rhys Bevan. "I'm just on my way to the Usher Playhouse." Fleur airily waved a gloved hand, and went on to say, "The masquerade ball arrangements, you know." She began to walk past them, then, as if as an afterthought, said to Glynis, "You'll find your talented niece inside, awash in costumes."

Then Fleur, with a studied gesture, opened her fringed parasol and strolled up Fall Street, while both Glynis and Rhys Bevan stood looking after her. Glynis wondered what was going through the agent's mind, since his expression didn't reveal a thing.

Up the road, Grandy Fox emerged from the telegraph office. He hesitated on the front stoop, glancing up and down Fall Street, then, apparently spotting Rhys Bevan, he started toward them. On the way he passed Fleur Coddington, who, from Glynis's vantage point, seemed to ignore the agent as she turned onto the river bridge. For a moment, Grandy stood looking after her. Then he shrugged and continued on toward the dress shop, calling out, "Rhys! Just the man I need to see— wire came in for you a few minutes ago."

When he reached them, he handed the telegram to Rhys Bevan, then grinned at Glynis. "Good day, Miss Tryon. Hope *you* aren't going to snub me too." He gave a significant look toward the bridge, where Fleur Coddington's retreating figure was still visible. "I assume Mrs. Coddington is put out because I don't sharpen her scissors anymore. But there didn't seem any reason to continue the peddler role, not after the entire town witnessed my cover being blown sky high."

Glynis tried to smile, but was defeated by her concern for Zeph, and what potentially devastating news the wire might hold. She stood there tensely while Rhys Bevan scanned it before she asked, "Is it about Harper's Ferry?"

"No, no, it isn't," he said, appearing somewhat distracted. "Seems I'm being recalled to Washington."

Glynis felt a sense of alarm. It might be coincidence, but

since Rhys Bevan's arrival there had been no more murders. "So you'll be leaving Seneca Falls soon?"

He nodded. "Looks like it. I notified Treasury that the flow of bogus money had all but dried up in the past several weeks. I think the perpetrators have moved on, probably because they felt we were getting too close. So it's back to Washington to wait until they surface somewhere else."

"But the killer hasn't been found yet," Glynis objected.

"Finding killers isn't my job," he replied. "But Grandy, I don't think you and I should both leave at the same time. The counterfeiters, if they've simply been lying low, could start up operations again."

Grandy nodded. "I agree. I should stay for at least a few more weeks—see what happens. I'll wire Treasury to that effect."

Glynis sighed in relief. When both men looked at her, she said in embarrassment, "I confess to being glad one of you is staying. Although perhaps the murders were tied to the counterfeiting ring, and there's nothing more to worry about now." As she said this, however, she failed to convince herself it was true.

Rhys Bevan turned to Grandy Fox. "I've got a few things to clean up yet today, so when you wire Washington, tell them I'll leave on the first train out tomorrow."

"Right." Grandy's face crinkled into a pleasant grin as he said to Glynis, "Constable Stuart and I will man the fort until we're sure the killer has gone elsewhere. And Rhys is needed more in Washington than here right now."

Glynis watched Grandy head back toward the telegraph office, then realized Rhys Bevan was looking at her with what seemed to be an assessment. Why? To see how afraid she really was? So afraid that she'd confide in him—but about what? Glynis couldn't even guess at what he suspected her of concealing. To her surprise, all he said was, "I should be on my way, Miss Tryon. It has been a very great pleasure meeting you." Instead of walking away, however, he continued to study her, and seemed to be expecting a reply.

"Mr. Bevan, I'm afraid you think I've been evasive. But if

I knew something that would help, I would tell you. I hope you believe that.''

He shook his head. ''I'm afraid I don't. I'm convinced you think that Fleur Coddington is involved with the counterfeiters in some way, but you won't say how.''

''Why do you think that?''

''Because of the concern you've showed about your niece working in there,'' he answered, motioning toward the shop. ''I know for a fact that you stay there every night until she leaves—except on those nights when Mrs. Smith is with her.''

Glynis swallowed hard. He was right, of course. And it was fortunate that Lacey Smith *was* working many extra hours on the masquerade ball costumes with Emma.

Her face must have revealed this, as Rhys Bevan smiled again, saying, ''Yes. And I think you're wise to be cautious.''

If he intended to unnerve her, he'd succeeded. She stood there, biting her lower lip, trying to decide what to say to this man. How could she tell him about Cullen's interest in Fleur Coddington? After all, she didn't know absolutely that Cullen suspected Fleur of participating in counterfeiting. Or how could she tell Rhys Bevan that she had become increasingly concerned that Emma, too, was concealing something. She couldn't. But she would confront Emma herself, tonight.

''You'll be going tomorrow, then?'' she asked him, trying to ignore the hollow feeling in the pit of her stomach. ''Are you going to tell anyone else that you're leaving?''

''Everyone that needs to know. And Grandy will be here.''

''Yes, and I'm relieved because . . .'' She broke off, not certain she wanted Rhys Bevan to know how disturbed she really was; as they'd been standing there, she'd been growing more anxious by the minute. Not that she could put her finger on why.

She just shook her head, although he was obviously waiting for her to say more. He reached out to take her hand, and held it lightly. ''I have a feeling we'll meet in the future, Miss Tryon. And again, it will be to my great pleasure.''

He held her gaze until Glynis felt her color rising. As she dropped her eyes, he pressed her hand and said, ''Another favorite author of yours said, 'In every parting there is an image of death.' ''

Glynis, had she expected anything at all from him, would have guessed he'd come up with something witty or breezy, but not this. "Yes," she answered, "my very great favorite, George Eliot."

Rhys Bevan, still holding her hand, grinned. "These women authors do like their Georges, don't they? Ah, Miss Tryon . . . Glynis . . . I shall miss you. No one else plays this game half as well as you. By the way, I hope you'll think to add a large cigar to your George Sand impersonation. That would really make the town sit up and take notice."

"I'm afraid it would!" Glynis finally laughed, and realized she'd not extracted her hand from his. "But here's another, Mr. Bevan: 'All farewells should be sudden.' ''

He gave her another long look. "The man knew what he was saying, and I'll wager a month's pay it *was* a man."

"And you'd be right; it was Byron."

"Another George! Well, I shall heed his advice." He dropped her hand, and turned to leave. But he said over his shoulder, "Just one more, from you-know-who: 'Parting is such sweet sorrow.' Though that never did make sense to me."

And he walked away. Glynis felt an inexplicable pang of regret. She quickly attributed it to the odd sense of abandonment she was experiencing, along with her worry about Zeph. She watched Rhys Bevan's easy rhythmic strides up Fall Street for a brief moment, then mounted the steps to La Maison de Fleur.

She found Emma, much as Fleur had portrayed, awash in near-finished gowns, cloaks, skirts of inconceivable variety, and hats from feather-trimmed leghorns to demure bonnets. Glynis assumed the sagging rack along the wall held finished costumes, as they were shrouded in white muslin, while yards of fabric and lace and ribbon covered every visible surface. In the midst of this, Lacey Smith sat calmly hemming a pair of gold velvet trousers that Glynis guessed might belong to George Sand.

Emma jumped to her feet, sending a shower of ostrich feathers into the air. "Aunt Glynis, thank goodness you've come. I just remembered, I haven't quite finished your redingote. Let me find it—I know it's here somewhere!''

Emma began to painstakingly sort through the capes and coats and jackets draped carefully over a long table. Lacey chuckled. "Emma, child, how can you keep track of all that stuff?''

"I can't!'' Emma wailed. "How will I ever finish in time when the ball's just three days away? Oh, Lord!''

Glynis glanced at Lacey, who was shaking her head and laughing. "She'll make it,'' the woman said. "Never saw no one person could work so fast as that child.''

"Here it is!'' Emma cried, separating from the rest a gold velvet coat. She held it out to Glynis. "You're going to look so elegant, Aunt Glyn. With that cream, lace-trimmed silk blouse under this coat, you'd make the real George Sand green with envy. And wait until Rhys Bevan sees you—I just bet he and Constable Stuart end up fighting a duel!''

Glynis refused to rise to this bait. She slipped into the coat, marveling at what Emma had done to modify the redingote's characteristic looseness, making it fit closely over the shoulders and bust before the skillfully placed gores flared it to ankle-length. A thin silk lining slithered under the rich golden pile of the velvet, and for a moment Glynis disregarded the afternoon's distress, and sighed with pleasure.

Lacey smiled broadly. "I have to tell you, I thought this trouser-and-coat business was a bad idea. But I surely have changed my mind. Miss Tryon, you do look a beautiful sight. Set a whole new style, you will.''

"Of course you must wear your short black boots, the ones with square heels,'' Emma declared, pushing up the redingote sleeves and pinning them rapidly, "and we have to do something with your hair.''

"My hair?''

"You can't keep it in that bun, Aunt Glynis—not and wear *my* George Sand outfit, you can't! Besides, everybody would know you immediately. The whole point is to disguise yourself so you can't be recognized.''

For no apparent reason, Glynis felt something unpleasant streak down her spine. She tried to ignore it by saying, "Then why did you tell Rhys Bevan who I was going as, dear Emma?''

Emma stopped pinning and looked astonished. ''I didn't—that is, not exactly. He *was* trying to worm it out of me, Aunt Glyn, and he was so persistent, I just said . . . what *did* I say?''

Lacey grinned. ''You says, 'Mr. Bevan, you wouldn't know if I tells you.' And then, you says, 'An author and she dresses like a man.' ''

''You said *that,* Emma?''

Emma nodded, looking unconcerned. ''He wouldn't know who I was talking about, Aunt Glynis.''

''Oh, Rhys Bevan certainly would. He did. Well, it doesn't matter now—he won't be at the ball, anyway.''

''He won't?'' Emma rocked back on her heels. ''Besides sending him an invitation, Miss Usher asked him, personally, to come. She'll be beside herself if he doesn't show up!''

''Got her cap set for him, she has,'' Lacey added.

''But I'm really sorry, Aunt Glynis, for spilling the beans to Mr. Bevan. And after I've been so *careful* not to tell what anyone is wearing. I haven't even told you. In fact,'' Emma said, grinning, ''you don't know what *my* costume is.''

''Or mine, either,'' said Lacey. ''Course it'll be hard to miss me and Isaiah.'' Her face beamed, and Emma smiled broadly when Lacey added, ''We'll be the ones holding up the moon.''

She and Emma gave each other a telling look. ''Lacey, you're not supposed to tell!'' Emma said, still smiling. ''Miss Usher will lay us both out in lavender if she hears.''

''Hears what?'' Glynis asked.

Emma turned her back and picked up something from a nearby table. When she turned around she held in front of herself a close facsimile of a Roman toga, but one covered completely with layers of green peacock feathers, sprinkled with small glittering silver beads. And now Emma clambered up onto a chair and struck a pose, head up, left arm extended with right arm pulled back and bent at the elbow. Her right fingers held an invisible object next to her ear. ''See my silver bow and arrows?'' She wiggled her fingers. ''Just call me Diana!'' she laughed. ''Diana—mighty huntress! Goddess of the Moon!''

She jumped down from the chair, while Lacey, laughing, shook a finger at her. "Emma, child, your aunt breathes a word of this to Miss Vanessa, you and me best get on the next train out of town. 'Cause if we don't, that lady going to *ride* us out on a rail."

She and Emma seemed to find this uproariously funny. Glynis looked around for an empty spot to sit and wait out their laughter. Failing to find one, she stood against the wall until calm had been restored. Although bewildered, she had to smile herself; it was nearly impossible to believe that this young woman rocked with mirth was the same one who, just five months before, had been so withdrawn she would barely speak.

When they finally quieted, Glynis asked, "Now what was that all about?"

"Oh, Aunt Glynis," Emma gasped, wiping her eyes. "It's been just too funny. But you can't tell anyone!" She waited until Glynis nodded before she said, "Do you know why Miss Usher picked *this* particular Saturday night for the ball?"

"No, I don't know why," Glynis answered.

"Well, course you don't," Lacey said. "Who *would* know? 'Cepting Miss Usher, that is." She broke off as her voice started to shake, and Glynis was afraid the two would be set off again before she found out the cause.

"Emma, what is significant about Saturday night?"

Emma, clearly making a great effort to keep her face straight, answered, "It's the *hunter's moon,* Aunt Glyn! That's what Miss Usher came up with as the ball's theme—the hunter's moon. And Lacey and I think it was all because—" she threw her ally a grin "—because Miss Usher wanted to go hunting." Emma caught her breath and then blurted, "Hunting for Rhys Bevan!"

And now, all restraint cast aside, the two women sank to the floor and howled with glee.

Glynis, however, did not feel in the least like laughing. What she felt was dread, a sense of something lying in wait, brooding, just beyond the reach of understanding. For some unknown reason, the train trip from Rochester suddenly came back to her, and, along with it, the dying Barrymore's words when he'd dropped the pouch into her lap. He'd said something like, "The trouble's in Seneca Falls."

She suspected now that Rhys Bevan had been dangerously mistaken. The killer had not left town with the counterfeiters. His agenda must be different from theirs—Sally Lunt's murder had pointed to that. Did it mean there would be another murder in Seneca Falls?

And now the theme of the masquerade ball held for Glynis a starkly menacing significance: *the hunter's moon.*

TWENTY-TWO

❧

Dress was the one unfailing talisman and charm used for keeping all things in their places. Everybody was dressed for a Fancy Ball that was never to leave off.
—CHARLES DICKENS, *A TALE OF TWO CITIES* 1859

MIDWAY ACROSS THE river bridge, Glynis reined in the livery-rented, dapple-gray mare, then pulled off her mask to gaze at the luminous disk riding just above the horizon. The immense hunter's moon looked close enough to pluck from the sky. Vanessa Usher had chosen this night for the masquerade ball with her intuitive genius for drama, regardless of what Emma and Lacey speculated about her motives. Even the weather cooperated. Despite a killing frost several days before, the night held the balmy warmth of Indian summer.

While she admired the moon, Glynis smoothed the nap of her velvet trousers. The unrestricted freedom of movement they permitted was more than enough reason for women to throw off forever their hoop skirts and corsets. This freedom, in fact, had persuaded Glynis not to hire a carriage, but to ride the mare instead. And why not? She had become, during the year in Springfield, a competent rider. Also, she was unescorted, a circumstance usually forbidden a woman attending a social function of mixed company, but one which the masquerade's peculiar circumstances made possible; no one would know who she was—no one, that is, except Emma and Lacey, and livery owner John Boone. And he knew only because, despite the mask, he'd recognized her voice. At least this had warned her to be more careful. Although caution was not especially characteristic of George Sand.

Reluctantly, Glynis took one last look at the moon, then replaced the white domino half mask and nudged the horse's sides with her heels. The mare started forward, only to shy

seconds later when a sudden blare of hunting horns exploded
from the Usher Playhouse. Another dramatic touch from Vanessa. Glynis could now see colored lanterns strung along the
sides of the theater and on down the path to the canal, where
partygoers were arriving in packet boats.

Her stomach knotted as it had done numerous times since
she'd left the Peartree house. Once again, she checked to make
certain Jacques Sundown's walking stick was securely tied to
the saddle and within reach. Although it made her feel somewhat less vulnerable, it would afford scant protection if the
killer learned that she knew his identity. And Glynis now
thought she did know.

The tangled skein had begun to unravel the afternoon Rhys
Bevan had announced he would leave; the same afternoon
Glynis had a final fitting of her George Sand outfit at La Maison
de Fleur and finally, *finally,* remembered the dying banker's
words in the train from Rochester. Once those words had been
recalled, subsequent events began unwinding from her memory
to form a pattern, the overall design of which, if it proved to
be correct, was one of diabolic dimension.

The mortally wounded Barrymore had told her, she came to
realize, not only where to look, but for what to look. And until
now Glynis had entirely ignored the clues with which he had
pointed to his murderer: his words and the contents of his tobacco pouch.

She supposed it did no good to further berate herself for
being so blind. No one else had seen the significance either,
although if they had it might have saved several lives. And
even now, she couldn't be absolutely certain. There were loose
threads she hadn't as yet tied into the overall tapestry of greed
and treason and murder. But tonight might unmask a killer, and
nothing could serve that purpose better than a masquerade ball.

Thus she would be compelled to temporarily put aside her
gnawing fear for Zeph, from whom no one had heard. In the
past several days most of the members of John Brown's band
had been identified—those who had been killed or captured
alive at Harper's Ferry. Neither Zeph nor his cousin was among
them. Not so far. However, there remained little hope that any
of the men were still at large. The dragnet had apparently pulled

in with relentless speed those few who'd initially made their escape.

She couldn't think about that now. Nor could she afford to reflect further on the abrupt departure of Rhys Bevan, who might come to regret his ill-conceived exit. But she could not ignore what had become her single greatest fear. The very real possibility of another murder.

Now, taking several deep breaths in a useless attempt to calm herself, Glynis urged the little mare along the towpath. As the sloping path that led to the theater appeared, another blast of hunting horns made her gaze with longing at the remote and silent moon.

AFTER GLYNIS HAD tethered the mare, she followed a group of recent arrivals to the entrance of the Usher Playhouse. She felt herself being scrutinized, but without apparent recognition. Nonetheless she did see, below the half masks, several broad smiles of what appeared to be frank approval from, of all things, the men in the group. Perhaps they couldn't see the trousers under the redingote. Or, more likely, they thought her to be a man! Yes; her hair was down, pulled back softly with velvet ribbon, so to them she might be an eighteenth-century courtier. In any event, she began to believe her disguise was reliable—it certainly was liberating—until recall made her stomach knot again.

She waited while those ahead of her entered the theater. Then she followed them through the playhouse doors—and into a web of moonbeams. They floated in ghostly splendor among towering white trees whose branches reached for an immense pearly disk, a mirror image of the one hanging in the night sky. For a moment Glynis yielded to wonder and allowed herself to believe she had entered an enchanted forest.

A forest made real by Vanessa Usher's imagination. The theater seating had been removed to create a vast room, across which wide scarves of white silk hammocked, swinging gently from hooks placed high on the walls. The nearly full-grown trees had been placed in tubs at intervals under the high ceiling, and appeared to be catching the moonbeams in their white-washed branches. And the moon itself? Glynis had to walk

directly beneath it to see fishing line holding the huge, translucent alabaster plate; a form of gypsum, she recalled from
some obscure library reference, appropriately named selenite
from *selene,* meaning moon.

She heard a deep chuckle, and turned to find a red-turbaned
Negro woman with enormous hoop earrings and flowing gold-
and-red-striped kaftan. A Nubian princess? But even the half
mask could not disguise Lacey Smith when she chuckled.

"What a moon, Lacey!" Glynis said, relieved not to have
to alter her voice. "Did Isaiah make it?"

"Sure did." This came from a masked Nubian prince in
multicolored robe who appeared beside Lacey.

"Isaiah, everybody knows your voice," Lacey said indig-
nantly. "So what good's a mask unless you hush up?"

Isaiah laughed, and motioned for Glynis to turn around so
she faced the stage, which, she found, had been transformed to
a forest glade encircled by slim birch saplings. Tall ferns and
ivy and white camellias—no doubt originating in the Usher
conservatory—carpeted the stage floor. To one side of the glade
a harpsichord nestled in the greenery. Opposite stood an alabaster sculpture of a young woman in Roman toga, poised with
bow and arrow.

"Was Emma your model for that Diana?" Glynis asked Isaiah.

"Promised not to tell."

"Well, it's beautiful."

Isaiah and Lacey both smiled the disembodied smiles of the
half-masked. Glynis glanced around the forested room, lit with
white candles in wall sconces, floor-standing candelabra, and
chandeliers. A host of frosted lanterns swung from the tree
branches. As more partygoers arrived every minute, the theater
began to fill with an exotic collection of characters, ones both
historically real and fictional.

Queen Elizabeth stood holding court near the entrance doors,
the tiny black domino mask clearly not intended to conceal
Vanessa Usher—who else as Elizabeth?—in characteristic
large lace ruff and black velvet gown, the skirt of which was
made monstrously wide by the frame beneath it. Glynis then
searched for someone with substantial girth, surely impossible

to hide. She at last spotted an ample gentleman in black judge's robe and white powdered wig who was undoubtedly Jeremiah Merrycoyf—in the persona of his admired jurist, Chief Justice John Marshall. At least Glynis hoped it was Marshall and not Sir William Blackstone, whose belief in the inferiority of women had delivered married females of the English-speaking world clear back to the Middle Ages.

Neva Cardoza-Levy had required coaxing—in truth, browbeating, Glynis conceded—to make her attend. It was, after all, a benefit for *her* refuge, everyone who knew her had argued; Vanessa Usher just incidentally happened to be the patroness. Thus Neva now stood, clearly impatient and icily cordial, in the near vicinity of Queen Elizabeth—but not too near. Dr. Cardoza-Levy wore a simple long white gown with red cording on neck and sleeves. This was meant to be symbolic, she explained, of all the ancient women healers whose names had been written out of the historical records maintained by men. In vivid contrast, her husband Abraham was in a colorful floor-length robe and almost as long a beard, which Glynis assumed portrayed the biblical Abraham. She had to smile, thinking that Neva must be enjoying her and her husband's embodiment of the thunderous clash of science and religion, its clamor just that year increased tenfold by the publication of Charles Darwin's *On the Origin of Species.*

Glynis now ran her eyes over the new arrivals. "Lacey, have you seen Emma?"

"No, I been looking for her, too. She said she'd be late, though—she and her young Mr. MacAlistair—'cause she had to pick up some sewing supplies in case some of the women popped the seams of their gowns! Just you imagine that!"

"No, I can't. I'll have a hard time getting back into any kind of gown, much less a tight one, after these trousers. So Emma meant to go to the shop, then? With Adam?"

"That's what she said. Funny, I don't see Mrs. Coddington here either."

"Would you know her if you saw her, Lacey? Oh, of course—you must have helped make her costume." When Lacey nodded, Glynis asked, "What about Constable Stuart? Did you make his?"

"He's not coming in costume. Least that's what he said."

"Did he say why not?"

"He said he don't believe the law should travel in disguise."
Lacey pursed her lips, rolling her eyes behind the slits of the
mask. And Glynis had to agree. Cullen was becoming very
staid—or had he always been that way? No; that wasn't fair.
With five murders as yet unsolved, and the murderer still at
large, he needed to be visible.

She felt Lacey tugging at her sleeve, motioning to the couple
who had just come through the entrance doors. "That's Mrs.
Stanton and her husband," Lacey whispered. "We did her costume—know who it is?"

Glynis noted the absence of voluminous petticoats, and the
soft drape of Elizabeth's blue silk gown. The simple style had
a high waist with black velvet ribbon under the bust, and another fastened with a cameo around Elizabeth's neck. "I'd
guess she's a mid–eighteenth century woman, possibly French
or English, Lacey. But who of that time would Elizabeth Stanton choose to—of course! She's Mary Wollstonecraft, isn't
she?"

Lacey gave her a quizzical look as she nodded. "But how'd
you know? None of us in the shop had ever heard of the lady."

"Oh, but Elizabeth Stanton knows her well, figuratively
speaking. Wollstonecraft was a pioneer, an Englishwoman who
wrote a trailblazing essay on the rights of women. How clever
of Elizabeth. But does her husband Henry know whom she's
portraying?"

"I don't think so," chuckled Lacey.

"No, I don't think so either," agreed Glynis.

Silver trays had now appeared in the hands of servers, and
the smell of wine and whiskey came with pungent force across
the room—the temperance reformers would be more than unhappy. Not that Vanessa would care; she would simply tell
them if they didn't like it, they didn't have to drink it. Moreover, steaming cups of hot chocolate, coffee, and tea followed
in the alcohol's wake. And Isaiah, his head swiveling toward
the trays, motioned to his wife.

As the couple moved away, Glynis peered into the growing
crowd for someone she might be able to identify. Her niece's

costume should be simple enough to find, but Glynis still didn't see her. Emma surely should be there by this time. But if Adam MacAlistair was with her, Glynis supposed she shouldn't worry. Still, she would need Emma—and would need her soon. She was the one person who could identify at least some of those there by their costumes. And Glynis knew the one she believed guilty had been invited; she'd made certain of it. Although as a result she had owed Vanessa a debt of unknown magnitude.

But where, in the meantime, was Cullen? Without a costume he should be easy enough to see. Then it occurred to her that he might also be at La Maison de Fleur. She felt a sharp prick of apprehension. Cullen did not yet know of her suspicions. And he didn't know either that she'd at last succeeded, just that morning, in wresting from her niece that which had been so disturbing Emma: the money she'd accidentally discovered sewn into the gowns at Fleur Coddington's shop. Another loose thread in the grim tapestry.

A firm tap on her shoulder made her turn to confront a hooked nose in full face mask, the thin slash of mouth grinning down at her. "Who am I?" came a guttural voice from behind the grin. The voice defied recognition. As did the appearance.

Glynis took a step back from the figure, who stood wrapped in an oddly patched, fur-trimmed velvet robe. A crown perched at a rakish angle above the mask. "Well, a king seems to be rather obvious," she answered. "A British monarch? I'm afraid those are the only ones I know anything about." She felt a fool to remain there addressing a leering mask.

The figure turned to one side, pointing toward his back. Glynis saw with discomfort that a hump rose between his shoulder blades. Why masquerade as someone so deformed? Ah, yes! "I'd guess," she said now, "that you might be Richard the Third. At least from Shakespeare's point of view."

The figure skipped around her in a circle, which made her doubt her conclusion, since Shakespeare's Richard was lame. But the crown now bobbed toward her as she received a bow and a round of applause from her mysterious companion. Who could be hiding behind this grotesque disguise—and why come to the ball as one of the most hated monarchs in history?

Glynis by now had decided, however, that this man was not the killer. No matter how great the vanity of the true criminal, surely few would risk mocking fate in this way: Richard the Third was known as a murderer! And while the killer might believe the rules which applied to ordinary mortals did not apply to him, he would hardly trumpet that fact by portraying Shakespeare's villainous king. Therefore, she reasoned, the man before her probably was the one person here tonight—of those she did not recognize—least likely to be the killer. Or so she hoped.

But as she turned away from the grinning mask, the guttural voice behind her said: " 'And thus I clothe my naked villainy . . . And seem a saint when most I play the devil.' "

Glynis froze in place. It sounded like a threat. By the time she'd recovered enough to whirl around, the figure had melted into the growing crowd. But the jolt he'd provided had been enough to make her limbs weak.

There seemed to be a sudden bustle around the stage. Glynis shook off her apprehension and looked up to see Vanessa Usher, her Elizabethan gown flattening the greenery as she swept to stage right. There she stood beckoning with impatience to her unseen vassals. Moments later musicians with violins, lute, flute, and cello emerged from backstage to arrange themselves around the harpsichord. And as if lured by sirens' song, eager couples darted across the floor to form their dance figures. Glynis slipped through them and made her way toward the theater entrance. She heard behind her the first stately strains of an Elizabethan pavane.

She had begun to truly worry about Emma. Could her niece possibly still be at La Maison de Fleur? But just then, to her immense relief, Cullen came through the doors.

She hurried to him, saying, "Cullen, I'm glad you're here." Then, seeing his sudden frown, she remembered and moved closer to whisper, "It's Glynis."

He drew back in surprise, and looked her up and down. "Glynis," he said quietly, "you certainly do look different in trousers."

"Well, yes, that's the point."

"Who are you supposed to be?"

"Cullen," she said, ignoring his question, "have you seen Emma? Perhaps on your way here?"

"No. Why?"

"Because I think she should have arrived by now. Lacey Smith said Emma had planned to go to La Maison de Fleur first with Adam MacAlistair, but still—the party started over an hour ago."

"If she's with Adam, why are you concerned?" Cullen asked as he continued to eye her trousers with obvious reservations, if not disapproval.

"I suppose you're right about Emma," she said reluctantly, "but, after all, it hasn't been entirely safe in Seneca Falls lately."

"Are you adding your voice to the growing criticism of the constable's performance?" he asked and his voice carried an unmistakable edge.

"No, of course not," Glynis protested, and then wondered why she had bothered. He was clearly out of sorts again. She glanced around, but no one seemed close enough to overhear them.

"Cullen, I have to ask you this. Weren't you escorting Fleur Coddington here tonight? And if so, where is she?"

"No, I wasn't escorting her." He sounded even more irritated, and then added, "And I don't know where she is. Why?"

Glynis decided she couldn't spare the time to explain, so she said, "It just seems odd that both Fleur Coddington and Emma have not—"

She broke off as the entrance doors flew open and Emma, a wild-eyed Diana, rushed inside. Close on her heels was Adam MacAlistair in glittering chain mail hauberk, complete with sword and shield. Glynis barely noticed him; she was too concerned with her niece's obvious distress.

"Aunt Glynis!" Emma cried. "Oh, Aunt Glyn!"

She threw herself at Glynis, who had a sudden terrifying premonition of what her niece would say. "Emma, please come back outside," Glynis urged, "so we don't send everyone here into an uproar." She pulled Emma in her shimmering feathered toga back out the doors with Cullen and Adam right behind them.

The moon had made day of night, and its brightness now lent an incongruous gaiety to the tense scene.

"What's happened?" Cullen demanded. Adam threw him a scowl and with the sword at his side clanking loudly, he clasped Emma's trembling shoulders. But she shook him off, as she was plainly making a great effort to compose herself. She ignored Cullen as well and in a shaky voice said to Glynis, "I don't know how to tell you this, Aunt Glyn, but it's poor Mrs. Coddington. She's dead. She's been murdered."

No, surely not Fleur! Glynis looked to Adam for confirmation. He nodded, while Cullen, as she would expect, went a ghastly white.

"Are you sure?" he said hoarsely to Adam.

"We're sure. There was no heartbeat. And she had bruises on her neck, same as you said Tom Bingham did. We found her on the floor in the back room of the shop. You know, it scares the hell out of me that Emma, if she'd gotten there any earlier, might have been—" He left off, his voice losing strength.

"All right," Cullen said, "tell me what happened—from the beginning." Despite his shocking pallor, he sounded nearly normal; no mean accomplishment, Glynis noted with respect.

"I didn't get there until just after Emma did," Adam began.

"No, you didn't, so why not let me tell this?" Emma said, casting Adam a distraught but determined look. "I went to the shop for some last-minute things," she explained, "and I went in through the front Fall Street entrance. Mrs. Coddington had said she'd be there, but when I didn't hear her moving around, I just thought she'd already left for the ball. Adam was to meet me there and . . . and . . ." Here Emma's voice faltered.

"Naturally, I went in the front entrance," Adam went on. "And Emma and I were there together for five, maybe ten minutes."

"How long had you been there before Adam arrived?" Cullen asked Emma.

"Just a minute or two."

"So you didn't hear anything out of the ordinary while you were there?" he prodded.

"Of course not. Do you think if I had I would've stayed?"

"Emma," Glynis said quickly to cut off Cullen's retort, "at some point you must have gone to the shop's back room—and that's when you found her?"

"Yes," Emma answered, her voice ragged. "We went to the back to pick up my bow and arrows."

"All right," said Cullen heavily. "Did you leave . . . leave everything as it was?"

Both Emma and Adam nodded. "But I didn't want to just go off and abandon her," Emma said, shooting Adam an accusatory look.

"There was no alternative," Adam responded. "I couldn't let Emma stay there by herself. And I couldn't let her come here alone either."

"O.K. I'm leaving now, but I want to see you both after I've been to the shop," Cullen ordered. "So take Miss Tryon home, Adam, and wait for me at Peartree's."

To Glynis's surprise, Emma drew herself up ramrod straight and announced, "I'm not going home. Not yet."

Adam's mouth opened and closed several times before he said, "Emma, what are you talking about—of course you're going home. Right now. You've been through enough tonight."

"I've also worked very hard for this night," Emma said, her voice holding a quaver—in spite of which she appeared resolute. "I'm not leaving here without at least seeing the costumes."

At this, Glynis felt a surge of gratitude, as well as a sense of relief. Although Emma unquestionably did need rest, Glynis needed her niece's knowledge, and Emma knew it. But Adam protested, "No! Emma, I can't allow you to subject yourself to more strain."

"You don't have anything to say about it, Adam. I mean to stay. And Fleur Coddington would want me to."

Glynis would have found Adam's expression worthy of some study if she hadn't been so concerned about Cullen. He didn't even seem to have heard this exchange. He'd simply walked off. Her heart ached for him, but she doubted she could offer any comfort, not at this point. She watched him head toward the horses, then followed him for a few steps.

"Cullen, please come back as soon as you can. I think we'll need you here."

Again, the words didn't seem to register. He just kept walking. Glynis debated with herself, then went after him. "Cullen, please listen to me. It's important."

"I can't now, Glynis, I have to go. You don't know . . . you just don't know what's been going on."

"I know that Fleur Coddington was probably involved, in some way, with the counterfeiting business," Glynis said evenly, regretting that she had to say this to him now, in this way, but deciding she did not have a choice.

He turned to her, his jaw rigid. "This is not the time to talk about it! But if you know that much, then you know I'm at least partly responsible for what's happened. I've suspected her of passing counterfeit banknotes for some time. Through her, I thought I could find the actual counterfeiter, but I put her at risk. Just by being seen with me."

"You couldn't have foreseen this happening, Cullen." She hadn't seen it either, had thought the next victim, if there was one, would be male. "I know you're terribly upset," she said, "and yes, I know this isn't the time, but—"

"You're right, it's not."

She reached for his arm. "Cullen, please listen."

"Leave me alone, Glynis—I mean it!" He jerked his arm away and turned to mount his horse.

The loathing in his voice, despite her insight that it was mostly for himself, brought Glynis close to tears. It was all she could do to get out the request, "Cullen, would you at least send Liam Cleary back here?"

She didn't know if he heard her. He just rode off. Exactly as Jacques Sundown might do. And in her distress, Glynis questioned why she seemed fated to care for these silent stubborn men.

THEY STOOD TOGETHER under Isaiah Smith's moon, she and Emma, at the end of a column of long groaning tables, laden with every imaginable variety of rich food: oysters on the half shell, cold poached salmon in aspic, wheels of cheese the size of dinner plates, sirloins of beef, flocks of ducks and chickens and partridge, and roasted pig, complete with a New York Northern Spy apple wedged in its mouth. And that was just the first two tables of six.

"That pig makes me ill," Emma said, keeping her eyes well averted. "I'll never smell pork again without wanting to throw up."

While Glynis echoed this sentiment, she couldn't allow herself, or her niece, to be distracted. In the past hour, Emma had stood there stoically, identifying all those masquerading in costumes made at La Maison de Fleur. Thus, in combination with a process of elimination, Glynis estimated they had managed to sort through probably two-thirds of those at the ball. It was the men, however, who were important.

The only woman in whom she'd been interested was Margaret Taylor. "Yes, I think I'll be able to spot her," Emma had said some time earlier, "because she bought the fabric from me—though she acted very secretive and wouldn't say what it was for. She must have planned to make the costume herself. But I'd know that forest green wool anywhere."

Glynis believed this. "But can you find Margaret Taylor *in it?*"

"I've been trying. But there's so many people milling around. Oh, wait—I think she's there, Aunt Glyn. Over by that tree near the stage. She's wearing trousers like you!"

Glynis tried to swing around casually. But she was finding it difficult to peer at people without looking obvious. Fortunately, everyone else was doing the same thing; it was, after all, the nature of a masquerade.

"Are you certain that's her, Emma?"

"It's the green wool, I'm certain of that!"

"Whom do you suppose her costume is meant to portray?" Glynis considered aloud. "I wonder if it's Robin Hood?"

She saw with surprise that Emma was nearly smiling. "You're so good, Aunt Glynis. What if you weren't a librarian, and you didn't know all that stuff?"

If she didn't know "all that stuff," Glynis thought, then perhaps she wouldn't find herself so often in unpleasant circumstances. She looked again, and now, the more she studied Robin Hood, the more she convinced herself it was Margaret

Taylor. The domino mask and tilted brim and feather of her soft felt hat hid the woman's features some, but the height and weight looked right. Still, if she hadn't seen Margaret without her glasses that day, she never could have identified her.

Glynis now had to keep her eyes on both the people approaching the food tables and the outlaw in forest green.

After another half hour, during the course of which her niece looked increasingly pale, Glynis relented. "All right, Emma. Let's move back out of the mainstream and take stock."

As they went toward the far side of the room, a short-bearded friar, with large round-brimmed felt hat, sandals, and a burlap robe tied at the waist with a length of hemp, came toward them. The most remarkable thing about this friar was the stuffed bird perched on his shoulder. Glynis sincerely hoped it was stuffed, as it had a distinctly predatory cast to its yellow eyes.

"Good evening, ladies," the friar said, standing squarely before them and grinning with obvious enjoyment. "May I say that you are without question, Miss Emma, the most fetching nymph here tonight."

Emma ducked her head. But her domino mask couldn't conceal the blush creeping up over her cheeks. "How did you know it was me?" she asked.

"By the angry-looking young knight over there who can't take his eyes off you," the friar replied. "Did you banish Sir MacAlistair for trifling with your bow and arrows?"

Glynis, who had recognized Grandy Fox's voice several minutes earlier, commented, "I wouldn't think you'd approve of bows and arrows, my good friar."

"Oh, so you know who I am."

"Possibly. Francis of Assisi?"

"Very good, Miss Tryon! You were tipped off by my handsome bird, I assume? Almost as handsome as your outfit. No doubt *you* are some literary figure—say, perhaps, the fabled Anonymous?"

Glynis smiled. "So far," she replied, evading his question, "you're one of the few men here who, once they discovered I was female, haven't viewed my trousers with outrage."

"They're afraid, that's all," Grandy said with a grin. "What would happen if all you women started wearing pants? How would we know who was supposed to be in command? Oh, fair Mistress Emma, here cometh your faithful knight-errant—charging into the fray with his sword and shield.''

Emma smiled with weak effort, Glynis noticed, and her concern grew. However, Adam MacAlistair, coming across the floor at a fast clip, must have seen her niece fading. Or had seen Grandy Fox.

"Don't you think you've had enough, Emma?" Adam asked. He ignored completely Friar Fox, who, giving Emma a wink and a smile, disappeared into the crowd at the food tables.

"I am tired," Emma admitted, "and I feel so terrible about Mrs. Coddington. But do you still need me, Aunt Glyn?"

Glynis tried to prepare herself for Emma's and Adam's departure. And they *had* found nearly all the men she'd most needed to identify. Attorney Cyril Doggett, a round-shouldered, gaunt-faced wraith in pointed beard and black jurist robe which, together with long-bladed scythe, portrayed either Father Time or, conceivably, Robespierre. Failed bank vice-president Valerian Voss, whose ermine robe and casket of gold clutched under his arm labeled him King Midas—under the circumstances, such a damning or tasteless characterization that Glynis almost dismissed him from consideration on the same grounds as she had Richard the Third. And dentist Alan Fitzhugh, foppishly dressed as Beau Brummel, so Emma said. He had draped on his arm yet another jewelry-laden woman; thus Beau Brummel or Casanova, it mattered not—unless Alan Fitzhugh proved, in truth, to be Bluebeard.

So now, only Colonel Dorian de Warde remained elusively disguised.

This time Adam appeared resolute. Emma was going home! She did not seem disposed to argue with him, and she remained deeply affected by the death of Fleur Coddington. Adam took Emma's hand and led her away unprotesting.

Glynis looked around as she all of a sudden realized she hadn't seen Richard the Third since their initial encounter. Emma had had no knowledge of this character, and now Glynis wondered if, contrary to her earlier guess, the Shakespeare-quoting monarch might have been Colonel de Warde.

*   *   *

GLYNIS STOOD BY the front doors of the playhouse. After several more hours of eating and dancing, she guessed it must now be close to midnight. She again scanned the crowd, which had begun to thin due to the lateness of the hour, and experienced a moment of utter panic; she had lost sight of Robin Hood, whom she'd been watching so diligently. In the minute or two she took her eyes off the figure to say good-bye to Neva and Abraham, Margaret Taylor seemed to have vanished. Glynis stood casting frantically about—and now discovered that another of those she'd been watching also seemed to have disappeared. It was almost as if they'd been waiting for her attention to be diverted.

She told herself, in trying to slow her racing pulse, that she was leaping to an irrational conclusion. They couldn't possibly know what she suspected. How could they? However, she was also acutely aware that Liam Cleary had not yet appeared. Either Cullen hadn't heard her request, or he had ignored it.

She went quickly toward the stage where the dancers were circling, and as they went round she scanned them in near desperation. But then, just as she was losing hope completely, she caught from the corner of her eye a flash of forest green. A side door then swung closed behind it.

She reached the door in seconds, glancing back to make certain no one observed her. Then she carefully pushed the door open a crack. The moonlight made it no effort to see Robin Hood just untying one of the horses. Glynis waited until the horse had been mounted and headed south in an easy canter, before she herself slipped through the door.

TWENTY-THREE

ॐ

Behold, a pale horse; and his name that sat on him was Death.
—REVELATION 6:8

GLYNIS GUIDED THE dapple-gray mare through the trees at the foot of a drumlin hill, while keeping a safe distance between herself and the bay horse that Margaret Taylor rode. Forced to trail far behind in order to remain unseen, Glynis had twice, when crossing open fields, lost sight of the woman entirely. By this time, her nerves felt as taut as bowstrings.

She knew—once she located the North Star—that they traveled southeast and had been ever since leaving the playhouse, but it was all she knew, except that, if they continued in the same direction, there were no villages ahead. They might have covered three or four miles by now, which meant they should soon reach Painter Creek. Beyond that lay Cayuga Lake.

Just once, as they came over a rise, did she catch sight of the horse that Margaret Taylor was following, and then only because the horse was white, a small pale speck in the distance. Glynis thought of them now as a ghostly trio passing through the quiet moonlit countryside: the white horse and its deadly rider; Margaret Taylor on the bay; and, behind them, she and the gray mare. Although she had repeatedly looked back over her shoulder, she could see no one following *her*.

Glynis pulled up hard on the reins as she suddenly realized the bay horse ahead had come to a standstill. The trees had thinned, and she could see, some way beyond, the rise of another drumlin. She glanced up at the North Star again to satisfy herself their direction hadn't changed. Her horse pawed the ground and snorted softly. Although seeing the frosty mist of the mare's breath made Glynis shiver, the chill barely penetrated the velvet redingote and trousers. She wondered if she would have attempted this in full skirt and petticoats. And she decided she would not have. This in turn made her consider whether in putting on George Sand's bold clothing she'd been obliged to put on the woman's persona as well.

It certainly would have been wiser not to do this alone. She'd regretted almost immediately her impulse to follow Margaret Taylor. But what else could she have done? When she saw Margaret leave the ball, Glynis believed, from what she had recently learned, that the woman meant to track a killer. The question remained as to what Margaret intended to do when she found him. After all, the man had murdered everyone he thought necessary to protect his identity. But if that wasn't obvious to Margaret Taylor, Glynis hardly felt in a position to point it out. Nor, under the circumstances, did she think it would do any good.

Since he had killed Fleur Coddington, it seemed almost certain the man would leave Seneca Falls directly. He could well be planning to do so tonight. Thus all Glynis could hope for now was confirmation of her suspicions; Rhys Bevan and the Treasury could take over from there. She just prayed she could manage it without being discovered. Now she peered ahead, and since Margaret Taylor's horse didn't appear to be moving, Glynis tried to wipe the grit from her eyes, then reached over to pat the mare's shoulder. When she looked again, the bay horse had vanished.

She stood in the stirrups and frantically searched the landscape ahead. Nothing, anywhere, moved. It was as if the ground had yawned open and consumed Margaret Taylor and the bay horse in a single swallow, leaving behind not a trace of them. The only logical answer to their disappearance, Glynis saw when she forced upon herself some restraint, lay beyond the drumlin hill.

But the moonlight gave objects no depth of field, much like the ancient maps that pictured a flat earth; this made it almost impossible for her to judge distance. A dozen or more trees stood between her and the drumlin, so at least there would be some cover. There seemed only one alternative to going forward and that was to turn back. George Sand would no doubt have thought this impasse exhilarating.

Glynis reluctantly tapped the mare's sides with her heels and they started forward. Except for the occasional cry of an owl overhead, she and the horse traveled quietly through the trees. They might as well be on the moon, Glynis thought, for all the vast stillness around them. Still except for her heart thudding in dread of a gunshot exploding in the night, or of someone leaping out from behind a tree. She almost lost heart, then, and turned back. But she had to acknowledge the voice within her that said she would likely never be safe, and neither would Emma, if the killer even so much as dreamed they suspected him. Surely it would be better to make certain now that she had the right man, than to spend the rest of her life looking over her shoulder.

As she drew closer to the hill, she could see the large boulders strewn at its foot. A few were as tall as a man. Someone could easily be concealed behind them, and the iron-shod hooves of the mare announced her coming like drumbeats. Glynis pulled up on the reins. She would have to go the rest of the way on foot. She assured herself that when she reached the far side of the hill, she would see Margaret and the bay horse well beyond.

After she'd tied the mare to a sapling, she turned toward the boulders and took a few steps toward them, and then remembered. She quickly returned to the mare and removed Jacques's walking stick from behind the saddle; grasping it tightly, she again crept forward. Her freedom of movement in the trousers gave her some courage, and if she managed to survive this, she would chafe in skirts forever after. Staying as low to the ground as possible, she reached the first boulders and dropped to a crouch. She could hear the sound of water running over rock. It must be Painter Creek.

Glynis stayed where she was, listening for something other than the water. Nothing, not even hoofbeats. The others must be well ahead. She moved cautiously around a few more boulders. Gaining confidence, she moved faster, too fast, and lost her balance, catching her boot between smaller rocks. She fell to her knees but, bracing herself with the walking stick, kept from plunging headlong against a boulder. After pulling the boot free, she sat back to rub her ankle. It ached somewhat, but otherwise seemed all right. It was then a shadowed fissure some short distance away caught her attention. She stood up, gingerly testing the ankle. When she decided it was sound, she moved closer to the shadowed area and realized it was not merely a narrow cleavage between the rocks but a large opening in the side of the hill.

She had heard there were caves along the Finger Lakes' shores, but one this far inland? She didn't know how close Cayuga Lake might be—maybe only a mile or two—and it was fed by Painter Creek. She supposed at one time the lakeshore might have been here when the ice sheets began to retreat.

She had to climb over some smaller rocks to get within several yards of the cave entrance. It was wider than she'd first thought, and high enough for a man on horseback to pass through. Somewhere in her mind a warning began to sound; she'd read about counterfeiters' caves in the material Mr. DuBois had sent her. The warning became an alarm. She took a fast step backward, readying to turn and run.

It was too late.

The male voice coming from inside the cave sounded almost apologetic. "I was afraid it might be you, Miss Tryon. Can't contain your curiosity, can you? Not even when your life depends on it!"

Glynis stood there, unable to see him yet, and unable to move for the fear that coursed through her. The familiar voice sounded so casual she might even have believed, for a split second, that she was not in danger. The reality of what he had already done immediately stripped her of this fantasy.

Where was Margaret Taylor? Probably a mile beyond by now, maybe even as far as the lake. Unless, unless . . . Glynis struggled to reject the notion that Margaret Taylor just might be in league with this man.

"Come on inside, Miss Tryon—or shall I call you Glynis? Under the circumstances, I think we can afford to do away with formalities, don't you?"

Once inside the cave she would be trapped; outside she might have a chance to run. She still couldn't see him clearly, so she didn't know if he had a weapon, and she shook her head. A sharp click reached her, and now she saw the silhouette of his revolver as he stepped outside into the moonlight.

"I'm in somewhat of a hurry, Glynis. There'll be a train coming by not too far from here fairly soon. I intend to get on it. Get on it alone—except for a great deal of money. So come along." He pushed aside a lock of hair that had fallen over his forehead and Glynis saw the steadiness of his hand. The man appeared to have no nervousness, no feelings at all, he who was about to kill again.

Her mouth was so dry, she wondered if she could still talk. It occurred to her that if Margaret Taylor was still close by, she might be overhearing this. He had said he was leaving alone, which would indicate the woman wasn't mixed up in the crimes. Or it could mean that he'd already killed Margaret before she herself got there.

"You can't think," she began, "that you'll get away. There are too many people who know." She stopped as the revolver was raised again. At the same time, a numbness seemed to be crawling up her spine. She wondered if, when it reached her brain, she would even care if she died.

"I'm through being patient," he said sharply, "now get in here!"

Again she heard the click as he cocked the hammer. It jolted her out of the initial shock, and she took several short steps toward him. Anything was better than just standing there while he played with her fear.

"There's a good girl," he said, backing up until he stood inside the cave. Glynis saw flickers of lantern light behind him as he motioned with the gun. "Come on, get in here."

She followed him through the cave entrance. Once inside she smelled mold and damp earth—along with another odor, pungent and vaguely familiar, and out of place there. The dirt and dim light began to make her eyes water. When she started to wipe them, she suddenly realized the walking stick was still in her hand. Her fingers were so numb she'd forgotten she had it, and apparently he hadn't seen it. Or he didn't care; what use was a stick against a revolver? She slowly moved the hand holding it farther behind her back.

The lanterns hung from hooks nailed into several upright railroad ties abutting the cave roof. "So, what do you think of the workshop, Glynis? Nothing fancy, as you see." He gestured toward the rear of the cavern, even though all she could see was a chasm of darkness. "Printing press is back there—too heavy to move in one piece, so the engraver just left it." He laughed lightly and shifted so that he stood next to a lantern. His masquerade costume had been replaced by denim trousers and jacket. He didn't need the hemp rope anymore. Not after he'd used it to kill Fleur Coddington. She had guessed it had been his weapon the moment she'd recognized him at the ball.

"Now we can see each other better," he said easily, his body as relaxed as a cat stretched out in the sun. A cat . . . cat urine, that was the pungent odor, Glynis thought remotely, as she backed against a side of the cave and watched the gun in his hand. Then he added, "You knew, though, didn't you?"

Glynis looked straight into his eyes and said, with as much confidence as she could feign, "I don't believe you can get away. Rhys Bevan will be after you in a flash when you turn up missing. To say nothing of the trail of bodies you'll have left behind."

Grandy Fox gave her his most winsome grin, and reached down to grasp a leather saddlebag lying on the cave floor. Shaking it for her benefit, he grinned even more broadly at the jingle of coins. Glynis, in the meantime, scanned the cave for signs of Margaret Taylor. The numbness had begun to grant her an icy sort of calm—perhaps this was what men underwent, those who calmly faced a firing squad. The walking stick she now held behind her with both hands, while trying to twist the wolf head without his noticing. She counted on his vanity to convince him he had nothing to fear from her. Moreover, that vanity was what she needed to keep him talking—it just might keep her alive.

"Grandy, how long have you been a double agent?"

He dropped the saddlebag and straightened abruptly, and for a terrible moment she thought she had miscalculated. But he merely smiled. "You're a smart one, aren't you? I knew early on you were going to be a problem, but your friend, Colonel de Warde, insisted you weren't to be, shall we say, damaged."

"And Colonel de Warde is a friend of yours?"

"Of recent vintage, to answer your first question. Did you figure de Warde out, too?"

"I think he's engaged in some sort of espionage for Britain, yes. Whatever it is involves counterfeiting. What was the plan, Grandy? To flood the country with worthless money to debase American currency, like my Great-Grandfather Tryon did during the Revolution?"

Grandy laughed, a sincere-sounding laugh she heard with revulsion. "You mean 'colonial uprising'—*revolution*'s too lofty a term. So Governor Will Tryon was your ancestor. As the colonel would say, 'What a charming coincidence.' You know, my smart but too-curious lady, you might have made an outstanding criminal—it sometimes runs in families, I hear. But how did you know I was a double agent?"

He leaned against one of the railroad ties to fish a thin British cigar out of the pocket of his denim jacket. When he reached for a match, he had to fumble in the pocket, and while he searched, Glynis took the opportunity to retwist the wolf head. Perspiration made her hands slippery, and she didn't know if she'd turned it enough. She would have only one opportunity to find out—if she'd have even that.

He had lit the cigar and now watched her, waiting for a response.

"When did I guess you were a double agent? Partly when I realized you worked in disguise," she answered. "That was a revelation—and it came from the costumes for the masquerade ball. Disguises would explain how just one man might appear to be several places at almost the same time. For instance, playing fiddle at the Rochester public market while keeping an eye on poor Barrymore, and attacking him in the market a little while later; it took only a switch from straw hat to cap and false mustache, followed by another quick change on the train. You must have earlier stashed the black hat, jacket, and false beard in the baggage car. Except for the fact that the beard shed black fibers on those clothes you left behind, I must say, Grandy, I was impressed when I realized what you'd accomplished."

Glynis felt her hope increase one tiny notch when he very nearly preened. "That's my specialty—the Maestro of Disguise, the colonel calls me. But you still haven't answered my question."

"Oh, yes," she said quickly, "the double agent. Well, you couldn't know it, but Barrymore managed to whisper a few words to me before you killed him. He said—or rather I *thought* he said—'the trouble's in Seneca Falls.' Of course, what he'd actually said was 'the *double's* in Seneca Falls.' He'd figured out it was you involved with the bogus notes drawn on his bank, didn't he? And he must have discovered that you, a U.S. Treasury agent, were also working for the British."

She stopped as Grandy smiled around the cigar. "Come on, you didn't figure out 'double agent' from *that*," he chuckled.

"No, not from that alone. But combined with the gold eagle he dropped I did. The coin proved to be genuine, which was important because I came to see that he'd picked it purposefully—so that it wasn't associated with his bank's counterfeit notes. It was, you see, a *double* eagle."

"I think Treasury should hire you," Grandy said expansively. "Although you'd make more money as a crook. But believe me, you're better than most of the agents they've got down there in Washington." He paused and added, "Except for Rhys Bevan. I worried a lot about him. Thought for sure he was on to me a couple of times. But then, when he left town, I knew I was in the clear. He's just not quite as smart as me, old Rhys isn't."

And then, from somewhere nearby, came an odd low-pitched sound. The rumble of a train, Glynis guessed, with rising panic. But surely a train couldn't be heard inside the cave.

"Did you hear that?" Grandy said, tossing away the half-smoked cigar.

"No, I didn't hear anything. Why?"

He shot her a look of disbelief, and pulled a watch from his trouser pocket. "That's funny," he said, frowning, "it's not time for the train yet." He cocked his ear toward the cave mouth, then shrugged at the silence.

Trying to distract him, Glynis said quickly, "But I still haven't figured out why you killed Sally Lunt. Was that really necessary?"

"Afraid so. She discovered we were using Fleur Coddington's shop as a distribution hub for the bogus notes. That was really a thing of beauty while it lasted—the clothes were shipped to passers all over the state. When Sally stumbled on it, she made exactly the wrong move.''

''The wrong move?'' Glynis repeated. She thought, however, that Adam MacAlistair had already given her the answer. ''You mean Sally went to Cyril Doggett with the information?''

''Can you imagine that?'' Grandy snorted. ''Doggett's a bigger crook than I am.''

And for the first time, Glynis considered the possibility that Grandy Fox was mad. Not only a man with no conscience, a man evil enough to mow down whatever stood in the path of his greed, and with vanity sufficient to outshine the sun—but also mad.

Just as she was about to ask another question, she heard it again—the soft rumbling that seemed too near to be a train. She spoke loudly, hoping to cover it before he noticed. ''So Cyril Doggett is part of the counterfeiting operation?'' she asked.

''*Was* part of it. *Was*. It's over now, at least in this part of the country. The best engraver in the United States was right here in western New York, but Brockway's left. Things were getting too risky, he told the colonel.''

''You said he's gone, this Brockway? What will the others do without him?''

Grandy gave a sharp laugh. ''Good for you—you figured them out, too! How?''

''I decided there were too many good suspects—and finally came to realize that, indeed, all those suspects *were* good. That you were *all* involved! But I don't know which came first. Did Colonel de Warde first recruit you, and then the others—or did you find them?''

''Glynis, Glynis, you disappoint me. Of course I came first. But you were close. I knew about Doggett from the Treasury investigation. The colonel found him in New Haven—then they both helped spring Doggett's friend Brockway from Auburn Prison. Figured we might as well set up shop right here—convenient small town and all. After that, it was just a matter of finding a couple others in, shall we say, advantageous positions. I set up most of it—de Warde's in espionage, he didn't know anything about counterfeiting!''

Glynis nodded. "So you found a greedy bank vice-president, and a dentist with expensive habits who could get gold without much suspicion: Voss and Fitzhugh. But you said Brockway's left the area?"

"He's long gone. So's the colonel—gone back to merry old England. He got what he wanted from Brockway. And then some. Down south of the Mason-Dixon line the stew of war is being stirred, Glynis. Stirred by Yankee dollars. It'll boil over soon, anytime now."

Glynis caught her breath. "Do you mean John Brown's raid at Harper's Ferry? You people had something to do with *that?*"

"Just put a little fire under the pot!"

He was obviously very taken with his metaphor, Glynis thought, her fear begun to shade into anger. The arrogance of these men! Toying with lives—with Zeph's life—as if it were a game.

Grandy shifted his weight against the railroad tie. "Britain wants war in America. This country is still 'the Colonies' to them—a babe of Mother Empire as far as they're concerned. And they'll do what they can to get the baby back. They *need* that southern cotton."

He stopped talking and seemed to be listening. And when he glanced at his watch again, his casual manner was gone. His shoulders stiffened and he spoke more rapidly. "It's about time to go, Glynis. Too bad you didn't stay clear of me, and I'll have to answer to the colonel for this. But he's not here. There's just the two of us, and that's one too—"

He broke off, cocking his head, this time toward the rear of the cave. "What the hell—I hear something!"

Glynis heard it, too; the soft rumble became a growl. Grandy stepped away from the tie, pivoting to squint into the black cavern behind them. He leaned forward on the balls of his feet, neck muscles knotting, and then a deep snarling roar made the cave floor seem to shake.

Grandy took several steps backward. At the same time, Glynis saw a figure in forest green dart through the cave entrance. Margaret Taylor had a rifle in her hands—but did she know Grandy had a revolver? As Margaret raised the rifle, her scream of "You bastard!" made Grandy swivel toward her.

Glynis swung the walking stick around and snatched off the head to uncover its razor-sharp blade. But she was too slow to match Grandy's lightning response. As Margaret aimed the rifle, he fired. When she staggered backward, hand at her breast, the rifle discharged, sending the bullet ricocheting off a rock wall and on into the rear of the cave.

Glynis raised the stick and brought the blade down on Grandy's gun hand, feeling the impact of steel against bone. With a scream Grandy dropped the revolver as blood spurted from the gash, and he whirled toward Glynis. His eyes bright with pain and fury, he grabbed with his good hand for the stick. She managed to jerk herself sideways toward the gun, straining to reach it. But Grandy leapt toward her. Holding the stick with both hands, she swung it at him again. He jumped out of the way, and as she took an unbalanced step backward, her boot came down on the outstretched leg of Margaret Taylor. Glynis tottered, throwing up her arms to keep from falling. Grandy rushed at her, striking her so hard she fell backward, and he yanked the stick from her grasp with a force that sent him staggering backward into the rock wall.

She scrambled to her feet, managing to circle and move clear of the still-breathing woman. But now, even as blood flowed from his slashed right hand, Grandy lunged at her with the blade, driving her before him and forcing her farther and farther back into the recesses of the cave. Toward the beast that had made that chilling sound.

She didn't dare turn her back on him, but with every step she expected to collide with the rock wall. She kept her eyes on the knife, praying Grandy would lose strength with the loss of blood. He didn't even seem to notice it—but his one-handed thrusts were wild as he came after her, or she would have been bayoneted. And now, from the corner of her eye, Glynis saw a stork-like cast-iron object standing several yards away—the printing press?—and wondered if she could get behind it.

She backed toward it, but in shrinking away from another of Grandy's furious lunges, one shoulder banged hard into an unyielding iron surface. His next thrust compelled her to jerk backward, and she fell full force against a cracked front leg of the printing press. She felt the leg give way as she crumpled to the cave floor. As Grandy began to raise the knife over her, she rolled to one side—and saw the press rocking just before it toppled forward with a thundering crash, throwing Grandy Fox face down with his legs pinned underneath a tangle of cast iron.

And suddenly, from out of the darkness, a great tawny shape hurtled forward, splitting the air with a roar of fury.

The enraged mountain lion landed beside the trapped Grandy Fox. While Glynis huddled in terror against the cave wall, the lion raked the prone torso again and again with its deadly claws. Then the large canine teeth bared and it bit unerringly into the back of the man's neck at the base of his skull. A terrible scream was cut off abruptly, but still it echoed throughout the cave.

Glynis struggled to pull her feet under her so she could rise, at the same time watching Grandy Fox's arms jerk spasmodically, slower and slower, under the creamy belly of the lion. The hindquarters of the big cat were toward her, its long heavy tail switching inches from her face. Glynis dug her fingernails into the rock wall as she climbed to her feet and began to slide along the side of the cave toward the light. A high-pitched cry from behind her made her stop instantly. She stood frozen in place. Then she slowly turned her face toward what had become a piteous mewing. Two small furry shapes had bounded from somewhere deeper inside the cave, and now were making for what must be their mother.

Glynis stood as still as death. It was, she knew, a question of how much a threat the lioness judged her. A soft rumble came from deep within its throat, and the kittens tumbled to a halt a few feet from the body of Grandy Fox. Then, to Glynis's horror, one of the kittens bounced toward her. It looked just like an overgrown tame kitten, Glynis thought, her heart pounding, the kitten's buff-brown body sprinkled with dark spots and silvery eyes glittering with mischief. It had come to within a few feet of her when the lioness growled again. The kitten ignored the warning and pounced on Glynis's boot. Then it jumped back and crouched, hindquarters quivering as it prepared to attack the boot again.

The lioness turned from her kill, and padded over to her

offspring. With one swipe of its front paw, claws retracted, the mother sent the kitten rolling toward the back of the cave. Protesting loudly, it picked itself up and ambled off into the darkness beyond.

Glynis didn't know what would anger the lioness more, if she looked straight into the unblinking gold-brown eyes or averted her gaze, or if she moved slowly but deliberately away. This animal could kill her as easily as it had the much bigger man, yet for no good reason Glynis began to feel less afraid of it than she had of the mad Grandy Fox. However, she didn't move.

She stood there, motionless, for what seemed like hours. Her leg muscles began to tremble with fatigue, and she could feel a cramp moving up her calf. As her head began to swim, from somewhere close by the second kitten gave a forlorn whine. The short rounded ears of the lioness swiveled toward the sound. Its eyes blinked once, slowly, and with a soft throaty growl it moved past Glynis, so close she could feel the heat of its body. Its teeth closed on the loose folds of the kitten's neck, and the lioness glided with her offspring into the far recesses of the cave.

Glynis found she was panting, and perspiration rolled off her face. She couldn't bring herself to look at what remained of Grandy Fox—and then she remembered Margaret Taylor. She ran toward the mouth of the cave, and with a rush of relief found the woman seated, her back against the wall. Her eyes flicked open when Glynis reached her. There didn't seem to be much blood on the green jerkin.

She knelt beside the woman. "Are you badly hurt?"

"The bullet grazed my shoulder," Margaret Taylor answered. "Fox must have seen you coming at him with that bayonet, because his aim was bad. I'm just groggy now from banging my head when I fell." She winced a little as she moved her shoulder, but no new blood appeared.

"Then we'd better get out of here," Glynis said, glancing over her shoulder. "There's a mountain lion back there with her kittens. For some reason she left me alone. But she went right after Grandy Fox—" she swallowed hard "—maybe because she smelled blood."

"Is he dead?" Margaret's voice was eager.

"Very dead," Glynis sighed.

"Good. Although I'd like to have done it myself," Margaret said harshly.

Glynis rose, jarred by the woman's tone and her fierce expression. But she understood why and said nothing, just reached down and helped Margaret to her feet.

With Glynis's arm around the woman's waist, they stumbled together out into the moon-washed night. After putting some distance between themselves and the mouth of the cave, both collapsed on the nearest flat rock.

"How long were you out here?" Glynis asked. "I thought you'd ridden on by."

"I had. Then when I didn't see you behind me anymore . . ."

"You *knew* I was following you?"

"I come from hunt country, Miss Tryon"—Margaret exaggerated her light southern drawl—"and I can track pretty well. I surely do know when something's behind me. But," she admitted, "I went on past here because I didn't see his horse, not until I looked back for you. It's over there, tethered behind that big boulder."

Glynis straightened up and began to wipe perspiration and grit off her face, then flinched in pain.

"You've got a bad bruise on your cheekbone," Margaret offered. "Your coat's torn in a dozen places—or maybe it's slashed—your elbow's scraped raw, sticking through a hole in the sleeve, and your trousers are ripped over the left knee. You do not look like the composed Miss Tryon. You look like you've been in a fight." Her mouth curved upward, and Glynis realized it was probably the first time she'd seen the woman smile. And certainly the most she'd ever heard her say. But then, this was no longer the same woman.

"I know your maiden name was Taylor," Glynis said, "and I believe your married name is Fairfax?"

The woman gave her a brief nod. "My given name is Margaret, though I never used it until I came north. Call me Meg." She gestured toward the cave. "The bastard killed my husband. But I think you know that."

"Your husband was a Treasury agent, wasn't he?" Glynis asked. "John Fairfax?"

Meg nodded. "How did you find out?"

"I began to guess something was amiss the day I brought the telegram to you. You looked completely different without your glasses—which you didn't need—and with your hair down. It occurred to me that you'd been deliberately disguising yourself. Of course I didn't realize, at the time, that disguise would become a key element in this tragedy, but I did begin to think about it. Then later, when I found out who Rhys Bevan was, I put two and two together." Glynis told her about Mr. Grimes's ready comments at the telegraph office.

"Ah, the privacy of a small town," Meg commented, but her voice held humor. "I wired Rhys several times to see if the Treasury had any leads on who killed John. Miss Tryon— Glynis, do you mind?—Rhys said that you questioned him about me."

"I did, but I'd already determined who you were. When Cullen Stuart found your husband, he also found a portrait miniature of a woman. After the telegram episode I asked to see the miniature, recognized you, and Rhys Bevan later confirmed it. I'd already noted your interest in Grandy Fox."

"I just wanted the constable to check on Fox," Meg said, "that's all. I didn't know he was the one who killed John. I'd never seen him until I came here. And then Rhys Bevan arrived and announced that Fox was another Treasury agent—God, what a cover for him! I felt sure, though, that the killer was here somewhere. A week before he was killed, John wrote that he was about to crack the counterfeiting ring. Here in Seneca Falls."

"And Grandy Fox found out and killed him." Glynis gazed with sadness at the cave entrance. Meg Fairfax wouldn't know that her husband had likely spent his last hours there, given the counterfeit bill clutched in his hand when Cullen found his body nearby.

"My husband wasn't the only one the bastard killed that night. I was six months pregnant when I got the wire from Treasury about John. I lost the baby."

Glynis knew anything she could say would sound trite. For

a time, she said nothing. "When Rhys Bevan showed up," she said at last, "we all assumed we were wrong about Grandy Fox. I certainly did. It still makes me angry to think how Grandy must have enjoyed waiting for trial, knowing the Treasury would be notified about the counterfeiting angle—and that someone would show up and clear him. Although he said something in the cave that made me think he wasn't happy it was Rhys Bevan who appeared."

"Rhys shouldn't have gone back south," Meg replied. "I guess he—"

She left this unfinished and they both sprang to their feet at the sound of galloping hooves. Two figures on horseback were racing toward them across the moon-swept landscape.

"One of them is Cullen," Glynis said as they drew nearer. "And the other . . . the other is Rhys Bevan!"

"Rhys Bevan! How *can* it be—how did he get back here so fast?"

"I don't think he ever left," Glynis said, smiling to herself.

The men obviously saw her tethered gray mare, because they pulled up their horses just short of the boulders. Both leapt to the ground and immediately began searching the rocks. That's right, Glynis thought, don't ask questions—just jump right in, hell-bent-for-leather. A little late.

And, indeed, Meg said dryly, "Our heroes."

Glynis laughed, and both men's heads came up.

"Glynis?" yelled the voice of Rhys Bevan. "Glynis Tryon, is that you? Are you all right? Damn it, answer me!"

SOME TIME LATER, when they made ready to leave, Rhys suggested that Glynis and Cullen switch horses, as the Morgan and Rhys's own rented livery gelding had been ridden hard. Cullen could then ride ahead with the rested gray mare and take Meg Fairfax to Dr. Cardoza-Levy. Even though Meg maintained that her shoulder was tolerable, Rhys insisted. Thus when they left the cave, Meg was on the bay and Cullen the mare, leading the white horse with Grandy Fox's body. The two men had retrieved it from the cave without encountering the mountain lion, although both had gone in with revolvers drawn.

"I'm thankful you didn't have to shoot her," Glynis said now, as she and Rhys Bevan started off at a slower pace with the flagging Morgan and the gelding.

Rhys Bevan gave her a sidelong glance. "Lion's a friend of yours?"

"I told you that she spared me," Glynis answered, "although I can't understand why that Brockway man would work in a cave with a lioness in residence."

"She probably wasn't there then. These lions move their kittens around all the time. Keeps them away from predators. Out of harm's way and out of mischief."

He slowed his horse and motioned for Glynis to do the same, although now they dropped even farther behind the others. But she had no resources left and was grateful for a more leisurely pace. When Cullen looked back at them over his shoulder, Rhys waved him on.

The hunter's moon was lowering in the western sky, and in the clear air the North Star shone with a steady light. Though the night held a chill, Glynis found it at least kept her from falling asleep. When she glanced over at Rhys, he looked as if he regularly rode through the countryside at five in the morning.

The silence was as soothing now as it had been threatening before. And it was some time before Rhys said, "All right, Miss Tryon, alias George Sand. I admire the trousers by the way. As well as the woman in them, although she could use a bit of patching up—but then, that's to be expected if you insist on brawling. Now then, I have a few questions for you."

"*You* have a few questions? You, who passed yourself off as Richard the Third?"

"So you *did* know it was me."

"I wasn't certain until Grandy Fox appeared dressed as Francis of Assisi—*Saint* Francis! I also finally decided only you would dare come to a ball dressed as Richard the Third!"

"I hoped you'd understand that quote about the saint and devil. Although, you're one of the few Americans I've met who would." He glanced at her with a grin.

Glynis smiled. " 'And seem the saint when most I play the devil.' Very clever, Richard. But couldn't you have been a little less roundabout?"

"No. I just wanted to warn you off. I was worried you suspected Fox, and didn't want you doing something dangerous, such as confronting him. That certainly was a lost cause, wasn't it? But we had no solid proof against him—at least that's what I thought then. And it's exactly why I didn't tell Meg Fairfax that I was on to Fox. I knew she'd go after him. And so who ends up taking out double agent and killer Grandy the Fox? Not the chief detective of the U.S. Treasury; not the constable of Seneca Falls, former member of Pinkerton's Detective Agency. Two women and a lioness! But *why* did you do it, Glynis? He would have killed you without so much as a moral twitch. You must have known that."

"I did. But all I wanted was to be sure it *was* him. Then I would have wired you—you who were *supposed* to be in Washington. Believe me, I wouldn't have followed Meg Fairfax if I'd known what would happen. Now *I* have a question, Mr. Rhys Bevan, chief detective. *What on earth took you so long to get here?*"

Rhys grimaced slightly. He said nothing.

"What is so mysterious about it?" Glynis persisted. "When I asked that earlier, you mumbled something about the time it took to track us, but there were *three* sets of prints to follow! You never actually did answer me—but you were at the ball, Rhys, and must have seen Meg and myself leave. I rather counted on that, you realize. That you'd come after—"

"I know, I know. Are you really going to insist on an answer? Make me shame myself before you? Become an object of your scorn and pity?"

Glynis tried not to smile. But then she remembered the terror of the cave. "Yes, I guess I will insist."

"You're a heartless woman. All right! I couldn't find a horse."

"What?"

"A horse. You know: 'A horse! a horse! my kingdom for . . . ' and so on and so forth."

"*What* are you raving about? How can you make light of something so serious?"

"I am not making light of anything. I couldn't find a horse to ride. I'd rented a carriage along with this gelding for the masquerade, hoping, just hoping, that perchance Richard the Third might persuade you to let him drive you home.''

He shot her a sideways look.

''I lost track of you and Meg,'' he went on when she didn't respond, ''while I was outside looking for Cullen Stuart—I didn't know, then, what had happened to Fleur Coddington. When I got back inside, I didn't see you—or Meg. Then I began to worry. After all, the whole point of my so public and heralded return to Washington was to take Fox off his guard. That wire I got from Treasury was bogus, by the way—I sent it to myself.''

Glynis, determined not to smile at this cheerful confession, shook her head. ''How long had you suspected Grandy Fox?''

''Long. Too many things kept going awry. Crooks getting away. Too damn many people getting killed when Fox was in the vicinity. And he had way too much money to throw around. I just couldn't cut loose from Washington long enough to prove it—of course, we'd never lost two agents before. But good, I see you aren't interested in your embarrassing inquiry anymore.''

''Oh, yes, I am. Go on—so you'd lost track of Meg and myself.''

Rhys sighed, and lit a British Philip Morris cigarette he'd dug out of his jacket pocket. Glynis shuddered, recalling Grandy Fox's last cigar.

''You're cold? Here, take my jacket.'' He'd stripped it off before Glynis could explain.

''I'm not cold,'' she said weakly as he pulled the gelding in closer while he wrapped his jacket around her.

''Too bad, it's a warm jacket. Now, where were we? I finally realized the two of you were not in that theater. I combed the place thoroughly. When I got back outside, I saw the gray mare you'd ridden was gone. Found the tracks, though, so I *was* going to follow you. I didn't want the carriage, and I'd just started to unhitch this gelding—and some drunk comes weaving out of the theater and accuses me of stealing *his* horse. He does this very loudly and abusively. Do not laugh, Miss Tryon, it was not humorous.''

''Go on,'' she said, smiling in spite of herself.

"I was labeled a horse thief! Which is a very serious offense around here, I take it, and a number of your civic-minded males, all inebriated, decided I should answer for it. They held me at gunpoint while someone went after The Law! Being as how they were all three sheets to the wind, I should have known better than to resist—but I was damn worried about you. To make a long story short, I got shot at, chased to the canal and back, nearly lynched, and otherwise mistreated before I made good my escape. By that time, Stuart had arrived. And here I am!"

Glynis was laughing now.

Rhys Bevan stared at her. "I bare my soul, confess my failure as your protector, and you laugh. That's why I didn't want to tell you. I knew you would be unsympathetic."

Glynis, still smiling, gazed off to the west, where the hunter's moon had set—and well it should set on such a bloody night as this had been, she thought, her smile fading. To the east the line between land and sky had been drawn, and the first gray of dawn inched upward. "Look, it's nearly morning," she said. "Shouldn't we go a little faster? Cullen and Meg are barely in sight."

Rhys Bevan's mood had changed; Glynis could feel it. She'd seen this before, seen him move from bantering to seriousness in the flick of an eye. Now he seemed reluctant to talk at all. "One last question," he said finally.

Glynis shrugged, and realized she was still inside his jacket. It smelled like strong soap and tobacco and coffee and gunpowder—reminding her that his was a dangerous profession. That he would be going back to it soon. "One question," she said.

"I've figured out what Cullen Stuart feels for you. But how do you feel about him?"

"You are, without doubt, Rhys Bevan, the most forward man I have ever met! And that is none of your business. Why would you ask me such a thing?"

"You know why. Besides, I told you before—I haven't got much time. But if you're as annoyed as you sound, why are you smiling?"

Glynis threw her hands in the air, nearly lost the reins, and urged the Morgan to a canter.

"And what's more," Rhys said, bringing the gelding up close beside her, "I think George Sand would have answered me."

TWENTY-FOUR

⟐

The usual quiet of our domestic affairs has been interrupted by a singular attempt to excite a servile insurrection in Virginia. . . . On the night of October 16, [John Brown] made a descent upon the Town of Harper's Ferry—a place containing about 5000 inhabitants, with a United States arsenal in which more than 100,000 stand of arms are usually stored.
—HARPER'S NEW MONTHLY MAGAZINE.
1859

NOVEMBER 1859

GLYNIS PUT THE new issue of *Harper's* down on her library desk. She had already read through the three-column article twice, looking for Zeph's name among those of John Brown's band who had been taken prisoner. The men who had died were recorded in *Harper's* under "the names and fate of the persons engaged in this mad undertaking." Glynis had found among the dead the names of John Brown's sons Oliver and Watson, and his secretary of war, John Henry Kagi. There were seven others as well. The article also reported that a few men had escaped the military dragnet, but their names were as yet unknown. Although this last offered some hope, it wasn't much. If Zeph *had* escaped, he surely should have returned by now. According to all the newspapers, the Virginia town had been in a state of panic for days following the raid, thus there could well have been others killed who were still unidentified.

John Brown and the surviving members of his raiding party had been charged with inciting slaves to insurrection, with treason, and with murder. The ensuing trial had been held quickly because the Virginia governor's prosecutor told the court that he feared a mob might break into the jail and lynch Brown, or that some prisoners might die of their wounds before they could be hanged.

The trial had lasted three days, with Brown found guilty on all counts and sentenced to be executed on the second day of December. *Harper's* contended that: "As to the treatment he [Brown] had received on his trial, it had been more generous than he could have expected." And Brown himself had written his family, the article stated, that if it was necessary for the ends of justice that his life should be taken, he was content.

Glynis glanced again at her calendar. The past days had been so rushed that she barely knew what day it was. The calendar said it was now November 30th; indeed, the library windows framed flurries of snow. Still there was no Zeph.

She had read that repercussions of John Brown's fiasco in Virginia continued to be felt even as far away as there in western New York. Letters and documents found in a Maryland farmhouse following the raid had implicated a number of wealthy Northern abolitionists as contributing to Brown's cause. The identities of these men, if in fact they were identified, had not been released. However, Elizabeth Stanton's cousin Gerrit Smith, said by the family to be suffering a nervous breakdown, had voluntarily committed himself to the Utica Lunatic Asylum, and Rochester's abolitionist newspaper editor, Frederick Douglass, had fled to England.

By far the most ominous consequence was the declaration by southern politicians that the northern abolitionist and anti-slavery parties had not only applauded but subsidized Brown. This proved, the southerners said, that the North was determined to free the southern slaves by violent means. Thus talk of war could now be heard daily, even in as small a town as Seneca Falls. And because of a single extremist act, it seemed as if war had suddenly become almost inevitable; the only question that appeared to remain was when. Perhaps, Glynis prayed, men's tempers would cool following Brown's execution. That, as Grandy Fox had so blithely predicted, the "stew of war" would not boil over.

Glynis looked up as the library door swung open. Emma and Adam MacAlistair came dashing in, laughing and sprinkled with snow, and their cheeks ruddy from the brisk wind.

"Back from Waterloo so soon?" Glynis asked.

"Oh, Adam insisted on racing," Emma said. Her small mea-

sure of pique with him, Glynis guessed, was feigned, as her
niece looked extremely happy. "Of course," Emma went on,
"the carriage we had couldn't possibly win against Rhys
Bevan's horse."

Glynis smiled. "Well, is the trial over?"

"It's over," Adam said, unwinding from his neck a long,
colorfully striped knit scarf that Emma had finished a few days
before. "And my former associate, Cyril Doggett," Adam continued, "will spend the rest of his dreary days in Auburn
Prison. After less than an hour's deliberation, the jury convicted
him of counterfeiting, and as accessory to the murder of Sally
Lunt. So that's all of them."

Several days before, Valerian Voss and Alan Fitzhugh had
been tried for counterfeiting. Both had been convicted.

"We thought you'd want to know, Aunt Glyn. Oh, on the
way here we stopped for mail," Emma said, handing her several items. "Who do you know in England?" She gestured to
a heavy white envelope.

Glynis shook her head. It clearly hadn't come from the book
dealers she dealt with, as it had an imposing and official-
looking seal. She reached for the letter-opener.

> Office of War and the Colonies of Great Britain
> London, England
> November 1, 1859

My dear Miss Tryon,

It was with some interest that I received information regarding a mutual acquaintance of ours, one United States
Treasury Agent Granville Fox. It would seem that Mr. Fox
met with an unpleasant demise, although, if my reports are
accurate, it surely was one he richly deserved. The details
are somewhat sketchy; however, I have reason to believe that
you, dear lady, had some small part to play in his undoing.
Please be assured that there will be no lingering resentment
whatsoever on the part of those who once were acquainted
with the late Fox.

Should you ever find reason to visit London, Miss Tryon,
I should like to offer my assistance in making your stay an

enjoyable one. You may contact me through the office stated above. In any event, I am quite certain that we will meet again before too long a time passes. Until then,

I remain your faithful and admiring servant,
Colonel Dorian de Warde

Glynis looked up from the letter to see Emma and Adam watching her closely.

"Well?" Emma said. "Aunt Glyn, you look rather strange."

"I *feel* rather strange. I'm apparently being informed that I needn't worry about retaliation at the hands of the British War Office."

"*What?*" This from both Emma and Adam.

Glynis wasn't sure she should laugh, but she certainly felt like it. "This letter is from Colonel de Warde—you do remember Colonel de Warde! Rhys Bevan assures me the man is one of Britain's foremost espionage agents. This letter from him seems to be a compliment of sorts, although there's a subtle element of warning implied."

"I don't believe that man wrote to you!" Emma declared. "Why would he?"

"I'm not certain I care to speculate."

"I never quite appreciated," Adam said, "that the life of a librarian could be so intriguing."

Now Glynis did laugh.

"We have more good news," Emma said. "I mean more than about those horrible men. Adam and Mr. Merrycoyf found the note that Fleur Coddington had given to Grandy Fox, with the papers in her safe. The note that says she borrowed the money from him to buy the shop next door and to finance the renovations of La Maison de Fleur."

Glynis nodded. Cullen had told her his first suspicions of Fleur had come from her sudden and mysterious wealth. He knew she had been denied a loan from Farmers and Merchants Bank—by vice-president Valerian Voss. Undoubtedly, Glynis surmised, it had been because she was a woman; a woman in business by herself, and without a male partner or a husband. Glynis felt herself becoming angry all over again. So Fleur had obtained the money from Grandy, and was then forced into the counterfeiting operation—although that could have been Voss's purpose from the start.

Cullen said he believed that after Sally Lunt's murder, Fleur had been frightened enough to consider confessing. She had said, the day of her death, that she was ready to tell him something, and would do so that night. But Grandy Fox, ever vigilant, had reached her first. Cullen still felt responsible.

"Aunt Glynis! Are you listening?"

"I'm sorry, Emma. Just thinking about Fleur Coddington."

"I know, it's awful," Emma agreed. Then her practicality prevailed, and she announced, "So now Adam says Fleur's note to Grandy is void because . . . because . . ."

"Because it was supported by a criminal act," Adam finished. "So the title to the shop is clear. The place will be up for sale."

"And Adam's figuring out how I can get the financing to buy it," Emma bubbled, her face flushed with excitement.

"Naturally, it would be a simple matter if you were married," Adam said, smiling broadly.

Emma turned pink, and she said tartly, "Adam, I've told you that I'm not ready to do that. You have to find another way to get me the money."

Adam MacAlistair's self-confident smile never wavered.

GLYNIS AND RHYS Bevan stood halfway up the library steps, the snow flurrying off and on as clouds raced over a watery sun. "You're leaving, then?" she asked. He had returned to Seneca Falls to testify at the counterfeiting trials.

Rhys nodded. "Have to catch the late train about an hour from now. I'm supposed to be back at the Treasury tomorrow. So, Miss Tryon, when are you coming to Washington?"

"What makes you think I plan to do that?"

"Because *I'm* there—and I'm inviting you. George Sand would accept with alacrity."

"Rhys, it may have escaped your notice, but I am a librarian with a library. I can't just go running off."

"Why not? You did it before. Went to Springfield for a year. What's Washington compared to that?"

Glynis shook her head. "It's not the same, and you know it. It's . . . it's . . ."

"If you say *unseemly,* I shall make the most unseemly scene you've ever been part of, Glynis Tryon. Now say you'll come. Or do I have to travel all the way back here and abduct you?"

"There's no reason why you can't come back here."

"Glynis, it may have escaped *your* notice, but Seneca Falls is not exactly the hub of the Republic."

"Well, there you are," she said, hoping against hope her eyes wouldn't fill. But it did seem unlikely they would meet again.

"Meg Fairfax would be delighted to have you visit her in Maryland," Rhys persisted. "And you said you have a friend in Richmond as well. Neither are far from Washington—on a good horse." He grinned. "Believe it or not, I *have* a good horse." The grin disappeared with his next words: "And don't tell me your resistance is because of Cullen Stuart."

Rhys, until now, had mentioned Cullen only once after the night of the hunter's moon, and then he'd said, "If Stuart has known you for as many years as you say, and still doesn't know what to do with you, far be it from me to tell him. And that goes for your roaming Indian, too!"

The man was forward.

Glynis said to him now, "I'll consider a visit."

"Do more than consider. Time may be getting short for coming south. To paraphrase our benefactor the Bard, John Brown 'opened the purple testament of bleeding war.' "

"I hope you're wrong."

"So do I. Look, I have to leave now, Glynis. Promise me you'll come south before the year is out."

"I can't do that. But perhaps later . . . I'll see. That's *all* I can promise."

"For now, that's enough—my letters will persuade you. And so, Miss Tryon, in the tongue of your ancestors: *Ffarwel!*"

"Farewell?"

Rhys nodded, and put his hands on her shoulders. Glynis drew back; he was so audacious, he might intend to kiss her right there on Fall Street! Before she could object, however,

Rhys Bevan had leaned forward and lightly brushed her cheek
with his lips. "That's for *now*," he said.

He took the remaining steps in a swirl of flakes. When he
got to the road, he turned and shouted at what seemed the top
of his lungs, "Next year in Virginia, George!"

Glynis drew in her breath, and quickly looked around. The
audience consisted solely of an Irish setter shaking itself of
snow. She started down the steps to her library, smothering a
smile. Then, as she reached for the door, she heard someone
call to her. Not Rhys, but someone else. Her heart lifted as she
whirled toward the voice and saw a man coming toward her
through the snow. He was thinner, and looked older than he
should, and he walked with a limp, but it was Zeph.

Glynis opened her arms as she went up the steps to meet
him.

EPILOGUE

ON THE SECOND day of December in the year of our Lord 1859, Henry Wadsworth Longfellow wrote in his diary:

This will be a great day in our history; the date of a new Revolution—quite as much needed as the old one. Even now as I write, they are leading old John Brown to execution in Virginia for attempting to rescue slaves! This sowing the wind to reap the whirlwind, which will come soon.

And above the tiny hamlet of North Elba, high in the snow-covered woods of northern New York, Annie Brown walked slowly out of the log house. She thrust her hands into the frayed pockets of a man's jacket. The frosted ground crunched under her second-hand leather shoes. When she got to the edge of the stream, she climbed onto a large boulder, and stood looking out at the vast silent mountains.

They would always be there.

HISTORICAL NOTES

❦

AUBURN PRISON

Located in the city of Auburn, New York, Auburn Prison was built in 1816 and is the oldest operating maximum-security penal institution in the country. Its name was changed in the 1950s to the Auburn Correctional Facility.

BROCKWAY, WILLIAM (1822–1920)

William "Long Bill" Brockway's activities—the earliest of which are recounted in the body of the novel—began during the decades prior to the Civil War known as the Golden Age of American Counterfeiting. Brockway's extraordinarily successful career in this arena resulted in his being considered the "King of the Counterfeiters" by two directors of the United States Secret Service. The early records of the Secret Service are inexact, but it appears that Brockway was seized somewhere in upstate New York in the 1850s and sentenced to a short term in Sing Sing Prison. After that, Brockway seems to have been for the most part a fortunate and elusive thief. If he was a lucky counterfeiter, however, he was unlucky in love; his infrequent brushes with the law were almost exclusively the consequence of his entanglements with women. The interested reader will find Brockway in any work dealing with the history of United States counterfeiting.

BROWN, ANNE (1845–?)

John Brown's daughter Anne—or Annie, as her father referred to her—moved to California in the 1880s, where she married a man named Adams and bore six children. Her letters to John Brown's biographers indicate that she was an intelligent and compassionate woman whose recollections of the days prior to the Harpers Ferry raid remained clear throughout her life. She wrote complimentarily of the men who followed John Brown, "my invisibles" as she called them: "taking them all together, I think they would compare well with the same number of men in any station of life." Her involvement with Brown's articulate, idealistic secretary of war, John Henry Kagi, is the author's conjecture based on Anne's particularly admiring description of Kagi.

BROWN FAMILY

John Brown's second wife, the self-sacrificing Mary Anne, moved to California with the remaining family members (all but John Jr.). The pregnancy of Anne Brown's sister-in-law Martha ended tragically: both Martha and the baby died shortly after the disaster at Harpers Ferry. Some years later, Anne's brother Salmon committed suicide. John Brown himself is buried—with the two sons and several other followers who died at Harpers Ferry—near the farmhouse at North Elba in the Adirondack Mountains. The John Brown farm is today a New York State Historic Site.

CARR'S HOTEL

This tavern and inn, originally called the Clinton House, was built in Seneca Falls sometime around 1850. Thomas Carr, an Englishman, purchased the property in 1856 primarily to serve travelers on the stagecoach, railroad, and canal. After changing hands once again in 1866, the hotel burned in the "Great Fire" of 1890. It was rebuilt by Norman Gould of Gould Pumps and, as the Hotel Gould, subsequently changed hands a number of times. Although it still stands on Fall Street, its future at this writing is sadly uncertain.

DUBOIS, WILLIAM E. (1810–1881)

Assayer of the United States Mint until shortly before his death, William DuBois was himself a coin collector and the author of numerous articles on currency, as well as a co-author of *A Manual of the Gold and Silver Coins of all Nations, Struck Within the Past Century,* published in 1842. DuBois also instituted the Mint Cabinet, a collection of coins which still exists at the Philadelphia Mint.

DULCIMER

Easier to transport than its bulky cousin the piano, the hammered dulcimer traveled west with the pioneers, and was used as accompaniment for both folk singers and dancers, as well as religious services. Dulcimers were played at picnics, parties, contests, or at any event at which rural and small-town peoples were gathered. Most pertinent to *Through a Gold Eagle,* however, is the fact that, during the decade of the 1850s, the center of American dulcimer production was Chautauqua County, in western New York.

GOLD EAGLE

The large number of foreign coins in circulation in colonial America made transactions among banks, merchants, and individuals difficult—many of the coins were of uncertain value and authenticity. The 1792 Mint Act not only provided for the establishment of a mint, but also set up a system of weights and measures for gold, silver, and copper coinage. America's first gold coins—half eagles and eagles—were struck in 1795.

HARPER'S NEW MONTHLY MAGAZINE

One of the most successful of numerous nineteenth-century magazines, *Harper's* carried fiction and poetry as well as essays, news articles, travelogues, biographical sketches, and fashion writing. A popular feature proved to be the novels that were presented in monthly installments, such as Thackeray's *The Virginians*, which ran in 1859. Bound volumes of *Harper's* can occasionally be found in rare-book stores. *Harper's* offers a fascinating, detailed glimpse of life in the nineteenth century.

REMINGTON ARMS COMPANY

The company's founder, Eliphalet Remington, built the first of his legendary rifles in 1816. Thus the Remington Arms Company, located in the town of Ilion, in New York's Mohawk Valley, is the oldest continuously operating gun manufacturer in the United States. The factory and a museum are open to the public, and provide an interesting look at America's relentless romance with firearms.

SMITH, GERRIT (1797–1874)

Politician, abolitionist and philanthropist, Gerrit Smith also championed women's rights, temperance, prison reform, international peace, and land reform. Although he denied unto death that he had anything to do with the Harpers Ferry raid, there is evidence in his personal correspondence that he was a close acquaintance of John Brown (and had owned the land on which Brown's farm was located), and was the single largest financial backer of Brown among the conspiratorial "Secret Six." (These prominent abolitionists included a physician, an industrialist, and two ministers.) Scholars have disagreed over whether Smith's "insanity" was genuine. However, there is no question that his residency in the Utica Lunatic Asylum prevented his arrest following Harpers Ferry. The diagnosis of his condition given by the asylum was "acute mania," and was probably what is commonly referred to today as manic-depression. Smith resided at the asylum for approximately eight weeks; he returned to his home in Petersboro, New York, four weeks after John Brown's execution, and thereafter resumed his public life.

Items that appeared in the Historical Notes sections of *Seneca Falls Inheritance, North Star Conspiracy,* and *Blackwater Spirits* have not been included in the above, although some notes may also be pertinent to *Through a Gold Eagle*. Since there is frequent historical overlap, this choice was made to prevent these sections from eventually becoming longer than the novels themselves.

Claire gets what she wants. . . .

Claire allowed herself a moment of smugness. By the end of this day the group would have broken down into its component couples. Zoey would have found a place to be with Lucas, Aisha with Christopher, Nina with Benjamin. Only Claire and Jake would be wandering alone, unattached. But with a hot tub, a clear starry night, a fireplace, the warm, mellow afterglow of a day on the slopes . . .

It was a pity to have to manipulate him this way, but it was his own fault for being stubborn. She loved him, he loved her. Just because he seemed determined to screw that up didn't mean she had to let him.

Look for the other books in this romantic series.

BOYFRIENDS
GIRLFRIENDS

CLAIRE
GETS
CAUGHT

KATHERINE APPLEGATE

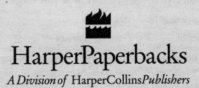

HarperPaperbacks

A Division of **HarperCollins***Publishers*

For Fran Lebowitz and, as always,
for Michael

This is a work of fiction. The characters, incidents, and dialogues are products of the author's imagination and are not to be construed as real. Any resemblance to actual events or persons, living or dead, is entirely coincidental.

HarperPaperbacks *A Division of* HarperCollins*Publishers*
10 East 53rd Street, New York, N.Y. 10022

Copyright © 1994 by Daniel Weiss Associates, Inc.,
and Katherine Applegate
Cover art copyright © 1994 Daniel Weiss Associates, Inc.

All rights reserved. No part of this book may be used or reproduced in any manner whatsoever without written permission of the publisher, except in the case of brief quotations embodied in critical articles and reviews. For information address Daniel Weiss Associates, Inc., 33 West 17th Street, New York, New York 10011.

Produced by Daniel Weiss Associates, Inc.,
33 West 17th Street, New York, New York 10011.

First printing: June 1994

Printed in the United States of America

HarperPaperbacks and colophon are trademarks of HarperCollins*Publishers*

10 9 8 7 6 5 4 3 2 1

"This is it," Claire said. "This has to be the end. It's either me or Wade. One of us had to lose and . . ." She took a deep breath. ". . . He's already lost all he could."

"Claire—"

"No, don't, all right?" she said harshly. "This is hard enough. I really do care for you, and I know you care for me, so don't make me any sadder by saying it. There's just too much history between us. And to tell you the truth, I'm not a person who can go around for long feeling guilty. I'm sorry about what happened two years ago. I'm sorry you can't deal with this without trying to destroy yourself. But you can't. Which leaves only one solution."

His arms tightened around her, holding her close. She pressed her cheek against his shoulder and blotted her tears on his shirt.

He took her face with his hand and forced her to look at him. He kissed her for a long, still moment.

Then she took another deep breath. She let the emotion run out of her, turning her thoughts away. She thought of her widow's walk. She thought of *how much she liked to be up there, watching the lightning illuminate the darkness, watching snow drift down to settle on the little town below.*

She had always been able to do what she had to. And now she pulled away, leaving the warmth of Jake's arms. She turned, and with dry eyes, walked away.

Claire left the dance, the sound of the music dying away behind her as she left the campus and headed down through the town, past the darkened storefronts and bright restaurants. It was a crisp, chilly evening and she walked briskly, her heels loud on the sidewalk.

It had gone pretty well, if she said so herself. Right now Jake was realizing what had happened: that she had given him up to avoid hurting him anymore. He was also realizing that he was all alone, staring at a room full of couples.

"I'm sorry you can't deal with this without trying to destroy yourself," she repeated under her breath. Perfect. Just the right touch of condescension.

Now to let him enjoy life without her for a while. See how much he liked it when he got what he *thought* he wanted. And then, she would simply wait until the right opportunity presented itself.

Claire smiled. It was unfair, it was dishonest, and it was certainly manipulative. But more important, with a little luck, it would probably work out just fine.

Zoey Passmore

I found the quiz in <u>Seventeen</u> or <u>Sassy</u> or <u>YM</u>, one of those, and tore it out. "How Well Do You Know Him?" with the word <u>Him</u> in bright pink letters. You're supposed to fill it out on your own first, guessing what your boyfriend's answer will be. Then later you ask your boyfriend, and if his answer is what you guessed it would be, great. If not, then you don't know him as well as you thought, right? Not that I take quizzes all that seriously. Still, I figured there had to be some validity to it or they wouldn't print

it in a serious magazine
like . . . like whichever one
it was in.

Anyway. The first ques-
tion was,

1 On the issue of sex, your boyfriend will say he is willing to: (A) Put it off until you are married; (B) Wait until you feel the time is right and not pressure you till then; (C) Pressure you to do it because once you try it you'll like it; (D) Leave you and go out with someone else if you keep saying no; (E) Not applicable, we're already having sex.

Well. Kind of cuts right
to the heart of things,
doesn't it? First of all, we
can eliminate E right away.
I am not sleeping with
Lucas. I've never done it
with anyone. Not that I
haven't thought about it.
A lot. Especially when he's
kissing me and his hands
are . . . See? I'm thinking
about it right now.

But no. I don't know why, but that's like a step I'm not ready for yet. I think Lucas respects that. He doesn't respect it a lot; I mean, he's not thrilled by my saying no. Sometimes he's <u>very</u> not thrilled. But he wouldn't answer D. He also wouldn't answer A. I'm thinking he'll come down somewhere between a B and a C. Call it a C-plus. Although what he'll actually answer on the quiz is B, because he'll think that's the answer I want him to give.

LUCAS CABRAL

Forget E, unfortunately. If the answer were E, I

wouldn't be taking really cold showers every night after I say good night to Zoey. If the answer were E, I wouldn't be bouncing off the walls and waking up remembering dreams that, believe me, you don't want to hear about. Nope. Not E.

Not A, either. D is a possibility; I mean, if this goes on forever. Seriously, say we're talking ten years, we're both in our late twenties? It's like well into the twenty-first century and I'm still not getting laid? I don't think so.

The true answer is C. Of course. But I have to answer B. I'm not an idiot.

Nina Geiger

Let's just set question one aside for a moment. Benjamin and I aren't even in the same room as that question. At least I'm not. I guess I don't know about him, given that we've only really had one date, which happened to be the first real date I ever had with anyone. I'm not exactly the Source of True Wisdom on this subject.

2 Your boyfriend's idea of a perfect date would be: (A) Going out for burgers and a movie; (B) Having a picnic on the beach and watching the sun go down; (C) Attending a rock concert; or (D) Hanging out with a big group of your mutual friends.

Easy. He'd like the concert, of course, over a movie. Benjamin's blind and he's big on music. But the answer he'd give if you asked him is B. Get it? Blind guy watching the sun go down? That's Benjamin's idea of funny. Mine too, actually.

BENJAMIN PASSMORE

B.

Aisha Gray

Question one, C. Christopher isn't shy about asking. But then, I'm not shy about saying no. Question two, I'd guess B because B would give him the best chance of getting back to question one.

Ah, question three. How appropriate.

3 Will your boyfriend say that (A) You are both free to see other people; (B) He can see other girls but he expects you to be faithful; (C) He'll be faithful to you but he understands if you want to go out with other guys; (D) Let's just see how it all works out.

There it is, the question I never asked but should have. But would Christopher have given me an honest answer?

That's the problem with quizzes. They all depend on how honest he is, how honest you are, and how prepared you are to see the truth. I'm guessing he'll answer A. But I'm guessing what he really means is B.

Christopher Shupe

I'VE BEEN LIVING IN AISHA'S
HOUSE WHILE I RECUPERATED FROM A
VERY UNFORTUNATE RUN-IN WITH
SOME GUYS WHO DIDN'T APPRECIATE
THE COLOR OF MY SKIN. I'M HAVING
MEALS COOKED FOR ME BY AISHA'S
MOTHER, AND BOOKS BROUGHT TO ME
BY AISHA'S FATHER. AISHA'S
LITTLE BROTHER COMES AROUND AND
PLAYS VIDEO GAMES WITH ME. I
WOULD HAVE TO BE A BIGGER TOAD
THAN I AM TO ANSWER A UNDER
THESE CIRCUMSTANCES, KNOWING HOW
AISHA FEELS. I GUESS IF YOU
REALLY TWISTED MY ARM, I'D SAY
MY HEARTFELT ANSWER WOULD BE B.
BUT I DON'T KNOW ANYMORE. AISHA
HAS STUCK BY ME BIG TIME. THAT
COUNTS FOR A LOT. I ALSO HAPPEN

TO LIKE HER MORE THAN ANY GIRL
I'VE EVER MET.

MY ANSWER IS D. I GUESS. ASK
ME AGAIN LATER WHEN I'M TOTALLY
BACK ON MY FEET.

One

The waves were more gray than blue, and when Lucas stood up on his board, his longish blond hair was the only splash of color in a tableau of sea and sky that could almost have been a black-and-white photograph.

Zoey Passmore pulled the cowl neck of her sweater up over her chin and ears and slid her hands up inside the sleeves. The beach sand had lost all of the warmth from the sun that had shone so encouragingly earlier in the day, and she kept to the blanket. She'd collected driftwood from the beach and fallen limbs from the pine trees behind her and piled them with ex-Girl Scout expertise in a nice little pyramid. But she didn't want to light the fire until Lucas was with her for fear she'd burn up all her stash of fuel before he finally got tired of surfing.

Lucas fell from the board, diving into the water headfirst and surfacing moments later to shake the water from his hair like a dog. He grinned and held up a single finger, indicating one more wave.

She watched him reclaim his board and paddle back out, black rubber tight on his legs and butt, his feet bare and probably frozen by now. But she couldn't begrudge him the opportunity. There were rarely surfable waves on Chatham Island. This was a fluke, the result of a major storm far out over the Atlantic. It had brought them just the skirts of its clouds and enough of a surge to send Lucas scrambling to wax his old board and squeeze himself into a wet suit he'd clearly outgrown.

He caught a wave and had a good, long ride, bringing the board within a few feet of the narrow beach before he tumbled.

But he kept his word and emerged from the surf, lifting his board free of the foam that surged to within a couple of yards of Zoey's feet.

"Quick, light the fire!" he yelled. "I'm numb."

Zoey smiled. His hair was wet and tousled, his body outlined in perfect detail by the tight wet suit. She felt a definite twinge. He looked incredible. Too incredible for Zoey's own good. She fished in her bag for the matches, but without taking her eyes from him.

She tore her eyes away and found the matches. He planted his surfboard upright in the sand and flopped onto the blanket beside her, smelling of salt and laughing in sheer delight.

"Damn, I'd forgotten how much I loved that." He pulled the zipper halfway down his chest and inhaled deeply. "If only I'd been able to breathe. I guess I'll have to break down and buy a new suit."

Zoey struck a match, but it was instantly blown out by the wind. *Don't say it*, she warned herself. *Don't say it.*

Then she said it anyway. "I think that suit looks pretty good on you." Her voice wobbled a little and she concentrated on lighting a second match, cupping it in her hands. She touched the flame to the dried grass kindling. It crackled loudly and caught fire.

Lucas rolled toward her and without warning stuck his hands under her sweater, pressing them to her bare stomach.

Zoey squealed and tried to push him away, but he held on. "Get those icicles off me!"

"I can't wait for the fire," he said. "I need warmth now. My hands are numb."

"I warned you it was freezing out there. You're the one who said 'Don't worry, I'll be plenty warm in my wet suit.'"

Lucas slid his hands around her back and drew her against him. Then he rolled onto his back, still holding her tight. "My lips are numb, too."

Zoey lowered her mouth to his and kissed his cold lips. She closed her eyes and kissed him again, more deeply, a vision of him rising from the surf still firmly fixed in her mind. Within seconds his lips were as warm as her own. She kissed his cheeks and pressed her hands to them. She kissed his eyelids and his neck.

"Now are you warm?" Zoey asked.

"Mmm. Now even other parts of me are warm," he said.

"Don't be crude."

"I meant my feet."

"Sure you did," Zoey said. She gave him a light peck on the lips and rolled off him. "Are you hungry?"

"That depends. Is there anything *else* on the menu? I mean besides food. You know, maybe something for some *other* form of hunger?"

"We have hot dogs and we have s'mores. That's what's on the menu."

Lucas sighed. "Okay, then I guess I'm hungry." There was no mistaking the pouting tone in his voice.

"Lucas, I thought we were going to give that topic a rest," Zoey said testily.

Lucas sat up and wrapped his arms around his knees. "I'm sorry. But you know, one thing kind of leads to another. We make out, we touch each other, first thing you know, I'm thinking about the next step. It's like . . . like saying hey, we'll get all dressed up, we'll drive to a fancy restaurant, we'll sit down and order this great meal, only, surprise, we're not going to eat anything."

Zoey was silent for a moment while the fire snapped and spread a glow around them. "You're using a food example. You must be hungry."

"I'm starving," he admitted ruefully.

"Look, Lucas, if every time we make out you're going to say I'm leading you toward sex,

15

then what am I supposed to do?" She held up her hand quickly. "Scratch that question. My point is, I really, really like kissing you. Really, really. But I'm not going to be able to enjoy it if you keep saying step one has to lead to step two has to lead to step three when I'm not ready for step three. You know?"

Lucas shrugged and looked away. Then he looked back at her, dissatisfied but not angry. "So if I want one and two, I have to shut up about three."

Zoey sighed heavily. It wasn't like she never considered step three. They weren't all that different, not really, she and Lucas. Except that it was more complicated for her than for him. It must be nice to be a guy and have everything be so simple and straightforward—just be led around by your hormones and never have to think about consequences. "Lucas, don't you want this to be a choice I can make for myself, one way or the other, and that I can feel good about?"

He absorbed that for a moment and winced. "Yeah, yeah," he said, making no attempt at sincerity.

Zoey smiled and hugged him. "We can still do some more of steps one and two."

"Okay. But first, we eat."

Zoey said good-bye to Lucas as night fell over Chatham Island and the tiny village of North Harbor. He went off toward his home, tired from the surf and, Zoey was sure, still a bit disgruntled and unsatisfied. She herself was feeling edgy, as she often did after making out with Lucas. She'd intended to go straight home and finish the journalism class assignment that was hanging over her head, but she didn't feel like concentrating. She was full of pent-up energy. She waved her arms back and forth at her sides, realizing how strange it would look to anyone who might be out on the streets and saw her.

She decided to stop by Nina's house. Zoey hadn't talked to her since the night before at the homecoming dance. Normally Nina could be counted on to drop by on just about any day of the week, especially a weekend day. But so far the day had been Nina-less.

Zoey walked the length of Center Street, crossing to walk through the parklike center of the circle. An island car, muffler blasting, front bumper held on by string, came rattling by and Zoey waved. Mrs. Gray, Aisha's mother. There were few of the island's three hundred permanent residents Zoey didn't recognize.

She reached Lighthouse Road, the northern edge of the island where cobblestones, low picket fences, and neatly tended gardens ran into sharp-edged, slick-wet rocks and sudden explosions of ocean spray. She went in through the gate of the Geiger house and instinctively looked up at the widow's walk, a railed deck atop the third story of the old house. Sure enough, there was Claire Geiger, Nina's sister. She was wearing a bright yellow rain slicker. Her long, voluptuous black hair streamed out from under an incongruous yellow rain hat.

"Damn," Zoey said under her breath. She herself was still wearing just a sweater, no coat.

Claire peered down, leaning casually on the rickety-looking railing. "Hey, Zoey."

"Hi, Claire. It's going to rain, huh?" Zoey yelled up at her, craning her neck.

"Zoey, we are completely blanketed with nimbostratus."

"Uh-huh," Zoey said.

"Rain clouds. Nimbostratus. But forget these." She waved a hand dismissively. "This is nothing. What's great is that there's a monster Canadian cold front rolling down toward upstate New York and Vermont."

"Yeah, that's cool, all right," Zoey said dryly. If Claire hadn't had the good luck to be very beautiful and endowed with a natural elegance that emerged even from beneath a rain slicker, she would have spent her life as a nerd. Yet because she was the person she was, her fascination with weather, her natural solitude, her distant reserve all added to a sense that she was a unique individual, not to be judged by anyone's standards but her own. Whatever *those* might be.

"Snow," Claire said, her eyes glowing as if she were announcing the advent of universal world peace. "There's a serious possibility of major

18

snow in Vermont. Say, around . . . Killington? And next weekend is a three-day weekend?"

Zoey clicked. "Ski trip? Are you thinking ski trip?"

Claire smiled her infrequent smile. "Very likely. I'll let you know."

"Excellent," Zoey said enthusiastically. She and Claire didn't share much (except for some ex-boyfriends), but they did both like to ski. And even though the school year was less than two months old, Zoey had been feeling hemmed in lately. A road trip would be just the thing.

She had no idea whether Lucas would like the idea. He'd never mentioned skiing. But snowboarding was very similar to surfing.

And yet, it brought up the question of spending a weekend with Lucas away from family.

"Where would we stay?" Zoey yelled up.

"My dad knows a guy with a condo there. This early in the year he won't have rented it," Claire said. She smiled knowingly. "Don't worry, I'm sure there will be plenty of beds for whatever arrangement you want."

Zoey knocked at the front door and went on in. She followed the sound of the Red Hot Chili Peppers up the stairs to Nina's room. She banged on Nina's door.

"Qué día tan hermoso!"

She went inside and found Nina Geiger

19

lying on her back on the bed, feet up on the wall, holding a Spanish textbook above her head. She was shouting phrases over the music, singsong Spanish intermingling with the cheerfully defiant obscenity coming from the stereo.

"Cree usted que hara buen tiempo mañana?"

"Nina!" Zoey yelled at the top of her lungs.

Nina looked alarmed, then smiled. "Zoey. *Chiquita. Como está?"*

Zoey sat on the bed and stretched to turn down the music. She and Nina did not share musical tastes. In fact, on a surface level they shared almost nothing. Nina was a year younger, louder, funnier, stranger, more vulnerable despite everything, and tended to dress like a refugee from Seattle by way of a rest stop in New York. The two of them had been best friends for years.

"I just stopped by to say hi," Zoey said. "You didn't come over today."

Nina shrugged and looked away evasively. "I am so behind on homework, Zoey. In history class I'm behind by an entire war. And in Modern Media I'm just media-ocre."

Zoey made a disgusted face at her pun. "Don't tell me you're hiding out because you have homework. Do I look dumb enough to believe that?"

"I thought it was worth a try."

"Come on, Nina. You didn't come over because you didn't want to run into Benjamin."

Nina rolled over and searched for her purse.

20

"That's not it," she said. "That would be silly and immature, and as we both know, I am the model of maturity."

"Things didn't go too well between you guys?" Zoey asked reluctantly. She had promised herself she would not, under any circumstances, get involved in the tentative relationship between her best friend and her brother. But this wasn't getting involved, exactly. She was just making conversation.

"Things went fine," Nina said. She continued to avoid Zoey's gaze, searching through her purse. She found a pack of Lucky Strikes and stuck one in her mouth, as always leaving it unlit.

"Look, you can tell me. Nothing you say will embarrass me."

"Okay, Zoey, since you asked. After the dance Benjamin and I stripped naked and made love like animals in the mud in the middle of the football field."

For a split second, Zoey's heart stopped. Then she sighed. "Okay, there *are* some things you could say that might embarrass me," she admitted.

Nina looked pleased with herself, as she always did when she managed to get a reaction out of someone. "Actually, it was no big deal."

"It was your first date, Nina."

"Didn't Benjamin already tell you what happened?"

"I don't talk to my brother about his love

life," Zoey said. "I talk to my best friend about my brother's love life. Now, I promise I will never get involved again, in any way, or even ask so much as a single question, but come on, Nina. I mean, this was a big thing for you."

After years of silence Nina had recently accused her uncle of molesting her as a child. One of Nina's deepest scars from that experience was a lingering fear of the opposite sex. Zoey knew that what would have been just a date for most girls was an act of courage for Nina.

"Well, we danced."

"I know. I saw that part," Zoey said patiently. "I was there."

"We held hands. It was sort of like you told me it would be. Only my hands kept getting sweaty, and I never knew when we were supposed to stop, or after we stopped when we should start again."

"That's good, though," Zoey said, feeling a wave of affection for her friend. "You got through it, right?"

Nina nodded. "Yeah. But it was close. I mean, when we kissed—"

"You what?"

"We went outside and, you know . . ."

"Is this another joke?"

"No. I kissed him, all right? Jeez. I guess I should have taken pictures."

"Where did you kiss him?"

"Outside?"

"You know what I mean," Zoey said.

22

"On the mouth. Actually, I missed on the first try and kissed his nose. But the second one was full lip contact. No tongue, though," she added helpfully.

This detail was just half a step too far for Zoey. "Okay, there is something sick about this. I mean, if it were any other guy, I'd be asking for all the gory details. But it's *Benjamin*."

"Yeah." Nina smiled wistfully. She nodded. "It was nice. I mean, a couple of times all the old stuff with my uncle started coming back, and I was getting panicky. A couple of times I was close to blowing punch and Doritos all over Benjamin."

"That would have been romantic," Zoey said, grinning at the image.

"But then I said, no, this is Benjamin, not someone else, and it's right now, not back then. And so then I was mostly liking it."

"Mostly?"

"Like papayas." Nina sucked thoughtfully on the cigarette.

"Papayas."

"You know, like it's unfamiliar, you haven't tasted it before, so you're cautious. It's not something you're sure of, like watermelon or apples. Then you start thinking, well, it's new and different, but it's not bad. I could see where over time I could develop a taste for this."

"That's good."

"Yeah." She looked up at the ceiling. "Yeah. Only . . . I don't know what Benjamin thought. I mean, he's tasted papayas before. He's tasted them with Claire, in fact. And she's a much more experienced papaya than I am."

"Oh, I get it. So you're worried about what Benjamin thought. Like did he enjoy it as much as you did."

"Or maybe it was just a pity date all along. And maybe he thought *no way*." She bit her lip.

"You shouldn't worry about him and Claire. I think that's over. It's Jake she's interested in now."

"Oh, *really*?" Nina said. "So how come she broke up with Jake at the dance?"

Zoey's mouth dropped open. "She dumped him? Poor Jake."

"Yeah, yeah, poor Jake. That's not what's important. Benjamin and Claire were *a thing* for a long time, as in years. Benjamin and I have been *a thing* for, let's see, almost twenty-four hours."

"I don't think Claire would go after your boyfriend, Nina," Zoey said, trying to sound convincing.

"Please. Claire would snatch a cookie out of the hand of a starving orphan. I'm not saying she would enjoy it, but if she felt she had to . . . I've tried to tell you," Nina went on, wagging her finger, "she worships Satan up there on that widow's walk. In fact, Claire gets Satan to do her homework for her. Last week he slept over and they made popcorn and stayed up all night watching reruns on

24

Nick at Night. Satan is especially fond of *F Troop*, it turns out."

"Are you done?"

"Yeah, I think so."

"Look. If you're worried about how Benjamin feels, you could just ask him," Zoey suggested.

Nina looked half-troubled and half-sly. "Or maybe someone else could find out for me." She batted her eyes.

"Oh no. I am not getting in the middle of you and Benjamin. No way."

Nina shrugged and fell serious. "I guess we'll work it out. I mean, Benjamin and I are good friends no matter what, right? One date, one kiss won't suddenly change everything. Will it?"

Probably, Zoey thought. "Everything will be fine," she said out loud.

Two

Christopher Shupe was living in greater luxury than he had ever seen outside of a movie or *Lifestyles of the Rich and Famous.* The bedroom was twice the size of any normal bedroom. It would have been possible to fit the entire two-bedroom project apartment where he'd grown up into this one room. The high, plush four-poster bed, as big as it was, with flowery draped fabric, voluminous matching down comforter, and some form of pillow covers that Aisha's mother insisted on calling shams, looked tiny in the overall space.

The floor was polished dark wood, partly covered with thick rugs. The walls were papered, trimmed in little flowery decals. The curtains were heavy and multilayered. He had a couch and a love seat and a coffee table. He had a tall oak dresser and a curved, oak-framed mirror.

And that was just the bedroom. He also got a separate dressing room, whatever that was about. And a monstrous closet that made his few articles of clothing look paltry.

But it was the bathroom that was truly amazing. There were endless miles of tiled countertops and a stalled shower, but by far the coolest feature was the raised whirlpool bath. He could lie in the whirlpool up to his chest in hot, foaming currents, and look out the window, down over the lights of North Harbor.

At the moment he was doing just that, though his attention was drawn to the small color TV showing a late-running football game. The remote control was on the tile beside him, alongside a cold soda.

It was a fine life, although very temporary. Too bad it had come as a consequence of getting beaten up. He still had to keep his bandaged arm and stitched face out of the water, but the heat felt wonderful on the bruises covering his legs and stomach and back.

Christopher heard a distant knock on the bedroom door and Aisha's voice.

"Come in!" he yelled.

The door opened. "Are you in the bathroom?"

"Yeah. But I'm jacuzzing. Don't worry. I won't show you anything you don't want to see."

Aisha Gray appeared, framed by the bathroom door, tall, thin, graceful, topped by a volcano of bouncy dark curls. "Stay in the water," she warned. "My mom wants to know if you think you can make it downstairs for dinner. If not, she'll bring you something up here."

"I can more or less walk up and down stairs," Christopher said. "But I don't know if your mom and dad and Kalif want to stare at my face through dinner." He indicated the stitches and the blood redness in one eye.

"You don't look so bad," Aisha said. Sweetly, it seemed to Christopher. She sat down at the far edge of the raised tile platform. "Besides, Kalif would love it. He thinks stitches are tough. He wants some of his own."

"Let's hope not, huh?" Christopher felt the cloud forming over him again. Suppressed rage and frustration that could only be kept under control by concentrating on the revenge he had promised himself. He forced a smile. "With all this luxury, you guys are going to have a hard time getting rid of me."

"I told my mom to put you in one of the cheap rooms," Aisha said. "But this room is her pride and joy. You know, in summer this rents out for two hundred and fifty dollars a day, not counting tax. Of course, a continental breakfast is included."

"Your mom is very cool," Christopher said with feeling. As soon as she'd learned of the beating Christopher had taken, Mrs. Gray had offered the facilities of the bed-and-breakfast as a place for him to recover. He had no family in the area, and no family capable of helping anywhere.

"She has that nurturing thing going big time," Aisha said fondly. "But I told her not to be stuffing pastries down you, making you fat."

Christopher nodded. "How about you,

Aisha? No nurturing instincts?"

"Why? You need additional nurturing?"

"I *need* you to come over here and kiss me."

Aisha gave him a dubious look. "You're taking a bath."

"So close your eyes."

Aisha slid closer but stayed just out of reach. "I don't know, Christopher. It's not like we've settled everything between us. We were broken up before this whole thing happened. And I seem to remember that it was your fault."

She wasn't exactly saying no. More like she was looking for some reassurance. "Aisha, do you really believe that I'm thinking about any girl but you right now?"

"Maybe not *right now,*" Aisha said. "But five minutes from now?"

"Are you going to kiss me or not?"

Aisha looked him over thoughtfully. She had an uncanny way of slipping into an observational mode that reminded him of a scientist watching bacteria through a microscope. It was part of what made her so interesting—she was always precariously balanced between cool, skeptical reason and blind, impetuous romance.

Aisha bit her lip and shook her head ruefully, and Christopher knew that romance had gained the upper hand. For the moment, at least. She moved closer and put her hand to his bruised cheek. Her fingers were cool. She lowered her face toward his, closing her black eyes slowly. Her lips met his.

He returned the kiss, feeling it spread throughout his body like a painkiller. Her lips were so soft. Her touch so gentle. Her hair fell around his face, almost closing off the outside world.

Why couldn't he just tell her that he would be faithful? And mean it? She had been at his side the instant she knew he was hurt. She was at his side now. She was beautiful and passionate and he had never, with any other girl, felt the way he did at this moment with Aisha.

He opened his eyes and saw that hers were still closed. Through her curls he caught a glimpse of the TV, and of the L.A. Rams cheerleaders.

Still, he reminded himself, there were so many girls in the world. Why should he accept limits? Even the delicious limits imposed by Aisha's full, soft lips?

Aisha pulled away, but only an inch. "I do love you," she whispered. "I wish I didn't, but I do."

What should he say? Did he love her back? Yes, he did love her. Yes, of that he was certain. It *was* love. But should he say it? Would she think it was some sort of vow?

The hesitation was fatal. She drew back, pushing her hair out of her face.

"Aisha . . ." he began.

She stood up, keeping her eyes averted. "Dinner is in about fifteen minutes," she said. "I'll have my mom bring it up to you."

Claire climbed down the ladder that led from the widow's walk back to her room, feeling wet and elated. The storm hadn't been much more than a lazy drizzle. A disappointment, as she'd been hoping for some good lightning. But Zoey had jumped at the idea of a road trip to Vermont. And Zoey would convince Nina to come along, and what Zoey and Nina did, Aisha could be convinced to go along with. That would mean all four girls, plus of course Lucas, who would certainly come with Zoey; Christopher, if he was well enough and getting along with Aisha by then; even Benjamin, if Nina hadn't found some way to alienate him on their one date. Benjamin and Nina. Claire shook her head. She might get used to that concept eventually, but it would take time.

Anyway, if the entire contingent of island kids went away for the weekend, wouldn't Jake want to go, too? Jake was the most fanatic skier of the group. Of course he'd go—as long as it looked like a nonromantic, noncouple, group sort of thing.

Claire shucked off her raincoat and hat and hung them on the closet hook. She spread a towel under them to soak up the dripping rainwater.

She would have to make clear to Jake that she considered it over between them. It wouldn't be about the two of them being together. It would just be about enjoying some

31

early snow and being off the island. A group thing. And the trick would be getting someone else to invite him.

Then if, while they were off at some romantic mountain hideaway, things very innocently developed between Jake and Claire . . . Well, it would be Jake's own choice, wouldn't it?

Claire quickly changed her blouse and started downstairs toward the aroma of clam chowder and Janelle's homemade corn muffins.

She ran into Nina and Zoey on the second-floor landing.

"What are you grinning about?" Nina demanded, looking suspicious. "You look like you're up to something."

"Are you going to stay for dinner, Zoey?" Claire asked, ignoring her sister and wiping the telltale smile off her face.

"No, I'm heading home. But thanks."

The three of them descended the stairs. "Have you told Nina about the snow?" Claire asked.

"No. We were talking about . . . other stuff," Zoey said cryptically.

Benjamin, Claire realized with a surprising pang. *Stupid*, she told herself sternly. It was absurd to be planning to win back Jake while at the same time feeling a sense of loss every time Benjamin's name came up. Chatham Island was getting too small. Too many former boyfriends lying around.

"What about snow?" Nina asked.

"We're thinking road trip this weekend," Claire said. "There's supposed to be a snowstorm moving through Vermont, and with that, plus the man-made snow, Zoey and I were thinking maybe we'd head to Killington. Me, Zoey, and I assume, Lucas."

"Well, Nina, you'd come, too, wouldn't you?" Zoey said quickly.

Claire fought the urge to smile. The mental image of just the three of them—Zoey, Lucas, and Claire—hadn't set too well with Zoey. She wanted Nina along, too. But Nina was looking dubious. "Oh, Nina doesn't want to come," Claire said.

"You don't want me along, Claire? I'm hurt," Nina said.

They paused in the entryway. "It's not that I don't want you along, Nina—" Claire let the sentence hang. Of course she *did* want her sister along, if Nina could bring Benjamin and add to the sense it was just one big happy island family. But Nina would do the opposite of whatever Claire wanted.

"If you guys are going, *I'm* going," Nina announced.

"You don't even ski," Claire pointed out.

"Maybe I'll learn. I'm a work in progress, Claire. I intend to do lots of things in my life that I haven't done before. Be a roadie for Pearl Jam. Get a tattoo on my left butt cheek. Shave all your hair off while you're asleep some night.

It's a busy life, but I could probably find the time to learn to ski."

"You might even enjoy it," Zoey suggested helpfully.

"Don't push it, Zo," Nina said. "No offense, but only an idiot could enjoy hurtling uncontrollably down a slope while their ears freeze and break off."

"So, you're in," Claire said, trying to sound annoyed. Easy enough, really, since Nina had a natural talent for annoying her.

"Yeah."

Claire sighed and headed toward the dining room. Now, with her back turned, she could allow herself an impish smile. Easy. So easy.

"Well, then I guess one of you two should invite Benjamin," Claire called over her shoulder.

Claire Geiger

Well, what an interesting question. It would be even more interesting if I were sure who, my boyfriend was. In my mind it's still Jake, though technically I broke up with him at the homecoming dance. But it isn't that simple. I mean, I broke it off because that's what he needed me to do. He couldn't reconcile being in love with me and blaming me for the death of his brother, Wade, two years ago. It was tearing him up, and me pressuring him to get over it wasn't helping.

So I told him it was over. I think the military phrase for it is <u>tactical</u> <u>retreat</u>.

Which of the following ten descriptions would my boyfriend agree apply to me? I'll give it a shot, though I'm not sure when or if I'll ever be able to get Jake's answers.

1. Manipulative. Yes, Jake would have to go along with that. And what can I do? Deny it? That would seem even more manipulative.

2. Vain. No.

3. Beautiful. Yes. And no, that does not prove I'm vain.

I know I'm attractive, but I honestly don't care that much. Although it can be useful.

3. Giving. That might be stretching the facts a little.

4. Friendly. That would also be stretching the facts a little.

5. Romantic. More than people think, but I doubt Jake would answer yes to it. I genuinely am in love with Jake. Sure, I'm willing to be a little manipulative in pursuit of some happiness, but that doesn't make the emotion any less sincere. So, yes, I am a romantic.

Just not one who thinks romance is all about heavy sighs and soulful looks. Jake would answer no.

6. Intelligent. Yes. And Jake would say yes as well. In fact, I think he's a little intimidated.

7. Sensual. Less than most people think. I have the sense that people have an incorrect opinion of me here. Probably. I wouldn't really know because I don't spend a lot of time trying to guess what people are thinking about me. It would be interesting to see Jake's answer to this one, though. I imagine, like most guys, he would hope the answer is yes.

8. Funny. I don't know. I'm not Nina, obviously. And I don't remember Jake and me ever laughing much. We had a relationship that had about one good week before it entered this sort of continuing crisis. The Cold

War, Part Two. Right now he'd answer no to this, just to annoy me.

9. Loyal. Another tough one. I don't think any of the guys I've gone out with would say yes to this. Which I guess is too bad. I suppose the truth is that my main loyalty is to myself, and despite everything I've tried to do to show my loyalty to Jake, I doubt he would give me a point here. Someday, maybe. Not yet.

10. Good. Ah, there's a deceptively sneaky one from the old quizmaster. Am I a good person? Benjamin once told me that deep down inside I was fundamentally decent, and could be counted on to do the right thing. And Benjamin is a perceptive person. But he's also still in love with me, so perhaps his judgment is wrong. I don't think Jake thinks of me as a good person, though I know he's still in love with me as well. All I can say is that I always try to do what's right. As long as the right thing is also the thing that works.

Three

"What am I supposed to do? Do I sit with you? Do I sit with him? Do I say hi to him, then come sit with you? Do I ignore him unless he says hi to me, or unless he sits with me? I don't understand any of this. Isn't there a book somewhere that explains it all? *The Big Book o' Relationships*?"

Nina found the pack of Lucky Strikes in her purse and stuck one, unlit, in the corner of her mouth. The chill sea breeze fretted her dark hair, stinging her cheeks and eyes. She drew her jacket around her, comforted by the warmth and the satisfying groan of the leather. She glared across the deck of the ferry at Benjamin, who was listening to music through earphones and hiding his blank eyes behind black Ray•Bans.

"I am absolutely *not* going to get involved in your relationship with my brother," Zoey announced firmly. "I meant what I said yesterday. That was it. Never again." She was sitting beside Nina on the bench, shivering because, as usual, she had not dressed warmly enough. She'd spent nearly her entire life in Maine but still clung to what Nina thought was an inappropriate optimism about the weather. Now Zoey was holding her wispy blond hair down with her hands, trying to keep her ears warm. "What you do with Benjamin is your problem, and his. I'm not advising, I'm not passing information back and forth, I'm not spying for either of you."

Nina gave her a dirty look. "Zoey, why do you have bare legs when it's this cold? You're a senior; figure it out. It's cold. And it's distracting, having to talk to someone who is turning blue and rattling. Especially someone who doesn't understand that girl-girl solidarity transcends mere sister-brother solidarity."

"*You* have bare legs," Zoey said. "I mean, those tights aren't exactly warm."

"Yes, but I have hot legs. I always have. My upper body gets cold, but my legs are unnaturally hot. At night sometimes I have to stick them out from under the blankets."

"I never knew that about you," Zoey said dryly.

"Oh, yeah. Hot-leg Nina—new from Mattel. I'll be Barbie's newest, coolest friend."

Zoey laughed. "See, this is why I can't give you advice. I have my own selfish interests. I mean, if you start sitting with Benjamin every day, who'll sit with me and keep me from doing my homework on the way in to school?"

"I notice Lucas doesn't always sit with us," Nina pointed out. "So I figured maybe there was some *thing* I didn't know about. Some secret agreement everyone but me knows about that says boyfriends and girlfriends don't sit together at certain times. A state law or something. Like at lunch it's always just you and me and Aisha. And Claire, whenever she feels like hanging with her inferiors."

Zoey shrugged. "These things just work out. I mean, I spend lots of time with Lucas. He's over every night. Wait, backspace—every *evening*. He's over every evening."

"Hey, Eesh," Nina said, reaching around Zoey's back to poke Aisha.

Aisha looked up from her notebook, where she'd been busily scribbling calculus problems. "What?"

"I just wanted to see if you were conscious," Nina said.

"I'm trying to get my calc done so I don't have to do it during lunch."

"Hmm," Nina said, nudging Zoey. "Aisha is behind on her homework. That's fact number one. And fact number two is that Christopher is now living with her. Do I sense a connection there somewhere?"

Aisha slapped her pen against her pad. "He is not living with me. I happen to live in a B&B. Strangers often stay there. It's the whole point of a B&B. Christopher is no more living with me than any of the old fart couples who come and spend a weekend."

"Touchy, isn't she?" Nina said gleefully.

43

"How is Christopher doing?" Zoey asked.

"He's recovering pretty well. Mostly he's living it up while my mom stuffs the latest recipe from *Gourmet* magazine down his throat."

"Do you think he'll want to go skiing?" Nina asked.

"Do I think he'll want to go skiing?" Aisha repeated. "Yes, Nina. That was the very first thing he asked for this morning when he woke up. He said, 'Hey, I'd like to go skiing.'"

"Ha," Nina pounced. "So you were there with him *when he woke up.*"

"It was a figure of speech." Aisha closed her notebook with an air of resignation. "Christopher is unfortunately still a partial toad. He's an injured toad I am helping take care of out of the goodness of my heart, but he's still a toad."

"Huh. So, you guys don't want to go skiing?" Nina asked.

"What is this with skiing?" Aisha exploded.

"Claire says it's going to snow in Vermont," Zoey said.

Aisha threw up her hands. "It's like having a conversation with Beavis and Butt-head. Would one of you explain to me what you are talking about?"

Nina raised her hand. "Can I be Butt-head? Zoey's the blond."

"We're thinking about taking a road trip over to Vermont this weekend," Zoey explained. "It's supposed to snow, and Claire says she can get

44

us all a condo at Killington. Claire and I both like to ski."

"It's an excellent way to make yourself into a paraplegic," Nina said.

Aisha shrugged. "I don't think Christopher would be up for skiing by then. Besides, I really doubt he skis."

"Lucas doesn't either, but I figured since he likes to surf, he'd probably get into snowboarding."

"I don't do either," Nina said. "I just drink hot chocolate and sing 'Walkin' in a Winter Wonderland' over and over until people threaten to kill me."

"Sounds like fun," Aisha said dubiously.

"First it has to snow," Zoey said. "Then we have to get all the parental units to go along."

"Are you asking Benjamin?" Aisha asked Nina.

"Sure," Nina said with more confidence than she felt. "I'll ask him later. Unless Zoey would just be a good friend and ask him for me."

"This looks like a boyfriend-girlfriend situation, *not* a brother-sister situation," Zoey said.

"Except for Claire, who is currently boyfriendless," Aisha noted.

Nina nodded thoughtfully. "Yeah. Unless for some reason Jake decides to come along." She glanced across the deck at Claire, who was sitting alone, reading a book. A shadow of suspicion crossed Nina's mind. This whole trip was Claire's idea.

But no, not even Claire was that subtle.

*　　　*　　　*

Benjamin ran his finger along the curved brass railing as he descended the stairs from the top deck to the bottom deck. One, two, three . . . fifteen stairs, counted off almost without thinking. He turned a sharp right, advanced to the next railing, and, so naturally that a casual observer would not have known he was blind, he trailed a finger along the painted brass to the gangway.

Once on the dock he needed a landmark to locate himself. The ferry landing was imprecise, and he needed precision. He unfolded his cane, swung it in a short arc and quickly found the bench he was seeking. Now, in a line with the bench, it would be fifty-two paces to the curb at the end of the dock.

He heard a person fall into step with him and guessed from a host of almost imperceptible clues that it was Nina.

"Hi, Nina," he said with a smile. "You can't fool me just because you change brands of soap."

"Damn," Nina said. "I went from Dove to Irish Spring. It's manly, yes, but I like it, too."

"Yeah, but you stayed with Lucky Strikes. The smell of tobacco but no smoke. Dead giveaway. Plus Doc Martens make a certain sound. So do tights when your legs rub together." He put on a cocky swagger. "Don't mess with me, Nina. I have powers far beyond anything you puny earthlings could comprehend."

"Oh yeah? What color underwear do I have

on? And my legs do not rub together."

"White. All cotton."

There was a long silence. "Okay, I give up," Nina said.

Benjamin grinned. "Just a lucky guess."

"Okay. Try this. How many fingers am I holding up?"

"One. The middle one. That was too easy." He was rewarded by the sound of Nina's laughter, a sound that conveyed a sort of unforced, childlike delight. It was a sound that always touched a soft spot in Benjamin.

Laughs were telling, he had discovered. Claire's was rare and dryly appreciative. Bestowed like a pat on the back for a job well done. Zoey always sounded surprised, as if she hadn't been expecting to laugh but wow! now she was and she was glad about it. Aisha had two—a restrained, moderate one that was partly just politeness, and a wilder one that broke out like an escaped animal she couldn't quite get under control.

"So, look, Benjamin," Nina began in the awkward way she had of shifting into a serious topic. "I was wondering. I mean, usually on Monday after school I come over and read to you."

"Yes."

"Well, do you want me to come over and read to you today as usual?"

"Sure. Why not?"

"No reason. I was just asking."

They reached the curb and Benjamin turned

toward the crosswalk. In a corner of his mind the count went on, a subliminal reassurance that he knew where he was, could place himself in the invisible world. "I still want you to keep reading, unless you decide you don't want to."

"Do you *want* me to decide I don't want to?" Nina asked.

"No, I want you to decide that you *do* want to. Unless you really don't want to."

"I want to."

"Which? Keep reading? Or not?"

"Whichever you want," Nina said.

Benjamin groaned. "Nina, this isn't supposed to happen. Even though we went out together, we're supposed to go on being friends. Friends first. That was the deal."

"So . . . so you're saying the other thing, that was just the one time?"

"Is that what you want?" Benjamin asked.

"No fair. I asked you first. Come on, light's green."

They crossed the street. Benjamin could hear the idling car engines on his left and the electronic click as the light went to yellow. Some distance ahead he could hear Zoey's voice, raised in conversation with Lucas.

"I had a good time the other night," Benjamin said.

"Me too," Nina said guardedly. "The music was pretty bad, but it was fun anyway. I mean, dancing and all."

Was Nina trying to tell him something? Had

48

she been turned off by the kiss they had shared? It was certainly possible. She was just starting to deal with the corrosive aftermath of the situation with her uncle. Maybe she hadn't felt good about kissing Benjamin. Maybe she wasn't ready to go that far.

Or maybe she just didn't like *him* in that way. Maybe it wasn't some general thing, maybe it was specific. She'd avoided coming over on Sunday. And just now, on the ferry, she hadn't even come over to say hello.

"Yeah, dancing," Benjamin said, distracted by his own thoughts.

A silence descended that lasted several minutes. "So. I'll come over this afternoon and read for a couple of hours," Nina said.

Was she sounding relieved? No, that wasn't quite it. But she sounded strange. "That would be great," Benjamin said.

Four

"There is no doubt but that as we move into the electronic environment of the near future we will see changes in the craft of journalism," Mr. Schwarz said. "But the basics will still be much the same. It will still be a matter of conveying the facts, giving those facts context, and—"

The bell rang, ending first period. Instantly books were gathered up, feet shuffled, desks scraped on the floor.

"—I guess I'll leave you all in suspense until tomorrow," Mr. Schwarz said. "Zoey? Can you stay for a moment? The rest of you, take off. But don't forget I want your assignments on my desk by Thursday, no excuses."

Zoey hung back as the rest of the class rushed past. She picked up her books and papers and went up to the desk, wondering if she'd done something wrong or blown some test. But as she searched her memory, she couldn't imagine what it might be.

"What did you want, Mr. Schwarz?" He was, without a doubt, the best-looking teacher at Weymouth High: tall, fairly young for a teacher, with brown rock-star hair.

He wiggled his eyebrows suggestively. "I got a call from Lisa Soo at the *Weymouth Times*."

Lisa Soo was the assistant style editor at the city newspaper, which put her in charge of the twice-a-month youth section, written by students from all the high schools in the area. Zoey had done articles for her during her junior year.

"What did she do, find a misspelled word from one of my old stories?" Zoey asked, not wanting to seem too eager.

"No, she has an assignment for us, and I suggested you'd be the person for the job."

Zoey felt a thrill of anticipation. It was just the youth page, but it was for a real paper. Those kinds of clips, along with her contributions to the high school paper, would help get her on the student paper when she went to college. And that was an important step toward landing a serious reporting job when she graduated from college. Not the White House beat for the *Washington Post*, maybe, but a good starting job that might *lead* to the White House beat at the *Washington Post*. Followed by some time overseas covering wars and natural disasters. Then, after she'd proven herself as a serious journalist, a move to TV. Say, ABC bureau chief in Paris or Tokyo or Jerusalem. And during her spare time, she'd write steamy romance novels under a wittily chosen pen name. Only her closest friends would realize that the queen of romance and the serious, Pulitzer-prize-winning foreign correspondent were the same woman.

"Zoey?"

She snapped back to reality. "Sorry."

Mr. Schwarz smiled. "How far gone were you? *New York Times*?"

Zoey blushed. "I'd only reached the first Pulitzer prize."

"Uh-huh. Listen, this is a serious story, and she wants your best effort."

"What is it?"

"There are rumors of illegal drug use on our varsity football team. You go out with someone on the team, don't you?"

"I used to," Zoey said, feeling her heart trip.

"Are you still on speaking terms with this person?"

Zoey shrugged. "I think so. But I doubt if he'd know anything about it. Jake isn't into that at all." She hoped that was true. The night of the homecoming game Lucas had made some remark about Jake being high, but then, Lucas and Jake had never gotten along very well.

Mr. Schwarz nodded. "Still, it would give you a place to start."

"Yes, I guess it would."

"Give it your best shot. If you get a story, it could move right off the youth page onto the front page." He shook a warning finger at her. "But source everything. And triple check everything. No off-the-record quotes unless you talk to me first and clear it. This is serious stuff, and we don't want to make accusations unless we have it totally nailed down. This is not something I want you to hurry on. Take all the time you need. You understand?"

"Absolutely," Zoey said seriously. "All the time I need. Very careful." Her mind was already racing, trying to figure ways to get at the story. Ways that would bypass Jake, should it turn out that he was involved.

"Okay, take off. And don't let me down."

She turned and started off, deep in thought. Then she paused. "Mr. Schwarz?"

"Yes?"

"Thanks for giving this to me. I really appreciate it."

He winked. "Just tell me this—in the Pulitzer daydream, you're not some airhead anchorwoman, are you?"

"No way. Foreign correspondent. Trench coat and the whole thing."

She stepped out into the hallway and hurried toward her next class, practically buzzing with excitement. A real story. At least potentially a real story. Football and drugs. It would be hard to beat that combination for getting the reader's attention.

Jake McRoyan had set his alarm for four A.M. that morning. He had gotten up and pumped iron hard for forty-five minutes, working his muscles to the limit with the free weights. Then he had taken a six-mile run, circling the northern half of Chatham Island twice till his lungs were screaming and his heart was racing.

He had cooled down by viciously pummeling

the heavy bag that hung on a swivel in the corner of his room. Afterward, sweating and flushed and so weary he thought he might not be able to stand, he'd showered and, in the full-length mirror, had checked his body, flexing the muscles, looking for signs of the weakness he knew must be there.

He had let the team down. He had let himself down. He had let the memory of his brother down. All because of Claire. All because, despite the lean, layered muscle in the mirror, he was weak. And no amount of pounding the punching bag would change that essential fact.

Even Claire had at last seen it. Why else had she dumped him at the dance?

That morning he had been alone on the ferry ride over to school. Alone on the walk up the hill from the dock to school. And for the first time in his life, he had entered the school feeling that he had to avoid the gaze of the people he met.

So many people would get pleasure out of ragging on him. So many people would enjoy pointing out the hypocrisy of straight-arrow Jake, suspended from the team for refusing to take a drug test.

He had waited for it to start in gym class, his second period.

And there *had* been some banter about the lost homecoming game, but no mention of the real reason—that the star running back had been hung over through the first half, and buzzed on coke through the last half.

No one had mentioned cocaine. No one had

even hinted at his suspension. Were people feeling sorry for him? Was that it? Or had it reached the point where no one cared whether Jake McRoyan or anyone else used drugs? No. Weymouth, Maine, wasn't exactly Detroit or Chicago. Here, an accusation that a football player was using was still worth a pretty good scandal.

They ran a basketball drill in gym class, not Jake's best game, especially with sore, bunched muscles and a profound weariness from lost sleep. But although there had been one or two slams at his less-than-elegant hook shot, the dreaded word *drugs* had not been spoken.

Hell, if the situation had been reversed, *he* would have thought of plenty to say to an athlete who had blown an important game because of his own personal problems. Plenty. But there had been nothing. It was just strange.

He was leaving the locker room on his way to third period when BeeBee Hoyt fell in beside him. BeeBee was a sophomore who played tight end on the football team. Jake braced himself. Now it would start.

"Hey, Jakester. What's this I hear about you doing K-berger?"

Jake was utterly nonplussed. "What?"

"You and Louise Kronenberger, dude. After the game Friday. Is that why Claire Geiger split on you at the dance? Inquiring minds want to know."

Jake frowned. "I was at a party where she was." He concentrated. The party was a blur in his memory. It had come right after the game, right after he'd been suspended. He had drunk a great deal of beer, he remembered that. A great deal. Much later he'd managed to stagger to the water taxi and get back to the island. The next thing he'd known, he was waking up in Claire's guest room, sick and in pain.

"Tad Crowley's telling people you got faced and pranged the K-berger."

Jake hardened his expression. "Yeah, well, I guess it's open season on me now." Flashes of memory: sitting beside Louise on a couch. She had looked good. But that was all. Wasn't it?

"So, you're saying you didn't?" BeeBee pressed.

"What's it matter, BeeBee? Who the hell's going to believe anything I have to say about *anything*?" Jake demanded bitterly.

BeeBee half-closed his eyes and affected a bored look. "I don't know what you're talking about, dude," he said carefully.

"Screw you, BeeBee. You know what I'm talking about."

"No. I don't. Coach says I don't, so I don't. I'm clueless. I wasn't even there. I was in some other state."

Jake stopped and gripped the smaller boy's arm. "What are you talking about?"

Now BeeBee looked a little scared. He tried to pull away. "Chill, big Jake. Coach said it stays in the team. No one says anything to anyone about him suspending you. Ever. He doesn't want a bunch of parents on his back, I guess."

"Are you telling me no one outside the team knows about this?" Jake tightened his grip urgently.

"Coach said he'd cut the balls off the first guy who said anything. Jeez, you're breaking my arm, man."

Jake released him. He drew what felt like his first real, deep, honest breath in days. Coach was keeping things covered up. He didn't want to hurt Jake's chances of getting into a college athletics program. Plus, like BeeBee said, he probably didn't want a lot of parents running around screaming about drugs.

The secret wouldn't hold forever, though. No matter what the coach said, some guys would tell their friends, others would tell their girlfriends. But this way it would come out slowly. And dribbling out bit by bit like a piece of gossip, most people probably wouldn't believe it. After all, if anyone had a clean rep at Weymouth High, it was Jake.

"Sorry," Jake said, absently patting BeeBee's arm where he had squeezed it. "I'm a little tense, I guess." Then he shook his head in relief and amusement. "Forget that crap about me and K-berger. I'll admit I was drunk that night, but I'm not that stupid."

Jake felt a little flicker of life returning to him. A week from today he could take the drug test, pass it with flying colors, and be back on the team. He would stay sober. He would get himself back in shape. He would be up and ready for the game after next. All the crap of the last few weeks would be behind him.

Five

"This is very close to something that a human being could eat without having to run to the bathroom clutching her throat," Nina said, chewing a bite of the food from her tray. "Very close. I can't say it's good, but it doesn't make me gag."

Claire raised a skeptical eyebrow and looked across the round cafeteria table at her sister. "Are you just saying that, hoping I'll try some?" she asked.

Nina made a heart-crossing gesture. "It's honestly not awful."

Claire hesitated, waiting for either Zoey or Aisha to try a bite. Aisha obliged first.

"Huh," she said. She chewed slowly, with a thoughtful look in her eyes. "I wonder what it is?"

"It's tan, or you might prefer beige," Nina said, "with forest-green highlights that may be a type of vegetable material."

"It could be . . ." Zoey rolled her eyes to the ceiling. "I'm getting a sense of vegetables. Possibly spinach. Also, there's a hint of meat."

Claire tried it. It wasn't bad. It wasn't identifiable, but it wasn't bad. Very likely she didn't really want to know what it was. She shrugged and had a fleeting image of an entire school being hauled away in ambulances. "So. Chances of snow in the mountains have gotten better since yesterday," she said. She focused on Zoey. "Have you asked Lucas yet?"

Zoey looked uncomfortable and began playing with a tendril of hair. "Not yet. Actually, I was starting to have doubts about the whole thing. I mean, it's such a long drive and all."

"Long drive? It's like two hundred miles, even if we stick to the highway," Claire said. "We catch the seven-forty ferry on Saturday, we load up your folks' van, and we're making our first run by noon. Ski all afternoon. All the next day. Ski the morning after that, and we're back by dinnertime on Monday."

Zoey nodded agreement but still looked unconvinced. "Well, what's this condo like?"

"Why? You suddenly need five-star accommodations? It's a nice condo. Two or three bedrooms plus a living room, a fireplace, a Jacuzzi out on the deck."

Again Zoey nodded guardedly. "So, like how many beds are there?"

Claire smiled wryly. "Oh, so that's what you're worried about. Huge surprise. Look, there are enough beds and rooms and everything that I'm sure we can work out *whatever* arrangement you want."

"It would be easier with just two bedrooms,"

Aisha weighed in. "Then it would be guys in one, girls in the other. Three bedrooms brings up other possibilities."

Claire drummed her fingers impatiently. "Look, it's not like anyone is going to have much privacy. We're not talking No-tell Motel here. I mean, if everyone comes, it will be eight people in one condo." The second the word *eight* was out of her mouth she wished she could call it back. But no one had taken any notice.

"I guess you're right," Zoey said, "but what are the guys going to think? If I go to Lucas and say, Lucas, do you want to spend a weekend in the mountains with me? he's going to think . . . you know. And lately . . . well, anyway." She started eating again, keeping her eyes down.

Claire groaned inwardly. Good grief. So Lucas was getting a little frisky. Big deal. All Zoey had to do was say no. Or yes. Or whatever.

"I know what Christopher would think if I asked *him*," Aisha said. "I mean, he'd interpret it his own way, regardless of what I said. Besides. I'm not sure I really want to spend a weekend with Christopher."

"He's living right in your own house," Claire pointed out. Why was everyone being so difficult? This should have been easy—a big group trip would make it seem only natural that Jake come along, too. After all, even though he wasn't with her anymore, he was still part of

60

the group. And then, away from the island, with absolutely no pressure from her, the natural course of events would bring together the only two unattached people. Simple, really.

"I know he's living in my house," Aisha argued. "But so are my mother and father and my little brother. If we're all at some ski lodge, I have no one around but you guys. And anyway, that's not the only thing. I'm not even sure Christopher and I *are* Christopher and I. He has a whole different idea about how things are supposed to be than I do. At least I think he does."

"Maybe he'll come around more to your point of view," Claire said, trying to sound interested. The truth was, she didn't much care if Christopher and Aisha were together or not, except that the plan really only worked if it looked like the whole Chatham Island group was going, guys as well as girls. She certainly couldn't convince Jake to come if it was just the four girls and him. That would make it like a *girl* thing, not a *group* thing.

Aisha snorted derisively. "Christopher suffers from hound syndrome. I don't think there's a cure."

"So you guys are bailing? It's down to me and Nina?" Claire said distastefully.

"That's a horrible thought," Nina agreed. "It would end up like *The Shining*. I'd be going around saying *redrum* and she'd be chasing me through the snow with an ax."

"I could do that at home," Claire muttered. "What did Benjamin say?"

Now it was Nina's turn to look away. "I sort of forgot to mention it to him."

Claire threw up her hands. It was a clean sweep. Perfect. Now no one was going. Zoey didn't want to give Lucas the wrong impression. Aisha was trying to put distance between Christopher and her. And Nina? God knew what idea had gotten into Nina's head about Benjamin.

"Well, *I'm* still going," Claire said flatly. "By Saturday noon I will be there." *And so will the rest of you and your various boyfriends,* she vowed silently. *And Jake, too.*

Whether any of them liked it or not.

Jake's last period of the day was study hall, time he could use to go to the library, see his guidance counselor, or do homework. He had arranged his classes with a last-period study hall so he could work out in the gym and get ready for football practice. It wasn't technically an acceptable use of study hall, but no one had ever objected.

But this was to be a week without football. Which meant that study hall was . . . whatever he wanted it to be. The study hall teacher barely knew Jake's name. He was free.

It was an unusual sensation. Football had been a big part of his life ever since Wade had made the team, back when Jake was still in eighth grade. After Wade's death, Jake had followed in his footsteps. It seemed utterly strange to think that all the guys would be out on the field this afternoon, running plays without him. His first instinct was to go out and at least watch the practice. But that would have just been pathetic. And he had been pathetic enough recently.

The depressing memories crowded in on him as he escaped from history class. Drunk before a vital practice, Claire sobering him up with coffee and a shower. Drunk after the game, waking up freezing on the North Harbor dock, surrounded by the faces of his friends—some worried and sympathetic, like Zoey, others, like Lucas, barely able to conceal their disgust.

He tried to shake off the memories and walked faster. He wanted to evade Zoey and Lucas and Benjamin, who were all in the same history class. Zoey had indicated that she wanted to talk to him after class, but he had very little to say to her. She was either going to say something sweet and encouraging about his breakup with Claire, or, despite the coach's warnings, some rumor about his suspension from the team had already leaked out. Either way, he didn't want to talk to her. He had loved Zoey for a long time. Had imagined a future of them together. Her pity now, however well intentioned, would be impossible to bear.

He plowed smoothly into the anonymous hallway crowds of noisy underclassmen. A group of freshmen trying desperately to look tough were swaggering down the hall in front of him, but sensibly parted at his approach.

"Jake!"

A female voice. Jake decided to pretend he hadn't heard. It didn't sound like Zoey or Claire, but he couldn't be sure.

A soft hand touched his arm, and he had no choice but to turn and meet the person it belonged to. He fixed a scowl on his face.

"Well, you look fierce," Louise Kronenberger said, smirking at him.

Instantly he felt uneasy. BeeBee's insinuation was fresh in his mind. What were *not* fresh in his mind were the details of the party at Tad Crowley's apartment after the game. He half-tried to remember. He had a clear flash of sitting beside Louise on a couch and noticing that her skirt had ridden so far up that he could see her panties. But that was about it.

"Hi, Louise," he said, feeling something close to panic.

"Hi, Louise." She mimicked his nervous tone perfectly. "Don't want to be seen with me, huh?"

Louise glanced over her shoulder, took his hand, and drew him into a recessed doorway. She opened the door and peeked inside. Then she pulled Jake after her into the gloomy, vacant chemistry lab and closed the door behind them. To Jake's astonishment, she put her arms around his neck, raised herself on tiptoes, and kissed him on the mouth.

"What was that for?" he gasped. It had been a nice kiss, but it scared him. He was wobbling on the edge of a cliff, about to lose his balance.

"That was for Friday night," she said suggestively. "I didn't want to say anything to you at the dance, what with you being there with almighty Claire Geiger." She laughed her carefree, amused laugh, a sound that struck new chords of memory in Jake's brain. Why did that laugh sound so familiar?

"I guess we had a good time Friday night," he said guardedly.

Louise made a pouting face. "You *guess*? I know I enjoyed it," she said. "Except for the times when you'd blurt out Claire's name." She erupted in another round of amusement.

Jake felt the blood draining from his face. "Louise . . . Look, I was awfully drunk that night." Plus, coming down off two rounds of cocaine, a football game, emotional depression, a suspension from the team . . .

"We were both pretty well blitzed." She peered at him closely, looking a little disappointed, as if he were a dunce stubbornly refusing to get a very funny joke. "You're not going to go into the whole regrets and second-thoughts thing, are you?"

Jake rubbed his hand over his face. It was hot and his hand was moist. "I don't know how to say this, but did something happen between us? I mean, something more than flirting on the couch?"

Louise stared at him, dumbstruck. Then a slow smile began to spread. "Are you b.s.'ing me? Are you telling me you don't remember?" The grin gave way to a delighted laugh. "Your first time and you don't even remember? It *was* your first time, wasn't it? You said it was, and guys don't usually lie about how *little* experience they have."

"Are you . . . Is this true? Because, you know, it would be a pretty sick joke to play on someone."

Louise made a wry smile. She began to pull down the neck of her sweater, revealing some of her left breast. A red, puckered mark lay against the white flesh. "Want to match the hickey to the mouth?" she asked. "I'll bet it's like snowflakes, or fingerprints—no two hickeys exactly alike."

Jake rocked back on his heels. Oh God, it was true. What BeeBee had told him. It was true. Fragments of disturbing—and explicit—memory were racing across his consciousness now.

"Don't heave a kidney, Jake," Louise said. "It's not that big a deal. I mean, it wasn't *my* first time. And it was my idea as much as it was yours."

"God, Louise . . . I . . . I was so drunk that night." His breath was coming short and fast. He gulped hard. What was he supposed to say? Thanks, I'm sure I had a good time? "I didn't mean to do it. Really. I mean, that's not me. I don't believe in . . . I don't know what to say."

Now Louise was looking annoyed. "Oh, grow up, Jake. I said you weren't my first. And, not that I want to break your heart or anything, but you won't be my last."

"Who have you told about this?" he demanded. Claire? Did Claire know?

She shrugged. "The people at the party had to know. Those who were sober enough to notice anything at all."

Jake shook his head despairingly. The day had begun with an unexpected reprieve, the news that Coach was covering up the drug suspension. Now it was ending with this.

What had he come to? It made him sick just to think of it. It was as if his life were spinning further and further out of control.

And worst of all was the fear that when Claire learned of this, any remote chance of their getting back together would be over.

5 Will your boyfriend say that he tells you the whole truth (A) All of the time, even if it reflects badly on him; (B) Most of the time, unless it reflects badly on you; (C) Only when it's something you need to know; (D) Only when it suits his purposes. (Try to get your boyfriend to answer at least this question honestly.)

Claire

Of all the guys I have ever known, Jake is the only one I think can honestly answer A. Possibly because he's never done anything he's ashamed of.

Benjamin will tell the truth and the whole truth . . . but only when he chooses. In other words, he's fundamentally honest, but he'll save up the truth for the time when it will do him the most good.

When I was going with Lucas, I don't know how much truth either of us ever told. He keeps his secrets. And so do I. Of course, that was two years ago. He may have changed. You'd have to ask Zoey that.

I have _not_ changed. Jake has been through some bad times lately, but I don't think he's changed, either. I'm a D and he's an R. Probably that means we're not a very good match, but I don't live my life according to magazine quizzes.

Aisha

Too easy. The answer is D. If I could get Christopher up to a C, I think I could live

with that. Anything more than
that would involve transplanting
a different brain into Christopher's body. Which might not
be such a bad idea. I myself
am a B. I'll tell anyone the
truth as long as it isn't something that would really hurt
their feelings. For example, I do
tell Christopher he's immature.
He is, he needs someone to tell
him, and anyway he thinks
it's just one of his cute character traits. I don't tell him
his singing makes birds fall
down dead out of the trees. That
would hurt his feelings.

So I'm saving that for a
time when I really need to
unload on him.

Nina

I believe it was the immortal
Curly who asked, "what is
truth?" Or maybe it was "what
is truth, nyuk, nyuk, nyuk?"
Anyway, the definition of truth
has haunted the great thinkers
and philosophers down through
the ages. Now it's my turn to
deal with it, so we may start
seeing some progress.

Does Benjamin tell me the
truth, the whole truth, and
nothing but the truth? I
certainly hope not. Like I want
him saying, Gee, Nina, your
breath smells of Velveeta and

peanut butter, you sicken me?
No. I think not. If he were an
A, I don't think we'd last long
as a couple. Not that we're
likely to last long as a couple
anyway, because I'm not sure
we ever were a couple in the
full sense of couplehood.

As usual with Benjamin, no single answer works. He's halfway
between B and C. A C-plus, let's
say. I hate to screw up his
GPA like that, but maybe there
will be a makeup test later.

Zoey

I think Lucas is very
honest. At least about the

things that involve us as a couple. He's certainly up front about where he wants the relationship to go, and how soon he'd like it to go there. And I'm equally honest about telling him that I have a slightly different vision of the direction and speed.

Yes, I trust him to be honest. That's not the problem. The problem is when he's honest, and I'm honest, and there doesn't seem to be any way for us to agree. Then what? Either someone gives in, or both people go separate ways, or you end up like some old couple who hate each other but are staying together for the sake of the kids.

Six

Claire waited until Wednesday afternoon to act. She had been waiting for two things. First, the weather. There was no point in going ahead with what she was privately calling *The Plan* until it was certain that the weather would cooperate.

And beginning at two a.m. on Wednesday, a Canadian cold front dumped an early blanket of snow from southern Quebec to western Massachusetts. At the lower elevations it melted away, but above a thousand feet it lay across mountain slopes like a big goose-down comforter. Between this natural snowfall and the man-made snow, Killington was in business.

Second, she had waited for some evidence that Zoey and Lucas, Aisha and Christopher, and Nina and Benjamin had come back around to the idea of the road trip.

The evidence was not good. On Tuesday morning Aisha complained that now that she was spending more time under the same roof with Christopher, she was beginning to think he wasn't as good-looking as she had once thought. On Tuesday evening Benjamin had called the house wanting to speak to Nina, and Nina, who had once quivered every time Benjamin entered a room, told Claire to tell him she was out. Then, just this morning, Zoey had shown all the signs of pouting after some sort of fight with Lucas, who was showing all the signs of pouting right back.

At lunch Claire had learned that Zoey, Aisha, and Nina were going to the mall after school. They had asked her along, but she had declined.

Instead, she rode the ferry home with Lucas, Benjamin, and Jake—all three of them former boy-friends, though she hoped Jake was less *former* than the other two.

She sat down beside Benjamin. He stiffened as he recognized her and pulled the earphones off his head with a deep sigh.

"What are you listening to?" she asked.

He made a self-deprecating gesture. "Opera, believe it or not. It's the only area of music I haven't gotten into before. I'm getting so I like it. It's so extreme."

"Opera," Claire repeated. "I don't think you want to go around spreading the word that you listen to opera."

"Oh, I don't know. Maybe I'll set a new trend. A year from today, MTV might be doing blocks of opera. Pavarotti could have a whole new career as a VJ."

"Uh-huh. Have you tried any of it out on Nina?"

Benjamin smiled impishly. "You know, that was really quite subtle. I like the way you were able to work with whatever conversation was available, even opera. A very smooth segue from what you are pretending to talk about into the actual reason you came over here to sit by me."

Claire gritted her teeth. She was beginning to remember one of the reasons she'd broken up with Benjamin. "You're getting to be a suspicious person, Benjamin."

"I know. It's a serious character flaw. I'll try to do better in the future. So, what about Nina?"

"Well, I know my credentials as a big sister may be a little in doubt—"

Benjamin laughed in overly quick agreement. "—but I am still the little psycho's only sibling. And I was just wondering what you had decided about the ski trip."

A blank look. "What ski trip?"

"She didn't even tell you?" Claire tried to sound shocked. "We're all going this weekend over to Vermont. Me. Zoey and Lucas. Aisha and Christopher. And supposedly you and Nina."

Benjamin looked thoughtful. He hunched forward and began pressing his fingertips together. "Okay, I give up."

"What?"

He sat up straight. "I give up. I can't figure out what you're up to."

Claire forced an innocent laugh. Benjamin

was pound-for-pound the biggest pain in the butt around sometimes. He should think about a career with the CIA. "I'm just the one who has to make the arrangements for the condo. I want to know how many people are coming. Also, if there's some problem between you and Nina, well, she's totally inexperienced, you know, and I thought maybe I could help."

Benjamin did a double take. "You know, for a minute there I thought I heard you say you wanted to help."

Claire sighed. "Listen, Benjamin, you can think what you want about me, but I *do* care about Nina. I don't make a big thing of it, but I do care. She comes straight off the showdown with our uncle and plunges into her first big dating experience with a guy she's had a crush on for years but who, until recently, didn't even really know she was alive and treated her like his little buddy."

She was pleased to see Benjamin wince. *Take that, smart guy. I can play the guilt card as well as anyone.*

Now Benjamin looked genuinely uncomfortable. "Okay, not that I'm buying you as a concerned big sister, but the truth is I don't know what's going on with Nina and me. I thought everything was great at the dance. Then she blows me off all day Sunday. I see her on Monday and it's like she's sending signals that it was a onetime thing. She comes over and reads to me that day, but it's very stiff. And yesterday I call your house and . . . well, you were there, obviously . . . she claims she's out. You tell *me* what's going on," he ended in outright frustration.

Claire absorbed this information, none of it really surprising. "I think she's just new to all this boyfriend-girlfriend stuff," Claire said soothingly. "She doesn't know what is supposed to happen after a first date. But come on, Benjamin, she's been mooning over you for a long time."

"Maybe the reality didn't live up to the expectation," Benjamin said glumly.

"I'll feel her out. Find out what she's thinking. It's probably just nervousness and inexperience. If that's the case, do you want to go skiing with all of us?"

"Claire, just how in hell could I go skiing?" He grinned. "I'll admit it would be funny watching me try. Even better would be coming back to school afterward, telling people I'd spent the weekend skiing, and see who had the nerve to ask for an explanation."

"It's going to be a big group thing, Benjamin. You know, island kids only. It wouldn't be the group without you."

He nodded. "I'll come along for the ride. I can read and listen to music and go out with you guys at night. But I still don't get it. Eventually I will figure out what you're up to, but I have to admit, I don't see it yet."

Claire suppressed the desire to laugh in triumph. It was such a rare pleasure, manipulating Benjamin. After him, the rest would be easy. "It is remotely possible that I just like going skiing, isn't it? And that at the same time I want to see my little sister happy?"

"Yeah, right."

Claire leaned over and gave him a kiss on the cheek. "You need to lighten up, Benjamin."

The smile dropped instantly from his face as she kissed him. And, to her surprise, his reaction was not unlike her own.

Yes, there was still something there between them. But it would fade, she assured herself. It would fade.

Seven

Lucas got off the ferry and headed through the town toward his house, the image of Claire kissing Benjamin fresh in his mind. It hadn't looked like much of a kiss, more like a Hollywood *hello* kiss; still, it was the kind of thing Zoey would want him to tell her.

It was extremely annoying, the habit people seemed to have of revealing their secrets to him. Louise Kronenberger had told him at the dance about sleeping with Jake. Lucas didn't *need* to know that, didn't *want* to know that, and didn't want Zoey finding out that he knew that and somehow twisting it around to look like he was keeping things from her.

Zoey had already reamed him out over the time when he had known Christopher was getting different girls' phone numbers. Like it was Lucas's job to tell Zoey, so that Zoey could warn Aisha. Like it was Lucas's fault that Aisha had walked in on Christopher and some girl practically in the act.

And lately the secrets kept piling up and growing in importance. The worst was that he knew the idiot skinheads who had beaten up Christopher. But if he dropped a dime on the guys involved, Lucas feared they might get back at him by hurting Zoey. So he'd kept his mouth shut. Not an easy decision, or one that gave him any satisfaction. Few things would have given him as much pleasure as seeing Snake put back behind bars.

Then Christopher had asked Lucas to obtain a gun. As if Lucas knew where guns could just be picked up. As if he were crazy enough to get one for Christopher so Christopher could try to hunt down the guys who beat him up. The very guys whom Lucas was shielding so they wouldn't hurt Zoey who, if she learned any of this, would lay on a guilt trip of such epic proportions that Lucas would be left feeling like untreated sewage and no longer be allowed to kiss Zoey's foot, let alone anything else.

Yes, it would be nice to get through the rest of the year without learning any more secrets. The responsibility was too much.

He reached his house but hesitated about going inside. Yesterday his mother had told him that Christopher had called while he was out. It wasn't hard to imagine why Christopher had called. Christopher would probably keep calling. Unless he could change Christopher's mind.

With a sigh, Lucas started up the winding road that led up along the crest of the hill. It was a steep ten-minute walk to the big bed-and-breakfast. Aisha made the walk every day. The girl must have steel knees.

Kalif, Aisha's little brother, opened the door and let him in, pointing the way upstairs to Christopher's room. Lucas knocked on the door.

"Come in," Christopher said.

Lucas opened the door and his jaw dropped. Christopher was sitting on the high bed like some ancient Persian prince, propped against a mountain of brightly covered pillows, a TV remote in one hand with the other resting near an artistically arranged fruit-and-cheese platter.

"Jeez, Christopher. Do I have to bow when I come into the room?"

Christopher grinned. "You peasants are so easily impressed. Would you care for a small wedge of Brie? Perhaps a fresh strawberry?"

Lucas walked around the room and peeked into the bathroom. "Oh, man. This makes me sick. My whole room could fit in your shower."

"How is everything going down in the village?" Christopher asked. "I so enjoy hearing of the comic antics of the simple folk."

Lucas pointed to an antique-looking chair. "Can I sit in that?"

Christopher waved a magisterial hand. "Yes, I'll just have the servants clean it afterward."

Lucas sat down and looked Christopher over closely. "You seem like you're doing better."

"I am. A little stiff here and there, but I managed to do some sit-ups and push-ups this morning." He smiled at the memory. "It gave me a good excuse to lie in the Jacuzzi for an hour afterward. Actually, I'm probably eighty percent back. I'd be doing my paper route again, only I'm letting Kalif take it for a week and keep the money."

"How about your seventy other jobs?" Christopher had graduated from high school in Baltimore, moved away from his ravaged family, and set about earning enough money to go to college. He delivered papers, cooked for Zoey's father at Passmores' Restaurant, was the equipment manager for the school's athletics department, and did fix-up work everywhere around the island.

"Everyone's being very cool about it. I figure after this coming weekend, I'll be back at it. Sort of a forced vacation, here."

Lucas looked down at his hands. "Any word from the cops on the guys who jumped you?" he asked casually. If the damned cops would just catch the creeps, then Lucas's worry and guilt would be over.

Christopher's smile disappeared. His eyes, normally quick and inquisitive, went dull as steel. "No. I didn't really think there would be. Zoey wasn't able to make an identification. And I never really saw them. But I *will* see them. Sooner or later I'll find out who it was and take care of them. That's why I called your house yesterday. I still need what we talked about that night at the hospital."

Lucas shook his head. "Christopher, I don't think that's the way to go."

"Yeah? Why is that?" Christopher asked belligerently.

"Look, I spent two years in YA, and probably half the guys in there are there because they got into some revenge or payback situation. Either their parents did something they didn't like, or else their girlfriend cheated on them, or some guy didn't give them respect. I mean, payback keeps jails and prisons in business."

"So I'm just supposed to shrug it off?" Christopher bristled angrily. "Some skinhead Nazi sons of bitches try and kick my teeth in and I just go, well, too bad, let's get on with life like nothing happened? I don't think so, man. Nobody does that to me and just walks away laughing."

"Okay, fine. I can't argue with that. They ought to pay. But first, you don't even know who these guys are, and second, they didn't *kill* you, right? Justice does not say they should die for what they did."

"So I'll just injure them," Christopher sneered. "Would that be more just? I'll put them in a hospital. They can have my old room."

"With a gun? Guns are for killing. You don't *injure* someone with a nine millimeter. And what about the other thing? You don't know who these guys are. Are you just going to shoot people without even being sure they're the ones who popped you?"

"Maybe," Christopher snapped.

"Christopher, look, you and I haven't known

each other all that long, but I don't see you as being a guy who goes around just shooting people. And I'm real sure I'm not the kind of person who is going to help you get a gun."

"I can get one without you," Christopher said. "I'm over eighteen. It's legal."

"Yeah. But it would be stupid. I mean, you're supposed to go to college next year, right? You want to make it prison instead?"

"I have no choice," Christopher said in a more subdued voice. He met Lucas's eyes. "What would you do if it was you who'd been stomped in some alley?"

Lucas had expected the question, but he didn't have an easy answer. "I don't know. I guess if I knew who the guys were and for some reason the cops couldn't deal with them, I might do just what you're thinking about doing. Only you don't know who the guys are. You don't know who to go after."

Lucas could see Christopher's angry resolve beginning to disintegrate. He swallowed and looked away, and when he spoke again, Lucas was shocked and embarrassed to hear a rough trembling in his voice. "I just keep thinking if I could have got up off the ground . . ."

"Zoey said they caught you on the back of the head first. You were stunned. You were outnumbered." Lucas shrugged. "No one wins every fight. Sometimes all you can do is take your beating and try to survive."

Christopher looked like he was fighting back

tears. He bit his lip and with sudden savagery said, "Easy for you, Lucas. What beating have you ever had to just take?"

Lucas smiled a twisted, sad smile. "The one my old man gave me with his fists about twice a week until I went off to the YA." He tried to stave off the wave of anger and bitterness that rose like a volcano inside him whenever he remembered those days. "Like I said. Sometimes you just take your beating and survive."

Lucas left Christopher behind in his regal convalescence and started down the hill. It had grown dark out, and through breaks in the trees Lucas could see the brightly lit ferry gliding across unusually smooth water on its way back from Weymouth. The six thirty. It would be at the dock in another fifteen minutes, give or take. If Zoey was on it, she'd be back at her house shortly after that.

Lucas decided to wait for her there. He felt sick at heart and desperately needed some time with Zoey. She would make him forget the memory of Christopher, trying so hard to sound tough, trying to cover a fresh pain that hadn't yet begun to heal.

Watching Christopher deal with that had just brought back all the similar feelings Lucas had so often experienced. He wondered if he was doing the right thing, not turning the two skinheads over to the cops. He hoped he'd at least convinced Christopher not to go the way of a gun. But sometimes life seemed to go off into a sort of hopeless area where there were never any good answers. Just a lot of choices between bad and worse.

He paced the gravel in front of Zoey's house, growing more morose by the minute and more anxious for Zoey to come and dispel his bad mood.

"Hey, Lucas. Want to come inside and wait?"

Lucas turned and saw Benjamin, appearing to look out of his open ground-floor window. Maybe his gaze was off a point or two, but it was close. And he had *known* it was Lucas. "You're not really blind, are you, Benjamin? This is all some elaborate practical joke you've been playing."

Benjamin got the self-mocking cocky look he put on when he knew he had impressed someone. "It had to be you, Lucas. Who else would be lurking in our front yard, muttering under his breath and pacing back and forth?"

Lucas went to the door and on inside into the warmth and the light. Benjamin met him in the hallway. "You smell like potpourri," Benjamin said.

"Is that those bowls of like wood chips and stuff people leave out to smell up a room?"

"Yeah, that's the stuff."

"I've been up seeing Christopher. He's living like King Tut up there. Jacuzzi. TV. Free food. Potpourri. Real hard-core suffering."

Benjamin led the way toward the family

room. "Is he going to be able to go on this road trip, do you think?"

"A road trip?"

"You know. The big skiing weekend thing in Vermont. Everyone's going, although no one bothered to tell me until just this afternoon."

"I have no idea what you're talking about."

"Aha!" Benjamin held up a finger as if he had just made a major point.

"Aha, what?" Lucas flopped onto the couch and unzipped his jacket. Zoey's house always seemed hot. Maybe his own house was just cold.

"I don't know aha what. Yet. But I will," Benjamin said craftily. "So you're saying you don't know about the ski weekend in Vermont."

"No. Why would I be going to Vermont?"

"That's what I'd like to know," Benjamin said.

Mrs. Passmore came in, carrying a cup of coffee. Lucas liked Zoey's mother. She was about ten light-years cooler than his own mother. In fact, both of Zoey's parents were from different worlds than his own folks. And looking at Zoey's mom made him think maybe twenty years from now Zoey would still be beautiful.

"Hi, Lucas," Mrs. Passmore said. "Where's Zoey?"

"Mall day," Lucas said. "I thought she might be on the six thirty and I'd just wait here for her to get home."

"You don't need an excuse to come over," Mrs. Passmore said. "You're nicer than my own kids."

"Good shot, Mom." Benjamin slapped a hand over his heart. "Aren't you late getting down to the restaurant?" he asked. "We can't start the big drunken party till you leave."

"I know, I know. Never trust anyone over thirty, as we used to say many years ago."

"You're not over thirty, are you?" Lucas asked disingenuously.

"Not in dog years, maybe," Benjamin said under his breath.

"See what I have to put up with?" Mrs. Passmore asked Lucas. She checked her watch. "Actually, I am late. There's some veal stew left over from the lunch shift in the frig. You two can nuke it up if you're hungry. Bye."

"Bye, Mom."

"Bye, Mrs. Passmore." Lucas waited till she was gone. "So, are you going to explain this Vermont thing?"

"According to Claire, everyone is going to spend next weekend at this condo she's lined up. In Killington. And as part of the *everyone*, your name came up."

"You mean, like I know about this?" Lucas asked. "Like I've said I'm going?"

"Exactly. Supposedly it's me and Nina, you and Zoey, Aisha and Christopher."

"Christopher didn't say anything about it."

"See? Claire is up to something," Benjamin said thoughtfully.

"Still, it could be fun," Lucas said. *Him and Zoey*. Him and Zoey and a condo a long way from any parental types. It was hard to see where there was anything terrible in that.

Of course. That's why Zoey hadn't said anything about it.

Well, she was being kind of selfish. Just because she didn't want him to have a chance to . . . to spend some private time with her.

"Maybe it's Zoey who's up to something," he said under his breath. Oh, this was going to be excellent.

I've got you, my pretty, and your Gap bag, too.

The line from *The Wizard of Oz* popped up in Lucas's mind as soon as he saw Zoey, trundling in, looking flushed from the chilly night air and carrying a bag from The Gap.

"Hi, babe." Lucas got up and took the bag from Zoey's hand and gave her a chaste kiss on the cheek.

"Hi," Zoey said, glancing at Benjamin on the couch. "What have you guys been up to?"

"We've been discussing whether quantum theory has any implications for broader epistemological questions," Benjamin said without missing a beat.

Lucas nodded agreement. "Also, we were wondering what kind of person would actually buy a Mariah Carey CD."

"I have a Mariah Carey CD."

"Yeah, but we decided you're okay anyway."

"How generous," Zoey said, sweetly sarcastic. "Come on. You can carry my bag."

Lucas followed her upstairs, barely containing his excitement. He had her. He had her good. Ms. Open and Honest. Ms. You-should-have-told-me-Christopher-was-a-hound. Ms.—

Inside the door to her room, Zoey turned and put her arms around Lucas's neck and pulled him down for a real kiss. Instantly Lucas forgot that he was supposed to be playing it cool and standoffish. Then he remembered and started to pull away, but Zoey put her tongue in his mouth and he forgot again.

"I missed you," Zoey breathed.

This was the moment for a stern, disapproving look, but instead Lucas lay back on her bed and pulled her on top. It was several moments later that the first "uh . . . uh," was sounded by Zoey, and Lucas reluctantly stopped doing what he was beginning to do.

Damn. He'd had the moral high ground and he'd given it up. Now whatever he said, he would end up sounding petulant.

Zoey gave him the consolation kiss she always bestowed after she'd flashed her STOP sign. "So what did you do this afternoon without me?" she asked.

"Went up to see Christopher."

"How is he?"

"Fine." The memory of his conversation with Christopher brought back all the guilt he'd felt at hiding secrets from Zoey. Which, in turn, brought back the justifiable outrage he felt on learning that she'd been hiding something from him.

Only he would have to be very cool. Very subtle, or he would just look like he was pouting, or else like all he was after was a chance to get her away to a private condo with a private bedroom and no parents and probably a king-sized bed or possibly a Jacuzzi out on the deck under starry skies which would get Zoey into a bathing suit . . . at most. Subtlety. That's what was required here.

"So what's this about a ski trip you didn't tell me about?" he blurted.

Zoey looked surprised and, to Lucas's infinite gratification, embarrassed. Her throat was beginning to turn red, the blush easing up into her cheeks. She looked away. "Who told you about that?"

Well. He hadn't needed subtlety after all. "Benjamin told me. Obviously you decided *not* to tell me." *Fine, now don't overdo it,* he warned himself. But it was too good to resist. "Ms. Honesty. Ms. No Secrets. Ha."

Zoey gave him an appraising look. "I suppose you think you've really got me, don't you?"

"Cold. Signed, sealed, and delivered. After all the crap you gave me over Christopher and that blond chick. After that whole honesty lecture, and how between us we'd never need secrets. There's really only one thing I can say—nah nah nah nah nah nah."

"Lucas, the reason I—"

"Nah nah nah nah nah nah. Hypocrite."

"Are we going to discuss this like intelligent people?" Zoey demanded.

Lucas held up a finger. "One more. Nah nah nah nah nah nah."

"Are you done?"

"For now," he said, holding his head at a cocky angle. "Although I reserve the right to fire another *nah* or two if necessary."

"Look. The reason I didn't mention the ski idea was that I really didn't think you'd want to go."

"Yeah, right."

"Also, *I* didn't really want to go."

"You told me you love to ski," Lucas said, shaking his head in contemptuous disbelief.

"Yeah, but *you* don't even know how to ski."

"I surf. If you can surf, you can easily learn to snowboard. You should never lie, Zoey. You are so lame at it."

Zoey took a deep breath. "Okay, you *know* the reason I didn't want to go. I didn't want you to get the wrong idea."

Here it was, Lucas realized, like a gift from God—the moment when he would get to trot out one of Zoey's favorite lines and destroy her with it.

"What you mean is, you don't trust me," he said in a sad little voice. He saw her wince. Yes! She was down. The referee had started the count.

Zoey sucked in air as if she really had been

93

punched. "You enjoyed that, didn't you?"

"Yes, I did."

Zoey nodded. "Well, I guess I deserved it. I was a hypocrite."

Lucas grinned beatifically. Ah, life was sweet.

"So, uh, Lucas. How would you like to drive over to Vermont this weekend?"

"Gee, I think that would be fun," he said enthusiastically. "Almost as much fun as actually winning an argument with you."

Zoey gave him a dirty look. "Enjoy it while you can. You won't be winning the argument you're hoping you'll win this weekend."

"Let's hear it one . . . more . . . time . . . Nah nah nah nah nah nah nah."

6 First, rate your boyfriend's looks and attractiveness on a scale of one to ten, with one being equal to, say, Senator Jesse Helms, and ten being a melding of John Kennedy Junior and Denzel Washington. Then rate yourself. Finally, have your boyfriend rate you and himself on the same scale.

Zoey

First of all, whoever wrote this quiz is showing her age. JFK Junior and Denzel Washington could practically be my dad. Dads. Well, if they were melded, one dad. A cute dad, don't get me wrong, but still a slight bit aged.

Second of all, I don't really approve of concentrating on looks as being all that important. Although I guess the point is to see whether you and your boyfriend have some wildly different numbers. Like say you think you rate a nine, but your boyfriend says you're only a four. That might be revealing, I guess.

So I'll answer, but I'm answering under protest because I don't think this is a very feminist question.

I'd give me a six and Lucas a nine.

No, I don't have a poor self-image; I'm just being realistic. I have nice hair and my face is okay, except that my eyes aren't perfectly lined up. But I don't exactly have major breast development. Not that I'm saying a girl's self-image should be based on the size of her breasts.

I'm just saying that's one of the things society, and especially the male half of society, seems to get obsessed with.

Although why should I let society bully me into having a poor self-image? Really?

So, let me change those numbers. I'll give myself a seven. Lucas is still a nine. The only reason he isn't a ten is because I don't want him to get too full of himself.

LUCAS

Zoey's a ten. No question. I'm maybe a seven or something, especially since her previous boyfriend was Jake. That guy looks like someone from a Soloflex ad, whereas

I look more like I should
be a bass player for some
alternative rock band.

   But Zoey's perfect. I
mean, her face, her hair,
her legs, her . . . not to
mention her . . . whew.
Never mind. Don't want to
start thinking that way.

                Claire

Oh, who cares?

                Aisha

   Okay, Christopher would
say I'm an eight or a nine.
See, he wouldn't want to
insult me, but at the same
time he wouldn't want to
make me think I was too good
for him. Also he'll say he's

like an eight, maybe, although
what he believes is that he's
off the scale —a twelve or
something. Infinity.

In reality, I am probably an
eight. I think my eyes are too
far apart and also my legs are
kind of bony. Christopher, too,
is an eight. He'd be a nine or
even a ten except there's that
huge bulge in his head where he
keeps his extra ego.

Christopher

AISHA'S A NINE. I'M A TEN. THAT
PUTS ME UP BY ONE, WHICH IS FINE.
YOU NEED THAT EDGE WORKING IN
YOUR FAVOR. IF AISHA WERE A TOTAL
TEN, SHE'D PROBABLY TELL ME TO
TAKE A WALK. GIRLS GET THAT WAY
WHEN THEY'RE TOO PERFECT. LIKE

CLAIRE, FOR EXAMPLE, WHO IS A TEN
BUT WHO I WOULDN'T GO NEAR IF
YOU PAID ME.

Nina

Can we use fractions? Because
I'm just not sure I could be
accurately represented by an
integer. I feel the need for
fractions, which is odd because I
don't normally crave fractions.
Or perhaps a radical. Perhaps a
square root. Or maybe we should
employ parentheses in some way.
(Parentheses are very popular in
every math class I've ever taken,
she adds parenthetically.)

To be serious, I'd have to say

that I'm probably x squared minus
y. Or the other way around.

   But the real mystery is, how
would Benjamin answer this
question? All he can go by is
what people tell him. Zoey has
probably told him I'm a ten.
Claire has probably told him I'm a
two. That averages out to a six.

   As for Benjamin, Benjamin is
perfect. If Benjamin could see,
he probably wouldn't have
anything to do with me.

Eight

Jake slapped the alarm clock, sank back down on his pillow for a second, then forced himself up. He threw back the covers, stood up, and stumbled to his bathroom. When he came back, he began stretching out methodically: neck, shoulders, legs. He dropped to the floor and did fifty push-ups, rolled over and did fifty stomach crunches, then repeated the sequence twice more.

He had always enjoyed exercise, but it had taken on a new meaning lately. In his mind it had become the antidote to everything that had gone wrong in his life. The antidote to the depression and the inner conflict between what he saw as his duty and his fatal desire for Claire. It was the antidote to drinking and all that drinking had led to—cocaine to recover from his hangover, the loss of self-control that had gotten him kicked off the team and landed him in bed with Louise, a girl he cared nothing about.

It was a miracle he hadn't caught anything, he realized. A dose of clap or crabs would have just about topped off the week.

He looked down at himself suspiciously. So far, so good.

Jake dressed quickly in shorts, sleeveless T-shirt, and running shoes. He went out through the sliding glass door and across the patio and began running down the driveway to the road. It was still fairly dark. Not black, but a deep blue, with the moon long since gone. He ran south along the concave arc of the beach. As he turned eastward from Leeward Drive onto Pond Road he could see the horizon, already bright pink. And by the time he had joined the coast road that followed the eastern shore of the island, the brilliant crescent of the sun had peeked over the rim of the earth.

He pounded on, stride long and regular, over cracked pavement and drifting sand, arms high, his breathing not yet labored, past the shuttered, boarded-up summer homes. He could see the church spire and the familiar buildings of North Harbor, a picture of brilliant gold where the sun touched and deep night shadows that had not yet been driven off.

He ran the perimeter of the island past the Geiger house, trying but failing to stop himself from looking up and noticing that the light had not yet been turned on in Claire's room. She was still asleep, luxuriant black hair spread across her pillow, dark, serious eyes still closed.

He forced the image from his mind and accelerated the pace past the harbor, waving to the fishermen emerging from Passmores' with steaming paper cups of coffee. Zoey's father, Mr. Passmore, was standing with his own cup, dressed in kitchen whites, outside the back door of the restaurant, seemingly contemplating a spilled trash can.

Jake gave a nod and Mr. Passmore raised his cup in acknowledgment.

Another complete circuit of the island and he would have had a good workout. Down the western shore as sunlight ignited the glass and marble facades of downtown Weymouth, along the north shore of Big Bite pond past the still-sleeping homes there, up along the rugged, rocky beaches of the eastern shore.

He should turn through the town, avoiding the Geiger house altogether. But, he reasoned, it was easy to get a foot caught on the cobblestones. Safer to stick to the main road. He didn't even have to think about her as he passed. Didn't have to look. Just run and feel the slow burn in his legs and chest.

Claire saw him come past the second time. She had collected a cup of coffee from the kitchen and climbed up onto the widow's walk, as she did most mornings to watch the sun climb the sky.

She sipped the French roast and tightened the cord of her bathrobe against the breeze, a breeze that blew down from the distant and now snow-covered mountains.

Would he look up? she wondered. Yes, almost certainly. He'd be trying not to, but he would look.

He turned onto Lighthouse, moving with an easy grace that was surprising in someone so large. Claire smiled and felt a little twinge deep inside. He was such a powerful-looking creature, unstoppable, uncontrollable. He looked like he would never tire. Like he could keep running forever.

He kept his eyes firmly fixed on the road ahead, and Claire felt a momentary, perverse sense of gratification that he had proven her wrong. But then, just as he was passing by below, he turned his head and looked up, scanning up the side of the house, finding her with his eyes.

Claire sipped her coffee and gazed calmly out to sea, giving no sign that she had noticed him at all. He ran on, then looked back over his shoulder.

Well, Claire thought dryly, maybe not entirely uncontrollable.

Five blocks away, Lucas, too, was having a morning cup of coffee and enjoying the crisp air. He stood on the deck behind his house, leaning against the railing. He caught a glimpse of Jake through a gap in the buildings and trees, shook his head in amusement, and returned his closer attention to Zoey's house, just below his on the hill.

He could see straight into her kitchen and

the breakfast nook. Both were brightly lit. Mrs. Passmore was sitting with her back to him, reading a paper. From this angle he could just see Benjamin's left hand resting on the table. Zoey was in the kitchen, wearing the Boston Bruins jersey she wore to bed, white legs, and bare feet. She was fixing a bowl of cereal. She went into the breakfast nook and sat down between Benjamin and Mrs. Passmore.

Now he could see part of her face whenever she leaned forward to take a bite of cereal. One foot was curled up under her.

Lucas sighed. He felt it was somehow pathetic that he should get such profound pleasure out of watching her eat Grape-Nuts, but he couldn't help the way he felt. Seeing her this way, when he could just watch and not have to act cool, not have to exchange banter, just soak up every detail of the way she sat, the way she moved, the way God-help-him that she chewed her cereal and her tousled, uncombed blond hair lay against her neck . . .

He was disgustingly in love with her. He wanted her like he wanted life. More at times.

She laughed at something and slurped milk down her chin. She caught it with her finger and then licked the finger clean, still laughing.

"Here." Mrs. Passmore handed her daughter a paper napkin. "You still have some on your chin."

Zoey wiped her face. "I have to get going."

She took her bowl to the sink, ruffling Benjamin's hair affectionately as she passed.

She went upstairs and opened her closet door. Her eyes rested on a dress that had always been one of Jake's favorites. She was hoping to find an opportunity to approach Jake about the drug story she'd been given, and it probably wouldn't hurt to wear something he thought was attractive.

"No, Zoey," she chided herself, ashamed of the thought. That would be manipulative. If she was going to get Jake's help with the story, she'd get it honestly or not at all.

Except for the fact that *not at all* was just not an option.

She decided against the dress Jake liked and instead picked out an outfit Lucas liked.

She was climbing under the hot shower when the memory came back. A dream. Or at least a piece of a dream.

She had been skiing down a long slope. Lucas had been standing at the bottom, waiting impatiently for her. She had tried to veer off, but she found she couldn't avoid running into him. And yet it hadn't been a frightening dream. In fact, it had reminded her of flying dreams she'd had. More thrilling than scary.

That was all she remembered. Whether she'd managed in the dream to glide safely past Lucas . . . or not . . . she didn't recall. Either way, it didn't take Sigmund Freud to figure out the meaning.

She toweled off, replaced the outfit Lucas liked on the hanger beside the outfit Jake liked, and grabbed a sweater that neither of them liked.

Aisha was up, showered, and dressed earlier than usual. Which was to say that she would not have to make a mad run for the ferry. As she finished her breakfast she noticed her mother preparing a tray for Christopher. Aisha knew for a fact that Christopher was almost fully recovered and perfectly capable of coming downstairs for breakfast. But it was like some weird conspiracy between her mother, who seemed to enjoy treating Christopher like visiting royalty, and Christopher, who, of course, had no objection to breakfast in bed.

"I'll take it up," Aisha volunteered.

"It's no trouble," Mrs. Gray said cheerily.

Aisha got up from the table and lifted the tray. "He needs to start getting readjusted to real life," she said. She removed one of the two sweet rolls her mother had added and two of the four strips of bacon. "Besides, you're going to make him fat."

She carried the tray up the stairwell lined with colonial-era prints. The door of the room had a painted wooden plaque reading *Governor's Suite*. Aisha kicked the door lightly with her toe, rattling the plaque. No answer. She struggled to free a hand to open the door.

Inside, the curtains were still drawn and the room was dark. Christopher was obviously still asleep. She tiptoed over to set the tray down on the sideboard.

Aisha started to leave, but curiosity won out over good sense. She tiptoed over to the bed, nearly tripping on one of the rugs.

He was breathing heavily, his bare chest rising and falling slowly and, quite frankly, Aisha had to admit, attractively. It was impossible not to wonder what he had on beneath the quilt.

Too bad you're such a dog, Christopher, she thought. *If you weren't a two-timing, faithless weasel of a human being, you would be very, very fine.*

She leaned over and kissed him with feather-light lips. He groaned softly, but didn't open his eyes.

Was that for me, or for someone else? she wondered.

His food was going to be stone cold if he didn't wake up. Her mother would hate the idea of her food being eaten cold. Aisha leaned over him again, this time giving him a real kiss. A very real kiss.

A faint smile formed on his lips. His eyes were still closed. He moaned in a dreamy, not-yet-conscious voice. "Aisha?"

Aisha stood up and moved swiftly toward the door. When she reached it, she looked back. He was stirring, becoming conscious.

Aisha, he had said, still in his dream of being kissed. Aisha smiled in satisfaction. *Aisha,* not any other name.

That had to count for something.

Nine

The ferry pulled away, carrying Nina toward another day of the garbage disposal of the soul that was eleventh grade. She stuck a Lucky Strike in the corner of her mouth and inhaled the smell of tobacco. On the bottom of the box it said "L.S./M.F.T." She'd heard somewhere that it stood for "Lucky Strike Means Fine Tobacco." Actually, the fine tobacco stung her chapped lips. It might be wise to switch to not smoking a filtered cigarette. It might be wiser just to break the habit altogether, only as long as she didn't light up, it was harmless enough. And it annoyed so many people whom she enjoyed annoying.

Suddenly the gentle conversation beside her took a nasty turn.

"When exactly was this big decision being made?" Aisha demanded in a loud voice. "The last I heard it was a dead issue. None of us was going skiing."

Zoey was looking uncomfortable in the hideous sweater that no one, aside from her, liked. "I know, but Lucas found out about the whole thing, then it was like I was trying to hide it from him."

"You *were* trying to hide it from him," Aisha said, cocking an angry eyebrow at Zoey.

"Benjamin told Lucas," Zoey said.

Nina sat bolt upright, dropping the cigarette on her lap. "Benjamin?"

"Yeah, so actually, if anything, it's Nina's fault," Zoey said to Aisha. "She was the first to cave."

"I didn't cave anything," Nina protested. "I never said a word about any of this to Benjamin. Now he knows? He'll think I didn't want him to go."

"You *don't*," Aisha said. She was acting exasperated.

"That's not the point," Nina wailed. "It'll be like I'm dumping him or something. I don't want to dump him. I'm not even sure he's my boyfriend yet. I can't dump him in advance like that. It would be preemptive dumping. That's illegal."

"So who told Benjamin?" Zoey wondered.

"Oh, man," Aisha groaned, still giving Zoey a dirty look. "So now Claire's going, you're going with Lucas, Benjamin is probably going . . . How am I supposed to keep this from Christopher?"

"I have to ask him," Nina said, feeling panicky. "I have to ask Benjamin like it was my idea all along. I have to ask him to go and spend a *weekend* with me up on some *mountain* somewhere. And I don't even ski. I don't even like people who do ski."

"You could take lessons," Zoey said helpfully. "Or you could just hang out in the condo or the lodge with Benjamin."

"He doesn't even like me, I don't think," Nina said. "Now we're spending a weekend together?"

"Of course he likes you," Zoey said reassuringly.

"Did he say that?" Nina pounced greedily.

"I'm *not* going," Aisha said stubbornly.

"What did Benjamin say about me?" Nina persisted.

"He didn't say anything," Zoey said. "But you know he likes you."

Nina was far from satisfied with that answer. But what was she supposed to do? It would seem like a total slam not to ask Benjamin to go after Zoey had asked Lucas. She was trapped. Either she asked him, risking total, abject humiliation if he blew her off, or she didn't ask, in which case he would be hurt and think she was no longer interested in him.

And she *was* interested. Unless he *wasn't*.

She practically jumped up from the bench and made her way over to the spot where Benjamin was sitting, head back, sunglasses raised toward the sky.

"Benjamin," she said a little shrilly. "It's me, Nina."

He nodded. "Nina, you know you don't have to identify yourself to me. I know when it's you."

"Uh-huh," she said. "So. All set for the big ski trip?"

He turned his head, aiming the shades at her in his very convincing mimicry of a sighted person. "Ski trip?" he asked blankly.

What? He *didn't* know? Well, it was too late to change direction now. "Yeah, yeah. Big road trip. I figured you knew. It snowed in the mountains and like we were all going to get a condo and then Zoey and Claire can ski and the rest of us can sit around roasting marshmallows in the fireplace and take them to the hospital after they break their legs."

"Are you inviting me?" Benjamin asked.

"Of course I am. You're my . . . I mean, we're . . . you know."

"Friends?" he suggested.

It was not exactly the word Nina would have liked to hear. "Yeah. I mean, you know, Zoey asked Lucas, and I think Aisha's going to ask Christopher."

Benjamin shrugged. "Well, if everyone is going, I guess I'll go, too."

"Good," Nina said, feeling deflated. There it was again, that total lack of any of the feeling that had been there the night they'd kissed. Now it wasn't even like it had been, back when they were just good buds. "I'll tell Claire you're in."

She got up, relieved to be away from him. A feeling that did not promise much for the weekend. She found Claire downstairs, reading her Latin textbook and talking under her breath.

"You know that trip?" Nina asked without preamble.

Claire looked up from the book. "What about it?"

"I'm going," Nina said, feeling trapped and annoyed.

Claire nodded. "Good."

Nina did a double take. "Good?"

"Sure. Benjamin's coming, so I'm glad you're coming, too."

"Wait a minute, how do you know that Benjamin's coming?"

"I mentioned it to him yesterday and I got the impression he wanted to come."

"*You* mentioned it." *Of course. Who else?* Nina thought darkly.

"Yes. See? You say I never do you any favors. I knew you were kind of nervous about asking him, so I took care of it."

Nina's eyes narrowed in suspicion. "So you were being nice to me."

"Mmm." Claire returned to her book, but Nina caught the hint of a satisfied smile.

Nina nearly reeled from the implication. It was incredible, but there was no other reasonable explanation. Certainly not the lame explanation that Claire was trying to be nice. No. No, it was obvious what Claire was really up to.

Claire was after Benjamin. And judging from the way Benjamin had lied about his knowledge of the trip, Claire might already have been at least half-successful.

Zoey tossed the ball up over her head, drew back the racket, and brought it swiftly down. It

114

missed the ball by six inches. The ball fell on her head and bounced off.

"Excellent serve," Aisha said.

"The sun got in my eyes," Zoey explained.

"It's overcast," Aisha pointed out. "And what kind of overcast is it?" she asked rhetorically. She raised her voice to yell down to Claire who was on the far side of the court. "Claire! What kind of clouds are these?"

"Scattered cumulus. Is one of you going to hit the ball over here at some point or can Louise and I go change?"

"I'm trying," Zoey said. She threw the ball up again and this time managed to hit it with the racket. The ball flew up and, assisted by a tailing wind, sailed over the chain link fence that surrounded the tennis courts.

"Much better," Louise Kronenberger said. "Now we don't have to play."

"One of us should go get the ball," Zoey suggested.

"Why?" Claire asked.

"Claire's right," Louise said. "Coach Androgyny isn't around. And if she comes back, we just play dumb. Tell her we thought the match ended if someone knocked the ball over the fence."

The four girls drifted toward the net, cradling their rackets and looking around warily for signs of Coach Anders. On adjoining courts, other groups of girls played on, ranging from competent to very good.

"This is so dumb," Aisha said. "Who exactly was it who had the brilliant idea to put off our gym requirement till our senior year? We could have done all this *last* year and be free right now."

"Tennis beats basketball, anyway," Louise said. "I mean, later in life we can play tennis at the country club while our husbands are off at work."

Zoey rolled her eyes. "Are you planning on doing some time travel back to the 1950s, Louise?"

"No, I'm just planning on marrying a millionaire. It's much easier than having to work and support yourself. He goes off to his office and does his job, I go off to the country club and do the tennis pro." She laughed. "Who'll be having more fun ten years from now? Me, or you—Zoey Passmore the intrepid reporter, worrying about where to put a comma in a story about the problems of the clam-shucking industry?"

"Zoey will," Claire said, unexpectedly coming to her defense. "Louise, you'll have had three brats, be living on welfare, and hanging with some guy who rides a motorcycle."

"Huh," Louise said, completely unfazed. "So what's this biker look like?"

"Like you care?" Aisha muttered under her breath.

"Actually, I am pretty open-minded." Louise smirked. "Although lately I've been trying to decide which type I like more—the big, muscular, jock type"—she gave Claire a long look—"or the wiry, sensitive, bad boy." She fluttered her lashes at Zoey.

Zoey felt herself getting steamed. Louise wasn't just kidding. At the homecoming dance she'd been all over Lucas every time she got a chance. But there was no point in letting Louise see that she'd struck a nerve. Louise enjoyed getting under the skin of girls like Zoey. "The wiry, sensitive, bad boy will be spending the weekend with me at a ski lodge," she retorted.

"No! Don't tell me you're giving up your *virtue*! Not Zoey Passmore!"

Zoey felt a blush and realized too late she'd gotten teased into a pointless situation that was just going to get more embarrassing. What she should do was let it go. But with Louise mocking her, it was impossible. "No, I'm not *you*, Louise," she said. "We're all going skiing, *just* skiing. All of us together," she added.

"Oh. You mean all you virgin islanders?" Louise held up a hand. "Sorry. You're not *all* virgin islanders."

Zoey wanted to ask what she meant, but of course that was exactly what Louise wanted her to do. Besides, if Louise knew something—or thought she knew something—about one of the island kids, it was really none of Zoey's business.

Unless it was about Lucas. She narrowed her eyes in dark suspicion. Lucas had been homecoming king to Louise's queen. Had they somehow shared more than a dance?

"So, all of you are going skiing, huh?" Louise

said. She sighed. "Sounds like fun. Is your friend Christopher going, Aisha?"

Now Zoey saw Aisha's eyes growing suspicious. "I haven't decided . . . um, I mean, yes. Yes, Christopher is going. With me."

"And Jake?"

Silence. Zoey glanced at Claire, who just looked bored by the conversation. Certainly there was no sign that Claire cared one way or another about Jake. Evidently it really *was* over between the two of them. Poor Jake.

"Damn, here comes Coach," Aisha said.

The four of them wandered back toward their corners of the court.

"She was just yanking you," Aisha said to Zoey. "You know Louise—she's on a one-girl mission to spread insecurity around."

"I'll bet that's not all she spreads around," Zoey said in a voice that Louise might just be able to hear.

118

Ten

The idea occurred to Zoey while she was changing from gym clothes back into her normal clothes. She dismissed it as unworthy.

But during homeroom the next day the idea came back, slightly changed so that it seemed not quite so unworthy.

By lunch she had grown more used to the idea, but she had to talk to Claire about it first and Claire had not joined them for lunch.

It wasn't until her fifth-period American Literature class that Zoey saw Claire. By then Zoey had grown comfortable with the fact that her idea was partly self-serving. True, but was also a good thing to do regardless.

She was standing in the hall waiting for Claire to arrive when Jake passed by. He smiled in the distant way he'd adopted since their breakup. She smiled back, turning up the brightness level a little, and telling herself it certainly wasn't unethical to be nice to Jake.

"Hi, Jake," she said.

"Hi, Zoey," he said. "How's it going?"

"Great. How about you?"

He smiled ruefully at some private joke and said, "Couldn't be better," in a tone loaded with irony. He walked away and Zoey saw Claire approaching.

"Hey, Claire." She took Claire's arm and moved her out of the stream of traffic. "I wanted to ask you something."

Claire waited patiently.

"It's about Jake."

Claire drew a deep *why me?* breath and looked at Zoey skeptically.

"Look, I know you two just broke up and all. But you know, this whole road trip to Vermont . . . I mean, if Aisha decides to ask Christopher, and I think she probably will, you know, if she gets over being pissed off at him, well, it will be all of us. You, Nina, Eesh, me, Lucas, Benjamin, Christopher . . ."

Claire glanced toward the classroom door, clearly impatient to get into class. "So?"

"It's like everyone on the island *except* Jake," Zoey said.

Claire sighed a long, slow sigh.

"I just thought it would be nice to invite him to go, too," Zoey said. "Unlike everyone but you and me, Jake actually does ski."

Claire turned up her mouth in a faint grimace. "Are you asking my permission to invite Jake along?"

Zoey shrugged. "I just thought it would be polite to see if you minded very much."

Claire tilted her head, considering the question. "I guess it might be a little awkward, but more for him than for me. I'm just going to ski, and I don't see how his being around would keep me from skiing."

"So you don't mind?" Zoey said eagerly. The final bell rang.

"If he wants to go, I'm not going to stop him," Claire said with weary disinterest.

Zoey followed her into class and went to her desk. Jake had glanced over, but not at Zoey. His eyes had darted to Claire and then away.

Poor Jake, Zoey thought sadly. *I wonder if he knows how little Claire cares.*

It would be a good thing for him to come along to Vermont. Getting off the island and especially getting back to being part of the group would do him good. Maybe Zoey and he could patch up some of the lingering bad feelings between them. Maybe they could become friends again.

And then Zoey could ask him about the rumors of drug use on the football team. Not that that was her motivation for asking him along on the trip. No, in her heart she was sincere in wanting to reunite the group, to smooth over the rough edges that had formed in the last couple of months.

But when all that had been accomplished in a spirit of total sincerity and friendship . . . then it would be perfectly normal for her to ask for his help with her big story.

*　　　*　　　*

121

Jake spent the class paying almost no attention to what the teacher was saying. Instead he occupied his time by wondering what Zoey and Claire had been talking about out in the hallway.

That it involved him seemed certain. He was sure he had seen Zoey mouthing the word *Jake* several times. The *J* was very distinct.

Then Claire had come into the room wearing that nearly invisible smile, followed by Zoey, who had looked somewhat troubled.

Had one or both of them learned about the drug suspension? Was that secret out already? Or, worse yet perhaps, had they learned what had gone on between him and Louise?

A thrill of fear went up his spine. *They were in the same gym class with Louise!* That was it. That had to be it. That's why Claire was smirking. That had been a smirk of contempt. And Zoey had looked troubled because . . . well, just because she was nice and didn't like seeing people do dumb things.

When the bell rang at the end of class, Claire made a beeline out the door. Zoey hung back, waiting for him like a defensive lineman who was determined to keep him from running the ball.

Great. She probably wanted to talk about it. Ask him *why* and *how,* and whether he needed someone just to talk to. He steeled himself. He would handle it with dignity and honesty. Or else he'd just lie and say Louise was a dishonest slut and no way would he ever have slept with her. No matter how drunk and depressed he was.

"Jake, um, do you have a minute?"

"Sure," he said, summoning up an insouciant cheerfulness. "What's up?"

"Well, there's this idea that maybe we'd all drive to Vermont and go skiing this weekend," she said. "You know, all the old gang. Me and Nina and Lucas and Eesh and Claire and Christopher and Benjamin."

Jake nearly burst out laughing with relief. "Sounds like fun," he said.

"Anyway, it wouldn't be the group without you. So I was wondering if you'd come."

This was definitely better than getting cross-examined about Louise or his suspension. But a weekend road trip? With Zoey and Claire? And why was Zoey asking him? That was a very interesting question. He looked closely at her familiar face. Once he had been hopelessly in love with that face. It was still a very pretty face.

"I don't know," he stalled. "Where were you thinking of going? I don't think Sunday River's even open."

"We were going to go to Killington. Someone has a condo that Mr. Geiger knows or something." She waved her hand vaguely.

So. Zoey was asking him to go to Vermont for the weekend. *After* she had talked to Claire. Which meant either that Zoey had asked Claire's okay, *or*—aha!—Claire had asked Zoey to ask him.

Either way it could be trouble. He was *not* interested in spending time with Claire. Nor was he interested in Zoey any longer. In fact, he was getting used to being alone. Totally alone. No team, no girlfriend . . .

Just the same, though, he did enjoy skiing. And this was a *group* thing. He'd always been proud of the way the island kids tended to stick together.

"I don't have anything better to do," he said. "And if everyone else is coming, I guess I will, too."

7 How does your boyfriend feel about the other people in your life? Try to guess whether your boyfriend will say he (A) really likes; (B) somewhat likes; (C) is indifferent to; (D) somewhat *dislikes*; (E) can't stand: your closest friends, your mom and dad, your siblings, and your previous boyfriend, if applicable. Then compare your guesses to your boyfriend's actual answers.

Zoey

See? This is why I think sometimes these quizzes are a good thing. I've never really thought about how Lucas feels about all this stuff. I think for the most part that my friends are also his friends. Only to a lesser degree. For example, he likes Nina, but probably not as much as I do. Same for Aisha. I would say Lucas somewhat likes them. As for Claire, I know he doesn't trust

Claire because there's a lot of history between those two most of it bad. I won't say he can't stand her, though. More like D, somewhat dislikes.

He's barely talked to my dad, but I know he likes my mom. I think he sort of likes the idea of my parents. The way they're close and work together and are basically pretty cool. Sometimes cooler than I, personally, would like. And I know Lucas really likes Benjamin, although it's not like the two of them are best friends.

As for Lucas and my previous boyfriend, Jake . . . there's a lot of history between those two as well. They stay clear of each other, mostly. Polite but not friendly. Closest to a C.

Claire

My closest friends? I guess that would be Zoey and Aisha. I don't really know how Jake feels about Aisha; more or less indifferent, I guess. As for Zoey, I'm not one of those people who think that love, once it is formed, ever really goes away entirely. I think Jake still cares for Zoey. I also think Benjamin still cares for me. I even think Lucas, deep down inside, still has affection for me. And of course I still, from time to time, have feelings of tenderness for both of them. That's only natural. Things aren't always black and white. Usually they're shades of gray.

As to Jake and my father? Indifference. On both their parts. Jake and Nina? There's a healthy mutual dislike there, and always has been.

Jake and my "previous" boyfriend? That would be Benjamin, of course. And it's an interesting question. Jake and Benjamin are polar opposites. Jake is physical, Benjamin is intellectual. Jake is direct, Benjamin is subtle. Jake is all about passion and duty and living out some ideal vision of what a "man"

should be, and when he fails he's a
wreck. Benjamin is brilliant, ana-
lytical, cool, with his emotions kept
under such control that you wonder
how long he'll be able to keep it up.

I doubt they'll ever be close.

Aisha

How can I answer any of
this question? I'm not even
sure how Christopher feels about
me. All I can say is he <u>seems</u>
to really like my mom and dad
and Kalif. He <u>seems</u> to like my
friends. But who knows how he
likes them? For all I know,
Christopher is trying to calcu-
late some way to go after Loey
or Claire or Nina. I don't

<u>know;</u> that's the problem. I have the feeling Christopher is the kind of guy who would have been happy being a pirate, being dashing and ruthless and always in pursuit of something or someone.

As for previous boyfriends, I don't have anyone who would qualify. I went out with other guys before, guys who would have been happy to be faithful to me, to be open and honest with me, guys I could trust. But Christopher was the first one I ever really fell for.

And I'm supposedly smart. Right.

Nina

Benjamin and my best friend get along great. Of course, they are brother and sister. Benjamin and my dad get along great, too. They got to be friendly back when Benjamin was my sister's boyfriend. Benjamin and my sister? They don't get along as well as they used to, but I still have my suspicions about them. I mean, think about it. Why would Claire dump Benjamin for _Joke_? And the flip side is, why would Benjamin be happy with _me_ if he ever got the chance to get Claire back? Jeez,

when I put it that way, it's
enough to really make me
insecure. There's only one
possible solution—kill Claire in her
sleep. A stake through the
heart should do it, but it will
have to be sometime when the
sun's up and her evil power is
weakest.

Eleven

After school on Friday, Zoey, along with Claire, Aisha, and Nina, went to the multistory parking garage where islanders kept their "real" cars. Real cars were the cars that were parked on the mainland. They were the usual assortment of automobiles, ranging from the Geigers' Mercedes to the Grays' more humble Taurus to the Passmores' big van, and generally came with luxuries like brakes and windshields. Unlike "island" cars, which were used only for putting around the island's few roads and were pitiful piles of junk.

They decided to take the Passmore van, since they planned to hit the mall for everything they might conceivably need on a ski trip to Vermont. But to Zoey's surprise, the van was gone from its usual space.

"One of my folks must have come over," she said, explaining the obvious.

"I'm not supposed to take my dad's car unless I clear it with him first," Nina said.

"You're not supposed to take it anyway, unless *I'm* driving," Claire pointed out.

The three of them looked at Aisha.

"Sure. Why not? I have the keys. Only, if I do decide to buy a pair of skis, where are we going to put them?"

"We'll strap them on top," Zoey said. "But you shouldn't *buy*. Wait and rent equipment when you get there. You may not even like skiing."

Aisha made a face. "I'll either be skiing or stuck in the condo with Christopher. I have no choice but to like it."

"You'll enjoy it," Claire said with atypical cheeriness.

They searched out Aisha's car and headed toward the mall, stereo blasting, Claire and Zoey in the back, Nina in the passenger seat in full recline mode.

"How did Christopher react when you invited him?" Zoey yelled from the backseat.

"Not as excited as I'd expected. I think he feels a little insecure about it. I mean, he's from the projects of Baltimore. Very little skiing goes on there."

"Did he ever skateboard?" Zoey asked.

Aisha shrugged. "No idea."

"Similar skills. But if he's still bruised, he might want to take it easy."

"He'll have a great time," Claire said, still eerily upbeat. Suddenly something caught Zoey's eye. She turned quickly. "Hey. There goes our van." She wrinkled her brow. She was sure she'd seen her mother behind the wheel, but there had also been a glimpse of someone beside her. It wasn't Benjamin, since he, Lucas, and Christopher had planned their own guy version of a shopping trip. And her father would be at the restaurant on a Friday evening.

She shrugged it off. She opened her purse and looked at the check register. Enough to pay for gas and for food when they got to Vermont, but not a lot left over for shopping. Unless she were to use her handy ATM card to raid her savings account, sin of sins.

There were certain things she needed. For a start, she couldn't sleep in her usual Bruins jersey. She needed something a little more substantial than that. Something substantial, but not frumpy. Somewhere about halfway between Sears and Victoria's Secret.

She took a small spiral-bound pad from her purse and jotted a note.

"What's that?" Nina asked. Reclining the way she was, her head was practically in Zoey's lap.

"My list."

"You and your lists," Nina said, mocking her.

"Hey," Aisha said. "Don't make fun of lists. I have a list. If I didn't keep lists, I'd never get anything done."

Nina slapped her forehead. "So *that's* why I never accomplish anything. I remember once I'd been planning to find a cure for cancer, only I never wrote it down on a list. Sure enough, I forgot."

"So what's on your list?" Aisha called back over her shoulder.

"Oh, the usual. Little sample bottles of

shampoo and conditioner so I don't have to carry big bottles."

"I have that, too," Aisha said.

"Me too," Nina added. "In my head. My head list."

"Actually, this is just a small part of my bigger list, which is the list of stuff to bring with me tomorrow," Zoey admitted. "Clothes, makeup, and all that."

"Black lace teddy?" Nina asked.

"No. In fact, I was going to shop for something warm. Flannel, maybe."

"You could get pajamas with feet in them, like when you were little," Nina suggested. "That would stop Lucas dead in his tracks."

"This is not about Lucas," Zoey said. "It's about staying warm. We don't know how well heated this condo is, or if there are enough blankets."

"Or enough beds," Nina said with a leer.

Zoey grabbed Nina's jacket and placed it over Nina's head.

"It's a fully stocked condo," Claire said reassuringly.

"So you think we'll see the guys at the mall?" Aisha wondered.

"If we do, it will only be for a brief moment as they race past in perfectly straight lines, buy whatever they came for, and take off," Zoey said. "You know how guys shop. Speed shopping."

"That's because they never buy anything," Nina said, her voice muffled under her coat.

"Whereas I"—she produced a gold American Express card—"have the power to buy anything I want."

"Where did you get that?" Claire demanded.

"I asked Dad for it," Nina said, pulling her jacket off her face. "I told him I was thinking about changing my look entirely. I showed him a picture from a J. Crew catalog. You know, all clean and preppy looking. Sort of a blazer-chinos-pennyloafers look." She laughed. "Out came the old Am Ex."

"That's very devious," Claire said. "I'm proud of you. And as long as I get to use it, too, I won't even tell Dad how you manipulated him."

Trip Purchases: The Girls

Zoey

1 flower print flannel nightgown (JC Penny's)
1 3-pack of cotton underwear (JC Penny's)
1 R.E.M. CD
2 pairs L.L. Bean heavy woolen socks
1 pair ski pants
1 blue satin nightshirt (Victoria's Secret)
1 Swiss army knife
3 books: *First and Forever, Fireworks,* and *Sweet Savage Love*
2 rolls 35-millimeter film
1 sample-size shampoo
1 5-pack of razor blades
1 ChapStick

Claire

1 pair ski boots
2 pairs ski pants
1 leather miniskirt (Filene's)
1 wool-blend sweater (The Limited)
2 pairs L.L. Bean heavy woolen socks
1 sample-size shampoo
1 pound French roast coffee
2 books: *Amo, Amas, Amat and More* and *The Last Wilderness*
1 ChapStick

Aisha

2 books: *Skiing for Beginners* and *The New Guide to Skiing*
3 pairs L.L. Bean heavy woolen socks
1 pair gloves
1 Ace bandage
1 bottle Advil
1 pair ski pants
1 pair green satin pajamas (Filene's)
1 sample-size shampoo
1 sample-size conditioner
1 sample-size Crest
1 small loofah sponge
2 magazines: *Ski* with article on Killington and *Mademoiselle* with article "Why Men Lie"

Nina

1 Porno for Pyros CD
1 large bag peanut M&M's
2 pairs men's boxer shorts
4 pairs L.L. Bean heavy woolen socks
1 Barney the Dinosaur mask (Spencer's Gifts)
1 sample-size Afta Shave
3 temporary tattoos
1 Thighmaster
1 ChapStick

Trip Purchases: The Guys

Jake

1 new binding
1 pair new poles
1 pair sunglasses
1 hand-grip exerciser
1 bottle Afta Shave
1 ChapStick

Christopher

2 books: *Skiing for Beginners* and *The New Guide to Skiing*
1 pair gloves
1 bottle Listerine
1 bottle Safari cologne
1 box Trojan sensi-ribbed condoms

Benjamin

3 CDs: B.B. King, Blind Melon, and Mozart
2 books on tape: *A Morning for Flamingos*
    and *The Wine-Dark Sea*
1 scarf (hopefully black)
1 bag Jolly Rancher watermelon candy

Lucas

1 bottle Scope
2 Tic-tacs
1 box Mentor condoms

Twelve

Zoey and the girls returned to Chatham Island on the last ferry and arrived back at nine twenty-five. Zoey said good-bye to her friends and went straight to the restaurant. It was Friday, and with Christopher not available to pick up shifts yet, both her parents would be working late.

Her father was in the kitchen, cleaning it up after the evening dinner business, leaving out only what he would need to send the occasional order of steamed shrimp or nachos out to the bar.

"Hi, Dad," she said, setting her several bags of purchases on the stainless steel counter. She gave him a kiss on the cheek.

Mr. Passmore wore his hair pulled back in a ponytail fastened with a twist tie from a bread bag. He wore a faded Albert Einstein T-shirt under a food-stained white apron. He was nursing a cup of coffee to one side, while he stretched plastic wrap over a steel tub full of what looked like soup.

"No one on this island appreciates a good gumbo," he said. "Lobstah, steamahs, sometimes a good chowdah," he said, mimicking the Maine accent.

"So, you guys will be eating gumbo all week-end, I guess," Zoey said.

"What, you won't eat it, either? Oh, yeah. I forgot. The big road trip." He smiled. "Brings back memories of when I was your age and the road trips we used to take. Three of us drove from Dayton to Santa Fe in two days because we heard you could get peyote legally." He made a face. "Which is probably *not* the story I should have been telling you."

"We're just going skiing, Dad."

"Cool. But your mother wants to have a little talk with you."

Zoey let her shoulders sag expressively. "No drinking and driving, no drugs, no picking up hitchhikers—like there would be any room."

"Yeah, all that," her father agreed. "And my fatherly addition—if the red oil-pressure light goes on in the van—"

"Pull over immediately."

"Mmm. How much money do you have?"

"Well, I just went shopping."

Her father dug in his pants pocket and pulled out a handful of cash. "Looks like fifty-three dollars. Here. And don't tell your mom I gave you any. That way she'll give you some out of the register."

Zoey went out through the swinging doors into the dining room. She said hello to the waitress and found her mother behind the bar, waiting on half a dozen people.

"Dad said you wanted to give me a lecture before I took off," Zoey said.

"Well, you're not going now, are you?"

"First thing tomorrow morning. We're going to catch the seven forty. I figure you guys will still be asleep."

"Good guess." Her mother surveyed her customers. "Anyone ready? Tom?" When she got only negatives, she pulled Zoey aside into a corner of the dining room. They sat down at one of the tables.

"I just want to get a few things out on the table before you take off," her mother said.

"No drunk driving, no shooting heroin, no hitchhikers, and if the little red oil light comes on, I just keep driving till the van burns up."

"I know you know all that, Zoey, but I'm serious. No one drives drunk. Not you, not anyone. Even just one beer, you don't touch the key. Are we totally clear on that?"

"Mom, do you even realize that I don't drink?" Zoey asked.

"You don't? Ever?"

"I've had one or two beers in my whole life."

"Wow," her mother said. "I mean, that's good."

"I'm not the kind of person who would do something dumb like drive halfway across the country looking for peyote," Zoey said, batting her eyes.

Her mother nodded. "I know you're not. Anyway, just because *we* were stupid when we were young doesn't mean we're going to put up with *you* being stupid." She looked down at the tablecloth, picking at a spot of dried-on food with her fingernail. "Are you sleeping with Lucas?"

Zoey rolled her eyes and fervently wished she could just slip quietly from the room. She shifted position in her chair. "No, *Mother*. Of course not."

"Well, that's good," her mother said without much conviction. "I mean it really is. It was different when I was your age. All we had were crabs and clap and syphilis. We didn't have venereal diseases that were fatal at all, let alone a hundred percent fatal. Hell, we didn't even have herpes. At least I never heard anything about it, let alone AIDS. Man."

"Is that all you wanted to tell me?" Zoey said hopefully.

"Look, I'm just saying that if for any reason you *do* decide to sleep with anyone, use condoms."

Zoey felt the heat in her face, but with luck, in the dimly lit room the blush wouldn't be noticeable. "Mother, I know all that."

Her mother reached across the table and laid her hand on Zoey's arm. "Of course you do. But I'm telling you again because I want you to remember. I know it sounds like I'm being a hypocrite, but the truth is I'd be happier if you didn't start having sex at all yet. I can't control what you do or don't do, I know that. So, all I'm saying is, *if* you decide to do it, use a damned condom because that way at least you greatly *reduce* the odds of catching anything *and* the odds that I'm going to become a grandmother."

"Yes, Mother," Zoey said, gritting her teeth. "By the way, did you give this same lecture to Benjamin?"

"No, your father took care of that. After I twisted his arm a few times."

"Oh." Zoey was disappointed. She'd been hoping to at least catch her mother being sexist. "Anything else?"

"Yes. When you use a public toilet, flush it with your foot and don't sit all the way down."

Zoey smiled. "Got it."

Her mother looked at her and shook her head a little wistfully. "You're a good kid, Zoey. I don't know how your father and I ever managed to have two such great kids."

"Benjamin and I can't figure it out, either," Zoey said. "Hey, I saw you driving around when I was on my way to the mall. Who was with you?"

Her mother's eyes flickered. Then she shrugged indifferently. "There wasn't anyone with me."

"I thought maybe it was a hitchhiker," Zoey said accusingly.

Her mother made a face. "Go on, get out of here. Take some money from the register. And have fun. Just not too much."

Zoey lay in her bed, looking up at the low, sloping ceiling. She should get some sleep because she would have to do at least some of the driving tomorrow and she hated driving with a lot of people in the car. She had a vivid imagination and always conjured up images of driving into a train, killing or injuring everyone but herself. That way she would have to be alive and healthy and go around visiting all the people she had hurt in the hospital.

She wondered how Claire dealt with knowing that she had been driving and was responsible, at least in large part, for the death of Wade McRoyan. She herself would never have been able to handle the guilt. But Claire was a different person than she was. Everyone was different.

Like in the way they dealt with guys—Claire, always so in charge and in control, dumping one, grabbing another. Like the way she had just blown off Jake with hardly a second thought.

Claire was like Louise Kronenberger that way—always cool, no matter what.

Although there were some big differences. Like, for example, Zoey was pretty sure Claire had never done it.

She smiled up at the dark ceiling. That's because guys were too scared of Claire to ask.

Unfortunately, Zoey did not seem to have the knack of being in control. She couldn't be imperious like Claire. And she certainly wasn't going to be easy like Louise.

What had Louise meant with that crack about not all of them being virgin islanders? Had she meant Lucas?

Zoey shifted onto her side and pushed down the covers. Suddenly she was hot. The dreamy, philosophical mood had evaporated. Sex, sex, sex. It was like there was some huge conspiracy—Lucas, pushing and pleading and practically begging; her own mother, ready to hand her a box of condoms; every magazine on the stands, with one article or another about better sex, or more sex, or different sex.

The whole world wanted her to have sex. Even *she* wanted herself to have sex a lot of the time. It would make Lucas so happy and so grateful. And it wasn't like there weren't times when she thought about it, and even played out various scenarios in her mind. Just doing it would put an end to the whole battle of wills between her and Lucas.

But she had experienced many of these same thoughts when she had been going with Jake. Jake had been no more subtle than Lucas. And back then she had thought about how it might be fun with Jake, and how happy he would be, and grateful, and how it would put an end to the test of wills.

She loved Lucas. She felt she loved Lucas even more than she had once loved Jake. And yet, what if she had slept with Jake and then they'd broken up? And what if, somehow, some way, she and Lucas ended up breaking up?

She shifted onto her other side and looked out the dormered window to see silver moonlight on the bare branches of the trees. Tomorrow morning—or maybe it was technically morning already—she was going off, for the first time, on a weekend trip, more or less alone with a guy. A guy she loved, who loved her. Only he wanted the love to be physical.

And the only question was, in the end, should she say yes or no?

*   *   *

A few blocks away, Claire was also awake. But when she'd realized she wasn't falling asleep, she had pulled on a warm parka and climbed up to the widow's walk. With chilly fingers she'd reached around the brick chimney to the one loose brick, pried it out, and found her diary. She huddled with her back against the railing and tilted the pages toward the light of the moon. Reading was impossible, but she could see well enough to write in a straight line.

Temperature: 41 degrees. Almost no wind. Clear.

Tomorrow's the big ski trip. My plan has worked so far. Jake will be there alone. I'll be there alone. I'm hoping that, a week of solitude and believing he's lost me will help him get past all the stuff that's happened between us.

And then what? True love and

happiness? I have no idea. I'd like to think so, but I have to take things one step at a time. First, get Jake back. Then decide what that means for the longer term. Tomorrow's the big day. I've never gone away with a guy before. Although having six other people along keeps it from being a honeymoon exactly. I'm a little nervous about it all. Surprising, since there's really nothing to be nervous about.

Claire closed the diary and slid the pencil back in the spine. Nothing at all to be nervous about. Except, if Jake still rejected her, it would mean . . . being alone, but that didn't bother her.

It would mean that he hadn't forgiven her. That she still wasn't free of a night not unlike this one, two years earlier.

8 Will your boyfriend say it is okay for him to (A) look at other girls as long as it is totally innocent; (B) look at other girls, deliberately make eye contact, and smile; (C) look at other girls as much as he wants as long as he doesn't actually ask them out; or (D) never look at other girls when he's with you.

Nina

Okay, <u>next</u> question.

Zoey

I guess I don't mind it when Lucas looks at other girls. Just looks. If he was like Christopher, looking with serious intent, getting phone numbers and all, then I'd be very upset. And I think Lucas and I are in agreement on this. I think he'll answer A. If he answers B or C, I'd be

Kind of not all that thrilled. But I'm not so insecure I'd want him to answer D. I guess that would be asking too much.

Although I never look at other guys when I'm with Lucas. Almost never.

Claire

I'm not bothered by guys looking at other girls. I look at other guys, so it's only fair that I should extend that same right to Jake. Besides, I'm not the kind of person to get all worked up into an insecure, jealous frenzy like a lot of girls. Either there's nothing to worry about, in which case it's a waste of mental

energy, or there is. And if there is,
then the relationship is over anyway.

Aisha

I wouldn't mind guys looking at other girls if they could
at least do it with a little subtlety. You know, like the way
we girls look at guys: quick,
discreet, yet comprehensive.
With guys it's like they're
trying to memorize everything
when they look at a girl. Like
they want to be able to remember every tiny detail later on.
Personally, I don't even want
to think about why they're
that way, but they are.

Now, Christopher would say
he's free to look all he wants

and go get the girl's number.
Which is why I'm not so
sure I should even be taking
this quiz, because I'm not so
sure I have a boyfriend. But
as for just looking, that's no
big thing.

Wait a minute. Yes, it is. I
can't lie. It pisses me off.

It PISSES me off. Only I
can't do anything about it.

Yet.

Thirteen

THE DRIVE

weymouth

From Weymouth to Portland, Zoey drove and Nina took the front passenger seat. In the second row of seats, Aisha sat beside Christopher who sat beside Claire, who was wearing the leather mini she had purchased the day before. In the cramped space, her leg was pressed against Christopher's leg. Aisha was annoyed. Christopher glanced several times at Claire's legs, annoying Aisha still more.

Lucas, Jake, and Benjamin all sat in the far back, their shoulders cramped together. Lucas and Jake looked out their windows in opposite directions, having very little to say to each other.

Nina controlled the stereo and played the Porno for Pyros CD she'd bought the day before. This got on Benjamin's nerves because he was sitting back by the speakers. It also annoyed Zoey, who hated driving with other people in the car. One wrong turn could lead to a lifetime of guilt and regret.

Outside Portland, Nina insisted they make a pee stop at a McDonald's.

From Portland to Portsmouth, New Hampshire, Claire drove. Zoey moved to the back, thinking it would put her with Lucas, but when Lucas came back from the McDonald's, he grabbed the relatively roomy front passenger seat. So Zoey ended up sitting between Benjamin and Jake.

Aisha and Christopher were still together, with Nina beside Christopher. Nina was wearing faded, baggy pants and boots, and Christopher showed no signs of looking at her legs. So Aisha relaxed. Until she realized that Christopher could, from his angle, look up at the rearview mirror and get a fairly scandalous view of Claire's legs.

Claire, however, was using the rearview mirror herself, to watch what looked like Zoey and Jake in friendly conversation. Lucas ate an Egg McMuffin and channel-surfed the radio endlessly, driving everyone crazy.

Nina wondered darkly if Claire's frequent glances in the rearview mirror were aimed at Benjamin.

In Portsmouth they lost their way trying

to find Highway 4, resulting in a babble of helpful and conflicting suggestions that drove Claire, as soon as she had finally found the right road, to pull into a 7-Eleven and demand that someone else drive.

From Portsmouth to Concord, Jake drove, always a competitive event for him. He played highway tag with a car from Massachusetts, at one point rolling down the driver-side window to tell the other guy he was, in the phrase Mainers reserved for drivers from Massachusetts, a *Mass*-hole.

Benjamin sat in the passenger seat and, out of sheer perversity, played an opera CD until a group vote that he be forced to stop.

Nina, Zoey, and Aisha sat in the middle seat. Claire was in the back, sandwiched tightly between Christopher and Lucas, a situation that annoyed Jake, Aisha, and Zoey simultaneously. Snappish behavior began to break out all around, with arguments over music, how much the windows should be open or closed, heat, and driving style.

Nina suggested they should all join together and have a sing-along. She launched immediately into the Barney theme song, in which no one else joined.

Just past Concord, Aisha made a pee stop request, but Jake refused to stop. Zoey joined in the pee stop request. Benjamin, who was grumpy over the defeat of his opera, backed Jake. Nina joined Aisha and Zoey. Christopher lined up with the other guys and an argument on bladder differences between the sexes and its meaning in the world of sports, the military, and big business ensued.

At last Claire spoke up, told Jake in her quietly authoritative voice to pull over at the next rest stop, and he did.

Aisha drove from the rest stop to Lebanon, climbing into altitudes where snow clung to tree limbs and many of the cars were carrying full ski racks. Jake got the passenger seat. He turned to a rock station that faded in and out.

Christopher ended up in the far back with Zoey and Lucas. Lucas and Zoey held hands beneath the jacket draped over his lap. Christopher wished he could hold hands with Aisha, but Aisha was driving and, anyway, they didn't seem to be getting along all that well.

In the middle seat, Benjamin was stuck between Nina and Claire. Nina calculated the degree to which he was in contact with her versus the degree to which he was in contact with Claire. It *seemed* he was sitting closer to Nina, but there was no way of telling what was going on in his head. He might be paying much more attention to the contact with Claire.

They hit another McDonald's in Lebanon and Nina took over driving duties, because while no one had much faith in her driving, no one stepped forward to tell her so. Zoey took the seat beside her, watched the map, and clutched the dashboard fearfully each time Nina turned around to talk to someone in the back. The landscape had grown whiter all around as they climbed ever higher, but the roads remained clear.

Now Claire was in the middle seat next to Jake, both of them carefully ignoring each other, though Claire let her skirt creep up her thigh and Jake kept leaning forward to rub his forehead in a way that let him glance at her and then hate himself for glancing.

Benjamin sat behind Nina, wondering why she seemed to smell of Afta Shave.

Aisha was in the backseat, not objecting to the fact that Christopher had made room for his shoulders by putting his arm around hers.

Lucas sat on the other side of Aisha, trying not to notice Claire's hair, draped back over her seat so that it fell across his knees.

By the time the van pulled parked in front of the cluster of wood-frame, two-story condominiums, everyone was exhausted.

Killington

Fourteen

Claire breathed a sigh of relief as she surveyed the condo. They had made it. They were here. The Plan was working. And Jake had been mooning over her all the way up in the van. Except for that brief period when he'd seemed to be enjoying talking to Zoey.

The condo looked great. Upstairs were two bedrooms joined by a balcony that overlooked the tiny village of Killington. The downstairs featured a huge living room, a kitchen, and a second long deck with a redwood hot tub. From the deck the view was straight up the side of the mountain, a vast, rising expanse of frosted fir trees crisscrossed by dozens of white ski runs and the little red daisy chains of gondolas, looking like Christmas ornaments.

Zoey came up behind Claire and grabbed her arm as she was admiring the view. "There are only two bedrooms," she hissed in an urgent whisper.

"There's a fold-out couch there in the living room," Claire pointed out. "One bedroom has two double beds, and the other has one double. Altogether, with the couch, that's sleeping for eight people. What did you want? Bunk beds?"

"How are we going to divide up?"

Claire shrugged impatiently. "I assume it will be girls with girls and guys with guys. At least, *I* don't have any more exciting plans."

"Well, neither do I," Zoey said.

"Fine, so what's the problem? You share with Nina, I'll share with Aisha. Great. Now, let's get changed and hit the slope. I want to get back in shape quick. Before we leave, I want to be ready to try a black diamond trail."

"You're on your own, then," Zoey said. Trails were ranked in order of difficulty from green circle to blue square to black diamond. *Double* diamond trails were for professional-level skiers or the suicidal. "You're no better a skier than I am."

"Hey." Lucas, looking unsure of himself with hands in pockets, accompanied by Christopher. Benjamin had found a La-Z-Boy and had it in full recline. "Everyone's wondering where we should put our stuff," Lucas said.

"We figured guys sleep with guys, girls with girls," Claire said confidently.

Lucas and Christopher exchanged a shocked look and shuddered visibly. "Sleep with a guy?" Christopher said. "Not in this lifetime."

"You're just sharing a bed," Claire said.

"Who's sharing a bed?" Jake asked, arriving and slinging his bag onto the couch.

"Me and Nina," Zoey said, "Claire and Eesh. Then you guys work out whatever arrangements you want."

"Wait a minute," Jake said. "Like I'm going to be *in the same bed* as Christopher or Lucas? In what universe?"

"What's the problem?" Claire demanded. "*We're* sharing beds."

"You're girls," Lucas said. "Guys don't sleep with other guys."

Zoey gave him a dirty look. "Well, you can forget the other alternative."

"So can *you,*" Aisha told Christopher in the same tone of voice.

"That's not what this is about," Lucas grumbled.

"Uh-huh."

"Right. There's some *other* reason," Aisha said. "You guys cooked this up together, didn't you?"

"Actually," Benjamin said, speaking for the first time, "it's just something that guys don't do. We don't wear pink. We don't use the word *cute*. And we don't sleep with each other. We're manly men."

Claire felt herself doing a slow burn. What was the matter with all these people? She was trying to set up a nice romantic weekend here and get in some skiing, and between Zoey's outraged chastity and the guys' terror of homosexuality, they couldn't get past stage one.

"Look. Here it is," she said. "Two of you guys have to volunteer to sleep on the floor."

"So *all* the girls get beds, but only half the guys," Jake summarized. "Nice try."

"Jake," Claire said, striving to keep her voice mellow, "the girls are willing to share, two to a bed. You guys *won't* share, so two of you get beds and the other two get six feet of carpet."

Jake shook his head. "Uh-uh. We all draw straws or cut cards or something. Four people get beds. Four get floor."

Aisha planted her hands on her hips. "I'm not sleeping on the floor just because you insecure males are terrified you might wake up in the night and discover that your hand is accidentally on another guy's butt."

Bad tactic, Claire realized. Very bad tactic. All four guys had looked panicked by that mental picture.

"Look," Zoey said. "It's you guys who are the problem here. If you'd share beds, we could *all* have beds."

"*We* are not the ones with the problem," Lucas pointed out. "See, maybe it's you girls with the problem. After all, you're the ones who won't share a bed with a *guy.*"

Christopher gave Lucas a high five, but Claire noticed that neither Jake nor Benjamin joined in.

"Fine," Claire snapped. "Let's draw lots or whatever. Four people win. Then those four people can invite or not invite one of the remaining four to share. For my part, if I win, I'll sleep with Zoey or Aisha."

Nina chose that moment to come wandering in from the bathroom. "Excuse me? Claire? Is there something you've been hiding from me all these years?"

"Let me have your pack of cigarettes," Claire demanded.

"Smoking *and* sleeping with girls?" Nina asked archly. "Boy, you sure change when you get away from home."

Claire snatched the pack from the pocket of Nina's jacket. She extracted eight cigarettes, ignoring Nina's protest. She broke four of them in half, throwing away the excess, leaving her with four long and four short cigarettes.

"You know, you could have done that with just six cigarettes," Aisha pointed out. "Four long, break the other two in half and use both halves."

"Thanks for that math update. Here. Choose. Long gets a bed. Short gets floor. I'd like to get up the mountain sometime before next month." She stuck the cigarettes out toward Jake. He pulled a long one.

In quick succession Nina, Lucas, and Christopher pulled long ones.

"Unbelievable," Zoey complained, staring at her short cigarette. "Three out of the four guys. That means two of the girls are on the floor. What are the odds?"

"Arrangements could be made for some lucky girls," Christopher said with a leer.

"What do you mean, *two* girls are on the floor?" Nina demanded. "I count three."

"One of the girls can sleep with you," Zoey explained. "Namely, me."

"Ha. I don't think so. I won fair and square. Besides, I contributed the cigarettes. You losers are on your own."

*   *   *

The seemingly endless bed debate had been followed by a nearly as long bed*room* debate, with tempers, particularly Claire's, flaring. To Benjamin, she seemed once again to have some hidden agenda that she was impatient to pursue. But then again, maybe she just wanted to hit the slopes.

Finally, Benjamin found himself on the lower deck listening to the receding crunch of boots on snow, the voices growing fainter with distance. He trailed a finger through the hot water of the tub and felt the icy breeze on his face. He felt he could sense the awesome weight of the mountain towering above them. Could imagine the detail, filling in remembered colors, almost as if he were painting a picture. It might not be identical to the reality, but it was a good picture anyway.

Then he heard someone coming through the sliding glass doors, stepping out onto the deck. Nina. He should have realized that Nina hadn't left with the others. Instantly his mood darkened. She was trying to be nice, of course, but he didn't want her to be nice.

All the others had gone. The three confirmed skiers, Zoey, Claire, and Jake, had headed off at last to the lifts. Lucas, Christopher, and Aisha had gone off to sign up for either snowboarding or skiing lessons, figuring to try whichever was easier. Nina had stayed behind to be *nice*. The word for that kind of nice was *pity*.

Damn it, if anyone should know better, it was Nina. She knew him well enough. But maybe now that their relationship had changed, she was no longer ready to give him the rough, egalitarian treatment that he appreciated from her.

He didn't mind the being left behind. The simple fact was that there were limits on what a person could do without being able to see. He would never be an airline pilot, he would never be a marine rifleman, and he would never be a serious skier. Being the person he was, he wasn't thrilled about having to close off possibilities, but he had adjusted. He dealt with it without self-pity.

But other people inevitably felt sorry for him. Felt they had to find ways of including him in things. And it was that pity that burned.

"What are you still doing here?" he asked as gently as he could manage.

"I don't ski," she said simply. He could hear her climbing up to look down into the hot tub.

"Neither does Aisha. You could learn, though." Nina was trying to be nice, he reminded himself.

"I'm not all that into physical stuff. I mean, I can barely dance, as you know."

"You dance fine," he said tersely. Surely she should be getting the message by now.

"That doesn't mean I can ski. Besides, I'd rather just hang—"

"Look, Nina," he snapped suddenly, "I'm a big boy. I can amuse myself. I don't need a baby-sitter."

He heard her sharp intake of breath. What surprised him was the prolonged silence that followed it. As it stretched on it became more unsettling. Was she looking at him? Ignoring him?

At long last, "Screw you, Benjamin." A voice with tears in it.

"Nina, I'm not trying to be a jerk, but I don't need you to hold my hand for me."

"Yeah? You know what, Benjamin? Just because you're cranky from the drive up here, and just because you wish you'd never gone out with me, that doesn't give you the right to dump on me."

"Wait a minute, what are you ranting about? This is about you feeling sorry for me because I can't go and ski."

"No, that's *not* what it's about. I know better than to ever show anything like pity for The Great Benjamin Passmore, Sightless Wonder Boy."

"Fine, then you understand. So go off and enjoy yourself."

"You know, you're right. I was under the stupid impression that I might enjoy myself by being with you. But that was before I realized what a jerk you are."

He heard the door slide open.

"You said whatever happened, we'd always still be friends, Benjamin. But all it took to put an end to that was one lousy kiss. Yeah, one *lousy* kiss!" He heard the door slam, and then the ringing emptiness of the vast open spaces.

KILLINGTON SKI AREA

KILLINGTON VILLAGE—REST AREAS, LODGING, CONDOS, PARKING, ETC.

WEST GLADE
GLADES TRIPLE CHAIR
EAST GLADE
HIGHLINE
DOUBLE DIPPER
KILLINGTON PEAK DOUBLE CHAIR
ESCAPADE
OVATION
SUPERSTAR QUAD CHAIR
SUPERSTAR
SUPERSTAR
SKYE LARK
BITTERSWEET
JUGGERNAUT
NEEDLE'S EYE
NEEDLE'S EYE DOUBLE CHAIR
KILLINGTON GONDOLA
SOLITUDE
PIPE DREAM
SKYEBURST
THE JUG
DREAM MAKER
DREAM MAKER
BEAR CLAW

Fifteen

Claire felt the familiar rush of anticipation as the chairlift scooped them up, lifting their skis free of the snow, holding them in a careless grip as it drew them up the side of the mountain, swaying and wobbling high above the skiers below. It was an environment in which she felt so at home—cold, clear, quiet. Private, except for Zoey alongside her on the two-person chair.

They rose over birch and fir trees whose branches drooped under the weight of snow. And as they rose the panorama expanded, widening out across a dozen rounded mountain peaks, blazing sun winking and dancing along the wide white avenues of ski runs. Back down the mountain, the cars in the parking lot, the base lodge, the pristine village had all been reduced to Matchbox toys, or some too-perfect-to-be-realistic model.

Ahead a few dozen feet was Jake, ignoring the other person sharing his chair.

Claire allowed herself a moment of smugness. By the end of this day the group would have broken down into its component couples.

Zoey would have found a place to be with Lucas, Aisha with Christopher, Nina with Benjamin. Only Claire and Jake would be wandering alone, unattached. But with a hot tub, a clear starry night, a fireplace, the warm, mellow afterglow of a day on the slopes . . .

It was a pity to have to manipulate him this way, but it was his own fault for being stubborn. She loved him, he loved her. Just because he seemed determined to screw that up didn't mean she had to let him.

They reached the top after a fourteen-minute ride. Claire readied herself, slipping her gloved hands through the straps of her poles. Ahead Jake was obviously not waiting around to be friendly. He was already making his way toward the head of a trail, weaving confidently around other skiers. Claire muttered under her breath.

"What?" Zoey said.

"I said, there he goes." She grinned. "Race you to the bottom, Passmore."

Before Zoey could answer, Claire launched herself in pursuit of Jake. Jake had always been a more powerful skier, but Claire had greater finesse. She thought she could probably catch him, even pass him. If neither of them took a spill first.

Jake was schussing straight down the fall line, gathering speed down the particularly steep early part of the trail. Claire dropped into a tuck position and went after him.

The suddenness of acceleration took her breath away, literally, and it occurred to her that she hadn't skied in seven months, that she was badly out of shape, out of practice, and trying to chase a guy with unbreakable knees down a challenging trail. The smart thing would be to take her time, get readjusted, get warmed up, practice a few moves, and *then* get serious.

But Jake was getting serious *now*. It had become a challenge. Jake was trying to get away. And she wasn't going to let him.

They were halfway down the slope when she saw Jake lose it in a mogul field, making a wrong turn that sent him tumbling. She laughed out loud, a sound instantly snatched away by the wind. That would teach him to be a hotdog.

Should she stop and help him retrieve the loose ski that had escaped into the trees, or just coolly fly on by with a superior smile? Or maybe the best thing—

She felt something wrong. Felt the skis flying out from under her. Hit hard on her right shoulder, rolled, twisted, skidded, slid out of control on her behind, tried to dig in her heels, misjudged, flipped forward, and came to a final halt with her head buried in the snow, limbs splayed.

She pulled her head up and spit compacted snow out of her mouth. Snow was packed behind her sunglasses, and she cleared it with her clumsy gloved fingers. And a healthy handful of snow was down her back, out of reach. She would just have to wait for it to melt.

"Are you okay?" Jake, sitting just a few feet away, leaning back against a birch tree.

"Aside from feeling like an idiot? Yeah."

Jake went back to reseating his boot in the binding of his runaway ski. "You know, you're not actually supposed to stop by using your face that way."

Claire was crawling forward to retrieve her own skis, which had stopped in the trough of a mogul. "Go ahead and laugh," she said sourly.

Jake grinned. "I think I will. I mean, that was a bad fall. I thought you might have snapped your neck. But then I realized you were just demonstrating the new 'ostrich' stop, where you stop by suddenly sticking your entire head into the snow."

Claire laughed despite herself. "I was trying to beat you to the bottom."

"I might have been showing off," Jake admitted. "And it was going pretty well there up until I went airborne."

"Oh, great," Claire said. "Look at this." Zoey was gliding calmly past in a shallow traverse, giving a nonchalant wave. She yelled something and grinned.

"What did she say?" Jake asked.

"'Tortoise and the Hare,'" Claire said. "You know, the kids' story about the race between the rabbit and the turtle, where the turtle wins because she doesn't try to show off when she's totally out of shape?"

Jake used his poles to push himself up. He came over and, after planting himself firmly, gave Claire a hand up.

"You know, if we cut across here we can catch

a nice, gentle trail," Jake suggested, sounding almost shy.

"After you, tortoise," Claire said happily.

It was going better and faster than Claire had hoped. She had spent the afternoon skiing with Jake. Sometimes they ran into Zoey, but without any spoken agreement or acknowledgment between them, Claire and Jake had become partners for the day. Riding the lifts together, always staying within sight of each other, challenging each other with stunts that rarely ever worked.

But she was aware that it was a shaky truce. She had caught him watching her admiringly from time to time, but that didn't mean much. The question had never been whether Jake was attracted to her. The question was whether he was ready to let go of the past and get on with living his own life.

In other words, to do what she wanted him to do.

By the time the sun began to drop below the peaks, they were both worn out and chilled. They spotted Zoey a distance away, heading toward the ski school, and caught up with her.

"Hi," Zoey said. "You two champions do any more of that trick skiing you were demonstrating earlier?"

Claire gave her a dubious look. "I suppose you didn't fall once."

"Not more than six or eight times," Zoey said. "Never face first though. I prefer the popular butt fall. Let me ask you this—are your shins killing you?"

"You need to lean against the front of your boot more," Jake suggested. "I always used to tell you . . ." He let the sentence drift away. Claire knew he'd been the one who'd taught Zoey to ski. They'd gone fairly often, back when they were boyfriend and girlfriend, sometimes with Jake's parents, once or twice with the Passmores.

"You were a great teacher," Zoey said sincerely. "I was lucky to have you."

Had there been an emotional subtext there of some kind? Claire wondered. Probably not. Zoey had a low threshold of subtlety. She was just being nice, telling Jake that she was still his friend. And that was good. Probably.

They came to the base of the novice slope and Zoey shielded her eyes, looking around for Lucas.

"There's Aisha and Christopher," Claire said, pointing. Christopher was sidestepping stiffly up a gentle rise while Aisha was snowplowing down, looking nervous about moving at just over walking speed.

"Let's race over and make them feel like rank, pathetic amateurs," Jake suggested, grinning wickedly.

"That would be rude," Zoey said. "Let's do it."

The three of them got up what speed they could and stopped just short of Aisha, throwing up as much snow spray as possible.

"Show-offs," Aisha muttered.

Christopher schussed woodenly down toward them, unable to stop until he was several feet past them. He looked back over his shoulder. "So this is what white people do for a good time, huh?"

Jake shrugged. "There has to be at least one sport white people are better at."

"For now," Christopher said. "Let me get a few more lessons and then we'll see. So far, all I know how to do really well is fall down."

"You'd have a long way to go before you could fall any better than Claire did," Jake said with a laugh.

Claire slapped his arm with her glove. "You went first."

"Where's Lucas?" Zoey asked.

"He just left a little while ago," Aisha said.

"Oh. He didn't like it?"

"Huh. He went nuts. He decided to do snowboarding and he's just been crazy. It's like he found religion or something. Bouncing around on those humpy things—" She made a wavy motion with her hand.

"Moguls," Zoey supplied.

"I think he wore himself out. He took off for the condo to thaw out his feet."

"Which is just what I'd like to do," Christopher said. "I'm not totally back up to a hundred percent . . ."

"Excuses, excuses," Aisha teased him.

"Let's all head back. Thaw out, then go see about food and nocturnal entertainment," Jake suggested.

"Nocturnal entertainment?" Christopher repeated, adding an exaggerated lascivious leer.

"Absolutely," Aisha said with a wink at Claire. "Too bad you're not a hundred percent, though. I couldn't be very entertained by a guy who was just, what, seventy percent?"

"There's a club for kids who don't have fake IDs," Jake said. "It's usually full of freshman scrotes, but we could just ignore them. And the music is okay."

"We're there," Claire said. A little music, a little dancing. Yes, she was truly a genius. It was all going like clockwork.

Sixteen

They arrived back at the condo, laughing and teasing, and ran into a stony wall of bad temper. Benjamin was in the living room doing the frostily polite routine Claire remembered well. She guessed it was possible Benjamin felt left out of the day's activities, but that wasn't like him at all. He knew what this was going to be like. It was more likely that he was pissed off by Nirvana, pounding from the floor above.

Claire went upstairs and found Nina, listening to her CD boom box and looking like a storm cloud. Nina glanced up at her resentfully and went back to reading a magazine.

Claire peeled off her ski clothes and began digging in her bag for something warm and soft. She found a heavy gray felt bathrobe and slipped into it gratefully. "Have a good time today?" she asked Nina.

Nina's response was a sneer. *Okay,* Claire thought, *trouble in paradise.* She went over and turned the music down to a more reasonable level.

"Turn it back up," Nina snapped.

"Nina, not that I want to sound like Dad, but

there are other people around, and other people next door, too."

"What, did *Benjamin* ask you to come up here and turn down the music?"

"No, actually Benjamin didn't have much to say."

"He had plenty to say to me," Nina grumbled.

"I'm guessing there was a . . . disagreement?"

"No. No disagreement. We agree. We agree totally."

Claire sighed. Her muscles ached and various parts of her body were tender and bruised. Plus, the familiar cold-induced lethargy had begun to steal over her, making her dopey and thick. "Why don't you two work it out? I'm going to go jump in the shower."

She headed for the bathroom.

"I have nothing to talk about with that weasel! Maybe *you* should talk to him, Claire!" Nina shouted after her.

Ten minutes later, feeling somewhat more alert, Claire went back to check on Nina. Not that she cared about Nina's spat with Benjamin, but she did want to keep things running along smoothly.

But back in the room she found Nina deep in passionate conversation with Zoey and Aisha. Zoey was interrupting every few minutes to say, "Look, I can't get between you and my brother."

Aisha was listening impatiently. "So why don't you just grab him, sit him down, and say hey, what the hell is the deal with you, Benjamin? Cut to the chase."

"Oh, like you do with Christopher?" Nina pointed out.

"That's different," Aisha claimed. "Benjamin's easy to talk to."

"You know something? I'm tired of hearing about what a saint Benjamin is," Nina said. "Everyone thinks he's perfect. But I'll tell you, he can be pretty snotty when he wants to be. And rude. And mean, too."

"Benjamin, mean?" Zoey asked disbelievingly. Then she held up her hands. "Sorry. I'm not involved."

"He should just come right out and say—" Nina suspended her sentence when she realized that Claire was in the room. "Never mind."

Claire sighed and slipped out of her robe.

Nina gave her a dirty look. "And I wonder why Benjamin isn't really interested in me," she said pointedly. "He's still pining for the lost ice princess and her twin icebergs."

Claire pulled a sweater on over her head. "Leave me out of it, Nina. This sounds like it's between you and Benjamin."

Nina looked away, obviously embarrassed by having come right out and been vocal about her jealousy. "Yeah, right," she muttered.

Claire pulled on pants and a pair of new socks. "Nina, why don't you just go and apologize to Benjamin for whatever idiotic or annoying thing you did to make him mad. Tell him it's just the way you are, that you're some-

179

how genetically programmed to be a pain in the ass. He'll believe that. I know *I* do."

Lord, she thought as she headed down the stairs. *You try to arrange a simple little seduction and it has to turn into a three-ring circus.*

Aisha felt slightly ridiculous, standing in front of a sliding glass door just inches from darkness and below-freezing temperatures when she was wearing nothing but a bathing suit. But she couldn't wear a parka into the hot tub and, having never experienced a hot tub outside, and being sore from a day of skiing lessons, she was determined to make the run.

The only question was shoes. It was only about five steps to the tub, but the wooden deck was covered with tracked, dirty slush. The problem was, if she put on shoes to run to the tub, she would have to pause to take off the shoes, and that would leave her exposed, bare flesh to the wind for extra seconds.

"Go for it, Aisha," Lucas said, leaning over her shoulder to look out. "I'd join you, but I'm afraid Zoey and Christopher might both get the wrong idea."

"It's cold out there. Normally I don't wear a bathing suit when it's twenty degrees."

"Soon as you hit the water you'll be fine," Lucas assured her.

Aisha took a deep breath and slid open the door. "AHHHHH!"

She ran on tiptoes, scampered up the side,

and plunged neck deep into the steaming, churning water.

Lucas stuck his head out the door. "Of course, what I forgot to mention was that the real problem comes when you decide to get out." He gave a smile and went back inside.

Get out. Yes, Aisha realized, that could be painful. Still, for now it was heaven. She moved weightlessly around the tub until she located a strategically placed jet. Ah, yes. This *was* good for the tired muscles.

She leaned her head back against the side and looked off toward the mountain. Night had fallen, but the moon was still trapped behind the mountainside, backlighting the peak with a silvery luminescence. Overhead were more stars than Aisha had ever seen before, sharp and unblinking in the crystal mountain air.

A steady foot traffic moved from the nearby condos toward the base lodge and other restaurants and night spots. A group of middle-aged types in bright down parkas came walking past and gave her a friendly, mittened wave. She raised a hand from the warm water to wave back but instantly lowered it again. Yes, getting *out* would be the tough part. She might just have to stay in here forever.

She heard boots crunching on snow and pried open one eye to look. It was a guy following the same path as the middle-aged group, only this one was much younger. He smiled as he drew near.

"Is good night for this thing, yes?"

Aisha smiled, partly because she was just feeling good, and partly because his accent was sort of sweetly comical. "It's a beautiful night, yes."

He stopped and looked over the railing at her. "I am Pyotr. Peter."

"Aisha," she said. He seemed harmless enough, and she didn't want to be rude to a foreigner.

"Isha?"

"Aisha," she repeated her name more slowly.

"Peter," he said. "But in my country, Pyotr."

"Nice to meet you," Aisha said. It was a strange circumstance for meeting someone for the first time, but Pyotr-Peter seemed nice and was definitely cute, accent or no. He couldn't be more than eighteen or nineteen, she estimated. "What country are you from?"

"Estonia."

"Oh." She had no clear idea where Estonia was, but had the sense that it was in Europe somewhere. "Well, nice to meet you, Pyotr."

"Very pleasant meeting you also, Aisha. Shall you be going to a club or disco, I hope?"

"A little later, maybe," she said.

"Then if I have the luck, I will see you later." He smiled and headed off down the path toward the lodge.

Estonia. Now where on earth was Estonia? And what was a very cute Estonian doing in Vermont?

The glass door slid open and Christopher stuck out his head. "Why didn't you tell me you were coming out here? I would have joined you."

She cocked a finger at him. "You've just answered your own question."

"Funny. Come on, we're all going to get something to eat."

"I can't get out," she said.

Christopher's face lit up. "You mean you're . . . you don't have any clothes on?"

Aisha rolled her eyes. "Little one-track minds," she muttered under her breath. Were guys in Estonia like this? Probably not. They probably spent all their time wondering where on earth they were. "Actually, no, Christopher, I don't have anything on. And I'll get out, but I want you to close your eyes and not peek."

"Okay," he said quickly. "No problem."

"You *swear*?"

"Cross my heart. Jeez, Aisha, I'm not some slimeball."

"Okay. If you swear. Close your eyes."

He did, covering them with his hand. Aisha stood up and dashed toward the door, dripping water that would be ice in a matter of seconds.

"You have a bathing suit on, you liar!" Christopher yelled in outrage.

Aisha ran past him and jumped inside. "How would you know, since you swore not to look?" She left him to think of an answer, slid the door shut on him, and threw the lock.

9 Will your boyfriend say that his dreams about you are usually rated G, PG, PG-13, R, or X? How about your dreams of him?

Zoey

Okay, who wrote this stupid quiz? I mean, I know it's a quiz for girl-friends and their boy-friends, but honestly, with some of these questions I don't even want to know the answers. And I certainly don't want Lucas knowing all of my answers.

I think dreams are pri-vate. What your subcon-scious comes up with isn't something you should be telling people about. Really. It's just not anyone else's busi-ness. Not even Lucas's business.

Besides, I don't think dreams mean anything. Just because in a dream maybe you're . . . well, never mind. It's no one's business.

LUCAS

There is A very useful saying I learned while I was in jAil—I respectfully refuse to Answer on grounds that it may incriminAte me.

Aisha

I think dreams are out of your control, so they tend to be about a lot of different things, all mixed together. Sometimes a person shows up in your dream and it's like he's just part of the crowd. Other times, maybe he's the star

player. But if you averaged
them out, I guess my dreams
wouldn't rate anything more
than a PG. No biggie. There
aren't any demons hiding in
some dark corner of my brain.

As for Christopher's dreams,
I hate to think. I guess,
being realistic, that I do show
up there sometimes in his
subconscious. Sometimes I may
just be the UPS delivery
driver or something. Other
times, who knows? Who wants
to know?

Okay, I'd like to know. But
not if he knew that I knew.
That would be sick.

Christopher

THE TRUTH IS, I VERY RARELY

REMEMBER MY DREAMS. THE ONES I DO REMEMBER ARE USUALLY MORE LIKE NIGHTMARES, AND WITH THOSE I'D JUST AS SOON FORGET.

THE GOOD ONES FADE AS SOON AS I OPEN MY EYES, WHICH IS A DRAG. I THINK IT WOULD BE COOL TO BE ABLE TO HAVE REALLY GREAT, OUT-THERE DREAMS—MAYBE A _SPORTS ILLUSTRATED SWIMSUIT EDITION_ MEETS THE _FORBES_ LIST OF THE 400 RICHEST PEOPLE AND I'M AROUND NUMBER SIX ON THE LIST AND MOVING UP DREAM. COME TO THINK OF IT, THAT'S MY MOST FREQUENT DAYDREAM.

ANYWAY, I HOPE I'M HAVING GREAT R- AND X-RATED DREAMS BECAUSE I'D LIKE TO THINK THE OLD SUBCONSCIOUS IS HAVING A REALLY GOOD TIME, EVEN IF I'M NOT.

Nina

My dreams are all about fuzzy bunny rabbits. I believe that Benjamin also dreams about fuzzy bunny rabbits. Now is this quiz over with yet?

Okay, honestly, I used to have recurring nightmares. They were about what happened with my uncle, and they were not fun. I have them less now, but occasionally they'll still come bubbling up out of my subconscious. They're rated D for disgusting.

But I'll bet Benjamin has really cool dreams. I doubt that I'm in any of them, except maybe as a minor supporting actor. You know, like I could be the person watching helplessly as he falls . . . falls . . . FAAAAALLS! Aiyee!

But if he did happen to dream about me, I think it would be like a G-rated thing. You know, okay to see with your parents. Bring the kids. When he dreams of Claire, it's probably more like a PG-13, you know, but for sheer horror, not for sex.

BENJAMIN

In my dreams I can often see. Sometimes I can "see" people I've never seen in real life, people I didn't ~~nkow~~ know back then. Or I see these people changed, grown older or something. Sometimes these visions are so extraordinarily compelling that I can't help but believe them. I've "seen" Zoey this way, older than I remember her from when we were little and I was still sighted. I've seen Claire and Nina, too. All of them—Zoey, Claire, Nina—are very beautiful in my dreams. Maybe they're beautiful in real life, too. Or maybe I just have an artistic and optimistic subconscious.

But I don't have R-rated dreams, ~~tle~~ let alone X, because I'm simply too decent and mature and gentlemanly a guy for that.

And if you believe that . . .

Claire

There are a lot of storms in my dreams. Tornadoes and hurricanes and thunder. I'd love to see a real tornado someday. Be as close as I could get, hear it and feel it . . . I find those dreams very exciting. But they're G rated. And those are about the only dreams I remember. Sometimes a dream about my mom,

but those are just sad. Sorry. Nothing
very exciting here.

As for Jake? He probably dreams
about football.

JAKE

I have two kinds of
dreams—R-rated dreams,
which make me kind of
spacey all the next day,
and football dreams, where
I can't make my legs run
and the defensive linemen
are all huge brutes who
are going to crush me into
the dirt and stomp me
with their cleats.

Mostly I prefer the R-
rated dreams.

Seventeen

Full of burgers and potato skins and nachos, they arrived at the club. Nina had been expecting the worst. She figured that an underage club in a ski area would be playing a mix of weenie tunes. And in her present mood, a single Michael Bolton song could cause her to run amok. Instead, they walked into a good sound system with Aerosmith blowing through "Big Ten Inch Record."

"Good sign," Nina said. The first good thing to happen all day long.

"What?" Zoey yelled, cupping her ear.

"I said, thank God they're not playing the kind of stuff *you* like."

Zoey gave her a nasty look but decided against a comeback. Nina was near the edge and creeping closer all the time.

Lucas took Zoey's arm and led her away toward the dance floor. Aisha and Christopher followed them. Claire spotted a booth just emptying out and made a dash toward it.

A group of younger kids arrived at the booth at the same time, prepared to put up a fight. But then Jake went up, jerked a thumb over his shoulder, and the younger kids slunk away.

"You're such a big bully," Claire told Jake. "It's very useful."

They sat down, Nina separated from Benjamin, who ended up on the far side, sitting beside Claire. *Coincidence?* Nina wondered. *Yeah, right.* She didn't believe in coincidence where either Claire or Benjamin was concerned.

Suddenly she felt depressed. Maybe it was the music, which had shifted into a bluesy Robert Cray song. The lyrics were all about mistrust— *". . . but I suspect foul play . . . I suspect foul play."*

Oh, yes. She suspected foul play, all right. She suspected the whole reason behind this stupid trip was to give Claire an excuse to be with Benjamin.

". . . sitting here and thinking back, it all starts making sense . . ."

Claire nudged Benjamin's shoulder and whispered something in his ear. At first he looked a little confused, or even embarrassed, but he slid out of the booth and let Claire lead him to the dance floor.

Nina followed them with her eyes. Oh, yes, maybe you could say hey, no big deal. Why shouldn't they have a dance? People danced with other people without it meaning anything. Out on the dance floor, Zoey was now dancing with Christopher and Lucas with Aisha. No biggie. Except that again, with Claire and Benjamin, nothing was ever innocent, no matter how innocent it looked.

Nina glanced at Jake. He looked like he was arguing with himself. His eyebrows twitched from time to time, and his mouth even moved in muttered, unheard conversation.

Suddenly he looked over at Nina. His expression showed a half-formed, unwilling intention to ask her to dance. Nina shook her head no and Jake looked relieved.

The song ended and segued into some Pearl Jam. Zoey went over and danced with her brother. Christopher headed off to the rest room and Aisha came over and grabbed Jake, who went along meekly.

Claire sat down at the booth and took a long drink of her soda without acknowledging Nina.

Nina realized she was boiling. She'd been pissed off at Benjamin all day long. After storming out of the condo she'd wandered around the village, bored, which had just made her more resentful. Then, at dinner, when Claire had actually fed Benjamin one of her French fries, she'd gotten really steamed. Now she was so angry that she was unable to keep still, leg bouncing, hands drumming the tabletop. It probably just looked like she was responding to the music, but that wasn't it. Eddie Vedder's anger was just feeding her own, giving it shape.

It was a strange feeling. An unknown feeling. Not that Nina had never been mad before. But she had never been this kind of mad. There was a new element added, something desperate. Something that twisted her insides.

Not just anger. She knew anger. For years she had denied her anger at her uncle. Had denied her anger at her father for putting her in the position of being used by her uncle. Denied, especially, her unjustified but still real anger at her mother for having died.

No, not just anger. It was jealousy, Nina had to admit. That was the feeling. Rotten, soul-chewing jealousy.

Claire had had her chance. Nina had waited and hidden and suppressed her feelings for Benjamin for all sorts of reasons: from fear, from self-loathing, from guilt. But at last, she had gotten past some of that stuff, *enough* of that stuff that she had taken the huge emotional chance of telling Benjamin how she felt about him.

She had gone to homecoming with him and basically announced to the world that she was no longer the person everyone had known. She'd crossed the damned bridge, taken the risk, *kissed* him! And now . . . now it was like it all had never happened. Benjamin couldn't even seem to stand having her around. And Claire was the cause. She was certain of that. At least *part* of the cause.

"What did you and Benjamin talk about?" Nina demanded. The sound of her own voice surprised her.

Claire cocked a disdainful eyebrow at her. "Am I supposed to report to you?"

"I just want to know what happened."

195

"No."

"Damn you, Claire."

Claire looked surprised. It was dawning on her that this time her little sister wasn't just playing around. "What is the matter with you? Having a PMS attack?"

Nina's hand was trembling as she lifted her Coke to take a drink. There was no point, she told herself. She couldn't win a fight with Claire. And she didn't want to fight. What was she fighting *for*? For a guy who'd kissed her exactly once and then blown her off? The reasonable thing to do was just—

Only she wasn't feeling reasonable. "I know you're after Benjamin. I know that's what this whole stupid trip is about. You think you're so damned smart, Claire, but I know you set this all up."

Now Claire looked alarmed. She shot a glance toward Jake, returning with the others to the booth. Claire bit her lip, cursed under her breath, and quickly slid out of the booth.

"Running away, Claire?" Nina snapped.

Claire whirled. "I don't want to have a family fight in front of everyone. Outside."

Nina hesitated only a moment. All right. They'd do it outside. She jumped up and brushed past Zoey, ignoring her greeting.

Outside, the air was still and shockingly cold. Claire was waiting in the parking lot, arms crossed over her chest, looking, in the unnatural bluish lights, like Morticia in a bad mood. The bass from the music filtered out from the club but seemed to leave undisturbed the more profound, underlying silence.

"You want to run that by me again?" Claire said.

"You know what I said. You set this whole weekend thing up so you could go after Benjamin. I know you're still in love with him and you won't let him go. You think you're so brilliant, but I caught you, Claire. I figured out your game."

Claire pointed a finger. "Nina, I think you should calm down."

"I don't want to calm down!" Nina cried, her voice suddenly ragged.

"Look, you need to get a grip." Claire's voice had dropped to a low, deliberate calm. "This is kind of new to you, I know. The whole boyfriend-girlfriend thing. And you are overreacting."

"I am not," Nina said. Tears filled her eyes. "I'm not stupid, you know. I know Benjamin likes you better. Everyone likes you better. Big surprise. But I really—" Her voice choked.

Claire moved closer. Nina turned away, defeated and humiliated by the tears that were flowing freely.

"You're wrong about people liking me better," Claire said. "You're wrong about everything you just said, and what you suspect."

"Forget it," Nina muttered.

"Look, Nina, here's the truth. Of course there is still something between Benjamin and me. Yes, I still look at him and think he's attractive. And, yes, I guess . . . no, I *know* he hasn't completely forgotten his feelings for me."

"At least you're being honest," Nina said in a tired voice.

"Things don't just end cleanly and completely between people who've been in love."

Nina nodded. "Yeah, well, it's not like I can compete with you. You decided to get him back; what the hell can I do?"

"I did not decide to get him back," Claire said.

Nina risked a glance at Claire's face. She looked annoyed. Annoyed was Claire's version of sincere.

Claire sighed and glanced back toward the door of the club. "Okay, I'll tell you, Nina. But for once in your life, you keep your mouth shut. I mean *shut*." She sighed again. "I didn't set up this weekend to get back with Benjamin. I set it up to get back with Jake."

Nina frowned. "You just broke up with Jake."

"Well . . . Look, he was all bent because he thought by being with me he was forgetting about Wade. And since I seemed to be trying to force him to forgive me, he'd gotten himself backed into sort of an emotional corner. You understand?"

Nina nodded, although she was mystified.

"So I dumped him. That way I knew he'd start missing me. Human nature—you can reject what's easily available, but you always want what you can't have."

"So . . . you pretended to dump him. You acted like you couldn't care less, and he—"

"He realizes what he's missing, finds a way to make peace with himself, and then, all that's necessary is"—she held out her hands, encompassing the dark mountains, the starry sky, the warm light of the village—"the right time and place. And with a loud popping sound he'll pull his head out of his butt."

Nina digested the information and felt the pieces falling into place. "You *were* flirting with Benjamin . . . but only to make Jake feel insecure."

"Very good, Grasshopper," Claire said sarcastically.

"Oh, you *are* rotten." Nina laughed suddenly. It was breathtaking. "You're more manipulative than even I ever realized."

Claire smiled her infrequent smile. Naturally, she thought Nina had just complimented her. "See, it's about me and Jake. Not about me and Benjamin. Although I will say one thing." Her voice softened and the smile grew wistful. "You picked a good guy to fall in love with when you picked Benjamin."

Nina nodded mutely. "I just don't think it goes both ways."

"You're on your own with that, little sister. The only advice I can give you is—think about getting your own head out of your butt and telling him how you feel. Be direct."

"*Direct?* Why? You aren't."

"I'm me. You're you," Claire said with weary condescension. "You have to work with what you have."

Eighteen

Aisha had danced a few dances with Christopher and one with Jake, just because she felt like dancing and he was available at the moment. Then she'd danced with Benjamin and Lucas, being democratic about it. Then, feeling guilty because she'd neglected Christopher, she went looking for him.

She found him holding court, telling a small group of kids, a guy and two girls, a story about Baltimore. Looking more closely, she saw that one of the girls was wearing a silk Baltimore Orioles baseball cap. It went well with her tissue-paper-sheer top and long, bare, presumably cold legs. Possibly it was all just innocent talk about Christopher's old hometown, she told herself. Only Ms. Orioles kept touching Christopher's arm whenever she asked a question.

Yet she didn't want to go stomping up like THE GIRLFRIEND, acting all proprietary about Christopher. Especially since they weren't even officially boyfriend and girlfriend.

"Hi. Is me, Peter. You recall?"

Aisha turned and saw him smiling at her.

The dorky hat he'd been wearing was gone and so was the parka. Definite improvements.

"Estonia, right?"

He smiled, showing a nice lineup of pearly whites. "Do you enjoy to dance?"

"Sometimes."

"Maybe you have a boyfriend?" he asked tentatively.

"Funny you should ask," Aisha said. She glanced at Christopher, who was leaning in to hear something Ms. Baseball had to say. "If you're asking me to dance, the answer is yes."

They danced two songs. Peter wasn't a great dancer. Not embarrassing, but not great. He seemed to know it and made clumsy, self-deprecating remarks in fractured English.

Aisha checked on Christopher, but no, he hadn't moved. He hadn't come looking for her. In fact, he was asking Ms. Baseball to dance.

Fair enough, Aisha told herself. She herself had danced with Peter. Although Peter wasn't quite the dancer Ms. Baseball was.

"So, Peter, what's the deal with you?" Aisha asked. "What are you doing in Vermont?"

"Oh, we are living here now, in Ohio America. I am Russian from Estonia. In Estonia is not good to be Russian. Estonia people don't like us very good."

"So you're like a minority there."

"Yes. Like Negro people in America."

"African-American. Or black. Mostly we don't say Negro."

"I offend?"

"No, not at all. I'm the ignorant one. To be honest with you, I don't even know where Estonia is."

He shrugged expressively. "You know where Ohio is, yes? That is my home now."

"So you're just here skiing, like everyone else. Are you any good?"

"Not so good."

Aisha sensed he was just being modest. "How *not so good*?"

He grinned. "I am maybe to be on the Olympic team for America." He waved a hand dismissively. "Probably not."

"No way. That's so cool."

"Very cold, sometimes, yes. You must have proper clothing."

Aisha laughed. "No, I meant *cool* as in—"

But he gave her a wink. "I was making joke. Do you ski?"

"I've taken one lesson." She held up a finger. "I can turn around in a big circle by plopping my skis down one after the other, I can go down a really gentle slope, sometimes even without falling down, and that's it."

"Then I must give you lessons," he said promptly.

"You? I don't think I could exactly afford to pay for an Olympic-level teacher."

"You teach me to dance"—he made a brushing gesture with his two hands—"and we are even."

*   *   *

202

"So where do you think Nina and Claire were running off to?" Zoey wondered aloud, taking a long swallow of her drink. She was hot from dancing.

Jake shrugged. "Who knows, with those two? They're the siblings from hell. With Claire and Nina together on this trip, you had to know there'd be bloodshed sooner or later."

"Where's Aisha?" Christopher asked as he returned to the booth. He scanned the dance floor, looking perturbed.

Zoey made a *who knows?* face. "I already lost Lucas in here somewhere." The club was wall-to-wall now, with bodies in motion to the music.

"This place is all right," Jake said into Zoey's ear.

She smiled her agreement. They were getting along, almost like old times. Well, actually, *not* like old times. In the old days they would have been here as a couple, making out, dancing most dances together, holding hands under the table. Now it was like they had begun to be friends again.

And it was all right to talk to old friends, Zoey told herself. About the weather . . . about mutual friends . . . about whether anyone on the football team was using drugs . . .

She made a face. Why did the idea of asking Jake about the story make her feel grubby? It was what reporters did, and if she wanted to be a reporter someday, she'd pretty well have to get used to asking people questions, wouldn't she?

On the other hand, another part of her wanted to write romance novels. It was that part of her that felt uncomfortable using a former boyfriend as a source. Maybe the two careers weren't as compatible as she hoped. Maybe *relentless reporter* and *queen of the love story* didn't go all that well together.

"You know, I'm glad we don't hate each other anymore," Jake said.

Zoey was touched. "I never hated you, Jake."

He nodded. "I know. I was just kidding."

"We're friends, right?" she asked.

He winked. "Absolutely."

Claire came back, as always managing by some magic to make a path through the close-packed bodies, like Moses parting the Red Sea. Nina was behind her, looking abashed and somewhat confused. Zoey saw the two Geiger sisters so often, in such familiar circumstances, that she seldom noticed how much alike they were. But when you saw them together, they looked like . . . well, like sisters, obviously. Both with luxuriant dark hair, though Claire managed to use hers to greater effect; both with startling, almond-shaped eyes, though Nina's were lighter; both with a natural grace that Claire exploited and Nina seemed determined to conceal. Despite Nina's insecurity, Claire wasn't so much more beautiful. And yet the crowd parted for Claire and guys' heads swiveled around to watch her pass, while Nina had to push and shove to keep up.

Claire slid in beside Zoey. Nina sat beside Benjamin and affected an intense interest in what was going on out on the dance floor. She was drumming her fingers and biting her lip.

Suddenly she turned on Benjamin. "So you want to dance, or what?"

"Sure," he said.

"How about you, Claire?" Jake asked, sounding almost timid.

"I'd like to," Claire said neutrally. "But I have to hit the girls' room."

"Be prepared for a major line," Zoey warned her.

The DJ was onto an En Vogue song that Zoey liked and she looked around again for Lucas.

"How about you and me?" Jake said. "I saw Lucas in deep conversation with some guys with purple hair. Snowboarders. You know, you've created a monster getting Lucas into that."

Zoey rolled her eyes. "I'm starting to realize it. That's all he's been talking about." Well, almost all he'd been talking about. She got up and walked with Jake out onto the floor. They danced a fast dance and then, more tentatively, a slow dance.

Holding each other only as close as was proper between friends, Zoey realized she nevertheless felt terribly awkward and uncertain. Not enough time had gone by for her to reach the point where she could touch Jake and feel nothing at all. She wished Lucas were around, but at the same time, she wasn't sure how he would react to seeing her with Jake.

The music had softened enough for conversation. But Zoey's mind was not on chitchat. The time was right. It was now, or maybe not for a long time. And she wanted to at least be able to tell Mr. Schwarz that she had gotten a good start on the story.

"Guess what?" she said brightly.

"What?"

"I got another assignment for a story for the *Weymouth Times.*"

"Cool. I'm proud of you."

"Yeah."

"So what is it? Another story on cafeteria food? I loved that one."

"No, actually, it's kind of a more serious story," she said, feeling a renewed wave of grubbiness at beating around the bush this way.

"Sounds impressive."

"It's about . . . well, I guess there are some rumors about drug use. On the football team."

Jake froze. His hands dropped away from her. His expression grew hard. He shook his head in shock. "Unbelievable."

"It's just a story," Zoey said, talking fast but not fast enough. The damage was done.

"Am I the biggest moron on earth?" Jake demanded bitterly. "I think we're getting back to a point where we're friends, and thinking, okay, this is nice because you know, even if it is over between us, I still really like Zoey. She's a cool girl."

"Look, forget it, Jake. I know *you* probably wouldn't even know if anyone on the team *was* using. I mean, I know you. That's not you at all."

"Nice try, Zoey, but even I'm not *that* dumb." He pushed her away and headed back to the booth, leaving her feeling appalled and ashamed.

Claire had just arrived back from the girls' room. Lucas wandered back and was sipping a drink, giving Jake, and then Zoey a cold, suspicious look.

"I'm out of here," Jake announced.

"I'll go with you," Claire said instantly. She hurried to catch up with him.

"Have a nice time with Jake?" Lucas demanded.

"Not exactly," Zoey said.

Nineteen

"Okay, so we're back in the condo," Benjamin said in a *playing along with a lunatic* tone. "Now can you tell me what this is all about?"

Nina paced the floor of the dark living room, biting her thumb and wondering, quite frankly, what the answer to Benjamin's question was. She had dragged him out onto the dance floor, and then, still feeling edgy and dissatisfied and weirdly excited by Claire's strange confession, she'd dragged him back to the condo. She'd had an image in her mind at the time, something having to do with Claire's injunction to be direct—the queen of manipulation telling her to be direct!—but right now, alone with Benjamin, absolutely alone, no friends, no parents, nothing whatsoever standing between them . . . she had sort of lost the image. Or at least it had become bogged down with frustrating tendrils of reality. The worst of which was Benjamin refusing to play the role she had imagined for him.

Be direct!

"You want to tell me what the hell is the

matter with you, you creep?" she demanded suddenly. Well, it *was* direct.

"The matter with *me*?"

"Yeah. Like . . . like why did you give me all that crap this afternoon? What was that all about?"

Benjamin made a frustrated sound. "Look, you know I don't like people feeling sorry for me."

"I wasn't feeling sorry for you. You twisted scrotal sac."

"Bull. Why were you hanging around here with me, then?"

"How about because I'd rather hang out with you than do anything else?"

Benjamin started to answer, then hesitated. "You're just saying that," he said at last.

"Oh, good retort," Nina said sarcastically.

He pushed his shades back up on his nose and exhaled slowly. "It can't be true that you just really wanted to be with me," he said. "Because, see, if that's true, then I was a real butthole." He shifted his jacket uncomfortably on his shoulders. Then he made a wry smile. "Of course, I don't think I was exactly a *twisted scrotal sac*."

Nina moved closer. He *was* a jerk, maybe, but when he smiled, when he looked at her, near her, in her general direction, whatever was the right phrase for what he did . . . he still made it hard for her to stay mad.

"I thought you were blowing me off," she said. "I thought . . . you know. All that."

"I thought you were, you know, signaling me to back off," he said.

"No."

"Me neither."

"Oh. Really?"

"Really."

"Really?"

"Really," he said.

"Benjamin . . ."

"Yes?"

"I, uh, I know you're not like in love with me, so don't say you are because I know you aren't, at least not yet, and that's cool." She twisted her fingers together. Be direct. Fine. Direct. "But I really do love you," she blurted in a rush.

He reached toward her. She waited while his hand found her face, stroking her cheek. His fingers touched the tear that had run down it. "Could I kiss you?"

Nina nodded, forgetting, as she sometimes did, that he couldn't see. But he drew her to him, with nothing but the light touch of his gentle fingers trailing down from her cheek to her neck.

This time she had no fears that old memories would come between them. The only memory she had was of their first kiss. And as his lips met hers it was an instant made up of sweetest pleasure and utter relief.

"Let's see if in the future we can't both just say what we're really thinking," Benjamin suggested.

Nina kissed him again.

"You know," she said with a confessional laugh, "I thought Claire set this whole weekend up because she was trying to get you back.

That's why I was so insane tonight."

Benjamin shook his head. "Nah. She set all this up so she could get *Jake* back."

Nina held him out at arm's length. "You *knew* that?"

"Oh, sure. But I let her think I hadn't figured it out." He grinned hugely. "Claire gets such pleasure out of thinking she's outsmarted everyone."

"You're as bad as she is."

"Probably," he admitted. "Maybe that's why even though Claire and I will always have . . . *something* . . . Maybe that's why we both need to have someone nicer and sweeter than ourselves."

"Like me?" Nina asked.

"Exactly like you," Benjamin said. "Except . . . you know, with better taste in music."

Nina kissed him again and drew him slowly down to the couch.

For the second time in the evening, Claire found herself outside the club. Some strange uncontrollable fate seemed to want to keep her out of the warm, welcoming interior and out in the frosty night.

She chased Jake, who was marching forward on his long legs, apparently oblivious to the breeze, which had begun to pick up, cold air tumbling down the slope. She had to run to catch up over ice and snow and between parked cars.

"Hey, wait up!" she called out. "I'll break my neck running after you."

He marched on several paces, but then relented and waited, still staring fixedly ahead.

"Thanks," she said.

He set off again, looking, especially with the steam coming out of his nostrils, like an angry bull.

"You want to tell me what happened between you and Zoey?"

Apparently not. At least not until they were halfway back to the condo, where he stopped so suddenly she ran into him.

"You know, Claire, I have to apologize," he said at last. "I always thought *you* were manipulative."

"Me?" Claire said in a reasonable facsimile of innocent astonishment.

"But I've come to find out Zoey's the one who really plays that game."

"Zoey?" This time it was genuine astonishment.

Jake stopped and turned to face her. "She set me up. I think she set up this whole trip just to loosen me up and get me off my guard."

"Really? Zoey?"

He nodded. He looked grim. "I guess maybe she already told you. I guess you already know about everything."

Claire shook her head cautiously. "I don't think I do, no."

"About my being suspended."

"Suspended . . . from what?"

"From the team."

Claire was shocked. "You were suspended from the team?"

"You didn't know?"

"No. I haven't heard anything about it."

"I wasn't in the game last night. Supposedly I have a pulled hamstring. That's the story. At least until people find out I was skiing over the weekend."

Claire shrugged apologetically. "I don't pay all that much attention to football."

He seemed at least partly relieved. "So maybe it's just Zoey. And the team. And a few others. Zoey probably told Lucas, too. But Lucas doesn't have many friends, so he probably didn't say anything." He started walking again, now at a more reasonable pace, hands deep in his pockets, hunched down inside the collar of his jacket.

"Maybe you could let me in on what's happening," Claire suggested.

He shrugged. "Maybe I should. Maybe you're exactly the person I should tell."

Claire waited patiently, listening to the sound of their footsteps on crisp snow.

"I did up a couple of lines of coke during the homecoming game," he said.

Claire tried to cover her sharp intake of breath by pretending to cough.

"I was hungover and out of it. You saw. I totally blew the first half. Someone . . . no point dragging him into it, but someone said I could do a little coke and straighten up. It worked for a while. We scored some points. Only the coach from the other team wasn't stupid. He told our coach he'd better do something about it. Coach basically told me I could take a piss test right there, and if I was positive I was gone for good from the team. Or—" He made a grim, cynical smile. "I could refuse the test and be suspended until I could take it and pass it. Then Coach covered the whole thing up, told the team to keep quiet." He rolled his eyes. "I pee on Tuesday."

"God, Jake. I had no idea this was going on." There it was again—that unfamiliar feeling of guilt she so disliked. While she had been playing out her clever plan, Jake had been in real, deep trouble. And she hadn't known. In fact, she'd dumped him the day after the team suspended him. Wonderful timing.

"Mmm. Well, Zoey tells me tonight that oh, guess what? She has a story assignment. From the *Weymouth Times*, no less." He waved his hand airily in mimicry of Zoey's nonchalance. "A story about drug use on the team. And oh, by the way, would *I* happen, by any strange coincidence, to know *any*thing about it? Not that *I* would be involved in any way, oh no."

Claire almost burst out laughing, but stifled the urge. The notion of Zoey as ruthless interrogator was just so bizarre. Zoey probably *didn't* know Jake was involved. Knowing Zoey, it would have been a major moral dilemma for her even to bring it up with Jake.

"So you think she arranged this whole trip just to get next to you?" Claire asked.

"Now that I look back. I mean, *she* was the

214

one who invited me. Plus she's been extremely nice to me the whole time."

Claire nodded sagely. She would have liked to clear Zoey of his suspicions, but there wasn't any way to do that without confessing the truth. Oh well, Zoey would survive.

They reached the condo and, by unspoken agreement, stopped outside at the bottom of the deck. "I guess it's not really Zoey I'm mad at, though," Jake said in a low voice. "I'm the one who screwed up. Drinking. Doing coke." He shook his head in disbelief. "I have become a first-class screwup."

Claire stepped closer, not too close, just within the aura of his warmth. "Maybe I had something to do with all of that," she said. "I knew you were feeling, you know, conflicted."

"Nah, it's me. It's me. I can't blame anyone else. No one else forced me to hit the beer as hard as I did. That was me raising the bottles. That was me who let the team down. Me who . . . did other things."

"Everyone makes mistakes," Claire said. "Even the best people. And you are the best, Jake."

Jake bowed his head. "Yeah, I guess everyone does make mistakes. But it's easier to deal with your own mistakes when you haven't been a self-righteous jerk. Telling other people . . . how to live their lives. Refusing ever to forgive . . . other people . . . for the things they did wrong."

Claire held her breath. She hadn't made the connection until that moment. But Jake had.

"I know you didn't mean to—" He struggled to control his voice. "I know it was an accident. You know, with Wade. I just wanted someone to blame. First it was Lucas. Then you. But like you said, *everyone* makes mistakes. Even big dumb straight-arrow jocks like me."

Claire slid her arms around his waist. "You're not so dumb."

"Yeah, I am," he said with feeling. "Any guy who would let you go, no matter what the reason was, is too dumb to believe."

Claire looked up into his eyes. "Jake, I am more sorry than I could ever tell you for what happened with Wade." Her own words, intended only to clinch the moment, suddenly struck home. It occurred to her that she was telling the truth. "There are just two things I deeply regret. One is that I never knew what my uncle was doing to Nina so I could protect her. The other is what I did to you and your family."

She brushed at a tear, amazed to discover it trickling down her cheek.

"I'm freezing," Jake said. "Let's go inside to continue making up. I don't think anyone's back but us."

Claire nodded. "Yes, let's make up for a couple of hours, at least."

Arm in arm, they climbed onto the deck and eased open the sliding glass doors. Claire heard a loud gasp. She turned on the light and saw Nina and Benjamin, clothing rumpled, faces flushed, lying on the couch still wrapped together.

"I'm . . . uh . . . I'm being direct," Nina said, blushing pinker.

"For the first time ever, she does what I tell her to do," Claire said to Jake, shaking her head. "Next I'm going to try telling her to leave home and join a cult."

Twenty

"People are disappearing around here at an alarming rate," Zoey shouted over the sound of more Aerosmith. "I haven't seen Nina or Benjamin in a while. And now Claire and Jake are both gone, too." She *knew* why Jake was gone, but as to the others . . .

"And I haven't seen Aisha in half an hour now," Christopher said, obviously frustrated.

"Did you piss her off?" Lucas asked.

"No, I didn't piss her off," Christopher said sharply. Then less confidently, "At least, I don't think I pissed her off. We were dancing. Then I happened to hear these people talking about Baltimore, so I got to talking with them about the old hometown and all."

"And these were *guys* from Baltimore?" Lucas asked.

"Some of them were guys. I mean, there was one dude. But it's not what you're thinking. They weren't even all that cool-looking or anything. The one was a total head-bag situation."

"I'm sure I didn't really hear you say that,"

Zoey said, shooting Christopher a withering look.

"Personally, I don't approve of that kind of sexist talk," Lucas said. He put his arm around Zoey. "I'm much too enlightened."

"I'm going to go look for her some more," Christopher said. "Maybe she went back to the condo." He got up and melted into the crowd.

"Great, now everyone will be back at the condo," Lucas said darkly. "No privacy at all for us. What if we want to discuss the meaning of life?"

"I'll bet that's just what you want to discuss," Zoey said. But Lucas was right. The condo would be way too crowded for Zoey to have to worry about anything happening. Which was especially good, because after the disastrous encounter with Jake, romance was about the last thing on her mind.

Lucas looked disappointed, almost glum. Then a light came on in his eyes. "So you want to get out of here?"

"Shouldn't we wait for Christopher and Eesh?"

"They're semi-adults. They can find their own way back."

They got up and walked out into the night. As they neared the condo they heard a strange, compelling sound—a brilliant soprano voice soaring from one impossibly high note to the next.

"I'm guessing that's Benjamin," Lucas said.

Zoey grinned. "No, Benjamin's a tenor."

They found Benjamin with Nina in the hot tub, the portable CD player belting out opera.

"Quick, Zoey," Lucas said. "The pod people have taken control of Nina."

Nina splashed a handful of water toward him, missing. "Hey, shut up, this is my favorite *area*."

"Aria," Benjamin corrected.

"Are I *what*?" Nina came back, laughing in appreciation of her own wit.

"No, that's not a pod," Lucas admitted. "It's still Nina."

Zoey pulled him away. "I don't think they want *us* hanging around," she whispered.

"Oh, yeah. Look, um, where are your keys to the van? I sort of left something out there."

Zoey found her purse and Lucas hurried away, looking like a naughty child planning a prank. She went upstairs and found one bedroom door closed. She considered knocking, but decided against it. From inside there were indistinct, low murmuring sounds that didn't sound like an invitation.

She went into the other bedroom and flopped back on a bed. The bed was slated to be either Lucas's or Jake's. She didn't much care, since neither of them was around. She wondered what was going on in the next room. Obviously it had to be Jake and Claire. Unless, by some weird twist of fate, it was Jake and Aisha. That seemed pretty unlikely, but then, unlikely things had become commonplace lately, ever since Lucas had returned to Chatham Island and she and Jake had broken up. It really wasn't all that strange that Jake and Claire would be back together, having just broken up exactly a week earlier.

Lucas was in the doorway. "That's *Jake's* bed, you know."

Zoey shrugged. "I was tired. I flopped on the first soft flat surface I saw."

"Well, uh, look, I have a kind of surprise for you."

"A surprise?" She tried to sound excited, but she really was weary. The run-in with Jake had punctured her good mood. Jake thought she was ruthless enough to try to use him for her own selfish reasons. And he wasn't far from being right.

"Come on." Lucas took her hand and pulled her to her feet. As often happened, his touch revived her, at least a little. She slipped her arms around him and gave him a kiss.

"Not here," Lucas said conspiratorially. "Any second now Nina or Aisha or Claire or someone will come barging in."

"You have a better place?"

"Ha. It happens I do."

He kept her hand in his and led her swiftly down the stairs and out the front door to the parking lot. The van was running, exhaust billowing.

Lucas opened the side door, climbed in, and drew her after him. He'd had the heat running and it was perfectly warm. The seats had been reconfigured to make a little open area, just big enough for the two of them to lie side by side on the unzipped sleeping bag he'd laid out.

Zoey laughed appreciatively. "You went to a lot of trouble."

"Nothing but the best for you," he said. "At least it's private."

"Except for the windows."

"We'll just have to steam those up," he said.

With some reluctance, Aisha had accepted Peter's offer to run over to his hotel for a minute. First, she barely knew the guy. Second, she couldn't find Christopher to tell him she was leaving. Third, it was the kind of thing that Christopher, with his one-track mind, might misinterpret.

On the other hand, she'd reminded herself, when last seen, Christopher had been dancing with Ms. Baseball and keeping a very close eye on her every move. And Peter seemed like a nice enough guy. What were the odds he was a crazed Estonian ax murderer? But in case he was, she decided maybe she'd just wait in the lobby.

They had spent their time sitting on the over-stuffed lobby chairs, looking through a small photo album he had. Pictures of Mom and Dad. Pictures of his three sisters. Pictures of the old home back in Estonia that brought tears to his eyes. Pictures of the new home in Ohio.

That was it. No ax murdering. Not even an attempt to kiss her. He was just a sweet, polite guy who'd wanted her to have a cup of hot tea with him and look at pictures of the old, lost homestead.

Then, when she'd begun to yawn, he'd insisted on walking her back to the condo.

As they walked, it was impossible for Aisha

not to compare Peter with Christopher. One gentle, the other brash. One modest, the other with half the world's supply of ego. Peter even had a girlfriend back in Estonia that he had been faithful to until she had written him to say she was dating a bus driver.

He didn't have the effect on her that Christopher had, didn't make her want to kiss him the way Christopher did. Didn't make her feel crazy the way Christopher always had and probably always would. But he was nice. It was like a reminder that nice, cute, gentle, sweet guys (who, if they skied competitively, probably had bodies like steel) were still out there in the world.

In other words, there was a world beyond Christopher.

The condo was dark and Aisha realized, with a shocked look at her watch, that it was very late. The moon had set and there was no sound except for a car engine idling in the parking lot.

"I had fun, Peter."

"I like you very much," Peter said.

"Maybe I'll see you tomorrow."

"Please, yes."

To her surprise he leaned close and gave her a chaste peck on the cheek. "Good night, Aisha."

"Night." She climbed the steps to the deck as quietly as she could. Maybe she could get through the living room and upstairs without waking anyone up. But before she could put her hand on the sliding glass door, it opened.

"Where *the hell* have you been?"

Christopher. "Sorry, I hope I didn't worry anyone," Aisha whispered. "I kind of lost track of time."

"Why should I worry just because you disappear for hours and turn up with some guy who kisses you right out there in front of me?"

"Like I said, I'm sorry. But you're not my father, all right?"

"Where did you go with him?" Christopher demanded.

Aisha pushed past him into the warmth of the living room. In the dark she sensed another person, but peering around, she could see no one. Christopher was still fully dressed. Obviously he had been waiting up for her, no doubt fuming the entire time.

Well, well. So *he* was jealous.

"I went to his hotel room to look at some things he wanted to show me," Aisha said. Yes, she could have chosen her words a little more carefully, but why not let Christopher imagine the worst?

"You . . . You . . . to his . . ." Christopher sputtered. "Just what did he show you?"

"Is there someone else in here?" Aisha asked.

"Benjamin's on the floor," Christopher said. "He's asleep."

"Yeah," a voice said, "and I can't hear a thing."

"Look, don't try and change the subject," Christopher said angrily.

"Fine. Same subject. What were you and the Baltimore Areolas talking about?"

"Can you clarify that?" Benjamin asked.

"Some girl wearing a Baltimore Orioles T-shirt," Aisha said.

Benjamin chuckled. "That's pretty good, Aisha."

"Thanks."

"Okay, fine," Christopher said. "You don't want to tell me, cool. You don't have to."

"Good," Aisha said brightly. "Good night."

"Wait! Where are you going?"

"Up to bed."

"You really *aren't* going to tell me what you did with that dude? Don't you think I have a right to know? Don't you think you owe me some honesty?"

Aisha smiled contentedly as she climbed the stairs. Sometimes life just worked out so well.

Twenty-one

The van windows had been well steamed.

They had made out for what seemed to Zoey a long time. Not that she was complaining. Only it didn't seem like Lucas was getting tired, and she was.

"Maybe we should go inside," she suggested.

"Too many people in there," he said. He kissed the hollow of her neck, something that never failed to send shivers through her.

"Mmmm. Yes. Only, look, we have to get some sleep."

"Do we? I'm not tired."

She shoved him playfully. "You're never tired. You're the Energizer Bunny when it comes to making out."

"Don't you like it?" he asked.

"Of course I like it. Have I been acting like I don't?"

He shook his head. "No. But see, I don't want to go to sleep. I . . . look, Zoey. I want to make love. I even bought condoms because last time you said it was rotten of me even to suggest it unless we were protected and all." He fumbled around in the corner behind the front seat and pulled out a string of condoms, holding them up as evidence.

Zoey recoiled, scooting back away from him. Then, realizing how ridiculous her reaction had been, she started giggling.

"I don't think this is funny," Lucas said.

But Zoey couldn't stop now. She was giggling herself into hiccups.

"Damn it, Zoey," Lucas said sharply. "Don't laugh at me."

Obviously his feelings had been hurt, but still Zoey couldn't stop laughing. She was beginning to get alarmed.

He touched her, but she shook off his hand. He sat back, his eyes furious. At last Zoey got the spasms of laughter under control.

"I'm sorry," she said in a choked voice. "I wasn't laughing at you, Lucas."

"Yeah, it's real funny that I love you, isn't it? Big laugh."

"Lucas, that's not it," Zoey said. "I was just . . . I don't know, I was tense or something. It's been kind of a bad night. Jake and I—"

"*Jake?* What about Jake?"

"Nothing, nothing." She waved a dismissive hand.

"Look, Zoey, we're here together, we're alone, your mom or dad isn't suddenly going to show up . . . I mean, if we're not going to do it now, when are we going to?"

Zoey felt a wave of weariness mixed with

frustration sweep over her. This day had started with the nerve-wracking drive, followed by arguments over beds, followed by too much skiing on out-of-shape muscles, followed by having Jake make her feel like a jerk. The best part had been the last hour, here with Lucas. Only now he seemed determined to ruin even that.

"Lucas, I told you. I don't know. I love you. I think you're amazingly hot. But I'm not ready yet to start having sex."

"Why? Can you just tell me that? Why?"

"Lucas, look, I've thought about this lately. I've been thinking about it a lot. I know a lot of people our age are doing it and all, and I know *you* want to. But, see, the thing is, I used to think about doing it with Jake, too, back when we were together. He used to be the one asking, and I was saying no. If I had slept with him, and then we'd broken up the way we did . . . I mean, it's not like it's just going to be one time, with one person. You think it will be, but if I'd slept with Jake, and then with you, that would be two guys right there, and I'm only seventeen."

"So I'm nothing more to you than Jake was," he said coldly.

"That's not what I'm saying," she protested. "But okay, how about this? If we slept together tonight, what about tomorrow night? What about every night from now on? It's not like you'd get tired of doing it. It would take over our lives. That's all our relationship would be about."

"You know, it is at least *slightly* possible that

you might enjoy it, too," Lucas said.

"It's very possible," Zoey said softly. "Of course I would. Of course I'd enjoy being closer to you than I've ever been with anyone else, Lucas. I enjoy *everything* we do together, even the things where I tell you to stop. But whether I enjoy something isn't the only thing to consider. You're not the one who has to worry about getting pregnant, for example."

"I would always stand by you if something like that happened," he said fiercely.

"Oh, Lucas, see? That's what I mean. It's not something *you* have to think about as seriously as I do. First of all, if I got pregnant and *if* I decided to have the baby, are you going to support us? And pay for a baby-sitter so I can still go to college? On what? Minimum wage?"

He nodded slowly, but not as a sign of agreement. "In other words, we will never have sex."

"I'm not saying that."

"Then when? Give me a date or a time or something. The turn of the millennium? Next time Halley's Comet passes by? When? I mean, I thought when we decided to do this little weekend trip, that meant you were ready to be more grown up."

"I never said that. I never promised you; in fact I told you just the opposite."

"Fine. Not tonight, then. Tomorrow night? When?"

Zoey buried her face in her hands. "Damn it, Lucas."

"When?"

Her self-control snapped. "When I'm ready, that's when," she spat. "When *I* say that *I'm* ready."

"You know something, Zoey? Screw you."

"Lucas . . ."

"You're a very smart girl. You can come up with a million reasons why you don't want to make love to me. But I'm not going to wait around to hear them all. See, the hard fact is, I don't have to wait for you to make up your mind. If it's not you, then it will be someone else, Zoey. When you decide you're ready, you let me know. I *may* still care."

He slid open the van door, jumped out, and slammed it shut violently behind him. The inside of the van rang with the silence. Zoey slumped against the side wall and drew the sleeping bag up around her. She felt stunned, too stunned to think or analyze. It had all happened so suddenly. One minute they were bantering, the next kissing, and in an instant, *an instant,* it was all over.

All over with the guy she loved with all her heart.

Twenty-two

It was almost morning before Zoey got out of the van. She'd had to turn off the engine for fear of getting gassed by the exhaust, and after that the temperature inside had dropped dramatically.

She had spent hours, sometimes crying, sometimes imagining one scenario after another—Lucas would come out and say he was sorry, that he hadn't meant it, that it was all some male equivalent of PMS. Or, alternately, she would go to him, crawl into his warm bed, and make love to him so gently and quietly that no one else in the room would even know.

But she knew neither scenario was going to happen. And after a while she cried no more, just stared blankly, feeling drained of all energy, grim, and utterly depressed.

As she stretched her cramped limbs and climbed out of the van, the stars were still visible in the sky, but the mountains could now be seen as darker masses against a somewhat lighter sky. Soon the sun would begin peeking through the valleys, and Zoey wanted to be gone before then.

She went into the condo, grateful for the

warmth. Christopher was breathing heavily, sprawled in a dream across the couch. Benjamin was rolled tightly in a sleeping bag on the floor. As silently as she could, she went to Benjamin and knelt beside him. She could hear the pattern of his breathing change. He knew she was there.

"Hi," she whispered.

"What's up?"

"Look, um, I've decided to go home early. They have a bus that runs from the village. It's not that expensive or anything."

In the gloom she could see his blank eyes searching, as though they might somehow see something. "What's the matter?"

"It's too complicated to go into, Benjamin."

"Oh. You and Lucas break up or something?"

"Something. I guess we did break up." Even now she couldn't keep the quiver out of her voice.

"I'm sorry, kid," he whispered. He found her and gave her a hug. "You don't have to leave, though."

She sighed deeply. "Lucas hates me. Jake hates me over something else. It wouldn't be any fun for me or for them."

"I still like you," Benjamin said.

"You're my big brother. You have to." She pressed the keys to the van into his hand. "Tell everyone to stay and have fun. Especially you and Nina. Okay? I'll be fine. And make sure you get my skis home."

She hugged him tightly again and got up to go, feeling more alone than she had ever felt before.

10

Will your boyfriend say you and he will still be together a week from now, a month from now, a year from now?

Claire

Jake would say yes, yes, and yes. But then, Jake is a romantic. I don't like trying to guess the future—it never, ever works. Which is why life is interesting.

Aisha

If he's honest, I'm afraid he'd answer yes, yes, and no. I guess I'd rather it was either three straight yeses or three straight no's. I'd like to just know, one way or the other, so I could concentrate on more important things.

Nina

Benjamin would answer who knows? who knows? and who knows? For my answer I would have to call the Psychic Friends Network.

Zoey

~~I know Lucas and I feel the same about this~~ ~~yes, yes, and yes.~~

Twenty-three

The bus ride took forever. Killington to Boston, then a change of buses to go to Portland and a second change to get back to Weymouth. On the ride she slept a little and cried some more, hoping with what energy she could muster that Lucas would bitterly regret being such a jerk.

It was late afternoon before she caught the familiar ferry and saw the comforting silhouette of Chatham Island approaching. She was exhausted beyond belief, caught in an endless, gray dream of remembered conversations, secret wishes, and resilient hopes that clung to life despite everything.

She got off the ferry and briefly considered stopping in at the restaurant. But at this time of day her father would be in the kitchen and her mother would be at home, sleeping in preparation for the Sunday night bar shift. Showing up back home a day early would just worry her father. This was more a mother-daughter type of thing.

She slogged through the streets and almost collapsed with relief on reaching her home. A good, long night of sleep and the events of the trip would all seem much clearer. Maybe Lucas would call and say all the things she still desperately hoped he would say. Maybe he had already caught the next bus and was on his way to her. Maybe.

She went in quietly, not wanting to wake her mother earlier than necessary. She dropped her bag at the foot of the stairs and made her way up.

At the top landing she heard a sound. Her mother's voice, a low murmur.

She went to her parents' bedroom door. It was open several inches.

"Mom?"

She heard a muttered curse. A rapid shuffling, another curse, this time a man's voice. A figure flashed past the open door. Running, pulling on a shirt in a frantic rush. A man.

A man, not her father.

Not *her* father.

But a man she had recognized beyond a shadow of a doubt.